Praise for

A KING'S RANSOM

"A panoramic retelling of the tumultuous last years of Richard the Lionheart's life . . . Penman has absorbed herself so fully into the heart and mind of her protagonist that an undeniably flawed but refreshingly human Richard virtually walks off the pages. This atmospheric fictional biography showcases the author's mastery of all things medieval while providing some refreshingly new twists on the life and times of a hallowed hero."

—Booklist

"Detailed down to the last flagon of wine, Penman's work will please serious fans of historical fiction. . . . Seven years of sieges and battles, confrontations in castles and on horseback are lovingly detailed. . . . Penman's latest is a massively entertaining work of historical fiction for dedicated fans."

—Kirkus Reviews

"A well-researched and impressively detailed narrative displaying a strong commitment to historical accuracy and richly drawn, sympathetic characters. Penman has a rare gift for making the complicated political world of medieval Europe accessible to today's readers, and her many fans will be well rewarded by this latest offering."

—Library Journal

"There's betrayal, war, illness and intrigue . . . [Penman] includes everyday details that get you right into the story. . . . Once you start reading you won't want to stop."

—British Weekly

"*A King's Ransom* [is] historical fiction of the first order, a narrative synthesis of the royal marriages and petty rivalries, the personal slights and gestures of loyalty, the grand deeds and simple twists of fate that shape events. . . . Instead of history that reads like a novel, Penman achieves something greater: a novel that reads like history."

—Willamette Week

Praise for

LIONHEART

"As in her previous historical novels [and] mysteries, Penman expertly weaves well-researched historical events into her fast-paced revisionist story. Certain to appeal to historical fiction fans interested in the medieval era."

—*Library Journal*

"She ably captures the political intricacies of the time. Readers will eagerly await the next installment, which will focus on Richard's capture and ransom on his way home."

—*Publishers Weekly*

"The richly imagined dialogue and story are intercut with snippets from primary sources. The truth of the events makes the novel all the more fascinating and worthy of several reads."

—*BookPage*

"The great Crusader King Richard . . . comes alive in all his complex splendor in this masterpiece of a medieval tapestry."

—*New York Times* bestselling author MARGARET GEORGE

Praise for

DEVIL'S BROOD

"For those who like their historical fiction as complex and tightly woven as a medieval tapestry, this book cannot fail to please. Highly recommended."

—*Library Journal*

"Teaming with characters and authentic period detail, the novel is part splendid pageant and part history lecture."

—*Booklist*

Praise for

TIME AND CHANCE

"Here, as in many of her other novels, Penman combines an in-depth knowledge of medieval Europe with vivid storytelling, re-creating the complex events and emotional drama of the twelfth century. Recommended for historical fiction collections and where Penman's other books are popular."

—*Library Journal*

"Perfect for fans of battles lost and won, on the field and in the boudoir, by a vivid cast of characters doing their best to make history live."

—Kirkus Reviews

BY SHARON KAY PENMAN

A
KING'S
RANSOM

A
KING'S
RANSOM

SHARON KAY
PENMAN

Ballantine Books Trade Paperbacks
New York

2015 Ballantine Books Trade Paperback Edition

Copyright © 2014 by Sharon Kay Penman
Reading group guide copyright © 2015 by Random House LLC

All rights reserved.

Published in the United States by Ballantine Books, an imprint of Random House, a division of Random House LLC, a Penguin Random House Company, New York.

BALLANTINE and the HOUSE colophon are registered trademarks of Random House LLC.

RANDOM HOUSE READER'S CIRCLE & Design is a registered trademark of Random House LLC.

Originally published in hardcover in the United States by G.P. Putnam's Sons, a member of The Penguin Group, in 2014.

ISBN 978-0-345-52833-9

Printed in the United States of America on acid-free paper

www.ballantinebooks.com

2 4 6 8 9 7 5 3 1

Book design by Gretchen Achilles

To Dr. John Phillips

CAST OF CHARACTERS

As of 1192

ROYAL HOUSE OF ENGLAND

RICHARD (b. September 1157), King of England, Duke of Normandy and Aquitaine, Count of Poitou and Anjou

ELEANOR (b. 1124), his mother, Dowager Queen of England, widow of King Henry II, Duchess of Aquitaine in her own right

BERENGARIA (b. c. 1170), Richard's queen, wed in Cyprus in 1191, daughter of Sancho VI, King of Navarre

JOHN (b. December 1166), Richard's youngest brother, Count of Mortain

JOANNA (b. October 1165), Richard's youngest sister, widowed Queen of Sicily

LEONORA (b. 1161), Richard's younger sister, Queen of Castile

HENRY (Hal) (1155–1183), Richard's deceased elder brother

GEOFFREY (1158–1186), Richard's deceased younger brother, Duke of Brittany by his marriage to Constance of Brittany

MATILDA (Tilda) (1156–1189), Richard's deceased older sister, Duchess of Saxony and Bavaria by her marriage to Heinrich der Löwe, mother of Richenza, Henrik, Otto, and Wilhelm

RICHENZA (b. 1171), Richard's niece, wife of Jaufre, Count of Perche

OTTO (b. 1177), Richard's nephew

WILHELM (b. 1184), Richard's nephew

PHILIP (b. 1181), Richard's illegitimate son

ENGLAND, NORMANDY, POITOU

GEOFFREY (Geoff), Richard's older half brother, Henry's illegitimate son, Archbishop of York

WILLIAM MARSHAL, one of Richard's justiciars, wed to Isabel de Clare, Countess of Pembroke

HUBERT WALTER, Bishop of Salisbury, accompanied Richard on crusade

GUILLAUME DE LONGCHAMP, Bishop of Ely, Richard's chancellor

GAUTIER DE COUTANCES, Archbishop of Rouen

ROBERT BEAUMONT, Earl of Leicester, accompanied Richard on crusade

RANDOLPH DE BLUNDEVILLE, Earl of Chester, second husband of Constance, Duchess of Brittany

ANDRÉ DE CHAUVIGNY, Lord of Châteauroux, Richard's cousin, accompanied him on crusade; wed to heiress Denise de Deols

MERCADIER, Richard's notorious mercenary captain

BRITTANY

CONSTANCE, Duchess of Brittany, widow of Geoffrey, now wed to the Earl of Chester

Her children by Geoffrey:

ARTHUR and ELEANOR (Aenor)

ROYAL HOUSE OF FRANCE

PHILIPPE CAPET (b. 1165), King of France

LOUIS CAPET, Philippe's father, first husband of Eleanor, deceased

MARGUERITE CAPET, Philippe's half sister, widow of Richard's brother Hal, now wed to Bela, King of Hungary

MARIE, Countess of Champagne, half sister to Philippe and Richard, Eleanor's daughter by Louis Capet, mother of Henri of Champagne

HENRI, Count of Champagne, Marie's son, Richard's nephew, now wed to Isabella, Queen of Jerusalem

ALYS CAPET, Philippe's half sister, betrothed to Richard in childhood

PHILIP DE DREUX, Bishop of Beauvais, Philippe's cousin

ROYAL HOUSE OF THE HOLY ROMAN EMPIRE

HEINRICH VON HOHENSTAUFEN (b. 1165), Holy Roman Emperor

CONSTANCE DE HAUTEVILLE, his empress, daughter of a Sicilian king

KONRAD VON HOHENSTAUFEN, Count of the Palatine, Heinrich's uncle

CONRAD, DUKE OF SWABIA, Heinrich's younger brother

OTTO, COUNT OF BURGUNDY, Heinrich's younger brother

PHILIP, briefly the Bishop of Würzburg, later the Duke of Tuscany, Heinrich's youngest brother

GERMANY

HEINRICH "DER LÖWE," former Duke of Saxony and Bavaria, wed to Richard's deceased sister, Matilda

HENRIK, his eldest son

OTTO, RICHENZA, and WILHELM, his other children, raised in England

BONIFACE, Marquis of Montferrat, brother to the slain Conrad of Montferrat

MARKWARD VON ANNWEILER, Heinrich's seneschal

COUNT DIETRICH VON HOCHSTADEN, Heinrich's vassal

LUDWIG, current Duke of Bavaria

ALBERT, Bishop of Liege, assassinated that November

Soon to be in rebellion against Heinrich:

BRUNO, Archbishop of Cologne

ADOLF VON ALTENA, his nephew, Provost of Cologne Cathedral

KONRAD VON WITTELSBACH, Archbishop of Mainz

HEINRICH, Duke of Brabant

HEINRICH, Duke of Limburg

OTTOKAR, Duke of Bohemia

AUSTRIA

LEOPOLD VON BABENBERG, Duke of Austria

HELENA, his duchess

FRIEDRICH, his eldest son

LEOPOLD, his youngest son

HADMAR VON KUENRING, Leopold's *ministerialis*, castellan of Durnstein Castle

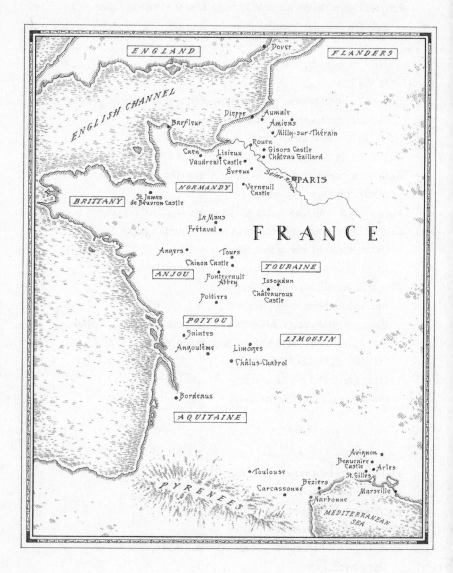

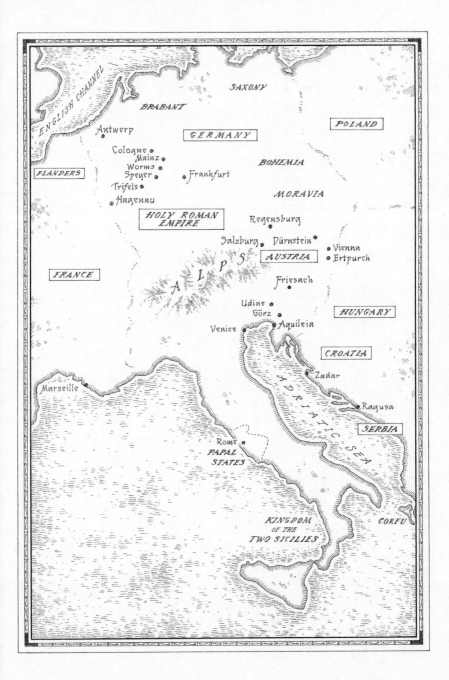

A
KING'S
RANSOM

CHAPTER ONE

❧

They were dangerously close to the coast of North Africa, so the ship's master had warned his crew to keep a sharp eye out for pirates. When the sailor perched up in the rigging shouted, men instinctively dropped hands to sword hilts, for they were battle-seasoned soldiers, returning home from Outremer after a three-year truce had been made with the Sultan of Egypt, Salah al-Din, known to the crusaders as Saladin. They crowded to the gunwales, but they saw no sails upon the horizon, only the slate-grey sea and a sky mottled with winter clouds.

Finding no sign of pirates, the knights glanced toward the man standing in the prow of the ship. He would always attract more than his share of attention, for he was taller than most men, his hair and beard a striking shade of red-gold. But he was in need of a barber's shears, and the costly wool mantle draped about his shoulders was frayed around the edges, stained with sweat and sea salt. While these weeks at sea had taken their toll, his hollowed cheekbones and pallor testified to his near-fatal bout with quartan fever. He might be almost invincible in hand-to-hand combat, but he'd not been able to stave off the deadly maladies and miasmas that stalked the Holy Land. Twice he'd come close to dying from sickness in Outremer, the fate of their crusade rising and falling with his every labored breath, for all knew they had no chance of prevailing without him—even the French lords, whose loathing for Saladin paled in comparison to the intensity of the hatred they felt for the Lionheart, Richard of England.

The animosity between the kings of England and France had burned hotter than any Saracen flame. Unable to match Richard's battlefield brilliance or utter fearlessness, Philippe Capet had broken the oath he'd sworn to God and abandoned the crusade after the fall of Acre, returning to France with his honor in tatters and his heart filled with bile. He soon began to conspire with Richard's younger brother John, hoping to take advantage of the English king's absence to lay claim to his domains in Normandy. When he learned of their treachery, Richard was desperate to get home, to save his kingdom while he still could. But he'd remained in Outremer, bound by a holy vow that fettered him more tightly than any chains could have done, and after he'd managed to retake the crusader city of Jaffa from a much larger Saracen army, Saladin was ready to discuss peace terms.

Richard won some significant concessions. When he arrived in Outremer, the Kingdom of Jerusalem had consisted of the city of Tyre and a siege camp at Acre. When he departed sixteen months later, the kingdom stretched along the coast from Tyre to Jaffa, Saladin had lost the powerful stronghold of Ascalon, and Christian pilgrims could once again worship in the Holy City. But they had not reclaimed Jerusalem from the Saracens. The most sacred city in Christendom still flew the saffron banners of Saladin, and even before he'd left Outremer, Richard's enemies were declaring the crusade a failure.

What they did not know was that he, too, believed he had failed. He'd been one of the few to refuse to visit Jerusalem and pray at the Holy Sepulchre, confiding to his queen that he'd not earned that right. He'd promised the new ruler of Jerusalem, his nephew Henri of Champagne, that he would come back as soon as he'd dealt with the unscrupulous French king and his faithless brother. And on that October night as his ship headed out into the open sea and Acre receded into the distance, he'd whispered a fervent prayer that God would keep Outremer safe until he could return.

The ship's master was conducting a shouted dialogue with the lookout in the rigging, translating for the English king's benefit. Turning toward his knights, Richard tersely informed them that a storm was nigh. A muted sound of dismay swept through their ranks, for most men were convinced it took more courage to set foot on the wet, pitching deck of the *Holy Rood* than it did to ride onto a hundred battlefields. So far they'd been lucky, not having encountered any of the fierce gales that made winter travel so hazardous. But they all had vivid memories of the violent storms that had battered the royal fleet on their way to Outremer, and many of them now hastily made the sign of the cross.

It was said that sailors could predict bad weather in their very bones, and this one's forecast was not long in proving true. The wind began to rise, catching the ship's sails and rippling the dark surface of the sea with frothy whitecaps. Black clouds gathered along the horizon, and the day's light was soon blotted out. The crewmen scrambled to obey their master's commands, the helmsman hunched over the tiller like a priest at his altar as he struggled to keep the bow headed into the waves. The Bishop of Salisbury and some of the others sought the dubious shelter of their canvas tent. Richard remained on deck, for he always chose to face his foes head-on, and so his Welsh cousin Morgan ap Ranulf and the Flemish lord Baldwin de Bethune stayed loyally by his side, holding tight to the gunwale as the ship dropped down into troughs and battled its way up again. The ship's master had told them that their local pilot said there was a safe harbor up the coast at Sciacca, and as they raced the storm, more and more men sought out the clerics on board, asking to be shriven of their sins while there was still time.

By now the wind was howling like a wolf pack on the prowl. They'd reefed the sails, but the *Holy Rood* continued to heel dangerously. When they tried to lower them, one of the downhaul lines started to come loose. With courage that left even Richard dumbfounded, two sailors scrambled up into the rigging and somehow managed to reattach it. With both masts bare, their ship was still propelled by the force of the wind on the hull and rigging, but it no longer skimmed the waves like a bird about to take flight.

Rain had begun to fall, needle-sharp against their skin; within moments, all on deck were drenched. They'd not be able to reach Sciacca, the master told Richard, shouting to be heard above the roaring of the wind, and were heading for a cove a few leagues below the town. The men on the *Holy Rood* had often faced down Death. Most had thought themselves doomed at Jaffa, caught outside the city walls by an army seven times the size of theirs. Richard had saved them, though, gaining a victory that should have been impossible. As joyful as they'd been by that miraculous reprieve, they felt even more grateful when their ship at last dropped anchor in a small inlet that offered shelter from the worst of the storm, for they feared death by drowning more than being slain by an enemy's blade.

They awakened at dawn to a Sicilian sunrise that tinted the sky a pale gold, the occasional cloud spangled in copper and bronze. With the prospect of a fair day for sailing, spirits rose and they made ready to break their fast with bread, cheese, and figs. But it was then that a warning yell came from the rigging, and they soon saw the lateen sails of two large galleys heading toward the cove. The ship's master, a grizzled Pisan who'd lived most of his life on the deck of a ship, started to curse under his breath. Had they encountered pirate galleys in open water, they'd have had a good chance of outrunning them, but their sails had not yet been hoisted, making them a tempting target for sea rovers, who were now maneuvering to block the entrance to the bay.

Richard had joined the older man at the gunwale, his gaze fixed upon the wind-whipped flags flying from the galley mastheads. And then he smiled. "Not pirates," he announced to his watching men. "They are King Tancred's galleys." Turning to the master, he gave the order to run up the banner of the English Royal House. The galleys were close enough now for them to see the reaction of the men aboard, the easing of tension as they realized the *Holy Rood* was not a threat. The largest of the ships was soon within hailing distance, and after getting confirmation that the King of England was indeed a passenger, they invited Richard to board their galley to confer with their lord, the Count of Conversano. He gladly accepted, hungry for news of his kingdom and his enemies, and, taking the Bishop of Salisbury and two Templar knights, he jumped into their longboat and was rowed across to the galley.

Aboard the *Holy Rood*, there was relieved laughter; no man who'd taken part in Richard's attack upon a huge Saracen ship off the coast of Tyre was eager to experience another sea battle. Morgan ap Ranulf helped himself to a chunk of bread smeared with honey and watched as his cousin the king boarded the galley and was given a respectful welcome. He was soon joined by a crusader comrade and friend, Warin Fitz Gerald, and obligingly broke off a piece of the loaf for the Norman knight as they joked who was more wretched, a knight on the deck of a ship or a sailor on horseback. Warin had a ribald sense of humor and he was soon speculating who would be unhappier, a virgin in a bawdy house or a whore in a nunnery. Morgan elbowed him in the ribs, reminding Warin of their mock pact not to speak of women whilst they were stranded on shipboard, having an itch but no way to scratch it.

Such talk turned Morgan's thoughts to the woman he loved, the Lady Mariam, who'd sailed from Acre on Michaelmas with the king's sister, Joanna, widowed Queen of Sicily, and the king's wife, Berengaria of Navarre. Surely they'd safely reached Sicily by now, intending to continue their journey overland, for Joanna was very susceptible to mal de mer; when she'd sailed for Sicily at age ten to wed William de Hauteville, she'd become so seasick that they'd been forced to land at Naples and travel the rest of the way on horseback. That homesick little child-bride was now a stunningly beautiful woman of twenty-seven, and Morgan, who was very fond of his cousin, wondered what fate would await her upon her return to Richard's realm. She'd be a rare marital prize, and he hoped the English king would choose a man who was worthy of her.

Royal marriages were matters of state, of course, and compatibility was not a concern when diplomatic alliances were at stake. But if they were lucky, a high-born husband and wife could find contentment together. Morgan thought Richard seemed content enough with his queen, who'd traveled from her small Spanish kingdom with Richard's formidable mother, the celebrated—some would say notorious—Eleanor of Aquitaine, joining Richard in Sicily and wedding him in Cyprus on their way to the Holy Land. Morgan suspected, though, that Berengaria would never lay claim to the king's heart in the way that Mariam had laid claim to his. Richard revered his mother, who was as astute as any ruler in Christendom, but Morgan did not think women mattered all that much to the Lionheart, who seemed more at home in an army camp than in any of his palaces.

Both men turned as Warin's squire, Arne, approached, carefully balancing two cups of wine. He lingered afterward, until Morgan, who liked the boy, gave him an encouraging look. "May I ask you a question, my lords?" Taking their consent for granted, for he was optimistic by nature, he squatted down beside them. "I am puzzled," he confessed. "This Tancred is the King of Sicily. He took the throne after Queen Joanna's husband died? And then he seized her dower lands and imprisoned her in Palermo? So why is King Richard friendly with this man?"

Warin rolled his eyes, for Arne's habit of making many of his sentences sound like questions both amused and annoyed him. Morgan was more indulgent, for the boy had spoken no French at all upon his arrival in the Holy Land. He'd come to the siege of Acre with Duke Leopold von Babenberg, squire to a knight of the Austrian *ministerialis*, Hadmar von Kuenring. The duke was a devout crusader, having taken the cross twice. But he was a very proud man and after a quarrel with Richard that left his pride in shreds, he'd abandoned the crusade and returned to Austria in high dudgeon. Arne's knight could not accompany the other Austrians, though, for he'd been stricken with Arnaldia, the malady that had almost killed Richard.

The camp doctors had held out no hope for him, and Arne was encouraged to sail with his countrymen and his irate duke. But he would not desert his lord, tending the man faithfully until his death. The crusaders were touched by the boy's loyalty and the Flemish baron Jacques de Avesnes had accepted Arne into his household. After Jacques's death during the battle of Arsuf, Warin had taken the boy on as his squire. He'd turned out to be conscientious and cheerful, and once they were safely back in Richard's domains, Warin and Morgan meant to ask Richard for funds to pay for Arne's return to Austria, if that was his desire. Richard was very openhanded, as befitted a great lord, and since he liked the boy, too, they thought he'd consent.

Now it was Morgan who took it upon himself to explain the intricacies of Sicilian politics to Arne. "What you say is true, lad. King Tancred did indeed hold Queen Joanna in confinement and took her dower lands, for they controlled the roads from the alpine passes, the route the Holy Roman Emperor would have taken when he led his army into Italy." He started to tell Arne that the Emperor Heinrich had claimed the Sicilian throne after the death of Joanna's husband, for their only son had died and the heir was therefore the king's aunt, Constance de Hauteville, Heinrich's wife. He remembered in time that Arne likely knew that, for the Austrian duke was one of Heinrich's vassals.

Taking another swallow of wine, he offered the cup to Arne, who accepted it happily. "Tancred bore Lady Joanna no ill will, and made sure that she was treated well in captivity, holding her at one of her own palaces. He'd feared to release her because of her close bond with the Empress Constance, but he was given no choice when King Richard swept into Sicily like one of their hot *scirocco* winds, demanding that his sister be freed at once and her dower restored to her. Tancred wisely sent her to Richard in Messina and offered gold for her dower rights."

Arne was listening with interest, his head cocked to the side. "Thank you, Sir Morgan. But how did Tancred and our king become so friendly?"

Morgan noted the boy's use of "our king" and wondered if Arne would even want to return to his Austrian homeland. Those who'd fought alongside the Lionheart in the Holy Land had been bedazzled by his bravura exploits, for in their world, nothing was more admired than prowess on the battlefield, and so it made sense that this Austrian youth would have been bedazzled, too. "Tancred and King Richard found they had much in common, lad. They are both soldiers, both men who are accustomed to speaking their minds, and both hold the French king in great contempt."

Arne grinned. "Who does not?" he asked cheekily, and all within earshot laughed, for Philippe Capet had done irreparable harm to his reputation by deserting the crusade; even his own French lords had refused to accompany him back to France, putting their crusaders' vows above their fealty to their king. In light of what transpired, Morgan thought it would have been better had they followed Philippe, for the men he left in command, the Duke of Burgundy and the Bishop of Beauvais, would prove to be as much of a danger to Richard as Saladin's Saracens. Burgundy had paid the ultimate price for his treachery, dying at Acre just before the peace terms were agreed upon, but Beauvais had sailed for home in September, spreading lies about Richard in his wake, accusing the English king of every sin but the murder of the sainted martyr Thomas Becket in his own Canterbury Cathedral. And if Richard had not been just thirteen when his father had uttered those heedless words that would result in the archbishop's death, Morgan did not doubt that Beauvais would have blamed him for that, too.

Guillain de l'Etang wandered over, suggesting a dice game while they awaited the king's return, and they cleared a spot on the deck as he dug in his scrip for the dice. Not all of the knights had liked Guillain at first, for he was so taciturn that strangers sometimes thought he was mute. His size was intimidating, too, for he was even taller than Richard, with shoulders so broad that men joked he had to enter doors sideways and powerfully muscled arms that a blacksmith might have envied. He'd kept to himself, seeming aloof and even arrogant. But then he'd attracted Richard's attention by lifting a Cypriot soldier over his head and throwing him into a horse trough during the fighting in the streets of Amathus. When they saw that he had the king's favor, the others began to show him greater friendliness, and discovered that he was not haughty, merely shy, with a placid, easygoing nature and a very dry sense of humor. He still was not much of a talker, and he was observing Warin's antics with quiet amusement as the Norman knight loudly bemoaned his bad luck and offended Richard's chaplain by asking him to bless the dice.

They were beginning another game when a sailor signaled that the king was coming back. Getting to his feet, Morgan was brushing off his mantle when he glanced toward the men in the approaching longboat and felt a sudden unease, for both Richard and the bishop were as impassive as statues carved from stone, their faces utterly blank. If the king was employing his court mask, that meant the news he'd gotten was not good.

❧

RICHARD HAD BEEN GIVEN a wine cup, but he set it down, untasted, as his men crowded into the tent. "We dare not land at Marseille," he said abruptly, for he knew no other way than to say it straight out.

His words stirred a startled ripple, one of alarm and confusion, for Marseille was under the control of an ally. They exchanged baffled glances and Warin Fitz Gerald exclaimed, "Why not, my liege? I thought you and the King of Aragon were friends!"

"So did I," Richard said, with a tight smile that held no humor. "Whilst we were in the Holy Land, some of you may have heard a Saracen proverb: 'The enemy of my enemy is my friend.' Well, that cuts both ways, for 'The enemy of my friend is my enemy, too,' and it seems that Alfonso has become friends with the Count of Toulouse."

The mere mention of the count's name was enough, for they all knew that Raimon de St Gilles was an inveterate foe of the English Royal House. The dukes of Aquitaine had long advanced their own claim to Toulouse, and Richard was more than England's king; he was also Duke of Aquitaine and Normandy, Count of Poitou and Anjou. They still did not understand why King Alfonso would have chosen to deal with the Devil, but they waited for Richard to answer that unspoken question.

"St Gilles is a cankered, malevolent weasel," Richard growled, with a vitriol he usually reserved for the French king and the Bishop of Beauvais. "When that treacherous whoreson balked at taking the cross, I knew he meant to take advantage of my absence to ravage my lands in Aquitaine, and that is indeed what he did. He got those malcontents the Count of Périgord and the Viscount of Brosse to rebel after my seneschal took ill. Fortunately my queen's father came to my aid, sending his son Sancho to put down the rebellion. Sancho had such success that St Gilles realized he had to take Navarre off the chessboard, and so he approached the King of Aragon, whose rivalry with the Navarrese king proved stronger than his friendship with me. Alfonso accepted St Gilles's offer to ally with him against Navarre, which means that the entire southern coast of France is barred to me, as are Barcelona and the other ports in Aragon."

"Where can we land, then?" Richard's admiral, Robert de Turnham, was not a man easily shaken, but he could not keep the dismay from his voice. He was more familiar with maps than most, and was quicker, therefore, to realize that their options had just narrowed dramatically and dangerously.

"A very good question, Rob," Richard said, with another of those mirthless smiles. "The Count of Conversano says that I cannot land at any Italian port, for that hellspawn on the German throne has the Genoese fleet patrolling the coast in search of our ship. Moreover, Heinrich has made a new pact with my erstwhile allies at Pisa in preparation for his invasion of Sicily, so it is out, too. And needless to say, we cannot sail directly to England or Normandy or any ports in Aquitaine."

There were nods of agreement, for even those with a weak grasp of geography understood that much. To attempt to pass through the Pillars of Hercules out into the Atlantic Ocean would be utter madness. The currents in the straits flowed toward the east, with a speed no ship could hope to match, and beyond lay winter storms of unbelievable savagery, with waves towering as high as sixty feet.

A stunned silence settled over the tent as they began to comprehend the full extent of their peril. The three de Préaux brothers conferred in whispers, and then Jean cleared his throat. "Sire . . . it might be best to pass the winter in Sicily, at King Tancred's court. You'd be welcome there and that would give us time to find another route home."

Several of the men winced, for there was a glaring flaw in Jean de Préaux's plan and their king's temper could be as combustible as sun-dried straw. Richard surprised them by saying without anger, "If I did that, Jean, there would be no kingdom waiting for me when I did reach home. My brother and the French king would thank God fasting if I gave them such an opportunity, claiming I was dead and John the legitimate heir to the English throne."

Morgan understood why Richard had reacted with such unusual patience. If it was true that the Lionheart never forgot a wrong done him, it was also true that he never forgot a kindness, and Guilhem de Préaux had saved his life in the Holy Land. Richard had delayed his departure beyond the point when it was safe to sail as he sought to ransom Guilhem from Saladin, and Morgan was sure the de Préaux family would be basking in royal favor until the English king drew his last breath. He glanced at the Préaux brothers and then back toward his cousin. "What mean you to do, my liege?" he asked, sure that Richard already had a plan in mind, for he'd never known another man so quick-witted or coolheaded in a crisis, one of the reasons for his spectacular successes on the battlefield.

When Richard looked over at the Bishop of Salisbury, Morgan saw that they'd discussed this, either during their visit to the Count of Conversano's galley or immediately upon their return to the *Holy Rood*. "We have few choices open to us," Richard said bluntly, "since we cannot land in France or Spain or Italy. After studying the count's map, it was obvious that we must turn back. We will have to sail up the Adriatic coast, land at a port where I am not likely to be recognized, and then try to reach my nephew and brother-in-law's lands in Saxony."

There were a few gasps and then an eerie quiet as the men tried to come to terms with their new reality. It was not easy, for they'd been just a three-day sail from Marseille, and now suddenly they found themselves facing a sea voyage that could last for weeks, at a season when even experienced sailors like the Genoese and Pisans did not venture far from port, and then a long and danger-ous overland winter journey through territories hostile to their king.

One of the Templars, Sir Ralph St Leger, asked if they had a map and Rich-ard's clerk produced one, unrolling a parchment sheet that offered only the bare outlines of the lands bordering the Greek, Ionian, and Adriatic seas. "I agree that Saxony would offer us a safe haven," the Templar knight said slowly. "Your brother by marriage and his son are in rebellion against the Emperor Heinrich again. But how do we get there?"

Richard drew his dagger and leaned over the map, using the blade as a pointer. "By way of Hungary, whose king is my kinsman by marriage, and then Bohemia, for its duke would never do Heinrich a good turn." He paused, smoke-grey eyes moving intently from face to face. He saw what he expected to find; they looked troubled but resolute. He'd known they would be loyal, theirs a brotherhood forged on the battlefields of Arsuf and Ibn Ibrak and Jaffa; they'd fought with him and bled with him and would die with him if need be. His throat tightening, he summoned up a smile, saying, "But if any of you have a better idea, for God's sake, speak up now." None did, for what was there to say?

As they rose to go, Richard told the Bishop of Salisbury and his Welsh cousin to remain. Once they were alone, he studied Hubert Walter in silence for a mo-ment, knowing the prelate would not like what he was about to say. "I want you to return to Tancred's court with the Count of Conversano, Hubert. He'll pro-vide you with an escort to Rome."

Caught by surprise, the other man shook his head vehemently. "I want to ac-company you, my lord king!"

"I know you do. But I have greater need of you elsewhere. I want you to confer with the Pope, do what you can to stiffen the man's backbone. Now that he's fi-nally offered papal recognition to Tancred, I do not want him to renege for fear of Heinrich. And then I want you to get to England as quickly as you can. My lady mother will be doing her best to rein my fool brother in, but that's no easy task, not with Johnny bound and determined to entangle himself in Philippe's web. You ought to be safe enough, traveling under the Pope's auspices, and the protection Holy Church offers a man who's taken the cross should serve as your shield." White teeth flashed in what was not a smile. "It ought to protect me, too, but I'd as soon not put it to the test."

Hubert looked unhappy, but he did not argue, knowing it would be futile. Richard was already turning toward his cousin. "I'd say you got more than you bargained for when Joanna beseeched you to keep me out of trouble on our journey home."

Morgan had not realized Richard knew of Joanna's entreaty that he sail on the *Holy Rood*. Ostensibly her concern was for her brother's health, as he was still recovering from the quartan fever, but Morgan knew she was also worried that Richard would not be traveling with their cousin, André de Chauvigny, who seemed to be the only man able to curb Richard's more reckless impulses.

"I fear, sire, that would be a task beyond my capabilities." Richard assumed he was joking, but he was speaking nothing less than the truth, for the king's family and friends did not understand how a man so careful with the lives of his soldiers could be so careless with his own.

"The count did have some good news midst all the bad," Richard said, with a sudden smile. "My sister and my wife landed safely at Brindisi, and were given a lavish welcome by Tancred and his queen, doubtless trying to make amends to Joanna, as well he should. It happens that the Count of Conversano, Hugh Lapin, was Joanna's gaoler in Palermo. He'd treated her well, though, and he said, in great relief, that she was very gracious when he arrived at Brindisi to escort her and Berengaria to Tancred's court. . . ."

Richard paused, for Morgan was beaming, and it occurred to him that this might be the last real smile any of them would see for some time to come. After dismissing both men, he sank down on his bed, grateful for this rare moment alone. He'd put up a brave front for his men, but he was shaken, too, by this sudden downturn in their fortunes. How many more weeks would they be at sea now? His memories of their stormy voyage to the Holy Land were still so vivid that he'd declared sailors ought not to be allowed to testify in court, for they were clearly quite mad. The *Holy Rood* crew had laughed uproariously, taking his jest as a great compliment. But Richard's knights saw too much truth in it for humor, for none of them understood how any man could choose to spend more time on shipboard than absolutely necessary.

Richard lay back on the bed, thinking grimly of the winter trek that they'd face, assuming they landed safely at some Adriatic port. He was not as confident as he'd sounded when he'd insisted that the Hungarian king would be friendly. It was true that Bela's queen was the widow of Richard's elder brother. But Marguerite was also the sister of the Lady Alys, the French princess who'd been betrothed to Richard in childhood and repudiated so he could wed Berengaria of

Navarre, and he supposed she might feel that Alys had been treated rather shab-bily. Would her feelings matter to her husband? He had no way of knowing. At least Bela was known to be very hostile to the Duke of Austria and no friend to the Holy Roman Emperor. His bleak musings were interrupted by the entrance of Fulk de Poitiers, his clerk of the chamber, and he sat up hastily.

Fulk frowned at the sight of the map, which had fallen to the deck. Retrieving it, he gave Richard a probing look, but said nothing, carefully putting the map away in a coffer and then beginning to straighten its contents. Richard watched with a smile, for he knew the other man well; Fulk had been in his service before he'd become England's king. "You may as well say it, for I know you're busy contemplating all the ways we can come to grief," he gibed. "What are you envi-sioning? The *Holy Rood* going down in a gale? Taken by pirates? You see me buried by an avalanche in a German mountain pass? Or rotting in one of Hein-rich's dungeons?"

The clerk was unperturbed by the sarcasm. "Those are all possibilities," he said, "although you left a few out. We could encounter bandits on those moun-tain roads. You could end up in a Viennese dungeon, too, if we stray across the Austrian border, for their duke is said to bear you a bitter grudge."

Richard had heard that, too, and was puzzled by it, for his quarrel with Duke Leopold had been a minor matter, not worthy of a vendetta. "Tell me, Fulk, do you ever allow yourself to believe that the worst is not a certainty? Just for a change of pace?"

"We balance each other out, my liege, for you can never conceive of defeat."

Richard didn't deny it. "Well, you know what the Romans said. 'Fortune fa-vors the bold.' And the lucky. You will admit that I am lucky, Fulk?"

The older man glanced up from the coffer. "Aye, you've been lucky, my liege," he agreed, before adding, "so far."

Richard shook his head, torn between amusement and exasperation. But they both knew he valued the dour Poitevin for the very trait that could be so irksome—his candor. He always got from Fulk de Poitiers what kings were rarely given—unsparing honesty.

BY NOVEMBER 11, the *Holy Rood* was approaching the island of Corfu. The sight of its mountains and lush greenery was both welcome and disheartening. The men were thankful to have crossed the open waters stretching between

Sicily and Greece, but they could not help remembering that they'd landed at Corfu just a few weeks ago, never dreaming they'd see it again so soon. On their earlier visit, they'd dropped anchor at Kerkyra, where a small town had grown up around the castle; this time they meant to avoid the Corfu Channel and sail up the west coast. Corfu, notorious as a pirate's den, was also honeycombed with spies and they did not want word to spread that the English king's ship had been seen in the Ionian Sea.

They would have to stop hugging the shoreline before they reached the castle of Angelokastro and the ship's master decided to halt in a small cove and replenish their supply of fresh water. The anchors were thrown overboard and as their longboat rowed toward the beach, the passengers took advantage of this brief respite from the waves and wind to amuse themselves. Martinmas in their homelands was usually chilly and wet, offering a foretaste of the coming winter, and so they were all enjoying the warm sun and mild air, many of them stripping off their mantles as they watched Guillain de l'Etang take on another challenger. A trestle table had been set up on deck and the Norman was locking arms with Hugh de Neville, an English knight. The wagering had stopped, though, for Guillain had already defeated two of the Templars and a burly sailor and now no one was willing to bet against him. Hugh put up a valiant fight, but his hand was soon forced inexorably down onto the table. It ended quickly, as the other matches had done, and Hugh mustered up the unconvincing smile of a man trying to be a good sport.

Glancing around for another contender, Warin Fitz Gerald grinned as his eyes lit upon the man leaning against the gunwale. "What of you, sire? Why not teach Guillain a lesson in humility? We do not want him to get too puffed up with pride, do we?"

Richard was tempted. But he'd learned that few men were willing to defeat a king, be it at chess, arm wrestling, or jousting, and the only thing he hated more than losing was being allowed to win. Deciding that Guillain was too honest and too honorable not to give his best effort, Richard was reaching for his mantle's clasp when their lookout yelled, "Sail ho!"

The game forgotten, the men squinted and shaded their eyes against the sun's glare until they spotted the galleys heading their way. The ship's master spat out an oath, for no merchant would choose a galley to carry his wares; they were seagoing weapons of war. There were three of them—sleek ebony hulls riding low in the water, triangular sails the color of blood, bronze spurs meant for ramming glimpsed each time they rode the crest of a wave. No flags flew from their mastheads and they were close enough now for those on the *Holy Rood* to see that the men on deck were holding crossbows, swords, axes, and grappling hooks. But Richard had already given the command, "To arms," for one glance had been enough for him to discern their predatory intent.

His young squires, Jehan and Saer, were awaiting Richard in their tent, and hurried to help him don his gambeson, the padded tunic worn under his hauberk. Other knights were crowding into the tent to retrieve their armor, carefully packed away in coffers to protect it from the corrosive sea air. Once he'd buckled his scabbard and fastened his helmet strap, Richard snatched up his crossbow and hastened back on deck.

The anchors had been hauled up and the sailors were unfurling the sails; on the beach, the stranded crewmen were dragging the longboat onto the shore, apparently hoping to hide from the pirates if the *Holy Rood* was taken or sunk. Richard's arbalesters were awaiting his orders, their crossbows spanned and bolts aligned. Some of the knights had not taken the time to put on the mail chausses that protected their legs, although all were wearing their hauberks and helmets. They were combat veterans, but unlike his sailors, they had no experience in sea warfare. Glancing around at their tense faces, he pitched his voice so all could hear. "Defending a ship is no different from defending a castle, lads . . . aside from the risk of drowning, of course." As he'd hoped, that dispersed some of the tension; soldiers usually responded well to gallows humor.

Morgan pushed his way toward the king. He was still fumbling with his ventail, seeking to draw it across his throat. He usually felt more secure once he was clad in mail; now, though, he could not help thinking that if he slipped on the wet deck, it would drag him down like an anchor. Richard was studying the pirate ships as intently as he studied battlefields, and Morgan hoped he was formulating a strategy for another unlikely victory; the odds were not in their favor.

He reached his cousin just as Richard beckoned to the ship's master, saying that he needed a man who spoke Greek. The Pisan nodded, for that was the native tongue of half a dozen members of the seventy-five-man crew. Before he could summon any of them, Hugh de Neville offered another candidate. "What of Petros, sire? You remember—the sailor from Messina. He acted as translator when your ladies were shipwrecked on Cyprus and proved to be very useful. He might even know some of those cutthroats, for I heard him boasting that he has a cousin on a pirate ship out of Kassiopi."

"Get him."

The words were no sooner out of Richard's mouth than a youth materialized as if by magic before him. Petros's black eyes were shining, for he was never happier than when he was the center of attention. "You ask for me, lord king? I speak Greek from the cradle, but my French . . . it is very good. When we were in Cyprus—"

"I need information about these pirates. Do they know about Saladin? The war in the Holy Land?"

"Of course they do, lord! They care about the recovery of Jerusalem, too. Why, some have even taken the cross. A man can be a pirate *and* a good Christian."

"Have they heard of me?"

Petros grinned. "I daresay they've heard of you in Cathay, lord. After what you did at Jaffa—"

Richard usually enjoyed hearing his battlefield prowess lauded, but now he cut off the sailor's effusive praise with a gesture. "I hope you are right, Petros. I want you to tell them that this is the *Holy Rood* out of Acre, commanded by the English king."

Petros blinked in surprise. He obeyed at once, though, calling out to the closest of the pirate galleys. A reply soon came echoing across the waves. "They ask why they should believe that, lord."

Richard had expected as much. Turning to the ship's master, he told the man to raise his banner and, within moments, the royal lion of England was fluttering proudly from the masthead. The knights were murmuring among themselves, uneasy about the king's decision to reveal his identity. "Now tell them this, Petros. Say the English king is called Lionheart because he does not know how to surrender. He will never yield to them. To take this ship, they will have to fight to the death."

For the first time, Petros hesitated. "They are proud men, lord. I do not think they can be—"

"Tell them," Richard said, and Petros did. His message appeared to stir up a lively debate among the pirates. Richard waited a few moments, and then nodded again to Petros. "Now tell them this—that it need not come to that. There is a way by which we both benefit and with no blood being shed. Tell their chieftain that I would speak with him."

As Richard had anticipated, that was a challenge no pirate could refuse, and Petros was soon negotiating a meeting, while the knights clustered around their king, the bolder ones expressing their misgivings, fearing that he would agree to meet the pirate chieftain on his own galley, for they well knew Richard was quite capable of such a reckless act. He shrugged off their protests, and it was eventually agreed that he and the pirate would meet at midpoint between the two vessels. Their longboat was summoned from the beach, and much to the dismay of Richard's men, he and Petros were soon being rowed out toward the approaching pirate longboat.

Morgan and Baldwin de Bethune stood at the gunwale, never taking their eyes from the tall figure in the prow of the longboat. They'd both been loyal to the old king, Richard's father, had stayed with Henry until he'd drawn his last anguished breath at Chinon Castle, and while they were pragmatic enough to recognize Richard as their lawful king, they'd been wary at first of this man they knew only by repute. But that was before they fought beside him in Messina, Cyprus, and the Holy Land. Now they watched anxiously as he conferred with the pirate within range of the latter's crossbowmen; that the pirate was taking the same risk was no comfort to them. The conversation was an animated one and Petros was kept busy translating from French to Greek and back to French again. It was not long, though, before a reassuring sound drifted back on the wind—laughter. Morgan and Baldwin exchanged glances, marveling that once again Richard had managed to snatch victory from the jaws of defeat.

CLIMBING THE LADDER, Richard swung himself over the gunwale and grinned at the men crowding the deck. "It is all settled. I have hired two of their galleys and crew for two hundred marks."

There was an immediate outcry, exclamations of shock and alarm and bewilderment. Raising his hand to still them, Richard explained that he was known to be sailing on the *Holy Rood* and his enemies would be on the lookout for it. Switching to the galleys was one way to throw them off his trail. That made sense to his men, but they did not find it as easy to trust in the word of a pirate chieftain as Richard apparently did. None voiced objections, though, for kings were not to be questioned.

Richard headed for the tent, with Baldwin and Morgan right on his heels. The others watched, hoping that a highborn lord and a kinsman might dare to do what they could not: express their misgivings about this new alliance with sea rovers. Jehan and Saer had already begun to remove the king's hauberk. He was in good spirits and answered readily enough when Baldwin asked how he could be sure these pirates could be trusted.

"Petros was right. They do care about the fate of the Holy Land, and for the past few months, soldiers have been passing through Corfu on their way home, all of them carrying tales of the French king's perfidy and the battles we fought against Saladin. At the risk of sounding immodest," Richard said with another grin, "I come off well in those stories and Captain Georgios and his men are eager to hear my own account of them. They still want the two hundred marks, mind you, but they also want to help us escape our enemies. Georgios was actually indignant to hear of my plight, pointing out that men who'd taken the cross are under the protection of the Church. Ironic, is it not, that a pirate should have more honor than kings or emperors?"

Baldwin's qualms were assuaged, for he believed Richard to be a good judge of character, a survival skill for those who wore crowns or commanded armies. Morgan was still shaken, for he'd just spent an hour fearing for the king's safety and wondering how he was going to tell Joanna that he'd merely watched as her brother went off alone to meet with pirates. "But you did not know this Georgios was a man of honor when you got into that longboat," he blurted out. "Are you never afraid for your own life?"

Richard's eyebrows shot upward in surprise. "Surely you've not forgotten that Good Friday storm that scattered our fleet after we left Sicily? Need I refresh your memory, Morgan? The wind keening like the souls of the damned, the waves higher than church spires, all of us sure we'd breathed our last. Or the tempest we encountered in the Gulf of Satalea, where our ships were blown backward by the force of the wind. You show me a man who claims he was not afraid during those storms, and I'll show you a liar."

That wasn't what Morgan needed to know; he'd taken it for granted that Richard feared storms at sea, not being insane. He'd gone too far to retreat, though. "But what of the battlefield? I've seen you take chances that . . ." He paused, then said simply, "Do you never fear for your own safety?"

Richard was quiet for a moment, considering whether that was a question he wanted to answer. He suspected it was one many a man had long wanted to ask, although the only person who'd ever dared had been his wife. It was easier just to brush the query aside. But he liked his Welsh cousin and knew that Morgan's concern was genuine. "Well," he said at last, "when a man's blood is running hot and his heart is racing, it can be difficult to tell excitement from fear."

There was a silence and then Baldwin said, very dryly, "Passing strange, for I have no trouble at all telling them apart."

Richard laughed, handed his gambeson to one of his squires, and then made one final effort to explain what seemed to him quite obvious. "It is simple, really. In a storm, we are utterly helpless, at the mercy of the wind and waves. But on the battlefield, my fate is in my own hands. What happens is up to me."

Morgan agreed that a lack of control would be frightening to any man, especially a king. But he was convinced that Richard was surely the only one on God's earth who felt in control of events on the battlefield. Seeing that there would be no satisfactory answer to a question he ought not to have asked in the first place, he changed the subject and asked when the switch from the *Holy Rood* to the pirate galleys would occur.

"On the morrow. I need to provide our men with enough money to make their way home. The *Holy Rood* will take them to Brindisi, where they can choose to travel overland, pass the winter in Sicily, or even take passage on a ship sailing for one of the ports that are barred to me. They are not the quarry in this hunt, after all."

Seeing that Baldwin and Morgan were confused, Richard explained that he was only taking twenty men with him, heading off any objections with some blunt speaking. "We do not have enough men to keep us safe, just enough to attract unwanted attention. The only chance I have to reach Saxony is to travel as fast and as inconspicuously as possible."

Their first reaction was to protest, horrified by the very thought that their king would be venturing into enemy territory with only twenty men. Their second was a reluctant realization that Richard was right. Their third was to insist that they both be amongst the twenty men. Richard feigned displeasure that they were overstepping themselves, but he was touched that they were so willing to follow him into the frigid, far reaches of Hell, the German empire of Heinrich von Hohenstaufen.

❧

THE MASTER AND CREW of the *Holy Rood* were obviously relieved that they'd be spared a harrowing voyage along the Adriatic coast. But Richard's knights and crossbowmen and men-at-arms responded as Baldwin and Morgan had done, all clamoring to accompany him. "You are daft, the lot of you," he said huskily, "for no man with his wits about him would choose snowdrifts and bad

German ale over Palermo's palm trees and bawdy houses." But he did not let sentiment influence his selection of the twenty men, hardening his heart against the tearful pleas of his own squires and choosing those who he thought would be most formidable in a fight, calmest in a crisis. He made exceptions only for his chaplain, Ancelm; his clerk of the chamber, Fulk de Poitiers; and—much to the boy's delight—Arne, whose ability to speak German was sure to be an asset. The others chosen were Morgan, Baldwin, Hugh de Neville, Warin Fitz Gerald, his admiral Robert de Turnham, Robert de Harcourt, Guillain de l'Etang, Walkelin de Ferrers, four Templars, and his five best arbalesters. They would be facing dangers, hardships, deprivation, and possible death, but they reacted as if they'd been given a great honor, any fear they may have felt firmly tethered by pride.

Of all those who'd not been chosen, none were as devastated as Guilhem de Préaux. While the other men lined the gunwales to watch as Richard sailed away on a pirate galley, Guilhem retreated to the tent to rage and pace, tearful one moment, cursing the next. "How could he have left me behind?" he cried as his brothers, Pierre and Jean, followed him. "How could he ever have doubted my loyalty?"

"He did not, you fool," Pierre said, and left it to Jean to console Guilhem, for Richard had entrusted them with the care of his squires and they were now in need of solace, too. As Pierre withdrew, dropping the tent flap to give them a small measure of privacy, Jean rummaged around until he found a wineskin and tossed it to his brother.

"Pierre is right. The king would never doubt your loyalty or your courage. You ought to know better than that."

"Then why would he not take me with him?"

"Why do you think, Guilhem? Your loyalty cost you nigh on a year of your life, and whilst you rarely talk of it, we know you had no easy time in confinement. It is true that we owe a debt of fealty to Richard, our liege lord. But he would not have you pay that debt twice over."

Guilhem studied his brother's face, then took several deep swallows from the wineskin. "I would have paid it gladly."

Jean reached over, clasping him on the shoulder. "I know, lad," he said quietly, "I know. And so does the king."

"Did he say that?" Guilhem challenged, his head coming up sharply at the unexpected confirmation.

"He did. When he charged us with looking after his squires, he said,

'Guilhem has already been a guest of the Saracens.' He made a grim jest, then, about Heinrich being a less gentle gaoler than Saladin."

It had been intolerable for Guilhem, thinking that the king had judged him to be unworthy. But now that he knew better, he found it brought him little comfort, for the king's need had never been greater and he would be hundreds of miles away, unable to help. When he slumped down on a coffer chest, Jean squeezed his shoulder again and then left so he might have some time alone.

Guilhem did not linger long in the tent. Draining the wineskin, he followed his brother back on deck, where he shoved his way toward the gunwale. There he stood, neither moving nor speaking, watching until the pirate galleys had disappeared from view.

CHAPTER TWO

❖

Richard was accustomed to living on familiar terms with Death, but never had it been so close, so insistent. His body was as bruised as if he'd been absorbing blows from Saracen maces and he could still taste blood in his mouth after he'd been slammed to the deck as the galley heeled suddenly. Their tent was no protection against the stinging rain, for the canvas was being shredded by the wind. They huddled together for warmth and for protection, clinging tightly to one another to avoid being swept overboard. One of the pirates had lost his footing and would have gone over the gunwale if not for Guillain de l'Etang's strength; he'd grabbed the man's ankle and held on until other crew members could haul him back onto the deck. All of the men had become violently seasick once the storm struck, even the sailors, and the tent reeked of vomit, sweat, and fear.

As the *Sea-Wolf* rode the crest of another wave, the men tensed. Georgios, the pirate chieftain, had told them that they had a chance as long as Spyro, the helmsman, could keep the galley from being hit broadside. But it was terrifying to slide down into a trough, blinded by the flying spray, drenched by the cold water breaking over the galley. Each time it happened, there was a frozen moment in which they were sure they'd continue their downward plunge. When the ship continued to fight the sea, rising up again, they exhaled ragged breaths and thought of their God, their women, their homelands.

Richard found himself remembering a delirious night at Jaffa after he'd been stricken with quartan fever; he'd begun hallucinating, convinced his dead brother Geoffrey was there, laughing in the shadows beyond his bed. Closing his eyes now, he could hear echoes of Geoffrey's lazily mocking voice. *Face it, Richard, you'll never make old bones. Other men lust after women. You lust after Death, always have. You've been chasing after her like a lovesick lad, and sooner or later she'll take pity and let you catch her.*

"No," he said suddenly, "that's not so!" He did not lust after Death, did not want to follow her into the black depths of this frigid, hungry sea. Those nearest to him turned at the sound of his voice, their eyes questioning, hopeful, for they hung on his every pronouncement, as if he alone could save them. Men had been depending upon him like that since his twenty-first year, when he'd taken the impregnable Taillebourg Castle, proudly proving to the world and his father that he understood war the way a bishop understood Scriptures. On the battlefield, he had answers, knew what to do. But on the pitching deck of the *Sea-Wolf*, he was as helpless as young Arne.

"Lord king!" Petros lurched into the tent, followed by the pirate chief, who squatted down as the sailor from Messina translated for him. Georgios hadn't yet lost all of his bravado, but it was fraying around the edges and his dark eyes were somber even if his manner was blasé. "He wants me to tell you," Petros said, "that his helmsman still cannot head for shore. As long as the night and storm obscure the coast, he does not know where we are." As unwelcome as his words were, none thought to challenge him, for they'd seen the sheer cliffs to starboard earlier in the day; unless they were sure there was a harbor or cove hidden by the darkness, the galley would be dashed to pieces against those rocks if it ventured too close to land. Georgios spoke again, Petros cocking his head to listen. "He's never seen a storm as fierce as this one, lord. He says that every sailor knows women and dead bodies are bad luck on shipboard. But he never knew kings could be bad luck, too."

"That's passing strange," Richard said, "for I was just thinking the same thing about pirates." When his reply was conveyed to Georgios, the pirate smiled, but it was a pale imitation of his usual cocky grin. Before he could respond, they heard a shout out on the deck. The other men stiffened, for although none of them understood Greek, they'd learned what that alarm meant—another monster wave was looming.

The ship shuddered, like an animal in its death throes. Its prow was pointing skyward, so steep was the wave, and the men desperately braced themselves, knowing the worst was to come. The galley was engulfed, white water breaking over both sides, flooding the deck. And then it was going down, plunging into the trough, and there was nothing in their world but seething, surging water. Richard heard terrified cries of "Jesu!" and "Holy Mother!" Beside him, Arne was whimpering in German. The bow was completely submerged and Richard was sure that the *Sea-Wolf* was doomed, heading for the bottom of the Adriatic Sea.

"Lord God, I entreat Thee to save us, Thy servants!" Richard's voice rose above the roar of the storm, for he was used to shouting commands on the battlefield. "Let us reach a safe harbor and I pledge one hundred thousand ducats to build for Thee a church wherever we come ashore! Do not let men who've taken the cross die at sea and be denied Christian burial!"

Waves continued to crash onto the deck, soaking the men and stealing their breaths. But then the galley's prow was coming up again, battling back to the surface, and they realized that they would not drown just yet. They slumped against one another, chests heaving as they sought to draw sweet air into their lungs. Petros tugged at Georgio's arm, pointing at Richard and murmuring in Greek. The pirate's eyes widened and then he began to laugh. "He says," Petros reported, "that you have saved us, lord, for how could the Almighty resist such a vast sum, veritably a king's ransom."

Richard knew better than to claim a victory while the battle still hung in the balance. He didn't bother to point that out to Georgios, though, for his stomach was roiling again. He had nothing left to vomit up, but he could taste bile in his mouth and fumbled for the wineskin at his belt, taking a swig and then flipping the wineskin to Arne, who looked as if he was greatly in need of it.

His clerk was staring after Georgios, his mouth set in a hard line. "That man," he said coldly, "is a blasphemer."

His disapproval gave Richard some grim amusement. "He's a pirate, Fulk. They are not noted for their piety."

Fulk did not see the humor. "They are damned, the lot of them," he insisted and no one had the inclination or the energy to argue with him. The rain had eased up, but the sea continued to rage, tossing the galley violently. Through the rips in the tent, they could see the sky was beginning to lighten, shading from ink black to a dark leaden grey. And then Petros was back, his olive skin no longer blanched, his cheekbones flushed with color.

"Spyro has recognized a landmark—Mount Srd!" he cried. "He says we're not far from the harbor at Ragusa!"

COMING OUT ON DECK, Richard was relieved to see the second pirate galley in the distance, for they'd been separated when the storm broke and he'd feared that his ten men aboard the *Sea-Serpent* had been lost. As the night retreated, the coast was coming into focus. Ahead lay a heavily wooded island that Petros said was called La Croma, and beyond it was the city of Ragusa. The sea was still churning and waves were pounding against the white cliffs of La Croma, sending spume high into the air. Richard's knights had joined him at the gunwale, gazing yearningly toward the harbor that would be their salvation. But then one of Georgio's crewmen pulled him aside, obviously agitated, and when the other pirates clustered around their chieftain, Richard felt a sudden disquiet.

"Petros! What is wrong?"

The young sailor hastened toward them, surefooted even though the deck was awash and bucking like an unbroken horse. "We're taking on water in the bilge, lord. The helmsman says we cannot reach Ragusa, so he's going to try to land on La Croma."

Richard drew a sharp breath, for the island looked like a fortress, its limestone crags ready to repel any intruders, and the closer they got, the more foreboding it seemed. The pirates were not panicking, though, straining at the oars as the helmsman manned the tiller, and as they rounded the tip of the isle, Richard saw a beach below the cliffs. It was strewn with rocks, some of them the size of boulders, but it offered their best chance for survival.

The surf was so wild that it looked like a boiling cauldron and the galley rocked from side to side as the crewmen rowed toward that rocky beach. But the helmsman kept it on course, and as soon as they reached the shallows, the sailors leapt out and began to drag the galley up onto the island. Richard and his knights splashed into the water to help. It was rough going and by the time they'd safely beached the galley, they were all exhausted. As they sprawled on the stony ground, the second galley drew closer, its men shouting and pointing toward Ragusa to indicate they were heading for the harbor a half mile away. Once they were sure the *Sea-Serpent* was going to make it, the men stranded on La Croma reluctantly struggled to their feet, for they were soaked to the skin and had to find shelter as soon as possible.

"We need to get a fire started," Richard said, looking toward the tangled groves of pine and laurel that bordered the beach. "Does anyone live on this island, Petros?" The words were no sooner out of his mouth than he had his answer. A light flared in the dark of the woods, moving so erratically that it could only be a lantern or torch. Richard and his knights dropped their hands to sword hilts, watching that swaying flame. Hooded figures were visible through the trees now, cloaked in black. At first glance, they seemed spectral and ghostly, even sinister. But then they emerged onto the beach and the shipwrecked men exchanged sheepish smiles, for these otherworldly wraiths were Benedictine monks.

Richard moved to meet them. He had no idea what language was spoken in Ragusa. Hoping that at least one of the monks had some knowledge of Latin, he said, "We are pilgrims returning from the Holy Land. Can you give us shelter?"

He was surprised to be answered in Latin as good as his own, as several monks assured him that he and his men would be welcome guests of their abbot. He thanked them courteously and then began to laugh. The monks had rescued other shipwreck survivors and since men often reacted emotionally after coming so close to dying, they saw nothing strange in Richard's mirthful outburst. They had no way of knowing the real reason for his amusement—that this small, secluded community of monks would be the beneficiaries of his extravagant vow to God. With one hundred thousand ducats to spend, their isolated little island would have a church to rival the spectacular cathedrals of Rome, Palermo, and Constantinople.

⟡

RICHARD AWOKE WITH A START, torn from a dream that had not been a pleasant one. Arne was sitting cross-legged on the floor by his straw-filled mattress. Sitting up, he glanced around, but the abbey guest hall was empty. Where were his men? "What time is it, Arne?"

"You're awake, sire!" Arne's smile was bright enough to pierce the shadowed gloom of the hall. "I heard the bells ringing for None not long ago, so it is just past the ninth hour of the day."

Richard frowned. Three o'clock? He'd meant to rest for a brief while. How could he have slept for more than six hours? "Why did you not awaken me?"

Arne was flustered by the sharp tone. "You ... you did not say ..." he stammered, "and ... and you needed sleep?"

That was precisely the problem—that he had needed the sleep. To Richard, it was troubling proof that he'd not fully regained his strength, that his body was still weakened more than two months after his bout with quartan fever.

Cutting off Arne's apology, he said, "Never mind, lad. Do I have anything dry to wear?"

The boy nodded eagerly, saying they'd retrieved their coffers from the *Sea-Wolf*, and hurried to fetch braies, chausses, a shirt, and a tunic. All of their clothes were damp and wrinkled, smelling faintly of mildew after so long at sea, but they were still an improvement over the sodden garments Richard had peeled off before falling into bed. He rarely had the patience to allow his squires to assist him in dressing, for he could do it more quickly himself, and he waved Arne away as he pulled the braies on and then drew the shirt over his head. He was belting the tunic while Arne hovered nearby, eager to help, when the door slammed open and Baldwin and Morgan hurried into the hall.

"My liege, the Count of Ragusa and their archbishop are in the abbot's great hall, asking to see you!"

Richard didn't like the sound of that, thinking this was a rather exalted welcoming committee for ordinary pilgrims. Joanna had told him that her husband had often personally taken a hand when shipwreck survivors turned up in Sicily, and he wanted to believe this was a similar act of Christian charity. But good soldiers developed sharp survival instincts, and his were beginning to tingle. "They asked for me?" he said, trying to recall the name he'd given the abbot.

Morgan had an expressive face, not meant for secrets, and his concern was obvious. Baldwin was more phlegmatic, rarely revealing his inner thoughts. Now, though, he looked as troubled as the Welshman. "They asked for the king of the English," he said grimly.

Richard caught his breath and then swore, cursing the pirates in language that added substantially to Arne's growing list of French obscenities. When he turned to demand his sword, he saw the boy was already holding out the scabbard.

"What will you do, sire?" Arne was not surprised when Richard did not reply, for what could they do? They were trapped on the island. They could not flee and he did not see how the king could resist, either, with just ten men at his back. No, nine and a half, he amended unhappily, knowing how little help he could offer in a fight. Scurrying after Richard as he left the guest hall, Arne caught up with them in time to hear Morgan ask if Ragusa was an ally of the Holy Roman Empire. He could not repress a shiver, for he knew their fate might well turn upon the answer to that question.

Richard hesitated, trying to recall all he knew of Ragusa, which was not that much. "It is a city-state like Venice or Genoa. I was told that it recognizes the suzerainty of Constantinople, but the Greeks do not meddle in its governance. I do not think it has ties to the Hohenstaufens, at least not formal ones. For all I know, though, their count could be Heinrich's cousin," he said bitterly, remembering his surprise upon learning that the Duke of Austria claimed kinship to Isaac Comnenus and bore him a grudge for deposing the Cypriot despot.

By now they'd reached the abbot's great hall. For one of the few times in his life, Richard did not have a plan of action. He could deny he was the English king or try to shame them into honoring the Church's protection for men who'd taken the cross, but neither of those options seemed likely to carry the day. He'd rarely felt so uneasy and he sought reassurance by dropping his hand to the hilt of his sword. As his fingers closed around the haft, the familiar feel of it was comforting, and he found himself remembering something he'd once read, that pagan Norsemen believed they could not enter Valhalla unless they died with sword in hand. And then he straightened his shoulders, raised his head, and shoved the door open, crossing the threshold with a deliberate swagger.

The hall was crowded. All of the monks were there, murmuring among themselves. The abbot was standing with two men who could only be the count and the archbishop. They made an odd couple, the former tall and so thin he appeared gaunt, the latter short and rotund, both of them elegantly garbed, though, with jewels flashing on their fingers. There was a hush as Richard entered and then an excited buzz swept the hall. Abbot Stephanus hastened toward Richard, moving with surprising agility for one no longer young.

"My lord king," he said in impeccable Latin, and bowed. "I had no idea so illustrious a guest was being sheltered under our roof. May I introduce Count Raphael de Goce and Archbishop Bernard."

Both men made respectful obeisances. The count opened his mouth to speak, but the archbishop was quicker. "We are honored to welcome the renowned and redoubtable king of the English to our city. Your war against the infidel Saracens has made you a hero wherever people embrace the True Faith. I never thought I'd have the opportunity to hear of these battles from the victor of Jaffa himself!"

When he paused for breath, Count Raphael seized his chance. Casting a glance toward the archbishop that revealed the rivalry between the two men, he said reprovingly, "Jaffa was indeed a great victory. But surely we'd be remiss, my lord archbishop, if we did not speak of the king's greatest achievement in the Holy Land. Because of his efforts, Christian pilgrims can once again pray in the sacred city of Jerusalem." Beaming, he turned and beckoned to a woman nearby. "May I present to you my lady wife, the Countess Marussa. We want to invite you to be our honored guest during your stay in Ragusa."

"My lady," Richard said, and she blushed and giggled when he kissed her hand, for he could play the gallant when he chose; he had grown up at his mother's court in Aquitaine, after all. Any doubts he may have harbored had disappeared as soon as he saw the countess; the count would hardly have brought his wife along if this were a trap of some sort. Once again his luck had prevailed, shipwrecking them in probably the only place along the Adriatic coast where the Lionheart legend counted for more than the enmity of the German emperor and the French king.

❧

RICHARD'S MEN LIKED RAGUSA so much that they joked it was a pity he'd not agree to stay and become its king. The weather was much milder than November back in their homelands and it was a pleasure to walk on ground that did not shift under their feet. The city itself was very prosperous and its streets were cleaner than any they'd seen. There were public baths, allowing them to soak off the accumulated dirt of the past seven weeks. They were able to get their clothes washed and mended, buying what they needed in the town's thriving markets, for the Ragusans carried on an active trade with their Adriatic neighbors. Best of all, the people were very friendly, treating them like heroes.

Even communication was not as troublesome as they'd anticipated. While the official language of Ragusa was Latin, the citizens also spoke dialects of Italian and Slavic, and what they called "Old Ragusan." Richard, his chaplain, Anselm, Fulk, and Baldwin de Bethune could converse easily in Latin. The others either had a smattering of it or none at all, but Ragusa had been briefly under the control of Sicily and some of its citizens had learned the French spoken at the Sicilian court. Petros was in his glory, for he could understand the Italian heard in the city streets and so his services were in great demand. Petros passed most of his days in an agreeable alcoholic haze, for the knights enjoyed frequenting the local taverns, where men were eager to buy them drinks in order to hear their stories of the crusade. Life in Ragusa was so much more pleasant than life on shipboard that the men hoped it would take a while for the pirates to repair the *Sea-Wolf* and for Richard to arrange a loan to honor his pledge.

There was a snake in this Adriatic Eden, though. Richard had warned his men to stay away from the local women. They understood the logic behind his order, but some of the female Ragusans were very pretty and very flirtatious. They were delighted, therefore, when Petros discovered that the taverns down by the harbor offered more than wine. Richard and Baldwin were dining with Archbishop Bernard, and the Templars declined because of their vows of chastity, but Warin and Hugh de Neville recruited so many of the others that they joked they ought to ask for a group rate.

While Morgan had been hesitant at first, he'd managed to convince his conscience that the Lady Mariam would understand under the circumstances. Warin included young Arne, too, embarrassing the boy by declaring loudly that it was time the lad learned where his sword ought to be sheathed. Georgios kept his men under a tight rein in ports like Ragusa, for the pirates wanted to be able to come back on future voyages. But several of the crew had slipped away and joined the knights, so it was a boisterous and cheerful bunch who trooped into a wharf-side tavern called the Half-Moon.

They were surprised to find that prostitution in Ragusa was run by women. The bawd, a handsome redhead in her forties with a practiced smile and hard eyes, told her hirelings to turn away other customers, for she calculated that men so long at sea would be so eager for female flesh that they'd pay well for the privilege. Some haggling ensued, but when she summoned the youngest and the prettiest of her whores, the men decided that her price was reasonable. It was then, though, that Morgan learned something that quenched his lust as thoroughly as if he'd been drenched with cold water. He'd been admiring a girl with blue eyes and wheat-colored hair—seeking one utterly unlike the sloe-eyed, golden-skinned Mariam, who was half Saracen—when the bawd casually mentioned that Ludmila was new, having been bought from slave traders just that past summer.

Morgan had been taken aback by the slave markets in Sicily, Cyprus, and the Holy Land, for slavery was no longer known in the domains of the Angevin kings. But those slaves had all been Saracens, infidels. This girl would have looked at home in any European city. The bawd, puzzled by his questions, told him that Ludmila came from Dalmatia, as did most of Ragusa's slaves, and conceded that she was Christian, although she added dismissively that Dalmatians followed the Greek Orthodox Church, not the Church of Rome, and so their faith was suspect. Not to Morgan, though, who was shocked that the Ragusans

would be willing to enslave their fellow Christians, and he politely declined
Ludmila's services, feeling he'd be somehow complicit in her enslavement if he
did not.

The bawd was surprised and then scornful, although she tried to hide it. His
companions' astonishment quickly turned to amusement, and Morgan knew
he'd be enduring their mockery for weeks to come. But his easygoing demeanor
masked a strong will, and he remained adamant. He'd wait in the tavern whilst
they went abovestairs, he declared, deflecting their ridicule with a sardonic gibe,
saying he was sure he'd not have to wait long. They laughed, offered a few more
playful insults, and began to pick their bedmates from the assembled women. It
was then that Arne amazed them all by announcing that he did not feel right
about swiving a slave, either, and he would wait with Morgan.

Even Morgan was startled, although he welcomed an ally and defended
Arne's decision until the others lost interest and let their whores take them
abovestairs.

Back in the tavern common room, Morgan ordered wine and found a corner
table for them. They drank in silence for a time, but he sensed Arne had something on his mind and after several cups of surprisingly good wine, the boy had
quaffed enough liquid courage to make a confession.

"If I confide in you, Sir Morgan, will you promise not to tell the others?"

"If that is your wish, Arne. Does this secret of yours have something to do
with your refusal to go abovestairs with one of the whores?" Arne was regarding
him as if he had second sight, but he'd suspected there was more to the boy's
reluctance than an aversion to slavery; he was still young enough to remember
how powerful hungers of the flesh could be for a lad of Arne's age.

Arne nodded, then ducked his head to stare intently into his wine cup. "I
have been lying, Sir Morgan, lying to the king, to you all," he confessed, flushing
so deeply that even the tips of his ears turned red. "You think I am sixteen, but I
am not. I was born at Michaelmas in God's Year 1178."

"You are only fourteen, lad?"

Arne nodded again. "When I entered my lord's service in Austria, my uncle
told him I was fourteen. It was not so—I was twelve—but I was big for my age
and I'd be one less mouth for my uncle's family to feed. . . ."

Arne's diffidence made more sense to Morgan now; a green lad of fourteen
was more likely to be skittish his first time, and to be fearful he was committing
a mortal sin. Arne confirmed that by mumbling a rambling story he claimed
to have heard about a youth who'd been taken by his brothers to a brothel and

then shamed himself by being unable to perform. "Not only was he the laugh-ingstock of the village when the whore told his brothers that he'd spilled his seed ere he could even get into bed, but their priest heard and warned him that thinking of a sin was as bad as doing it and so he'd still go to Hell! How fair is that, Sir Morgan?"

Morgan quickly brought his wine cup up to hide a smile. This was definitely not how he'd expected his evening to go—tutoring this fledgling in the ways of carnal lust. Ordering more wine, he did his best, assuring Arne that there was no hurry, no need to rush into sin. His own body would tell him when he was ready, and whilst it was natural for a man to be somewhat nervous his first time, a naked woman did wonders to dispel any anxieties or qualms. And although the Church did indeed preach that fornication was a mortal sin, many men—King Richard amongst them—felt that it was a venial sin at worst, for certes not as serious as adultery or breaking a holy vow of chastity. Arne cheered up to hear that Richard thought fornication to be a minor matter, for he was convinced that the English king's most casual comment was to be taken as Gospel. He was fur-ther reassured when Morgan reminded him that the point of confession was to wipe a slate clean.

"Most soldiers I know admit they are sinners, find a confessor to lay light penances, and make sure that they are shriven ere they go into battle—or set foot on a ship like the *Sea-Wolf.* You could do worse than to follow in their foot-steps, Arne." Adding with a grin, "And if Warin and the others tease you about abstaining tonight, just tell them you'd heard a rumor that the Ragusan whores were poxed. That will shut them up!"

Arne laughed and was soon chattering happily as they finished a second flagon. Morgan drank his wine, listened, and marveled at the vagaries of fate—that a Welsh knight and an Austrian stripling should be sharing wine and confidences in this shabby, wharf-side tavern, far from home and all they held dear. The ways of the Almighty truly were beyond the understanding of mortal men. So many crusaders had left their homes and families for God and glory, only to find lonely graves in foreign lands. He fervently hoped it was the Al-mighty's Will that they'd be luckier than the thousands who'd been stricken by pestilence, struck down by Saracen swords. He was convinced that Richard had God's favor. How else explain why he was still alive, as reckless as he was with his own safety? He would get them home if any man could. But as Morgan sig-naled for another round of drinks, Wales had never seemed as far away as it did on this early December eve in Ragusa.

THE RIVALRY BETWEEN RAGUSA'S COUNT and archbishop had become even more intense now that they had a genuine prize to compete for—the favor of a king. Richard had taken a liking to Archbishop Bernard, who was enthralled by his stories of the campaign against Saladin. The portly prelate had a keen sense of humor, too, laughing heartily when Richard joked that he was remarkably bloodthirsty for a man of God. Count Raphael's company was less enjoyable, for he tended to be pompous and long-winded. It was politic to keep his goodwill, though, so Richard did his best to divide his time between the two men, although he complained to his friends, only half in jest, that he'd begun to feel like a bone caught between two hungry dogs. The tension would ignite at a lavish feast given in Richard's honor on his last day in Ragusa. But when it happened, Archbishop Bernard and Count Raphael would be unlikely allies, united against the abbot of the Benedictine monastery on La Croma.

Richard was seated on the dais with the count, archbishop, members of the city's great council, and their wives. He'd insisted that Abbot Stephanus be seated at the high table, too, while his own men were scattered at the lower tables, all enjoying the rich fare, so different from the rations they could expect once they were back at sea. They were savoring the latest dish—roast swan—when raised voices attracted their attention. The count was on his feet, red-faced, pointing an accusing finger at the black-robed abbot. The latter pushed his chair back and rose, too, apparently giving as good as he got. Morgan and Warin did not have enough Latin to follow the argument, but they watched with interest as the abbey's prior and monks moved from their lesser seats to join the abbot, like soldiers rallying around their commander, for theirs was the stoic demeanor of men knowing they faced overwhelming odds but determined to resist, nonetheless.

By now the quarrel had reached the stage where all were clamoring loudly and no one was listening. Richard was leaning back in his chair, arms folded, looking bored, which Morgan and Warin knew meant that he was fast losing patience. They grinned and nudged each other when he finally stood and shouted for silence. Once the hall quieted and he was sure he held center stage, he began to speak, at one point rebuking the count as he tried to interrupt. By the time he was done, men had begun to exchange glances, reluctantly nodding their heads. The archbishop now acted as peacemaker, moving forward and holding out his hand to the abbot. This earned him a resentful look from Count

Raphael, but after his wife leaned over and whispered in his ear, he joined the other two men, and the hall erupted in relieved applause.

Richard's knights could only speculate among themselves as to the reason for the uproar, but their curiosity was not satisfied until the conclusion of the meal. As the trestle tables were taken down and musicians entered the hall, Richard sauntered over and explained what they'd witnessed but not understood.

"The highborn citizens of Ragusa were not happy that Abbot Stephanus and his monks were to receive such a windfall. They argued that so large a sum of money was best spent on rebuilding their cathedral, not 'wasted' on a church that none but monks would see. The abbot balked, insisting it was clearly God's Will that the church be built on La Croma, since that is where we came ashore."

"You seem to have resolved the dispute, sire," Morgan pointed out, "for they are no longer hurling insults at one another. How did you do it?"

"I told them that I was willing for the money to be spent on renovating the cathedral, but only on two conditions. First, the Pope must consent to the change, for it was a holy vow, after all. Second, some of the funds must be used to rebuild the abbey church. And as a sweetener for the abbey, I suggested that the abbots of La Croma be allowed to say Mass in St Mary's Cathedral every year at Candlemas to honor this generous concession."

Richard's mouth curved in a faint smile. "The best way to tell if a compromise is fair is if both sides are dissatisfied with it. In this case, there was some disappointment, but they could see the justice in my proposal, for they'd all benefit by it, too. It helped, of course, that the Ragusans are reasonable men. In other words, not French."

They laughed, even though they knew there was no humor in that joke; Richard would never forgive his French allies for doing all they could to sabotage the crusade. Warin seized this opening to advance a supposition of his own.

"I've been thinking, my lord," he began, jabbing Hugh de Neville in the ribs when he pretended to reel back in shock. "I know we've been worrying about the lies that the Bishop of Beauvais has been spreading about you on his way back to France—that you were conspiring with the Saracens and never wanted to retake Jerusalem, nonsense like that. But the Cypriot pirates and the citizens of Ragusa did not believe it, for they'd heard the truth from soldiers returning home. Is it not possible that the truth will prevail over the slanders even in Germany and France?"

Richard was surprised by the other man's naïveté. "Philippe already knows the truth about what happened in Outremer, but that will not stop him from trying to brand me as a traitor to the Christian faith. As for Heinrich, he is as indifferent to truth as he is to honor. But if it is true that a man is judged by the enemies he's made, I must be doing something right."

They laughed again and their last evening in Ragusa ended on a grace note, all grateful for this brief respite from the harsh reality that awaited them on the morrow, when they left the city's sheltered harbor for the open sea.

AFTER TAKING THE SEA-WOLF for a trial run, Georgios had concluded it was still not seaworthy, and so he took command of the Sea-Serpent, leaving some of his crew behind to recaulk the Sea-Wolf's hull. Most of Ragusa's citizens turned out to bid Richard farewell, cheering as the pirate galley unfurled its sails and raised its anchors. Richard waved from the stern, laughing and promising to come back to hear Mass in their splendid new cathedral. But he felt a chill when a cloud suddenly blotted out the sun, casting shadows onto the deck of the Sea-Serpent, for he sensed that it would be a long time before he saw such friendly faces again.

They were heading for the Hungarian port city of Zadar, about 175 miles up the coast, and Georgios said complacently that it ought to be an easy voyage, for a galley could cover a hundred miles a day if the winds were right. The more superstitious among Richard's men thought that he'd jinxed them by such arrogance, for once they left Ragusa behind, the wind became fitful and they were soon becalmed. They were forced to drop anchor and await favorable winds. Instead, they awoke the next morning to find themselves shrouded in thick, smothering fog. It was unsettling and eerie, for all sounds were oddly muffled and they felt like blind men, trapped in a wet white cloud. The fog did not disperse until the third day, and they felt a surge of relief as the Sea-Serpent got under way. Once they reached Zadar, they would not have to set foot on an accursed ship again, at least not until they had to cross the Narrow Sea that lay between England and France.

Richard had not decided if he ought to identify himself openly in Zadar and seek a safe conduct from King Bela. Their passage through Hungary would be much easier with Bela's official blessing. If only he could be sure that Bela's queen would not seek to poison her husband's mind against him. Marguerite was not likely to think well of him. His brother Hal's widow, she was also

Philippe's half sister and a full sister to the Lady Alys. He hadn't thought of Alys in a great while. They'd been betrothed in childhood and she'd grown up at his father's court. She was pretty enough, but as tame as a caged songbird, lacking spirit or fire, or any of the qualities that might have caught his interest. Conventional women had always bored him. He supposed his wife could be considered conventional, too, for the Spanish raised their women to be deferential and biddable. For certes, Berenguela had a strong sense of duty and she was almost too pious at times. But she would be loyal to him till her last mortal breath and there was steel in her spine. She had shown her courage time and time again during their voyage to the Holy Land and in the months that followed, and there was nothing he admired more than courage. He'd not have traded Berenguela for Alys even if that meant he'd have been welcomed at the Hungarian court like Bela's long-lost brother.

Georgios guessed they were less than a hundred miles from Zadar now, raising their spirits. But the dawn sky the next morning was redder than blood and by midday clouds were gathering along the western horizon. The *Sea-Serpent* was soon wallowing in heavy swells and, sure that another storm was brewing, the pirate chieftain cut a roll of parchment into strips, had Richard's chaplain ink in the names of saints, and shook them into his cap. The crew and passengers each chose one and promised to say a Mass for that saint when they safely reached shore. Georgios had exempted Richard from the drawing, saying with a glimmer of mischief that the king had already paid his dues, since one hundred thousand ducats could buy a lifetime of Masses. He then ceremoniously cast the saints' names into the sea and they all breathed easier, at least for a while.

The storm that hit hours later was not as savage as the one that had stranded them on La Croma, but it proved to be longer-lasting. For three days, the *Sea-Serpent* was battered by the waves and wind, pelted with sleet. The men slept little, ate less, gulped syrup of ginger to calm their heaving stomachs, and prayed—not just to the saints they'd drawn, but to every saint they could remember. The wind was cold and fierce and Spyro, the helmsman, told them it was a bora, which swept down from the inland mountains and wreaked havoc during the winter months. Shivering in their wet clothes, Richard's knights crouched miserably in the tent and longed for Zadar the way they'd been told infidels yearned for Mecca.

They'd been driven far out to sea by the bora, had not seen land for two days. When Richard demanded to know how much farther to Zadar, Georgios reluctantly admitted that the port was lost, far behind them. Unnerved by the English king's volcanic outburst, which put him in mind of Sicily's Mountain of Fire, he assured Richard that there was another Hungarian port at Pula and they could put in there once the winds decreased and Spyro could use his navigational aid, a magnetized needle stuck in a sliver of cork that, when floated in a bucket of water, always pointed north. Sailors relied upon the stars and landmarks to chart their course, he reminded Richard, neither of which were now available to Spyro. As soon as the weather cleared, they would land at Pula or they could sail back to Zadar if that was the king's wish. He sounded very matter-of-fact and confident, but he had no answer when Richard asked what would happen if the storm did not slacken soon.

On the third day, they finally glimpsed land, only it was on the larboard side of the galley. As they realized they were gazing at the Italian coast, the men were shocked that they'd been swept so far off course. That distant shoreline soon disappeared and once more they could see nothing but sea and sky. Georgios promised again that they would head for a Hungarian port after they escaped the bora's accursed clutches. He made the wind sound like a malevolent entity, capable of malice, and few of Richard's men would argue with him at that point.

When the storm was finally over, the men on the *Sea-Serpent*, passengers and crew alike, were too exhausted to rejoice; the most they could muster was numbed relief. Spyro consulted the sailing needle and adjusted the ship's course. But they did not have long to savor their reprieve, for a few hours later, calamity struck. The first indication Richard had that something had gone very wrong was a sudden shout, followed by a burst of profanity; even though he spoke no Greek, there was no mistaking the tone. Hastening out on deck, he found the pirates clustered around the tiller, all talking at once in an obvious panic.

"Petros! What has happened?"

The young sailor usually thrived on danger and chaos. Now, though, he just looked scared. "God help us, lord, for we've lost the rudder! It is not responding to the tiller!"

Petros went on to say that it must have been damaged by the constant pounding of the waves, or else it had become entangled in seaweed or a fishing net. Richard was no longer listening, for an alarming image was flashing before his eyes—a crippled Saracen ship, floundering helplessly after some of his sailors had dived into the water and tied ropes around its rudder, disabling it so their galleys could attack. Without its rudder, a ship was unable to steer, at the mercy of the waves and wind.

FOR ANOTHER DAY, the *Sea-Serpent* was carried along by the current, the men aboard praying, for there was not much else they could do. But the next morning Spyro woke them by yelling for Georgios, and Petros told them that there was land ahead, explaining that the changing color of the sea meant a river estuary. They clung to the gunwale, staring intently at the horizon, cheering when they heard the distant echoes of the surf. At last the shoreline came into view, greenish grey under an overcast, dull sky. The pirates were manning the oars again. As soon as they reached the shallows, they plunged into the water to beach the galley. The ground was marshy and they sank into it almost to the tops of their boots, but even a quagmire seemed like Eden to them after their ordeal on the *Sea-Serpent*.

The pirates were positioning the anchors to keep the galley from being caught in the next high tide and cursing among themselves as they confirmed that the rudder had indeed broken off. The wind had a bite and the men began to shiver. A silence fell as they looked around at the most barren, bleak landscape any had ever seen. No trees. No vegetation, just salty marsh grass. No sounds but the surging of the surf, not even the cries of seabirds. No signs of life.

Richard spoke for them all when he said at last, "Where in God's holy name are we?"

CHAPTER THREE

❧

They'd had to trudge several miles inland to find solid ground and fuel. By then, it was dark and once they got several fires going, the men rolled into their blankets and slept, too exhausted for hunger. The next morning, they were heartened by fleeting glimpses of the sun, the first time in days that the sky had not been smothered in storm clouds. After consulting with the *Sea-Serpent*'s helmsman and studying their best map, Richard sent several men in search of civilization, and then they settled down to wait.

Richard was seated cross-legged on the ground, staring intently at the map as if it would provide the answers he needed if only he studied it long enough. He glanced up briefly as Warin and Morgan joined him, then resumed his scrutiny of the map. Warin leaned closer to see. "Are you sure Spyro is right about where we are, my lord?"

Richard's shoulders twitched in a shrug. "He claims his sailing needle always points to the north, and so he concluded we've come ashore somewhere between Venice and Aquileia."

They both peered over his shoulder at the map. They already knew the route they would be taking—east toward Hungary. Assuming they could find horses to buy. Assuming they did not run into any enemy patrols, for they were in hostile territory now. Unlike Ragusa, the writ of the Holy Roman Emperor ran here. To keep from dwelling on these troubling thoughts, Morgan asked, "Do you know what the pirates intend, sire?"

"Petros says they will replace the rudder and patch up the *Sea-Serpent* as best they can, then hug the coast to Venice, where they'll get her recaulked and re-pair the sails. They are not willing to brave the winter storms by taking her out into the open sea, so they'll likely pass the next few months whoring and drinking in some safe harbor port." Richard gave them a quick smile that never reached his eyes. "So if any of you want to turn pirate, I'll understand."

"The whoring and drinking sound tempting, I admit," Morgan agreed, striv-ing to match his cousin's bantering tone. "But I'd sooner take holy vows ere I set foot on shipboard again."

Warin could never resist a game of one-upmanship and started to say he'd drink goat's piss ere he'd sail again, but he'd lost his audience. Richard was get-ting to his feet as Petros and Georgios approached.

Petros kept his eyes averted and his head down, putting Richard on the alert. "Lord . . . Georgios thinks you ought to pay more than the two hundred marks. He says he did not expect that both of his ships would be damaged on this voyage."

"Well, I did not expect to be set ashore in a Godforsaken bog," Richard coun-tered coolly. "Does this look like Zadar to him?"

When Petros translated the English king's reply, the pirate chieftain scowled. He started to argue, but Richard's expression was unyielding and, instead, he turned on his heel and stalked off. With an apologetic glance over his shoulder, Petros followed.

Once they were out of earshot, Richard confided, "I do not really blame him for this," waving his arm to take in their desolate surroundings. "How many pirates can part the seas like Moses, after all? He did the best he could, and I decided at Ragusa that he'd earned extra recompense."

Warin and Morgan shared a puzzled look. "Then why did you refuse him, sire?"

"Because he demanded it of me, Morgan. Had I agreed, he'd have seen it as a sign of weakness. Now when he does get it, he'll appreciate it all the more."

Morgan nodded, amused that Richard sounded somewhat impatient, as if he were belaboring the obvious. He'd learned that those who had this special gift—the mastery of other men—seldom realized how rare a gift it was. He'd seen it in Richard's father and brother Geoffrey. For certes, not in his brothers Hal or John. A king who lacked it was a king doomed to failure, like England's King Stephen, who'd been courageous on the battlefield and charming in the great hall, but whose reign had been known as "the anarchy," a time "when Christ and his Saints slept."

A sudden shout from one of their sentries turned their attention toward the road that wound through the woods toward the west. When these riders were identified as their own, they felt a surge of hope, for they'd not expected their men to return so soon—or mounted.

Richard had chosen Anselm and Arne for their skills in Latin and German, sending along Guillain de l'Etang and two of the Templars as protection. They were mobbed as soon as they dismounted, pelted with questions about what they'd found and jokes about their horses, none of which was a worthy mount for a knight, much less a king. Richard finally silenced them and signaled for Anselm to speak.

The chaplain was a young man, well liked by the others, for he was cheerful, good-hearted, and more forgiving of the foibles of mortal men than many priests, too much in awe of Richard to lay heavy penances for royal sins. He looked understandably pleased with the success of their mission, but Richard knew him well enough to detect the unease behind his smile, and he was bracing for the bad even as Anselm delivered the good.

"There is a village called Latisana not far from here, sire. At first we were at a loss, for their priest did not know enough Latin to converse with me, and all the townspeople we met spoke some sort of Italian dialect. But we eventually found a blacksmith who understood German, and he directed Arne to a man with horses to sell. We bought all he had, even that one," he said, gesturing toward a wall-eyed, sway-backed gelding. "I thought we could use him for a packhorse. The horse trader told us that we could buy more horses in the town of Görz, east of Latisana."

Arne could keep silent no longer, for he'd greatly enjoyed his first stint as translator. "The people were friendly, my lord, once they learned we were pilgrims on our way home from the Holy Land. They have a hodgepodge of languages here, like in Ragusa—Italian and Slavic dialects. But many of them speak German, too, and I'll be able to interpret for you in Görz, for their lord's name is a German one—Engelbert."

Richard's eyes flicked from the boy to Anselm. "Tell me about this Lord Engelbert," he said, already sure he would not like what he was about to hear.

"He is the Count of Görz, sire, sharing power with his brother, Meinhard. His lord father died last year, so he's not been ruling all that long. But from what we could glean in Latisana, he seems well regarded by the people. He is a vassal of the Holy Roman Emperor, of course. . . ."

"And?" Richard prompted, his voice sharp, and Anselm confirmed his suspicions by giving him an unhappy look.

"He is also the nephew of Conrad of Montferrat, sire," he said reluctantly, and in the dismayed silence that followed, his words seemed to echo ominously on the chill December air. Conrad, an Italian-German lord and adventurer, had been slain by members of the feared Saracen cult known as the Assassins, just days after he'd been chosen as the next King of Jerusalem, and the Bishop of Beauvais and the Duke of Burgundy had sought to put the blame upon Richard, accusing him of procuring Conrad's murder. Richard had been contemptuous of the charge, insisting that no one who knew him would heed such a slander. But would Conrad's kinsman believe it?

PETROS WAS VERY PLEASED with his bonus. He'd claimed he meant to return to Messina in the spring, but Richard suspected that he was tempted to try his hand at piracy and, after thanking the youth for his services, he said, only half in jest, "Go back to Sicily, lad. You'll be less likely to get yourself hanged there."

He moved then toward Georgios. He'd already paid the pirate chieftain the agreed-upon two hundred marks, but now he flipped a leather pouch into the air. "It is probably less than you want and more than you deserve," he said dryly, "but it ought to cover the cost of repairing the *Sea-Wolf* and *Sea-Serpent*. Share some with Spyro, for he earned every denier with that landing on La Croma."

Pride kept Georgios from opening the pouch then and there, but he was reassured by the heft of it, and grinned. "No regrets. I'll never have to buy another drink again, not with the stories I'll have to tell about my voyage with the king called Lionheart."

He and Petros were soon joined by Spyro and they stood watching as Richard and his men headed east, toward Görz. Arne looked back once and waved, and then the road curved into the trees and they disappeared from view. Spyro started to turn away, muttering under his breath, "God help them."

Petros heard and frowned. "He'll make it," he insisted. "Fortune smiles on him."

Georgios was counting the coins in the pouch, but he glanced up at that. "He'll need more than luck," he said, and this time Petros did not argue.

☙

THE CASTLE AT GÖRZ dominated the valley, situated on a hill overlooking the town, the pale winter sky behind it stabbed by snow-crowned alpine peaks. Ringed by thick stone walls and deep ditches, it looked as if it could withstand a siege until Judgment Day, not a reassuring sight to the men standing in the street below. Morgan was the first to speak. "Let's just hope we do not get to take a tour of its dungeons," he said, and started up the path, followed by Anselm and Arne.

They gained admittance without difficulty, but Count Engelbert was holding court in the great hall, hearing petitions and complaints and resolving local disputes, so it was not until late afternoon that they were ushered into his presence. He was seated at a trestle table with a scribe perched on a stool nearby, his writing utensils spread out on a small lap desk. The count was younger than they'd expected, under thirty. If not for the high-quality wool tunic, the fur-trimmed mantle, and the garnet ring on his finger, he'd have attracted no attention, for he was thin of face and stoop-shouldered, his hair a nondescript shade of brown. But his gaze was direct, even piercing, dark eyes revealing both intelligence and the suspicion of strangers that was so common in their world, for most people never strayed far from the places where they were born.

"So . . . you are pilgrims on your way home from the Holy Land." Either his command of Latin was limited or he preferred to converse in his own tongue, for he addressed himself to the one German-speaking member of their party. "Who are you?"

Suddenly nervous, Arne hesitated, but after getting encouraging smiles from Anselm and Morgan, he took a step closer to the table. "We are led by the Flemish lord Baldwin de Bethune, and our master, Hugh, who is a merchant in fine silks back in his homeland." The words of his rehearsed story were coming more easily now. "We are traveling, too, with some Templar knights. They ask, my lord count, that you issue a safe conduct allowing them to pass through your domains, in the name of Our Lord Jesus Christ, for whom they fought."

The count's face could have been carved from the same stones as his castle for all the emotion he showed; they had no idea what he was thinking. "Did you get to see Jerusalem?" he asked after an uncomfortably long pause. When Arne said they had, he nodded, almost imperceptibly. "So you visited the Holy Sepulchre?"

Getting another confirmation from Arne, he reached for the silver wine cup at his elbow and took a sip. "And did you stop in Ragusa?"

Arne gaped at him. "No, lord! We put in for supplies in a town called Pula." He added hastily that they'd been heading for Trieste, but had been blown off course by the contrary bora winds.

This was met with another silence, and he glanced imploringly toward his companions. Although they'd been unable to follow the conversation, Anselm and Morgan sensed that it was not going well. Deciding it was time to reveal to the count just how much his cooperation would be worth, the chaplain reached for his scrip and passed its contents to Arne. The boy squeezed it tightly for luck and then set it on the table with a flourish, thrilled to be able to hold something so valuable, however briefly.

As it reflected the torchlight, the ring seemed to catch fire, its massive ruby glowing in a setting of beaten gold. "This is a gift from my master, the merchant Hugh," Arne declared proudly, "to show our appreciation for your goodwill and hospitality, my lord count."

The count's eyes had widened at first sight of the ring. He did not pick it up, though, and instead turned and abruptly dismissed his scribe. Leaning back then in his chair, he regarded them pensively. "Your master's name is not Hugh," he said at last. "You serve the English king."

Arne gasped, too stunned to respond. But Morgan had a good ear for languages and he'd picked up a little German from the boy during their months together. Recognizing the words *"englische"* and *"könig,"* he found it all too easy to interpret the horrified expression on Arne's face, and he began to laugh loudly. His companions were quick to comprehend and Arne and Anselm hastily forced laughter, too. "Tell the count," Morgan directed the boy, "that our master will be greatly flattered that he could have been mistaken for a king. But we can assure Count Engelbert that he is a mercer and pilgrim, no more than that."

When Engelbert reached for the ring, they held their breaths. He inspected it without haste, running his thumb over the flaming jewel, the intricate gold leaf design done so lovingly by a Pisan goldsmith. And then he slid it back across the table toward them.

"I cannot accept this. Tell the king of the English that I respect his vow and his struggle to free the Holy Land from the infidel Saracens. But tell him this, too—that he is in grave peril and must leave Görz at once, for I cannot guarantee his safety should word get out of his presence here. The Emperor Heinrich will richly reward any man who delivers your king into his hands."

AFTER FINDING AN INN, Richard and his men had eaten their first hot meal in over a week. He'd then sent Arne and Baldwin to buy horses, and they'd delighted Görz's horse traders by buying the best animals the town had to offer. Arne was then dispatched with Anselm and Morgan to seek safe conducts from the count, and while he awaited their return, Richard went to the stable to inspect Baldwin's purchases. They were not as bad as he'd feared, although he soon concluded that Baldwin had been overcharged. When the other man glumly admitted as much, Richard found a smile, assuring Baldwin that paying too much for horses in Görz was not likely to cost him any sleep.

"Sleep." The word had taken on the sweetness of honey, for none of them had gotten a full night's rest since leaving Ragusa. They were alone in the stable, the grooms having gone off for their evening meal, and so they could at last talk freely, having remained mute for most of the day, not wanting to draw attention to themselves by speaking French. Stooping to examine a roan gelding's foreleg, Richard straightened up with an effort, feeling as if he'd aged twenty years overnight.

"I never paid beds much mind unless one had a woman in it," he admitted to Baldwin, "but right now the pallets back in that filthy, flea-ridden inn are looking better to me than the royal palace at Acre."

Baldwin nodded, and pointed toward the shadows where one of the Templars had dozed off while still standing. "We'd best have the innkeeper awaken us in the morn, or else we might well sleep past Christmas. How long dare we stay?"

"That will depend upon how successful Morgan and Anselm are. If they cannot get in to see the count or if he balks at giving safe conducts, we'll have to leave at first light. But if that ring buys his goodwill, I think we can risk a day or two here. God knows we all need a chance to rest up—"

Richard checked himself, having heard footsteps in the front of the stable. Baldwin tensed, too, and reached over to awaken the Templar, who was instantly alert, his a soldier's reflexes. The king's admiral, Robert de Turnham, and Guillain de l'Etang were hurrying toward their stall, their faces taut and troubled, and behind them, Richard caught a glimpse of Anselm and Morgan, trailed by Arne, whose puppylike energy seemed suddenly sapped. It was obvious that Robert and Guillain already knew what had transpired at the castle, but they both stepped aside once they reached Richard, deferring to his chaplain and cousin, and he realized that he was about to receive yet more bad news.

"Are we alone?" Anselm asked in Latin, catching himself from adding "my liege," for it was not easy to stop using the acknowledgments of rank. "Can we talk here?"

When Richard nodded, Anselm and Morgan exchanged glances and then the Welshman said bluntly, "Count Engelbert . . . He knows who you are. When we presented him with the ring, he said . . ." Morgan paused for breath and to recall the count's words precisely. "He said, 'Your master's name is not Hugh. You serve the English king.'"

"Christ Jesus," Richard said, very softly. "How could he . . ." He stopped then, for that did not matter. "How did you get away?"

"Did you lead them back here?" Baldwin's tone was accusing, and both Morgan and Anselm bridled.

"No!" they said in unison, speaking at once and drowning each other out as they tried to explain. Richard held up a hand for silence, pointing then at Morgan to continue. "He did not arrest us. He would not even accept the ring. He said that he respected your vow and what you'd done against Saladin."

Richard considered this, for once doubting his fabled luck. Could he really have found an honorable man midst Heinrich's lackeys and lickspittles? "And he said nothing about Conrad?"

Morgan shook his head and Anselm confirmed it. "Nary a word, sire."

"He did mention Ragusa, lord," Arne interjected, "asking if we'd stopped there. I said no, of course."

"But he warned us that we must leave Görz straightaway," Morgan said bleakly. "He said you were in great danger, that Heinrich has cast a wide net and men will be on the lookout for you everywhere since you could be anywhere."

Richard was silent for a moment, weighing his rapidly dwindling options. He could not remember ever being so tired or so disheartened. Turning toward the Templar, he told him to fetch the men who'd gone to a tavern across the street from the stable, and sent Arne back to the inn to gather up their belongings. And then he gave the command his aching body and weary brain dreaded, the command they *all* dreaded, saying grimly, "Saddle up."

❧

METHILDIS OF ANDECHS, former Countess of Pisino and current Countess of Görz, was not happy with her husband. He'd been tossing and turning for hours, making it impossible for her to sleep. It was like sharing a bed with a river eel, and when he rolled over again, this time jabbing her in the ribs with an elbow, she'd had enough.

Sitting up in bed, she shook his shoulder. "You may as well tell me what is troubling you, Engelbert. Neither of us will be getting any sleep this night unless you do."

He sat up, too, running his hand through his tousled hair. "As you wish, my dear," he agreed, so readily that she felt a suspicion spark, wondering if he'd deliberately awakened her so they could talk; usually she had to coax him into unburdening himself. He surprised her greatly by what he did next, calling out sharply to his sleeping squire, ordering the befuddled boy to fetch a flagon of wine from the buttery. He was usually an indulgent master, sometimes too indulgent in his wife's opinion, and the squire was obviously shocked to be torn from sleep and sent off on an errand in the middle of the night. Shivering, he dressed with haste, clutching his mantle tightly as he stumbled toward the door. As soon as they were alone, Engelbert jerked the linen hangings back, allowing the blackness of their cocooned bed to be diluted by the white-gold flames in the hearth.

By now, Methildis was feeling stirrings of alarm. "Engelbert, what is it?" she asked, all her earlier vexation gone from her voice. "What is wrong?" She wasn't sure what she was expecting. They'd been married for two years, time enough for her to learn he was a worrier by nature, given to conscience pangs and prone to second-guessing himself. But his next words took her breath away.

"The English king is in Görz."

"What . . . here? Are you sure?"

There was enough light now to see him nod his head. "He sent three of his men to me today, asking for safe conducts. They gave a false name, of course, claimed he was a merchant, traveling with other pilgrims on their way home from the Holy Land. I knew, though, that they lied."

Methildis was wide-awake now, and enthralled, already envisioning the imperial favor they'd be enjoying for capturing the emperor's hated foe. "How did you know, Engelbert? What made you even suspect them?"

"Two days ago a man came to me, someone who'd brought me useful bits of information in the past. He said he'd met a sailor in a dockside tavern in Aquileia, whose ship had arrived from Ragusa that past week. The sailor claimed that the English king was in Ragusa, being acclaimed by the count and townspeople as the savior of the Holy Land, and planning to build a great cathedral in their city. That seemed an unlikely story to me and I dismissed it as drunken tavern ramblings. But then these men came seeking safe conducts, and they were so obviously ill at ease that I remembered the Ragusa tale. When I mentioned Ragusa to the stripling who spoke German, he went whiter than a corpse-candle. I still had only suspicions, of course . . . until they gave me a ring as a token of their master's goodwill—the most magnificent ruby I've ever seen."

"Really?" Methildis breathed, for she dearly loved jewelry. As eager as she was to see it, though, that could wait. "I do not understand, Engelbert. Why did that confirm your suspicions?"

He smiled thinly. "Because no merchant, however wealthy, would ever have given up something of such value. That was a grand gesture only a king would make, a king accustomed to spending lavishly and bestowing largesse without counting the cost."

That made sense to Methildis. "What happened then? Did they try to deny it?" She doubted the English king was already in custody, for surely he'd have told her, told them all, if that were so. It was hard not to berate him for keeping this secret from her, but she swallowed her reproaches and asked instead if he'd forced them to reveal Richard's whereabouts. Even if they were still balking, they'd not be able to hold out for long. Her brother had once told her that there were ways of making the bravest man talk, and with so much at stake, Engelbert could not afford to be squeamish.

Her husband did not reply, though, instead giving her an odd look, one she could not interpret, and she had a sudden sense of unease. "Engelbert? What are you not telling me? Richard did not escape, did he?"

"No," he said, and she heaved a sigh of relief, until he added, "I let him go."

"You did *what*?"

She sounded so incredulous, so horrified, that color rose in his face. "I let him go," he repeated, this time sounding both defensive and defiant. "It was the right thing to do, Methildis. He'd taken the cross, was under the Church's protection. Nor had he done anything to deserve being detained. No state of war exists between England and the empire."

Methildis was so dumbfounded that she could only blurt out the first objection to come to mind. "How can you say he does not deserve to be detained? What about your uncle's murder?"

His mouth twisted down scornfully. "You did not truly believe that, did you? If there is any man in Christendom who'd do his own killing, for certes it is Richard of England. Conrad counted a day misspent if he did not make at least one new enemy, so he finally reaped what he'd sown."

Methildis opened her mouth, shut it again. She'd erred by mentioning Conrad. She should have known better, for he'd abandoned his first wife, Engelbert's aunt, when the opportunity presented itself to wed the sister of the Emperor of the Greeks in Constantinople. "Do you not realize what you've done, Engelbert? You've defied the Emperor Heinrich!"

"I had no other choice! The Holy Church's position on this could not be clearer. Men who take the cross to fight the infidels are not to be harmed. Suppose I attempted to seize him, he resisted—as, of course, he would—and he was slain? I could be excommunicated by the Pope, could face eternal damnation!"

"By the current Pope? That timid old man? He'd never dare to challenge Heinrich!"

"He might not have the courage to excommunicate Heinrich, I grant you that. But me? I'd make the perfect sacrificial goat. And I am not about to jeopardize my immortal soul just to keep Heinrich happy!"

"I cannot believe you truly think it is more dangerous to offend the Pope than Heinrich! You could not be that blind, that foolish!"

"I am done talking about this," he warned. "I followed the dictates of my conscience and no man can do better than that. I'll say no more on it—and hear no more on it from you. Is that clear?"

Methildis had a much more combustible temper than her husband; it kindled quickly and burned itself out just as quickly. Engelbert's rare flare-ups of fury were quite different, difficult to ignite and difficult to extinguish. She saw now that she'd poked and prodded a cold hearth until the ashes and embers caught fire, for she recognized that obdurate expression on his face. She'd learned that she could only wait for his anger to cool on its own. But time was the one luxury she did not have; every hour that passed would take the English king farther from Görz. She was a proud woman, the daughter of a count and the sister of a duke, and she'd never been one to play the role of a docile, biddable wife. With so much at stake, though, she had no choice.

Reaching out, she put her hand on his arm. "I ask your pardon, my lord husband. I was indeed in the wrong to speak to you so shrilly. Will you forgive me?"

He half turned toward her, and she could see surprise on his face, but suspicion, too. "You are not usually so quick to make amends," he said, sounding skeptical. He did not pull away from her touch, though, and she took encouragement from that. He was not as confident as he'd have her believe; if he was not harboring doubts, why had he been unable to sleep?

"I know," she conceded. "I can be a shrew, I admit it. But this is different,

Engelbert. We must face this danger together, united against it. I truly do understand why you acted as you did," she lied. "You are a far more honorable man than Heinrich. If you are unwilling to discuss this further, I will abide by your wishes—just as I will support whatever decision you make, as your wife and your countess. I entreat you, though, to answer two questions, just two. After that, I promise to hold my peace."

He drew back into the deeper shadows cast by the bed hangings and she could no longer see his face. "Very well," he said, after an endless silence that had her digging her nails into her palm. "Ask your questions."

"Thank you," she said, thinking that he'd owe her a huge debt for making her humble herself like this—mayhap that splendid ruby ring he'd been given; she loved rubies. "My first question is this: Do you think the English king will be able to escape capture, to make his way to safety in Hungary or Saxony?"

"No," he said, after another interminably long pause. "No, I do not."

"Nor do I," she agreed quickly. "And when he is taken prisoner, what do you think will happen then?"

"How would I know that?"

You know, she thought, *you are just loath to admit it.* She carefully kept any anger or resentment from her voice, though. "Once he is in the emperor's power, it will all come out. How you could have seized him in Görz and did not. When Heinrich learns that you let him go, do you think he will forgive you for that?" That was three questions, but she was sure he was no longer counting, for that third question went to the heart of the matter, was likely the one that had been robbing him of sleep.

He was quiet for so long that she feared he would try to avoid answering. But he finally said, very low, "No, I know he will not."

Methildis shut her eyes in a silent prayer of thankfulness that he'd regained his senses. "You followed your conscience and gave the English king a chance to escape. But now you must protect yourself, Engelbert. You did your duty as a Christian. Now you must do it as the emperor's liegeman. On the morrow you must send word to your brother, Meinhard, that Richard of England was reportedly seen in Görz. If he is captured elsewhere, it is not your doing and not your fault. He is in God's hands, as are we all."

She held her breath then, waiting for him to argue, to protest. When he did not, she felt such relief that she sank back, exhausted, against the pillows, feeling as if she'd staved off disaster by a hairsbreadth. Reaching for his hand, she gave it a squeeze. "You will send a messenger to Meinhard?"

"I will." It was little more than a whisper, but it was enough for her. It was quiet after that, and as his breathing steadied and slowed, she could tell that he was drifting toward sleep. She'd given him this peace of mind, she thought, a way to reconcile his conflicting loyalties. She was growing drowsy, too. But then she remembered.

"Engelbert. The ruby ring . . . Where is it?"

"Wha . . ." he mumbled, yawning. "I gave it back to them. . . ." He slid easily into sleep then, never hearing his wife's quick intake of breath, as sharp as any blade.

CHAPTER FOUR

❧

After fleeing Görz, Richard and his men took shelter that night in a charcoal burner's hut. The man and his family were terrified by the sudden appearance of these armed foreigners, and not comforted by Arne's attempts at reassurance. None of them drew an easy breath until the men rode on in the morning, and then they could only marvel at their good fortune, for the knights had left a generous sum for their reluctant hospitality, more coins than they'd ever seen. Laughing and hugging one another, they vowed to pray for these mysterious strangers, beseeching Saint Christopher, who was said to protect travelers, to keep them safe as they faced the perils of the mountain roads.

❁

THE ALEHOUSE WAS SMALL and shabby, its trampled floor rushes reeking of spilt ale and mouse droppings, its dingy walls yellowed by smoke and streaked with dirt. It was very crowded, for the day had been a cold one, the leaden skies threatening snow, and Richard and his men had trouble finding seats. The food was not any better than the surroundings, but they ate it without complaint, for hunger was a good sauce and this was their first meal since they'd left Görz.

During their brief stay with the charcoal burner, they'd concluded the danger was so great that Hungary was now beyond their reach, and they'd have to head north toward Moravia, ruled by the brother of Duke Ottokar of Bohemia, where they hoped to receive a friendly welcome. On their arrival in the town of Udine, they avoided the castle, not willing to risk another safe-conduct fiasco. After arranging to stable their horses, they took rooms in a nearby inn, and then went in search of a tavern or alehouse that served meals. As they scooped up the beans and salted herring with stale bread, they tried not to remember the four-course dinner thrown for them by Archbishop Bernard and Count Raphael; it was less than a fortnight since they'd sailed from Ragusa, but already it seemed a distant part of their past.

All around them swirled familiar sounds: laughter and good-natured squabbling and shouts for more ale to the harried servingmaids, who were kept as busy fending off groping hands as they were pouring ale. They could have been back in any alehouse or tavern in their own homelands if the language had not been German, occasionally interspersed with Italian dialects. They ate in silence themselves, not wanting to attract attention by speaking French, small, gloomy islands in a cheerful, boisterous sea of ale-soaked camaraderie. Arne had just gone to find the privy when Guillain de l'Etang rose and took the seat he vacated, settling onto the bench next to Richard.

"I think we are being followed," he said, very softly. "In the corner by the ale keg, the man in the green woolen mantle and felt hat."

Richard shifted slightly so he could see Guillain's suspect. He looked to be in his forties, of average height, his brown hair and beard closely clipped, with a thin white scar creasing his forehead above thick brows and heavy-lidded dark eyes. He was well dressed, obviously a person of means, and he wore the sword at his hip like a man who'd feel naked without one. He'd been nursing an ale while regarding the other customers with studied disinterest, but when Richard glanced his way, he drew farther back into the shadows.

"I saw him first at the stables," Guillain confided, pitching his voice for Richard's ear alone. "He was entering as we were leaving. I saw him next when we were looking for an inn, loitering in the marketplace. And then he turns up here. Udine is not Paris, but it is no small village, either, and it seems odd that every time we look around, there he is."

Richard agreed with him. After a low-voiced exchange with Guillain, he waited until Arne returned and then rose without haste, dropping coins on the table for the servingmaid. Following his lead, his companions drained the last of their ales and pushed away from the bench, trying to cloak their urgency in nonchalance. Once they were out in the street, Guillain slapped a few backs as if jovially parting from friends and disappeared into an alley that overlooked the alehouse. The others broke up into smaller groups and took different routes back to their inn.

A brisk wind had sprung up as the daylight ebbed, and the inn's sign was creaking and swaying with each gust. *Der Schwarz Löwe*. The Black Lion. The beast was crudely drawn and looked grey in patches where the paint had flaked away, but it was not a sight to give them comfort, for the black lion was the emblem of the House of Hohenstaufen. The inn itself was as dilapidated as its sign, and the innkeeper had been astonished and delighted when they'd taken two rooms, for privacy was a luxury few could afford and most travelers not only shared rooms with strangers, they shared beds, too. His curiosity and his avarice aroused in equal measure, he made a pest of himself upon their return, offering wine, more candles, extra blankets, even female company if they wished, swearing he could provide them with women who were young, pretty, and free of the pox. Having been so ill-served by his merchant disguise in Görz, Richard had decided to pass as a Templar, a more plausible identity for a man whose very walk had a soldier's swagger, and Arne finally got rid of the insistent innkeeper by telling him they were all Templar knights and sergeants, sworn to vows of chastity.

The rooms were small, and with all twenty of them crammed into one chamber, there was barely space to stand, much less sit down. They waited in a tense silence, broken only by the occasional hoarse coughing of one of the crossbowmen, and it seemed like years to them before Guillain rapped twice on the door and then slid inside. The news he brought was good, though. He'd kept vigil in the alley until the bells had chimed for Vespers, but the man in the green mantle had not stirred from the alehouse. "I suppose I was seeing shadows where there were none," he conceded, with an abashed smile.

Now that they were able to relax, the men could admit how tired they all were, and the Templars and crossbowmen soon departed for their own room. Richard's companions set about spreading out their blankets, taking off their boots, mail, and weapons, but planning to sleep in their clothes. Richard sat on the edge of one of the two beds, and began to study his map again, as he did whenever the opportunity arose, tilting the candle to avoid dripping wax onto the parchment. Anselm was thumbing through his psalter, Morgan was trying to patch a hole in his boot with leather cut from his belt, and Warin was grumbling as he used his knife to remove the stitches from the hem of his mantle; the money not stuffed into their saddlebags had been sewn into their clothes, but Warin had spaced the coins too close together and discovered to his dismay that he jingled when he walked. He was still bent over the mantle, awkwardly wielding a needle as the others began to snuff out their candles, lusting after sleep as they usually lusted after women. It was then that a soft knock sounded on the door.

Richard paused in the act of removing his boots and gestured to Arne. Most of the men assumed it was the meddlesome innkeeper making one last attempt to earn a few more coins, but they still sat up on their pallets, for they were learning to be as wary as stray cats. Yawning, Arne shuffled toward the door. *"Wer ist das?"*

"A friend." Those whispered words sent a chill through the listening men, for they'd been spoken in French.

Richard reached for his sword, always close at hand, and nodded at Guillain, who drew his dagger from its sheath and took up position against the wall. Arne then slowly slid the latch back, looking as if he expected to find a demon on the other side. The hinges shrieked as he pulled the door open to reveal the man from the alehouse. As soon as he stepped into the room, he found himself caught in a choke hold, Guillain's arm pressing against his throat, his dagger poised to slide up under the man's ribs.

"I am a friend!" the man gasped. "I swear it by the Blessed Mother!"

Richard signaled for one of the candles to be brought up to light the man's face. "Who are you?" he demanded, his voice as threatening as the sword he now leveled at the intruder's chest.

His response was a gurgle, for Guillain had inadvertently tightened his hold. When he eased the pressure, the man gulped air before telling them that his name was Roger d'Argentan.

Argentan was a town in Normandy, which explained his fluent French. "Let him go," Richard directed. Guillain did, but kept his dagger ready as he stepped back. "So why are you here, Roger d'Argentan?" Richard asked coldly. "It is an odd hour to be calling on strangers."

Roger did not object when Morgan reached out and relieved him of his sword. Instead, he knelt before Richard. "It is urgent that I speak with you, my lord king."

There were a few indrawn breaths. Richard gave away nothing, staring down at the kneeling man. "Are you daft?" he jeered. "When did you ever see a king staying in a sty like this? And for Christ's sake, get up. You're making a fool of yourself."

Roger stayed on his knees. "I am the sworn man of Count Meinhard. He was told that the English king might be coming his way and he dispatched me to find you, my liege, knowing I'd seen you when I'd returned to Normandy to visit my family. It was nineteen years ago, and you were just a lad of sixteen. But you've not changed much, sire. I knew you at once."

Richard shook his head impatiently. "You're either daft," he said again, "or drunk. Do you truly think the English king would dare to venture into the lands of the Holy Roman Emperor with a handful of men? He is said to be reckless, not mad."

Taking the cue, his knights chuckled. But Roger's eyes were filling with tears. "What do I have to say to convince you? Why would I dare to come here like this if I did not want to help you? Once I recognized you, I had only to return to the castle and tell Count Meinhard. You'd have awakened to find the inn surrounded by his soldiers. Instead, I sought you out, risking all to warn you. As God is my witness, if you do not heed me, you are surely doomed!"

There was so much raw emotion in his voice that Richard hesitated; could any man be such a good actor? "You say you're Count Meinhard's sworn man. Why would you 'risk all' for the English king?"

"Count Meinhard is indeed my lord," Roger said softly, "and he has been good to me. But I am Norman born and bred and you are my duke. I could not live with myself if I betrayed you."

Richard studied the other man's face intently. "I believe you," he said at last, and Roger drew his first unconstricted breath since entering the chamber. He got stiffly to his feet as Richard asked why Meinhard thought the English king might be in Udine.

"He got a warning this morn from his brother, Count Engelbert of Görz." Catching the startled looks the other men exchanged, Roger smiled. "Engelbert let you go. I knew it as soon as I heard, for he'd have been loath to harm a man who'd taken the cross. But that wife of his must have goaded him into protecting his arse afterward."

"I take it your lord does not share Engelbert's scruples," Richard said dryly.

"Count Meinhard is a good son of the Church. But he is also a vassal of the Holy Roman Emperor." Roger paused to cough, for his throat was still tender, and he hoped the inevitable bruises would not be too conspicuous. His huge assailant no longer regarded him as a threat, though, for he'd sheathed his dagger, and now asked how he'd found their inn, saying he was sure Roger had not followed them. "I already knew where you were staying. There are not that many inns in Udine and I'd been to all of them."

"So what now?"

"I will go back to Count Meinhard and tell him the report was false. I will say I found some pilgrims returning from the Holy Land, but Richard of England was not amongst them. That will gain you a little time. I made no mention of you, my liege, when I questioned the innkeepers and stable grooms, asking only about strangers. But word is already getting out. I overheard snatches of conversation in the alehouse and your name figured in some of them. The count will likely send others out to search, too, if only to be sure I was not mistaken. I think your greatest danger at the moment is that talkative innkeeper belowstairs. He was bedazzled by your free spending and if he hears the rumors, he'll be off to the castle in the blink of an eye."

Several of the knights had begun to bristle at the implied criticism, and Richard raised a hand to silence them. "We needed the privacy, for it was the only way we could talk amongst ourselves."

Roger nodded, for the grim truth was that no matter what they did, they put themselves at risk. "I looked your horses over, and they . . . Well, how can I put it?" With another faint smile. "Let's just say I've seen better. I want you to take mine, my lord king. I fetched him from the castle ere I came here and he's below in the inn courtyard, tied to their hitching post, a roan stallion with a black mane and tail. But you must go now. Get as far from Udine as you can, as fast as you can."

The men were already pulling on their boots, buckling their scabbards. Richard sent Warin to give the bad news to their sleeping companions in the other chamber, and then turned back toward the Norman knight. "Will the count blame you for our escape?"

"He'll be sorely disappointed, but I've served him loyally for twenty years and risen high enough in his favor to be given his niece as my wife. As long as he believes mine was an honest mistake, I'll be safe enough."

Richard hoped he was right. Reaching out, he put his hand on the Norman knight's shoulder. "You are a brave man, Roger d'Argentan. I will not forget you."

Roger's sore throat tightened and he swallowed with an effort. "Go with God, my liege."

❧

THEY HAD TO HURRY, for the town gates would close once curfew rang. They decided to split into two groups in hopes of attracting less attention. Leading the first one, Richard and his companions forced themselves to hold their mounts to a walk when their every instinct was to urge their horses into a brisk gallop. The streets were quiet and few people were out, driven indoors by the cold and the approach of dark. Lights gleamed through the chinks in shutters and the men cast yearning glances toward them as they rode by, for those modest houses held treasures they valued more than gold on this bleak December night—blazing hearths and beds.

When they saw the north gate ahead, they felt an easing of tension, for Udine would soon be disappearing into the distance. It was then that the door of a tavern burst open and men spilled out into the street. They were loud and rowdy, brandishing wine flasks and lanterns and even a few crude torches. Richard and his knights drew rein, sensing trouble, and sent Arne on ahead to find out what was going on; he was soon back, blue eyes wide with dismay.

"They are hunting the English king," he said anxiously, "having heard the rumors that he may be here in Udine. They think Count Meinhard will richly reward the man who finds him, and they plan to search all the inns for strangers."

No one spoke, but the same thought was in all their minds: if not for Roger, they'd have been trapped in the Black Lion, for this drunken mob would soon have drawn men from the castle. They glanced around, but they did not know the town and they could easily lose their way in the dark maze of narrow alleys and lanes. It seemed safer to stay on the main street and bluff their way out. They rode on, hands tightening on the reins, moving their mantles for easy access to their scabbards. The crowd was blocking the street. Some started to move aside, though, accustomed to giving way to horsemen. Echoing Arne's mumbled greeting, the knights muttered a guttural *"Guten Abend,"* all the while hoping fervently that these wine-soused brains would not wonder why men would be departing the city after night had fallen.

It was to be a forlorn hope. Some of the men were already staring at them, puzzlement quickly flaring into suspicion. Made bold by their numbers, several strode into the street to bar the way, hurling questions at them like weapons, and the belligerent tone made translation unnecessary. But submitting to an interrogation was not an option. They did not draw their swords, merely spurred their horses forward, and men scattered in all directions, screaming and yelling and cursing as they sought to avoid being trampled. Richard and his knights did not slow down, nor did they glance back at the chaos they left in their wake. Men were scrambling to their feet, groping for their fallen torches and lanterns as shutters up and down the street were flung open and heads popped out to see what was amiss. The guards had emerged from the gatehouse, and they, too, had to dive aside as the riders swept past them and galloped through the gate out into the night.

They had little time to savor their escape, though. They'd not gone far before they heard a new uproar behind them. Alarmed, for they'd not expected pursuit to be organized so fast, they reined in to look back at the town, and it was only then that they realized what was happening. The rest of their group had ridden right into the maelstrom and found themselves surrounded by an angry crowd.

Richard swore and started to swing Roger's stallion around. His men stared at him, horrified, but Morgan was the one to act. "No!" he cried, spurring his own horse into Richard's path. The roan swerved and it took Richard a few moments to get him under control.

"Have you lost your mind?" he snarled. Morgan had never borne the brunt of his cousin's royal rage before, and his mouth went dry. Before he could respond, Baldwin moved his own mount to block Richard's way.

"Morgan remembered Ibn Ibrak," he said, meeting Richard's eyes unflinchingly.

There was no need to say more, for they all knew what had happened at Ibn Ibrak. Squires foraging for firewood and their Templar guards had been ambushed by Saracens. Richard had been just two miles away, and when he'd learned of the attack, he'd sent the Earl of Leicester to the rescue while he hurried to arm himself. Upon his arrival at the battle, he'd found that it had been a trap and the crusaders were surrounded by a much larger force. His men had pleaded with him to retreat, arguing that he could not save the doomed knights. He'd retorted angrily that he'd sent those men out there, promising to follow with aid, and if they died without him, he did not deserve to be called a king. He'd then spurred his stallion into the fray, rallied his men, and managed a safe withdrawal from the field. His bravura actions at Ibn Ibrak had contributed to the growing legend of the Lionheart, but the memory only instilled fear in his knights outside the walls of Udine.

Richard's jaw muscles clenched. "I saved the men at Ibn Ibrak."

"Yes, you did," Baldwin agreed. "But that is not possible now. If you go back there, you will be killed or captured. Think, sire! The Templars could have slipped away when they saw what was happening. They could even have gone back to the inn, for they'd be safe enough with you gone. Instead, they acted to draw the mob's attention onto themselves and you know why—to give you the time you need to escape. You must honor their choice, my lord. You owe them that."

Richard wanted to argue. But when Baldwin urged them on, he gave in and turned Roger's roan stallion away from Udine and followed the Fleming. Once they were sure that they were not being pursued, they slackened their pace, sparing their weary horses as best they could. The day's clouds had begun to disperse and their way was dimly lit by the emergence of the moon and a scattering of distant stars. They felt the cold more after so many months in the Holy Land and their hands and faces were soon reddened and windburned. The jagged silhouettes of the alpine peaks that rose up on either side of the road only contributed to their claustrophobic sense of being hemmed in, surrounded by dangers, enemies, and hidden perils.

Richard had not spoken for hours and, knowing that they had no comfort to offer, his companions left him alone with thoughts as dark as the December night. Of all he had endured since being shipwrecked on the Istrian coast—the hunger, the cold, the lack of sleep, the indignity of being hunted as if he were a fox with hounds baying on his trail—nothing had shaken him as deeply as the capture of the Templars and crossbowmen, forcing him to admit just how powerless he was, how vulnerable. Fulk had accused him of being unable to conceive of defeat, and the Poitevin clerk was right; he did always expect to prevail over other men, confident of his own abilities and dismissive of his foes. But now he found himself assailed by rare doubts. How many more men would they lose? How could they hope to evade capture if the entire countryside was on the lookout for suspicious strangers? And if he was taken, what then? For the first time, he seriously considered the fate that would await him if he fell into Heinrich's hands, utterly at the mercy of a man who had none. England's king, God's anointed, cast into a German dungeon whilst his lands in Normandy were ravaged by that craven whoreson on the French throne and Johnny claimed his crown. If his misgivings were unfamiliar, so, too, was the emotion that now rode with him on this icy mountain road—fear.

THEY COVERED TWENTY-FIVE MILES before daring to halt at the Benedictine monastery of St Gall in Moggio. There they were accepted by the monks as pilgrims and were able at last to get a desperately needed night's sleep in the abbey guest hall. They'd hoped to make better time on the Via Julia Augusta, the Roman road that was the main route from Aquileia to the Alps, for it was over twenty feet wide and paved with stones. They soon discovered that great stretches of it were in disrepair, though, and the weather turned nasty; they found themselves riding through snow squalls that sometimes obscured the road altogether. They were in the duchy of Carinthia now, a wild, rugged land where strangers were always regarded with mistrust, bandits roamed the heavily wooded forests, and they'd not be likely to encounter another lord with principles or a transplanted Norman with divided loyalties.

They debated making a stop in the town of Villach, but caution prevailed and they rode on, seeking shelter at another monastery, a Benedictine abbey on the north shore of a vast lake called the Ossiach. The next day, they pushed themselves and their horses to cover more than thirty miles, an impressive feat on winter roads, and as daylight was fading, they were approaching the walled town of Friesach.

The monks at St Gall had told Anselm that Friesach was one of the most prosperous towns in Carinthia, for it was the site of a rich silver mine, which had attracted men eager to seek their fortune. That would make it easier to blend in, they agreed, but they'd already realized it was nonetheless a risk they had to take, for darkness was falling and they were urgently in need of food and rest.

They stabled their horses, but delayed looking for an inn until they were sure it was safe to stay overnight in Friesach. Finding a tavern across from the parish church of St Bartholomew, they ordered a meal while Arne ventured out onto the city streets to eavesdrop, observe, and judge the public mood. They felt oddly uneasy with him gone, so dependent had they become upon him in the past week; his ability to speak German was, they all agreed, truly a Godsend.

The tavern was crowded, the conversation loud and cheerful. From what they'd seen so far of Friesach, it was indeed as the St Gall monks had described— thriving, bustling, and populous. A good place to go unnoticed, certainly safer than Görz, Udine, or Villach. They pitched into a mediocre Advent fish meal with relish, grateful to be out of the cold and out of the saddle, and encouraged to hear other tongues beside German.

Richard had taken a seat in the shadows, trying to be as inconspicuous as possible. He knew men thought him arrogant and he supposed he was, but he was also capable of laughing at himself, and as he began to relax and thaw out, he could see the perverse humor in it—that for the first time in his life, he was hoping *not* to attract attention. With a little imagination, he could hear the amused voice of his cousin André de Chauvigny echoing in his ear, *You trying to seem modest and unassuming? You'd have a better chance of flying to the moon and back.* He and André had fought side by side for nigh on twenty years, and he'd have given a great deal to have his cousin here in Friesach. He smiled to himself then, for he'd never admit that to André, of course. Barbed banter was the coin of their realm and heartfelt admissions of affection were rejected out of hand as counterfeit.

Warin had noticed several heavily rouged and powdered women and he leaned over to call them to the other men's attention. His hopes were dashed, though, as they laughed at him and Fulk asked acidly if he meant to get roaring drunk and start a brawl after he'd gone whoring. He started to defend himself, only to be chided for speaking too loudly, and lapsed into a sulky silence, much to his friends' amusement. Anselm was growing concerned by their merriment, fretting that the wine was going to their heads after so many hours without food, and he was leaning over to whisper his concern to Richard when he saw the king set down his wine cup with a thud. Following the direction of Richard's gaze, he went rigid, too, for Arne was back, hastening across the crowded common room toward them, and he was ashen, so pale he looked bloodless.

They quickly made room for him on the bench, all their levity vanishing with their first look at Arne's face. "A lord named Friedrich von Pettau is at the castle," he said, so softly they had to strain to hear his voice. "He came all the way from Salzberg, bringing many knights and vowing to capture the English king. The people I spoke with said that rumors have been spreading like the pox. They thought it was a joke, saying the king must have wings for men are claiming to have seen him in dozens of places. But they said Lord Friedrich believes the stories and his men are everywhere, watching the stables, the taverns, alehouses, and, above all, the inns. They said a mouse could not gnaw through the net that has been cast over the town."

By the time he was done, Arne's halting words had trailed off into a choked silence. No one spoke after that. Nor did they meet one another's eyes. During their night at St Gall abbey, they'd come up with an emergency plan, one to fall back upon if all hope seemed gone. But none of them had ever expected to have to make use of it, and now that the moment was upon them, they were stunned.

For once, Richard was not the first into the breach. When he said nothing, Baldwin realized that it was up to him. "We know what must be done," he said quietly, his gaze moving from one face to another and then back to Richard.

"You must go now, leave the town straightaway. We will do what we can to attract as much attention as possible and keep this Lord Friedrich so busy that he will have nary a thought to spare for anyone but us."

For Richard, this was the nadir of their ordeal. He felt as if he were sacrificing his friends, violating a commander's paramount duty to see to the safety of his men. And though he would never have admitted it, even to himself, it was a daunting prospect to continue on into the heartland of his enemy's empire with only young Arne and one lone knight. Getting slowly to his feet, he glanced over at Warin and forced a smile. "It looks as if you'll be able to swive a whore or two tonight, after all."

Warin looked stricken, mumbling something inaudible. None of them knew what to say. Richard let his hand rest on Baldwin's shoulder for a moment. "Do not stint yourselves," he said, striving without much success for a light tone. "All know the English king is a hopeless spendthrift, after all." He turned away then, and headed for the door, with Arne and Guillain de l'Etang following close behind. None of them glanced back.

The silence was smothering. Anselm lowered his head to hide tears. Robert de Turnham was slowly clenching and unclenching a fist, muttering under his breath. Warin had already emptied his own cup and now reached over to drain Richard's. The usually phlegmatic Fulk was daubing at his eyes with the corner of his sleeve, grateful that none noticed, for each man was caught up in his own misery. Morgan was gripping his eating knife so tightly that the handle was digging into his palm. Standing up suddenly, he said, "I am sorry, I cannot do this. I know we agreed that only Guillain was to go with him. But the Lady Joanna will skin me alive if I stay behind in Friesach." Shoving his knife into its sheath, he fastened his mantle with unsteady fingers and then hurried after Richard.

Baldwin straightened his shoulders. "Well," he said, "I suppose we'd best get on with it." He clapped his hands and whistled to catch a servingmaid's eye, making the universal gesture for more drinks, and then turned back to his companions, beginning to speak French in a clear, carrying voice. The others followed his example, laughing too loudly, leering at the servingmaids, and it was not long before some of the tavern customers were casting curious and speculative glances their way.

CHAPTER FIVE

⚜

DECEMBER 1192

Duchy of Austria

They could not be sure where they were, for they did not know how far they'd traveled after fleeing Friesach, and they did not know the date, either, for the days had blurred, one into the other, since their shipwreck on the Istrian coast. Drawing rein on the crest of a hill, they gazed down at the vista unfolding below them—deep woods on either side of the road, and in the distance, shimmering like a Holy Land mirage, the silvery sheen of a great river, curving around a partially walled town, its church spires wreathed in the smoke plumes that were spiraling up into the grey, wintry sky.

For a time, there was silence as they absorbed what they were seeing. Arne was the one to speak first, pointing toward the gleaming ribbon of water. "Is that the Danube?"

He sounded hesitant, afraid to let himself hope, for if it was the Danube, that meant the town on the river's bank was Vienna, and they were just fifty miles from the border of Moravia and safety. It also meant they'd ridden nigh on a hundred fifty miles in the past three days and nights, a feat they'd have sworn beforehand to be impossible in the dead of winter on these mountain roads.

"It must be the Danube," Morgan said, with all the conviction he could muster. "Look how wide it is." Arne let out a jubilant shout, but the men were too exhausted to match his youthful exuberance, and they merely exchanged brief smiles. They decided to send Arne on ahead to confirm that this was indeed Vienna, and as soon as he and Morgan rode on, Richard and Guillain de l'Etang turned off into the woods.

They did not go far from the lightning-seared tree stump that was to serve as a landmark for Arne and Morgan, and once they felt sure they were not visible from the road, they dismounted and hitched their horses to a low-hanging branch. They settled back against the grey trunk of an ancient beech and prepared to wait. They didn't talk, each man alone with his thoughts, and soon Richard and then Guillain dozed off. They were jolted to wakefulness some time later by the sound of approaching riders and scrambled to their feet, shocked that they could have fallen asleep like that. They were gripping the hilts of their swords, making ready to unsheathe them, when they saw Arne and Morgan coming through the trees.

Both were grinning, but Morgan deferred to Arne, letting the boy be the one to break the good news. "That is Vienna and we went into the town and found a street peddler and brought back food for you!" Sliding off his horse, he triumphantly brandished a hemp sack. "We bought hot cheese tarts and roasted chestnuts, though they are not hot anymore. Sir Morgan and I ate ours in the town, but then we were challenged by men from the castle and . . ."

Arne finally ran out of breath, and Morgan took over the narrative. "Well, we do not know they were from the castle, but they were on the lookout for strangers, so we will have to seek shelter elsewhere. Vienna is much smaller than I'd expected and we'd have no chance of escaping notice."

That was disappointing to Richard and Guillain, for they'd hoped Vienna would be a good-sized city, large enough to provide cover. "What did you do when they confronted you?"

Morgan's grin came back and Arne laughed outright. "Sir Morgan was so clever, sire! He answered them in Welsh and they just gaped at him, not understanding a word he said!"

"I was tempted to try out my fledgling Arabic on them," Morgan said with a chuckle, "but decided Welsh was safer since some of them might have seen service in the Holy Land." His smile disappearing then, he said, "They were looking for strangers who spoke French. They had no idea what I was speaking, but since it was not French, they let us go."

It was alarming to find out that Vienna was under such close surveillance; they'd hoped the Austrians had not yet heard the rumors that the English king had been spotted in Carinthia. Richard's shoulders slumped as he thought of the long ride ahead of them. "So why do you both look so cheerful?" he asked, more sharply than he intended. "Your news does not sound very encouraging to me."

"Oh, but we found us a place to stay, sire! Since we have to avoid Vienna, we stopped in a village on the outskirts of the town, called . . ." Arne frowned, trying to recall the name, and Morgan supplied it.

"Ertpurch. It is not much to look at, but it has an alewife and she was agreeable to renting us a room. She's a widow with two sons, and she leapt at the chance to earn a few coins. She says we can stay in her bedchamber and she will sleep out by the hearth with her lads."

"And the blacksmith said we could put our horses in his stable," Arne chimed in again, "whilst the alewife said she would cook for us if we provided the food!"

The boy sounded as pleased as if they'd been invited to stay at a royal palace. But after what they'd endured for the past three days, the alewife's house in Ertpurch sounded good to Richard, too. "We're lucky that we sent you and Morgan on ahead to scout for us, Arne," he said, and the youngster grinned from ear to ear, blushing at the praise.

"Very lucky," Morgan said, but there was something in his tone that caused Richard to tense, suddenly sure there was more to their account of their visit to Vienna than he'd so far heard.

"Even if the townspeople were not so suspicious, we'd not have dared to enter Vienna." Morgan's dark eyes met Richard's grey ones steadily. "I knew that as soon as I saw the red-and-white banner flying over the castle."

"Leopold's," Richard said, sounding unsurprised, and Morgan nodded.

"It is pure bad luck that the duke is here and not at one of his other residences." Leaving unsaid the rest—that not only did Duke Leopold bear Richard a lethal grudge, he was one of the few men who would recognize Richard at once, making it impossible to dispute his identity should it come to that.

⚜

ERTPURCH WAS AS UNPREPOSSESSING as Morgan had described, a cluster of single-story cottages with thatched roofs, a church, a smithy, a baker's oven, a handful of shops, a cemetery, and fields that were covered now in snow. Beyond was the camp of men come to trade and sell horses; Arne explained that foreigners were not permitted to sell goods in Vienna and so did their business outside the town's walls. Now that he was back in his homeland, he was chattering nonstop, proud that he could tell them so much about Vienna and the duke. He'd never been to Vienna until today, he confided, and had always imagined it was a goodly city, but it seemed downright meager after he'd seen Acre and Jerusalem. He was eager to share with them all the gossip he'd heard about Leopold, evoking amusement when he revealed that the duke was known as "The Virtu-ous," but by then, they were approaching the alewife's cottage and he had to save the rest of his stories for later, for they dared speak French only behind closed doors.

The alewife, a thin, fair-haired woman named Els, welcomed them warmly, and they understood why as soon as they entered her modest dwelling; it was obvious that the widow needed the money. Her young sons watched, wide-eyed, as she escorted the men into the house's bedchamber. It was small and sparsely furnished, for she'd moved her bed out by the hearth, apologizing that she had so little bedding to spare. But it was the best shelter they'd had since escap-ing from Friesach and they had no complaints. She bustled about, finding a few blankets for them, a chamber pot, and several tallow candles, and then shared the leftovers from her family's meal: boiled cabbage, barley bread, and a pottage of turnip greens, beets, and onions, washed down with some of her ex-cellent ale.

They were grateful for her generosity, and Morgan played the gallant to great effect, kissing her hand and murmuring Welsh compliments that made her laugh even though she understood not a word of it. It was a huge relief, though, when she finally retreated, leaving them alone in the shabby bedchamber. Apart from the cheese tarts Arne had purchased in Vienna, they'd had nothing to eat for three days, and they fell upon the simple fare ravenously. Guillain cut trench-ers from the loaf of bread and Arne ladled the pottage onto them, but when he turned to offer the first serving to the king, he got no response. Richard had stretched out on his blanket, wrapping himself in his mantle, not even bothering to take his boots off. When Arne bent over to set the food on the floor beside him, he was taken aback to see that the older man was already asleep.

"He's not hungry?" he asked, looking to the others for guidance. "Should we wake him up to eat? It's been so long. . . ."

"Let him sleep, lad." But they all kept casting glances toward Richard as they ate, and when they were done, Morgan rose and leaned over the sleeping man, putting his hand on his cousin's forehead. He did not stir at the touch, and Mor-gan sank back on his haunches, nodding in response to Guillain's silent query. "He's feverish," he said, confirming what they'd both suspected and feared for several days.

Arne gasped in dismay. "What will we do? We cannot seek out a doctor!"

"No, we cannot," Morgan agreed grimly. "On the morrow, lad, you must go into Vienna, find an apothecary, and buy aqua vitae; I've always heard it is good for fevers. Buy blankets, too, for we're like to freeze in here without them. Chicken is the best food for the sick, but no vendor will sell it during Advent, so get eggs and bread and garlic."

"I will," Arne promised solemnly. "Is there anything else I can do?"

Morgan glanced again toward Richard. "He's more stubborn than any mule, and not only will he not admit he's ill, he'll insist upon getting on his horse tomorrow if we let him. But we cannot continue on until he is stronger, for another bout of the quartan fever could well-nigh kill him. So yes, there is something else you can do, Arne. When you go into Vienna, find a church and offer up a prayer for his quick recovery."

ARNE WAS GRATEFUL TO Morgan for keeping the secret of his real age. But he had another secret that he did not share with his companions, for he felt vaguely guilty about it. How could he be enjoying himself so much when he knew they were suffering? Oh, there had been some scary moments—especially on shipboard and when they had to fight their way out of Udine—but most of the time, his excitement was stronger than his discomfort or anxiety. He felt very honored to be trusted by the English king, to be treated like an ally by these renowned knights, and he sensed that he was taking part in history, for surely men would be talking of King Richard's bold escape for many years to come.

He was in high spirits as he rode into Vienna, feeling like a knight on a confidential mission for his king. He'd never had so much money before and it was easy to pretend he was a wealthy lord. He stopped to flip a coin to a ragged beggar and grinned when the elderly man cried, "Bless you, young sir!"

His first task was to find a moneychanger, for they'd spent most of the coins they'd changed in Görz. Fortunately, Vienna was a crossroads for men traveling to the Holy Land, for Russian traders and Italian merchants, and so there was a need for such services. He found a moneychanger's stall by St Stephen's Church, and smiled at the man's sudden interest at sight of the gold bezants he slid across the table. "I want to change these for pfennigs," he announced grandly, "and do not try to cheat me, for I am no ignorant foreigner, was born near Hainberg."

In truth, he had no idea what a bezant was worth, but he watched closely as the man counted out the coins, and tried to look as if he were accustomed to such dealings. He felt an unexpected tug of sentiment as he scooped up the pfennigs, for he'd not seen the small silver coins for several years, and they reminded him of the life that had once been his, back when he'd never imagined he'd see so much of the world or serve a king.

He went next to the apothecary's shop, where the apothecary noted his scruffy appearance and said curtly that aqua vitae was too costly for a lad like him. He changed his tune when Arne jingled his bulging money pouch, and after putting the aqua vitae phial in a sack, he brought out cinquefoil and wood sorrel, saying they were also very good for fevers. Unable to decide between them, Arne bought both.

It was not a market day, but he had no trouble finding a peddler's cart. Arne bought the peddler's best blankets, candles, and the lone pillow, pleased to find one for the king. He then bought soap and a wooden comb, thinking they'd want to tidy themselves up once they reached Moravia, a brass mirror and a pig's-bladder ball as farewell gifts for the alewife and her sons, a set of bone dice for Morgan and Guillain, a jar of honey for Richard, and some candied quince for himself.

He couldn't remember the last time he'd had so much fun, for never had he been able to spend without counting the cost. He got eggs from another peddler, two round loaves of bread from a baker, and then his eye was caught by a cook-shop sign across the street from the Judenstadt, where the town's Jews dwelled. Here, as at the apothecary's shop, he was eyed askance until he showed he had money, and then they were happy to sell him fish tarts, hot peas, and wafers drizzled with honey. Looking around the shop for delicacies to tempt the king's poor appetite, he remembered a tale Warin had told him about a wondrous creature called a barnacle goose; because it was hatched in the sea, men said it could be eaten on fast days when meat was forbidden.

"What a pity you do not have a barnacle goose," he said regretfully, eager to impress the cook-shop hirelings with the story of this legendary fowl. To his surprise, they were familiar with it, and told him that whilst they had no barnacle geese on hand, they did have a roasted beaver's tail for sale; since it was covered with scales like a fish, it could be eaten during Advent with a clear conscience.

Arne bought it at once, not even flinching at the price, delighted to be able to bring meat back to the king. As he emerged from the cook-shop, burdened with all his purchases, he was going to retrieve his horse when he remembered he'd not said a prayer for Richard yet. He paused, looking around for the nearest church. It was then that a hand clamped down upon his shoulder, spinning him around, and a gruff voice demanded, "Not so fast, boy. We have some questions for you."

❦

RICHARD AWOKE WITH A start, torn from sleep so abruptly that he felt disoriented. For a disquieting moment, he did not know where he was, for this deeply shadowed chamber did not seem familiar. But then Morgan came into his line of vision, holding a candle aloft, and he remembered. He'd slept for hours, gotten up in the night to pass water, finding it so cold that he thought his piss might freeze, and then rolled into his blanket again and sank back into sleep as soon as he'd closed his eyes. Sitting up, he winced, for every muscle in his body was aching. "Is it morning yet?"

"Actually, the day is well-nigh gone," Morgan said. "It is about two hours till sunset."

"Jesu, Morgan, why did you not awaken me? We lost an entire day!"

"We needed to rest, sire," Guillain said, quietly but firmly. "And so did the horses."

Richard had to acknowledge the common sense of that, for he knew he'd just about reached the end of his endurance. Morgan was putting down a plate, saying the alewife had brought them cheese, bread, and ale to break their fast, and they'd sent Arne into the town to buy food and blankets.

Richard sipped the ale but did not touch the food. His face was flushed, and they could see sweat stains on his tunic, perspiration beading his forehead. Picking up a second cup, Morgan handed it to the other man. "Drink this, sire," he urged. "It is barley water, which is said to be good for fevers."

Richard started to deny his fever, then realized that was pointless. Reaching for the cup, he drank the barley water, grimacing at the taste. He forced himself then to swallow some of the bread and cheese, feeling their eyes upon him. "You say Arne went into the town? Is that safe for him?"

"They're looking for knights, grown men, foreigners, not boys whose native tongue is German," Guillain said. "Why would anyone pay heed to him?"

Richard was silent, thinking of all the men they'd lost so far. "I'd give a lot," he said at last, "to know what happened back in Friesach."

"I can tell you that," Morgan said, so confidently that Richard paused with the bread halfway to his mouth. "They spent money like drunken sailors and mayhap even started a brawl if Baldwin thought it necessary to attract attention. When this Lord Friedrich arrived to interrogate them, they denied that the English king was amongst them and were highly indignant that men who'd taken the cross should be harassed or threatened. My guess is that Friedrich then put them under arrest. He must be in dread of Heinrich's disfavor if he raced all the way from Salzburg to chase down a rumor. But they will not be harmed, sire. They are under the Church's shield, and whilst some of Heinrich's lords might be willing to seize you in defiance of that protection, I very much doubt that they will risk excommunication for anyone else."

"I hope you are right, Cousin." Setting the bread down, Richard lay back on the blanket, covered himself with his mantle, and his even breathing soon told them that he slept again.

Morgan took out their map and, after positioning the candle, he began to study the route they would take into Moravia. Fifty miles, not far at all. Then Bavaria and Saxony and sailing for England from a North Sea port. Lying down on his own blanket, he wondered where Joanna and Mariam were on this December day. Probably in Rome by now. Mariam would not be pleased when she learned that he'd refused to stay with the others in Friesach, for she had no liking for the English king and would not want him to put his life in peril for Richard. But he'd rather deal with her resentment than face Joanna and tell her he'd abandoned her brother in the lion's den. He was very fond of his beautiful cousin, but she had a hellcat's temper. All the Angevins did, he thought with a drowsy smile. He was half asleep when the door burst open and Arne stumbled into the room.

Guillain gestured toward Richard, warning Arne not to speak too loudly. "He needs his sleep. What happened, lad? By the looks of you, nothing good."

His composure was both comforting and calming. Arne took several deep, bracing breaths, waiting until he could speak clearly and coherently. "I was stopped and questioned by men in the town. The moneychanger told them about my gold bezants. I was about to leave when they grabbed me. I was so scared . . ." he confessed, unable to repress a shudder.

Morgan handed him Richard's unfinished ale. "Drink it down, Arne, then tell us what happened. Were they the duke's men? How did you get away?"

Arne gulped the ale in several swallows. "No, I think they were the moneychanger's friends, for they interrogated me there in the street, not at the castle. They were satisfied with the answers I gave and let me go. I told them I had the bezants because my master was coming back from the Holy Land. I explained he had not returned with Duke Leopold and the other Austrians because he'd been very ill at Acre, but he recovered and fought under the Duke of Burgundy's command until the peace was made."

"So you gave them the name of the knight you'd accompanied to Acre. That was quick thinking, Arne."

Arne was too unnerved to appreciate the praise. "It was all I could think to say. My master had been a household knight of Sir Hadmar von Kuenring and I mentioned his name, too. What I said was true . . . except that my master did not survive, but I thought no one would know that. I told them he had stopped at Holy Cross Abbey in Heiligenkreuz to rest because he was ailing and sent me on ahead to buy supplies. And they believed me. The Almighty truly guided my tongue," he whispered, and shivered again. "But this is a dangerous place, Sir Morgan. Too many men are looking for the king, greedy for the reward they think they'd get from the duke. We need to leave here straightaway."

Morgan and Guillain looked at each other and then over at Richard's motionless form. "We cannot do that, Arne, not yet," Guillain said, keeping his voice low. "The king is still too ill to ride. He needs to rest for another day or two."

Morgan nodded in agreement. "As long as we take care, we ought to be safe enough here. Did you get the aqua vitae, lad? And the food?"

Arne pointed toward the sacks he'd dropped by the door. "Wait till you see all I bought! I've blankets and a pillow for the king and the aqua vitae and herbal potions and lots of food. . . ." He frowned suddenly, rooting about in the sacks. "It is gone! The beaver tail I bought for the king! Those wretches must have taken it whilst they were questioning me. . . ."

They had no idea what he was talking about, but it sounded so ludicrous that they both laughed. When Richard awoke hours later and was told the story of the stolen beaver tail, he laughed, too, and Arne considered the loss well worth it, then, for this was the first time they'd heard Richard laugh in days, not since he'd had to leave the rest of his men behind in Friesach.

⚜

THE NEXT DAY IT snowed and the men hunkered down in the widow's house. Richard passed the hours sleeping, Guillain and Morgan napping and playing hazard with their new dice, Arne doing chores for Els and telling her sons about the strange beasts called camels that he'd seen in the Holy Land. The next morning dawned cold but clear and Richard seemed better, too, so it was de-cided they would depart on the following day.

Els had told Arne this was the saint's day of Thomas the Apostle, just four days from Christmas, and he thought it would be a memorable one, for by then they'd have reached safety in Moravia. He was nervous about making another trip into Vienna, but they needed food. Richard was still sleeping, Guillain had gone to the smithy to groom their horses, and Morgan had offered to cut fire-wood for Els, so there was no one to see Arne off. Taking care not to awaken the king, he fastened his mantle and then looked around for Guillain's woolen cap; the knight had said he could borrow it for the ride into town. In his search through their meager belongings, he came across Richard's gloves and pulled them out to admire them. Gloves were still a novelty, worn only by churchmen or the nobility; this pair was made of fine calfskin, lined with vair fur, embroi-dered with gold thread. Arne couldn't resist trying them on and they felt so good that he was reluctant to take them off, for the air outside was so frigid that the village seemed encased in ice and men's breaths trailed after them like white smoke. He jammed Guillain's cap down upon his head—it was too big, but at least it covered his ears—and then checked to make sure Richard's sleep was restful; they were fearful that his quartan fever might come back, and each day without the telltale chills was a great relief to them all.

THE WIND WAS CUTTING and Arne urged his mount on, covering the few miles between Ertpurch and Vienna at a brisk pace. He was pleased to see that it was a market day, for that should make it easier to buy what he needed. He re-membered just in time to remove Richard's costly gloves, tucking them into his belt, and took care to avoid the moneychanger's stall. He gave a coin to the ragged beggar again, getting a blessing in return, then headed for the cook-shop, where he bought more fish tarts and wafers. After that, he browsed the market-place, looking for food they could pack into their saddlebags. He settled on loaves of bread, hard cheese, almonds, and strips of unappetizing salted herring, not bothering to haggle with the vendors, for he wanted to leave Vienna as soon as he could.

But then he saw the girl. She was admiring a peddler's merchandise, her blue eyes caressing his finely woven cloths, delicate lace, and bright ribbons, and Arne thought she was the prettiest sight he'd ever seen, her cheeks scarlet with cold, the tips of her blond braids peeking provocatively from beneath her veil. As if feeling his gaze, she glanced up and for a moment their eyes met; then she looked modestly away, but he was sure the corners of her mouth were curving in a smile. He sauntered over and casually began to examine the peddler's wares. Reaching for a ribbon, he held it up for her appraisal, murmuring, "This is the very color of your eyes."

"You think so?" She gave him a sideways glance, and this time he definitely saw a smile.

The peddler was in no mood to indulge their flirtation, though, sure that they hadn't a pfennig between them. Snatching the ribbon back from Arne, he growled, "Do not put your greasy fingers on the goods! As for you, Margrethe, you'd best be on your way ere I tell your father you were making calf eyes at this bedraggled knave."

Arne flushed darkly and glared at the man. "If this is how you treat your customers, no wonder you are doing so poorly!"

"Customers are people who buy things, boy," the peddler said with a sneer.

"Well, that is what I am doing," Arne snapped, grabbing the ribbon and several items at random. "I'll take these." The peddler named a price so high that several of the bystanders nudged one another and snickered, but Arne was too angry to calculate the true worth of the ribbons and lace. Pulling out his money pouch, he flung a handful of pfennigs at the other man, who looked so flustered that their growing audience laughed and applauded Arne. Only then did he realize that they'd drawn a crowd.

"This is for you," he said, with all the dignity he could muster, offering the ribbons and the square of lace to Margrethe. "Please accept it as an apology for involving you in this unseemly row."

She blushed, but reached out to take the gift as some of the bystanders applauded again. It was clear to Arne that the peddler was not a popular figure in Vienna. It was also clear to him that he'd attracted attention he could ill afford. Making the girl what he hoped was a courtly bow, he turned and began to push through the crowd. He was still flushed, but now it was embarrassment and not indignation that colored his cheeks. Thank God Almighty the king and the others need never know about this foolishness.

He'd gone only a few paces, though, before several men stepped in front of him, barring the way. "We do not often see a stripling who looks like a beggar but spends like a lord," one said. "How did you come by so much money, lad?"

Arne took a backward step, but people were thronging around him and there was no room to retreat. "I am no thief, if that is what you think," he said, as steadily as he could. "My master sent me into town to buy goods for him. The money is his, not mine."

"I doubt that your master told you to buy ribbons for pretty wenches. He ought to be told that his servant is so high-handed with his money."

Arne had won the crowd's favor by standing up to the peddler, and a few of them now came to his defense, telling the men to "let the lad be." Arne's interrogator scowled, but his companions seemed to be losing interest, one of them saying, "Get his master's name, Jorg, and let him go. It's colder than a witch's teat and if we stay out here much longer, I'm going to freeze the body part I'd least like to lose."

Some of the bystanders laughed and Arne began to breathe again. Jorg was still frowning, though, and reached for his arm. "Come over here, boy, and tell me more about your master." His grip was painful, hard enough to leave a bruise, and Arne instinctively recoiled. As he did, his mantle was caught by a gust of wind, revealing the gloves tucked into his belt. Most of their audience did not notice. Jorg did, seeing enough to spark his curiosity, and he yanked Arne's mantle back.

"Well, well, what do we have here?" Grabbing the gloves, he held them up so his companions could see the soft leather and fur lining, and that changed everything. Arne's throat constricted, cutting off speech. Surrounded by these predatory, cold-eyed men, he began to tremble, a lamb cornered by wolves.

❦

THIS TIME ARNE HAD fallen into the hands of the duke's men, for they took him straight to the castle and up into a chamber over the gatehouse. Shoving him down in a chair, they deliberately let the suspense build before Jorg said abruptly, "Are you ready to tell us about these gloves, boy?"

Arne had realized at once that he could not use his earlier cover story, for no knight or minor lord would have gloves like these. Nor could he claim he'd found them, for if he was suspected of theft, he'd be hanged. All he could think to do was to fall back upon Richard's original disguise, and he told them haltingly that he served a rich merchant and the gloves were his. "My master was taken sick and stopped at Holy Cross Abbey, sending me on ahead to Vienna to buy supplies for him. He . . . he is a kind man and let me borrow his gloves because it was so cold. . . ."

The words were no sooner out of his mouth than Jorg backhanded him across the face. His head whipped back, blood streaming from his nose as the knight reached out and grasped the neck of his tunic, shaking him roughly. "Do not lie to me, whelp. These are no merchant's gloves. They were made for a bishop . . . or a king."

Arne swallowed, tasting blood on his lips from his broken nose. He could not wipe it away for another of the men had seized his arms and was binding them behind his back. "I . . . I am not lying, I swear it. . . ."

Jorg used his fist now, burying it in Arne's stomach. Gasping for breath, he had to fight back nausea, and could only shake his head as Jorg snarled, "You serve the English king, churl, admit it!" His mute denial earned him another blow, this one to his face again. His head was spinning, and he'd never been so frightened. But when they demanded he tell them where the king was, he swore he did not know of any king, and sobbed, knowing he'd pay in pain for his loyalty. He could not betray Richard, though. Richard trusted him, and as the blows rained down, he clung to that, as his only lifeline in a world gone mad, that he must prove worthy of the king's trust.

"Let me have a try." This was not Jorg's voice. "Look at me, boy," he said, not unkindly. "We do not want to hurt you. But we know you're lying. How do we know? You're carrying a king's gloves. You have a pouch filled with coins, including bezants from the Holy Land. And word came from Friesach that the men arrested there had been seen with a German-speaking lad." He paused, and when Arne kept silent, he said, "You are being very foolish," sounding almost friendly. "What is your name?"

Arne could barely see this new interrogator, for one eye was already swollen shut and his other eye was blurred with tears. "Arne . . ."

"Well, that is a start. Arne, listen to me. You will tell us what we want to know. By being stubborn like this, you are only prolonging your suffering. Answer our questions and you'll not be hit anymore. We'll even fetch a doctor to tend to your hurts. Now . . . where is the English king?"

"I . . . I do not know," Arne croaked. "I do not know!"

Someone laughed harshly; he thought it was Jorg. The second man shook his head and shrugged. "So be it. He's all yours, Jorg."

Arne squeezed his eye shut, as if not seeing the horror might make it go away. But then Jorg grabbed his hair and wrenched his head up. "You see this, boy? Look at this blade. Damn you, look at it! If you do not start giving us honest answers, I swear I will take it and cut your lying tongue out!"

Arne was crying softly, hopelessly, and when Jorge put the dagger to his throat, he shuddered and sobbed again. When the blade sliced his cheek, he cried out. But he did not answer any of the questions Jorg was shouting in his ear, and a third man intervened, drawing Jorg away. Arne sagged against the ropes binding him to the chair, grateful for this brief reprieve from the pain. They were soon back, though. "One last chance, whelp." When Arne only whimpered, Jorg turned away to take something from the other man. Arne was suddenly aware of heat and he squinted to see a fire iron only inches from his face. His hair was being held again, his head pulled back, and then there was nothing but the sickening stench of burning flesh and agony and screaming.

RICHARD WAS REGARDING THE DISH in front of him without enthusiasm and Morgan hid a smile, sure this was the first time he'd ever eaten boiled cabbage, which was unlikely to have made an appearance on the royal table. "Els is getting very motherly," he said cheerfully, "for she insisted upon sharing some of the leftovers from her boys' dinner. She told Arne we were much too thin and needed to eat more hearty fare. I daresay she's right." He knew from the way his clothes fit that he'd lost weight in these past few weeks and he thought his cousin looked downright gaunt. When Richard put the dish aside, Morgan hoped it was because he found the cabbage's odor unappealing and not because of his fever. He had been taking the aqua vitae and herbs dutifully, even drinking the barley water, but Morgan knew what he really needed was a few more days of bed rest.

"Arne ought to be back from the town soon," he assured Richard, "with food more to your liking."

"That lad has been a blessing, for I do not know how we'd have fared without him. I will have to find a way to reward his loyalty. That goes for you, too, Cousin," Richard said, with a quick smile. "I'd offer you an earldom if I did not fear you'd take it as an insult."

Morgan grinned. "You're joking, but King Henry did offer my father an earldom and he turned it down. It became a family jest, for he'd say that a Welshman with an English earldom was as unnatural as a bull with teats." They both laughed at that and Morgan added lightly, "I had no choice but to accompany you, sire. I'd promised your sister that I'd not let you out of my sight and I feared her wrath far more than I fear Heinrich's!"

"As well you should," Richard agreed, with a grin of his own. "Joanna is a force to be reckoned with. She all but scorched my ears off when I told her I'd suggested to Saladin that we make peace by wedding her to his brother, al-Adil."

Morgan had been about to take a swallow of ale, and nearly choked. "You did what?"

"Ah, I forgot you did not know about that. I still think it was one of my better ideas. It would have made al-Adil a king and so he had to be interested, for he was being offered both a crown and a beautiful bride. I was sure Saladin would refuse, and thought that might cause some rancor between the brothers. Joanna did not appreciate my diplomatic deviousness, though, and told me in no uncertain terms that she was not about to join a *harim*." Richard was laughing now. "She reminded me that she grew to womanhood in Sicily, so she knew Muslims could have four wives. I then reminded her that she'd be a queen, so she'd have greater rank than al-Adil's other wives, and she threw a cushion at me!"

Morgan was as amazed as he was amused. "I cannot believe you were able to keep this scheme so secret. Good God, think how the French would have reacted if word of it had gotten out!"

"That would have been awkward," Richard conceded. "It was awkward, too, when Saladin accepted the proposal."

Morgan's jaw dropped. "He accepted it?"

"Yes, check and mate. I had to rewrite canon law, explaining that Joanna needed the Pope's approval for such a marriage, being a widowed queen, and offered my niece in her stead if they were not willing to wait for the papal consent. Over dinner with al-Adil, I suggested that we could resolve the problem if he agreed to convert to Christianity, and he parried by proposing that Joanna become a Muslim."

By now, Morgan was laughing so hard that he was on the verge of tears. "Passing strange," he said, once he'd gotten his breath back, "that you got along so much better with your Saracen foes than with your French allies!"

"That is easy enough to explain. Saladin and al-Adil were men of honor, whereas the French . . . Well, if they are not in league with the Devil, it is only because he does not want them." No longer laughing, Richard said pensively, "The terms I offered Saladin then were virtually the same as the ones he finally accepted after I'd retaken Jaffa—aside from Joanna's participation, of course. We'd have saved so many lives if we'd only been able to make peace that November instead of the following September. Not to mention that we'd have been able to go home months ago. As interesting as this adventure has been, Morgan, I could have gone to my grave quite happily without ever laying eyes upon Ertpurch."

Morgan agreed heartily and they shared a quiet moment, regretting what might have been. Soon afterward, Richard went back to sleep, and Morgan napped for a time, too; he doubted that any of them would ever take sleep for granted again. He was awakened when Guillain entered the chamber. There was no sign yet of Arne, he reported, but the horses had benefited from several days' rest and the farrier had discovered that Morgan's gelding was in danger of losing a shoe, which he'd replaced. They were keeping their voices low so Richard would not be disturbed, and frowned as sudden barking erupted outside. Richard did not stir, though, and Morgan began looking for the dice.

But the barking did not stop, was so loud now that it sounded as if all the dogs in the village were in full tongue. The two men exchanged uneasy looks and Guillain crossed to the window, unbarred the shutters, and peered out. "Holy Christ!" He slammed the shutters and whirled around, the blood draining from his face. "There are soldiers outside!"

Morgan reacted instinctively, crying out Richard's name and dashing across the room to bar the door even as he realized the futility of it. The urgency in his voice awoke Richard at once. "Soldiers, sire," Guillain said hoarsely and Richard was at the window in two strides. Opening the shutters just enough to give him a view of the alewife's yard, he saw crossbowmen and men-at-arms taking up position. Els and her sons were standing out in the street, looking bewildered, as her neighbors emerged to see what was happening. Several knights had dismounted and, as Richard watched, they drew their swords and began to approach the house, shouting his name and one of the few German words he knew, *"König"*—king.

Richard latched the shutters again. His heart was thudding, his breath coming quick and shallow as his body reacted to the danger, while his stunned brain still struggled to accept what he'd seen. Morgan and Guillain looked just as shocked. None of them had truly believed that they'd be caught, for Richard's self-confidence was contagious and they'd seen him defy the odds time and time again in the Holy Land. Now that his legendary luck had suddenly run out in this small Austrian village, it did not seem real to any of them, least of all to Richard.

He had his sword in hand now, but that was an unthinking response. For the first time in his life, he experienced what so many other men did in battle—pure physical panic. They were trapped, with no way out and only two choices— surrender or die. As he stared at the bedchamber door, hearing the thud of boots as the soldiers tried to kick it in, his emotions were in such turmoil that death seemed preferable to what awaited him outside this room.

Someone must have found an axe, for the wood suddenly splintered and the door's hinges gave way. The chamber was poorly lit and the intruders halted in the doorway, blinking as their vision adjusted to the shadows. Their eyes swept past Morgan—not tall enough—lingered for a moment on Guillain, and then fastened upon Richard; as dirty and shaggy as his hair was, it was still the color of copper, as distinctive as his uncommon height.

They were yelling at him, waving their swords. But none of them moved into the room, and as he looked from face to face, Richard was astonished by what he saw—fear. He and Morgan and Guillain were hopelessly outnumbered, as help- less as fish caught in a weir, with only one outcome if they resisted, yet these men were afraid of him. That realization proved to be his salvation. His brain began to function again. He did have some leverage, after all—his reputation. It had happened more and more toward the end of his stay in the Holy Land—Saladin's emirs and Mamluks, men of proven courage, veering away rather than cross swords with him. And these Austrian knights were no more eager to fight him than the Saracens. They respected his prowess, and that understanding gave him the courage to do what he had to do, to take that first, frightening step into the unknown.

"I will yield only to your duke," he said, greatly relieved that his voice sounded as it always did, giving away no hint of his inner anguish. They looked at one another, then flung more German at him, and he tried again, this time in Latin. When it was obvious they did not comprehend, he said, "Morgan," remember- ing that his cousin had picked up a smattering of German from Arne.

Morgan felt as if his brain had gone blank, but with a great effort, he managed to dredge up a few words. *"Herzog! Herzog Leopold!"* They reacted at once to their duke's name, and he added, *"Hier,"* gesturing around the room to indicate Leopold was to come here. They seemed to think this was a very good idea, for several were nodding and saying, *"Ja,"* with obvious enthusiasm. "They under- stand," Morgan said, with a sigh of relief. "They'll fetch Leopold."

The Austrians stayed by the door, swords drawn, but seemed content to wait. They were all staring at Richard, nudging one another, and he heard the word

"Löwenherz" being repeated. He'd guessed its meaning even before Morgan translated it as "Lionheart." Crossing to the bed, he retrieved his frayed, stained mantle and draped it around his shoulders as if it were royal robes of state.

The bravado of that gesture brought tears to Morgan's eyes. He'd initially been wary of Richard, for his allegiance had been pledged to Richard's brother Geoffrey and his father, the old king. But he'd come to know Richard well in the past two years, and now he felt the depth of the other man's desperation and despair, the proudest of the proud shamed before enemies he'd scorned. He did not doubt that Richard would have found it easier to be taken prisoner by Saladin. Watching as Richard braced for whatever humiliation and danger lay ahead, preparing to brazen it out, he found himself remembering Guilhem de Préaux, who'd claimed that he was Malik Ric to save Richard from capture. He would have made that sacrifice, too, had it only been in his power—not just because Richard was his king or his cousin, but because theirs was a bond only those who fought together and faced death together could fully understand.

He saw his own misery reflected on Guillain's face. There were tears in Guillain's eyes, too, as he said softly, "I am sorry, sire." Richard shook his head, letting his hand rest for a moment on the knight's arm. Morgan found his own mantle and untied his money pouch from his belt. He knew the soldiers would take every pfennig for themselves and he was determined to get the money to the alewife if he could; better she should have it than Leopold's lackeys. His eyes lingered for a moment on Arne's bedding. He hated to think what might have befallen the boy in Vienna.

Much too soon, they heard the noise outside that signaled Leopold's approach. Richard had never dreaded anything more than what was to come. This was likely to be their last moments alone, and he reached out to embrace Morgan, then Guillaume. "I'll be damned if I'll wait cowering, like a fox run to earth," he declared, sheathing his sword, and then starting toward the door. The soldiers moved aside to let him pass, so hastily that it was almost comical. *Like Moses parting the Red Sea,* Morgan thought irreverently as he and Guillaume followed close behind.

There was a crowd waiting as Richard emerged from the alewife's house into the pallid winter sunlight, soldiers, villagers, and a large contingent of knights who'd accompanied their duke. Leopold was mounted on a magnificent white stallion and was just as magnificently garbed, his hat and mantle trimmed with sable fur, his scabbard studded with gemstones, his hands adorned with several jeweled rings. His appearance did not fully match Richard's memory of him, and then he realized why: this was the first time he'd ever seen Leopold smile.

Leopold did not dismount at once, for that enabled him to look down upon the man who was some inches the taller of the two. "When they told me about the boy they'd picked up in the marketplace, I confess I had my doubts," he said, still smiling. "But by God, it is you."

Richard regarded him stonily, before saying tersely, "My lord duke." He stayed where he was until Leopold swung from the saddle, only then stepping forward and unsheathing his sword. Most of Leopold's men already had their weapons drawn, and they brought them up quickly then. Ignoring them, Richard held out his sword, hilt first, to his captor, saying nothing.

Leopold accepted the sword, then subjected Richard to a deliberate, slow scrutiny, taking in the tangled hair, long beard, mud-caked boots, and begrimed mantle, which only partially covered the once-white Templar's tunic, now streaked with dirt and sweat. "You do not look very kingly now, do you, my lord Lionheart? Indeed, you look like a man we'd expect to find in a hovel like this. How true that *Pride goeth before destruction and a haughty spirit before a fall.*"

Richard welcomed the fury that now surged through his veins, sweeping away all shame and fear. "Since you're quoting from Scriptures, you'd do well to remember another verse. *God is not mocked, for whatsoever a man soweth, that shall he also reap.* There will be no forgiveness for harming men who've taken the cross, neither from the Church nor Almighty God. You'd best think upon that whilst there is still time. Is this petty revenge worth eternal damnation?"

Hot color flooded Leopold's face and throat. "You've forfeited your right to Church protection by your crimes in the Holy Land!"

"I daresay I'd have heard had you been elected Pope. Celestine is the man on the papal throne and are you so delusional that you truly believe he'll agree with you? When pigs fly!"

They'd been speaking in French, so only Morgan and Guillain could follow the accusations they were hurling at each other. Knowing that Richard had never learned to guard his tongue, Morgan took a quick step forward. While he did not think Leopold was a man utterly without honor like Heinrich, he'd still been willing to lay hands upon a crusader. What might he do behind his castle walls if Richard continued to bait him like this? Judging it a good time to intervene, he said, "My lord duke," seeking to sound respectful and deferential. "What of Arne, the lad who was seized in the marketplace? Where is he?"

Leopold looked his way, seemingly debating whether the question deserved an answer. "I was told the boy was stubborn," he said after a long pause, "and had to be persuaded to talk. But I doubt that his injuries are serious."

Morgan forgot about placating the Austrian duke. "You tortured him?" Guillain was no less outraged and he glared at Leopold, calling him shameless and milk-livered, insults that, fortunately for him, were not heard by the duke, whose attention was focused upon the English king.

Richard was staring at Leopold with all of the considerable contempt at his command. "You are bound and determined to get to Hell, Leopold. The boy your men tortured took the cross, too, and is under the protection of Holy Church no less than we are."

Leopold was as angry as Richard, but he was coming to realize that it was not advisable to continue exchanging insults with the English king. Even if his knights and men could not understand what was being said, there was no mistaking Richard's defiant tone, and some might find it demeaning that he was allowing himself to be challenged by a man who was his prisoner, after all. "We are done here," he said curtly and ordered horses brought up for the three men. "Are you going to mount on your own or shall we have to drag you back to Vienna like a common felon?"

As he expected, Richard had far too much pride for that, and he and his companions were soon astride horses fitted with halters and leads instead of bridles and reins. Richard still found himself surrounded by riders with drawn swords, for Leopold was taking no chances with his prize prisoner. As they rode out of Ertpurch, the villagers clustered in the road to watch them go, astonished that such high drama had occurred in their peaceful little hamlet. Els was already the target of jokes about her boarder, the king of the English, but they were good-natured jests; her neighbors were thankful that she was not being punished for the inadvertent role she'd played in aiding their duke's great enemy. She said what was expected of her, expressed shock and dismay that she'd had such wicked men under her roof. But all the while, she could feel the money pouch hidden between her breasts, for Morgan had managed to slip it to her while gallantly kissing her hand in farewell. She did not doubt that Duke Leopold was a good man, a good ruler. She meant to pray, though, for the safety of the prisoners, a secret she'd share only with God. And she would pray, too, she decided, for the soul of her duke, for surely he would burn in Hell for what he'd done this day.

CHAPTER SIX

❧

DECEMBER 1192

Vienna, Austria

The chamber was little bigger than a cell, containing only a pallet, a chamber pot, and a wooden stool. There was a small, shuttered window, though, and several torches smoldered in wall sconces. For all of his bravado, Richard felt relief; at least he'd not been cast into the suffocating blackness of a frigid, underground dungeon. As spartan as his new surroundings were, they were no worse than what he'd endured in the eleven days since their shipwreck. All he wanted now was time alone, time to come to terms with this shocking spin of Fortune's wheel. But he soon saw that his guards did not intend to leave, that he was to be kept under constant surveillance by men with drawn swords. Under other circumstances, he might have seen the twisted humor in it; what did Leopold fear, that he could walk through walls or fly to safety like an eagle? Now he felt only a dulled throb of anger and despair. It did not bother him that he'd be watched even as he used the chamber pot; soldiers had no false modesty. But with so many eyes upon him, he could not let down his guard for even a heartbeat; he was determined that his enemies never know how deeply shaken he was by his capture.

There was no heat in the chamber and he was soon shivering. He was thirsty, too, for his mouth had gone so dry he had not even enough saliva to spit. But he'd be damned to eternal hellfire ere he'd ask them for anything. He'd not give Leopold that satisfaction. Unable to sit, he began to pace, and the guards kept bumping into one another as they sought to keep him at arm's length. They reminded him of the crowds flocking to a bear baiting, at once fascinated by and fearful of the chained bear. He did not doubt the bear would prefer to die fighting, lashing out at the hounds tormenting him as long as he had strength in those massive paws.

They'd come so close—just fifty miles from the Moravian border! If not for his accursed fever, they'd be safe now. How could his body have betrayed him like that? How could this be the Almighty's Will? He'd failed to take Jerusalem; he could not deny that. But he'd tried, Christ Jesus, how he'd tried, sabotaged time and time again by those French miscreants. And he'd stayed, he'd honored his vow even after learning that Philippe and Johnny were plotting to usurp his throne. He'd not given up and gone home as Philippe and Leopold had. What had he done to deserve this?

Minutes seemed to drag by like hours, hours like days. He thought he heard bells chiming in the town; calling parishioners to Vespers? Compline? When the door opened suddenly, he spun around, expecting that Leopold had come to gloat. But he found himself facing a grey-haired priest, flanked by two servants. As they moved into the chamber, Richard saw that they carried a tray of food and a pile of blankets. "I am Father Otto, the duke's chaplain," the priest said in quite good Latin, giving Richard one of those chained-bear glances and then looking quickly away. "I thought you might be hungry, my lord."

"What of my men? Have they been fed?"

"I . . . I am not sure. But I will look into it," the chaplain promised. He'd yet to meet Richard's eyes and Richard wondered if his unease could be due to embarrassment. Who would know better than a man of God the gravity of Leopold's transgression?

As he studied the priest, Richard realized that his pride had led him astray. By not protesting his treatment, he was making it easier for them. They'd dared to capture a king, so by God, he'd act like one. "What of the lad, Arne? Leopold admitted he'd been tortured to get him to speak. I want him seen by a doctor straightaway. He is under the Church's protection no less than my knights, for we all took holy vows. Tell Leopold for me that he is putting his immortal soul in peril for what he has done this day. Better yet, tell him yourself. You are his confessor, are you not? Then do not shirk your duty, priest. Speak up whilst there is still time for your lord to repent."

The chaplain ducked his head, his distress so evident now that it was obvious he was not happy with his duke's actions. Those who served both the Almighty and secular lords did their best to follow Jesus's teachings and render unto Caesar the things which were Caesar's, and unto God the things that were God's, all the while praying they'd never have to choose between the two. Richard had learned to read other men as a priest read his psalter and he doubted that Father Otto would have the inner strength to defy his duke. Would Leopold's bishops have more courage? But even if they spoke up, would he heed them?

"I will do what I can, my lord," Father Otto replied, still staring down at his shoes. Richard watched as he made a hasty retreat, hoping that the priest would at least intercede on behalf of his knights and Arne. He gave the food only a cursory glance; it was plain fare, a fish pottage not likely to be served at Leopold's table, but there was an ample helping of it, as well as a loaf of fresh-baked bread, and a cup of ale. He had no appetite, though. Picking up the ale, he crossed to the window, and his guards became agitated when he began to unfasten the shutters. A sharp word from their sergeant quieted them, and Richard understood why as he pulled the shutters back, for the window was almost as narrow as an arrow slit, offering no chance of escape. A blast of icy air struck him in the face, taking his breath, but he stayed by the window for a while, gazing up at the darkening sky. It looked like a black sea adrift with stars, far removed from the earthly troubles of mortal men.

❧

MORGAN AND GUILLAIN HAD been separated from Richard so swiftly that there had been no time for farewells. They tensed when they were taken into a stairwell, fearing that it led down to the dungeons. When their guards escorted them into a chamber lit by a single oil lamp, they were heartened at the sight of that flickering flame, for they knew dungeons were blacker than the pits of Hell. The door slammed behind them and they began cautiously to explore their new abode. It was large and windowless, with kegs lining the walls, and they soon concluded that they'd been locked in a cellar storeroom. The lamp cast only a small pool of light, the rest of the chamber swallowed up in darkness. They could hear scrabbling noises in the shadows and exchanged glances, hoping it was mice and not rats.

But then Morgan caught another sound, one that raised the hairs on the back of his neck. He stood very still, listening intently, and when it came again, he moved in that direction. A moment later, he was kneeling between two of the storage kegs. A body was crumpled on the floor, knees pulled up to his chest. He seemed oblivious to Morgan's presence, but he groaned when the Welshman touched his shoulder, raising his hand as if to ward off a blow. "Arne?" At the sound of his name, he whimpered again and tried to shrink farther back into the shadows. Morgan turned toward Guillain, but the knight was already moving to the wall recess that held the lamp. A moment later, he was back, and as he raised the lamp, both men braced themselves for what they would see.

The wavering light was feeble, but it was also merciless, revealing to them a face whiter than death, eyes swollen to bruised slits, nose crusted with dried blood, with red welts on forehead and throat, the burns so raw and blistered that they flinched from the sight. They'd seen wounds before, seen men gutted by sword thrusts, run through by lances, seen heads split open by axes. But nothing had horrified or outraged them so much as what they now saw in this Viennese storeroom, looking upon what had been done to Arne.

"Do not be afraid, lad. It's me," Morgan said gently. "You're safe now, amongst friends." He had no way of knowing if that was true or not, but it was what the boy needed to hear. Arne squinted up at him, unable to see the face but recognizing the voice, and began to weep. They could make out little of his speech at first, broken bursts of German, interspersed with sobs. When he finally was able to recover some of his French, they heard only one word, mumbled over and over: "Sorry . . . sorry. . . ."

Morgan had never known a fury like this, the killing kind. Guillain, a man of few words, now found them in abundance, and he began bitterly to curse Arne's abusers, then Duke Leopold, Emperor Heinrich, King Philippe, and the Austrians, Germans, and French who served them. Morgan gathered the boy to him, and held Arne as he wept, murmuring words of comfort that he doubted Arne even heard.

They had no way of judging time, leaping to their feet when the door opened and men entered with torches and drawn swords. The guards were followed by a priest and servants bringing food, blankets, a chamber pot, and another sputtering oil lamp. The priest seemed polite, even sympathetic, but they did not have enough Latin to follow what he was saying. Handing Morgan a glass phial of dark liquid and a clay pot that smelled of goose grease, he gestured toward Arne, and they understood that he was offering something for the boy's pain and burns. As his lantern's light fell across Arne's face, he averted his eyes and made the sign of the cross. When he turned to go, Morgan called out, *"König Richard?"* The priest paused, gazed at him sadly, and then slowly shook his head.

Once they were gone, Morgan and Guillain did their best for Arne, smearing the salve upon his burns and coaxing him into swallowing some of the liquid. He refused to eat any of the food, though, and continued to shiver even after they'd swaddled him in blankets. "Will . . . will he ever forgive me?" he whispered, his hand tightening on Morgan's arm.

"Forgive you, lad? Richard will most likely knight you!"

Arne's bloodied lower lip began to quiver. "He'll not hate me?" They assured him that Richard admired courage above all other virtues, that he'd not be blamed for breaking under torture, that he had nothing to reproach himself for, and for the first time since he'd been caught in the marketplace, Arne felt the faintest flicker of hope. "What will happen to him?" he asked softly, and they assured him again that Leopold would not dare to harm the King of England, the man who'd defeated Saladin at Acre and Jaffa. They could not tell if he believed that. But they did not know if they believed that, either.

❧

RICHARD HAD NOT EXPECTED to be able to sleep, but physical exhaustion prevailed over emotional angst. The next thing he knew, Father Otto was bending over his pallet, apologetically explaining that he'd been summoned by the duke, giving Richard another hard lesson in life as a prisoner—at the beck and call of a man he'd disdained. He was grateful to see that the chaplain had brought a washing basin and a towel, so at least he could clean his face and hands. He suspected that Leopold had it in mind to display him before his barons and bishops, bedraggled and dirty and, as Leopold had gleefully put it, "not at all kingly." Such an ordeal would lacerate his pride, but he vowed silently that none of them would ever know it and splashed cold water onto his face before breaking his fast with a few swallows of bread and cheese. Only then did he turn to the nervously fidgeting priest and say coolly, "Let's go."

But as soon as he emerged from the keep, he saw that he'd misread Leopold's intentions. It was very early, too early for a gathering of Austrian nobles; stars still glimmered overhead and only a faint glow along the eastern horizon hinted that dawn was nigh. As he followed the chaplain and guards out into the bailey, he glanced around and then came to an abrupt halt at the sight of the riders coming from the stables. Yawning and blinking, they were clad in mail, armed with swords, lances, and shields. Knights ready for war—or to escort a highborn prisoner.

Leopold was standing several yards away, giving instructions to a man who looked as if he'd spent most of his life soldiering; he had the sharp-eyed, dispassionate gaze of one who missed little and was beyond surprising. Seeing Richard then, the duke gestured for a waiting groom to bring up a bay gelding and then strode toward the English king.

"I am sending you to one of our most impregnable strongholds—Dürnstein," he announced in lieu of greetings.

Richard was thankful that he'd long ago mastered one of a king's most useful skills—the ability to camouflage his emotions. "Better Dürnstein than Hell," he said, and had the fleeting satisfaction of seeing Leopold's mouth tighten and a muscle twitch under his eye.

The other man did not lash out, though, regarding Richard with the deliberation of one who'd resolved beforehand not to lose his temper. "Dürnstein is fifty miles from Vienna. If you give me your sworn word that you'll not try to escape, you need not be bound. Do you agree?"

Richard was tempted to point out the inconsistency in Leopold's position. How could he be willing to trust in the honor of a man he'd accused of betraying Christendom? "I do *not* agree. I'll not aid and abet you in this abduction or make it seem less than what it is—as much a crime as any ambush by roadside bandits."

Leopold's jaw jutted out, but he said only, "Your pride will be your undoing, Lionheart."

When the soldiers approached him with ropes, Richard held out his wrists, for that would be less painful than having his hands tied behind his back—and he'd not be quite so helpless. They began fumbling with the ropes, but they had so much trouble with the knots that the sharp-eyed soldier shook his head impatiently, waved them off, and completed the task himself.

The groom was waiting with Richard's horse, but an awkward silence fell as they belatedly realized he would have difficulty mounting now. It was the same knight who stepped forward again, leading the gelding over to a mounting block and then helping to boost Richard up into the saddle. Richard found it profoundly humiliating, and although he kept his face impassive, he could not keep hot color from burning across his cheekbones.

As soon as Richard was mounted, Leopold turned away, heading toward the great hall. But Father Otto lingered, saying quietly, "You need not fear for your men, my lord. They'll not be maltreated, for they have done nothing wrong."

"Then why are they being held? There is no legal justification for not freeing them at once, and with the money that was taken from me in Ertpurch. Or does your duke plan to add theft to his growing list of sins?"

The priest winced. "If I may speak plainly, my lord? I understand your anger. But you must learn to govern your tongue."

"Must I, indeed?"

"Yes, sire," the older man insisted earnestly, "for your own sake, you must."

Richard did not reply, but the chaplain still remained out in the bailey, watching until the English king and his guards rode through the gateway and disappeared from view.

⟨⟡⟩

AFTER CROSSING THE DANUBE, they headed west along the river. They encountered few other travelers, for most people preferred to detour off the road when they spotted a large band of armed men in the distance. The knights were commanded by the man with the detached demeanor and cynical eyes; by now, Richard had learned his name was Gunther. He spoke neither French nor Latin, but he managed to communicate with Richard when need be, using the universal language of soldiers—gestures, sardonic smiles, and the instinctive understanding of men who'd shared the same experiences, albeit on different battlefields.

They set a fast pace and by sunset, they'd covered more than thirty miles. Richard never knew the name of the small town where they passed the night, taking over a ramshackle inn that reminded him of the Black Lion in Udine. Once they were settled in, Gunther directed men to take turns guarding Richard and then removed the ropes. They grumbled among themselves; Richard guessed that they were complaining they'd not have to keep watch if he was kept tied up, but none of them protested to Gunther. Richard ate little of the meal provided by the innkeeper, and slept even less, lying awake as most of the knights snored loudly and his guards watched him with the intensity of cats at a mouse hole. Had he spoken any German, he could have told them that they were worrying for naught. He was well aware that escape was an impossibility, although that did not stop him from occupying those long, wakeful hours by considering each and every one of those impossible escapes. Better to do that than to think about what awaited him at Dürnstein, or the men he'd lost since their shipwreck, or how the news of his capture would affect those who mattered the most to him: his mother, sister, wife, his cousin André, his young son back in Poitiers.

The next morning, Gunther paused, holding out the ropes and raising an eyebrow questioningly. Richard understood what was being asked and very much wanted to agree; it had not taken long for him to regret spurning

Leopold's offer. But pride would not let him retreat from his defiant stand and he shook his head. Gunther shrugged and lashed his wrists together, although Richard thought he could detect a reluctant gleam of respect in the knight's eyes, the sort of admiration men reserved for behavior that was stubborn, brave, and foolhardy.

Clouds were gathering as they continued on the next day, and the air had the feel of coming snow. As the temperature plunged, so did Richard's spirits. He'd begun to fear that his fever was spiking again, that he might be vulnerable to another attack of quartan fever. He could not imagine anything worse than to be gravely ill and helpless in the hands of his enemies; he'd always found it difficult enough to be ill amongst his friends. And if he did sicken again, God help him if he was thrown into a Dürnstein dungeon, for he'd not last long in a cold, dark, and damp cell. He'd been unable to forget Father Otto's somber warning, replaying in his mind his two tense encounters with Leopold. For certes, he'd not given the Austrian duke any reason to think kindly of him. Would Leopold seek to take revenge now that he was away from public view? Had he been treated harshly in Vienna, word would have gotten out, and Leopold was already on very precarious ground with the Church. But who would know what happened behind the stone walls of a remote, inaccessible fortress like Dürnstein?

Govern your tongue, the priest had said. God knows he'd not done that, he thought ruefully, and a memory suddenly surfaced—listening as their father rebuked his brother Hal for some forgotten misdeed. Hal had been making matters worse, of course, blustering and trying to put the blame on others until Henry had interrupted, saying that when a man fell into a deep hole, it was usually a good idea to stop digging. The memory was so vivid and so unexpected that it evoked a brief smile, albeit a grim one. He would indeed do better to put his shovel aside. He knew that full well. But he knew, too, that pride was his only shield, all that he had to fend off fear and utter despair.

❧

BY LATE AFTERNOON, they could see castle walls in the distance. Even before Gunther pointed toward it and said, "Dürnstein," Richard knew that he was looking at Leopold's "impregnable stronghold." It cast a formidable shadow over the valley, perched high on a cliff above the Danube, as rough-hewn, ominous, and impassable as the surrounding mountains. Richard would normally have assessed it with a soldier's eye, seeking its weaknesses and weighing its strengths. Now he saw only a prison.

❧

DÜRNSTEIN WAS TO HOLD several surprises for Richard. The first one was waiting in the outer bailey to greet them, for he was a man Richard knew— Hadmar von Kuenring, an Austrian knight who'd accompanied Leopold to the Holy Land. Richard had shared a meal with him one hot July night before Acre fell, and he remembered swapping bawdy jokes with Hadmar, something he could not have imagined doing with Hadmar's prickly, proper duke, Leopold the Virtuous.

Hadmar was a *ministerialis*; when Richard had first heard that term, he'd assumed it meant Hadmar was a court official. He'd been astounded when Hadmar had confided over several flagons of wine that *ministeriales* were of the knightly class but they were unfree. They served their lords in a variety of ways just as English and French knights did, and some of them—like Hadmar— enjoyed noble status. But they could not wed without their lord's permission, nor could they leave his service, for they were bound to him in the way that an English serf was bound to the land. Upon recognizing Hadmar, Richard's unease intensified, for how could a *ministerialis* heed his own conscience?

Hadmar seemed slightly uncomfortable and Richard wondered if he remembered that night in the siege camp at Acre, too. "My lord king," he said, with a wry half smile. "I'd usually say 'Welcome to Dürnstein,' but that seems ridiculous under the circumstances. I suppose we'll just have to muddle through this as best we can. You must be tired and hungry—"

He broke off then, for he was close enough now to see Richard's bonds. Drawing his dagger, he cut through the ropes, and then gave Gunther a look as sharp as his knife blade. After rubbing his wrists to restore the circulation, Richard swung from the saddle, saying, "Sir Gunther was merely following the duke's orders, Sir Hadmar."

They'd been conversing in Latin, but Gunther seemed to understand that the English king had just come to his defense, for as their eyes met, he nodded, the corners of his mouth twitching in what was almost a smile. Hadmar was frowning, clearly taken aback to learn that Leopold had ordered Richard bound, but then he nodded, too, and said briskly, "Whatever needs to be said can be said

inside, by a fire. Come with me." And he turned, starting to walk toward the
inner gatehouse, taking it for granted that Richard would follow.

RICHARD'S SECOND SURPRISE WAS the room where he was to be confined,
for it was a bedchamber much more comfortable than he'd have dared to expect.
It had a real bed, one laden with pillows and fur-lined coverlets, a charcoal
brazier heaped with smoldering coals, woven wall hangings to block out the
December chill, a trestle table and two chairs, an abundance of candles and
several oil lamps, even fresh floor rushes. Glancing around, he wondered who'd
been evicted from this chamber for his benefit, and he wondered, too, how Leopold would react to Hadmar's generosity.

As he moved farther into the room, he stopped so suddenly that one of his
guards bumped into him, astonished by what he saw in the corner behind the
bed: a large wooden tub, with padded rims and a stool. The rest of his guards
had followed him into the chamber, so he assumed he was to be kept under constant surveillance here, too. They did not interfere as he prowled the confines of
his new prison, watching him with more curiosity than hostility, not objecting
even when he unshuttered one of the windows. It offered a spectacular view of
the mountains and the swift flowing waters of the Danube, but no chance of
escape, not unless a man was desperate enough to commit self-slaughter, ending
his earthly suffering, but at the cost of eternal damnation. Richard closed the
shutters and was warming his hands over the brazier when a knock sounded on
the door and his guards admitted servants lugging large buckets of heated water,
an armful of towels, and even a bowl of liquid soap. Thinking that Hadmar von
Kuenring was deserving of an English earldom, Richard began to strip off his
clothes.

Having done his best to scrub off several weeks of grime, he was still soaking
in the tub, luxuriating in the feel of the hot water upon his aching, constricted
muscles, when Hadmar entered. "No offense meant," he said with a slight smile,
"but I assumed you'd be in dire need of a bath by now."

"No offense taken, for I was."

"I'll send a barber to you tomorrow to cut your hair and beard." Hadmar
beckoned to another servant, who deposited a pile of clothing upon the bed.
"We'll find you something suitable to wear, but for now these garments will have
to do. You're too tall to wear any of mine." Looking down at the filthy tunic,

shirt, braies, and torn chausses that Richard had scattered about the floor, he said, "With your permission, I'll get rid of these. I doubt you'll want to see them again, much less wear them."

Richard almost asked if Leopold would like them as keepsakes, like a wolf pelt or the antlers of a slain stag, but he caught himself before he reached for the shovel and suggested that Hadmar's almoner could find a use for them. The Austrian was clearly trying to make the best of a difficult situation, forced into the dual role of host and gaoler, and so when he turned to go after saying a meal would be sent up soon, Richard gave him what he would never have offered Leopold—courtesy. "Thank you," he said, as if he were a guest expressing his appreciation for Hadmar's hospitality, and the other man smiled, looking pleased and relieved that they'd been able to evade the first pitfall in a road strewn with them.

⚜

RICHARD WAS KEPT ISOLATED from the members of Hadmar's household, seeing only the guards who watched him day and night and Hadmar himself, who paid brief visits to make sure his needs were being met. He was provided with the best meals he'd eaten since leaving Ragusa, clothing, even a few books and a lute, for Hadmar had remembered that the English king was a musician. While he was appreciative of these amenities, they were ointments offered for a bleeding internal wound. He could not imagine how his mother had endured sixteen years of confinement with her wits intact. After just a week, his nerves were fraying like well-worn hemp. Not knowing what his future held was intolerable. He did not try to interrogate Hadmar about Leopold's intentions, feeling that would be a poor way to repay the older man's small kindnesses. Even if Hadmar knew what Leopold had in mind, he'd hardly confide in his prisoner, so such a conversation would only embarrass him.

Richard had not realized Christmas had arrived until he was served a dish of roast goose, signifying Advent was past. When he asked to attend Christmas Mass in the castle chapel, Hadmar had reluctantly refused, obviously following Leopold's orders, not his own inclinations, for on his next visit, he brought a set of Paternoster beads. Richard dutifully recited fifty Ave Marias each evening, but prayers could not drown out the insidious inner voice whispering that God had turned His face away, deaf to his pleas.

He passed most of his days thinking about his tomorrows. Surely Leopold must mean to ransom him? Leopold could not keep him confined indefinitely, no matter how great his grievance, and word of his plight would get out; too many people knew about the hunt for the English king. Nor did he believe the Austrian duke would dare to put him on trial for his alleged crimes in the Holy Land. Heinrich might, though—a chilling thought. And Philippe would not even bother with the farce of a trial. If he was turned over to the French king, he'd never see the sun again.

On the Monday after Christmas, Richard was struggling with a new enemy—boredom. He was accustomed to constant activity, physical and mental, and this enforced solitude was in itself a form of torture. He flipped at random through one of Hadmar's books, unable to concentrate, and finally sprawled on the bed to play a plaintive melody on the lute. After a time, he began to try different chords, creating his own song, one that expressed all he could not put into words. He was so intent upon the music that he did not hear the steps approaching the door and was taken by surprise when it opened suddenly, for Hadmar rarely visited him in the evening.

The guards were startled, too, staring at the two youths poised in the doorway. Richard sat up, interested in this unexpected development. The boys looked so similar that he guessed they were brothers or cousins; he put their ages at about sixteen or seventeen. He assumed that the Austrians and Germans followed the same practices of England and France, sending highborn youngsters to apprentice as squires in noble households. But as he watched them argue with the flustered guards, he decided they might well be Hadmar's own sons, for they had the easy assurance of those favored from birth. When the nervous guards continued to protest, one of the boys moved closer and Richard heard the clink of coins as pfennigs were exchanged. That did the trick; the guards stepped back, and the youths approached the bed.

They seemed wary and he thought again of that chained bear. But their eyes were shining with excitement. "I am Leo," one said, in schoolboy but understandable Latin, "and this is my brother, Friedrich. We wish to talk with you."

Friedrich seemed to think his brother had been too brash, for he added quickly, in better Latin, "Will you speak with us, lord king?"

In his present mood, Richard would have welcomed any diversion. "Why not?"

They needed no further encouragement, pulled a coffer closer to the bed and perched on it, putting Richard in mind of birds about to take flight. Setting the lute aside, he said, "What do you want to talk about?"

"About the war in the Holy Land," Leo said promptly, and his brother nodded in agreement. "We would hear about Jaffa and the march to Acre. We've heard stories from soldiers coming home, but we know soldiers like to boast, to make small skirmishes sound like great battles, so we were not sure how much to believe."

"How do you know I'll not boast, too?"

Friedrich seemed perplexed by the question, but Leo flashed an impudent smile. "Men already call you Lionheart," he said, "so why would you need to boast?"

Richard was amused by the lad's cockiness. "What would you hear first?"

"About Jaffa," they said in unison and listened raptly as he told them. After concluding that Jerusalem could not be taken, their army had withdrawn to Acre. He'd been planning an assault upon Beirut, the only port still in Saladin's hands, when word had reached them of a Saracen surprise attack upon Jaffa. The French had refused to help, even though there were wounded French soldiers recuperating at Jaffa, so Richard sent his nephew, Henri of Champagne, south with their army whilst he sailed down the coast. But they'd been becalmed and could not reach Jaffa for three days. They'd anchored their galleys offshore, waiting for dawn to see if the town and castle still held out. And as the dark retreated, they saw the saffron banners of Saladin streaming in the wind.

That had been one of the worst moments of Richard's life. Losing himself in the retelling, he could feel again his anguished rage. Jaffa held over four thousand men, women, and children, who were now dead or doomed for the slave markets in Damascus, all because the wind had dropped, keeping him from getting there in time. He'd lingered offshore, listening to the taunts of the jubilant Saracen soldiers, sick at heart. But then a priest had jumped from the castle wall and swum out to his galley.

"The castle had not yet fallen," he told the boys, "so we still had a chance." When his red galley, the *Sea-Cleaver*, headed for the beach, the Saracens watched in astonishment, unable to believe their greatly outnumbered foes would dare to land. Richard had been the first one ashore, a sword in one hand, his crossbow in the other, his knights loyally splashing after him even though they all expected to die there in the shallows. "But our crossbowmen cleared the beach, and I knew a back way into the town. There we finally encountered serious resistance and there was fierce fighting in the streets—until the castle garrison raced out to join us. Caught between my men and the garrison, the Saracens either died or surrendered."

The expression on their faces was a familiar one. He'd often seen youngsters look like that, enthralled and eager to experience the glory and gore of battle, although they thought more of the former than the latter. "So you do not think I am boasting," he said with a hinted smile, "I must tell you that Saladin had lost control of his men, that many of them were more interested in looting than fighting, which is why we were able to prevail despite being so outnumbered. Soldiers expect to gain booty in war, whether they be Muslim or Christian, and Saladin's men had grown war-weary after years of conflict." But they were not interested in the unromantic realities of war, only the bloody splendor of it, and they urged him now to tell them of the second battle of Jaffa four days later.

He did and, for a brief time, his words intoxicated all three of them. The cold December night gave way to the searing heat of Outremer. The boys could feel the blazing white sun on their skin, see the harsh grandeur of the land under a copper sky, and they hung on Richard's every word. "Jaffa stank like a charnel house, for towns taken by storm are shown no mercy. We'd pitched our tents outside the crumbling walls, and when Saladin learned that our army had been halted at Caesarea, he decided to strike, sure that if I was killed or captured, his war would be won. And if not for a Genoese crossbowman who'd risen early to take a piss, we'd have been caught sleeping. But he saw the sun reflecting off their shields. I had only fifty-four knights, four hundred crossbowmen, two thousand men-at-arms, and just eleven horses, whilst we later learned that Saladin's army numbered over seven thousand. There was no time to retreat into Jaffa, and even if we had, it was too damaged to hold off an assault. So I had our men anchor their spears in the ground and kneel, with our crossbowmen standing behind them, sheltered by their shields. As soon as one arbalester shot, he'd be handed another spanned crossbow, so the firing would be continuous. I assured our men that the Saracens' horses would not charge into a barricade of spears, and I was right. Again and again, they veered off at the last moment. We held fast for more than six hours, and when their repeated, failed charges had them bone-weary and frustrated, my knights and I charged and swept them from the field."

"How did you think of such a tactic? That was truly inspired!"

"It was not original, Friedrich. I borrowed the tactic from the Saracens, for I've never been too proud to learn from an enemy."

Leo leaned forward, resting his hands on his knees. "Tell us about the march from Acre," he said, and Richard did. They'd moved the coffer closer to the bed as he'd talked, wanting to know if it was true men died from the scorching heat of the sun—it was—and if the Holy Land had poisonous stinging vermin called scorpions—it did—and if he'd been wounded by a crossbow bolt in the days leading up to the battle at Arsuf—he had.

They'd all lost track of time, the boys enthralled by these stories of combat with infidels on the sacred ground where the Lord Christ once walked, Richard grateful for the chance to escape the stone walls of Dürnstein, if only in his imagination. When one of the guards cleared his throat meaningfully, that broke the spell, reminding them that it was growing late. "We must go ere we are missed," Friedrich said reluctantly. "Just one more question. We were told that at Jaffa you rode up and down alone in front of the Saracen army and not one of them dared to accept your challenge to combat. Surely that cannot be true? It would be quite mad!"

Richard grinned. "I daresay it was, Friedrich. But it seemed like a good idea at the time."

They stared at him and then burst out laughing. Their laughter stopped abruptly, though, as if they'd realized they'd let their guard down too far, been bedazzled into forgetting that this man was the enemy. Leo jumped to his feet, glaring at Richard with sudden hostility. "I do not understand you," he said, his voice rising. "You are a great warrior, as brave as Roland, and you were willing to die for Our Saviour. So how could you treat our father so shamefully?"

Richard blinked in surprise. "I had no quarrel with Had—" He broke off then, belatedly realizing the truth. "Are you the sons of Duke Leopold?"

Friedrich was on his feet now, saying proudly, "We have that honor. I am Friedrich von Babenberg, my lord father's firstborn, heir to the duchies of Austria and Styria, and this is my brother, Leopold."

Leo had assumed a defiant stance, chin jutting out, hands clenching into fists, and Richard wondered how he'd not seen the resemblance sooner, for the boy was the veritable image of Leopold in high dudgeon. "You shamed our father," he said accusingly. "At Acre, your men tore down his banner and you let it happen!"

Richard did not want to criticize the duke to his own sons, but neither was he willing to lie to them. "They were acting on my orders. When I was told he'd hoisted his banner, I told them to take it down, and I make no apologies for it. The French king and I had agreed that each of us would have half of Acre, and by flying his banner, your father was staking a claim to the city and its spoils. He was in the wrong, not I."

This argument carried no weight with Leo. "He fought with his men to take Acre, so why should he not have a right to share in the spoils? He was your ally and you treated him as if he were some lesser lord, of no account. But he is the Duke of Austria, and now you'll learn to your cost just what that means!" He turned on his heel and stalked out then, slamming the heavy oaken door resoundingly behind him.

Friedrich did not follow. "I do not understand, either," he said, but without his brother's belligerence. "My lord father is a proud man and you shamed him needlessly. When your men snatched his banner and flung it down into a ditch, they were trampling upon his pride, his honor, Austria's honor."

Richard was not happy with the unexpected turn the conversation had taken, discovering that Friedrich's reproaches were harder to deflect than Leo's accusations. "I did not know the banner had been thrown into a ditch."

"If you had known, would you have punished your men for it?"

Richard paused for a moment to consider. "No," he said honestly, "most likely I would not have. As I said, they were following orders."

"You claim my father was in the wrong for flying his banner. Even if that is so, what you did was far worse, for you forced him to leave the army and return home."

Richard scowled. "I most certainly did not. It was his choice to abandon the war, and a shameful one it was, for he'd sworn the same holy vow that I had, that we all had, to stay in Outremer until we'd recaptured Jerusalem from the infidels."

"But you made it impossible for him to stay. You truly do not see that? All of his men knew what happened, knew you'd treated the banner of Austria as if it were a worthless rag. How could he stay after being shamed and humiliated like that? His only way to save face was to depart, even though it grieved him greatly to do so. This was the second time he'd taken the cross. On his first visit to the Holy Land, he'd even been given a splinter of the True Cross by the King of Jerusalem and, as precious as it was to him, he presented it to the abbey at Heiligenkreuz, saying it belonged in a House of God. He cared for the fate of the Holy Land as much as you did, my lord. Had you only shown some concern for his honor—which he had every right to expect—he'd never have left, and you might not be here at Dürnstein this December eve." Friedrich turned then, apparently confident he'd gotten the last word, and walked with dignity to the door.

After they'd gone, servants brought up Richard's supper, but he ignored it. He'd initially dismissed Leopold's complaint as an annoyance, but when the duke sailed with the French king, he'd felt for the Austrian the same searing contempt he harbored for Philippe, unable to understand how they could so easily dishonor a vow made to Almighty God. Until tonight, he'd never tried to see Leopold's side. As reluctant as he was to admit it, there was some truth in what Friedrich had said. It would have been hard for such a proud man to remain after being humbled by the English king.

Lying back on the bed, he called up memories of that fateful confrontation. With all he had on his mind, Leopold's grievance had seemed of minor importance, and he'd had no sympathy for the duke's indignant protests. Losing patience, he'd started to turn away when Leopold had dared to grab his arm, and that fired his own temper. He remembered the other man's face, so deeply flushed he looked sunburned, his mouth ringed in white, a muscle twitching in his cheek. He remembered, too, telling his wife, sister, and nephew about it afterward. Henri had offered to intercede with Leopold, "to smooth his ruffled feathers," but he'd said not to bother, that Leopold "could stew in his own juices." Henri had considerable charm when he chose to exert it; could he have placated the irate duke? If he'd not been so indifferent to Leopold's wounded pride, might their meeting in Ertpurch have gone differently? Yes, Leopold was Heinrich's vassal, but he was no man's puppet, and if his son was right, he'd been very serious about taking the cross, unlike Philippe. Might he have been loath to seize a man under the protection of the Church, like Count Englebert in Görz? Would he have chosen to honor his vow to God above his fealty to the Holy Roman Emperor?

He was still brooding over his encounter with Leopold's sons when Hadmar made an unexpected appearance. "I thought you should know that Duke Leopold arrived late this afternoon. He said that he will be speaking with you on the morrow."

"Thank you for telling me," Richard said, and then, as the other man turned to go, he called out impulsively, "Sir Hadmar, wait. Do you blame me for removing your duke's banner at Acre?"

"Of course I do. By treating our banner with such disdain, you showed disdain for Duke Leopold, for our duchy, and for all Austrians."

Richard had not expected such an uncompromising response. "I appreciate your candor," he said, and Hadmar nodded stiffly, then withdrew, leaving Richard to try to reconcile this glimpse of a cold, implacable anger with the respectful treatment he'd so far received in Hadmar's care. He could only conclude that whilst Hadmar shared his duke's resentment over the banner, he did not approve of harming a man who'd taken the cross, who'd fought for Christ in the Holy Land.

❧

LEOPOLD SEEMED IN NO hurry to speak, standing in the middle of the chamber, arms akimbo as his gaze moved from Richard to the guards to the furnishings of the bedchamber. "I see that Sir Hadmar has provided you with lodgings befitting your rank," he said at last.

Richard regarded him challengingly. "Is that likely to change?"

"No." Leopold fell silent again and then raised his head, squaring his shoulders. "In Vienna, your chamber was not . . . suitable for one of high birth. Whatever you have done, you are a king, God's anointed. I was justly angered, but even so . . ." It was obvious he did not find it easy to admit this. His arms were now folded across his chest and his mouth tautly drawn, but he met Richard's eyes unflinchingly as he spoke.

The last thing Richard had been expecting was an almost-apology. It was a telling moment, though, revealing that the Austrian duke believed himself to be a man of honor, bound by a code of ethics that compelled him to acknowledge his mistakes, however distasteful he found that admission. "And what of my men?"

"They have been moved to more comfortable quarters. And a doctor has tended to the boy's injuries."

Richard would have choked before he'd say "Thank you." He settled for, "I am gladdened to hear that."

Leopold shifted position, glancing toward a coffer as if he meant to sit, then changed his mind. "My wife, the Duchess Helena, has accompanied me to Dürnstein, as have my sons, my brother, my nephew, and several clerics, including my cousin, the Archbishop of Salzburg, and the Bishop of Gurk. Sir Hadmar has planned a feast for this afternoon in honor of our arrival."

Richard did not understand why Leopold was telling him this, so he said nothing, watching as Leopold began to move restlessly about the chamber, picking up and discarding items at random. "Several of them have expressed a desire to meet you," the duke said, after yet another prolonged silence.

Richard stared at him, incredulous. "You are asking me to dine with you?"

A slight flush had begun to warm Leopold's face and throat. "No, that would be . . . awkward."

"I daresay it would. Since you have men guarding me with drawn swords day and night, I rather doubt I'd be trusted with a knife. Though I suppose you could assign a servant to cut my meat?"

Leopold ignored the sarcasm and continued doggedly on. "After the meal, my chief minstrel, Reinmar von Hagenau, will entertain us. I thought you might join us then." He paused, swinging back to face Richard. "I realize I cannot compel you, that the choice is yours. If you do accept the invitation, I would hope that we could agree to be . . ." He paused again, searching for the right word.

"Civil?" Richard suggested helpfully, his eyes gleaming. "By that, I assume you'd prefer that we avoid controversial topics like Cyprus, the Holy Land, and Hell."

Leopold was looking grim by now. "Clearly this was a mistake," he said, and started toward the door.

"I accept," Richard said, stopping the duke in his tracks.

"You do?" He sounded more suspicious than pleased, and Richard had to bite back a smile.

"Well, I happen to be free this afternoon. . . ."

Leopold studied the other man intently. "Very well, then. Sir Hadmar will escort you to the great hall after Sext has rung."

"I am looking forward to it more than I can say," Richard murmured, delighted to see the sudden unease in his gaoler's eyes. This was going to be a very tense afternoon for Duke Leopold; at least he hoped so. After the duke departed, Richard startled his guards by laughing aloud. This was a God-given opportunity and he meant to make the most of it. Isolation was a danger. The more contacts he could have with the outside world, the better, especially if those contacts included princes of the Church.

🙟

THE DUCHESS HELENA LOOKED to be a year or two younger than her husband, who was Richard's age—thirty-five. The daughter and sister of Hungarian kings, she was the only one besides Leopold who spoke any French, flavored with an appealing Hungarian accent. But language was not an obstacle, for most of the men were able to converse in Latin and a youthful archdeacon was able to translate into German for the women. Eufemia, Hadmar's wife, was considerably younger than her husband, and their two sons made only a brief appearance, considered too young to join the festivities. Friedrich and Leo were there, though, and when Richard acted as if this was their first meeting, Leo shot a barbed look at his brother and said Saint Friedrich's guilty conscience had caused him to confess all to their father. Friedrich scowled at Leo and muttered something in German under his breath that did not sound flattering to Richard. Their brotherly spat reminded him of his own squabbles with Geoffrey, for at that age neither had missed any opportunities to harass the other. Yet he sensed that Leo and Friedrich were allies as often as they were rivals, and that had not been true with Geoffrey or Hal. For whatever reasons—which had never interested him in his youth but which he sometimes pondered as an adult—the Angevin House had always taken Cain and Abel as role models.

Leopold's younger brother Heinrich was introduced to Richard as the Duke of Mödling, a duchy he'd not even heard of, but Leopold's teenage nephew Ulrich stirred some unpleasant memories of Friesach, for he was the Duke of Carinthia, a region Richard hoped never to have to see again. The other guests included Leopold's cousin Adalbert, the Archbishop of Salzburg; Dietrich, the Bishop of Gurk; and the Cistercian abbots of Stift Zwettl, which had been founded by Hadmar's father, and Stift Heiligenkreuz, which had figured in Arne's desperate cover story. Richard had hoped that Lord Friedrich von Pettau would be part of Leopold's entourage, for he yearned for information about the men arrested in Friesach, but their gaoler was not among those mingling in Dürnstein's great hall.

Richard would later look back on that afternoon as a truly bizarre experience, but one he'd enjoyed more than Leopold. The duke kept his distance, leaving it to Hadmar to act as the English king's host, and Richard could see that Leopold was on edge, not sure how long his unpredictable prisoner would remain on his good behavior. He was indeed tempted, for he knew a public argument about Leopold's likely descent into Hell would have mortified the duke in front of his family and friends. But that did not serve his interests, and so he set about doing all he could to charm these highborn guests. He gallantly kissed the hands of Helena and Eufemia, paying them the sort of courtly compliments he'd long ago learned in his mother's Aquitaine. He pleased Archbishop Adalbert by respectfully kissing his ring and, remembering Friedrich's story, he asked the abbot of Heiligenkreuz's Holy Cross Abbey to tell him about their sacred fragment of the True Cross. This was not only an inspired topic of conversation with clerics, it put Leopold in a favorable light, and Richard hoped the listeners would take note of his generosity of spirit, praising the man who was his gaoler.

He was not long in realizing why they'd been so eager to meet him. In part, it was natural curiosity, for he was a renowned soldier, one of the most celebrated kings in Christendom. But it was Jerusalem that was the true draw, and he soon found himself answering questions about desert battles in Outremer, the future of the Holy Land, and the man who fascinated much of Europe even if he was an infidel, Salah al-Din.

Leopold's brother and nephew and the other men present were most interested in the war; although he'd never show it and maintained a dignified silence, Richard was sure that the duke, too, yearned to hear of the march from Acre, of Ibn Ibrak and Jaffa. Had circumstances been different, he and Richard would have been fighting side by side against the Saracens, men doomed to Hell, of course, but worthy foes nonetheless. The clerics wanted to hear of the biblical holy sites and were visibly disappointed when Richard told them that he'd been one of the few not to make the pilgrimage to Jerusalem after the peace treaty was made. But when he explained that he did not feel he'd earned the right, having failed in his vow to retake Jerusalem from Saladin, he could see that they approved his resolve to keep faith with the Almighty, even found it admirable. That had indeed been his reason for denying himself the spiritual joy of seeing the Holy Sepulchre, the rock upon which the body of the Lord Christ had lain, the room where the Last Supper had taken place, all the sacred sites exalted in Scriptures. But he had no scruples about using his refusal to gain himself some goodwill amongst Leopold's bishops.

His love of music served him well, too, when Reinmar von Hagenau came forward to entertain, for he had some knowledge of the German troubadours called minnesingers, and he was able, therefore, to request one of Reinmar's songs by name. He graciously yielded to the women's coaxing and joined Reinmar in performing one of his own songs, although highborn poets in Aquitaine preferred to have their compositions sung by joglars and jongleurs. He even managed to turn the afternoon's one awkward moment to his advantage. Leo had been noticeably sulking, and taking advantage of a break in the conversation, he'd asked in a loud, carrying voice if it was true that the English king and his brothers were known as the Devil's brood. Both Leopold and Helena were dismayed by their son's rudeness, but Richard merely smiled and cheerfully shared his favorite family legend—Melusine, the Demon Countess of Anjou, who'd wed an Angevin count, only to reveal herself to be the Devil's daughter. He and his brothers had often joked about Melusine, taking a perverse pride in having such a scandalous ancestress. But seeing that some of the guests were shocked and the abbots were making the sign of the cross, he quickly reassured them that such stories were nonsense, of course, tales told by their enemies to discredit the Angevin House.

All in all, he was quite pleased with what he'd accomplished on this Tuesday in late December. Hadmar personally escorted him back to his tower chamber, with the guards much more conspicuous now that they'd left the hall. The Austrian bade Richard a polite good evening, pausing at the door to say, "You're a clever man."

Richard did not pretend to misunderstand him. "I'd take that as a compliment if you did not sound so surprised," he said dryly. "Your duke and I had no time to talk this afternoon. But we will need to talk . . . and soon."

Hadmar nodded. "You will," he promised, and for the moment, Richard had to be content with that.

LEOPOLD DID NOT RETURN until several hours after darkness had fallen. Richard was encouraged to see he was accompanied by a servant who placed a wine flagon and two gilded goblets upon the trestle table, pouring for both men before making a discreet departure. Leopold took a sip, keeping his eyes upon Richard all the while. "I think that went well," he said, as close as he could come to thanking the English king.

You mean I did not make you look like a fool in front of your family and vassals, Richard thought, reaching for his own wine cup. Leopold was showing signs of tension again, drumming his fingers absently upon the wooden table. "I regret my son's bad manners earlier today."

"He is young," Richard said with a shrug. "Besides, I like the lad. He has spirit, reminds me of my own son."

Leopold looked startled. "I did not know you had a son. I'd not heard that your queen was with child."

"Philip is not Berenguela's," Richard said, taking a swallow of the wine. "He is eleven, born long before my marriage." He was not surprised to see the other man's brows draw together, for how likely was it that one known as Leopold the Virtuous would have begotten any children outside of his marriage bed? But Leopold's frown was puzzled, not disapproving, as his next question proved.

"I thought your queen's name was Berengaria."

"It is, but only since our marriage. Her given name is Berenguela, but that was too foreign-sounding for my subjects. I prefer it myself, though, so we agreed that she would be Berengaria in the court and Berenguela in the bedchamber."

A silence fell then, as they both became aware of the incongruity of this moment, speaking so casually, almost intimately, of family, the sort of conversation a man might have with friends. Richard had mentally rehearsed what might well be one of the most important discussions of his life, but now he heard himself saying something utterly unpremeditated. "I did not know that my men threw your banner into a ditch until Friedrich told me last night."

"It was a sewer," Leopold said flatly.

Wonderful, Richard thought. *Next the man would reveal it had then been eaten by pigs.* "Friedrich asked me if I'd have punished my men had I known that. I said no, for they were following my orders, even if they did take it further than they ought. And if I had it to do over again, Leopold, I would still give that order. But I would have talked with you afterward about it. That we did not talk, I do regret."

Leopold's dark eyes were unreadable. "That sounds almost like an apology."

Richard smiled. "I'd say it is rather late for apologies. And under the circumstances, surely my sincerity would be suspect."

The Austrian duke gave no indication that he'd caught the ironic undertones. "Yes, it would," he agreed, confirming Richard's suspicion that the man had no sense of humor whatsoever.

Taking another swallow of wine, Richard leaned across the table. "Let's talk not of the past, but of the future, then. As I see it, we have a choice of two roads to take. We can let bygones be bygones and I ride out of here on the morrow, ideally with a safe escort into Moravia, whilst you give the order to set all of my men free, too. Or we can discuss a ransom. Naturally, I prefer that first road. But I'm willing to travel down the second one if need be. If it is to be the first option, I will give you my sworn word that I will seek no vengeance, will nurse no grievance against you, for I now understand that I was not as blameless in this matter as I first thought. If it must be the second, I am sure we can reach an accommodation satisfactory to us both. So, which will it be?"

Leopold was no longer meeting his eyes, staring down into the depths of his wine cup. "It can be neither."

That came as a shock, for Richard had convinced himself he'd be able to talk sense into the other man, having seen subtle signs that Leopold might be regretting grabbing a lion by the tail. A day ago, he'd have erupted in rage, reminding the duke that he'd be cast into eternal darkness if he persisted in this madness, demanding to know if any grievance was worth putting his immortal soul at risk. But a seventeen-year-old boy had done something few others had managed to do: he had gotten him to see a viewpoint other than his own. Setting his wine cup down carefully instead of slamming it to the floor, he said, "Leopold, you are making a fatal mistake. Whatever happens to me, you'll suffer a far worse fate. We both know the Holy Father will excommunicate you for so great a sin. But it is not too late. There is still time to undo what has been done."

Leopold pushed his chair back, got slowly to his feet. "You are wrong, Lionheart," he said somberly. "We no longer have the luxury of choosing our own fates. You see, I was honor-bound to send word of your capture to my liege lord, and Emperor Heinrich has commanded me to bring you to him at Regensburg. We depart on the morrow for the imperial court."

CHAPTER SEVEN

❧

JANUARY 1193

On Road to Regensburg, Germany

This time Richard agreed not to attempt an escape in order to avoid being bound. Hadmar gave him the excuse he needed by telling him it was one hundred fifty miles to Regensburg, but the truth was that he'd have done almost anything to avoid arriving at Heinrich's court trussed up like a Michaelmas goose. He was disappointed that the Archbishop of Salzburg and the Bishop of Gurk did not accompany Leopold, for he'd hoped he might get a chance to talk to one of them privately. But neither prelate nor the Cistercian abbots were part of the duke's retinue. Leopold kept a deliberate distance, offering Richard no opportunity to speak with him. He did manage one brief conversation with Hadmar and, figuring he had nothing to lose, he asked if the Austrian clerics approved of his captivity. The other man surprised him by how readily he answered. "Of course they do not. The duke is defying the Church and that is of great concern to them. But they are loyal to him, nonetheless, and will remain so, even if the Pope were to inflict the ultimate punishment upon him." Not what Richard wanted to hear.

They covered about twenty miles a day, a respectable distance for winter travel, staying at castles, once at a monastery, and once at an inn where their arrival sent the innkeeper into a tizzy. Richard was always lodged in comfortable quarters, but kept isolated and under heavy guard, which gave him too much time to think about what awaited him at the imperial court.

He'd never met Heinrich von Hohenstaufen, but what he knew of the other man was not reassuring. Heinrich was twenty-seven, very well educated, said to be fluent in Latin and, like Richard, a sometime poet. He was also said to be

ruthless, inflexible, unforgiving, and haughty. Richard's brother-in-law, the former Duke of Saxony, and his nephew had nothing good to say of him. Neither
had Richard's mother and wife.

Eleanor and Berengaria had an unexpected encounter with Heinrich and his
consort two years ago when they were on their way to join Richard in Sicily.
Heinrich and Constance were heading for Rome to be crowned by the Pope,
having learned of the death of Heinrich's father on crusade, and their paths had
converged in the Italian town of Lodi, much to the discomfort of its bishop, their
reluctant host. Lying on his bed in a German castle, doing his best to ignore the
guards encircling him with drawn swords, Richard recalled his mother's tren-
chant appraisal of the German emperor.

"Heinrich is clever, too clever by half. And cold. If he were cut, I daresay he'd
bleed pure ice. He had all the charm of a wounded badger." Eleanor had paused
when Richard laughed. "But he is a dangerous man, Richard, not one to be taken
lightly, for he has no scruples and a great deal of power. He'd make a very bad
enemy."

That was a damning indictment, but Richard found his wife's somber assessment to be even more troubling, for Berengaria was naturally inclined to give
others the benefit of the doubt and she was not one for drama or hyperbole. "He
does not appear regal," she'd said, "not like you or my brother Sancho, and at
first I wondered why men seemed to fear him so much. But his eyes . . . Richard,
I know this may sound foolish. But when I looked into his eyes, I felt that I was
looking into an abyss."

RICHARD DID HAVE ONE NIGHT in which he was free from his own dark
thoughts. Friedrich and Leo sneaked in to chat, bringing their cousin Ulrich,
the young Duke of Carinthia. They wanted him to tell Ulrich how he'd ridden
out alone to defy the Saracen army at Jaffa, translating freely for Ulrich, whose
Latin was shaky at best. Leo seemed to have thawed considerably since their last
meeting and Friedrich soon explained why, saying they were very glad that the
English king had apologized to their father for disrespecting his banner. This
came as a surprise to Richard, but as he listened to the youths chatter on, he realized what had happened. Leopold had taken his expression of "regret" for not
having talked at Acre and expanded it to cover the entire incident for the benefit

of his sons. Richard had no interest in salvaging Leopold's honor, but he liked Friedrich and Leo and saw no reason to deny them a lie that obviously brought them comfort. They seemed to think the worst was over now, that the emperor and he would agree upon a ransom and he'd soon be free to return to his own lands, but Richard put that down to the wishful thinking and natural optimism of the young. They were in high spirits and indiscreet, confiding that their mother had wanted to accompany them to Regensburg, for she was fond of Heinrich's wife, the Empress Constance. Yet their father had insisted she return to Vienna, which had sorely vexed her. Richard encouraged them to talk, wondering why Leopold would deny his wife a visit to the imperial court. He did not like the sound of that; did Leopold expect something to happen that he did not want Helena to witness?

As they rose to go, they conferred briefly and Leo declared that they had news to share. The emperor had ordered the king's imprisoned men to be brought to Regensburg, too. Count Meinhard was bringing the eight men he'd seized at Udine, Friedrich von Pettau was coming with the six men he'd arrested at Friesach, and their father had sent word to fetch the three prisoners he was holding back in Vienna. They watched Richard, smiling, clearly thinking this would please him. But this was the last thing he wanted to hear—that his men would be caught up with him in Heinrich's web. Leopold would have released them sooner or later, if only to soothe his conscience. Heinrich would see them as inconsequential.

⁂

ON EPIPHANY, GUNTHER REINED IN beside Richard, said, "Regensburg," and held up his fingers to indicate they were only ten miles from their destination. Richard was taken by surprise, therefore, when they halted at a castle after riding a few miles, for they could easily have reached Regensburg before nightfall. Like Dürnstein, this stronghold was perched on a cliff high above the Danube River, a stark, brooding silhouette against a winter sky bruised by snow clouds. Hadmar would later tell him it was known as Donaustauf, or Stauf on the Danube, owned by the Bishop of Regensburg. For now, he was given no explanations, merely escorted to an upper chamber. It was not until he unshuttered the window and saw Leopold and his retinue riding away that he realized he was being left behind while they continued on to Regensburg. He found that puzzling, even baffling; surely Leopold would be eager to display his prize at the imperial court? But there was no one to answer his questions, only his German-speaking guards. He'd always found it easy to banter with his soldiers, and he thought he'd have been able to establish a rapport with these Austrian men-at-arms, too, if not for the insurmountable language barrier.

He did not sleep well that night and was tense and restless the next day, expecting at any moment that Gunther would arrive to take him to Heinrich. It did not happen. By the second day, his emotional pendulum was veering wildly from frustration to fury to despair and back again. His guards watched him warily as he paced, murmuring among themselves, this constant surveillance rubbing his nerves so raw that he soon developed a throbbing headache. He went to bed early, for there was nothing else to do. No sooner had he finally fallen asleep, though, than he was jolted awake by a loud pounding on the door.

The guards hastened to lift the bolt and Hadmar strode into the chamber, snapping a command in German that had them gaping at him in astonishment. "You must hurry and dress," he told Richard, "for we are leaving tonight."

Richard sat up and stared at him. "Leaving for where? It is rather late for paying a visit to Heinrich."

Hadmar grimaced, growling another order to the guards. "We are not going to Regensburg. We are returning to Austria, so you must make haste."

"No," Richard said, so emphatically that the guards turned to stare at him even though they did not understand a word of Latin. "I am going nowhere until you tell me what has happened."

The other man scowled. "We've no time for this. The duke is waiting below in the bailey, wants us gone from here straightaway." When Richard did not move, he said impatiently, "You're not in a position to balk. Must I remind you that I can have you taken from here by force?"

"You think it would go well if you ordered your men to dress me and I resisted?" Richard jeered. "So unless you intend to drag me stark naked out into the snow, you'd best tell me what I have every right to know. What happened with Heinrich?"

Hadmar's hesitation was brief. "My duke and the emperor could not agree on terms for your surrender and Leopold began to fear that Heinrich might send men to seize you. He thinks it best if they continue the negotiations from a distance. Now, for the love of God, will you do as I ask?"

Richard nodded and swung his legs over the side of the bed, reaching for his clothes. Hadmar's answer was far from satisfactory, but his other questions could wait, for whatever Leopold's motivation, it was in his own best interests to get as far away from the imperial court as their horses could take them.

☙

THEY RODE FAST AND HARD, letting neither the cold nor a snowfall on the second day slow them down. Richard got no answers as the miles slipped away, for neither Leopold nor Hadmar ever ventured within speaking range. Even the duke's sons would no longer meet his gaze, quickly averting their eyes whenever he glanced in their direction. If he'd had any doubts that they knew something he did not, they were erased when he had an unexpected evening visit from the Austrian knight, Gunther. He brought a wineskin and the two men sat together for a while, passing the wineskin back and forth as Richard had so often done in the past, sitting by a campfire, drinking and joking and swapping memories of shared campaigns. With Gunther, there was no talk, of course, only what they could communicate without need of words. They drank in silence and then Gunther rose and departed, but that simple act of camaraderie gave Richard a small measure of comfort.

He actually felt a flicker of relief as Dürnstein loomed on the horizon, for in a world of foreboding shadows and shifting ground, it at least was familiar. And here he'd finally gotten some answers. It was well after dark when they arrived, but he awoke early the next morning to await his long-overdue talk with Leopold von Babenberg. As at Donaustauf, though, he was left alone to fume and fret as the hours passed. For a man with so little patience, waiting was an ordeal, one that forced him to face how powerless he was. The day ebbed away with excruciating slowness. Servants brought meals, then carried them away untouched. It was not until candles and oil lamps were lit as darkness infiltrated the chamber that his suspense was ended. He'd just about given up hope for the night when the door opened and Hadmar entered, followed by a servant carrying several large wine flagons and cups.

"The duke is gone," he said before Richard could speak. "He left for Vienna this afternoon, so you'll have to make do with me." He ordered the servant to put the tray on the table and then turned to Richard with a wide, sweeping gesture and a mocking bow. "After you, my lord king of the English."

Richard took a seat, glancing toward the flagons, which Hadmar was lining up between them. "This is a discussion that we cannot have whilst sober, then?"

"Sobriety is highly overrated," the other man said with a lopsided smile.

Richard had already noticed his flushed face, the slight slurring of his speech, and his suspicions were confirmed when Hadmar began to pour wine into their cups, his the exaggerated care of one not trusting his own reflexes. The *ministe-rialis* might not be drunk yet, but he was well on the way.

Sliding a cup across the table toward Richard, Hadmar took a deep swallow from his own cup. "As I told you at Donaustauf, my duke and the emperor could not agree on terms, and until they do, Leopold is not willing to give you up. Heinrich told him that there is a fortune to be made now that you are helpless in their hands, and Leopold wants to make sure that he gets his fair share."

Richard could not stop himself. Reaching for the shovel, he said scornfully, "So what began as wounded honor is now all about money." He at once regretted those intemperate words, not wanting Hadmar to storm out before he learned what had happened in Regensburg.

The Austrian did not appear to have taken offense, though. "So it would seem," he agreed equably. "Gold tends to bedazzle men as easily as beautiful women. Leopold quite sensibly puts no trust in the emperor's word and so wants safeguards in place to protect his interests. He also wants Heinrich to promise that you'll not be physically harmed whilst in his custody."

Richard set his wine cup down so abruptly that wine sloshed over the rim. "Does Leopold have reason to think my physical safety would be put at risk?"

Hadmar shrugged, drank again, and belched. "Knowing our esteemed emperor is reason enough, especially now that he has the blood of a bishop on his hands."

"What mean you by that?"

"We arrived at Regensburg to find Heinrich has embroiled himself in a scandal of monumental proportions. Nigh on eighteen months ago, the Bishop of Liege died on his way home from the Holy Land and two candidates soon emerged for his See. Albert of Louvain was an Archdeacon of Liege and, more important, the younger brother of the Duke of Brabant and the nephew of the Duke of Limburg. He was not yet thirty, the canonical age for consecrating a bishop, but oddly, no one bothered about that, not even the Pope."

He paused to drink again. "The second candidate was another Albert, the Provost of Rethel, whose primary qualification seems to have been that he is the maternal uncle of Heinrich's wife, the Empress Constance. He was backed by Baldwin of Hainaut, the Count of Flanders, who was not about to accept any man proposed by his rival, the Duke of Brabant. The first Albert won the election easily but the second Albert continued to protest, as did Count Baldwin, and the whole matter was referred to the imperial court. The emperor formed a committee of bishops and abbots to resolve it. They proved not to be the stuff of which martyrs are made, deciding Heinrich should declare the winner. He then proceeded to infuriate both sides and violate canon law by giving the bishopric to Lothar von Hochstaden, who happens to be the brother of Count Dietrich von Hochstaden, one of the emperor's battle commanders and probably the closest that Heinrich has ever come to having a friend."

In vino veritas, Richard thought. He was no longer angry at Leopold for his craven escape back to Vienna, for he'd never have gotten such wine-fueled candor from the duke. "So what happened then?" he prodded. "I'm guessing neither Albert raced to congratulate Heinrich's handpicked puppet."

"Indeed not," Hadmar confirmed, peering at Richard owlishly over the rim of his wine cup. "The first Albert headed for Rome to appeal to the Pope, whilst the second Albert, too old for such travel, stayed at home and sulked. The Holy Father submitted young Albert's claim to the papal curia and they voted in his favor. Apparently Celestine was willing to overlook a small matter like canonical age in order to vex the emperor, for he even honored Albert with the rank of cardinal and sent him off with a saddlebag filled with money and papal letters ordering his consecration."

Looking surprised to find his cup empty, Hadmar poured himself a generous helping and splashed wine onto the table as he sought to refill Richard's cup. "The Archbishop of Cologne enraged Heinrich by refusing to consecrate his choice, so he then dragged Lothar to Liege, where he forced the citizens to acknowledge him. Since the dissenters had their houses torn down, most rallied around Lothar. But Albert was now safe in French exile—or so the poor man thought—and there the Archbishop of Reims, who happens to be a papal legate and cardinal himself, was quite happy to consecrate Albert. This was last September. In October, three German knights arrived in Reims, claiming they were fleeing the wrath of Emperor Heinrich. They soon met Albert and won his trust. But this newfound friendship was short-lived, for on November 24, he agreed to go riding with them outside the city walls, and they promptly drew their swords and dispatched him to the afterlife. At least they had the decency not to slay him in a cathedral like your sainted Thomas of Canterbury. The killers then fled and guess where they sought refuge? Yes, indeed, straight as a crow flies to the imperial court."

While Richard could think of a few bishops he wouldn't mind dispatching himself to the afterlife—the Bishop of Beauvais came at once to mind—he was dumbfounded by the brutality and audacity of this crime. "Knowing what Becket's murder cost my father, how could Heinrich be so stupid?"

"That is the only plausible argument in Heinrich's defense," Hadmar allowed. "For whatever his other failings, he is not stupid. Of course, he is also one of the most arrogant souls ever to walk God's earth. You're as prideful as those lions you fancy, my lord king, but when matched against our emperor, you're a veritable lamb!" Hadmar seemed pleased with his wordplay, for he laughed loudly. "Heinrich denies any guilt, of course. But the slain bishop's kin have no doubts. The dukes of Brabant and Limburg are in open rebellion and the archbishops of Cologne and Mainz are expressing such outrage that they are likely to join the rebellion, too."

Richard leaned back in his chair, shocked that Heinrich could have blundered into such a quagmire, but very grateful for it. Hadmar watched him with a smile that held more sadness than amusement, and then shook his head. "You are thinking that Heinrich's troubles can work to your advantage, but just the opposite is true. There is nothing more dangerous than a cornered wolf and Heinrich sees your capture as a God-given opportunity to distract his subjects and to gain the money he needs to put down the rebellion. He even thinks he'll be able to use English or French gold to finance his invasion of Sicily, for he's still set upon claiming its crown in his wife's name. So he is desperate to get you into his hands and he'll do whatever it takes to make that happen."

Richard was no longer listening. "French gold?" he echoed, hoping against hope that he'd heard wrong.

Hadmar's smile vanished as if it had never been. "Heinrich told Leopold that he thought the English would pay dearly to ransom you. But King Philippe might pay even more to keep you entombed in a French prison for the rest of your earthly days."

"Heinrich would not dare turn me over to the French! He knows the Church would cast him into eternal darkness for so great a sin." Richard would have argued further, but he was silenced by what he saw now in the other man's eyes—pity.

Hadmar nodded to acknowledge the truth in that. "You are right. The emperor knows that even the aged, timid Celestine would have to take action then. That is why he told Leopold he intends to put you on trial."

Richard had a sudden and urgent need for wine and drained his cup in several swallows. "On what charges?"

"He means to accuse you of conspiring with Saladin to keep the Holy City in infidel hands and of arranging the murder of Conrad of Montferrat, but he may well come up with a few other charges, too. The Bishop of Beauvais visited the imperial court on his way back to France and he seems to have spent the time pouring poison into Heinrich's ear. The good bishop says you ought to be burned as a heretic, for you might well be a secret Muslim—"

"Lies, all arrant, despicable lies!" Richard raged. "I did all I could to recover Jerusalem, only to be thwarted by the French at every turn. Nor did I murder Conrad of Montferrat. Heinrich cares naught for the truth and he'll burn in Hell for that. But what of Leopold? Does he believe these lies? Do you, Hadmar?"

"Would I be sitting here now with you if I did?" Hadmar shot back, sounding testy for the first time. "Of course I do not believe these accusations. As for Leopold, I doubt that he does, either, for his grievance against you was always personal. He wanted to make you pay for humbling him in Acre and for deposing his kinsman in Cyprus, not to see you dragged before a German court—"

"I'll make no apologies for deposing Isaac Comnenus," Richard interrupted angrily. "He usurped the Cypriot throne and treated the people so harshly that they were only too willing to assist in his overthrow—"

Now it was Hadmar's turn to interrupt. "You need not defend your actions in Cyprus to me. I'd not have cared had you sent Isaac to the Cairo slave market instead of turning him over to the Knights Hospitaller. But Leopold felt obligated to object because his mother was a daughter of the Greek Royal House and thus a cousin to Isaac."

Richard had far greater concerns than Isaac Comnenus and he fell silent as he considered all that Hadmar had revealed. "It makes no sense," he said at last. "Heinrich told Leopold that he hopes to collect a large ransom. So why, then, put me on trial if his aim is to turn a profit?"

"Leopold asked that, too. Heinrich does indeed mean to demand a vast sum. But he knows that he'll be subjected to harsh criticism for holding you prisoner. Not only does your captivity violate the Church's protection, it breaches the rules of war, for no state of war exists between England and the empire. Leopold said that whilst Heinrich does not seem overly troubled by what the Pope might do, he does not want to add fuel to the rebellion or give German clerics an excuse to join the rebels. He thinks that once you are found guilty of betraying Christendom to the infidels—and you *will* be found guilty in his court—it will be more difficult for the Church to defend you and he'll have a free hand to do with you whatever he wishes, even if that means selling you to the highest bidder."

"If the highest bidder is the French king, it will be signing my death warrant. Heinrich would lose no sleep over that. Would Leopold?"

Hadmar did not answer at once, finally saying, "I think so. He knows you did not betray your fellow Christians in the Holy Land. Whether he'll admit it or not remains to be seen, though. He's a proud man and a stubborn one and he may well conclude that he's gone too far along this road to turn back now."

"Even if it means riding over a cliff? Hadmar, there is still time to stop this madness. From what you've been telling me, Leopold is not happy with Heinrich's plans for me. He fears—as well he ought—that his own honor will be stained. And he must fear, too, the wrath of the Church, for even if Celestine dares not excommunicate the Holy Roman Emperor, he'd have no such compunctions about a duke. Leopold will make the perfect scapegoat. Surely he realizes that?"

"I daresay he does," Hadmar admitted. "But he sees no way out now and so he figures he might as well profit by claiming half of the ransom. My duke is a practical man," he said with another sad smile. "He is half Greek, after all."

"If it is the accursed ransom he wants, he can have it. He can have it all. Convince him to forget about Heinrich and strike a deal with me. I told him I was willing to pay his ransom. I still am. I know he believes himself to be a man of honor. This may be his last chance to preserve that honor . . . and his peace of mind."

Hadmar reached for his wine cup and drank until it was empty. "Christ Jesus, Richard," he said softly, "do you think I have not already tried that? Leopold never bargained for any of this. He thought himself justified to hold you to account for the way you shamed him—shamed Austria—at Acre. But what Heinrich intends to do with you . . . That will gnaw away at him, poisoning his peace. Yet he sees no way out of this trap. He may not respect Heinrich, but the emperor is still his liege lord. To defy Heinrich and reach a private accord with you is beyond him. He'd see that as an act of rebellion, and he knows that Heinrich would, too. As horrified as he was by the Bishop of Liège's murder, he is not going to rebel against the man to whom he has sworn fealty and homage."

Shoving his chair back, Hadmar got unsteadily to his feet. "I thought you deserved to know the truth. I am sorry I cannot do more. I very much fear that what you call 'this madness' is not going to end well for any of us." Without waiting for Richard's response, he turned away, brushing aside the guard who sought to steady him as he staggered toward the door.

Richard did not move from the table. An eerie stillness seemed to have enveloped the chamber and he thought he could hear the dull thudding of his heart, the constricted rasp of his breath, even the sound of his own thoughts as they ricocheted around in his head. He poured more wine, only to set it down again quickly, for the sweet Rhenish wine tasted as bitter as wormwood and gall.

He was thirty-five and for nigh on twenty years, he'd been a soldier. By now Death was an old and familiar foe. He could not begin to count all the times he'd put his life at risk. Storms at sea, malarial fevers, sword thrusts that he'd parried just in time, lances that shattered against his shield, crossbow bolts and arrows that seared through the air with a lethal humming sound he sometimes heard in his dreams. Men said he was blessed in battle, but his body bore the scars of old wounds like any other man's. His nephew Henri had once told him, half admiringly and half in reproach, that he was easy to find on the battlefields of the Holy Land, for he was always in the thick of the fighting, usually surrounded by a sea of saffron, the colors of Saladin's elite Mamluk guard. He'd not denied it, for he believed that a king must lead by example, and he'd been the first to force his way into Messina, first to land upon the beach at Cyprus, and again at Jaffa. He'd long known that he did not feel the crippling fear that other men did in combat, had accepted it without question as God's gift, proof of divine favor.

But he no longer believed that he was Fortune's favorite, for he could make no sense of what had happened to him and his men in the past two months. Was God punishing him for his failure to take Jerusalem as he'd vowed? Had he angered the Almighty by breaking the Fifth Commandment and making war upon his father? What had he done to deserve this? How could he atone if he did not know how he'd sinned? He had no answers. He knew only that he'd never felt as desperate, as vulnerable, and as utterly alone as he did on this frigid January night at Dürnstein Castle.

CHAPTER EIGHT

❧

JANUARY 1193

London, England

She had been doubly blessed, born a great beauty and a great heiress. She would be the only woman to wear the crowns of both England and France, but history would remember her by the name of her beloved duchy—Eleanor of Aquitaine. She would prove to be as controversial as she was captivating, for she never accepted the constraints that their society and the Church imposed upon women, convinced that she could rule as well as any man. At thirteen, she'd wed the King of France, Louis Capet. While Louis had been bedazzled by his lively young wife, he'd been troubled by her strong will and worldly ways, for he'd been meant for the Church, pulled from the cloisters at age ten by the unexpected death of his elder brother. For her part, Eleanor had been heard to say that she'd thought to marry a king, only to find she'd married a monk. Theirs was a clash of temperaments and cultures. Eleanor was a child of the sun-splashed south, where the pursuit of pleasure was not sinful, troubadours were held in esteem, and women were not always demure, docile, and sweetly submissive, whereas Louis was a son of the more austere, staid, and conservative north.

Their marriage endured for fifteen years, though, even surviving the disastrous Second Crusade and the scandal that trailed in Eleanor's wake after their fateful visit to her uncle's court at Antioch, where she had attempted to end their union by making use of the tactic that kings had always employed to rid themselves of unwanted wives—arguing that their marriage was invalid because they were related within the forbidden fourth degree. Louis had her taken from

Antioch by force and his counselors tarnished her honor by whispering that it was unholy love for her uncle that had prompted such shocking, unwomanly behavior. It was a bitter lesson for Eleanor in the inequities of male and female power; it would not be her last.

What the marriage could not survive was her failure to provide Louis with a male heir. After the birth of her second daughter, he began to believe that the marriage was accursed in God's eyes, and ended it in March 1152. Eleanor at once returned to Aquitaine and barely two months later, she shocked Christendom by choosing her own husband instead of waiting dutifully for Louis to pick a man acceptable to the French Crown. Her choice could not have been more abhorrent to Louis, both as monarch and man, for she wed the Duke of Normandy, Henry Fitz Empress, nine years her junior, who already had a reputation for boldness and a good claim to the English throne.

If Eleanor and Louis had been mismatched, she and Henry were perfectly matched, two high-flying hawks who lusted after empires and each other. Within two years of their marriage, Henry had taken England and Eleanor was once again a queen. The Angevin domains far dwarfed those held by her former husband, stretching from the Scots border to the Mediterranean Sea, and to those watching in amazement, admiration, or dismay, Henry seemed to be riding the whirlwind. Eleanor proudly rode it with him. She'd failed to give Louis a son; she gave Henry five, four of whom survived to manhood, and three daughters, two of whom wed kings. For twenty years, they soared from triumph to triumph; not even the murder of an archbishop in Canterbury Cathedral dimmed the luster of the Angevin court. And then it all fell apart.

No one was more stunned than Henry when his three eldest sons rose up in rebellion against him, supported by their mother, his own queen. He prevailed, of course, facing untried youths and the militarily inept French king, but their rebellion had dealt him a heart's wound, one that never fully healed. His sons, he forgave, time and time again as the years passed. Eleanor, he could not forgive, for by blaming her for his estrangement from the sons he loved, he could avoid blaming himself. He concluded that Eleanor had been a jealous wife, resentful of his young mistress known as Fair Rosamund, and he did not believe her when Eleanor told him she'd rebelled because he'd laid such a heavy hand upon her beloved Aquitaine and refused to establish their sons in their own domains. His greatest weakness was an inability to relinquish any of his royal power and his sons chafed under a tight rein, while Eleanor remained his prisoner, held in English castles far from her homeland as summers turned to winters and then summers again, having to watch helplessly as her family tore itself asunder.

She once told Dame Amaria, the loyal maid who'd shared her long captivity, that she and Henry did not often make mistakes, but when they did, they tended to be spectacular. She had sixteen years to ponder hers, and during those long, difficult years shut away from the world, she developed a skill that neither her husband nor her sons had ever cultivated—the art of introspection. She also learned to live with her regrets, and that gave her the resilience to survive the tragedies she could not prevent.

Their golden boy, Hal, the young king, died in yet another rebellion against his father. Among Henry and Eleanor's failings as parents, they'd had obvious favorites—for Henry, it was Hal and then his youngest, John, and for Eleanor, it was always Richard. Geoffrey had been the forgotten son, and had been driven to rebellion by his father's failure to see that he and Richard were very different men from the feckless, charming, and irresponsible Hal. Geoffrey met a meaningless death in a tournament at the court of his new ally, the young French king, Philippe, who would prove to be as unlike Louis as granite and sand. Henry drove Richard away next, refusing to acknowledge him as the heir, thinking that would give him leverage over this strong-willed, fiery son. He succeeded only in convincing Richard that Henry meant to disinherit him in favor of John, and so he, too, traveled the same road as his brothers—to the French court. By then Henry was ailing, aging, and did not want to fight his son. But he was too proud to give Richard what he demanded—official recognition—and a life of brilliant triumphs would end in bitter tragedy. He died at Chinon Castle after making a humiliating surrender to Richard and Philippe, few doubting that the death blow had been the news that his beloved son John, for whom he'd sacrificed so much, had betrayed him.

Richard's first command as king was to free his mother from her confinement at Salisbury Castle. She was to be obeyed, he directed, in all matters, and so it was. Thus began perhaps the most satisfying time of Eleanor's life, for she was no longer a bird with clipped wings. She and Richard shared what Henry had so desperately wanted from his sons and never gotten: complete and utter trust. Her son was willing to do what Henry would not—make use of her formidable talents, the political instincts that had been sharply honed after more than fifty years on history's stage. Immediately upon Richard's accession to the throne, he prepared to honor his vow to free Jerusalem from the Saracens. It had been three years since he'd seen the white cliffs of Dover receding into the distance, confident that he could rely upon his mother to keep his kingdom at peace until his return.

Now in her sixty-ninth year, Eleanor was resisting aging as fiercely as she'd once fought against convention. After making a winter crossing of the Alps to deliver Richard's bride to him in Sicily, she'd returned to England to mediate between his volatile half brother Geoff, the reluctant Archbishop of York, and his unpopular chancellor, the clever, crippled, and prideful Bishop of Ely, Guillaume de Longchamp, and to keep a close eye upon his younger brother John, the Count of Mortain and a willing pawn of the French king. Eleanor had few good memories of England and yearned for the warmth and sophisticated splendor of her favorite city, Poitiers. She was determined, though, to remain on this accursed, rain-soaked isle until Richard returned from the Holy Land. As the weeks turned into months, other crusaders arrived home, most of them eager to relate tales of her son's bravura exploits on the battlefields of Outremer. But of Richard, there was no word, only an ominous, suffocating silence.

❦

THE CHAPEL OF ST JOHN THE EVANGELIST was the reason that Eleanor preferred to stay at the Tower of London rather than the royal palace at Westminster. The top floor of the keep was split into two large rooms, a great hall and a spacious bedchamber that offered a private entrance into the chapel. On nights when sleep would not come, Eleanor could wrap herself in a fur-lined cloak and slip silently into the oratory to be alone with God and her own thoughts. In her long life, she'd endured many a wretched Christmas—some as the bored, unhappy wife of the French king, many more as Henry's prisoner, unsure that she'd ever regain her freedom. But none had been as miserable as this past one, presiding over her Christmas Court with a composed demeanor and a brittle smile, daring one and all to believe the vile rumors her own son was spreading: that Richard was dead.

The stone walls of the chapel had been recently whitewashed and in the soft candlelight, they glowed like polished ivory. During the daylight hours, the sun turned the stained-glass windowpanes into resplendent jewels; now they gave off a muted shimmer, an occasional flicker of emerald or ruby or royal purple. The scent of incense hung in the air; Eleanor found it a comforting aroma, reminding her of the rich spices of Sicily and Poitou. Prayer cushions were scattered about on the gleaming tile floor, but her aging bones needed more cosseting and she'd had a wooden bench installed along the east wall. She sat down upon it now, easing an embroidered pillow into place against the small of her back. One of her greyhounds had followed her into the oratory, but she hadn't the heart to banish the beast. If the Almighty watched over even the sparrow, why should He not watch over dogs, too?

She'd not come to pray on this rainy January night; she'd already sent more prayers winging their way to the Almighty's ear than there were stars in the skies. "Ah, Harry," she said softly, "do they weep in Purgatory? Do they mourn their loved ones who've come to grief? I do not believe he is dead. I think I'd know if that were so. Surely I'd feel it?"

Yet would she? She'd had no premonitions for Hal or Geoffrey or her daughter Tilda, just the shock of hearing that she must bury yet another child. But she understood Richard as she'd not always understood his brothers. Theirs was a bond that went beyond blood. They shared so much—a deep, abiding loyalty to the duchy he'd expected to rule, a love of music and pageantry and distant, exotic places; risk-taking, too, although she'd learned to temper that urge with a dose of caution as she'd aged. She saw in Richard the best of her House, worthy heir to that long line of Dukes of Aquitaine, tracing their descent to the mighty Charlemagne. She saw in him, too, bittersweet flashes of his father, the young, dashing duke who'd seemed destined for greatness from their first meeting on a hot August day in Louis's Paris palace. No, if Richard were dead, she'd know.

But where was he? What had happened? Each passing day put his kingship more in peril, for if men believed that he'd not be coming back, they'd have no choice but to turn to John. She'd always thought she'd fight tooth and nail for the survival of their dynasty, but could she support John if he claimed the crown over his brother's dead body? She'd never fully forgiven him for betraying Harry on his deathbed. How could she forgive him now for betraying Richard, too? Suddenly she felt bone-weary, felt each and every one of her sixty-eight years. "What if we never know what befell him, Harry?" she whispered. "If his ship was caught in a storm at sea . . ."

"Madame?" Dame Amaria stood in the doorway, her anxiety conveyed in the stiffness of her posture and the slight quiver in her voice. "The Lord of Châteauroux is here, asking to see you. He apologizes for the lateness of the hour, but he says it is urgent."

Eleanor froze. André de Chauvigny was blood-kin, for his mother was her maternal aunt. He was far more than Richard's cousin, though; he was her son's closest friend, so close they could finish each other's sentences and communicate volumes with the exchange of a single glance, theirs the bond that Richard had lacked with his own brothers. But André had never set foot on English soil, joking that it had bad weather, worse wine, and virtuous women, all of which were good reasons to stay away. Yet now he'd braved a dangerous January crossing of the turbulent channel called the Narrow Sea. What had he heard? "Of course I will see him, Amaria." She still sat there on the bench for a few moments more, sensing that her world was about to change in ways she dreaded to contemplate.

By the time she emerged from the chapel, André had already been admitted to her bedchamber. He was soaking wet, his mantle sodden and travel-stained, his boots caked with mud, his disheveled state offering further evidence that his need to see her was indeed urgent. But Eleanor saw only his haggard, grief-stricken face.

"No, not Richard. . . ." That uneven, faltering voice sounded so unfamiliar she did not even recognize it as her own. The room suddenly seemed to tilt, her treacherous body betraying her as her God had done. She'd never fainted, had always prided herself on her calm response in a crisis. Now, though, she felt alarmingly light-headed, her knees threatening to give way. But André and Amaria were already there, hastily guiding her toward the closest seat.

As she collapsed into the chair, André flung himself onto his knees at her feet, grasping her hand in his two icy ones. "No, Madame, no! He is not dead!"

Her eyes intently searched his upturned face. "You swear it is so?"

"Upon the life of my own son. I'll not lie to you. It is bad, as bad as it could be. But he still lives."

She closed her eyes for a moment, looking so aged and frail that he found himself wondering how much of the truth he dared to tell her. But when she spoke, it was in the voice of the queen, not the anguished mother. "Tell me," she commanded. "Tell me all you know."

"Richard was captured several days before Christmas by the Duke of Austria's men, in a village near Vienna. Leopold put him under arrest and he is to be handed over to that hellspawn Heinrich, if it has not already happened."

Eleanor's hand clenched upon the arm of the chair. "How do you know this, André? How sure are you?"

"All too sure, Madame. I was going stark, raving mad at Châteauroux, waiting for word. I thought Archbishop Gautier would be amongst the first to hear anything, so I rode to Rouen after Christmas. I was still there when one of his spies arrived from the French court." André shifted uncomfortably, his body aching from hours in the saddle, and Eleanor gestured for him to rise. As he sank down upon a nearby coffer, he gratefully accepted the wine cup Amaria was offering. "Whatever the archbishop is paying his man, it is not enough. He somehow managed to make a copy of a letter Heinrich had written to Philippe, revealing Richard's capture."

"You have it with you?"

"I do, a copy of the original and a translation into French." Reaching into his tunic, he pulled out a leather pouch. "Here is the archbishop's letter to you, Madame, and here is Heinrich's." Not sure if she was familiar with Latin, an uncommon skill for most women, he handed her the French copy.

Eleanor waited until one of her ladies hurried over with a candlestick before she unrolled the parchment. The candle helped, but not enough. Eschewing false pride, she handed the letter back. "The lighting is too dim for my aging eyes. Read it aloud, André."

He rose and carried the letter toward a large iron candelabrum that was suspended from the ceiling. Clearing his throat, he gave Eleanor a quick glance, as if apologizing for what she was about to hear.

"*Heinrich, by the grace of God, emperor of the Romans and ever august, to his beloved and especial friend Philippe, the illustrious king of the Franks, health and sincere love and affection. . . . We have thought it proper to inform your nobleness that whilst the enemy of our empire and the disturber of your kingdom, Richard, King of England, was crossing the sea for the purpose of returning to his dominions, it so happened that the winds brought him to the region of Istria, at a place which lies between Aquileia and Venice, where, by the sanction of God, the king, having suffered shipwreck, escaped, together with a few others.*

"*A faithful subject of ours, the Count Meinhard of Görz, and the people of that district, hearing that he was in their territory, and calling to mind the treason and treachery and accumulated mischief he had been guilty of in the Land of Promise, pursued him with the intention of making him prisoner. However, the king taking to flight, they captured eight knights of his retinue. Shortly after, the king proceeded to a borough in the archbishopric of Salzburg, where Friedrich von Pettau took six of his knights, the king hastening on by night with only three attendants, in the direction of Austria. The road, however, being watched, and guards being set on every side, our dearly beloved cousin Leopold, Duke of Austria, captured the king in a humble house in a village in the vicinity of Vienna.*"

André paused then to take a swallow of wine, hoping to wash away the vile taste of the words in his mouth. *"Inasmuch as he is now in our power, and has always done his utmost for your annoyance and disturbance, we have thought proper to notify your nobleness, knowing that the same is well pleasing and will afford most abundant joy to your own feelings. Given at Rednitz on the fifth day before the calends of January."*

"It sounds as if Richard was trying to reach Saxony," Eleanor said after a very long silence. "He had obviously been warned that he dare not land at any Italian, French, or Spanish ports. But how did he come to have so few men with him, André? He was riding into enemy territory with less than twenty men? What happened to all the knights with him when he sailed from Acre?"

André shrugged helplessly, no less baffled. "Mayhap they drowned when he was shipwrecked. But surely we'd have heard of so great a disaster? Madame . . . there is more. The archbishop's spy was able to get his hands on a second letter, this one written by Philippe to Leopold after hearing Heinrich's news. He accused Richard of arranging Conrad of Montferrat's murder and cautioned Leopold that he was not to free Richard, not to do anything until they had a chance to confer." His mouth contorting, he said bitterly, "That accursed swine on the French throne means to put in his own bid for Richard, and if he does . . ."

There was no need to finish the sentence, for Eleanor understood the consequences fully as well as he did. She was sitting up straight now, no longer slumped back in the chair as if her bones could not bear her weight, and he saw that color was slowly returning to her cheeks; that sickly white pallor was gone. As he watched, it seemed to him that she was willing her body to recover, finding strength from some inner source that defied her advancing years, and he felt a rush of relief. It had shaken him to see her looking so fragile, so vulnerable, so old. She was on her feet now, beginning to pace as she absorbed the impact of the emperor's letter, and when she turned to face André, he saw that her hazel eyes had taken on a greenish, cat-like glitter, reflecting nothing at that moment but a fierce, unforgiving rage.

"They will not get away with this," she said, making that simple sentence a declaration of war. "We shall secure my son's freedom, no matter what it takes. And we will protect his kingdom until he can be restored to us, André."

That was exactly what André needed to hear. "I will leave for Germany as soon as I can make the arrangements, Madame, and I will find him, that I swear to you upon the surety of my soul—"

"No, André. Richard will have greater need of you here. Philippe will seek to lay claim to Normandy now that he knows he need not fear Richard's retaliation.

You and those men loyal to my son must hold it for him until he can deal with that 'accursed swine on the French throne' himself."

As much as André wanted to go to Germany on his own, to tear that wretched country apart in his search for Richard, he knew she was right. "I promise you, Madame, that Philippe will claim not a foot of Norman soil whilst Richard is gone." He hesitated then, for John was still her son, but it had to be said. "It will be a two-pronged attack—Philippe in Normandy, John in England. I do not know John's whereabouts, but he'll soon learn of Richard's capture and when he does—"

"John is in Wales, trying to hire routiers and not having much luck so far." Eleanor did not explain how she was so well informed about her youngest son's activities, instead giving André a level, almost challenging look from those mesmerizing green eyes. "You need not worry about John," she said coolly. "I will deal with him."

She turned then to Amaria, telling the woman to summon her scribe. "Word must go out on the morrow. Richard's justiciars must be told, especially Will Marshal. Thank God for Will. We'll have to send out writs for a great council, too. So much to do." She seemed to be talking to herself rather than to André, even though she glanced from time to time in his direction. "The ports must be put on alert and the royal castle garrisons strengthened. And we must begin laying plans to raise the ransom." Looking back at André, then, Eleanor was surprised to see that he was grinning.

"You remind me of Richard, my lady, planning one of his campaigns. You are sure that Heinrich will demand a ransom?"

"Had it been Philippe . . ." She shook her head grimly. "But Heinrich . . . Yes, he will seek to ransom Richard. He is in dire need of money, for he is facing a rebellion from his own vassals. The fool actually dared to kill a bishop, or at least made it appear as if he did, which makes me seriously reconsider my estimation of the man's intelligence. In a just and fair world, he'd be kept so busy fending off excommunication for that bloody act of lunacy that he'd never have dared to lay hands on Richard. But in a just and fair world, we'd not have a Pope so spineless it is a wonder he can walk upright," she said, so acidly that André saw she expected little help from Celestine in gaining Richard's freedom.

Eleanor crossed to André then and reached out, taking his hand in hers. "You look exhausted, Cousin. Did you sail from Barfleur to Southampton? So you've been on the road for days. My steward will find you lodgings here in the Tower. Try to get some sleep if you can. We will prevail, I promise you that."

"I believe you, Madame," he said, and he meant it, greatly heartened by the reemergence of the Eleanor of legend, the woman who'd dared to go on crusade, to choose her own destiny, to do what no other queen had ever done—rebel against the man who was her liege lord and husband. Richard's courage and boldness had not come entirely from his sire, he thought, but then his hand tightened on hers. "Madame . . . it cannot be allowed to drag out. Richard must be freed soon." He paused and then said, so softly that his words reached her ears alone, "A caged eagle does not thrive in captivity."

Eleanor was chilled to hear her own fears given voice so eloquently. But as her eyes and André's caught and held, she nodded, for this man knew her son as well as anyone on God's earth, possibly even better than she herself did. "I know," she said quietly. "But we must never forget this, André. Whilst Richard could not come back to us from the grave, he can come back from Germany. And he will."

⟡

AT FIRST, RICHARD'S QUEEN and his sister had been enjoying their stay in the Eternal City. The Pope had made them welcome and they'd soon been installed in the palace of the Frangipani family on the Palatine, the most famous of Rome's seven hills. Joanna had visited Rome on several occasions during her marriage to the Sicilian king, William II, and Berengaria had been there when she and Eleanor had traveled from Navarre to join Richard in Sicily. But Anna was keen to see all of the ancient sites and so the queens hired guides to take them to the Temple of Apollo, the Palace of Nero, and the underground crypts in the Baths of Diocletian, for indulging the girl called the Damsel of Cyprus had become a habit with them by then.

Anna was an object of considerable curiosity and gossip, for Roman society did not know what to make of her. It was known that she was the daughter of Isaac Comnenus, the self-proclaimed Emperor of Cyprus, who'd been deposed by Richard, and people were puzzled that she was neither a prisoner nor a hostage. It seemed obvious that she was now part of the royal household and Romans did not understand how this had come to pass. They did not know that Isaac Comnenus had been a father no girl could love, a man who'd been so hated by the Cypriots that they'd cooperated in his overthrow. Thirteen-year-old Anna and her stepmother, Sophia, had been happy to leave Cyprus and its bad memories behind, and she'd soon embraced her new life as the English king's ward.

On this January afternoon, Anna was playing tables with Alicia, the young girl Joanna had taken in after her Templar brother had been drowned in a shipwreck off the coast of Sicily. But she was finding it difficult to concentrate upon the game. Each time she glanced around the hall, she could see that the other women were just as distracted, too.

After nigh on two years in their company, Anna knew them all well by now. Her private name for Dame Beatrix was "the dragon," for the tart-tongued Norman had been with Joanna since childhood and she was not to be crossed. Berengaria's ladies were of little interest, for they spoke no French, just the Romance tongue of Navarre and the *lenga romana* spoken in Aquitaine, and they seemed boring and dull to the fifteen-year-old Anna. But there was nothing boring or dull about the Lady Mariam, whose family history was as exotic as her appearance. Her sun-kissed skin and slanting golden eyes proclaimed her Saracen blood, and although Anna knew she was a Christian, chosen as a companion for Joanna, King William's homesick child-bride, her mother had been one of the slave girls in the *harim* of King William's father. Her scandalous background made her a source of fascination for Anna, as did the fact that she'd been conducting a clandestine love affair with Joanna's Welsh cousin Morgan.

Anna wondered sometimes if Joanna and Berengaria knew of Mariam's trysts with Morgan. She was sure Berengaria would not approve, for Richard's queen adhered to a strict Spanish code of morality that made her seem older to Anna than her twenty-three years. Anna had been a bit bedazzled by Berengaria's husband, and she'd adopted the Saracen name for him—Malik Ric—because she knew it amused him. She did not think Berengaria was the best mate for such a man. She still liked Berengaria, though, for she had a good heart. Isaac Comnenus's daughter knew better than most how rare true kindness was in their world.

But it was Joanna whom Anna had come to love: Joanna, who was beautiful and worldly and had a mind and will of her own. She knew how to savor life's daily pleasures, too, and that was a lesson Anna had been eager to learn, for there had been little laughter at the Cypriot court, where her father had suspected mirth and stifled joy, fearful of losing his tenuous and illegal hold on power. So when her stepmother had chosen to stay in her native Sicily upon their arrival in Messina that past November, Anna had elected to remain with Joanna and Berengaria as they continued their journey on to the domains of the English king.

The game with Alicia forgotten, Anna found herself watching the other women in the hall. Berengaria was working on a delicate embroidery, as were most of the ladies-in-waiting, while Joanna read aloud to them from a book called *The History of the Kings of Britain*; Anna had heard Joanna say it had been written by an Augustinian canon named Geoffrey of Monmouth, but his name meant nothing to her. The book did not seem to be holding Joanna's attention, for she would occasionally pause, staring off into space before rousing herself to resume reading. Anna could not remember the last time she'd heard anyone laugh. It was almost as if this had become a house of mourning.

Alicia waited patiently for her friend to turn back to the game board. When it did not happen, she said softly, "I pray every day for King Richard's safe return." She'd meant to comfort, knowing how worried Anna was, how worried they all were, but Anna took it amiss and scowled.

"Of course Malik Ric is safe! How can you even doubt it?"

Anna's voice had carried and the adults in the hall glanced her way. None commented upon her passionate outcry, though, for the subject of the king's safety was a very sensitive one and certainly not to be discussed in the hearing of Richard's queen and sister. An uncomfortable silence fell, but they were accustomed to such fraught moments by now. The normal rhythms of a royal household had been utterly disrupted by the gradual, reluctant realization that the king was missing and could well be dead.

Berengaria smiled sadly as she watched Anna scold Alicia for her "lack of faith." Beside her, Joanna had given up any pretense of reading, the book lying open on her lap. She knew the bleak path that her sister-in-law's thoughts were following, for hers were keeping pace, both of them desperate for word of Richard's whereabouts. They never spoke of their apprehension, though, for they'd entered into a conspiracy of silence, acting as if there were no cause for concern, as if they could vanquish their dread by refusing to acknowledge it. They had done this once before, when they'd been stranded off the coast of Cyprus after the royal fleet had been scattered in a storm and Isaac Comnenus was threatening to take them ashore by force. Not once during that ordeal had either woman voiced her fear that Richard's galley might have gone down in that Good Friday storm, and their faith had been rewarded when Richard had arrived just hours before Isaac's ultimatum was to expire. But that had been only a week, albeit an endless one. Now it was more than two months since there'd been any sightings reported of the English king.

Groping for a safe topic of conversation, one that would not inadvertently lure them into discussing her husband's disappearance, Berengaria returned to their earlier discussion of the crime that was the talk of Rome—the shameful murder of the Bishop of Liege and the bloody footprints that seemed to lead right to Emperor Heinrich's throne. "I wish I could say I do not believe Heinrich capable of such a godless act, but I cannot, Joanna. There was something about the man that I found chilling. I feel heartsick for his wife. What will she do when the Holy Father casts Heinrich into eternal darkness? All Christians are duty bound to shun an excommunicate. But how can Constance do that? Do you think the Church will make allowances for her plight?"

Joanna cared deeply for Constance de Hauteville, who'd done so much to comfort her as she struggled to adapt to her new life in Sicily, and she hated to think of the misery that Constance had found in her marriage to Heinrich von Hohenstaufen. "I've never thought about how the wife of an excommunicate would cope," she admitted. "Fortunately, Constance will be spared that, for the Pope is not going to excommunicate Heinrich. My father was not excommunicated when Thomas Becket was slain, and the Church's outrage was even greater over his killing than the Bishop of Liege's murder."

"Yes, but Pope Alexander believed your lord father when he swore he'd never meant for those knights to act upon his heedless, angry words. The Holy Father knew him to be a good man at heart, one who truly mourned the archbishop's death. Can Pope Celestine say as much about Emperor Heinrich?"

"Mayhap not, but it will not matter. Whatever the Pope's suspicions about Heinrich's involvement in the crime, he has no proof." And he'd likely not act even if he had a confession written by Heinrich in his own blood. Joanna kept that cynical viewpoint to herself, though, for she was touched by her sister-in-law's innocent trust that justice would always prevail, be it in the papal curia or the king's court.

Berengaria was prepared to argue further. She knew, of course, that all churchmen were not pure and incorruptible. Some of them were truly loathsome individuals, their holy vows notwithstanding. She frowned then, thinking of her husband's enemy, the Bishop of Beauvais. But when the Church was confronted with such a shocking crime, the spilling of a bishop's blood, surely sordid political considerations would not prevent the guilty from being brought to judgment. Before she could continue, there was a stir at the end of the hall.

When she saw the tall, dignified figure being escorted toward them, Joanna jumped to her feet. "My lord bishop! How the sight of you gladdens our eyes!" She hastened forward to welcome Hubert Walter, with Berengaria just a step behind, for they'd both become quite fond of the Bishop of Salisbury during their time in the Holy Land. Joanna appreciated his pragmatism, Berengaria had been grateful for the spiritual support he'd given her when Richard seemed likely to die of the lethal malady called Arnaldia, and they both valued the bishop's unwavering loyalty to the English king.

Once greetings were exchanged and they were seated by the center hearth with wine and wafers on the way, Joanna was able to ask the question that had been hovering on her tongue from the moment she'd seen him entering the hall. "My lord bishop, when we left Acre, you were planning to sail with Richard. What changed your mind?"

"I did sail with the king, at least as far as Sicily. He insisted then that I disembark, for we'd learned that he was not going to be able to land at Marseille, and he said he wanted me to get to the Pope ere his enemies did, and then to hasten to England to help his lady mother and the justiciars rein in his brother. I arrived in the city last night and went to the papal palace this morning to pay my respects to the Holy Father. It was only then that I was told you were still in Rome, my lady."

"After listening to my sister-in-law's stories about their January crossing of the Alps," Joanna said, with a fond glance at Berengaria, "we decided to wait till the alpine routes were more passable in the spring. She said at one point the women had to be slid down the mountain slope on ox hides!"

Berengaria smiled at the memory, which was easier to do now that it was part of her past. Accepting a wine cup from a servant, she waited until the bishop had been served before saying quietly, "I realize you've heard nothing about my lord husband, for you'd have told us at once. But you can ease my mind on one matter. He'd not fully recovered from the quartan fever when we sailed from Acre. Was he well when you parted from him in November?"

Hubert stalled for time by reaching for a wafer he had no intention of eating. While he might normally have dreaded female hysteria, he knew both women well enough to be sure they'd not lose control. Knowing how devastated they'd be, though, by what he had to tell them, he wished he could delay the moment of truth even longer. "He was fit when I last saw him, Madame," he said, glad that he could at least assure Richard's wife of that much. "But I do have news of the king. Whilst I was still with the Pope, a courier arrived with an urgent message from the Archbishop of Cologne. I deeply regret that I must be the bearer of such ill tidings. King Richard was captured near Vienna by the Duke of Austria and, according to the archbishop, he will soon be turned over to the Emperor Heinrich."

Joanna had tensed with his first words of warning, and she thought she was braced for whatever he had to reveal. Now she discovered it was not so, for his news struck her like a physical blow. All the air seemed to have been expelled from her lungs and she found herself struggling for breath. When she glanced toward her sister-in-law, she suffered a second shock, for Berengaria was gazing raptly at the bishop as if he were one of God's own angels, her face glowing.

"Gracias a Dios!" She turned toward Joanna then, her smile radiant. "He is alive, Joanna, he is alive!"

"And a prisoner of the German emperor!"

"Not for long, though. The Holy Father will never tolerate such an outrageous breach of Church law. He will force Heinrich to release Richard and to make amends for daring to defy the Church and for treating a king, a man who fought for God in the Holy Land, with such disrespect." Berengaria reached over, covering Joanna's hand with her own. "I can confess now," she said, "how fearful I was. I kept remembering those savage storms, how the sea seethed and raged, how the gales were said to be even more violent during the winter . . . but I ought to have had more faith. The Almighty would never abandon Richard."

Joanna had opened her mouth, but she caught her words before they could escape. By now all in the hall had gathered around them as word spread, and Hubert related what little he knew—that Richard's ship had been driven onto the Istrian coast during a storm and he had apparently been trying to reach his nephew's lands in Saxony. "If he got as far as Vienna, he almost made it, too, for he'd have been safe once he'd crossed into Moravia. What I do not understand is why he had so few men with him. According to the archbishop, less than twenty, and only three with him when he was finally caught."

That horrified Joanna almost as much as the news of Richard's capture, for she had a vivid imagination and could envision all too well what those desperate weeks on the run must have been like for her brother. Mariam had drawn near and took advantage of the sudden silence to ask Bishop Hubert if the Archbishop of Cologne's messenger had known the names of those twenty men. When he shook his head, she said nothing, but she soon slipped unobtrusively from the hall, her passing noted only by Joanna, who knew she was terrified for Morgan's safety. She loved Mariam as a sister and was very fond of her cousin Morgan, but for now she could think of no one but Richard, facing the greatest danger of his life.

Berengaria withdrew as soon as she could politely do so, and as she exited the hall with her ladies, Joanna was sure she was going to the nearby church of Santa

Maria in Capitolo to give thanks for Richard's deliverance. Anna had accompanied her, as eager as Berengaria to believe the worst of Richard's ordeal was over, taking Alicia with her.

Their household knights began to break up into smaller groups to discuss this momentous news and what its ramifications would be. Finally Joanna found herself alone with Hubert Walter and Stephen de Turnham, the English lord who'd been entrusted by Richard with the safety of his women on their homeward journey. From the corner of her eye, she saw Beatrix hovering nearby, as she'd done for every crisis of Joanna's twenty-seven years, and she was grateful that she'd be able to turn to Beatrix for support, knowing Mariam, so often her mainstay, would be thinking only of Morgan. And she could expect no help from her sister-in-law, not as long as Berengaria clung to her belief that the Pope could bring a man like Heinrich to heel like a cowed dog.

She took her time, choosing her words with care, for she did not want to offend Hubert Walter, who was, after all, a prelate of the Church. "I fear I do not have as much confidence as my sister by marriage in the Holy Father's ability to influence the emperor."

"The Pope is indeed outraged, Madame, as are all at the Holy See. But if I may speak candidly, I very much doubt that he will dare to use the Church's most powerful weapon against Heinrich, and nothing less than excommunication and anathema will compel the emperor to set the king free."

Joanna rallied then, for to give in utterly to despair would be to fail Richard in his time of need. "Heinrich will seek to ransom Richard, as any common bandit would do. Whatever he demands, we will raise it. My mother will see to that." Forcing a smile, she said, "And I would back her against Heinrich any day of the week."

They smiled, too, as desperate as she for hope. But then the bishop showed Joanna just how much their world had changed by saying that it would be best if she and Berengaria remained in Rome indefinitely. It was too dangerous to pass close to the territories of the empire, for if they fell into Heinrich's hands, he could use their captivity to force further concessions from Richard. "We must not labor under the delusion that we are dealing with a man of honor," he said grimly. "There is nothing he will not do to enhance his own power, and we forget at our peril that he is utterly unfettered by scruples or moral boundaries."

Joanna bit her lip, knowing he spoke the truth. She found herself imagining what it must be like for Richard, at the mercy of such a man, and she could not suppress a shiver. So caught up was she in her own dark thoughts that she did not at first hear Hubert's question and he had to repeat himself. "I am sorry, my lord. You were saying something about letters?"

"I will be leaving Rome by week's end. I thought that you and Queen Berengaria might wish to give me letters to deliver."

"Letters . . . for my mother? Of course."

"No, letters for the king. I am not going back to England. I am going to Germany."

Joanna felt tears stinging her eyes. "Bless you for that."

He reached over and patted her hand. "You must never forget that there are men beyond counting who'd willingly offer up their own lives for the king."

"For certes, any man who ever fought beside him," Stephen de Turnham interjected.

Joanna smiled at them both, but her smile was as fleeting as that moment of hope. "Richard also has enemies beyond counting," she said, thinking of the French king and her own brother.

"Yes, he does," the bishop agreed, paying her the compliment of giving her the same brutal truth he'd have given to a man. "And now that they think he may have been dealt a mortal blow, the vultures will be circling."

Joanna's head came up, green eyes narrowing. "Let them. No vulture can bring down a lion." But the men knew better than that, and so did she.

❦

THE WELSH STRONGHOLD OF CARDIFF was over a hundred years old, built on the site of an ancient Roman fort. It had once been the prison of a king's brother; for thirty years, the Duke of Normandy had languished there at the command of the first King Henry. That was not a comforting thought to the current king's brother John, Count of Mortain, and he reminded himself that Cardiff was his now, come to him by his marriage to the wealthy Gloucester heiress.

Pushing away from the table and an interrupted chess game with one of his knights, Sir Durand de Curzon, John moved restlessly about the chamber before going to the window and unlatching the shutters. The storm continued unabated, rain slanting sideways, turning the inner bailey into a muddy quagmire, while the wind tested the castle defenses like an enemy army probing for weaknesses. John watched for a while longer before saying sulkily, "Does the sun never shine in this accursed country?"

His audience had no interest in discussing the weather. His mistress yawned and stretched like a sleek, pampered cat. Although it was midmorning, she was still abed. Sitting up, she let the sheet dip, giving Durand de Curzon a partial glimpse of her breasts. He was sure it was deliberate. He'd seen more beautiful women than Ursula, but never one who radiated such raw, smoldering sexuality. He doubted that even the most celibate of priests could look upon that wanton red mouth, those smoky grey eyes, that mane of lustrous flaxen hair, and that lush, ripe body without feeling the throb of forbidden desire. Hellfire and damnation, the woman was a walking, breathing mortal sin.

Feeling his eyes upon her, Ursula regarded him with indifference that he wanted to believe was feigned. But he would not have lain with her even had she been willing. As long as John was bedding her, she was off-limits, for there was too much at stake to risk it upon a tumble with a wench, no matter how enticing her carnal charms. Still, though, she bothered him, like an itch he could not scratch. He could not decide if she was the ultimate cynic, disillusioned and jaded, or simply dull-witted. Even with John, she seemed remarkably nonchalant. A royal concubine usually stroked her lover's pride as lovingly as his cock, hanging upon his every word as if they were as precious as pearls, laughing at all his jests, doing her best to make him believe she saw him as irresistible and clever and vigorous as he invariably saw himself. Not Ursula, though. Durand had never heard her compliment John, nor did she seem enthralled by his conversation, and his sardonic jests were as likely to earn an eye roll from her as an appreciative, sultry giggle. That John tolerated this dubious behavior only enhanced Durand's certainty that the woman must be scorching hot in bed.

John was still grumbling about the foul Welsh weather and Durand could no longer ignore him. He had many duties as a knight in John's household, some perfectly proper, others too dark to confess to any priest, but he was also expected to amuse his lord when called upon, to help John banish boredom, even if it meant playing endless games of chess or hazard or listening to John's musings about life, women, and how unfairly he'd been treated by his father. John was very defensive about his relationship with Henry, occasionally boring Durand almost to tears as he explained why he'd had no choice but to abandon his dying father and why anyone in his place would have done the same thing. Durand knew that few others saw this side of John, for John was not a man who easily gave his trust. But he'd begun to share some of his secrets with Durand, confident that they would be kept. What he did not know was that Durand had secrets of his own.

John had not yet moved from the window, careless of the cold, damp air he was allowing to invade his bedchamber. "If this keeps up much longer, we'll soon be building arks."

Durand decided it was time to contribute to the conversation lest John think he was not listening. "I've heard that many of the Welsh have webbed feet."

Unexpectedly, this stirred a rare flicker of curiosity in Ursula. "Truly?" When the men grinned, she scowled and sought to cover her faux pas by saying scornfully, "That sounds like the sort of nonsense you'd believe, Durand."

"It is not as far-fetched as that, my lady," he drawled. "Some people claim the English have long tails, but I've never had the opportunity to find out if there is any truth to it. Ah, wait, you were born in England, no? I daresay you've seen more naked Englishmen than I have. Any of them with tails?"

"I can tell you one English tail you'll never get to see, Durand—mine."

John turned from the window, clearly amused by their barbed byplay. "Now, now, children," he said, in the pitch-perfect tone of a parent reprimanding squabbling siblings. But when a knock sounded at the door, they were forgotten and he strode swiftly over to open it. It was one of his household knights, Geoffrey Luttrell, bearing a sealed letter. John reached for it eagerly, dismissed the knight with a careless gesture, and moved toward the oil lamp to read the letter. Geoffrey lingered long enough to shoot a hostile arrow of a look in Durand's direction. He knew the other knights resented his growing intimacy with John, had heard them grumbling about "those who got above themselves," for Durand's background, like his past, remained a mystery. A few days ago, he'd entered the hall just as one of them disdainfully called him "the count's tame wolf." They'd fallen silent when they realized he'd heard, for though they'd never admit it, there was something about Durand that other men found unsettling. But he'd laughed aloud, for he was not tamed, nor was he John's wolf. He was Eleanor's.

"It is from Hugh de Nonant," John said, casting the letter onto the table. "He's heard nothing about Richard. So why bother to send a messenger halfway across Wales just to tell me that?"

John seemed to be speaking the truth, but Durand would later see if he could manage to read the letter for himself, just to be sure. The Bishop of Coventry was as slippery as any eel, and while he'd so far proclaimed himself to be John's man, Durand thought he'd jump ship if Richard suddenly turned up, alive and well and ready to avenge himself upon those who'd been so quick to believe John's claim that he was dead.

"Do you want to continue the game, my lord?" he asked, gesturing toward the chessboard. John glanced at the ivory chess pieces, doubtlessly assessing his chances of victory. In many ways he was unlike his brothers, the dark one in a golden family, with a history of failures and misjudgments. At seventeen, he'd launched a rash assault upon Richard's Aquitaine, after an angry Henry had intemperately declared that Aquitaine was his if he could take it from his brother. He couldn't. At eighteen, his first command in Ireland had been an unmitigated disaster; he'd actually managed the impossible, uniting the Irish and the Norman settlers in their outrage against his misrule. He had timed his desertion of Henry correctly, though, making a private peace with Richard and Philippe while his father still lived. And he'd shown his first flashes of political skill by bringing down Richard's chancellor, Guillaume de Longchamp. Durand thought the chancellor had done himself in by his own arrogance and greed, but he had to admit that John had not made a misstep in his campaign to send Longchamp into exile. So far he had not displayed the same sure touch in his attempt to usurp his brother's throne, but Durand's months with Eleanor's youngest had taught him not to underestimate John's intelligence.

He was not surprised now when John said the game could wait, for he'd been maneuvered into an untenable position and in one way John was very much like the rest of his family; he hated to lose. "Have you further need of me, my lord?" Durand asked, hoping to be able to make his escape. But it was then that another knock sounded at the door.

Geoffrey was back, this time trailed by a travel-stained, weary messenger. "My lord, this man says he comes from the king of the French with an urgent message you must hear straightaway." He looked disappointed when John dismissed him before he could learn what it was, while Durand was allowed to remain. The courier was kneeling at John's feet, holding out a parchment threaded through with cord and sealed with wax that bore the imprint of Philippe's signet. But John paid more heed to the ring on the man's hand, an amethyst stone cut into octagonal facets, a secret sign that the message did indeed come from the French king.

He'd gotten other messages from Philippe, but never one accompanied by Philippe's own ring. Sending the courier away, he broke the seal. Durand watched intently as John read the letter, and when he heard John's sharp, indrawn breath, he could not hold his tongue. "Well?" he asked. "Is it good news or bad?"

John was studying the letter as if he could not believe what he'd just read. When he glanced up, his guard was down for the first time that Durand could remember, making him look suddenly younger than his twenty-six years. "It is good news for me," he said, "but bad news for my brother. It seems that Richard has managed to get himself captured by the Holy Roman Emperor."

Bleeding Christ! That would be a dagger through his queen's heart. Durand smiled, saying laconically, "How careless of him."

"Isn't it, though?" John agreed. He had his mother's hazel eyes; they were glowing now with light. "This changes everything!"

Even Ursula seemed interested in the news, for she'd risen from the bed, draping the fur coverlet strategically to cover her nudity. "What will happen now? Will the emperor kill your brother?"

"Not likely. Richard is worth far too much money to Heinrich." John laughed suddenly. "Although Richard has a rare talent for provoking otherwise sensible men into deranged rages. Philippe all but froths at the mouth when anyone even mentions the English king!"

Durand yearned to snatch the letter from John's hand, but he would have to be patient; unless John decided to burn it, he'd find a way to read it for himself later. With a surge of satisfaction, he realized that his services had become invaluable to the queen, for John had gone from being a minor threat to the peace of Richard's realm to a major one. Ursula had crossed to John's side, trailing her fur coverlet behind her, and he thought she was reassessing her own position, too, suddenly realizing she might soon be bedding a king.

"I do not see how this benefits you all that much, my lord," she said, "at least not in the long run. Yes, you'll gain valuable time to raise troops whilst the English king is being held prisoner in Germany. But sooner or later, the ransom will be paid and Richard will return to England to reclaim all he has lost, will he not?"

Durand thought that was a surprisingly astute observation from the apathetic Ursula, and he waited with interest to see how John would respond.

"Oh, I do not doubt that my lady mother will drain England's coffers to raise the ransom for her beloved Lionheart," John said, the corner of his mouth twisting down. "She'd see famine stalk the land and people begging in the streets without even blinking if that meant Richard's freedom. But what she does not yet know is that she'll not be the only player in this game. However much she is willing to pay to set Richard free, Philippe is willing to pay even more to see Richard rot in a dungeon for the rest of his born days."

Ursula had slipped her arm through John's. "Do you hate your brother so much, then?"

Durand was astonished that she'd dare to ask something like that. When John looked surprised but not offended, Durand decided his indulgence was proof that the woman must be even better in bed than he'd imagined. John actually seemed to be considering the question. "No," he said, after a pensive pause. "I would not say that I hate Richard."

Mayhap not, Durand thought, with a silent sneer, *but you're so bloody jealous of him that you're like to choke on it.*

Ursula was watching John with more curiosity than Durand had ever seen her show. "If you do not hate him, my lord, why do you want to see him 'rot in a dungeon for the rest of his born days'?"

John had turned away, opening a coffer and rooting around for parchment, quill pens, and ink. He had no scribe with him and did not trust the castle chaplain to inscribe the message he meant to send to Philippe, so he'd have to write it himself. But he straightened up at her question, regarding her quizzically. "Why would you even need to ask, woman? Because there is a crown in the offing, of course."

CHAPTER NINE

✣

FEBRUARY 1193

Oxford Castle, England

Eleanor was seated upon the dais in the great hall beside England's chief justiciar, Gautier de Coutances, Archbishop of Rouen. The members of the great council were finding seats on the wooden benches and she watched them closely, wondering how many of them would remain loyal to her son. The men in the first row were the other justiciars: Hugh Bardolf, William Briwerre, Geoffrey Fitz Peter, and William Marshal.

Beside them sat Richard's half brother Geoff. Eleanor knew he bore no love for Richard, but he loathed John far more, for he'd been fiercely loyal to the man who'd sired him, and had seen John's betrayal as Henry's death blow. Richard had honored Henry's dying wish and saw to it that Geoff was elected Archbishop of York, a post for which he was spectacularly ill-suited. Henry's insistence upon seeking for Geoff a career in the Church was, Eleanor thought sadly, further proof of how little he'd understood any of his sons, however much he'd claimed to love them. Geoff's brief tenure as archbishop had so far been a turbulent one, for he had inherited the Angevin fiery temper and had no qualms about excommunicating those who offended him.

One of those he'd excommunicated was sitting in the next row: Hugh de Puiset, Bishop of Durham. Hugh was one of those worldly prelates who saw the Church as a career, not a vocation. He was highborn, handsome, and affable. He was also luxury-loving, arrogant, quarrelsome, and indifferent to scandal; he had four illegitimate sons and a longtime mistress he'd never attempted to hide. He'd accumulated great wealth and when Richard was raising as much money as he could for the crusade, Hugh had purchased the earldom of

Northumberland for two thousand marks, prompting Richard to jest that he'd made a new earl out of an old bishop. Eleanor could not have imagined turning to Hugh for spiritual guidance, but his political skills might be useful in the coming struggle to free her son. Could he be trusted, though?

Close by were two other bishops who shared the same name. Hugh de Nonant, Bishop of Coventry, was believed to be hand in glove with John. Self-interest was his true religion and Eleanor thought he'd abandon John if it seemed likely that Richard would be returning to claim his kingdom. Yet if Hugh de Puiset and Hugh de Nonant were cynical wheeler-dealers, the third Hugh was that rarity, a powerful prelate who exuded a genuine odor of sanctity. Hugh d'Avalon's bishopric of Lincoln was a wealthy one, and he was no innocent Lamb of God midst the court wolves. He was not afraid to speak up in defense of his diocese or his Church, even if that meant facing down an angry Angevin king. But he was living proof that charm could be its own shield, for his boldness was tempered with humor, his candor infused with his innate understanding of human nature. Henry had become so fond of his vexingly independent bishop that gossip turned Hugh into another of the king's bastard sons. It was not so—Hugh was only seven years Henry's junior—but both men had been amused by the rumors and Eleanor suspected that her husband had half wished they were true. Whatever doubts she harbored about his fellow bishops, Eleanor had none about Hugh of Lincoln.

Her appraising gaze moved then from the princes of the Church to the barons of the realm. Hamelin de Warenne was Richard's uncle, one of Geoffrey of Anjou's by-blows. Henry had done well by his half brother, wedding him to a wealthy heiress who brought him an earldom, and Eleanor thought his loyalty to Richard was steadfast. She'd never been impressed by William d'Aubigny; although the earldom of Arundel was an important one, the man himself seemed to leave few footprints. Randolph de Blundeville was the grandson of a woman who'd been one of her closest friends, Maud, Countess of Chester, and therefore a cousin to Richard. He was also the husband of Eleanor's former daughter-in-law, Constance of Brittany, theirs a marriage of Henry's making, and one of mutual loathing if gossip was to be believed. He was young—only twenty-three—and so far he'd played no active role in the governance of the realm, neither taking the cross with Richard nor taking part in the downfall of Richard's chancellor, Guillaume de Longchamp. But his extensive holdings on both sides of the channel made him a great magnate and, therefore, a man to be watched.

Her eyes lingered for a moment upon the baron sitting to Chester's right. Like Randolph, he was young and of small stature. But Robert Beaumont, Earl of Leicester, had nothing to prove, for he'd been one of her son's closest companions in the Holy Land, and only Richard and André de Chauvigny had won greater fame for their crusading exploits. She'd had difficulty convincing him that he could best serve Richard by defending his domains, for he'd been as eager as André to set out for Germany. While he seemed composed now, there was a smoldering intensity about his calm that she found endearing, for she, too, yearned to rage and fume and curse the despicable, shameless men who'd dared to imprison her son.

Once all of the men were seated, they opened the council with a prayer, entreating the Almighty to keep the king safe and return him soon to his own realm. The Archbishop of Rouen then rose to his feet. "I regret to report that we have had no further news of our lord king, neither of his whereabouts nor his welfare. I can tell you, though, what we've learned of the Count of Mortain's actions. He apparently heard of the king's captivity about the same time that we did, for he soon sailed from Wales. Landing at Barfleur, he sought out William Fitz Ralph, the seneschal of Normandy, and other Norman lords." He glanced toward the Earl of Leicester. "You were present at that meeting, my lord. Will you tell the council what you told the queen and me?"

The young earl rose, nodding first to Eleanor and then the archbishop. "Count John claimed that King Richard is dead and demanded that we acknowledge John as the rightful heir to the English throne. We refused, of course, and he became very irate, warning us that he would not protect us against the French king unless we did as he bade." Leicester did not sound as if he'd been intimidated by John's threats, but Eleanor knew not all men would be as intrepid. Many would be loath to antagonize one who was likely to become their king if Richard died or remained a prisoner.

"We know," the archbishop resumed, "that Count John then rode straight for the court of the French king in Paris. He and Philippe apparently made some sort of pact. We have not yet learned the details of their Devil's deal, but we can safely assume that it will be to the detriment of our king."

Eleanor did not rise, but she raised a hand to draw attention to herself. "I have heard from my daughter, the Queen of Sicily," she said, pitching her voice so that all in the hall could hear. "She wrote that the Bishop of Salisbury was in Rome when word reached the Holy See of the king's plight. Bishop Hubert left for Germany at once. The Bishop of Bath was also in Rome and he paid a visit to my daughter and my son's queen, assuring them that he would leave straightaway for the imperial court to speak on the king's behalf. His mother is Heinrich's cousin and he seemed to think his kinship would gain him the emperor's ear." She knew she'd not been able to keep the skepticism from her voice, but she had little faith in Savaric Fitz Geldwin, another of those self-seekers with agendas of their own.

Godfrey de Lucy, Bishop of Winchester, was the next to speak. "Madame, my lord archbishop. Has there been any word from the Holy Father?"

Gautier de Coutances seemed to sigh. "No, my lord bishop, not yet."

The silence that followed his terse reply was fraught with all that none dared say. After a few moments, the archbishop began to speak of the need to defend Richard's kingdom in his absence. It was agreed that oaths of fidelity to Richard would be demanded throughout the realm and measures taken to protect the ports. They moved on then to the question of the king's ransom, although the discussion was tentative since they could not be sure a ransom would be demanded. Finally, they chose two men to travel to Germany and find their king, the abbots of the Cistercian abbeys of Boxley and Robertsbridge.

Eleanor did not know either man, but they seemed honored rather than daunted by the Herculean task that they had been given, and she took heart from that. It was heartening, too, to feel the outrage in the hall. She did not doubt that public opinion throughout Christendom would be on Richard's side, possibly even in France and Germany. Nor did she doubt that public opinion meant absolutely nothing to Heinrich von Hohenstaufen.

THE SOLAR WAS FILLING with shadows, save for a subdued spill of light cast by floating wicks in oil lamps and a brazier of glowing coals that did little to ease the chill of the chamber. William Marshal felt the cold more as he aged; he was in his forty-seventh year now, his youth long gone. He drew his mantle tighter, taking another swallow of wine as he watched his queen and the Earl of Leicester. They'd been talking for hours—or rather the earl was talking and the queen was listening. Will himself listened with half an ear, having heard Leicester's stories already. Eleanor was rapt, though, for he was telling her of Richard's time in the Holy Land, sharing with her the man a mother could not know—the battle commander, the soldier, the Lionheart. Will thought it only natural that Eleanor would be curious. But as he observed how engrossed she was in Leicester's words, it occurred to him that she was storing up memories of her son, memories to hold fast if he did not return from his German captivity. And he found that to be unutterably sad.

Will's destiny had long ago entwined with that of the Angevin House. He'd loved Hal, his knightly pupil, and it had broken his heart to see all that bright promise tarnished, to see what Hal became. He'd respected Hal's father, staying loyal to Henry until his death at Chinon Castle. He thought his own future died with the old king, for when they'd fled from Richard and the French king at Le Mans, he had publicly shamed Richard, unhorsing him to cover Henry's escape, and Richard was not a man to forgive a humiliation like that. Yet Richard *had* forgiven him, saying dryly that it was not in his interest to discourage loyalty to the king. Then Richard had given him the wife Henry had only promised, Isabel de Clare. Isabel was an earl's daughter, a king's granddaughter, and a great heiress. Even now, after more than three years of marriage, Will still marveled at his luck, for she'd brought him more than vast estates in England, South Wales, Normandy, and Ireland; she'd brought him a happiness he'd never known. Each time she smiled at him, each time he gazed upon the two sons she'd given him, he felt grateful to the man who'd made it possible, the man who was now held in a German prison.

But his deepest loyalties had always been to the queen. The younger son of a minor baron, he'd first met Eleanor and Henry while in the service of his uncle, the Earl of Salisbury. They'd been escorting the queen along the Poitiers Road when they'd been ambushed by the de Lusignans, a notorious clan of malcontents whose meat and drink was rebellion. They'd managed to gain Eleanor time to escape, but at a high price: Will's uncle was slain and Will taken prisoner. A penniless knight, he'd thought himself doomed—until the queen paid his ransom and took him into her household, setting him onto the path that would lead to Isabel de Clare. There was nothing he would not do for this woman. Her pain was his, her anger his, and her resolve to rescue her son his, too.

Leicester had at last exhausted his repertoire of crusader stories. Rising, he refilled their wine cups. "Do you think we'll hear soon about the French king's pact with your son, Madame?"

"I am sure of it. Archbishop Gautier boasts that he has an exceptionally skillful spy at the French court, and indeed he does," Eleanor said, and then her lips curved in a slight smile. "But I have an even better one."

Leaning back in her chair, she smiled again, warmly this time. "My son has been well served by the men who accompanied him to the Holy Land. I would ask one more thing of you, my lord earl. It is difficult to take the measure of a man without meeting him. I regret that I was denied the opportunity to meet the French king, for he sailed from Messina on the very day of my arrival. I would have thought he'd be curious to see the woman who'd been wed to his father," she said wryly, "but apparently not. So you have the advantage of me, Lord Robert." Her hazel eyes met his blue ones. "Tell me about Philippe Capet."

He'd been expecting such a question and had given it some thought. "Well . . . he has not yet reached thirty, but I think he was born old. He never gambles or curses. He is bored by hunting and disapproves of tournaments. He has no interest in music and you'll find no troubadours at the French court. I am not sure he is as craven as your son thinks, but he does have a nervous disposition and frets constantly over his health. He goes nowhere without bodyguards and he is the only man I've ever known who dislikes horses. He is quick to anger and whilst he may forgive, he never forgets. He is prideful, convinced that it is his divine destiny to restore the French court to greatness. And he is very cunning. We would forget that at our cost, Madame."

She knew his use of "we" was an attempt at tact; it was Richard he meant. Her son had a lamentable tendency to hold his enemies too cheaply. "What does he look like?"

"Not as tall as King Richard, not as short as Count John. Not so handsome that he'd be remembered if he were not a king, but for certes, not ugly. He has a ruddy complexion, the high color of those with hot tempers, and he used to have a full head of thick, unruly brown hair."

"'Used to have'?"

Leicester grinned. "When your son and Philippe sickened with Arnaldia during the siege of Acre, they both lost their hair; the doctors thought it was due to the high fever. Most of those stricken grew their hair back within a few months. King Richard did. But I've been told that Philippe did not, that he is now partially bald." He grinned again. "I have no doubt, Madame, that he blames your son for that, too. If he stubs a toe, if he awakens with a bellyache, if his horse throws a shoe, he blames King Richard."

"He hates Richard that much?"

"Oh yes, my lady. He is rather irrational when it comes to your son. He loathed being in the Holy Land, for he'd never wanted to take the cross. He hated the hot sun, the dust, the scorpions, the alien culture of Outremer. But above all, he hated the way King Richard overshadowed him at every turn. He surely knew he could not hope to compete with our king on the battlefield, but I do not think he realized that he'd be eclipsed in the council chamber, too, that he would be diminished on a daily basis. Nor did it help that King Richard held him in contempt and . . ."

He paused and Eleanor finished the sentence for him. ". . . and did not trouble to hide it."

He nodded. "Indeed, he did not, Madame."

Eleanor was quiet after that, not liking what she'd heard. She'd been able to "take the measure" of the Emperor Heinrich at Lodi, had marked him as a dangerous foe, ruthless and unscrupulous. Yet what she'd just learned convinced her that the French king posed an even greater threat to her son. Heinrich wanted to humiliate Richard and to profit by it. Since his hostility held no heat, he'd be guided by self-interest. Philippe's hostility was far more dangerous, for it was white-hot, intense, burning to the bone. Did Richard realize that, though?

⚜

LEICESTER HAD GONE OFF to bed and Will was about to ask the queen if she had further need of him, for she looked very tired. It was then that a knock sounded on the door and he crossed the chamber to open it. The man standing in the stairwell was young, tall, and dark, with black hair and grey eyes. Will did not know his name, but he knew who he was. Every royal court had men like this, shadowy figures who came and went on mysterious missions for their king—or their queen. He stepped back so Eleanor could see the identity of this new arrival and she at once beckoned him into the solar.

As he knelt before her, she leaned forward, tension etched into every line of her body. "Did you find Durand in Paris?"

"I did, Madame." He had been dreading this moment, knowing the pain he was about to inflict. "The news I bring is not good, my lady."

"I did not expect it would be." Gesturing for him to rise, she said evenly, "Tell me what you learned at the French court, Justin."

"Durand was able to give me the details of Count John's pact with the French king. He swore fealty to Philippe for Normandy and for all of King Richard's lands that he holds of the French Crown. He agreed to put aside his wife and wed Philippe's sister Alys. He agreed to yield Gisors Castle and to renounce any claims to the Vexin. In return, the French king promised to do all in his power to secure the English throne for Count John and to assist him in an invasion of England."

He'd forced himself to meet her gaze as he spoke, but once he was done, he glanced away, for he'd just delivered a damning indictment of treason against the man who was still her flesh and blood, a child of her womb.

Eleanor's face was a queen's court mask, revealing nothing. She thanked him before sending him down to the great hall, saying her steward would see that he had a meal and a comfortable bed for the night. She sank back in her chair then, looking so exhausted that Will's chest tightened. For a moment his eyes caught those of the queen's man, and a silent message flashed between them, one of anger and unease. For none who served Queen Eleanor wanted to see her hurt and none who knew Count John wanted to see him as England's king.

Will expected to be dismissed, too, and was startled when she said in a low voice, "I would have you stay a while longer, Will."

"Of course, Madame." As the door closed quietly, he took a seat beside her. He did not know what to say, what solace to offer. He tried to imagine how he would feel if his two small sons grew to manhood and turned on each other, as surely a vision of Hell as he could conjure up. Having no words, he was relieved to see that she expected none, that she sought only the comfort of his company. And so they sat together for a time, not speaking as night came on.

❦

AN EARLY MARCH SNOWFALL had powdered the inner bailey of Dürnstein Castle, and the noonday sun gave it a sparkling, crystalline sheen. Hadmar von Kuenring paused to watch as his two young sons pelted each other with snowballs, shrieking with excitement. Hadmar's smile faded, though, as he continued on toward the tower where the English king was held, for he'd grown weary of being a messenger of ill tidings.

He was in the stairwell when he heard the raised voices coming from Richard's chamber. Alarmed, he quickened his pace, taking the steps two at a time. Thrusting the door open, he came to a halt at the sight meeting his eyes. Richard and Eberhard, a tow-haired, good-natured youth half a head taller than his fellow guards, were seated at the table, hands gripped as each man sought to force the other man's arm down, while the rest were clustered around, laughing and cheering. They fell silent as soon as they saw Hadmar in the doorway and backed away from the table. Richard looked amused, but Eberhard went beet red and got to his feet so hastily that his chair toppled to the floor.

On several occasions, Hadmar had interrupted what appeared to be language lessons, with Richard pointing to various objects and his guards giving him the names in German. He hadn't commented on that, but arm wrestling was a bit too convivial for his liking and he thought it might be best to assign Eberhard to other duties—until he remembered that he'd soon be relieved of the responsibility for the English king's security.

Richard rose, clapping Eberhard playfully on the shoulder. The guard grinned sheepishly, but then addressed his lord, saying anxiously that he hoped he had not offended. Hadmar brushed aside the apology, regarding his prisoner with an ironic half smile. "I'll thank you not to suborn my men."

"We have to find some way to pass the time. They are as bored as I am by now." Richard gestured toward his vacated chair in a mocking parody of a host welcoming a guest. "Have a seat. You may as well be comfortable whilst you give me your bad news."

"What makes you think I bear bad news?"

"When have you ever brought me *good* news?"

Hadmar abruptly abandoned the bantering. "Nor is today any different. I have heard from my duke. He writes that he and Emperor Heinrich have agreed upon the terms for your surrender and he commands me to escort you to the imperial court at Speyer."

After two months of treading water, Richard just wanted to reach the shore, for he knew it was the waiting before a battle that eroded a soldier's confidence. It was never a good thing for men to have time to consider all that could go wrong. "Did Leopold tell you what they intend to demand of me?"

"No, he did not." Hadmar had not realized he was going to lie until he heard the words coming out of his mouth. It was not that he didn't believe the English king had a right to know, for he did. It was that he did not want to be the one to tell Richard what awaited him at Speyer.

※

RICHARD HAD EXPECTED to be taken directly to Speyer; instead, they headed for Ochsenfurt, a small town on the left bank of the River Main, where they were to await a summons from Duke Leopold. Heinrich apparently wanted to delay his appearance until his bishops and lords arrived for his Easter Court. Richard remembered reading how the Roman generals would bring their defeated foes back to Rome, and when they made their triumphant entry into the city, the captives would be dragged behind them in chains for the crowds to mock and jeer. He wondered bitterly if Heinrich knew about this ancient Roman custom; he was said to be well read.

Richard was being held in the guest hall of the Premonstratensian monastery dedicated to St Lambert, John the Baptist, and St George. He'd yet to meet the abbot, only occasionally caught a glimpse of one of the white-clad canons as they went about their duties. He did not see much of Hadmar, either, and time hung heavy on his hands. He tried to read and worked on a song he'd been composing about his captivity. Nothing he wrote satisfied him and he had to keep scraping the parchment clean and starting afresh, doubting that he'd be permitted to keep Hadmar's books and writing materials once they reached Speyer. He'd been surprised to discover that these minor indignities mattered so much, but they did—small, stinging reminders that he had less power than the least of his subjects, as defenseless as the Christian prisoners he'd freed at Darum. They'd been on their way to the slave markets in Cairo and they'd wept with joy at their deliverance. While he'd been glad that he was able to rescue them, he had not given it much thought after it was done. Now that memory was so vivid it occasionally intruded into his dreams.

He was lying on his bed, hoping to nap, when Hadmar came around the screen that had been set up to partition the hall. He was smiling. "You have guests."

Richard hastily sat up. For a moment, he thought it was Leopold, but he dismissed that at once, for Hadmar would not have announced him like that. He was getting to his feet as the Austrian lord stepped aside. Richard stared incredulously at the man standing behind Hadmar, and then a slow grin spread over his face. "I suppose you just happened to be passing by?"

Hubert Walter grinned, too. "Something like that," he said, and started forward. Richard was already moving toward him. Hubert would have knelt, but instead found himself embraced like a brother. By the time they stepped back, they both had tears in their eyes. It was only then that Richard saw the bishop was not alone. A second man had followed him, beaming and blinking back tears of his own. William de St Mère-Eglise was well known to Richard; he'd been Henry's trusted clerk of the chamber and soon after his coronation, Richard had named him Dean of St Martin's le Grand in London. His appearance seemed even more amazing to Richard than Hubert Walter's, and as soon as William knelt, he was raised up and embraced, too. By now they were all laughing and talking at once, not even noticing that Hadmar had discreetly disappeared.

"I'd gotten as far as Rome when I learned what had happened," Hubert was saying, "and, of course, I left for Germany straightaway. William happened to be in Rome, too, and he caught up with me on the road."

Richard felt a pang, for he was desperate for news from England and had hoped the bishop was coming from his island kingdom. His disappointment was forgotten, though, as soon as Hubert produced the letters. Snatching them up, he moved toward a wall torch and began to break the seals. There were four: one from his wife, one from his sister, one from Anna, the Damsel of Cyprus, and one from Stephen de Turnham, to whom he'd entrusted his women's safety. He read rapidly, then went back and reread them, smiling at Joanna's message and laughing outright at Anna's. "The lass says she has put some vile Cypriot curse upon all my enemies, promising that they'll be rotting away like lepers ere the year is out." But when he glanced again at his queen's letter, he shook his head, saying, "Berenguela's faith in that old man on the papal throne is truly remarkable." He'd once told his wife that her innocence was downright endearing; not so much now, though.

Putting the letters aside, he laughed again. He'd never thought he had a sentimental bone in his body and he was startled by how emotional he felt at the sight of their familiar faces. They had begun to tell him what they knew of the political ramifications of his capture, which was not much—that the Holy Father had been outraged by the news and he had an ally in the Archbishop of Cologne, who'd not only sent a warning to the Pope but had joined the rebels. Heinrich, they reported happily, was facing a serious rebellion.

Taking their cue from Hadmar, the guards were giving them some space, and when Richard asked for wine, impressing the clerics by doing it in German, it was soon fetched. Sitting at the table, they began to pepper him with questions. He answered readily at first, telling them about his encounters with the pirates and explaining his reasoning for choosing to take only twenty men with him on the pirate galleys. He had no trouble describing the first shipwreck at Ragusa and the second in that Godforsaken marsh, or their narrow escapes in Görz and Udine. But after that, the words did not come so easily. His memories of Friesach were like festering sores. And as he started to tell them about Ertpurch, he was dismayed to find it all coming back—their utter desperation, their exhaustion and hunger and cold, that damnable fever, and then the fear and shame of his capture. Relating it was like reliving it; he could even feel his body reacting as if he were back in the alewife's house, trapped and despairing, for his pulse had begun to race, his breath quickening, his throat constricting.

William was puzzled when Richard suddenly fell silent, but Hubert was quick to comprehend. He'd arrived at the siege of Acre nine months before Richard, and he'd often spoken to men who'd been held prisoner by the Saracens, some of them for years. What had struck him most forcefully was their uniform reluctance to speak of their ordeal and their obvious discomfort when they did. There was a great difference, he'd discovered, between the Saracen and Christian view of captivity. The first crusaders had made no effort to ransom their men, seeing a captive knight as a failure, his survival an embarrassment. Their attitude gradually changed, in part due to exposure to a culture in which it was seen as a duty to rescue one's own. But the stigma still lingered and so did the shame. If knights and men-at-arms felt it so keenly, Hubert imagined it would be even worse for a king, especially a king like this one.

"We'll have time to hear of your captivity later, sire," he said briskly. "For now, I think it best if we speak of Heinrich and what he hopes to gain by this outrageous crime." William seemed surprised, but Richard's fleeting look of relief confirmed Hubert's suspicion that this was still too raw a wound to be probed.

THIS THURSDAY BEFORE HOLY WEEK would prove to be a day of surprises for Richard. Only a few hours after the arrival of Hubert Walter and William de St Mère-Eglise, Hadmar ushered in two more visitors, men clad in the distinctive white cloaks of the Cistercians. They were exhausted, jubilant to have finally found their king, and mildly disappointed to see that they had not been the first to reach him. As fond as Richard was of the Bishop of Salisbury, he was even more elated by the arrival of these abbots from England, for their presence was proof that his plight was now known to his justiciars and his mother.

They brought more than news—a stack of letters so thick he thought every lord in his realm must have sent one. He read his mother's letter first, then those of his justiciars, and when he was done, he no longer felt so alone. Their outrage all but scorched the parchment, the pen strokes as slashing as sword blades as they railed at the blatant disregard of Church law and the laws of war. This was what he needed to hear, not his queen's pious certainty that Pope Celestine would prevail upon Emperor Heinrich to set him free.

"My lady mother says that you will tell me of my brother's conniving with the French king," he said, and they did, sharing all they knew of John's treason. Richard listened without interruption and then began to stalk back and forth as his anger caught fire. After Henry's death, men like Will Marshal had feared they'd suffer for their loyalty to the old king. But with fine inconsistency, Richard had rewarded those who'd stayed with Henry until the end and mistrusted those who'd been so eager to court his favor. Only John had not been chastised. Their mother had some misgivings about the generous provisions he made for John, and he still remembered his response, telling her that "Johnny deserves a chance to show he can be trusted if I play fair with him," adding with careless confidence that he did not see Johnny as any great threat.

Of course, he'd never expected that three years later, he'd be a prisoner of the Emperor Heinrich, unable to protect his own body, much less his distant domains. For the first time, he fully understood how his father must have felt upon being told that his best-loved son had betrayed him, and not for the first time, he wondered if the Almighty was punishing him for the part he'd played in Henry's downfall. But thoughts like that were reserved for those sleepless hours when he struggled to understand and accept God's Will. It was Johnny's treachery he must deal with now. Fortunately, he knew how to do that, knew what weapon would draw the most blood, would gash Johnny's pride to the bone. Mockery was the one thing Johnny could not abide.

Turning to face the other men, he smiled derisively. "My brother John is not the man to conquer a kingdom if there is anyone to offer the least resistance."

THIS WAS EASILY RICHARD'S BEST DAY since they'd sailed from Ragusa. While he was by nature an optimist, nearly three months in isolation had taken its toll. For all of his courtesy and occasional kindnesses, Hadmar von Kuenring was no friend, and Richard dared not forget that. But until Hubert Walter's unexpected appearance, he had not realized how lonely he was. Being able to speak freely to men he knew he could trust—and in French—did much to raise his spirits. After they departed, promising to return the next day, he was feeling cheerful enough to reach for Hadmar's lute. He could hear the music in his head and was strumming exploratory chords when he glanced up to find Hadmar standing several feet away. The Austrian's face was inscrutable; that in itself was warning enough. "I do not suppose you've come to tell me that my queen has arrived for a conjugal visit."

"I received a message from Duke Leopold," Hadmar said, his voice no more expressive than his face. "He said that we are to leave on the morrow for the imperial court." He waited for a response from Richard. Not getting one, he started to turn away and then stopped. "My duke did tell me that he was able to get the emperor to promise that you will suffer no bodily harm."

Richard deliberately picked up the lute again. "And we both know how much the emperor's promises are worth," he said, striking another chord. When he looked up again, Hadmar had gone.

THEY REACHED SPEYER three days later as dusk was falling. It was Palm Sunday and the great cathedral of St Mary and St Stephen was packed with worshippers, reminding Richard of how long it had been since he was shriven of his sins. He was expecting to be taken to the royal palace or perhaps to the bishop's palace, wherever Heinrich had been able to gather the largest audience for the spectacle of surrender. When Hadmar escorted him into the cathedral precincts and then to the chapter house north of the great church, he concluded that once again he was to be held offstage until Heinrich was ready for the circus to begin. But as soon as he crossed the threshold, he saw that he was wrong. It would seem that the emperor had chosen not to make their first meeting a public one.

Heinrich was seated in the ornate bishop's chair, flanked by Leopold and a stout, richly dressed man whom Richard assumed to be the Bishop of Speyer. There were others in the chapter house, but he was given no introductions to any of them. After Hadmar had gone to kneel before the emperor, Heinrich gestured for Richard's guards to bring him forward. Richard's first thought as he gazed upon his enemy was that Berenguela was right. There was nothing regal about Heinrich von Hohenstaufen. He was only of moderate height and slightly built, with a thin face, his pallor accentuated by blond hair and a sparse beard. But Berenguela was also right about his eyes. They were so pale they seemed colorless and Richard thought it was like looking into the flat, dead eyes of a snake.

Heinrich was holding a magnificent golden goblet studded with rubies. He drank, then set it down without haste upon the arm of his chair. "I expect men to kneel when they come into my presence." His voice was without inflexion, his Latin excellent.

"Well, we do not always get what we expect, do we?"

A faint smile touched those thin lips. "I could make you kneel."

Richard returned the smile. "No," he said, "*you* could not," giving the pronoun just enough emphasis so that there could be no mistaking his meaning.

Such an insult would have sent angry blood into Philippe's face. Heinrich did not react at all and Richard suddenly remembered his mother's caustic comment: that he had ice flowing through his veins.

It was Leopold who spoke up. "Can we get on with this?" That he would show such impatience told Richard that he was not happy to be here. It also showed he was confident that he had leverage with Heinrich, and Richard decided the Austrian duke was more of a fool than he'd first thought.

"Of course, Cousin." Heinrich smiled again, one of the most chilling smiles Richard had ever seen. "You may be the one to read the terms to the English king."

Leopold did not like that at all. When one of the emperor's scribes held out a parchment scroll, he took it with reluctance. Unrolling it, he glanced at it briefly and then back to Richard. "The Holy Roman Emperor and I agreed at Würzburg on the ides of February that I will deliver you, the king of the English, into his custody. You will be held at the emperor's pleasure until payment is paid of one hundred thousand silver marks. Half is to—"

"You cannot possibly be serious!" Richard was stunned. Even in his worst moments, he'd not expected a demand like this. One hundred thousand silver marks was twice the annual revenues of England and Normandy.

Leopold frowned. "If I may continue? As I said, you are to pay the sum of one hundred thousand marks. Half of this amount is to be the marriage portion of your niece, the Duchess of Brittany's daughter, who will wed my son Friedrich this coming Michaelmas. The remaining fifty thousand marks shall be paid at the beginning of Lent next year, and it is to be divided between the emperor and me."

He raised his eyes from the document to glare defiantly at Richard. "You will also give the emperor two hundred highborn hostages as surety that you will fulfill the terms of this agreement. The emperor is to provide me with two hundred hostages of his own as surety that if he dies before these terms are met, you will be returned to my custody. If I should die, my son is to act in my stead. If you die whilst in the emperor's power, your two hundred hostages will be released."

Thinking that Richard meant to protest, he raised his hand. "There is more. You must free my cousin, Isaac Comnenus, and return his daughter, Anna, to him. You must also provide the emperor with fifty war galleys and one hundred knights, and you must go in person with another one hundred knights to fight at the emperor's side in his war to overthrow the man who usurped the Sicilian throne."

Leopold paused then, as if to savor what was coming next. "There is one more condition for your release. The emperor will hold your hostages until you have persuaded the Pope to absolve me in the event that I am unfairly excommunicated for taking you prisoner."

It was one of the few times in Richard's life when he was speechless. He stared at them, thinking that he'd fallen in with madmen. One hundred thousand silver marks was a sum so vast that it beggared belief. And did they think the world would be fooled because they called it a dowry, not a ransom? The demand that he help personally to overthrow his ally Tancred was beyond vindictive and would reduce the King of England to the status of one of Heinrich's German vassals. The other terms were just as outrageous. Turn two hundred hostages over to Heinrich's mercy and wed his niece to Leopold's son? Free that whoreson Isaac Comnenus and give Anna back to him? Plead with the Pope on behalf of the man who'd abducted him?

"I think you have both lost your minds. I will never agree to any of this—never!"

Leopold flushed angrily, but Heinrich continued calmly sipping his wine. "Oh, I think you will," he said, with another of those frigid smiles. "You see, if you do not agree, then you're of no value to me, and I have no reason to keep you alive."

As a bluff, it was well played. But Richard knew it was a bluff, for these greedy lunatics were not going to kill him, not when they thought they could plunder England's coffers like Barbary pirates. "Well, then, we are at an impasse, for I would die ere I ever agreed to these terms."

His defiance did not seem to disturb Heinrich's composure in the least. "I will give you time to think it over." He gestured to the guards, who moved forward to encircle Richard again. Realizing he'd just been dismissed as if he were a servant, Richard felt a surge of hatred so strong that it momentarily blotted out all else; never had he wanted a sword in his hand as much as he did at that moment. He did not resist the guards, though, unwilling to give Heinrich that satisfaction. The emperor watched as they started toward the door, waiting until it had been opened before he spoke.

"There is one more matter. Your trial begins on the morrow."

CHAPTER TEN

❖

MARCH 1193

Speyer, Germany

Richard was back in the cathedral's chapter house, for Heinrich had decided that his trial would be held in the great hall of the Bishop of Speyer's palace. He was awaiting Hadmar's return and had begun to pace restlessly, while his Austrian guards tried to give him a little privacy by withdrawing to a corner of the chamber. He sensed their sympathy, but knew he'd be encountering a far more hostile audience when the Imperial Diet began, for Hadmar had already informed him that this was not to be a representative assembly of German princes. Since half of them were in revolt against Heinrich, they, of course, were conspicuously absent. The Austrian duke was present, with his brother, the Duke of Mödling, and his sons. Heinrich's closest kin were in attendance, too: his uncle, the Count Palatine of the Rhine, and two of his brothers: Conrad, the Duke of Swabia, and Otto, the Count Palatine of Burgundy. Hadmar had reported that the Archbishop of Trier was in the great hall, as were the bishops of Speyer, Worms, Passau, Freising, and Zeitz. So were the imperial *ministeriales*, led by Heinrich's marshal, Heinz von Kalden, and his seneschal, Markward von Annweiler, along with churchmen, envoys sent by the French king—and Boniface d'Aleramici, Marquis of Montferrat, younger brother of the man Richard was accused of murdering.

It seemed utterly unreal to Richard that he should be facing a trial, charged with betraying the Holy Land, and it felt like an eternity until Hadmar reappeared. "They are ready for you now," he said somberly. "You will not be entirely friendless, for the emperor has permitted the Bishop of Salisbury, the Bishop of Bath, William de St Mère-Eglise, and the abbots to attend."

The Bishop of Bath's presence was a surprise to Richard, and not an entirely welcome one, for he did not trust the man all that much. "But they do not get a vote, do they?"

Hadmar glanced at the guards and then lowered his voice, even though he knew they spoke no Latin. "May I offer you some advice?"

"I'd rather you offered me a fast horse and a head start," Richard said, with a tight smile. "But I'll take the advice, too."

"I think you ought to kneel to the emperor."

"I'd sooner jab a needle into my eye!"

Hadmar had been expecting such a reaction and raised his hand. "At least hear me out. After Emperor Heinrich's father drowned on his way to the Holy Land, much of the German army died when a plague struck Antioch. Heinrich's brother Friedrich eventually got the survivors to the siege camp at Acre, only then to die of a fever himself. Yes, I realize you know all this, but indulge me. When Duke Leopold and the Austrians arrived several months later, he took command of the Germans as the highest-ranking vassal of the emperor. So when you treated his banner with such blatant disrespect, you were insulting the Germans as well as the Austrians. Many of the men in the great hall think that you maligned Duke Leopold's courage and have contempt for all those of German blood."

"That is nonsense! I never accused Leopold of cowardice, just bad judgment. And my sister's sons and daughter, who are half German, are very dear to me."

"Nevertheless, this is what many believe and it is up to you to convince them it is not so. You can best do that by showing respect for Heinrich's rank, if not for the man himself."

"Even if I could assure them that I harbor no hatred of Germans, do you truly think that would affect their verdict?"

Richard knew Hadmar had tried in his way to be honest and he did not disappoint now. "No," he conceded, "most likely it would not. But it could not hurt, either." And with nothing more to be said, he signaled to the guards that it was time to escort the English king to face his accusers.

❧

THE BISHOP OF SALISBURY had been anxiously watching the doorway and as soon as Richard's guards appeared, he jumped to his feet and hurried toward them. They seemed hesitant, unsure if he should be permitted to approach the prisoner, but Hadmar said something in German and they stepped aside. Hubert had hoped to be able to alert Richard, but he was too late. His king was surveying the hall, his gaze moving from the men seated on the rows of benches to those on the dais. His audible, indrawn breath told Hubert that he'd spotted the man seated to Heinrich's left.

"I am sorry, sire," Hubert said softly. "We did not know the Bishop of Beauvais was here until this morning, or I would have gotten word to you somehow."

Richard was staring at the French bishop with loathing he made no attempt to conceal. "It might be for the best," he said at last. "I can hardly call Heinrich a liar to his face in front of his own Imperial Diet, but I'm free to expose Beauvais for the treacherous snake that he is."

Hubert felt a throb of relief, for he'd been troubled by his first glimpse of Richard; the deep shadows hovering under his eyes testified to a wakeful night. But he'd heard the English king sound like this before—coolheaded and composed, able to adapt his strategy to changing circumstances. This was the way he was on the battlefield, and Hubert thought he'd never faced a more daunting battle than he did on this March Monday in Holy Week.

There was a stir in the hall as the French envoys rose and, after bowing to the emperor, moved to intercept Richard. He knew one of them, Druon de Mello, for he'd been with the French army in the Holy Land. Richard had a favorable opinion of the older lord, seeing him as an honorable man often burdened by his king with tasks he found distasteful, and indeed, Druon did not look happy. "My lord Richard," he said, with another polite bow. "We bring you this from our lord, the king of the French."

Richard took the parchment, broke the seal, and read. When he glanced up, he saw that two of the envoys were regarding him challengingly, but Druon had averted his gaze. Without comment, he passed the letter to Hubert Walter, smiling grimly at the bishop's angry exclamation. Retrieving the parchment, he rolled it up and tucked it into his belt, and then, knowing he was the focal point of all eyes, he raised his head defiantly, determined that they'd see him show no unease.

The man Hadmar had identified as the Bishop of Speyer now rose to his feet and began to speak. When he was done, Hadmar said in a low voice, "The bishop says that they have found someone who speaks French so that you may understand the charges against you. He will also translate your responses into German."

"How magnanimous. Tell them it is not necessary. I prefer that you be the one to interpret for me. And I will be responding in Latin, not French."

Hadmar understood Richard's reasoning; he did not trust any interpreter provided by Heinrich. But when he stepped forward to address the court, Hadmar managed to make Richard's decision to speak in Latin sound like a courtesy, saying the English king knew that most of the men in the hall were familiar with that language. After a brief exchange with the bishop, he turned back to Richard, saying, "They have agreed to your requests."

"My requests?" Richard arched a brow in sardonic acknowledgment of Hadmar's tact, but the latter nudged him, and he saw that the bishop had beckoned a scribe to come forward. The hall had been buzzing since he'd made his entrance, but a silence fell now as the charges against the English king were read aloud.

Hadmar listened closely, waiting until the man paused so he could translate. "They say there can be no doubt that the Almighty wants you punished for your crimes, or else you'd not have fallen into the power of Duke Leopold. There are a number of accusations, including your ill treatment of the duke's kinsman, Isaac Comnenus, your lust for profit, and your arrogant conduct in the Holy Land. But the most serious charges are your alliance with the usurper King of Sicily, your complicity in the murder of Conrad of Montferrat, and your treacherous conspiracy with the Saracen Sultan of Egypt, Saladin."

It was what Richard had been expecting to hear and he nodded for Heinrich's spokesman to continue. This time the scribe spoke at some length, gesturing several times toward the Bishop of Beauvais. The audience leaned forward to hear, their gazes shifting from Richard to Boniface of Montferrat. A handsome, fair-haired man in his thirties, Boniface bore such a striking resemblance to his slain brother that Richard did not need Hadmar's whispered identification.

"You are accused of recognizing Tancred as Sicily's king whilst knowing full well that the crown belongs by right of blood to the emperor's consort, the Empress Constance." Hadmar would have elaborated, but Richard cut him off impatiently, wanting to know what had been said about Conrad.

"You'll not like it much," Hadmar warned. "It is claimed that you were Conrad's sworn enemy, that you did all you could to thwart his claim to the crown of Jerusalem. And when you saw that you'd failed and he would be king despite your efforts, you hired the Saracen sect called the Assassins to stab Conrad as he rode through the streets of Tyre. One of the Assassins was slain afterward, but the other one was captured and confessed to the Bishop of Beauvais and the Duke of Burgundy that the killing had been done at your behest."

Richard could feel the anger starting to stir, smoldering embers threatening to blaze into fiery life, but he fought it back, for rage made a man reckless. He shook his head, saying nothing, remembering how carelessly he'd once dismissed the charges by Beauvais and Burgundy, so proudly sure that none who knew him would ever give credence to them.

The scribe was continuing to make the case against him, having saved the most serious accusation for last, that Richard had betrayed his own Christian brethren by an unholy, heinous alliance with infidels. "The Bishop of Beauvais contends that from the day of your arrival in the Holy Land, you showed yourself willing to be beguiled by the Saracens. You at once sought to open negotiations with Saladin. You and he exchanged gifts and courtesies, for all the world as if you were dealing with another Christian king. You met with his brother on numerous occasions, once going off to feast in his tent. You formed friendships with some of Saladin's emirs and Mamluks. You even dared to knight several of them. And you refused time and time again to lay siege to Jerusalem. No matter how they entreated you, you remained adamant, and you managed to win the native-born Christians and the Templars over to your heretical views, somehow convincing them that Jerusalem could not be taken. You then proved that you were secretly in collusion with Saladin by making a shameful surrender, yielding the stronghold of Ascalon to the infidels, and abandoning the Holy Land to those sons of Perdition, a sin so great that you will surely burn for aye in the hottest flames of Hell."

"Is it my turn now?" When Hadmar nodded, Richard strode to the center of the hall. The silence was complete, even eerie. "I was born into a rank that makes me accountable only to Almighty God. But I do not fear the judgment of just men, and these accusations are so scurrilous and vile that I welcome this opportunity to defend myself against them. Be he an emperor, a king, or a knight, a man's honor is precious in his sight, for it is his legacy, how he will be remembered." Richard paused and then looked toward the dais. "So when I am done, mayhap the illustrious emperor of the Romans may wish to address those foul rumors that he had a hand in the murder of the Bishop of Liege."

Caught by surprise, Heinrich proved that he was not as invulnerable as he'd have others believe, for his hands tightened upon the arms of his chair and although his expression remained impassive, color crept into his face. As their eyes met, Richard felt a hot surge of pure pleasure. He knew the other man would not forgive him for that, but he did not care. If he was going down, by God, he'd go down with his banner nailed to the masthead. He was heartened, too, to see some smiles as he glanced around the hall—smiles hastily hidden, but smiles, nonetheless. So this carefully selected audience was not as partisan as Heinrich had hoped; even here there were men who doubted the emperor's innocence.

"I will respond to these charges in the order in which they were made. I arrived in Sicily to discover that my sister, Queen Joanna, had been detained in Palermo by King Tancred, who had also seized her dower lands. I secured my sister's freedom and after negotiations with Tancred, he agreed to pay twenty thousand ounces of gold as compensation for the loss of her dower, as well as another twenty thousand ounces that King William had bequeathed for the war against Saladin. So yes, I made a treaty with King Tancred, for there was no other way to get the money owed my sister or William's bequest. I understand why this would anger the emperor. But it was not done with malice. I was not pleased when I learned that the emperor had met the French king at Milan and formed an alliance that I knew would be to my detriment. Yet I did not question the emperor's right to make such a pact, no more than he can object to my right to act as I saw fit in my dealings with the King of Sicily. That is the way of statecraft, the prerogative of kings."

Richard paused again. They were listening intently, but he could not tell if his words were having any impact. "I am astonished that I should incur criticism for the actions I took against the usurper Isaac Comnenus, for I did no more than avenge myself for the wrongs done to my men, and in so doing, I was able to free the Cypriots from his oppressive yoke. When we sailed from Messina for the Holy Land, our fleet was scattered in a savage storm and several of our ships were driven ashore at Cyprus, including the ship carrying my betrothed, the Lady Berengaria of Navarre, and my sister Queen Joanna. Isaac imprisoned the shipwreck survivors and attempted to force my ladies to come ashore with threats, intending to hold them hostage. God willing, I arrived just in time to keep them from falling into his hands. Of course I sought to punish him for such an outrage; is there a man in this hall who would not have acted as I did?

"When Isaac then sought peace, I agreed, only to have him flee in the night rather than honor the terms of our pact. So I deposed this faithless, evil man, and I make no apologies, for he had refused to permit Christian ships to dock in Cypriot ports and was known to have ties to Saladin."

Richard turned then to face Leopold, who'd been given a seat of honor on the dais. "If the Duke of Austria is offended by these actions against his kins-man, I can only remind him that we all have family members who are an embarrassment—or worse. I would speak now of the insult I gave him at the siege of Acre, when I ordered his banner taken down. The initial fault was his, but I will admit I rebuked him too severely, for it resulted in his departure from Acre, and we could ill afford to lose a fighter of his stature. Surely, though, he has been well avenged for this injury by my detention and captivity."

Leopold was not looking like a man who'd been well avenged, though, his mouth tautly drawn, his color high, and his fists clenched at his sides. Richard took heart from the Austrian duke's discomfort, hoping it meant that he was making a convincing case on his own behalf.

"Nor did I seek to enrich myself at the expense of others; just the contrary is true. When King Tancred agreed to pay the forty thousand ounces of gold, the French king claimed half of that sum, arguing that we'd made a pact to share any booty won during our campaign. I agreed to give him a third, even though he could have no possible right to any of my sister's dower. But I did it so there would be peace between us. After I seized a rich Saracen caravan in Outremer, I gave fully a third of the plunder and livestock to the French, for that was their price for taking part in the raid; the rest I shared amongst my soldiers. Nor did I profit personally from the conquest of Cyprus. I sold it to the Knights Templar so we'd have it as a supply base for the Holy Land. And when the Templars de-cided they no longer wanted the island, I arranged for it to go to the King of Je-rusalem, Guy de Lusignan. The Templars had paid only forty thousand bezants and still owed another sixty thousand. I told Guy that if he repaid the Templars, I would waive payment of the sixty thousand. I did this to get Guy and his de Lusignan kindred out of Outremer, thus paving the way for Conrad, the Mar-quis of Montferrat, to become Jerusalem's king."

If possible, it became even quieter; the normal sounds in any assembly—shuffling of feet, coughing, throat clearing, and whispers—were absent. Richard glanced for the first time at Boniface of Montferrat. He was leaning back in his chair, arms folded across his chest, but his relaxed posture was belied by the nar-rowed eyes, the tightness of his jaw muscles.

"I admit there was no love lost between Conrad and myself. But our differ-ences were political, not personal. I did not believe he should be crowned King of Jerusalem, for I thought his claim was tainted by the circumstances of his marriage. For those of you who are not that familiar with the tangled rivalries of the Holy Land, Guy de Lusignan's claim to the throne was based upon his marriage to the Queen of Jerusalem, the Lady Sybilla, and when she died at the siege of Acre, he found himself in a precarious position. He argued that he was still a consecrated king, anointed with the sacred chrism, and should continue to rule. But many blamed him for the catastrophe the kingdom had suffered at the battle of Ḥaṭṭin, which led to the fall of the Holy City to Saladin, and few of the Poulains—the native-born Christians—wanted him as their king."

Richard swallowed with difficulty; his throat was getting dry. "I supported Guy for two reasons. The de Lusignans were my vassals back in Poitou, so I owed them my protection as their liege lord. And I was troubled by Conrad's actions in pursuit of that crown. Upon Sybilla's death, her younger sister, Isabella, had the strongest claim to the throne. But Isabella was wed to a man as unpopular as Guy was. Conrad convinced the Poulain lords that Isabella ought to leave her husband, Humphrey de Toron, and marry him. Although Isabella protested, not wanting to end her marriage, she was compelled to do so, for she was a young girl of only eighteen and without allies. I was not yet in the Holy Land, but my Archbishop of Canterbury was at Acre and he objected fiercely to this marriage, saying it would be bigamous and invalid. Had he not died of a fever, I think he may have prevailed. But as soon as he was dead, Isabella was wed to Conrad. One of the men most involved in this sordid affair was the Bishop of Beauvais, a man who never lets canon law or principles interfere with his own ambitions."

The French bishop had been slouched in his seat, feigning boredom, but at that, he straightened up and glared at Richard, who ignored him. "This is why I could not support Conrad, for I thought his claim to the throne was ill-gotten. When we sought at Acre to reconcile the competing claims of Guy and Conrad, that compromise satisfied no one. Conrad was so disgruntled that he even refused to take part in the campaign against Saladin and withdrew to Tyre."

Richard halted to allow Hadmar to translate his remarks into German for those who spoke no Latin. "Eventually I withdrew my opposition to Conrad, for I'd come to realize that it was not for us, who would be returning to our own lands, to choose a king for Outremer. We would go home, but the Holy Land *was* home for the Poulains, and the choice should be theirs, for they would have to live with it, not us. So I declared that I would accept whatever decision they made, and the Poulain lords unanimously elected Conrad. It was then that I acted to eliminate Guy as a threat to Conrad's reign, whilst sending my nephew Henri, Count of Champagne, to Tyre to notify Conrad that he was to be king. He was overjoyed and at once dispatched Henri to Acre to make arrangements for his coronation. But it was not to be."

Boniface of Montferrat had been given a seat on the dais, too, and the Bishop of Beauvais leaned over now to whisper something, but Boniface paid the other man no heed, keeping his gaze riveted upon the English king. His face was inscrutable; Richard had no idea what he was thinking.

"A few days later, Conrad went to dine with the Bishop of Beauvais, and on his way home, he was ambushed by two Assassins sent by Rashid al-Din Sinan, known as the Old Man of the Mountain. He was carried back, dying, to the citadel, where he instructed Isabella to yield Tyre only to me or to the rightful lord of the land. Would he have done that had he believed I was the one who had set the Assassins upon him? As little as he liked me, he knew I was not capable of such a vile act."

Richard had been moving about the hall as he spoke. He now approached the dais, his eyes meeting those of Conrad's brother. "This is a charge that is utterly foreign to my character. Not even my bitterest enemies have ever accused me of cowardice, and what could be more craven than to hire killers to strike a man down? Had I wished any man's death, I would have challenged him openly, just as I would challenge any man who dared to accuse me of such a cowardly, foul murder now—were I free to do so."

For the first time, Richard got a response from the audience; he could see some heads nodding at that, as if in agreement. "The captured Assassin was turned over to the Bishop of Beauvais, who would claim he'd confessed under torture that I had sent them to murder Conrad. This is an arrant lie. Moreover, the Assassins are not routiers, willing to sell their swords to the highest bidder, and anyone with any knowledge of the Holy Land would know that. But none of that mattered to the Bishop of Beauvais, who saw a chance to besmirch my honor and leapt at it."

Hot color scorched the bishop's face. He seemed about to speak, but Heinrich shook his head, and he sat back, giving Richard a look that was truly murderous.

Richard had wondered if he'd be interrupted or heckled, but apparently that was not proper protocol at an Imperial Diet and they'd so far heard him out in polite silence. Now, though, Boniface sent a murmur of surprise rustling through the hall. "So you are saying that the Bishop of Beauvais lied about it all?"

"The Bishop of Beauvais uses the truth the way other men use whores," Richard said, and there was a ripple of laughter at that, quickly stilled. "I would gladly swear upon my honor that I had nothing to do with your brother's murder, my lord marquis. But I daresay there are many in this hall who remain convinced I have no honor, for the good bishop has been slandering me the length and breadth of Christendom, blaming me for everything but the Great Flood. So to those of you who have swallowed the poison ladled out by the bishop, I can only tell you that men do not act against their self-interest. I am sure you all know that at the time of Conrad's murder, I was in danger of losing my kingdom because of the French king's plotting with my own brother, the Count of Mortain. The longer I stayed in the Holy Land, the more time I gave them to lay claim to my domains. I will freely admit I was desperate to get back to defend my realm. But I could not bring myself to break the vow I'd made to Almighty God, to abandon the Holy Land the way the French king did. I hoped that once Conrad was king, I could safely leave Outremer in his hands, for I knew his worth as a soldier."

Boniface studied him in silence for a long moment, his expression still unreadable. "If you are not the one responsible for my brother's death, who is?"

"I can only tell you what I was told by Balian d'Ibelin, Queen Isabella's stepfather, and the other Poulain lords. Your brother was a man of great courage and great abilities. But he was also reckless, strong-willed, and stubborn. I do not say that as a criticism," Richard said, flashing a sudden smile, "for those very words have been bandied about when my name has been mentioned. But I fear those qualities may have cost Conrad his life. He'd seized a merchant ship belonging to Rashid al-Din Sinan, and refused their demands to return the ship, its crew, and its cargo. Balian said that they'd warned Conrad it was dangerous to run afoul of the Assassins, that even Saladin had backed down after Rashid al-Din Sinan threatened to murder his family. Conrad just laughed. . . ."

Boniface said nothing, but Richard dared to hope that he may have convinced Conrad's brother of his innocence. At the least, he was sowing seeds of doubt where there had been only conviction. His voice was growing hoarse; never had he spoken at such length before, or with such passion. He was both surprised and grateful, therefore, when a servant appeared without warning, offering a cup of wine. *"Danke schön,"* he said, showing off his meager store of German, and drank deeply, wondering whom he had to thank for the wine. When the servant retreated, he nodded to a man in a front row, one who was a stranger to Richard.

"Of all the despicable lies told about me, none is more outrageous or shameless than that I would betray the Holy Land. I was one of the first princes to take the cross. I bear the scar upon my body from a Saracen crossbow bolt. I nearly died at Acre and again at Jaffa from the pestilent fevers that stalk Outremer. Even after learning that my own kingdom was in peril, I honored my holy vow and stayed. And now I find myself accused by the man who did not stay, for this campaign waged against me can be tracked back to Paris."

Richard had begun to pace, for he could feel the fury flaring up again. "I did seek to meet Saladin upon my arrival at the Acre siege camp, for I knew our only hope of regaining Jerusalem would be through a settlement of some sort. The Kingdom of Jerusalem is like a small island in a Saracen sea. The Christians are vastly outnumbered by the Muslims; at the battle of Ḥaṭṭīn, Guy de Lusignan could muster no more than twelve hundred knights. And, of course, I exchanged gifts and courtesies with Saladin, for these are the civilities which brave men share during war with worthy foes. Emperor Heinrich's own father, Friedrich of blessed memory, and Saladin sent gifts to each other, and none would dare to cast aspersions upon that great man for doing so."

He paused again for Hadmar to translate, taking deep breaths to get his anger under control. "Did I respect the Saracens? Yes, I did, for brave men are deserving of respect. I established friendly relations with al-Malik al-Adil, Saladin's brother, and with several of his emirs, hoping that they might influence the sultan to make peace. But I never forgot they were our enemies and infidels, even though many of them were men of honor.

"It is true that I refused to lay siege to Jerusalem. That was because I knew it could not be taken. When we made our march along the coast from Acre to Jaffa, my fleet kept our army supplied. But the Holy City is twenty-five miles inland. Saladin would have cut our supply lines to pieces; we would not even have been able to replace the horses lost. And the walls of Jerusalem are more than two miles in circumference, enclosing an area of over two hundred acres. We did not have enough men to surround the city, so we had no hopes of starving it into submission. The Poulain lords, the Templars, and the Hospitallers saw that we could not capture the city. Everyone saw that—save only the French. Even after we learned that Saladin had poisoned all the wells and cisterns within two leagues of Jerusalem, the Bishop of Beauvais and the Duke of Burgundy insisted that we could not lose because this was a holy war, sanctioned by God. But God was on the side of the Christians at Ḥaṭṭīn, and they still lost. The Almighty expects us to do our part.

"Nor did I surrender to Saladin. We reached a negotiated settlement, making a truce for three years. We did not achieve all that we hoped for; I do not deny that. But upon my arrival in the Holy Land, the Kingdom of Jerusalem consisted of the city of Tyre and the siege camp at Acre; all else had been lost to Saladin. When I departed, it stretched along the coast from Tyre to Jaffa, Saladin no longer held Ascalon, and Christian pilgrims were once again free to visit Jerusalem and worship at the Holy Sepulchre."

Richard moved toward the dais again. "My lord emperor, you have been misled. You believed what you were told by your French allies, but they have lied to you again and again. Let me tell you about these men you thought you could trust. I was not the one who violated his holy oath and abandoned the war with the Saracens. That was the French king. I am loath to say this, as he is my liege lord for Normandy and my lands on the other side of the Narrow Sea. But I knew I could not trust him and so I insisted that he swear upon holy relics that he would honor the protection the Church gives men who've taken the cross and wage no war against my domains whilst I was in the Holy Land. He very reluctantly agreed to do so and then tried to get Pope Celestine to release him from that oath, which the Holy Father, of course, refused to do."

This was the first mention Richard had made, even obliquely, to the fact that he was being held in defiance of Church law, for he'd seen no point in belaboring the obvious. But he thought it couldn't hurt to remind the Diet that Heinrich was no less guilty than Philippe in that regard.

"That still did not stop Philippe from conniving with my brother against me upon his return to France. And I believe that he instructed his French lords who'd remained in Outremer to thwart me at every turn. I have no other explanation for their conduct. I wanted us to strike at Saladin's base in Egypt, for that was the true source of his power, and if he thought it was threatened, he'd have been more likely to agree to favorable peace terms. They refused even to consider it. When we learned after our victory at Arsuf that Saladin was razing his stronghold at Ascalon to the ground rather than have it fall into our hands, I wanted us to sail to Ascalon and seize it ere it was destroyed. Again, the French lords balked. I later occupied the ruins of Ascalon and spent a small fortune rebuilding it. It well-nigh broke my heart that we could not persuade Saladin to let it remain in Christian hands. But he did agree that it should not be held by the Saracens, either, and that was no small concession on his part, for Ascalon had been the most formidable of his castles. Yet now I find myself accused of abandoning Ascalon by the very men who thwarted my attempt to take it!

"Nor did their bad faith and perfidy end there. After it was decided that we could not make an assault upon Jerusalem, most of the French withdrew from the army and retreated to Tyre, where they hatched a plan to capture Acre. I was then at Ascalon and only the fact that the Pisans defended the city fiercely until I could come to their rescue saved Acre from falling into the hands of the French.

Think about that. They were willing to make war upon their fellow Christians. How that must have delighted the Saracens."

Richard stalked back toward the dais, pointing accusingly at the Bishop of Beauvais. "This man sought only to sabotage me during our time in the Holy Land and he then slandered my name throughout Christendom. Yet those are not his greatest crimes. Scriptures tell us that we must forgive those who sin against us, for then we will be forgiven by the Heavenly Father. But I will never be able to forgive Philip de Dreux, the Bishop of Beauvais, for his refusal to help us rescue those trapped at Jaffa."

Richard's eyes swept the hall before returning to those on the dais. "I daresay you have all heard about the two battles that I fought at Jaffa. But you may not have heard of the treachery of the men who were supposed to be my allies. We had returned to Acre and I was planning to attack Beirut, the last port still under Saladin's control, when we received a desperate appeal from Jaffa. Saladin had launched a surprise assault upon the city and they did not know how long they could hold out. There were more than four thousand people in Jaffa, many of them soldiers recovering from war wounds—and a goodly number of them were French. Yet when we told the Bishop of Beauvais and the Duke of Burgundy that Jaffa was under attack, they refused to join the rescue mission. Their hatred of me mattered more than the lives of their own countrymen! Then they dared to accuse me of betraying my Christian brethren when the true guilt was theirs."

Beauvais had seemed on the verge of interrupting several times in the course of Richard's defense, but each time he'd been silenced by Heinrich. Now he started to rise to his feet, only to sink back in his seat at the emperor's terse command.

"There may be some in this hall who are loath to believe what I have said about the Duke of Burgundy and the Bishop of Beauvais. But you need not take my word for it. Sir Druon de Mello was with us in the Holy Land, and he is an honest man. If you ask, he will confirm what I've said."

Druon de Mello's head jerked up. He looked horrified to be the center of attention, and his obvious misery spoke volumes without a word being said. Hadmar was translating again, and when he was done, Richard drew the rolled-up parchment slowly and deliberately from his belt.

"But if you want further evidence that I've spoken the truth, I give you this. I would have willingly answered for any offenses I may have committed at the court of the French king, for he is my liege lord. He would never have dared to summon me, though. How do I know that? Because of this," he said, holding the parchment aloft so all could see.

"Philippe Capet has done everything in his power to destroy my honor and my good name, and now that I am entrapped in his web of lies, what does he do? At a time when he knows I am powerless to defend myself or my domains, he declares war upon England." Richard got the response he'd hoped for— expressions of shock and disgust on the faces of these German bishops and lords.

"But one of the accusations made against me by the French is true. They say that my war was a failure, and they are right. I have explained why I believed we could not recapture the Holy City. Yet that was the aim of our quest. I swore an oath to Almighty God that I would liberate Jerusalem from the Saracens, and I was unable to do it. My oath means more to me than the French king's oath did to him, though. So I promised Queen Isabella and my nephew and the Poulain lords that once I dealt with my faithless brother and treacherous liege lord, I would return to Outremer to fulfill my vow."

Looking about him, Richard was gratified to see that his words had resonated with the audience. "Now you have heard my account of what truly happened." He was tempted to end with a proud *Make of it what you will*. He realized, though, that arrogance was an indulgence he could not afford, and so he forced himself to strike a more conciliatory note. "I would hope that you give greater weight to my actions than to my enemies' lies and render justice this day to a man sorely in need of it."

There was a brief silence when he was done speaking, and then the hall erupted into applause and cheers. Men were standing and Richard soon found himself surrounded by Heinrich's lords and bishops, some of them with tears in their eyes. The stranger who'd sent him the wine introduced himself as Adolf von Altena, the Provost of Cologne's great cathedral, and showed himself to be a man of courage by saying loudly that the king of the English had been cruelly maligned. All of the bishops had joined the circle by now, even the Bishop of Speyer, and Richard had a fleeting moment to wonder if the prelates were seizing this opportunity to show their disapproval of their emperor's flouting of Church law. But then they were moving aside, clearing a path for Boniface of Montferrat.

The marquis came to a halt in front of Richard. "Do you swear upon the salvation of your immortal soul that you played no part in my brother's death?"

"I do so swear."

Boniface's pause was deliberate, for he shared Richard's flair for drama. "I believe you," he said at last, and that set off another bout of cheering.

Richard was dazed by his own success, for this had exceeded his wildest expectations. The small English contingent was laughing through tears and Hadmar had materialized at his side, a wide grin on his face. But Leopold remained seated, his rigid body language conveying his disappointment and anger. As Richard turned toward the dais, so did others, until the hall had grown quiet and all eyes were upon the emperor.

It was easy enough to read the emotions of the men flanking Heinrich. The Bishop of Beauvais looked as if he were in danger of strangling on his own bile. Heinrich's uncle seemed to share Leopold's dismay, while Heinrich's brothers were grinning behind his back, sibling rivalry apparently proving stronger than family solidarity. But Heinrich could have been carved from ice, so little did his face reveal of his thoughts.

When Richard started to walk toward the dais, it was so still that his footsteps echoed sharply on the tiled floor. For a long moment, his eyes held Heinrich's and then he knelt before the throne. There was a muted sound from the audience, almost like a collective catch of breath, which at once gave way to wild cheering. The hall quieted, though, when Heinrich got to his feet.

"We have been led astray by false tales. I see now that the English king has been unfairly accused and defamed." Reaching out, he signaled for Richard to rise and then, solemnly and formally, Heinrich gave the other man the kiss of peace.

The cheering began again, loudly enough to echo out into the city streets. Richard was not fooled by Heinrich's dispassionate demeanor. He was close enough to the emperor to see the frozen fury reflected in those ice-pale eyes, and he gloried in it. For most of his life, he'd made a habit of defying the odds, turning likely defeats into improbable triumphs. But never had he experienced a victory as sweet or as satisfying as the one he'd just won in the Imperial Diet at Speyer.

CHAPTER ELEVEN

❧

MARCH 1193

Speyer, Germany

The mood in the chamber was subdued, with most of the men taking their cues from their emperor, who'd so far said very little. Leopold was just as taciturn, lapsing into a brooding silence after saying morosely to Heinrich, "I did warn you. The man can talk as well as fight." Heinrich's brother Conrad was currently holding forth, disgruntled that he'd been assigned the duty of placating the enraged Bishop of Beauvais, but few were paying heed to his complaints.

Count Dietrich von Hochstaden finally lost patience with Conrad's grumbling and interrupted, his the confidence of one who stood close enough to the emperor to take such liberties. "I know who is to blame for this—Adolf von Altena. He was the first on his feet, the first to start cheering, and that set the other fools off. We ought never to have allowed him to attend."

The Bishop of Speyer heard that as an implied criticism and was quick to take umbrage, for Otto von Henneberg was a prince as well as bishop, and not about to accept a rebuke from one he regarded as his inferior. "We had no choice. He was sent here by his uncle, the Archbishop of Cologne, to negotiate on behalf of the rebels, and you know that, my lord count."

"'Negotiate'? Spying is more like it," Dietrich said with a sneer. "And since when do we negotiate with rebels? They deserve beheading, not cosseting."

Before Bishop Otto could retort, Heinrich's uncle rose to his feet. Konrad von Hohenstaufen had years of experience in navigating the sometimes stormy waters of imperial politics, and he was able to silence the squabbling merely by raising his hand. "This rebellion is not to be taken lightly, not when the Archbishops of Cologne and Mainz have joined it. What we must do now is to make sure that other prelates do not follow their example." For a moment, his eyes rested upon Count Dietrich, for he knew the other man was never one to advocate compromise or conciliation. "I have overheard some foolish men saying that the emperor ought to have ignored the verdict of the Imperial Diet instead of embracing it. Nothing would have been better calculated to swell the ranks of the rebels than such an arbitrary act. My nephew, the emperor, handled it wisely and prudently, and I, for one, was proud of his conduct this day."

He glanced then at Heinrich, marveling as always that the son should be so unlike the father. His brother, Friedrich Barbarossa, had been the embodiment of chivalry, a superb warrior, fearless in battle, shrewd, robust, genial, quick to laugh, and able to charm even his enemies, whereas Heinrich lacked all of those virtues. Heinrich did have an implacable resolve, extraordinary intelligence, and an unsettling ability to make decisions devoid of any emotional content, as Konrad thought he'd proved that afternoon in the Bishop of Speyer's great hall. He found his nephew both admirable and repellent, single-minded in his determination to defend and expand their empire, but utterly unable to identify with the needs and desires that drove other men. Konrad was not yet sure if that would make him a great emperor or a monster.

He was thankful, though, that Heinrich had been astute enough to see he'd been backed into a corner by the English king and disciplined enough to accept it. Had Heinrich not acted so swiftly and decisively, Konrad was sure he'd have made enemies of most of the men in the hall, those under the thrall of the Lionheart and those who were seeking any excuse to join the rebels. And Heinrich already had more enemies than he could handle, thanks to that bloody, botched murder of the Bishop of Liege. Konrad did not think his nephew had given the command to have the bishop killed. He thought it more likely that some of his lackeys had acted in the belief he'd be pleased, and Konrad's chief suspect was Count Dietrich von Hochstaden, brother of the man who'd contested that episcopal election. But he'd not asked Heinrich outright and knew he never would.

"I agree with the lord count," Speyer's bishop said firmly. "Word is already spreading of the English king's convincing defense before the Diet. Now that he has cleared his name, the Church will begin agitating for his release. I say we end this as quickly as we can, putting the blame on the French king and—" He stopped himself, but not in time.

"And me?" Leopold was on his feet, glowering at the prelate-prince.

"Well, you were the one who first laid hands upon a man who'd taken the cross."

"Because I was commanded to seize him by the emperor!"

The bishop shrugged and Heinrich's brother, who had no liking for Leopold and enjoyed muddying the waters, said snidely, "I doubt you will be able to prove that when summoned before the papal curia, so I'd think of another defense if I were you, my lord duke."

That outraged not only Leopold but all of the Austrians in the chamber. It also roused Heinrich from his private reverie, and he gave his brother a cold stare. Conrad had earned a well-deserved reputation at the imperial court for being truculent and difficult to deal with. He was not an utter fool, though, and the one person he never crossed was his older brother. He at once subsided, even mumbling a grudging apology when Leopold demanded it.

Heinrich shoved his chair back, saying, "We are done here for now." The others at once rose, made their obeisances, and began to file out. As he looked over his shoulder, Hadmar saw that Heinrich had kept his seat, signaling for his marshal, Heinz von Kalden, and his seneschal, Markward von Annweiler, to remain. Shutting the door upon this confidential colloquy, Hadmar felt a prickling of unease, but the sight of Heinrich and his most trusted *ministeriales* often invoked that sensation. The unholy trinity, he called them, although that was an indiscretion he confided to no one, not even his wife. With another speculative glance at that closed door, he hurried to catch up with his still-irate duke.

WILLIAM DE ST MÈRE-EGLISE was growing more and more nervous as the hours dragged by. Richard had been summoned to a meeting with the emperor and the Austrian duke, and he'd taken advantage of his improved status to insist that the Bishop of Salisbury accompany him. William had been left behind to pace and fret. They knew Heinrich would still attach conditions to Richard's release, but William felt confident that they would not be as outrageous as those demanded of Richard upon his Palm Sunday meeting with the emperor. The waiting was not easy, however.

When Hubert Walter finally returned, William began to pelt him with questions even before he'd closed the door. The bishop held up his hand as if to ward them off. "I will tell you all, I promise. But let me sit down first. I'd sooner bargain with the Devil's own than that lot."

William hastened over with a wine cup. "It was only to be expected that the emperor would be in a foul mood after the king's triumphant acquittal Monday."

"We did not see the emperor. He sent the bishops of Speyer and Bath to speak for him, although Leopold was there, and looking none too happy about it."

"The Bishop of Bath? Since when did he become the emperor's puppet?"

"He insisted he was the ideal choice, being blood-kin to the emperor and yet loyal to the king. But I doubt their kinship means much to Heinrich, and Savaric's loyalty is primarily to himself." Hubert took a swallow of wine and then another, realizing for the first time just how fatigued he was. "Are you ready to hear what they are seeking now? The emperor still wants that one hundred thousand silver marks, but this time around, it is being disguised as a 'fee' to reward Heinrich for brokering a peace between Richard and the French king."

William's jaw dropped. "He has no more chance of doing that than he does of earning sainthood!"

"I know, and so does he. That is why he has agreed that if he fails to reconcile the two kings, nothing will be owed to him."

William sat down on a nearby stool to consider this. "So . . . they are trying to save face now."

Hubert nodded, pleased the other man was so quick to comprehend. "That seems to be their primary concern, although they do want some tangible concessions, too. For Heinrich, that means Richard will provide him with fifty galleys and two hundred knights for a year's service."

"He is no longer demanding that Richard accompany him in person when he invades Sicily, then?"

"No, that was not even mentioned. Heinrich is proving to be a pragmatist, fortunately. He seems willing to settle for getting some military assistance in his war against Tancred whilst posing as the king's new friend, one led astray by those false, deceitful French. As for Duke Leopold, his price is the freedom of his kinsman and Richard's niece as a bride for his son. He was actually more obstinate than the emperor's spokesmen, most likely because he can see who is going to be the scapegoat when all the dust settles. But even he is not being utterly unreasonable. Richard said flatly that under no circumstances would he return Anna to her father, calling Isaac a lunatic and worse. So Leopold then came up with an alternative plan, that Richard's niece wed his eldest son and Anna wed the younger lad. Which is not a bad compromise when you think about it."

William nodded thoughtfully. "He'll need something substantive to point to when his duchy is laid under Interdict, something to show his unhappy vassals, and I suppose a royal marriage will have to do. What of the hostages?"

"They are being much more reasonable on that, too. Instead of two hundred, they are now willing to settle for sixty highborn hostages sent to the imperial court and seven sent to Vienna."

"And the king? How did Richard react to these more modest demands?"

Hubert smiled wryly. "After his rather spectacular vindication in the Imperial Diet, he does not think any demands at all should be made upon him."

"I understand that, I do. But these new terms are a great improvement over what they first tried to extort from him. I think we should accept them and get the king out of here as fast as horses can run."

"I agree," Hubert said, with another weary smile. "Now we need only convince Richard of that."

❧

RICHARD HEARD THEM OUT in a foreboding silence that made William de St Mère-Eglise and the Cistercian abbots uneasy, expecting his anger to erupt at any moment. Hubert Walter had come to know the king well during their time in the Holy Land and he interpreted that silence differently, seeing it as evidence that Richard had reluctantly come to the same conclusion as they had—that his first priority had to be regaining his freedom. Richard's common sense was their ally; it was his lacerated pride that they must win over.

"We understand why you are loath to consent, my liege. You have right on your side and thanks to your brilliant defense on Monday, you have demolished any possible legal justification for your detention. Yet none of this changes the fact that you are still in Emperor Heinrich's power, a man we know to be untrustworthy and dishonorable. They need to save face, and as much as I hate to say it, we need to let them."

"Bishop Hubert speaks the truth, my lord king," William said earnestly. "It is not safe to defy Heinrich, not until you are free again. Then you can pressure the Holy Father to move against them, as he ought to have done from the outset."

"There is another reason to accept their terms," Hubert continued. "The longer you remain in Germany, the more time that gives the French king and your brother to wreak havoc in your domains. Philippe has already led an army into Normandy and the queen's spy warned her that John hoped to gather a fleet at

Wissant to invade England. You can spare your subjects much suffering if you get home ere that happens."

Richard said nothing, but when he sat down in the closest chair, the slump of his shoulders and his bloodshot eyes spoke eloquently of his exhaustion, of the toll this was taking upon his body and his spirits. Hubert thought he was about to agree—until the Abbot of Boxley made the mistake of pointing out how much more reasonable the new demands were. Richard's head came up sharply at that, his eyes glittering. "I doubt that Tancred, the Cypriots, my niece, or Anna would agree with you," he snapped.

Dismayed to have blundered, the abbot looked to Hubert for help and the bishop did his best to provide it. "Tancred's fate will not rise or fall upon your providing Heinrich with fifty galleys. He has always expected Heinrich to launch another invasion and will be ready for it. Nor are the Cypriots at risk if Isaac regains his freedom. He is a broken reed, no longer posing a threat, for he lacks what any despot most needs—money."

"Nor are the marriages disparaging ones, my liege," William said quickly. "The Lady Aenor might do better, I admit, being the niece of England's king. But it is no disgrace to be the Duchess of Austria. Leopold's House is a proud one, with blood ties to many of the royal courts in Christendom. His mother was a Greek princess, his duchess the sister of a Hungarian king, and he can claim kinship to the Hohenstaufens, too. As for the Lady Anna, her prospects are not so promising, even if you were to provide a marriage portion for her. Isaac is disgraced and deposed, and he never had a legal right to Cyprus in any event. I suppose she might be welcomed by her mother's kindred back in Armenia, but few lords of high birth would see any benefits in taking her as a bride. So marriage to Leopold's younger son may be the best she can hope for."

"William is right, sire," Hubert said, just as quickly, wanting to head off any objections from Richard. "The girls could do far worse. Unless you object to Leopold's sons, fear that Friedrich and Leo will not do right by them?"

"No . . . they are good lads, both of them. I have no reason to think they would not be decent husbands to my niece and Anna."

Encouraged by this grudging concession from Richard, Hubert smiled. "We ought to remember, too, that not all betrothals lead to the altar. For certes, yours to the Lady Alys did not. And if my memory serves, your lord father and Emperor Friedrich were once talking of a marriage between you and one of the emperor's daughters, which came to naught."

"Thank God for that," Richard said fervently. "Had it come to pass, Heinrich would have been my brother by marriage." And when they laughed, he managed a thin smile of his own.

"So may we tell them on the morrow that you accept the terms?" Hubert would not have posed that question were he not already sure of the answer. He still held his breath, though, until Richard nodded, apparently finding the words themselves too bitter to the taste.

They were all greatly relieved to have it settled. Hubert suspected that Richard was, too, even if he'd never admit it. It was then, though, that the Abbot of Boxley made another error. "Let us drink, then, to the king's impending release," he exclaimed, and bustled over to the table to pour wine for them before Hubert could stop him.

Richard took a cup when it was thrust into his hand, but his eyes had darkened to a storm-sea grey. Hubert and William had too often seen the old king's eyes take on that same ominous shade just before the notorious Angevin temper ignited, and so they were braced for what happened next. The abbots and Richard's guards were not, and they all flinched and gasped when Richard's fist closed around the cup and he then flung it furiously across the chamber. It struck the wall with enough force to shatter, sending shards of glazed clay flying in all directions, while the wine splashed the whitewashed surface with splatters that looked eerily like bloodstains.

"I may have to agree to this odious extortion," Richard snarled, "but by God, I'll not celebrate it!"

❦

RICHARD WAS RECLINING IN the window-seat of his chamber in the Bishop of Speyer's palace, strumming a small harp; it was tangible evidence of his improved prospects, for as soon as he'd requested one from the bishop, it had been delivered to him within hours. He'd also been allowed to meet with some of the German prelates, and had even spent an enjoyable afternoon with the Provost of Cologne, Adolf von Altena, who'd given him an interesting update on the rebellion. But now that Easter was past, the men who'd attended the Imperial Diet had departed Speyer, and Richard's flood of visitors had ebbed to a trickle. He was pleased, therefore, when a knock sounded at the door, for after three months in semiseclusion, he welcomed Heinrich's open-door policy; isolation had been a punishment in and of itself for a man accustomed to being the center of attention.

He had new guards now that Leopold had formally surrendered him to the emperor, and one rose and moved casually to the door, admitting Hadmar and Leopold's two sons.

"We've come to bid you farewell," Friedrich declared, "for our lord father is returning to Austria today and so we might not see you again."

"Unless you come to our weddings," Leo chimed in, with a cheeky grin that Richard could not help returning.

"I expect I'll be too busy putting the fear of God into my brother and his French partner in crime."

"Well, you would be welcome," Friedrich assured him. "After all, when I wed your niece, you and I will be kin."

He sounded rather proud of that, and his brother elbowed him in the ribs. "Are you going to call him Uncle Lionheart?"

"Over my dead body," Richard said, and both youths laughed.

"Pay Leo no mind. I wanted to tell you," Friedrich said, with an attempt at adult gravitas, "that I am honored to marry your niece."

"He also wants to know what she looks like," Leo gibed, earning himself an indignant look from Friedrich.

"You are just as curious about the Damsel of Cyprus!"

Richard was amused by their playful rivalry, in such contrast to his own contentious relationship with John and his other brothers, and he surprised himself by thinking that whatever else might be said of Leopold, he'd proven to be a good father. "Well, I've not seen Aenor for over three years, and she is a little lass, only . . ." He paused to calculate rapidly. ". . . nine. But by the time she is old enough to be a wife, I daresay she will be pleasing to you, Friedrich. The women in my family are usually beauties."

"What about Anna? Is she pretty? How old is she?"

"Fifteen. And very pretty indeed, Leo, with long fair hair and blue eyes. She is also lively and quick to speak her mind, so if you expect a docile little lamb, you'll be disappointed."

"I fancy a lass who shows some spirit," Leo said loftily, for all the world as if he had vast experience with spirited girls, and Richard hid a smile. He was still angry at being forced to make these marriages, but it did help that both boys were so likable.

"You called her 'Aenor,'" Friedrich interjected. "I thought her name was Eleanor?"

"It is. Aenor is the Breton form. Geoffrey named her after our lady mother,"

Richard explained, thinking that this was one of the few times when he'd been pleased with his brother, for their father had been quite vexed by that, just as Geoffrey had intended.

"Breton?" Friedrich pondered that for a moment. "Is that what she speaks . . . Breton?"

"No, she speaks French, for that is the native tongue of the Breton dukes. I do not think her mother, Constance, speaks any Breton at all." For the first time, Richard thought about his sister-in-law's reaction to the marriage. She'd be furious, but he was not overly concerned about that. He had no fondness for Geoffrey's widow, thinking she'd proved herself to be quite untrustworthy during her marriage to his brother, urging him to ally with the French king and to lay claim to Aquitaine.

Leo had little interest in his brother's bride and wanted to know now what languages Anna spoke. He looked pleased when Richard said Anna spoke Greek and Armenian, and her French had improved dramatically since she'd joined his sister Joanna's household. "Very good! I speak some Greek, too. Our grandmother was the daughter of the Greek emperor in Constantinople and our father insisted that we learn it, saying we should be proud of that, being able to claim an emperor in our family."

Leo had straddled a chair, clearly planning to stay for a while, but he rose reluctantly to his feet when Hadmar reminded him that their lord father planned to depart within the hour. As they went charging into the stairwell like young colts, Hadmar lingered for a moment to say his own farewell to the English king.

Richard had not seen the Austrian *ministerialis* since he'd been transferred from Leopold's custody to Heinrich's, and he was pleased to have this opportunity for a few words. "You made my confinement more bearable than it might otherwise have been, Hadmar, and I will not forget that. I thank you for your courtesy, your kindness . . . and your advice," he added, with a slight smile. "I would hope that you've not lost favor with your duke because of it."

"He was not pleased with me after your trial, for he thought I welcomed your vindication too enthusiastically. But it passed, as he knows I would be loyal to him till my body's final breath. And he knows, too, that I do what few dare—I always tell him the truth, and every ruler needs such a man."

"Yes, they do, indeed." Richard found himself thinking of his own truthteller, Fulk de Poitiers. The Bishop of Speyer had assured him that his men would soon be freed, and he hoped so, for he'd missed his irascible, shrewd, and sarcastic clerk, a man as loyal to him as Hadmar was to Leopold. Did Heinrich have any such men? He very much doubted it.

Hadmar bowed, but then hesitated, his hand on the door. He had nothing that would justify his suspicions, much less constitute proof. It was just that he'd never known the emperor to yield so easily. But Heinrich had given the English king the kiss of peace, witnessed by every man present at the Imperial Diet. Would he dare to disavow that? Could he be so careless of his own honor? No, surely not. Why burden Richard with his own misgivings when they were likely no more than shadows and smoke?

"Godspeed, my lord Lionheart," he said, and moved into the stairwell after his duke's sons.

❦

HUBERT WALTER HAD BEEN horrified when Richard confided that for the first weeks of his detention, he'd been watched at all times by men with drawn swords, and the bishop was reassured now to see that his new German guards were playing a dice game, yet more proof that the king's circumstances had changed for the better. "I'd hoped they'd have been removed altogether," he admitted.

Richard had hoped so, too, but he merely shrugged. "They are polite and seem to think it is an honor to be guarding a king. The Bishop of Speyer even found one who speaks a little French; very little, if truth be told. Still better than my German, though." Gesturing toward the table, he said, "There are the letters I want you to take to England. William already has his. Did I tell you I have a scribe now? According to the bishop, the emperor thought it was not fitting that a king should be writing his own letters and kindly provided one for me."

Hubert smiled, for Richard's voice had been dripping with sarcasm. "I was trying to think," he continued, "who'd make a better spy than a scribe. Aside from a royal confessor, no one."

"Jesu forfend," Hubert said, only half jokingly, for violating the sanctity of the confessional was a serious sin. "I assume the letters are to the queen and your justiciars."

Richard nodded. "You'll be able to tell them all that I thought best not to commit to parchment." He gave the bishop a sidelong glance and a mischievous smile. "You'll be most interested, though, in one of the letters I entrusted to William, telling my lady mother that we need to address the vacant archbishopric of

Canterbury. It has been over two years, after all, since Archbishop Baldwin died at Acre. I'd say it is long overdue to fill it, no?"

Hubert nodded, hoping that his inner agitation was concealed beneath his matter-of-fact demeanor. As much as he yearned for the archbishopric, he'd never discussed it with Richard, too proud to campaign for a post that he might be judged unqualified for. Hubert had received extensive administrative and legal training in the household of his uncle, King Henry's chief justiciar, and had gained considerable experience serving as a justice of the Exchequer Court before Richard had approved his elevation to the bishopric of Salisbury. But he lacked the formal education expected of a prince of the Church, and was self-conscious about his inadequate command of Latin; he'd had to rely upon William's whispered translation in order to follow Richard's speech to the Imperial Diet. Fearing that if he asked Richard and was refused, it might damage a relationship he valued greatly, he'd never sought to plead his own case before the king. Nor would he do so now.

"I hope the monks of Christchurch Priory are more receptive to your choice this time," he said instead, for Richard's last attempt to select an archbishop had failed. He'd wanted the monks to elect the Archbishop of Monreale, having been impressed by the Sicilian prelate during his stay in Messina. But the Canterbury monks had balked and, finding it easier to defy the king at a distance, they'd declared they would not elect a "foreigner." Instead they'd chosen the Bishop of Bath, Reginald Fitz-Jocelyn, the uncle of the current Bishop of Bath, Savaric, who'd maneuvered to secure his uncle's election so he might gain the Bath bishopric for himself. The new archbishop had died within a month, however, and the post had remained vacant since then.

"I was very tactful—for once—in my letter to the Christchurch monks," Richard assured Hubert, "writing only that they are to hold an election with the advice of the queen and William de St Mère-Eglise. My mother will diplomatically inform them of my choice, but in such a way that they never realize they are being herded where she wishes them to go." He smiled, saying, "My mother is very good at that. My lord father, on the other hand, preferred a more direct approach. He actually wrote to the monks of Winchester that he ordered them to hold free elections, but forbade them to elect anyone but his clerk!"

Hubert joined in his laughter, but it sounded forced to Richard. A master of suspense—a trait he'd inherited from his father—he'd planned to drag the announcement out. Realizing how nervous the bishop was, though, he took pity. "I have told my mother that I want you as the next Archbishop of Canterbury."

Hubert had been bracing himself for disappointment and, for a moment, he could only stare at the other man. "I am deeply honored, my liege," he managed, "more than I can say."

"I do not want you to think that I chose you because you were willing to brave a winter crossing of the Alps on my behalf." Richard's mouth twitched and then he grinned. "Although I will admit it definitely did not hurt your chances."

Hubert's teeth worried his lower lip as ambition warred with conscience. The latter won, for the Archbishop of Canterbury was the head of England's Church. "I need to know that you are sure about this, my liege, sure that I am the right man. I feel compelled to tell you that there are others better educated than I, and my Latin is not as fluent as I would wish."

Richard started to joke about the advantages of not speaking Latin, stopping himself when he realized that Hubert was not responding with the modesty expected of a candidate for such a prestigious post, but was sincere. "I could find a hundred clerks who speak Latin as if it were their native tongue. I am not looking for a linguist, Hubert. I want a man of integrity, honor, courage, and intelligence—qualities you showed in abundance during our time in the Holy Land. I've known for months that you were the best choice, and had my voyage home been as uneventful as I'd hoped, you'd already have been consecrated by now."

"Thank you, my lord king!" Hubert would have knelt had Richard not stopped him.

"I have no doubts whatsoever that you will be a superb archbishop. Now . . . the sooner you get to England, the sooner you embrace your destiny and the sooner I gain my freedom." Richard smiled and then gave Hubert the same blessing he'd gotten from Hadmar von Kuenring. "Godspeed, my lord archbishop."

❦

THE CISTERCIAN ABBOTS HAD LEFT after Easter, but Hubert Walter and William de St Mère-Eglise had delayed their departure until the last day of March. Richard had not realized how much comfort he'd taken from their presence until they'd gone, and he had a restless night. He was not pleased, therefore, to be awakened early the next morning by Johan, the guard who spoke a smattering of French.

The youth kept stammering and repeating the words "the emperor," and Richard could only conclude that he'd been summoned by Heinrich. A knight was standing by the door, arms folded, and looked blankly at Richard when he spoke a few words of Latin. As much as he resented being dragged out of bed like this, he realized there was nothing he could do about it and he flung the covers back.

When he emerged into the garth, trailed by his guards, Richard saw that he already had an escort waiting, yawning as they slouched by their horses. He was surprised to see how early it was, the sky just beginning to lighten toward the east. He recognized the man in command, for Hadmar had pointed him out on several occasions: Sir Markward von Annweiler, an imperial *ministerialis* and Heinrich's seneschal. He came forward at once, introducing himself with a deferential bow and displaying the command of Latin that a court official would need. He was no longer young, into his fifth decade, but he appeared fit and energetic, his reddish-brown hair showing no grey yet. Unlike many of the Germans, he was clean-shaven, with striking moss-green eyes, and he had an unexpectedly charming smile. Richard thought cynically that he'd probably been able to seduce far more than his share of women with that smile—unless a woman had been vigilant enough to notice that the smile never reached his eyes.

"The emperor wants to see me?" Richard asked, and Markward confirmed it, signaling for a horse to be brought forward. There was so much that Richard had missed in the three months and ten days since his capture at Ertpurch. He missed having a woman in his bed, missed the easy camaraderie he'd enjoyed with his soldiers and the knights of his household, missed the people who mattered the most to him, missed his music and books and his favorite falcons, the sense of purpose that had driven all of his days. But he'd not expected how much he would miss riding a purebred stallion, that sensation of being one with a spirited creature eager to outrun the wind. The mount he was offered now was a horse he'd never have chosen for himself, a docile gelding that could not hold a candle to Fauvel, the magnificent Cypriot destrier that he'd ridden to so many victories in the Holy Land. This one had no bridle and reins, of course, just a halter with a lead attached, the ultimate symbol of his impotence.

Inwardly seething, he swung up into the saddle just as Markward told his guards that they would not be needed. Their disappointment was so obvious that Richard assumed they'd been looking forward to a rare opportunity to be called into the emperor's presence. "Consider yourself lucky, Johan," he said, but the young German did not understand, of course, and watched in puzzlement as the English king rode out of the precincts of the episcopal palace with his new guards.

The city was just coming awake and the streets were still deserted. Richard thought it passing strange that Heinrich should summon him at such an hour, yet he did not become suspicious until they turned into the street that led to the Old Gate, the main entrance to Speyer from the west. It was still barred, but a curt command from Markward sent the guards scrambling to open it. Richard took advantage of the brief delay to call the *ministerialis* by name, too loudly to be ignored. "I thought you said we were going to the imperial palace!"

Markward responded with another of those beguiling smiles. "Ah no, my lord king. You misunderstood. We ride to the village of Annweiler, where I was born."

"Why?"

"I do not question my emperor," Markward said blandly. "But I know your safety is of great concern to him. You are a very important guest of the empire, after all."

Richard's eyes narrowed on the other man's face. "I was told that I would be accompanying the emperor to his palace at Hagenau. Surely I'd be safe enough there."

The other man's shoulders twitched in what may have been a shrug. By now all of Richard's survival instincts were on full alert. None of this made sense to him, but he did not like it, not at all. The best soldiers had a sixth sense when it came to danger and he'd long ago learned to pay heed to his. "What sort of game is Heinrich playing?"

Those green eyes shone now with open amusement. "His favorite game, my lord king," Markward said cheerfully. "The one where he gets to change the rules."

❧

THEY TRAVELED AT A FAST PACE, reminding Richard of the urgency with which he'd been rushed to Dürnstein. He did not believe he was being taken to Annweiler; why would Heinrich want to send him to some paltry German village? The position of the sun told him that they were heading west, but he knew no more than that. With every mile they rode, though, his misgivings kept pace. His guards were of a different sort from the men who'd watched him at Dürnstein or the Bishop of Speyer's palace. He'd seen their ilk before, had hired some of their brethren himself—routiers whose swords were for sale to the highest bidder, untroubled by qualms of conscience and usually very good at what they did, which was to unleash hell at the command of the lord who'd paid them. He found it even more troubling that the lord giving those commands was Markward von Annweiler, for any man who'd gained Heinrich's trust was not one to be overly burdened with scruples himself. But no matter how he tried to untangle this Gordian knot, he made no progress. Heinrich had professed belief in his innocence in front of his own Imperial Diet. The German bishops and lords knew of the terms agreed upon for his release. Richard did not see how the emperor could disavow such a public commitment. So what did Heinrich hope to gain? Where was he being sent and—more important—why?

The road wound through a dark, primal forest that stretched as far as the eye could see. The patches of sky visible above the sentinel spruce and bare branches of silver beech were now splattered with clouds. Expecting to meet Heinrich at the imperial palace, Richard had chosen the more elegant of the two mantles he'd been given in Dürnstein, and he soon wished he'd selected the warmer one, for the April air had a wintry chill. They rode in silence, stopping only to rest the horses briefly and to allow the men to relieve themselves, and as soon as he'd dismounted, Richard found himself ringed by drawn swords again. His attempts to pry answers from Markward proved futile; the other man merely smiled, saying they had not much farther to go, that Annweiler was only twenty or so miles from Speyer. And with that, Richard had to be content.

The sun had begun its slow slide toward the west, haloing the clouds in crimson and gold, when the mountain peaks came into view, three rocky crags still glazed with snow at their summits. All three were crowned with castles, but only one held Richard's gaze, for it seemed to be floating on the mists swirling about its lower slopes. Backlit by the dying sun, its sandstone walls and towers rose up against the sky like a bloodred scar, and Richard's first thought was this was a fortress impregnable to assault, even more formidable than Dürnstein.

Markward signaled for a halt and then turned his horse, reining in beside Richard, who at once said sharply, "Do not tell me that is Annweiler."

"The town is below in the valley," Markward said amiably, "hidden in the mist. But you can see the castle quite clearly, even at this distance. That is Trifels. Mayhap you've heard of it, my lord?"

Richard had, for the notoriety of that red sandstone stronghold had spread well beyond the borders of Germany. Trifels was where prisoners of state and the most dangerous enemies of the empire were held.

CHAPTER TWELVE

❧

APRIL 1193

Trifels, Germany

Richard felt a surge of relief when he saw that he was not to be thrust into one of the castle's notorious dungeons, said to be black holes of Hell. But the best that could be said of his new lodging was that it was not an underground oubliette. The chamber was small and stark, containing only a pallet and a chamber pot. There were no windows, only several arrow slits, no source of heat, and a lone sputtering oil lamp. And he was again being guarded by men with drawn swords.

The chamber was cold, filling with the night mountain air, and when Richard sat down on the pallet, he saw that he'd been provided with one thin blanket. Leaning back against the wall, he tried to make sense of his plight. Ought he to have seen this coming? Yet how could he have imagined a betrayal of such magnitude? It was obvious now that Heinrich had been biding his time, waiting until the Imperial Diet had dispersed. But did Heinrich truly believe his treachery could be hidden away at Trifels? Why not, though? Only Almighty God knew what bloody secrets had been shrouded behind these stone walls. And how would anyone even know that he was here? His friends were on their way back to England, believing that terms had been struck for his release. How long would it be ere his disappearance became known? Weeks? Months?

When he rose from the bed, his guards at once went on the alert. They showed no overt hostility, but what he saw in their hard-eyed stares was worse—indifference. He did not know if they were routiers or unfree *ministeriales*, but he did not doubt that these were men who'd cut a baby's throat without qualms if told to do so by their lord. He'd had many bad moments since he'd looked out the window of the alewife's house in Ertpurch and seen the trap about to be sprung. But never had he felt as defenseless as he did now, utterly at the mercy of a man without honor or conscience or even prudence, a man so arrogantly sure of his own power that he'd dared to kill a prince of the Church.

Compline had been rung in the town's churches before a servant brought a tray into the chamber. He set it on the floor and hastily retreated. Richard stared down at the bread and cheese and ale, understanding that he was being sent a message with this meager meal, letting him know that his rank had been stripped away as soon as he'd ridden into the castle bailey. This was prisoner's fare, not what would be served a highborn hostage, much less a king. He forced himself to swallow a few mouthfuls, then pushed the plate aside. Not long afterward, Markward von Annweiler returned.

He was not alone. Richard's earlier introduction to the castle burgrave had been a terse one, for the *ministerialis* spoke neither Latin nor French. He was a big, burly man, the sort who might one day run to fat, with receding fair hair, watery blue eyes, and a stolid, phlegmatic mien; Richard had immediately assessed him as one who'd never disobeyed an order or had an original thought of his own. They were accompanied by more guards, so many that some had to wait out in the stairwell. Richard was already on his feet, intending to demand answers even if he did not expect to get them. It was then that he saw what one of the men was carrying—an armful of chains.

"You cannot think I will submit tamely whilst you put me in irons!"

"Actually, I did not," Markward conceded calmly, "so I asked the emperor what we should do if you resisted. He merely smiled. I took that to mean we can use as much force as needed. But I would hope it will not come to that. This is not a fight you can win, my lord king. Surely you see that. In your speech to the Imperial Diet—and a fine one it was, too—you argued convincingly that it would have been madness to assault Jerusalem when defeat was a certainty."

He nodded then to the burgrave, who uttered a command, and the guards began to fan out, with the obvious intent to encircle Richard. If they were daunted at the prospect of taking on such a celebrated soldier, it did not show on their faces; several were smiling as if they relished this opportunity. Markward was smiling, too, sounding almost friendly as he said, "You'll gain nothing by resisting. You'll merely prolong the inevitable whilst giving these lads a chance to brag in the local alehouse about subduing the English Lionheart. I am not a king, of course, but if I were one, I think I'd have too much pride to let myself be thrashed by lowborn louts."

Markward paused then to give Richard time to consider what he'd said. He could almost feel the rage radiating off the other man, but he could see that Richard was listening, and he was pleased by that. He was perfectly willing to give the command to beat the English king bloody, but he was practical by nature and preferred the easy way whenever possible.

"Suppose I make your cooperation worth your while," he said affably. "It has been a long day and I have a soft bed and a ripe wench awaiting me, so I would rather we do this sooner than later. If you submit to the manacles, I will forgo the leg shackles. What could be fairer than that?"

Richard did not trust himself to speak or even to move, sure that if he took so much as a single step, he'd launch himself at Markward's throat, consequences be damned. But the part of his brain not on fire realized that the German had spoken no less than the truth. Unless he wanted to force them to kill him, all he'd gain by resisting was pain and humiliation. And he was not yet ready to abandon all hope.

Interpreting his silence as surrender, Markward nodded again to the burgrave, who drew his sword, the signal for others to do the same. Only then did the guard with the chains come forward. Eyeing Richard warily, he handed the key to the closest man as he clapped the manacles onto the king's wrists, then reclaimed the key to lock them. Richard exercised all of the self-control at his command to stand motionless as this was done. He was caught by surprise, though, when the man then fastened the chain to a bolt in the wall. He'd not expected to be tethered to the wall like this, and as he looked accusingly at Markward, he realized how easy it would be for them now to fetter him with the leg shackles, too.

As if reading his mind, Markward grinned. "I do not make a habit of it, but I occasionally do honor my word, and fortunately for you, tonight is one of those times. I'm sure we can find use for the shackles elsewhere; we never seem to run out of prisoners here. Sleep well, my lord king." Opening the door, he smiled again. "Though I daresay my night will be a better one than yours."

◈

RICHARD SLEPT POORLY, for every time he shifted position, he was awakened by the tension in the chain. The manacles were made of iron and surprisingly heavy; they fit tightly and already his wrists were being rubbed raw. He did not

feel thankful that his ankles were not fettered, too, just a burning sense of outrage that a consecrated king should be subjected to such degrading maltreatment. He welcomed the fury, did all he could to feed the flames, clinging to his
anger as if it were a shield in a vain attempt to keep the shame at bay. Last night,
he'd told himself that he had no choice but to submit, that at least he could spare
his pride by doing so. In the cold light of day, it seemed to him that in salvaging
his pride, he'd sacrificed his honor.

Being chained up did not even rid him of the guards. There were only a few
now and they squatted in the shadows, passing the time by telling jokes, or so he
assumed, since they laughed often. But their continued presence salted his
wounds, for he'd not been alone for even a few moments since his capture on
December 21, not once free from prying, inquisitive eyes.

In midmorning, sounds from the inner bailey floated up through the arrow
slits. By listening intently, Richard concluded that Markward von Annweiler
was departing, doubtless returning to report to the emperor that he was securely
caged at Trifels. He felt no relief, though, that the *ministerialis* was gone. Now he
was surrounded by men who spoke not a word of French or Latin, unable to
communicate with any of them.

The hours dragged by. Richard passed the time by recalling every memory of
the past thirteen days, beginning with his first meeting with Heinrich in the
chapter house. There must be a pattern, something he'd missed. Heinrich was
not a man to act on impulse. He'd proved that by pretending to accept the verdict of the Imperial Diet. So what did he want? What did he hope to gain by this
betrayal? Did he think he could strike a new deal with a man desperate enough
to pay any price to escape Trifels? Or had he concluded that there was nothing
to be gained now that he'd been outwitted and outmaneuvered at Speyer? Richard could still hear that cool, dispassionate voice. *If you do not agree, then you're
of no value to me, and I have no reason to keep you alive.* Had he been sent to
Trifels to break his spirit? Or to suffer for daring to make a fool of Heinrich before his own court? He did not know the answer, but he would be given it by
day's end, and from an unexpected source.

He'd been served another scanty supper, a cup of weak ale, more bread and
cheese, when the door opened and the burgrave entered, followed by several
men carrying torches. The sudden brightness caused Richard to avert his gaze,
for once night had fallen, his cell quickly filled with shadows. When his eyes had
adjusted to the glare of those flames, he found himself looking into the face of
Philip de Dreux, Bishop of Beauvais.

The bishop was grinning. "Have I ever seen a sight so sweet? No, I think not. You're looking rather bedraggled, Lionheart, and it's only been two days. Imagine what a pitiful state you'll be in after you've enjoyed the emperor's hospitality for a month or two."

Richard got slowly to his feet. "I have you to thank for this, Beauvais?"

"I would love to be able to claim all the credit. But the emperor already had it in mind to send you here. He did not like how easily you beguiled his vassals and decided that you'd cause less trouble at Trifels. I agreed, of course. I explained, though, that it was not enough to keep you secluded, for you're stubborn, Lucifer proud, and badly in need of a few lessons in humility. Heinrich does not want you dead, if that be any comfort. He wants you broken, and time spent at Trifels usually breaks men like twigs. When you're ready to beg him for your freedom, then he may be willing to talk about new terms. As for me, I hope you hold out for a while. It gives me great pleasure to think of you cold, hungry, dirty, and fettered like a common felon."

"You are a dead man, Beauvais, I swear it!"

The bishop laughed. "I am quaking in my boots; can you tell? You still do not see, do you, Richard? Heinrich would sell you to the Caliph of Baghdad if the price was right. Yes, he wants you to be miserable during your stay at Trifels, but he wants the money even more. You think your mother and friends will empty England's coffers to rescue you, and I daresay you're right. But hatred is a far more powerful force than love, and my cousin Philippe hates you as much as I do. He was not happy to learn that Heinrich and Leopold had agreed upon terms for your release at Würzburg without giving him a chance to put in a bid of his own. I am going back to Paris on the morrow to deliver the good news that he now has another chance. Whatever the English can offer, he will match it and more, and not just for the pleasure of seeing you rot in a French dungeon. He is no fool and knows full well that it will be a lot easier to take Normandy and Anjou away from your brother than from you. So it is safe to say that he is greatly motivated to outbid your doting mother. Think on that during those nights when sleep will not come."

He waited to see if Richard would respond, and then signaled to the burgrave to open the door. "Farewell, my lord Lionheart," he said mockingly. "May the next time we meet be in Paris. And if you think these accommodations are lacking, wait until you see what awaits you in the royal dungeons of the French king."

RICHARD THOUGHT HE'D HIT his lowest point while having to endure the bishop's taunting. But the next day he began to cough and it got steadily worse. He was soon sure that he was running a fever, for the chamber no longer seemed as cold. He was already helpless in the hands of his enemies. If he was being punished for past sins, was that not enough? Must he sicken now, too, stricken with the chills and fever that had laid him low in the past? In the past, though, he'd been amongst friends and had doctors to tend to him. Even then he'd almost died of quartan fever at Jaffa. How long would it take for Death to claim him in this frigid, barren cell? Mayhap in time he'd come to see Death as an ally, but not yet. He was not ready to concede defeat, willing to suffer far greater deprivations than this to thwart those misbegotten, conniving caitiffs on the German and French thrones. Whatever he may have done to displease the Lord God, surely he was more deserving of Christ's mercy than Heinrich and Philippe.

RICHARD HAD BEEN TROUBLED for hours by coughing fits, but he'd finally fallen asleep after midnight. He was not sure what awakened him, for at first he heard only the snoring of his guards and the keening of the wind. Shivering, he reached again for his blanket and mantle. It was then that he heard it, a voice close at hand, telling him to wake up. The words were in French and the voice was very familiar. He sat up so abruptly that his chain jerked him backward. Peering into the darkness beyond his bed, he thought he could discern a figure standing a few feet away. For once, he was utterly at a loss. Feeling like a fool, he said dubiously, "Are you a ghost?"

The laughter was hoarse and raspy and familiar, too. "You'd think I'd have better things to do in the afterlife than haunt my ungrateful son, would you not? Yet here I am."

"No," Richard said, "you are *not* here."

"And you are not in a German dungeon," Henry shot back. "Let's assume that I got a safe conduct from Purgatory. I have something to tell you and for once I want you to heed what I say. Let's begin with that bastard Beauvais. Even a blind pig can turn up an acorn occasionally and he was right when he called you stubborn. That stubbornness will be your undoing if you do not start recognizing your new reality."

"And this reality involves chatting with a ghost?" Richard said dryly. "Well, why not? What should I be doing, then?"

"Start by admitting what you most fear."

Richard forgot that this had to be a dream. "I fear nothing!"

His father laughed again. "If that were true, your mother would be an even worse wife than I thought, for no blood son of mine could be such a fool. We both know what you most fear, Richard—what any man with half a brain would fear—that you could be turned over to the tender mercies of the French king."

He paused, as if daring Richard to deny it. "Say what you will of that German vulture, he is motivated by sheer greed. I daresay he is enjoying this chance to humiliate you, for you do have a rare gift for making enemies. But we're still dealing with basic greed, which is why the French king is so much more dangerous. Philippe hates you with the only spark of passion ever to inflame that shriveled soul of his. Oh, he would also like to put Johnny on your throne, realizing that Johnny is much easier prey than you. I confess to being grievously disappointed in that lad."

"So am I," Richard said, having discovered that he was actually enjoying his eerie, improbable conversation with this sardonic spirit.

"But it is Philippe's poisonous jealousy that would doom you. You do know what will happen if he ever gets you in his power, Richard? You'll never see the light of day again and when death comes, you'll welcome it."

"Of course I know that! But in case you've not noticed, I do not have much control over events these days."

"You have more control than you know, lad. Make the most of it. Do whatever it takes to keep Heinrich from selling you to the French."

"Even if that means swallowing every last shred of my pride?" Richard demanded, with sudden bitterness.

"Yes, damn you, yes! You owe this to me, Richard. Save my empire. Do not let my life's work become dust on the wind. Do not let Philippe and Johnny destroy it all." It was very quiet after that. When Henry finally spoke again, the raw passion was gone from his voice, as was the ironic, detached amusement. "There is something else you need to remember whenever this new reality of yours becomes more than you think you can bear. You cannot gain revenge from the grave. Trust me on this; I know."

Richard did not respond at once, for a fettered memory had just been set free—the last words his father had ever spoken to him. Compelled by Philippe to give his rebel son the kiss of peace, he'd done so, and then growled, *God grant that I live long enough to avenge myself upon you!* It was only then that Richard had realized Henry was truly dying.

"When I found myself a prisoner at Dürnstein, knowing I was facing a trial at Heinrich's court, charged with crimes I'd never committed, I began to think that mayhap I was being punished for other sins. At the time, I did not consider them sins. I thought I was justified in defending my birthright and my mother. Now . . . I am not so sure. Is this why God has turned His face away from me? Because of my sins against you?"

Richard waited tensely for Henry's answer. It never came. There was only silence.

THE NEXT MORNING, the dream was still so vivid that it unsettled Richard, for he remembered hallucinating at Jaffa in the throes of fever, convinced that Philippe and his brothers John and Geoffrey were at his sickbed. Could he be hallucinating again? He was not on fire with fever, though, and he took comfort from that, deciding it was only a dream, nothing more.

He had another bad day, for his coughing was now so persistent that he sometimes felt as if he were strangling. He finally gained a brief surcease in midafternoon when he fell asleep. But when he awoke, his fear of hallucinations came flooding back as he stared at the three men by his bed. The burgrave did not look as stoic as before; he was flushed and clearly ill at ease. A rail-thin youth with red hair, freckles, and a friendly gap-toothed smile was at the burgrave's side. And kneeling by the pallet was a man small and misshapen, cursed with a receding chin, flat nose, and crippled legs, so plain that his enemies cruelly called him "dwarf" and "imp" and "gargoyle," England's disgraced chancellor, Guillaume de Longchamp.

Richard struggled to sit up, for the chain had snagged on his blanket, limiting his range of motion. He still managed to touch the chancellor's arm, needing the reassurance that Longchamp was flesh and blood, not another phantom spirit. "Guillaume? How are you here?"

Longchamp's dark eyes shone with unshed tears. "God will punish them for this, sire," he said, reaching over to untangle the chain. "After your brother drove me into exile, I retreated to Normandy, but as soon as I heard of your capture, I set out for Rome and then Germany. When I got to Speyer, Heinrich had already left for Hagenau and no one knew your whereabouts. The Bishop of Speyer privately confided what the guards had told him—that the emperor's seneschal, Markward von Annweiler, had come at dawn for you. Bishop Otto insisted he'd had no part in it and did not know where you'd been taken. When I pressed him, though, he admitted it was most likely Trifels Castle."

This was not what Richard wanted to know, but he'd been too busy trying to suppress a cough to interrupt. "No . . . I meant how did you get the burgrave to let you in to see me? How did you even manage to communicate with the man? He speaks no French, no Latin. . . ."

"I had Arnold translate for me, sire. Ere I set out, I hired a German-speaking guide." Longchamp gestured toward the lanky redhead, who grinned in acknowledgment. "And the burgrave dared not refuse me. I told him that I am a papal legate as well as a consecrated bishop, and I swore a holy oath that if he did not admit me straightaway, I would excommunicate him then and there, cast his miserable soul out into eternal darkness."

Longchamp started to rise then, no easy feat, for he'd been lame in both legs since birth. But he waved the guide away when Arnold offered a helping hand, for he was fiercely proud. Once he was on his feet, he swung around on the burgrave, black eyes blazing. "Tell him this is a disgrace and an outrage, Arnold. The life of the English king is precious to the Almighty, and to the emperor, too—worth one hundred thousand silver marks, to be exact. If the king dies at Trifels, the emperor forfeits any chance to collect that ransom. And if he dies in this fool's custody, whom does he think will be blamed?"

He paused to let the guide translate, glaring at the burgrave all the while. "Tell him that as terrible as the emperor's wrath will be, how much greater will be the wrath of God. He will burn in the hottest pits of Hell for killing a man who took the cross, who fought for Christ in the Holy Land. All that the English king has suffered at his hands, he will suffer a thousandfold. Those cast into Hell are tortured by demons, drowned in rivers of boiling blood, trapped in lakes of fire. But as awful as these torments are, they are not the worst of the punishments inflicted upon the damned. The worst is that these doomed souls will never get to look upon the face of God."

By now the burgrave was the color of curdled milk, and even Arnold had paled. "He says he loves God, does not want to burn in Hell. What must he do?"

"Tell him to fetch a doctor or an apothecary from that village below to treat the king's fever and to do it now."

"He . . . he says he does not think it is permitted, my lord, that it has never been done."

"This has never been done, either!" Longchamp snapped, gesturing toward the chained man on the pallet. Limping toward the burgrave, he thrust his arm out, like a prophet of the Old Testament calling down celestial thunderbolts upon doomed sinners, and the burgrave retreated before him.

The guards were mesmerized by this extraordinary show, eyes round and mouths agape. When Longchamp began to spit out Latin imprecations, the German yielded and promised the apothecary would be sent for straightaway. And as he watched the huge, hulking burgrave wilt before his diminutive chancellor, Richard smiled for the first time since he'd been spirited away from Speyer to this isolated mountain citadel.

❧

THE APOTHECARY WAS ELDERLY and obviously nervous at being summoned to the castle, but he brought along a supply of herbs and instructed Arnold in how they were to be administered. Within hours, Richard's cough began to ease and his throat no longer felt so sore. He thought it helped, too, to have been served his first decent meal since his arrival at Trifels, a bowl of hot soup and bread that was not stale. He was even given a flagon of wine, at Longchamp's insistence. The apothecary's sleeping draught was beginning to take effect, and he smiled drowsily at his chancellor. "I am truly gladdened by your visit. And I'll take to my grave the memory of your turning that brawny burgrave into mush."

The older man shifted uncomfortably, for he'd insisted upon sitting on the floor next to Richard's pallet. "God has not forsaken you, my liege," he said earnestly, even imploringly. "You must not despair, for I am going to get you out of here."

Richard did not doubt the chancellor's sincerity, merely his ability to conjure up a miracle. "You cannot intimidate the emperor the way you did the burgrave, Guillaume," he said and yawned. "Heinrich would be right at home in Hell. . . ."

"Nevertheless, I will find a way, sire. I promise you that upon the surety of my soul." Richard didn't reply, his lashes drifting down to veil his eyes, and the even rhythm of his breathing soon told the chancellor that he slept. He planned to depart for the emperor's court at Hagenau at first light, so he knew he ought to be abed himself. But he found it hard to leave. Although he'd browbeaten the burgrave into giving Richard a second blanket, he could still feel the cold night air seeping through those open arrow slits, and he removed his own mantle, tucking it securely around the sleeping man.

His had not been an easy life, in some ways made more challenging because his disabled body housed a first-rate brain. He'd been brutally taunted as far back as he could remember, for theirs was an age in which physical deformity was often seen as the outer manifestation of inner evil. He'd soon realized that he was far more intelligent than his tormentors, and from an early age, he'd determined to show them all. Burning to prove himself superior to fools with handsome faces, healthy bodies, and empty heads, he'd looked to the Church as his only avenue of escape. Having neither charm nor good looks nor family ties to recommend him, he'd had only his exceptional intellect to rely upon, and it eventually earned him a clerkship with the old king's baseborn son, Geoff, and then a post in the chancery. His career would likely have stalled there if not for a chance encounter with Richard, then the young Duke of Aquitaine.

They could not have been more unlike—a prince blessed with the best their world had to offer and a puny misfit—but to Longchamp's amazement, Richard had been indifferent to his physical frailty, able to penetrate his cripple's guise and recognize the finely tempered steel of a blade-sharp mind. He had become Richard's chancellor and, when Richard was crowned, England's chancellor. Richard had elevated him to the bishopric of Ely, named him chief justiciar, secured for him a papal legateship, and entrusted his kingdom to Longchamp when he departed for the Holy Land.

Never had Longchamp's ambitions soared so high; he'd even dared to dream of the ultimate prize, the archbishopric of Canterbury. He'd taken advantage of his newfound power to provide for his family, to humble the enemies who'd scorned him for so long, and to give justice to those who so rarely received it whilst safeguarding his king's throne. But somewhere along that road, he'd lost his way. He'd antagonized men whose support he needed, let his disdain for the English and their Godforsaken isle show too nakedly, and then fallen into the trap set by the king's brother, who was far cleverer than he'd first thought. During his months in exile, he'd done little but reassess and relive his dizzying fall from grace, concluding that ungodly pride had led him astray.

Even more than his personal humiliation, he'd grieved for having let down his king, the one man who'd shown faith in him. His loyalty to Richard had long been the lodestar of his life, almost spiritual in its selfless intensity, rooted almost as much in Richard's acceptance of his physical flaws as in the tangible benefits of royal favor. It had not been tarnished by his disgrace; if anything, it burned all the brighter during the dark days of the past year. He yearned to make amends for his mistakes, knowing all the while that second chances were rarely given in this life, especially to those such as him. But he saw now that God had been more merciful than he'd dared hope.

"I failed you once, sire," he said softly. "I will not fail you again."

RICHARD KNEW BETTER THAN to take his chancellor's passionate promise as anything but what it was—a welcome expression of loyalty and outrage. But after Longchamp's visit, he was in better spirits. He'd been touched to find the bishop's mantle wrapped around him when he awakened the next day, and he was thankful for the timing of Longchamp's arrival, sure that the apothecary's potions had warded off a serious illness. Most important, the world would soon know that he'd been incarcerated in the emperor's notorious stronghold. However many bodies had been buried at Trifels, his would not be one of them.

He'd lost track of the days, but once he learned that Longchamp had reached Trifels on the eighth day of his imprisonment, he determined to keep count. Each morning, he managed to mark the wall by rubbing the edge of one of his manacles against it; he refused to let himself think a time might come when he'd have filled up all of the space within reach of his chain. He occupied his hours by composing songs in his head, compiling lists of men who now owed him a blood debt, and trying to anticipate what exorbitant and outrageous demands were likely to be made of him when he was eventually summoned by the emperor. He did not think it would happen for some weeks, though. If that weasel Beauvais could be believed, Heinrich would want to give him enough time to become desperate and in utter despair.

He was taken by surprise, therefore, on the sixteenth day of his captivity when the door opened and Markward von Annweiler sauntered in, followed by the burgrave. Richard got quickly to his feet; by now he'd learned how to maneuver his tethered chain. He thought the seneschal seemed relaxed and at ease, but that would probably be the case even if he'd been given imperial orders to slit the English king's throat.

"Well, now I have another reason not to forget you, my lord. You were the first king I'd ever escorted to Trifels and you are the first prisoner I've ever brought out."

Richard's reaction was great relief, for what could be worse than Trifels? "Where am I going?"

"To the imperial court at Hagenau. It seems that your chancellor has a golden tongue." Markward glanced over his shoulder and as the burgrave moved aside, Richard saw Guillaume de Longchamp hobbling in behind them.

"My God, Guillaume," he said incredulously, "you did it!"

Longchamp's smiles were usually sparing, but now he was beaming, dark eyes shining.

Turning to the burgrave, he held his hand out expectantly. The German slapped a key into his palm and he limped toward the bed. "If I may, my liege?" Richard grinned and extended his wrists as his chancellor inserted the key into the first lock. When he was finally freed of the manacles and chains, he thought he'd never heard a sweeter sound than the clank of the fetters striking the floor at his feet.

Markward had watched placidly, content to obey his emperor's commands, whatever they may be. "A bath is being heated," he told Richard, "and your chancellor has brought new clothes for you. When you are ready, your guards will escort you to the great hall."

As soon as Markward and the burgrave exited the chamber, Richard grabbed his little chancellor, lifted him up, and swung him around in an exuberant circle. "You truly did it!"

Longchamp actually blushed. "Sire, this is not seemly," he protested, and Richard set him down, remembering one time when he'd playfully slapped the chancellor on the back and nearly knocked him off his feet.

"Sorry," he said, laughing. "At least I did not kiss you! How did you do it, Guillaume? How did you change that hellspawn's mind?"

"I told him that I'd found you gravely ill. I may have exaggerated somewhat, for I made it sound as if you were lingering at Death's door. I told him, too, that he needed to know something the Bishop of Beauvais had kept from him— that you are susceptible to recurrent attacks of quartan fever, and you could well die if it happened whilst you were held a prisoner at Trifels."

He gave Richard a quick, searching look. "I hope you do not mind, sire, that I told him about your past illnesses. I had to convince him that there was a genuine danger in keeping you here."

"Hellfire, Guillaume, I'd not have cared if you'd told him I was a leper, not as long as it gets me out of this cesspit!"

"We know now that he truly does not seek your death. Of course, I pointed out that he had a great deal to lose were you to die at Trifels. Not only would there be no ransom, but his reputation would suffer irreparable damage once word got out that he'd sent you to the dreaded Trifels and thus caused your death. I also made sure to mention that I'd already dispatched couriers to the queen mother in England and to the Holy Father in Rome to let them know of your whereabouts. It had occurred to me that it was probably not wise to let Heinrich think I and I alone knew the secret of your incarceration here," he said dryly, and Richard saluted him with an approving smile, thinking that Heinrich might finally have met his match.

"I then expressed concern that sooner or later, word would reach the rebels and they would make good use of your plight to gain new followers. Even some of those who'd attended the Imperial Diet in Speyer might be receptive to the call to rebellion, having found the English king innocent of all the charges brought against him. I said this with great regret, of course."

"Of course." It was clear to Richard that Longchamp was going to draw out this account of his triumph; he'd never suffered from false modesty. But he did not care if the chancellor boasted of his spectacular success for years to come; he'd well earned that right. Something about this did not ring true, though. He could understand Heinrich being alarmed to learn his prize prisoner had almost died; his every breath was worth one hundred thousand silver marks. Yet Heinrich could have given the command to treat him more gently or even to send him to a less notorious prison. To go from Trifels to the imperial court at Hagenau was a dizzying turn of Fortune's wheel.

"What else did you tell him, Guillaume? What is missing so far from your narrative?"

Now it was Longchamp's turn to smile approvingly. "I implied that it might be shortsighted to make a bitter enemy of the English king. Alliances are as shifting as the tides, after all, and the day could come when the Holy Roman Empire and England might want to make common cause against France."

"Did you, indeed? And his response?"

"Oh, nothing was said outright. It was done by inference and insinuations. In other words, the lying language of diplomacy. You see, sire, I've made a study of our unholy emperor, and I've learned that he is not as keen on an alliance with the French as his father was. Heinrich has ambitions that go far beyond his own borders. He thinks in terms of what Germans call 'Weltherrschaft,' which we might translate as 'world empire.' The first step must be the conquest of the kingdom of Sicily, of course. But in time he'll start to seek expansion elsewhere, and France would be a natural target.

"Speaking of France, I borrowed a page from your book, my liege." Longchamp's smile was the closest he'd ever come to a jubilant grin. "The Bishop of Speyer told me how you'd cleverly heaped the blame on the French at your trial, thus giving the emperor a face-saving way out of his predicament. So I told Heinrich that you knew the Bishop of Beauvais was the one responsible for your ill treatment. I told him, too, that I know you far better than Beauvais does, and you were not going to break. No matter how long you were held at Trifels, it was never going to happen."

Richard said nothing, but color rose in his face as he stared down at the chains crumpled at his feet. Longchamp did not notice. "I also told Heinrich that I was authorized to negotiate on your behalf and I felt confident that we could reach terms that were mutually acceptable. I had to make him believe that it was in his own best interest to bring you back to court."

"And you did. What you accomplished was truly remarkable, Guillaume. You outwitted a master spider and I will never forget that you were the one to free me from his web."

Longchamp's face glowed. "I did have help, sire, from a kind and noble lady."

Richard's eyebrows rose, for he knew that Longchamp had the typical cleric's distrust of women, dismissing them as Daughters of Eve. "I would indeed hope that I have the Blessed Lady Mary on my side," he said, for that was the only woman he could imagine being praised by his chancellor.

Longchamp nodded. "You also have the Empress Constance on your side," he said, with the quiet pleasure of one making an astounding disclosure. "The emperor at first refused to see me and each day that he made me wait was one more day that you'd be trapped at Trifels. So I sought the empress out and she convinced Heinrich to meet with me."

Richard was astonished. This would bear thinking about, but for now, all he wanted was to leave Trifels in the dust. Sixteen days in chains had sapped his strength, though. His muscles were weak and he was light-headed when he took his first steps. His wrists had been badly chafed by the manacles, tingling painfully as he rubbed them to restore the circulation. He'd been moving around gingerly as he'd listened to Longchamp and he finally felt ready to tackle the stairs. "Let's get out of here," he said, but he came to a halt as his gaze fell on the discarded chains. Reaching down for them, he balanced their heavy weight for a moment and then he whirled and slammed them into the wall. The guards looked startled; they did not object, though, as Richard hammered the manacles until the locking devices broke off. Only then did he fling them to the ground and turn away, leaving the cell without a backward glance.

❧

RICHARD WAS SAVORING THE warmth of the sun on his face. Trifels was more than a feared prison; it had also been one of the favorite residences of Heinrich's father, with very comfortable royal quarters and a walled-in garden. Richard and his chancellor were there now, sitting on a wooden bench as his guards loitered nearby, looking bored. It had been decided to delay their departure for Hagenau until the morning, ostensibly because there were only a few hours of daylight remaining, actually to give Richard a little more time to regain his strength. He was eager to see Trifels receding into the distance, but for now he was content to breathe in fresh, untainted air and to watch fleecy clouds sweep like cresting waves across a sky as deep and blue as the Greek Sea.

"Think of all those poor devils caged up belowground," he said pensively. "Is it true that if a man goes years without seeing the sun or sky, he becomes blind as a bat?"

Longchamp had no interest in prisoners other than his king and he shrugged. He'd never dreaded anything so much as what he must do now. "Sire . . . I must tell you about the events that resulted in my exile from England."

Richard already knew. It had taken months for letters to reach him in the Holy Land, but eventually they did. Longchamp had been resisted from the first by men who scorned him for his low birth and misshapen body and arrogance, but it was his own misstep that would bring him down. Richard had commanded his brothers John and Geoff to stay out of England until his return, although he later relented at his mother's urgings. Longchamp had not believed Geoff had been released from his oath, and when the archbishop landed at Dover, the castellan of the great castle, wed to Longchamp's sister, had ordered his arrest. Geoff had taken refuge in St Martin's priory, and after a standoff of several days, he'd been taken out by force and imprisoned in the castle. Longchamp himself had not been in Dover at the time, and when he'd heard, he'd ordered Geoff's release. But by then, it was too late. People were horrified that an archbishop had been treated with such disrespect and the sanctuary violated, especially since it had been barely twenty years since the Archbishop of Canterbury had been slain in his own cathedral. The other bishops had united against Long-champ, John had proclaimed himself the champion of the half brother he'd always despised, and the chancellor's belated attempts to placate his foes were for naught. Stripped of his high offices, he'd had to take refuge in the Tower of London, and his chancellorship came to an ignominious end.

For Longchamp, even worse was to come. He'd always shown considerable courage for a man so physically vulnerable, but he briefly lost his nerve and sought to flee England in defiance of the great council's ban. Richard had heard several accounts of his disastrous escape attempt, one that he'd donned a monk's habit and the most popular version—that he'd camouflaged himself in women's clothing. But he'd been apprehended, his identity revealed, and the most virulent of his enemies, Hugh de Nonant, Bishop of Coventry, had circulated a scurrilous, hilarious letter that purported to describe Longchamp's misadventures on a Dover beach, accosted by a lustful fisherman who'd taken the disguised chancellor for a whore.

Whatever the truth of these stories, Richard had no intention of making Longchamp humiliate himself by recounting any of them. "I already know what happened, Guillaume. I will not deny that you made some grave mistakes. Nor was I happy to learn of them, although I never doubted your loyalty. But you were not entirely to blame; there is plenty of that to go around. It is clear now that my brother Johnny had it in mind to sabotage your efforts from the outset. As for my brother Geoff . . . well, that one will be arguing with St Peter at Heaven's gate."

Richard reached out and patted the other man on the shoulder. "What's past is past, and we need not speak of it again." But instead of the relief he'd expected to see, Longchamp's face showed only misery.

"Sire . . . there is more. I have long been slandered and defamed by my enemies. It is true I come from a modest background, but I am not the grandson of a serf, as the Bishop of Coventry claims; my father held a knight's fee of Hugh de Lacy. Nor did I disregard the advice of my fellow justiciars or live as lavishly as they say. They scorned me as an 'obscure foreigner' and detested me for not being English, but their real grievance was that I was not meek and obsequious and that I dared to challenge my 'betters.' I do not deny I sought to advance my kin and I may have relied too much upon my fellow 'foreigners,' filling posts with men from my native Normandy."

"I know of the complaints made against you," Richard said, somewhat impatiently, for he saw no reason to dwell upon this now.

Longchamp's cheeks had gone scarlet. "But you do not know of the worst accusations, my lord king, spread by that son of perdition, the Bishop of Coventry. I myself did not hear of them until recently. They are vile beyond belief. Hugh de Nonant and his lackeys say that . . . that I have committed the most grievous of sins: that I have taken young boys into my bed."

He'd been staring down at his clenched hands as he spoke, but he forced himself to look up now, to meet Richard's eyes. "My liege, I swear to you that these are wicked, despicable lies. I would never, never indulge in such a perversion, such a—"

"Enough!" Richard twisted around on the bench so he could look the other man full in the face. "See my hands," he said, holding them out, palms up. "Do you see the blood of Conrad de Montferrat on them? Need I swear to you that I did not connive with Saladin to betray the Kingdom of Jerusalem? Well, you need not swear to me of your innocence, either. I know there is no truth to these charges, for I know you."

Longchamp closed his eyes for a moment. Appalled by these accusations, which went far beyond any he'd ever anticipated, he'd found it mortifying even to give voice to them, but he'd felt honor-bound to let his king know that such rumors existed. "Thank you, my liege," he said, so low that his words barely reached Richard's ear.

"I agree that these charges are particularly foul, Guillaume, but you must bear this in mind—that they come from Hugh de Nonant. That in itself would cause men to doubt them, for his own sins are beyond reckoning. If even half of what is said of him is true, his only hope of gaining absolution will be to find a priest so drunken he'd shrive Lucifer himself. Few will believe him." Richard knew better, of course; salacious gossip spread faster than any plague. But that was the only comfort he could think to offer.

Longchamp grasped at it like a drowning man, so desperate was he to believe none would give credence to the Bishop of Coventry's slander. He even mustered up a wan smile at Richard's barbed jest. "Sire . . . there is something else we need to discuss ere we return to the great hall. In my life, I have met many sinful men—greedy, envious, spiteful, overly proud."

Richard cocked his head to the side, his smile quizzical. "If you are taking me to task for my own sins, it is not my fault that it has been so long since I've been shriven of them. And of the seven deadly sins, I refuse to claim more than three—wrath, pride, and lust."

"I was not speaking of your sins, my liege. We all sin; it is in our nature. But I have met only two men whom I would judge as truly evil. One is that despicable wretch Hugh de Nonant. The other is Heinrich von Hohenstaufen."

"I'd be the last one to dispute that. Where are you going with this, Guillaume?"

"When we reach Hagenau, Heinrich will want to discuss the new terms of your release. I have no doubts whatsoever that he will not agree to free you without payment of a very large ransom. I know how hard it will be for you to agree to this, but you truly have no choice, and I need to be sure you understand that."

Richard was silent for so long that the chancellor began to become uneasy. "I do," he said at last. Staring across the gardens at the red sandstone walls of the castle, he said grimly, "And that is not the worst of it. After Trifels, we know Heinrich cares naught about his own honor, which means that his word is worthless."

CHAPTER THIRTEEN

❧

Hagenau, Germany

As soon as he entered the great hall of the imperial palace, Richard felt all eyes upon him. There was no overt hostility, mainly curiosity, and he assumed word had spread of his exoneration in Speyer. Trailed by his guards, he started toward the dais, slowing his step so his chancellor could keep pace. Longchamp gave him a grateful, sideways glance, appreciative of these small acts of kindness that need not be acknowledged. As they approached the dais, Longchamp said a silent prayer that his king would be able to hold his temper, no matter the provocation.

Having vowed that he'd be damned ere he knelt again to this shameless swine, Richard compromised with a brief bow. Heinrich was regarding him with a cynical smile. "It pleases us to welcome the king of the English to our court. It is our earnest hope that we will soon be able to celebrate our friendship with a treaty of amity between England and the empire."

Richard bared his teeth in a smile of his own. "I value that alliance fully as much as you do, my lord emperor."

"Yes," Heinrich said complacently, "it is good that we are in such accord."

Richard turned then toward the woman seated beside Heinrich. Constance de Hauteville had married late in life, at age thirty-one, for her nephew, the King of Sicily, had been in no hurry to make a match for her. She was eleven years older than Heinrich and in the seven years they'd been wed, her womb had not quickened. Richard thought Heinrich would never put her aside as barren, though, for his claim to Sicily rested upon her slender shoulders. Joanna had told him Constance was lovely, but he thought she was too thin, the skin tightly drawn across her cheekbones, hers a mouth no longer shaped for smiles. He could see glimpses of the beauty she'd once been in the sapphire-blue eyes. Yet they were opaque, giving away nothing. She put him in mind of a castle long under siege, determined to hold out until the bitter end.

"Madame, it is my pleasure to meet you at last," he said, kissing her hand and getting a murmured courtesy in return. He was turning to greet Heinrich's uncle Konrad, the Count Palatine of the Rhine, when he was accosted enthusiastically by the Bishop of Bath.

"My liege, how it gladdens me to see you here at Hagenau!"

"I'd have been here sooner, but the emperor wanted to show me his castle at Trifels first."

While Richard got no response from Heinrich, he'd not expected one. He did catch interesting reactions from the others. An expression of surprise crossed Konrad's face. The corners of Constance's mouth curved ever so slightly. And Savaric Fitz Geldwin hastily averted his gaze. So Konrad had not known about his sojourn in Trifels. But the bishop did. Why would Heinrich have confided in this sly, pompous schemer?

Heinrich had leaned forward in his seat, his eyes intent upon Richard's face. "Now that we are to be allies, I have been thinking how best to demonstrate my goodwill. And then it occurred to me. I am in a position to do you a very good turn, my lord king."

Richard felt the brush of his chancellor's mantle as he edged closer. "And what is that, my lord emperor?"

"It has been called to my attention that your archbishopric of Canterbury has been vacant for more than two years. As it happens, I have the perfect candidate at hand—my cousin, the Bishop of Bath."

Richard's first reaction was not anger; it was disbelief. He stared at the other man, incredulous that even Heinrich would dare to meddle so blatantly in English affairs. "How kind of you to take such an interest in the English Church. I will give the Bishop of Bath's candidacy all the consideration it deserves."

"I knew you would appreciate my interest. But surely there is no need for consideration. My cousin is well qualified, after all. I will be pleased to provide you with my own scribe so that you may write to your justiciars in England, informing them of your wishes in this matter."

Longchamp surreptitiously touched his king's arm, hoping to convey a wordless warning. But one was already echoing in Richard's ears. *Do whatever it takes to keep Heinrich from selling you to the French.* "If it pleases my new ally, then it pleases me," he said tonelessly.

Heinrich nodded, with another of those hinted smiles. "It is good that we understand each other, my lord king. That bodes well for our future endeavors."

"Sire, how can I ever thank you?" Dropping dramatically to his knees before Richard, Savaric Fitz Geldwin gazed up euphorically at the king. "Such a great honor! I promise you that you will have no regrets. I will be loyal to you until my last mortal breath."

Richard looked down at Savaric's flushed, thrilled face, his own face expressionless. "You need not fear, my lord bishop. I know exactly what your loyalty is worth."

THE FOLLOWING TWO HOURS were very unpleasant ones for Richard. Many of those in attendance upon the emperor were eager to meet him or to renew acquaintances struck in Speyer, and he found himself having to smile and make small talk and act as if nothing were amiss. His new friends were primarily churchmen and he assumed they were grateful that they would not have to choose between allegiance to their emperor and their Pope now that he and Heinrich were supposedly reconciled. He did the best he could, but when he developed a pounding headache, he told Longchamp that he needed to end this farce straightaway.

Longchamp marveled that Richard had held out as long as this. "I will inform Heinrich that you are ready to depart," he promised, and limped off toward the dais. Despite his tactful phrasing, Richard knew what he was really saying—that they could go nowhere without Heinrich's permission—and that was just one more bitter drop in an already rancid drink. But as he waited for Longchamp to return, he noticed the empress standing a few feet away, conversing with the Bishop of Worms. As soon as the bishop moved off, Richard ended his own conversation with several archdeacons and crossed to Constance.

"Madame, may I have a word with you?"

"Of course, my lord king." Correctly interpreting the glance he gave her women, Constance added, "My ladies speak no French, so I rarely get a chance to make use of my native tongue."

Richard appreciated the subtlety of her assurance that they could speak freely. "My chancellor told me that you interceded on my behalf, getting him an audience with the emperor. If not for your kindness, I might still be enjoying the dubious comforts of Trifels. I wanted to tell you that you have a king in your debt—and I always pay my debts."

To anyone watching, Constance's smile was polite, impersonal, and as devoid of warmth as her husband's own smiles. But Richard thought he caught a spark in those extraordinary sapphire eyes. "You owe me no debt," she said softly, "for what I did, I did not do for the English king. I did it for Joanna's brother."

RICHARD'S CUTTHROAT TRIFELS GUARDS had been replaced immediately upon his arrival at Hagenau with men who were much more polite and personable. They'd made themselves as inconspicuous as possible during his time in the great hall and were escorting him now to his new quarters, which Markward von Annweiler had blithely assured him would be "more to your liking."

As they walked, Longchamp glanced at Richard from time to time. The other man was staring straight ahead, his face utterly blank. The chancellor knew he was still seething, though. "I am sorry, my liege. I never expected you to be ambushed like that." He got no response, but he was too troubled to keep silent. "Sire . . . is there any chance those Christchurch monks might actually elect Savaric?"

"No." After several more moments of silence, Richard said, "Heinrich provided me with a scribe at Speyer, too, but what he does not know is that I chose to write one letter myself, which William de St Mère-Eglise carried to London, in which I told my mother that I wanted Hubert Walter to be the next archbishop."

Longchamp felt an involuntary pang for the death of a dream, even though he understood now how unrealistic it had been. The Christchurch monks might well have elected him, for he'd been on excellent terms with them, but the English would never have accepted him. "I am relieved to hear that," he confessed, "for Savaric's accession to the archbishopric would surely be one of the signs of the coming Apocalypse."

"It would never have happened," Richard said flatly, "even if I'd not already sent that letter choosing Hubert Walter. My mother knows me too well. She'd have realized that any letter written in support of Savaric Fitz Geldwin would have been done under duress."

The chancellor gnawed his lower lip, understanding that Richard had never expected to do anything "under duress." "I think you handled that outrageous demand as well as could be done," he said, after another lengthy silence. "As long as we win the war, it does not matter if we lose a battle or two."

Richard came to an abrupt halt, turning upon Longchamp such a burning look that he could not help flinching, even though he realized the king's rage was not directed at him. "Good God, man, of course it matters!"

❧

HUBERT WALTER AND WILLIAM DE ST MÈRE-EGLISE traveled so swiftly that they reached London in just twenty days. They'd set such a fast pace that they'd arrived before the abbots of Boxley and Robertsbridge even though the latter had departed Speyer two days earlier, and so they had the pleasure of being the ones to bring the queen mother the news of her son's bravura performance before the Imperial Diet. Now they were dining with Eleanor in the great hall of her quarters in the Tower. Freed of the constraints of Lent, Eleanor's cooks had prepared an elaborate meal. As the season for roebuck had begun at Easter, the queen's table was graced with roast venison, as well as lamb stew, capon pie, sorrel soup with figs and dates, and Lombardy custard. The guests were serenaded with harp music and a sound Eleanor's household had not often heard in the past few months—her laughter.

"Had it not been his destiny to rule, your son would have made a superb lawyer," Hubert said with a smile, "for he addressed each and every charge against him and rendered them invalid, exposing them for the falsehoods they were. You'd have been very proud of him, Madame, for it was truly one of his finest hours."

"He must have put on a spectacular defense, indeed, if he forced Heinrich to back down," Eleanor said, with a smile of her own. "You and Dean William have brought me a precious gift this day, my lord bishop—hope." She devoted herself to the capon on her trencher then, but her mind was ranging far afield, weighing all that the bishop and the dean had shared with her in the course of the afternoon.

William Briwerre, the only one of the justiciars then in the city, began to tell Hubert Walter and William de St Mère-Eglise that John's rebellion had not gone as he'd hoped. His invasion with hired Flemish ships had not materialized, for Eleanor had called out the levies in the southeast. "The Count of Mortain then landed on his own, hired Welsh routiers to garrison the castles he'd seized last year, and dared to come to London, where he demanded that the justiciars swear fealty to him, claiming King Richard was dead. Of course, we refused, and he retreated to Windsor Castle, which is now under siege by William Marshal and the Archbishop of Rouen, whilst the Bishop of Durham is besieging his castle at Tickhill."

Eleanor was only half listening to Briwerre. The capon was perfectly seasoned, the pastry shell moist and flaky, but she was not fully aware of what she ate. Setting her knife down, she said pensively, "Heinrich is not a man to surrender his prey so easily and Richard's triumph does not change the fact that he remains in the emperor's power. I do not believe Heinrich will be satisfied with military aid for his Sicily campaign, no matter what he is saying now. I think we must assume that a goodly ransom will still be demanded ere he frees my son."

Glancing around the high table, she saw that the bishop and dean and William Briwerre were all nodding in agreement. "This means," she said, "that we need to make a truce with John."

William Briwerre turned so abruptly in his seat that some of his wine splattered onto the tablecloth. "But, Madame, we're on the verge of taking Windsor!"

"We cannot continue to expend large sums on besieging Windsor and Tickhill if we need to raise money for a ransom. And if the amount demanded is so large that we must impose a tax upon the people, how can we do that if the realm is in turmoil? No funds can be collected unless the kingdom is at peace—even if it is only a temporary peace."

Briwerre looked at her in dismay, for he was convinced that with enough time, they could capture both Windsor and Tickhill, and he wondered if a mother's protective instincts had impaired the queen's judgment; John was her son, too, after all. He would never dare to make such a suggestion, though, and he glanced toward the clerics, hoping that the bishop was willing to say what he could not. He was to be disappointed.

"I think you are right, Madame," Hubert said. "We need to give priority to securing King Richard's freedom, and if that means we must make deals we find distasteful, so be it."

Eleanor was relieved by Hubert's response, for she knew not all of the justiciars and council would agree with her, and it would help greatly to have the Bishop of Salisbury—soon to be the Archbishop of Canterbury—on her side. "What was Richard's reaction when you and the abbots told him of John's plotting with the French king?"

Hubert grinned. "He said, 'My brother John is not the man to conquer a kingdom if there is anyone to offer the least resistance.'"

A ripple of laughter swept the high table. Eleanor's eyes held an amused green glitter. "I think his response should be widely circulated," she said, with a cool smile that reassured William Briwerre somewhat; he still did not agree with her, but he no longer worried that maternal sentiment might lead her astray.

After servers brought in the last course, honey-drizzled wafers and sugared comfits, Eleanor gave her guests time to enjoy them before breaking the bad news. "I wish I could tell you that the French king has been no more successful than John. Alas, I cannot. Philippe has advanced deep into Normandy, accompanied by the Count of Flanders. He has gained control of the Vexin and he now holds Gisors and Neaufles."

Both clerics exclaimed at that, wanting to know how Philippe could have taken Gisors, one of the strongest of Richard's Norman castles. Eleanor's answer was a chilling one, for it raised the dangerous specter of treachery. "I am sorry to say," she said grimly, "that the castellan of Gisors, Gilbert de Vacoeil, betrayed the trust my son had placed in him, and surrendered Gisors and Neaufles to Philippe without offering any resistance whatsoever."

Hubert was a soldier as well as a churchman, and uttered a blistering profanity that would have done Richard proud. Unlike Richard, he at once apologized for such intemperate language. "What could be more dishonorable than abandoning his liege lord whilst knowing the king is a prisoner in Germany? There is surely a special circle of Hell reserved for such a foul self-server."

"And the loss of Gisors has disheartened men who might otherwise have shown more backbone. Several other lords then agreed to give Philippe's army passage across their lands, including three who fought with my son in the Holy Land." Eleanor's mouth set in a hard line. "And one of them was Jaufre, the Count of Perche, husband to my granddaughter Richenza."

Hubert and William de St Mère-Eglise exchanged glances. As troubling as this news was, it was not utterly unexpected, for these lords were vassals of both the Duke of Normandy and the King of France. Forced to choose between irreconcilable loyalties, they were likely to do whatever was necessary to safeguard their ancestral estates. Their actions would not be as harshly judged as the treachery of the castellan of Gisors, who'd not been protecting his own lands when he'd yielded the castles he'd been entrusted with by his king. Still, though, these were men of influence, and their defection might well inspire others to follow their example.

"This will greatly grieve the king when he hears of it," Hubert said somberly. "I know he thinks highly of Jaufre of Perche."

Eleanor did not want to imagine what it would be like for her son, a captive in a foreign land, learning that men he'd trusted had betrayed him. "I received a distraught letter from my granddaughter," she said quietly. "She was heartsick, but she said her husband had no choice, for Philippe is his king. Whilst there is truth in what she said, that will not make it any easier for my son to accept."

A pall had settled over the hall, threatening to smother their celebration of the good news brought by the bishop and dean. Eleanor was not willing to surrender hope so quickly, though. "We must remember that whatever my son loses in Normandy, he will regain upon his return. And he will be proud of the loyalty displayed by his English subjects, as well as the steadfastness of his ally, the Scots king. John attempted to lure King William into a war against Richard, doubtless remembering how eagerly he'd joined in the rebellion against my late husband twenty years ago. In the past, the Scots have never failed to take advantage of English turmoil and unrest. Not this time, though. Not only did the Scots king reject John's overtures, he sent us word that if Richard must pay a ransom to regain his freedom, the Scots will be willing to contribute to that ransom."

Eleanor accomplished what she'd hoped to do, for the mood lightened considerably after that. As a troubadour came forward to entertain, she was assuring the bishop that she and William de St Mère-Eglise would act quickly to inform the Christchurch monks of Richard's wishes for the archbishopric. Remembering Richard's wry comment about his father's command to the monks of Winchester, ordering them to hold a free election to elect only the candidate of his choice, Hubert related this story and Eleanor laughed heartily, saying she remembered that well. Hubert thought it was a sign of healing that she could find amusement and pleasure in memories of the man who'd held her prisoner for sixteen years.

It was William Briwerre who first saw the newcomer being escorted into the hall by the queen's steward. His travel-stained clothing indicated he was a courier and the fact that he'd not bothered to clean up before seeking Eleanor was significant in itself. As he drew nearer, Briwerre recognized him as one of the queen's men—utterly devoted to her, elusive, and at home in the shadows. "Madame," Briwerre said, but she'd already taken notice of her agent's approach.

"My lady," he said, kneeling. "Forgive me for interrupting your meal, but I have news you need to hear."

Eleanor regarded him calmly, while her hands clenched in her lap under the table. She'd dispatched him with a message for the seneschal of Normandy. But he ought not to have been back so soon. Nor did she see any sign of a letter. She hesitated, wondering if she should hear his news in private, then decided against it. Whatever was happening in Normandy, they all needed to know. Gesturing for him to rise, she said, "Tell me what you've learned, Justin. Did you meet with the seneschal?"

"No, Madame, I could not." He moved closer to the dais, his eyes never leaving her face. "I was unable to enter Rouen, for it is under siege by the French king and the Count of Flanders."

A shocked silence followed. No one spoke, for there was no need to say what was in all their minds—that if Rouen, the capital city of Normandy, fell to the French king, it could be a death blow to Richard's control of his duchy.

🦚

THE FRENCH KING WAS in high spirits, which he evinced by smiling from time to time. Philippe Capet's enemies claimed he had no sense of humor at all. This was not true, but it was somewhat feeble from lack of exercise. Philippe's view of the world was a sober one, which he attributed to his early accession to the French throne, at age fifteen. It had affected his education, too, for he had never mastered Latin and felt sensitive about that lack, all the more so because his nemesis, the English king, spoke it fluently. He had no false vanity and he knew he would always be eclipsed by Richard on the battlefield. He was quite competent when it came to siege warfare, though, for it played to his strengths, requiring a strategic sense and patience. And on this mild April afternoon before the walls of Rouen, he was already anticipating victory.

So far the month had been a blessed one for the twenty-seven-year-old French monarch. He saw Gisors Castle as a golden key, one that would open all of Normandy to him. Two days ago, the Bishop of Beauvais had returned from Germany, and when Philippe heard that the English king had been cast into a Trifels dungeon, he'd seen his enemy's suffering as divine retribution. Now, with a second chance to outbid the Lionheart's elderly mother, he was convinced that John would soon be on the English throne. And on the day that happened, he knew the accursed Angevin empire would be doomed.

His command tent was crowded, even though it was large enough to hold more than a hundred men. Trestle tables had been set up for a midday meal, draped with white linen and set with silver flagons and wine cups, and the dishes served were hot, savory, and worthy of a king. The wine in particular was of high quality, for Philippe enjoyed wine and hoped the time would come when he could lay claim to the famed vineyards of Aquitaine. Raising his cup, he said loudly, "Let us drink to Rouen's fall!"

The toast was enthusiastically echoed by the others in the tent, most of them of high birth, men eager for the booty such a campaign promised. Baldwin, the Count of Flanders and father of the French king's deceased queen, who'd died tragically in childbirth, was seated in the place of honor on Philippe's right, and the king's cousin, the Bishop of Beauvais, was sitting on his left. After the first course had been served, the bishop entertained his fellow diners by describing the sorry state of the English king, claiming Richard had begged him to intercede with the Holy Roman Emperor. Those who knew the Lionheart personally thought that rather unlikely, but Beauvais's account found favor with most of them, and there was much laughter when the bishop related the shameful circumstances of the English king's capture, saying he'd been found in a wretched inn little better than a bawdy house, where he'd sought to evade detection by pretending to be a kitchen scullion.

Not everyone found the bishop's stories amusing. Jaufre, the Count of Perche, never looked up from his plate, trying to ignore the curious stares cast his way, for all knew that he was wed to the English king's niece and his loyalties were therefore suspect. Staring down at the mutton stew, he found himself remembering his wife's tearful farewell. He'd done his best to make Richenza understand that he had no choice, that he had to obey Philippe's summons, reminding her that Philippe was his cousin and his king, reminding her, too, that he'd come back from the Holy Land deeply in debt and the Count of Mortain had promised to grant him Moulins and Bonsmoulins once he gained the English crown. Richenza had not been convinced, but Jaufre understood that women were emotional creatures and he knew she loved her uncle, having grown to womanhood at the English court. So he'd sought to be patient with her foolishness, especially now that she thought she might be breeding again; she'd already given him a son, born during his time in the Holy Land. He truly believed that he'd made the only decision he could. So why did it feel so wrong here in the French king's command tent?

Jaufre was not the only one to be discomfited by the Bishop of Beauvais's malice. Mathieu, the Seigneur of Montmorency, was hard put to hide his disgust. He hated Beauvais, unable to forgive him for forbidding the French from going to the aid of Jaffa. He never doubted that Beauvais and the Duke of Burgundy had cared more about denying the English king victory than defeating the infidels. And he'd reluctantly come to believe that was true for Philippe, too.

Mathieu had been just sixteen when he'd departed with his king for Outremer. He'd taken the cross with a youthful mixture of enthusiasm and piety and had been stunned when Philippe abandoned their holy war to return to France. Mathieu had not gone back with him, choosing to remain and honor his vow. In the Holy Land, he'd developed a deep admiration for the English king, the man who'd stayed whilst Philippe had fled. He had answered the French king's summons because Philippe was his liege lord, but he knew what they were doing was wrong and he feared that God would not forgive them for making war upon a crusader-king. As he glanced around the tent now, he felt alienated and alone, fettered by honor to obey a man he no longer respected.

"Do you think the town will surrender?"

Mathieu turned toward his seatmate, fourteen-year-old Guillaume, Count of Ponthieu. The boy had accompanied his uncle Hughes, the Count of St Pol, and he was so excited to be at a siege that he put Mathieu in mind of a kettle on the boil. Guillaume's father had died at Acre, and when Guillaume found out that Mathieu had been at Acre, too, the youngster was never willingly far from Mathieu's side. His uncle Hughes did not say much about his time in the Holy Land, he'd complained, and he was delighted that Mathieu was more forthcoming.

"Yes, I do think Rouen will yield to the king," Mathieu said, wishing he could take pleasure in that looming victory. At least some good might come out of this shameless assault, for Philippe's half sister, the Lady Alys, was being held in Rouen's great castle. Mathieu felt sorry for the French princess, a marriage pawn who'd become a prisoner. She'd been betrothed to King Richard when they both were children, but the old king had kept finding excuses to put off the wedding. Since Richard had no interest in wedding Alys, who'd initially been given a paltry marriage portion, he'd raised no objections. When he became king, he agreed to marry her upon his return from the Holy Land, but that had been a ploy to make sure Philippe honored his own crusader's vow. He'd actually had no intention of making Alys his wife and had arranged for his mother to bring the woman he did want to wed to him in Sicily.

Mathieu still remembered the confrontation between the two kings in a chapel in Messina. He'd listened, amazed, as Philippe accused Richard of bad faith, only to have the English king come back with a devastating response. He could not marry Alys, he'd said coolly, for she was rumored to have been his father's concubine and even to have borne him a child. When he proved that these rumors had been known at the French court, Philippe had been compelled to release him from the plight-troth, adding one more grudge to his hoard of grievances against the English king.

Mathieu did not know if the rumors were true, but it did not matter much. Whether King Henry had shamelessly seduced the girl who was his ward and his own son's betrothed or whether she was the innocent victim of vile gossip, the result was the same. Her honor was besmirched and her value on the marriage market plummeted. At least she would regain her freedom once Rouen fell to the French army. Not that Mathieu expected a warm homecoming for her. By now he had no illusions about the man who was his liege lord, and he was sure that Philippe saw Alys not as his sister, a flesh-and-blood woman who'd been ill used, but as an embarrassment to be disposed of quietly and quickly, most likely in a convenient nunnery. He still thought it was better to be a nun, even an unwilling one, than a hostage.

"So we will not get to fight?" Guillaume sounded so disappointed that Mathieu had to smile, feeling much older and more experienced than this eager, raw stripling. He was about to assure the boy that they might get to launch an assault upon the walls when Gautier, the French king's chamberlain, hastened into the tent. Leaning over, he whispered a few words to Philippe and the message was clearly a welcome one, for the French king actually grinned.

"Well," he said, "it looks as if Rouen will be ours by nightfall, for they are seeking to parley."

❧

As HE WATCHED THE approaching riders, Philippe was already savoring the sweet taste of triumph, for the city gates remained open, a sure sign that surrender was imminent. They were flying the white flag of truce, but a second banner caught the wind, too. He assumed it was the banner of the seneschal of Normandy, William Fitz Ralph, but then it unfurled and Philippe's smile vanished. As others recognized the coat of arms, there were muttered exclamations and curses. Young Guillaume tugged at the arm of his new friend, asking Mathieu what was wrong. Mathieu had no chance to respond, for Philippe was already striding forward to meet the emissaries from Rouen.

He nodded in response to the seneschal's greeting, but all of his attention was on the second rider. He was young and, even on horseback, it was obvious he was of small stature; he was also all too familiar to the French king.

"I was not aware that you were in Rouen, Leicester."

The earl smiled. "When I heard you might be stopping by, my lord king, I made haste to get here, eager to pay my respects. When did we last meet? Ah yes . . . it was at Acre. Did you have an easy trip back to your own lands? Such a pity your health would not permit you to remain. My king did the best he could in your absence. I daresay you've heard of his victories at Arsuf and Jaffa and—"

"This is not a social occasion, my lord earl!" Philippe glared at the other man, but he was irked with himself, too, for taking the bait. Unfazed by the rebuke, Leicester was acknowledging the men who'd fought with him in the Holy Land, blithely calling out greetings to the Count of St Pol, the Count of Perche, and Mathieu de Montmorency, but passing over the Bishop of Beauvais and his brother, the Count of Dreux, as if they were invisible. Philippe noted with displeasure that Jaufre and Mathieu were obviously discomfited and even St Pol looked somewhat uncomfortable.

"I am sure you have heard that the Count of Mortain met with me in Paris," Philippe said curtly, "where he did homage to me for this duchy and the other lands that are his by right as Duke of Normandy and England's king."

Leicester's eyebrows shot upward in a gesture all too reminiscent to Philippe of the English king. "Just as you confused Acre with Jerusalem, my lord, you seem to have confused the Count of Mortain with England's true king, who is currently enjoying the hospitality of your ally, the Emperor Heinrich."

"You are not a fool, Leicester, and only a fool would believe that Richard is ever coming back. John is to be your king, whether you like it or not. And as his liege lord, I have every right to enter Rouen. If you try to keep me out, you will greatly regret it. I have twenty-four trebuchets and—"

"Sire, you have been grievously misinformed! We have no intention of denying you entry to Rouen. Do we, my lord?" Leicester turned toward the seneschal, who nodded vigorously in agreement.

Philippe glanced from one to the other. "You are saying you surrender, then?"

"No, my lord king. I am saying that you are welcome to enter Rouen at any time you choose." Leicester flashed again the smile that Philippe was finding more and more irritating by the moment. "Look for yourself. The gates are open, are they not?"

Philippe scowled, angry but suddenly uncertain, too. "What sort of game is this, Leicester?"

"No game, my lord. I am inviting you into the city. I can safely say that it would please King Richard greatly to know that you were in Rouen."

Philippe could hear murmurings behind him as word spread among his men. His gaze shifted from the earl to those city gates, open and enticing in the bright April sunlight. Leicester was regarding him quizzically. Seeing that the French king was not going to respond, he made a gracious gesture of obeisance and then turned his stallion, calling back over his shoulder, "We'll be awaiting you, my liege!"

The seneschal spurred his horse to catch up with the earl, not drawing an easy breath until they had galloped through the gates. When he would have signaled for them to be shut, Leicester quickly countermanded him. "No, leave them open!"

William Fitz Ralph looked searchingly at the younger man. He'd thought the earl's plan was mad, but he'd been swayed by Leicester's rank and by the fact that he was one of the genuine heroes of the crusade. "Are you sure this will succeed, my lord?"

Leicester glanced back at the French army camp, which seemed to be in some disarray now, raised voices floating to them on the afternoon air. "I know Philippe Capet," he said. "I know how his mind works. He sees shadows at midnight and inhales suspicions the way the rest of us breathe in air. Nor is he one to lead the charge. Can you imagine our king or his lord father ever relying upon bodyguards? Philippe goes nowhere without them. Moreover, Queen Eleanor's spy sent her word that Philippe actually swallowed the rubbish Beauvais fed him, believing that our king hired Saracen Assassins to seek him out in Paris and murder him. Does this sound like a man who'd dare to venture into Rouen after I'd made him think he would be riding into a trap?"

"No, it does not," the seneschal admitted. "But even if he does not dare to accept your invitation, what is to keep him from sending his troops through those gates?"

"Pride. The fact that I called him out in front of his entire army. If he does not accept my dare, he loses face, and no commander can afford that. He does not have enough soldiers to surround the city, was relying upon threats to frighten the citizens into surrendering. Once he has had a chance to think it over, he will lead his men in search of easier quarry than Rouen."

The seneschal looked at the French army, all too visible through the open gates. Praying that the earl's bluff would work, he said, "I hope you are right, my lord."

He was not close enough to hear Leicester say, very softly, "I hope I am, too."

❧

WATCHING FROM THE TOWN WALLS, they could sometimes hear angry shouting wafting from the French king's command tent. Clearly there was dissension in the ranks, and the citizens of Rouen took heart from that. Leicester had gone to have a quick supper at a nearby cook-shop when he was hurriedly summoned by the seneschal. His heart pounding and his pulse racing, he took the steps up to the ramparts two at a time.

"Look!" William Fitz Ralph was grinning widely. "They are breaking camp, moving out! You did it, my lord earl!"

Leicester found himself mobbed by jubilant men and extricated himself with some difficulty before he could join Fitz Ralph at the wall. The seneschal was staring toward the west, shading his eyes against the glare of the dying sun. "What are those fires, though? What are they burning?"

When they realized what was happening—that the French king was burning his own siege engines—the men burst into amazed, raucous laughter as Leicester explained that Philippe had been guilty of such impulsive, angry acts before. For many years, the English and French kings had met to discuss their differences at an ancient tree known as the "peace elm." But after one frustrating session with King Henry, Philippe had instructed his men to chop the elm down. Hanging over the walls, the city's defenders hooted and yelled at the retreating French, but cried out in real outrage when they saw that their enemies were rolling kegs of wine toward the Seine and pouring it into the river rather than leave it for them.

The hero of the hour exchanged triumphant smiles with the seneschal. "Now," he said, "now we close the gates!"

❧

DAME MARTHE WAS GROWING frantic for she'd searched much of the castle without finding her mistress. While the Lady Alys was kept under discreet surveillance, she was not strictly guarded, the castellan treating her more as a guest than what she really was—a hostage. Marthe supposed she could have slipped out through a postern gate, but where would she have gone? Marthe had served Alys since she'd been sent to the English court at age nine, and could not have loved her more if she'd been Marthe's own child. That love did not blind her to her lady's nature, though. Alys was sweet and good-hearted and trusting, yet she lacked spirit, had nothing in her of the rebel. She would never have run away, never even have ventured out into the city on her own, no more than a bird bred in captivity would dare to leave the security of its cage.

Marthe had long known Alys would never be England's queen, for on the few occasions when she'd actually been in Richard's company, he'd shown her nothing more than polite indifference. She'd said nothing, though, for her lady remained convinced that the marriage would come to pass, and she realized that Alys needed that hope, needed to believe that she would have her happy ending. Alys kept faith long after another woman would have recognized the reality of her precarious position, right up until the moment when Marthe had to tell her that Richard had wed Berengaria of Navarre.

Having checked the great hall and the solar and chapel, even the kitchen, Marthe halted in the middle of the inner bailey, not knowing where else to look. She still remembered how Alys had wept, remembered trying in vain to comfort her, all the while cursing the men who'd failed her so spectacularly. But once Alys was forced to abandon her girlhood dream of a golden crown and a handsome husband renowned for his courage, she'd shown surprising resilience and embraced her new future at the French court as wholeheartedly as she'd once clung to her English destiny. She'd soon convinced herself that the brother she'd not seen since he was four years old would be her loving protector, that he would find a highborn husband for her, one worthy of a king's daughter. Once the English king—she no longer called him Richard—came back from the Holy Land, she would return to Paris and reclaim her life.

Marthe had no more confidence in the French king than she'd had in the two English kings. As before, she'd held her peace, though, not willing to deprive Alys of her dreams. But again, nothing had gone as expected. Instead of returning to England and setting Alys free, the English king was a prisoner in Germany. Only the Blessed Almighty knew when—or if—he would regain his own freedom, and Alys, now in her thirty-third year, was trapped with him as surely as if she, too, were Heinrich's hostage. She'd begun to despair—until a French army had appeared before the walls of Rouen.

Marthe suddenly knew where her lady was. She was no longer young and somewhat stout, and by the time she emerged onto the castle battlements, she was panting heavily. The sentries greeted her cheerfully, sharing wineskins to celebrate their town's reprieve. She soon saw Alys, a slender figure wrapped in a blue cloak, standing as far away from the guards as she could get. She did not turn, even when Marthe called her name, continuing to stare out at the abandoned French camp. Reaching her side, Marthe entreated, "Come inside, my lamb. You will take a chill out here."

Alys did not seem to hear. "They have gone, Marthe," she said, her blue eyes welling with tears. "They have gone and left me here."

❦

AFTER RETREATING FROM ROUEN, Philippe's army seized several important castles in quick succession, and gained some satisfaction in capturing Pacy-sur-Eure, for it belonged to the Earl of Leicester. It was not compensation, though, for his failure to take Rouen. Philippe was usually quick to anger, quick to forgive. But what he neither forgot nor forgave was being made to look like a fool, and he now bore Leicester a bitter grudge.

❦

RICHARD WAS PLAYING A dice game with his guards, mocking their comical efforts to speak French and his equally halting attempts to master German. His new warders were friendly, respectful, and curious, playful sheepdogs rather than the hungry wolves of Trifels; one of them could even string together more than a few words of French. But he knew they were Markward's spies, even if they did not see their duties in that light, and so he was determined to show no signs of despair or desperation before them. Since he had no money to wager, he told them he'd offer English knighthoods as his stakes, and they thought that was hilarious, calling one another Sir Herman and Sir Wilhelm with clumsy court bows. They joked in turn that they would smuggle in a whore called Lena for him, whose favors they all seemed to have enjoyed.

When Richard actually found himself half tempted by that offer, he realized he'd been far too long without a woman in his bed. That brought his wife to mind, for the first time in weeks. He felt confident that she was coping with his captivity, for her faith was unwavering, as steadfast as any saint's. He was more concerned for his mother and Joanna, thinking that memories of their own confinement would have been stirred up by his plight. And what of his son? Philip was twelve now, caught in that unmapped, alien land between childhood and manhood. He tried to remember how it was for him at twelve. How would he have reacted had his father been imprisoned? Surely with utter disbelief. But he'd have been able to turn to his mother for answers, for reassurance. Philip had no mother; she had died years ago.

In midafternoon, he was surprised and delighted to be given a letter; the seal was broken, of course, but any communication with the outside world was a cause for celebration. Once he read it, though, he was both saddened and shaken, for this unexpected death proved how little he understood what the Almighty intended for him. Leaning back in the window-seat, open to the warm May air, he struggled to comprehend the incomprehensible. Scriptures said that a man's heart plans his way but the Lord directs his steps. So God had guided him to this place, away from the Holy Land. But why? He watched as the letter slipped from his grasp, fluttering to the floor at his feet. Nothing made sense anymore.

A sudden knock at the door interrupted this brooding reverie. The guard dubbed Sir Wilhelm by his friends opened the door wide, admitting Markward von Annweiler. Richard tensed at the sight of the *ministerialis*, whom he'd always associate with that frigid cell at Trifels and those heavy iron manacles. But then the German was forgotten. "I do not believe it!" he exclaimed, jumping to his feet as Fulk de Poitiers followed Markward into the chamber.

The clerk quickly held up his hand. "If you must hug me, sire, try not to break a rib!"

Richard burst out laughing and embraced the older man joyfully, not as king and clerk, but as fellow shipwreck survivors, and when he stepped back, he saw the usually stoic cleric was actually blinking away tears. Markward had not lingered, sauntering out with a jaunty wave before they even noticed he was gone. Richard at once began to bombard Fulk with questions. Was he the only one freed? Where were the others? How had they been treated? Had he seen Guillain and Morgan, the lad Arne? Were they all well?

"You have to stop talking ere I can begin to answer, my liege," Fulk protested, with a fair imitation of his usual grumpiness. "I am afraid you'll have to make do with just me for now." The others were still in Regensburg, though they'd been promised they'd soon be released. Of course, promises were easy to offer, not always easy to spend. Whilst no one would ever mistake their German hosts for angels unaware, they'd not been maltreated. He'd been held with those arrested at Friesach, knew nothing of Guillain and Morgan or the boy. He had heard that the Templars and crossbowmen had been set free, though. He thought

Anselm would be the next one released, being a priest, but Baldwin de Bethune was likely to be held till the last, highborn enough to qualify as a hostage.

By now they were sitting in the window-seat and the sunlight was not kind, telling Fulk more about his king's captivity than any words could have done. "You do not look well, sire," he said bluntly. "I can see that you've lost weight, and sleep, too. That cocky German who escorted me here said you'd passed some days at Trifels Castle. Can that be true?"

"Sixteen days, to be precise," Richard said laconically, but he was willing to go no further than that. Fulk knew him well enough not to push, confident that when he was ready to talk about his ordeal, he would. That it had been an ordeal, Fulk did not doubt, for he was familiar with the sinister reputation of Heinrich's imperial prison. On the road from Regensburg, he'd been reassuring himself that the king's rank would have been respected, but that hope had vanished as soon as he'd heard the name of Trifels Castle.

"Obviously we have much to talk about," he said briskly. "I suspect you are better informed than us about what has been happening in England and Rome. I suppose it is too much to hope that the Holy Father has found the ballocks to take the emperor on."

Richard had rarely heard the words "Holy Father" invested with such sarcasm, and he laughed again, ridiculously happy to see his cantankerous clerk, hoping that his sudden sentimentality was a symptom of confinement and would not survive once he'd regained his freedom.

Fulk had noticed the dropped letter and instinctively reached for it, accustomed to taking charge of his king's correspondence. As he started to hand it to Richard, his gaze fell upon the salutation and he gave an exclamation of surprise. "You heard from the Doge of Venice?"

Richard saw no reason not to indulge his curiosity. "Go ahead, read it," he said, and Fulk at once held the letter up toward the light.

"*To his most serene lord, Richard, by the grace of God, King of England, Duke of Normandy and Aquitaine, and Count of Anjou, Enrico Dandolo, by the same grace, Doge of Venice, Dalmatia, and Cherum, health and sincere and duteous affection. Know ye that it has been intimated to me, from a source that can be relied upon, that Saladin, that enemy of the Christian religion, died in the first week of Lent. And one of his sons, whom he is said to have appointed heir to the whole of his dominions, is at present in Damascus, while the other one is ruling at Egypt and Alexandria. His brother is in the vicinity of Egypt with a numerous army, and the greatest dissension exists between them. Farewell.*"

When Fulk glanced up, Richard saw that he'd immediately grasped the significance of this momentous news. "With Saladin dead, my liege, and his empire in disarray, Jerusalem is a plum ripe for plucking."

"And if I'd not been compelled to make a truce with Saladin so I could return to defend my own kingdom, I'd still be in Outremer, Fulk. Without the French to hinder us, Henri and I could have taken Jerusalem back from the Saracens." Richard was on his feet now, striding back and forth. "The French king and my brother have much to answer for. And so does that scorpion on the German throne. Had I been able to reach England, it would not have taken me long to put Johnny and Philippe on the run. I could then have made plans to return to the Holy Land, just as I'd promised Henri and the Almighty. Now . . . who knows how long it will be ere I am free to fulfill my vow?"

He whirled suddenly, demanding of his clerk, "Does any of this make sense to you, Fulk? Why has God let this happen? Saladin's death offers a rare opportunity to regain the most sacred city in Christendom and yet I cannot take advantage of it!"

The easy answer would be to say it was not for them to question the ways of the Almighty. But Fulk was not one to offer easy answers, nor would Richard have accepted them. "I do not know what to tell you, my liege. I do not understand, either."

"Eventually Saladin's brother will prevail, for he is much more capable than his nephews. Now would have been the time to strike, yet here I am, thwarted not by the Saracens, but by another Christian ruler!" Richard spat out a few virulent oaths, none of which eased his frustration or his fury. Sitting down again, he slumped back wearily in the window-seat next to his clerk. "Saladin was a far better man than Philippe or Heinrich," he said at last. "A man of courage and honor. It is a great pity that he must be forever denied the grace of God."

Fulk sighed, thinking what Philippe or Heinrich would have made of such a statement. Sometimes it seemed to him that his king went out of his way to provide weapons for his enemies to use against him. Before he could respond, the door burst open and the Bishop of Bath hurried into the chamber.

"Sire, I have good news; wanted to be the one—" Savaric got no further, momentarily flustered by the unexpected sight of Fulk de Poitiers, for the two men had no liking for each other. "I did not expect to see you here, Master Fulk. My cousin the emperor must have forgotten to tell me you'd been released from custody."

Richard thought it might be possible to invent a drinking game based upon how often Savaric used the words "my cousin the emperor" in any of his conversations. Fulk made no attempt to conceal his distaste. "Not all men would be so proud to claim the king's gaoler as a kinsman, my lord bishop."

Savaric bristled. "You need to catch up with recent developments, Master Fulk. Our king and the emperor are steadfast friends now and Emperor Heinrich has sent a letter to England's justiciars in which he pledged lasting peace between our countries and vowed that from now on, he would look upon injuries done to King Richard as if they were done to him and the empire. Even your form of address is out of date, for I am soon to be Canterbury's archbishop."

Fulk's eyes were heavy-lidded and deep-set; now, however, they opened wider than gold bezants. "You—the Archbishop of Canterbury? When pigs—oof!" That exhalation was caused by Richard, who jabbed him sharply in the ribs and then asked Savaric about his "good news."

The bishop would have preferred to dwell upon his coming elevation to the highest ecclesiastical office in England, correctly assuming that Fulk was going to find it very difficult to accept. But now that they'd gotten that precious letter of support from Richard, he was eager to retain his king's favor. "Of course, sire. The emperor and the French king have agreed to meet next month at Vaucouleurs on the Nativity of St John the Baptist. I wanted to inform you straightaway, knowing you'd be pleased, for once the emperor convinces Philippe to make peace with you, your kingdom will no longer be in peril."

With Savaric's first words, Richard had stiffened, feeling as if he'd taken a physical blow to his midsection. He took several deep breaths, paying no heed to the bishop as he babbled on happily, saying he thought it likely his cousin the emperor would want him to attend this conference and he would be honored to act on behalf of his king. Fulk looked at Richard, then back at Savaric, and for once, held his tongue.

At last Saravic noticed that the conversation was utterly one-sided, and reluctantly took his leave, promising to return on the morrow. Once he'd gone, Fulk switched to Latin, even though he thought it unlikely any of the guards understood enough French to eavesdrop. "Sire, what is going on? Surely that puffed-up peacock is not to be archbishop! As for this upcoming conference with the French king, I do not like the sound of that, not at all."

Richard dismissed Savaric's prospects with a profanity, adding, "We'll see the Second Coming ere that fool ever wears the holy pallium. And you are right to be wary of this meeting. If it comes to pass, it will likely mean disaster for me. Philippe is eager to outbid my mother and my justiciars, wants Heinrich to turn me over to him instead of setting me free."

While this possibility had preyed upon Fulk's peace for the past five months, it was still chilling to hear it spoken aloud. "But it would still be easier—and less damaging to Heinrich's reputation—for him to accept an English ransom. And the queen mother will never be outbid, sire. Surely you know that?"

Richard had risen again, and as he paced the confines of his chamber, he put Fulk in mind of the caged lions he'd once seen at London's Tower. "If it were just a question of money, I'd not fear the outcome. But Philippe is in a position to offer Heinrich something that my mother cannot, something that could well tip the scales in his favor. When they meet at Vaucouleurs, he will likely promise to provide military aid in putting down the rebellion of Heinrich's lords. And if that happens, do you truly think Heinrich will refuse?"

Despite the warmth of the May sun flooding the window-seat, Fulk suddenly felt very cold. "Surely God would not let that happen," he said, without much conviction.

"It may be blasphemous to say this, but I cannot rely upon God to keep this meeting from taking place. No, if catastrophe is to be averted, I must do it myself."

"How will you do that, sire?"

"I do not know," Richard conceded, "at least not yet." And it seemed to him that he could feel his father's sarcastic spirit close at hand, nodding approvingly as he said, "I will find a way, though."

CHAPTER FOURTEEN

❦

MAY 1193

St Albans, England

Guillaume de Longchamp's return to England had so far been even more of an ordeal than he'd expected. After his ship docked in the estuary of the River Orwell at Ipswich, he'd sent word to Samson, Abbot of St Edmundsbury, letting him know as a courtesy that he would be traveling through lands held by the abbey. He was determined that none could accuse him of arrogance, a sin he now acknowledged he'd been guilty of in the past. Samson was not a friend. Longchamp was shocked, nonetheless, when the abbot responded by ordering a suspension of divine service in any town he passed through, and he'd endured the humiliation of entering a church only to have the priest halt the celebration of the Mass and stand mute at the altar until he'd departed. Longchamp's outrage was even stronger than his mortification, for he was no longer under a sentence of excommunication, which had been passed by the Archbishop of Rouen soon after he'd been sent into exile. Not only had the Holy Father the Pope absolved him, but Queen Eleanor had convinced the archbishop to lift his sentence of anathema. There was nothing he could do, though, except to push on toward London.

He'd hired mercenaries to see to his safety, but he decided he needed moral support, too, in light of the difficult task he faced; he could not deny that he felt very vulnerable in what he saw as a nest of vipers. All of his brothers had benefited greatly from his rise to a position of such power. He'd made Osbert and Henry sheriffs of Yorkshire and Herefordshire, secured for Stephen a post in Richard's own household, named another brother as Abbot of Croyland, and made Robert the Prior of Ely, with an even greater prize in mind—the abbacy of

Westminster. His downfall had dashed that dream, but at least Robert had not been deprived of his church post, unlike his brothers, who'd been stripped of their shrievalties by his enemies. His family remained loyal and, upon getting his urgent message, Robert had hastened to join him on his journey from Ipswich to London, bringing some good news. Their brother Henry had been arrested in the wake of Longchamp's disgrace and imprisoned at Count John's Cardiff Castle, but Robert was able to assure him that Henry was finally at liberty.

Worse was to come, though, for when they reached London, Longchamp found the gates barred to him. The hostility of the Londoners stung all the more because he'd given those ungrateful English dolts the right to elect their own sheriffs. Listening as they hooted and jeered him from the city walls, he thought he could right gladly turn his back on this accursed isle, never to set foot on its soil again—but not until he fulfilled his mission for his lord, the king.

HAVING LEARNED THAT QUEEN ELEANOR was meeting with the justiciars and the great council at St Albans, Longchamp headed north, girding himself for an encounter that he knew would be acrimonious. Robert glanced at his brother's profile as the Benedictine abbey of St Albans came into view. "Is there even one here who'll not want your head on a pike, Guillaume?"

"Well . . . the earls of Arundel and Surrey were my friends once, so they'd likely offer up a prayer for my soul as my head was separated from my body," Longchamp said dryly. He kept his eyes fastened upon the Norman tower, soaring well over a hundred feet into the Hertfordshire sky. "Whilst I'd not presume to call her a friend, the queen is not my enemy. She did me a great service last year."

Robert had not seen his brother since he'd been forced to flee England, and he welcomed this chance to learn the details of Longchamp's failed effort to regain power. "I'd heard that she supported your attempt to return from exile. Was that because she knew King Richard trusted you?"

"I think it was because she knew I'd tried to bribe Count John," Longchamp said, smiling at his brother's startled expression. "John had thought he'd be able to have his own way once I was eliminated. He was outmaneuvered by the Archbishop of Rouen, though, who produced a letter from King Richard, authorizing him as chief justiciar if I had to be removed from office. John had not bargained on that, and I hoped he might be amenable to an alliance with me rather than see Gautier de Coutances reign supreme. I was right, too. He agreed to back me if I paid him five hundred marks."

"But . . . but you detest and distrust Count John, Guillaume!"

"Yes . . . it was a Devil's deal, Rob. I convinced myself that I could better protect King Richard's interests if I were back in England, even if it meant making noxious concessions to John. I truly believed that I was doing it for the king, but I can see now that I was also loath to relinquish the power I'd enjoyed as his chief justiciar. Queen Eleanor's greatest fear was that John would be tempted into treason by the French king now that he'd returned from the Holy Land, and I suppose she saw me as a lesser evil than Philippe. With the queen and John on my side, I thought I could regain at least some of my authority."

"But . . . but John did not support your return!"

"No, he did not. When I landed at Dover, the queen sought to persuade the council to accept my offer to appear before them and answer any charges that had been made against me. They balked and sought John's opinion. I will say this for the man: he is remarkably honest about his dishonesty. He candidly told the council that I'd offered him five hundred marks for his support and invited them to better it. When they offered him two thousand marks, he cheerfully switched sides again. John never lets troublesome scruples get in the way of what he wants. So despite the queen's support, I was forced to return to Normandy, whilst she stopped John from joining Philippe at the French court."

Longchamp drew rein unexpectedly, turning in the saddle to look his brother full in the face. "But when I said the queen did me a 'great service,' Rob, I did not mean her efforts to end my exile. When I was forced to flee, Archbishop Gautier seized the revenues of my diocese of Ely. I retaliated by laying my own See under Interdict, and he and I excommunicated each other. I did him one better then by also excommunicating the other justiciars and my enemies like Hugh de Nonant, though the English bishops ignored my edicts."

He grimaced at that, for it still rankled that his fellow bishops had been so quick to abandon him. "When Queen Eleanor made a progress into Ely, she was appalled by the suffering of the people—my people—unable to bury their dead or celebrate the Mass or administer any of the sacraments other than baptizing children and offering the viaticum to the dying. She shamed me into lifting the Interdict, making me realize that in my need to punish Gautier de Coutances, I'd punished the innocent. There was a time when I'd have known that, Rob, but I let my hatred cloud my judgment. She then got the archbishop to return the Ely revenues to me and we absolved each other of our mutual excommunications. She is an extraordinary woman," he added, causing his brother to regard him in surprise, for Robert had never heard Longchamp speak with such admiration for one of the lesser sex.

Ahead of them loomed the great Norman gateway of the abbey and Longchamp reined in his horse again. "I feel," he confided wryly, "like Daniel entering the lion's den." But then he urged his mount forward, politely requesting admittance when once he'd have demanded it, and his brother began to wonder if he was that rarity—a man truly changed by his misfortunes, able to learn from his past mistakes.

LONGCHAMP'S APPEARANCE SET the council into an uproar. From the dais, where he was seated beside the queen and Hubert Walter, the Archbishop of Rouen recoiled as ostentatiously as a man who'd just found a snake in his bedchamber. The justiciars showed a bit more restraint, but their body language made it abundantly clear that Longchamp was an unwelcome intruder. His nemesis, the Bishop of Coventry, was already on his feet, as was the Archbishop of York. Bristling with outrage, Geoff stalked over to intercept Longchamp before he could approach the dais. As tall as his half brother Richard, and as hot-tempered, he towered over the undersized chancellor as he angrily challenged Longchamp's right to be there, saying scornfully, "I marvel that you'd dare to show your face again in England!"

"Run into any more lusty fishermen, Longchamp?" Hugh de Nonant said with a smirk, unleashing a wave of raucous laughter.

Longchamp flushed but stood his ground. Brushing past Geoff as if he were one of the stone pillars of the guest hall, he limped toward the dais. "Madame," he said, bowing deeply to the queen, who acknowledged him with a nod. Straightening up, he met Gautier de Coutances's cold stare without flinching.

"I come before you," he said, "neither as justiciar nor papal legate nor chancellor, but as a simple bishop and a messenger from our lord the king."

If he'd hoped to disarm his enemies with humility, he was to be disappointed, for his declaration was met with ridicule, his foes expressing disbelief that the king would ever trust him again. Normally it would have been for the chief justiciar to assert control, but it was obvious that Gautier de Coutances had no intention of coming to the aid of the man who'd once called him "the Pilate of

Rouen." It was Eleanor who put a halt to the mockery, merely by raising her hand. "You've seen my son?"

"I have, my lady. I found the king at Trifels Castle—" He got no further, for there were exclamations from all corners of the hall, from those who knew the sinister significance of that German mountain citadel. Eleanor paled noticeably and Hubert Walter gave an audible gasp. Taking advantage of the sudden stillness, Longchamp quickly assured Eleanor—for he was speaking only to the queen now—that Richard was no longer being held at Trifels, explaining that he'd been able to persuade Emperor Heinrich to return the king to the imperial court. There was some scoffing at that, but he did not care if they thought he was boasting; he was prouder of freeing Richard from Trifels than he was of anything else he'd ever done.

"I bring letters, Madame," he said, stepping forward to hand them to her. There was a private one from her son, meant for her eyes alone; one in Latin, meant for his justiciars and council; and then one from the Emperor Heinrich, sealed with the golden chrysobull used by the Holy Roman Emperors, claiming he and Richard were now "upon terms of concord and lasting peace," and pledging that he "shall look upon injuries done to King Richard as offered to ourselves and our imperial crown." And as Eleanor passed the public letters to the archbishop to be read aloud, Longchamp felt a savage satisfaction that these men who'd mocked him so mercilessly would soon hear their king describe him as "our most dearly beloved chancellor" and give him full credit for the escape from Trifels.

THE REST OF THE COUNCIL MEETING was not as contentious. When Longchamp relayed Richard's instructions for selecting the needed hostages, the Bishop of Coventry started to make a sarcastic comment about trusting him with other men's sons, only to be sharply silenced by Hubert Walter. Now that they knew a huge ransom would indeed be required to gain the king's freedom, they wasted no time. It was determined that a tithe would be assessed against laymen and clergy alike, a quarter of their income for the year, that each knight's fee would be charged twenty shillings, that the churches would have to contribute their gold and silver, and the Cistercians, who were forbidden by their order to possess costly chalices, must give their wool clip for the year. The money collected was to be stored in chests in St Paul's Cathedral, placed in the custody of

Hubert Walter, the Bishop of London, and the earls of Arundel and Surrey, under the seals of the queen and the Archbishop of Rouen. It would be a mammoth undertaking, imposing a great burden upon a kingdom already drained by the Saladin tithe, but Longchamp did not doubt the money would be raised—the queen would see to it. As he watched Eleanor coolly discussing what must be done to free her son, his private letter unopened on her lap until the council was ended, he thought that King Richard had been blessed by the Almighty in many ways, but above all in the woman who'd given him life.

ABBOT WARIN TOLD LONGCHAMP that the abbey's guest house and lodgings were already filled and he must seek shelter elsewhere. The chancellor supposed it might be true, for St Albans was overflowing with highborn guests summoned for the council. But he could not help remembering how differently he'd been treated when the king had visited St Albans the week after his coronation, how lavish the entertainment, how bountiful the abbot's hospitality. He made no protest, though, and sent his men to find rooms in the town. They eventually were able to rent a chamber in a private house, not up to Longchamp's usual standards of comfort. He was too exhausted to quibble and was making ready for bed when he received a message from the queen, summoning him back to the abbey.

LONGCHAMP WAS ESCORTED INTO Abbot Warin's parlor, where he found the queen attended by Hubert Walter, William Marshal, and her grandson Otto, the fifteen-year-old son of her deceased daughter, Tilda, the Duchess of Saxony. They greeted him with courtesy, if no warmth, and after a word from Eleanor, Otto offered his chair to the chancellor, sprawling then in a window-seat with the boneless abandon of the very young.

"My son told me in some detail how you convinced Heinrich that he should not be kept at Trifels. He was rather vague when it came to his own experiences there, though. I hope you will be more forthright, my lord bishop. I want you to tell me how bad it was for him."

Longchamp was relieved that Richard had not thought to swear him to silence, for there was no way he could have refused this tense, resolute woman;

he'd never seen eyes as penetrating as hers, could almost believe she was able to see into the inner recesses of his soul. "It was very bad, Madame," he said, and then proceeded to tell her exactly how bad. When he described how he'd found Richard, chained up and ailing, Hubert Walter and William Marshal expressed outrage and Otto's eyes widened in shock. But Eleanor neither flinched nor spoke, keeping her gaze unblinkingly upon Longchamp until he was done, until they knew the worst.

There was silence after he'd stopped speaking. He'd been telling himself that freeing the king was all that mattered, but he realized now that he needed them to acknowledge what a truly remarkable accomplishment his was. And he did get what he sought—from Eleanor's young grandson. "The Almighty must have sent you to Trifels," Otto exclaimed, "knowing how great my uncle's need was!"

Hubert and Will exchanged glances and they, too, then echoed the boy's praise; almost as if they were shamed into it, Longchamp thought sourly. Eleanor merely offered a simple "Thank you, my lord chancellor," but he was quite satisfied with her response. He'd argued that only King Richard could strip him of his office, yet he'd still been compelled to surrender the royal seal and his enemies insisted he was no longer England's chancellor. So to hear his title spoken now by the queen was to him a vindication of sorts, and he returned to his lodgings in much better spirits. Let the jackals nip at his heels. He had what they could only envy—the utter trust of his lord the king and the wholehearted gratitude of the queen mother.

THE OTHER MEN HAD not lingered after Longchamp's departure, for they'd been badly shaken to learn of Richard's ill treatment at Trifels. Will was highly indignant that a king should be cast in irons as if he were a common felon and Hubert was appalled by Heinrich's treachery, wincing to think how cheerfully he'd parted from Richard at Speyer, convinced that his release was ensured. Eleanor's grandson insisted upon escorting her back to the queen's hall built for royal visitors. Smiling, she rested her hand upon his arm as if he were a man grown. They did not have far to go, but as they approached the door, Otto's steps slowed.

"Granddame, I am quite willing to be a hostage for Uncle Richard. I'd do anything to help win his freedom. And I do not want you to worry about my little brother when we are sent to Germany. I will take good care of Wilhelm, and will do my best to keep him out of trouble, too," he promised, with the gravity that set so surprisingly on such young shoulders. He had inherited his father's dark coloring, but he was going to be taller than his sire, even as tall as Richard in time. Like his sister, he'd been blessed with a share of his mother's beauty, and his sudden, sweet smile never failed to remind her of her daughter, who'd died after a brief illness, only thirty-three.

"Keeping Wilhelm out of trouble will have you occupied night and day, Otto," she pointed out, and he grinned, kissing her on the cheek before he headed off toward the abbey guest hall. She stood by the door, watching him go. She'd become very fond of Otto, more like her daughter than his spirited sister Richenza and his mischievous nine-year-old brother. All three of them had been raised at the English court, arriving with their parents when Heinrich der Löwe and Tilda had been banished after falling out of favor with the Holy Roman Emperor, and remaining even after Der Löwe and Tilda and their eldest son, Henrik, had been permitted to return to Saxony three years later. Wilhelm, who'd been born at Winchester during his mother's exile, and Otto, who'd only been five when they'd left Saxony, spoke French rather than German as their native tongue, and when they reached Germany, they'd be strangers in a foreign land. Eleanor would have given a great deal to spare them that, but she knew she could not; Heinrich von Hohenstaufen was insistent that they be included, for their father and elder brother were among the rebels threatening his throne.

By now the sky was darker than midnight, stars glimmering like distant campfires in an alien world. Eleanor gazed up at those pinpoint white lights, hoping that her son was able to look upon them, too, on this tranquil spring evening. When she thought of his time at Trifels, shut away from the sun and sky and untainted air, she felt a tightness in her chest, a heaviness that would be with her until the day he regained his freedom. And if he did not . . . ?

Her ladies sensed her mood and remained subdued. She was sure she would not be able to sleep. Not knowing what else to do, she let them get her ready for bed. But as she feared, once the candles had been snuffed out and the bed hangings drawn, her control began to crumble and hot tears stung her eyes. She'd been living with fear for so long, from the day that Richard sailed from Sicily for the Holy Land. Many of his subjects had doubted that he'd ever come back, and there were dark nights when she'd shared their doubts. He'd somehow survived it all, though—the savage storms in the Greek Sea, the pestilent fevers, the bloody battles, even his own reckless need to be in the thick of the fighting—only to discover that he faced greater dangers on his way home than any in Outremer.

Once again she'd found herself holding a death vigil. Learning that he was a prisoner had kindled enough rage to keep the fear at bay—except at night. But then Hubert Walter had brought her news of Richard's triumph at Speyer and the fear finally retreated, shrinking away from this blazing, bright infusion of hope. She'd let herself believe that the worst was over, that her son would soon be home. So her defenses were down when she most needed them, blown apart by the mere mention of Trifels Castle.

No matter how she sought to summon sleep, she was at the mercy of her own memories. Her fears for her grown son were hopelessly entwined with mental images of the boy he'd once been. As she tossed and turned, she could see him at age twelve, coaxing his older brother, Hal, into letting him try the quintain and being knocked from his horse into the mud, only to bounce back up laughing, eager to try it again. She smiled through tears as she remembered the time he and Geoffrey had smuggled a snake into her bed. Closing her eyes, she could hear his voice, asking her to listen as he performed the first song he'd composed, insisting that she tell him the brutal truth, adding with a grin, *Unless you do not like it, Maman, then lie to me!*

She'd sometimes thought this was a curse peculiar to mothers, being condemned to grieve twice over—until Harry had confided that whenever he dreamed of their dead son Hal, he was always heartbreakingly young. They'd buried too many of their children, she and Harry. The loss of their firstborn had been the hardest to endure, for she'd had to watch helplessly as the little boy cried in pain and fought for breath, dying after a week of suffering, just two months from his third birthday. She'd not known when Hal was stricken with the bloody flux, not until he was dead. Geoffrey's tournament death had come as a shock, too. In the morning, she'd awakened thinking he was alive and well; by nightfall, he was gone, erased from her life if not her heart. She'd had no warning when a fever had claimed Tilda, either, not learning of her loss until six weeks after her daughter had breathed her last. Time had not blurred the sharp edges of that memory, nor the memory of having to tell Tilda's children. Richenza, newly wed to Jaufre of Perche, had been able to cry in her husband's arms, but it had been left to her to comfort Otto and little Wilhelm, too young to comprehend the awful finality of death.

Her mourning for Hal and Geoffrey had been steeped in guilt, too, for she was tormented by harrowing regrets for past mistakes and missed opportunities. She and Harry had often failed as parents, but she would not—could not—fail Richard now. She must not give in to despair, must remember that the endearing, youthful ghost haunting her tonight was a man of thirty-five, so fearless on the battlefield that she'd heard it said his men would wade through blood to the Pillars of Hercules if he asked it of them. A man capable of inspiring such loyalty was capable of surviving any ordeal that the German emperor could devise. But at what cost? She knew firsthand the wounds that captivity could inflict upon the soul.

No, she could not dwell upon these fears, for she'd drive herself mad if she did. She must somehow put from her mind those images of her son shackled and feverish and defenseless, must not think of the even greater horrors that might await him in a French dungeon. She would gain his freedom, and then she would help him take his vengeance upon the unworthy, cowardly men who'd dared to imprison a king. "I swear it, Richard," she said softly, "I swear it upon the life of your wretched, faithless brother."

She thought this night would never end; eventually her aging body yielded to exhaustion, though, and she slept. She awoke just before dawn, not able to recall her dreams, but knowing she'd found no peace in them, for her pillow was wet with tears.

❧

WHEN HEINRICH DEPARTED HAGENAU at the end of April, he had Richard escorted to the free imperial city of Worms, where he was given comfortable quarters in the palace, but kept under close watch. By mid-May, the emperor was staying at the Augustinian monastery of Mosbach on the River Neckar, which was only a two-day ride from Worms in case he needed to check upon his prize prisoner. On this mild Whitsunday evening, he'd been playing chess with his seneschal, Markward von Annweiler, when he was interrupted by a message from one of his Sicilian spies. He was not happy with what he read, for the man he called "that lowborn usurper" was continuing to strengthen his hold on Sicily. Tancred had gotten that gutless Pope to recognize his claim, and now he was negotiating a marital alliance for his eldest son with the daughter of the Greek emperor in Constantinople. Heinrich was disgusted that Emperor Isaac Angelus would agree to a marriage with a bastard's spawn, but he was concerned, too, for Tancred's attempts to legitimize his kingship were bearing fruit. Time suddenly seemed to be on Tancred's side, not his, for he could take no action until those accursed rebels were dealt with.

He'd gone back to the game, but he was unable to concentrate and Markward began to study the board carefully, seeking an unobtrusive way to throw the game, for his emperor did not like to lose. When a knock sounded on the door, Markward welcomed it. A squire hastened over and, much to Heinrich's surprise, his wife entered. He could not remember the last time she'd come to his bedchamber. Since the beginning of their marriage, he'd always been the one to go to her when he wanted to claim his conjugal rights; that way he could return to his own bed afterward, for he preferred to sleep alone.

Constance nodded coolly to Markward, who was not one of her favorite people, and then smiled at Heinrich. "My lord husband, this is Master Fulk de Poitiers, the English king's clerk." She stepped aside, revealing the man who'd followed her into the bedchamber. "I happened to be in the guest hall when he arrived from Worms, and when I learned he had an urgent message from King Richard, I thought you'd want to see him straightaway."

Fulk had actually sought her out and was impressed now by how smoothly she lied. He thanked her very politely and then knelt respectfully at her husband's feet. "I am here at my king's behest. He requests that you grant him an audience, my lord emperor, as soon as it can be arranged."

"What does he wish to discuss with me, Master Fulk?"

Hoping he could lie as convincingly as Constance, Fulk shook his head regretfully. "I do not know, my lord." He frowned, trying to look like a man vexed that his king had not confided in him. "He said only that it is a matter of great importance to you both." He held his breath then, waiting to see if Heinrich would take the bait.

Heinrich studied him dispassionately, but curiosity won out. Turning to Markward, he ordered the seneschal to go to Worms on the morrow and bring the English king to Mosbach. Glad to escape the chess game, Markward rose, offering to find the hosteller and get Fulk a bed for the night. Constance politely bade her husband farewell and would have followed the men had Heinrich not reached out and put his hand on her arm. "I will come to you later, my dear."

She did not show her surprise; she'd long ago learned to hide her true feelings from this man. "You are always welcome in my bed, my lord husband," she murmured, giving him a smile as meaningless as the life she led. She could remember a time when she'd been eager to pay the marriage debt, so desperate to conceive that she'd willingly have embraced Lucifer himself. Her hunger for a child was all-consuming in the early years of her marriage—not for Heinrich, but for Sicily. As much as she wanted her birthright—the Sicilian crown—she dreaded it, too, for she well knew that her beloved homeland would not fare well under her husband's iron rule. If only the Almighty had given her a son, even a daughter, there would have been at least a glimmer of hope for the Sicilians. But her own hopes had withered on the vine long ago, forcing her to face a bitter truth—she was that saddest and most useless of creatures, a barren wife.

HEINRICH WAS ATTENDED BY Count Dietrich, his brother Conrad, Markward, and his marshal, Heinz von Kalden, and Richard was accompanied by Fulk and his chaplain, Anselm, who'd recently been freed from confinement. Once the courtesies had been exchanged and wine served, the emperor leaned back in his chair, with the suggestion of a smile. "So . . . what is this 'matter of great importance,' my lord king?"

"It can fairly be said that you and I are in the same leaky boat, my lord emperor, for we both are facing challenges to our sovereignty. In my case, the threat is posed by my liege lord, Philippe Capet, and my own brother, a betrayal twice over. Your danger is greater, though, for even in captivity, I am still a consecrated king, whereas your enemies can do what mine cannot—elect another emperor. Indeed, I've heard that they intend to do just that, and since more than half of your vassals are now in rebellion against you, this must be a matter of grave concern to you. Were I in your stead, it would be to me, for certes."

Heinrich's complacent smile had vanished as soon as Richard had begun to speak. "I cannot believe you requested an audience merely to tell me what I already know, my lord. What is your point?"

"The longer this rebellion drags on, the more likely it is that other malcontents will join it. You need to take the initiative, to stop an insurrection from becoming a civil war, and I am in a position to help you do that." Richard paused to take a swallow of wine, keeping his eyes on Heinrich all the while. "If you are willing to make enough concessions, I think I can negotiate a settlement to end the rebellion ere it flares into a conflagration that could end Hohenstaufen rule."

"And why would they listen to you when they've so far spurned my offers to talk peace?"

Richard resisted the temptation to point out that he had greater credibility than Heinrich. "My brother by marriage and my nephew are amongst the leaders of the rebellion, and England has long enjoyed cordial relations with Cologne, an important trading partner for English merchants. Moreover, I think you will agree that at Speyer, I proved I can be quite persuasive."

Heinrich's brother Conrad and Dietrich did not like what they were hearing and, abandoning Latin for German, they both lodged what were obvious protests to Richard. The emperor ignored them. "Even if I did grant some concessions, what makes you think they'd be satisfied with that?"

"Because I can speak about combat with an authority that none could question. When I tell them that a battle commander's last resort ought to be an all-or-nothing war, they might well heed me. If I can convince them that their victory is not a certainty, they are likely to come to terms with you rather than risk losing everything."

Before Heinrich could reply, Dietrich launched another diatribe, speaking with considerable animation. By the time he was done, Heinrich's icy smile had come back. "Count Dietrich does not trust you and thinks you are up to no good. Mayhap you'd like to explain to him what you would gain from this, my lord king?"

Richard had no doubts that Heinrich knew full well what he'd gain. This challenge was meant to see how he'd respond, how candid he was willing to be. He took another sip of wine, thinking that words were his weapons now.

"Of course I expect to benefit. Had I claimed I was acting from pure benevolence or Christian charity, then Count Dietrich would have cause for concern." To his surprise, he caught an expression on Heinrich's face that looked like genuine amusement. It quickly passed, but he took it as proof that he was on the right road. "If I do this for you, I hope you'll conclude that the empire's interests are better served by an alliance with England and not France."

"And cancel that planned meeting with the French king at Vaucouleurs?"

With any other man, Richard would have demanded that as a quid pro quo before he'd ever have agreed to act on Heinrich's behalf. But an imperial promise would mean nothing, not when it was no more substantial than morning mist. Relying upon Heinrich's good faith was a fool's quest, yet he had no choice. "Vaucouleurs is a long way to ride if there is nothing to be gained at journey's end," he said with a shrug.

"Indeed it is," Heinrich agreed, his blasé tone belied by the eyes studying Richard with a hawk's unblinking intensity. "So you would have me believe that you truly do desire an alliance with the empire? If so, you have a most forgiving nature, my lord king of the English."

"No," Richard said, with deliberate coldness, "I do not. What I do have, my lord emperor, is the ability to separate the sheep from the goats. You have not given me reason to think kindly of you. Under other circumstances, I'd be nursing a grudge till my last mortal breath. But the grievances I have against you are no match for the wrongs done me by that Judas on the French throne."

"Yes, you made it rather clear at Speyer that you've no fondness for Philippe Capet. But even so—"

"You do not know the half of it! His treachery began well before we reached the Holy Land. When I seized Messina after the citizens rioted, Philippe offered to fight with Tancred against the English. I saw his letter myself. Yet even as he was betraying me behind my back, he was insisting that the French flag be flown over Messina once it was taken so he could share in the spoils. He then dared to demand half of my sister's dowry!"

Richard rose to his feet so quickly that his guards reacted with alarm, hands dropping to sword hilts. "Then in Outremer, he did all he could to make sure our holy war would end in failure. He abandoned the Almighty and his own allies and would have taken the French army with him had they not valued their oaths more than he did. But the Bishop of Beauvais and the Duke of Burgundy did his dirty work for him, sabotaging me at every turn, whilst Philippe tried to get the Pope to absolve him of his promise not to attack my lands as long as I was in the Holy Land. Last year he would have invaded Normandy if his lords had not balked. For those crimes alone, I'd see the bastard burn in Hell for a thousand years!"

It was a great relief to let his rage blaze up like this, to be able to speak the absolute truth for the first time in months. "And that only takes us through God's Year, 1192," he said bitterly. "Since then, Philippe and his lapdog Beauvais have done their best to destroy my reputation and my honor, with remarkable success. He has seduced my lack-witted brother into treason and even as we speak, a French army is laying waste to my duchy of Normandy. And as if that were not enough, he is now pressuring you to hand me over so he can cast me into a Paris dungeon. He'd not even have the decency to make my death a quick one. No, he'd want me to suffer . . . and all for what? Because I am twice the man that sniveling, cockless milksop could ever hope to be!"

They'd all been riveted by his outburst and when he finally paused for breath, Markward and Conrad grinned and applauded, while Heinrich summoned up another of his chilly smiles, saying dryly, "You really do not like the man, do you?"

"Can you blame me?" Richard reclaimed his seat and finished his wine in several gulps. His face was still flushed and his breathing uneven, for he'd not feigned his anger. To convince Heinrich, he knew he'd have to show passion that none could doubt, hatred hot enough to make it credible that he could overlook these months of captivity and humiliation, even Trifels Castle. For it was not enough that Heinrich agreed to let him try to make peace with the rebels. Even success would not be enough. Ending the rebellion was no guarantee of his safety, not with a man who knew no more of gratitude than he did of honor. Heinrich had to believe that his long-term interests lay with England, not France.

Heinrich signaled for a servant to refill Richard's wine cup. "Very well," he said. "I'll set up a meeting for you with the rebels."

"You will need to offer genuine concessions," Richard warned. "You must make it worth their while to end the rebellion. Are you willing to do that?" Dietrich frowned, obviously not liking that he dared to speak so bluntly to the emperor. But he could display the silver-tongued eloquence of God's own angels and it would count for naught if Heinrich would not offer terms the rebels could accept.

Heinrich did not reply at once. "Yes, I am willing," he said at last. "I want this over and done with." He smiled then, again without humor. "If you can make this happen . . . Well, let's just say that you hold your fate now in your own hands."

Richard smiled, too, for although it was clearly meant as a threat, it was not one to unnerve him. He'd held his fate in his own hands every time he'd ridden out onto a battlefield.

CHAPTER FIFTEEN

❧

MAY 1193

Frankfurt, Germany

It took over a fortnight to make the arrangements for the peace conference, as the rebels insisted that the emperor provide hostages as guarantees of their safety. It was eventually agreed upon that Richard would meet them at the imperial palace in Frankfurt while Heinrich took up residence at the castle of Hanau, ten miles away. Accompanied by his clerk, Fulk de Poitiers, his chaplain, Anselm, and his ever-present guards, Richard reached the riverside city on the last day of May. Several hours later a commotion in the inner court indicated the arrival of the rebel lords. Soon afterward, his door flew open and before the guards could react, his nephew burst into the chamber and embraced him exuberantly.

"Uncle, how glad I am to see you!"

Richard was very glad to see Henrik, too. It had been three years since they'd last met and the young man had matured considerably in that time. No longer a gangling clean-shaven youth of seventeen, he was several inches taller and now boasted a well-trimmed golden beard, for he was the only one of Tilda's children to inherit her fair coloring. He'd returned to Saxony with his parents when their exile ended, but he'd spent enough time in the Angevin domains to form close ties with his mother's family. He at once launched into an indignant attack upon Richard's gaoler, assuring him that most Germans were shamed by the emperor's outrageous maltreatment of a man under the protection of Holy Church.

"What of your father, lad? Is he here, too?"

"No, he refused to come. He said he'd sooner sup with the Devil than talk peace with a Hohenstaufen."

Richard's brother-in-law known as Der Löwe—the lion—had once been the most powerful of all the German lords, Duke of Saxony and Bavaria, a force to be reckoned with. But his feuding with the Hohenstaufens had proved catastrophic for his House. He'd been disgraced, exiled, and stripped of his titles and duchies. Richard could understand his bitterness. It did not make sense to him, though, for Heinrich der Löwe to hold out if all of his allies made peace with their hated enemy.

Henrik apparently didn't think so, either, for he said with a sigh, "I tried to convince him that he should at least hear what the emperor is offering. He was not willing to listen—to Heinrich or to me." His smile was rueful. "He has yet another grievance against the emperor now. I've been plight-trothed since childhood to Heinrich's first cousin. Agnes is the only child of Heinrich's uncle Konrad, the Count Palatine of the Rhine, so it was a brilliant match, and when he lost his duchies, my father took consolation from that, often saying that at least he did not have to worry about my future. Well, the marriage was forbidden by Heinrich, who wants to wed Agnes to Duke Ludwig of Bavaria. I admit I was very disappointed. Not only is Agnes a great heiress, she has a smile like a sunrise and we've always gotten along very well. But my father took it harder than I did. He hates the Hohenstaufens even more than you do, Uncle."

"No one hates them more than I do," Richard protested, with such mock outrage that Henrik laughed. "Does your father know you've come to the peace conference?"

Henrik nodded. "He knows that I am here only to see you. I'll not be able to join the others if you are able to cobble together a peace. I have to stand with him, even if it is not what I'd rather do." Relieved when Richard indicated he understood, Henrik straddled a chair, impatiently pushing aside the fair hair slanting across a sky-blue eye. "Uncle Richard . . . I have something to tell you, and you'll not like it. I had a letter from my sister, confessing that her husband took part in the French king's invasion of Normandy." Seeing Richard's mouth tighten, he said quickly, "Richenza says Jaufre felt he had no choice since Philippe is his king, but she is greatly distressed about it. When I write to her, what should I tell her?"

"Say I do not blame *her*," Richard said, with enough emphasis on the pronoun to tell Henrik that Jaufre was not so lucky. Richard was not truly surprised by Jaufre's defection, but it still stung, all the more because he was sure there would be others.

Henrik confirmed that now by giving him the names of several other barons who'd joined the French campaign, including two who'd fought beside him in the Holy Land. "And that is not the worst of it, Uncle. Richenza says that you lost Gisors Castle. The castellan betrayed your trust and surrendered it to the French king."

Richard had been expecting some defections, but not this. He slumped back in his chair, not sure whom he loathed more at that moment, the disloyal lickspittle who'd yielded up Gisors, the French king, who was as shameless as he was craven, or that hellspawn Heinrich.

Henrik hated being the bearer of ill tidings and so he'd deliberately held back Richenza's welcome news till the last, hoping the good would ease the rancid taste of the bad. "But the French king suffered a severe setback when he besieged Rouen, Uncle. The Earl of Leicester not only stopped him from seizing the city, he made a fool of Philippe in the bargain by opening the gates and challenging him to enter—if he dared. He did not and slunk away with his tail between his legs!"

Henrik's strategy worked; Richard roared with laughter. "What I'd not have given to see that!" He shared then with his nephew some stories of the Earl of Leicester's heroics in the Holy Land, and he was in much better spirits when the summons came to meet the German lords in the great hall. Rising, he beckoned to his guards as if he still had the right of command, silently vowing to show Philippe that, even as a prisoner, he was capable of thwarting the French king's treachery.

❧

ALL OF THE GERMAN REBELS except Richard's brother-in-law were present, but the leaders were clearly the Dukes of Brabant, Limburg, and Bohemia, and the Archbishops of Cologne and Mainz. Richard was predisposed to mistrust Heinrich of Limburg, for he'd not followed through on his vow to fight in the Holy Land, but he felt an immediate rapport with Limburg's nephew Heinrich of Brabant, and he was very pleased to see the Archbishop of Cologne's nephew Adolf von Altena; he'd been impressed by the cathedral prior's forthrightness and courage during his trial at Speyer. As he exchanged courtesies with Duke Ottokar of Bohemia, the irony of meeting under these circumstances was not lost upon him, for he'd initially hoped to find safety in Moravia, the duchy of Ottokar's brother. That was only five months ago, but it seemed as if it were part of the distant past, so much had happened since then.

Once they were seated at a long trestle table in the palace solar, Richard offered the services of his clerk, Fulk, as a scribe, and his chaplain opened the meeting with a prayer. He was encouraged that they'd been willing at least to hear him out. He knew, though, that he would need all of the eloquence at his command to convince them that they ought to make peace with a man they detested and distrusted.

He began by offering his condolences to the dukes of Brabant and Limburg, who were the brother and uncle of the murdered Bishop of Liege. Rather than splashing around in the shallows for a time, he chose to plunge into deep water straightaway, saying, "I want to be candid with you about my motives. I am not trying to end your rebellion because I have always yearned to be a peacemaker, and for certes, not because I wish to ease Heinrich's troubles. A peace settlement is very much in my own interest and I believe it is in yours, too. After I tell you why, I hope that you will agree with me."

He paused to assess the impact of his words. Hermann, the Landgrave of Thuringia, was regarding him with open suspicion, which was not surprising, for he'd long been an enemy of Richard's brother-in-law Der Löwe. The others seemed more curious than skeptical. "I am not sure if you've heard this yet. Next month the emperor intends to meet with the French king at Vaucouleurs." He could tell from their faces that most had not known of this.

"I'm sure you heard that the French king courageously declared war upon England just as I was put on trial at Speyer. Philippe is a most formidable foe—provided that his adversary is fighting for Christ in the Holy Land or hundreds of miles away in a German prison. He knows he cannot hope to defeat me on the field of battle. So he is willing to do almost anything to keep me from regaining my freedom. He has promised to match whatever ransom can be raised in England. But he realizes that it would be easier—and safer—for Heinrich to accept the English ransom, and it is my fear that when he meets Heinrich at Vaucouleurs, he will also offer military assistance in putting down your rebellion. In return for this invaluable aid, all Heinrich has to do is to hand me over to the French.

"If that happens, I am a dead man. But it does not bode well for any of you, either. You'd find yourselves facing the French to the west and Heinrich to the east, trapped between the two. At the moment, I'd say you do have a real chance of defeating Heinrich and possibly even deposing him. The Pope might actually muster up the resolve to recognize your new candidate if presented with a fait accompli. I believe that honor is to be yours, my lord," he said, with a nod toward the Duke of Brabant. "But if you add French troops to the mix, that changes everything and tips the scales decisively in Heinrich's favor. I've looked at maps and most of your castles are in the Rhineland, no? It would be all too easy for two armies to come at you in a pincer movement, and the consequences could be disastrous. In all honesty, neither Heinrich nor Philippe strikes me as another Caesar. But you'd be fighting a war on two fronts, which is every battle commander's worst fear. You'd likely be overwhelmed by sheer numbers."

Richard paused again. They were listening intently, most of their faces mirroring dismay, for they had enough combat experience to recognize the truth in what he'd said. "If this malevolent pact comes to pass, you're likely to find yourselves fighting not for victory, but for survival. You do have leverage now, though, and I propose that you make the most of it. Heinrich seems to be remarkably single-minded, and I get the sense that his planned conquest of Sicily is all that truly matters to him. He may be overweening and utterly bereft of honor. But he is no man's fool, and he knows Sicily is beyond his reach as long as his own empire is in turmoil. So he wants peace, and I think he'll be willing to make it on your terms."

They began to talk among themselves then, and since his own German was still rather rudimentary, Richard made no attempt to follow these fast and furious conversational outbursts. Henrik grinned and Adolf von Altena nodded approvingly when he caught Richard's eye. Feeling that he'd made the best case he could, Richard could only wait.

The Duke of Brabant was the first to direct his attention back to the English king, proving himself to be a pragmatist and proving, too, that he'd not really expected to become emperor himself. "It would not be enough for Heinrich to restore the lands and castles he's seized. He'd have to swear in public, preferably on holy relics, that he played no part in my brother's murder. Think you that he'd be willing to do that?"

After being forced to swear that he'd not been guilty of Conrad of Montferrat's murder, Richard found this role reversal very satisfying. By God's legs, let Heinrich see how he liked it. "Yes," he said, after a moment's thought. "I think he would agree." Adding with a grin, "Of course, I'd not want to be standing next to him when he did it—in case he drew down a celestial thunderbolt upon himself."

When that evoked laughter, Richard took it as an encouraging sign. Now, he decided, it was time to sweeten the pot. It would have to be carefully phrased so as not to affront anyone's pride. But if Heinrich and Leopold could disguise an extortion demand as a dowry, he ought to be able to make a bribe sound downright benign.

"There is something else I would like to discuss with you. I have to believe that Philippe Capet will not win and I'll not end my days in a French dungeon. I've discovered that hope is a prisoner's best armor," he said, and this time his smile was a bleak one. "I owe him a blood debt and I pass much of my time thinking of ways to pay it. I've been doing my best to convince Heinrich that England would make a more useful ally than France. But I want allies I can truly trust—men like you."

Bruno, the aged Archbishop of Cologne, took it upon himself to speak for the others, for his was one of the most prestigious of the German Sees. "What exactly do you have in mind, my lord king?"

"Once I'm back in my own domains, I mean to reclaim the lands Philippe has seized whilst I was held prisoner. I intend to make a two-pronged assault—one with a sword and one with a diplomatic noose. I want to tighten that noose around Philippe's neck, to watch him strangling for air, and the best way to do that is by alliances. I would like to offer money fiefs to you in return for your support against the French king. The benefits from such a formal arrangement are numerous. I get to put the fear of God into Philippe, to be sure that you will rebuff any overtures he may make, and to express my gratitude for your goodwill, for your endeavors to gain my freedom."

These were worldly men and they did not mistake his meaning, but there was nothing blatant about his offer, and their amused, approving smiles showed that they appreciated his deft touch.

"I for one would be quite willing to stand with you against the French king," the Duke of Brabant declared, making it easy for the others to follow his example. When they began to talk in German again, Henrik leaned over to murmur a playful "silver-tongued devil" that caused Richard to laugh aloud, for he was now sure that he was going to prevail.

It took several hours, but eventually they told Richard what he so urgently needed to hear—that they were willing to make peace with the emperor if he'd meet their terms.

"Very good," he said, smiling warmly at his newfound friends. "Now . . . tell me what you want from Heinrich, and I will do my utmost to get it for you."

❧

HANAU WAS A SMALL CASTLE protected by the waters of the River Kinzig. A hamlet had developed in its shadow, a handful of houses and a church, and that only enhanced its forlorn appearance, as if it were forgotten by the rest of the world, even by history. Its lord had been flustered by the unexpected arrival of the emperor and his entourage, uneasily playing host while fearing Heinrich had an ulterior motive for his visit. Why would he have chosen to stay at Hanau when his imperial palace was just ten miles away? The appearance of the English king shredded what was left of his composure. He nervously conducted his new royal guest and guards to the great hall, then hastily retreated.

A rainstorm had swept through the valley as night came on and a fire had been built in the hearth to keep the damp and evening chill at bay. Heinrich had been accompanied to Hanau by his uncle, his brother Conrad, his *ministeriales*, Count Dietrich, and Ludwig, the Bavarian duke hoping to lay claim to Henrik's betrothed. His uncle was reading, the others were playing chess and dice, and Heinrich's head was bent over a lute. It was a source of bafflement to Richard that a man so cold-blooded and callous could share his own love of poetry and music. It was like finding out that Satan secretly read Scriptures.

Heinrich struck a few more chords before he deigned to look up, as if just noticing the English king. "Well? What did they say?"

"They are willing to make peace." Richard unrolled a parchment and handed it to the emperor. "Here are their . . ." He almost said "demands," caught himself in time. "This is a written list of all their terms. I can tell you which ones are not open to negotiation. They want the return of those castles and lands seized from them and compensation for their losses. They want you to swear a public oath that you are innocent of the murder of the Bishop of Liege and find other bishops and lords willing to so swear on your behalf. You gave refuge to the men who killed the bishop, who are now to be banished from your court. Last, they want you to accept the election of the Duke of Limburg's son Simon as the next Bishop of Liege. He is only sixteen, well under the canonical age, but they assured me you ought to have no problem with that since your youngest brother, Philip, was chosen as Bishop of Würzburg at the tender age of thirteen."

Richard could not resist a sardonic smile at that. He need not have worried, though, for Heinrich's attention was utterly focused upon the document. The outburst came from Count Dietrich, who leapt to his feet, his face red with outrage. Richard could not follow his rant, but it was easy enough to guess the gist of it, for Dietrich was the chief suspect in the bishop's murder. Not only was he very close to the emperor, Heinrich had taken the bishopric from the two legitimate candidates and given it to Dietrich's brother Lothar. The Hochstaden brothers had suffered the most in the wake of the bishop's murder, for Lothar had been excommunicated by the Pope and Dietrich's lands had been razed by the rebels, all but one of his castles captured. It was only to be expected, therefore, that he'd be opposed to any peace settlement. Would Heinrich heed him, though?

To Richard's relief, the emperor seemed oblivious to Dietrich's diatribe, although it was loud enough to be heard out in the castle bailey. Watching closely as he read the list of terms, Richard could only hope that he was right in believing the conquest of Sicily mattered more to Heinrich than punishing the rebels. He felt a pang at the thought of a German army descending upon Tancred's domains, for he'd developed an unexpected friendship with the Sicilian king. Tancred knew another invasion was coming, though, and he'd be ready for it. Nor was Heinrich's victory a certainty. He'd tried to conquer Sicily once before, while Richard had been in the Holy Land, but his army had suffered greatly in the unfamiliar heat of an Italian summer, many sickening and dying during the siege of Naples. Heinrich himself had almost died of the bloody flux and had been forced to retreat back to Germany to recover. He'd foolishly or arrogantly left Constance behind in Salerno, where she'd been seized by the citizenry and turned over to Tancred. Richard could well imagine how Heinrich would have treated Tancred's wife had she fallen into his hands, but Tancred had received Constance more like a guest than a hostage, eventually releasing her into the Pope's custody. She'd managed to escape on her way to Rome, robbing Tancred and the Pope of a valuable pawn, but that had been her doing, not Heinrich's. His campaign had been an undeniable disaster, and Richard took heart from that now, reminding himself that Tancred was a far better soldier than Heinrich.

When Heinrich finally looked up from the list of demands, Richard suspected he'd been deliberately drawing out the suspense. "Leopold was right," he said, with one of the supercilious smiles Richard had come to detest. "You can talk as well as fight. I am impressed, I admit it. Their terms are onerous, but not outrageously so, and I can live with them."

Dietrich interrupted before he could say more, obviously protesting. Heinrich silenced him merely by turning to stare at him. Glancing back at Richard, he said, "You can return to Frankfurt on the morrow and tell them I will meet them at Koblenz in a fortnight to draw up a formal peace settlement."

"And you will want to inform the French king that you'll be too busy to meet him at Vaucouleurs." Richard sought to sound confident, all the while wondering if this was when he got the knife in his back.

But Heinrich merely smiled and said blandly, "Of course. There is no need for such a meeting now, is there?" He signaled to a servant, who hurried over to pour wine for them all, and they drank to celebrate the peaceful resolution of the rebellion, although Dietrich looked as if he were swilling soured milk. The wine did not taste much better to Richard, for he knew this new détente with Heinrich was a walk onto thinly frozen ice, hearing it crack under him with every step he took.

❦

WHILE RICHARD WAS very relieved that he'd been able to stave off that meeting at Vaucouleurs, he could take little pleasure from his accomplishment, even though he'd gained valuable future allies. It galled him greatly that he'd been compelled to act on Heinrich's behalf and he was unable to join in Fulk and Anselm's celebration of his success, for he did not feel like a victor, more like a pimp. He kept these dark thoughts to himself, for he did not expect them to understand. Yes, they'd shared his captivity, but they did not share his shame, for they were churchmen, not expected to hold their honor dearer than their lives, as a knight was—or a king.

❦

GUILLAUME DE LONGCHAMP WAS in need of wine, for he'd been talking nonstop for more than an hour and his mouth was getting dry. But he'd had much to tell his king: the truce struck with his brother John until November, the measures taken by the queen mother and the justiciars to raise the ransom and to select the hostages demanded by Heinrich, and the French king's successful Normandy campaign. He was glad to discover that Richard already knew of the loss of Gisors Castle and the defections, for he'd been dreading having to break such bad news. He'd not told Richard of his hostile reception in England or the new humiliations inflicted upon him, for he reasoned the king had troubles enough of his own without having to deal with *his* troubles, too. Instead, he did his best to sound positive, assuring Richard that Hubert Walter would have been consecrated as archbishop by now, stressing the loyalty of the king's subjects, and praising the queen mother so extravagantly that Richard joked he sounded smitten. But none of his news was as welcome as the letters he brought from Eleanor, Otto, Hubert Walter, the justiciars, and English lords.

Watching as Richard reread his letters, Longchamp wondered why he'd said nothing yet about his diplomatic triumph at Frankfurt. He thought that was a remarkable achievement for a prisoner, but he proceeded with caution in light of the king's silence. "I encountered Fulk in the Worms market ere I came to the palace, sire. He was haggling with a peddler over a surprise for you and he told me about your meeting with the German rebels. I wish I could be in Paris to witness the French king's chagrin and anger when he hears how you outwitted him!"

Richard appreciated his chancellor's diplomacy; he'd managed to hit upon the one pure pleasure of his Frankfurt feat—the misery it would give to Philippe Capet. Not wanting to talk about the meeting yet, he said instead, "Did I ever tell you how surprised I was when you and Fulk became such fast friends? When you joined my household, I fully expected the two of you to be at odds from the first day, given how prickly you both can be."

"True, neither of us suffers fools gladly. Nor are we celebrated for our tact. But that gave us something in common," Longchamp said with a smile. Taking the hint, he deferred discussion of the Frankfurt council until the king himself brought it up. "Sire . . . you said you had a new task for me?"

"Your arrival at Worms could not have been better timed, Guillaume, for we are about to negotiate a new agreement for my release. I will be relying upon you to keep Heinrich from draining my body of every last drop of my blood," Richard said, with a flippancy that did not disguise the bitterness, not to one who knew him as well as his chancellor did. "Afterward, I am sending you to France to meet with the French king. I want you to try to get him to agree to a truce. I hate the very thought of it, but there is no other way to keep him from swallowing Normandy whole whilst I am held prisoner here."

He'd just been given a huge challenge, one that would have daunted the most talented of diplomats. Longchamp thrived on such difficult missions, though, and he was promising Richard that he'd do his best when the door opened and Fulk hurried into the chamber. He was carrying Richard's "surprise," a caged green parrot that he'd hoped would prove entertaining, but the gift bird had been relegated to an afterthought by his second surprise.

"Sire, you'll never guess whom I just met below in the outer court!" Fulk's usually dour demeanor was utterly gone; he was beaming as he stepped aside to reveal Richard's new guests. Morgan and Guillain jostled each other in their eagerness to get through the doorway, and the German guards gaped at the jubilant reunion that followed, startled to see the English king embracing these knights like brothers, for they could not imagine their emperor ever showing such favor to men of lesser rank.

Richard was very familiar with the special camaraderie of soldiers, but he felt a particularly strong kinship with the twenty brave men who'd sailed with him on those pirate ships, and above all with Morgan and Guillain, who'd stood with him during one of the worst moments of his life. Once he'd assured himself that they'd endured their captivity as well as could be expected, he stepped back, frowning.

"Where is the lad? Was he not freed, too?"

"He was afraid to face you, sire," Morgan said sadly. "He thinks your plight is all his fault. We've tried to reassure him that you'd not blame him for breaking under torture. I thought we'd succeeded, but he lost his nerve again once we reached Worms." Morgan was reasonably confident that Richard would not blame the boy, but kings were not always tolerant of human frailties, and so he confided, "He is very young, my liege, even younger than we knew, not yet fifteen. . . ."

"Go find him, Morgan, and bring him here. If he balks, tell him it is a royal command."

It was only after Morgan departed that Richard noticed the parrot. He was very knowledgeable about falcons, but he knew nothing of pet birds and was regarding it dubiously as Fulk insisted it would be good company. He declared that it had potential, though, when Fulk stuck his hand in the cage and was promptly bitten. He and Guillain and Longchamp were laughing at the clerk's sputtering oaths when the door opened and Morgan half coaxed, half pushed Arne into the chamber.

The boy stumbled forward, sinking to his knees before Richard, his head bowed. Grasping his arm, Richard pulled him to his feet. "Look at me, Arne." For a long moment, he studied the youngster, his eyes tracking the crusted red welts that had been burned into his forehead and neck. "I am going to tell you something about courage, lad. It is not a lack of fear; it is *overcoming* fear. You endured great suffering for me, more than many men could have withstood. You have no reason to reproach yourself."

Arne's throat had closed up and he saw Richard through a blur of tears. Richard reached out, tracing with his thumb the worst of Arne's injuries, the one slashing from his eyebrow up into his hairline. "Others will look at this and see a scar, Arne. But they are wrong. It is a badge of honor."

Morgan and Guillain thought Arne seemed to gain in stature before their eyes, having had an oppressive weight finally lifted from his shoulders. "The king is right, Arne," Morgan said with a grin. "And that 'badge of honor' will serve you well in the future. When you go into a tavern and tell men how you got it, you'll never have to pay for another drink again."

"It will also prove useful when you want to impress a lass," Richard predicted, and when the men laughed, Arne joined in, awed that so much pain could be healed with a few well-chosen words. Their German guards watched, puzzled by the merriment, agreeing among themselves that the English truly were a strange breed.

❧

ON THE TWENTY-NINTH OF JUNE, Richard sat on the dais beside the German emperor in the great hall of the imperial palace at Worms as the terms of their agreement were made public. Heinrich's smile was triumphant and somewhat smug. It amused him to imagine the French king's dismay when he heard of this pact, especially since Philippe was responsible for his having gotten most of what he'd demanded from the English king; he could have no more effective weapon to hold over Richard's head than the threat of that Paris dungeon.

Richard had summoned up what he hoped was a smile of his own; it felt more like a grimace to him, the involuntary rictus seen so often on the faces of the dead. He was determined that none would know how much anguish this agreement had caused him. So he kept that smile steady even as the outrageous new terms were read aloud. His ransom had been raised to a staggering one hundred fifty thousand silver marks, and he would be freed only upon payment of two-thirds of that vast amount, one hundred thousand marks. He must provide Heinrich with sixty hostages and Duke Leopold with seven to guarantee payment of the remaining fifty thousand marks within seven months of his release. If he succeeded in making peace between the emperor and his brother-in-law, Heinrich der Löwe, the payment of that fifty thousand marks would be waived and no hostages would be required. But since the demands made of Der Löwe included his acceptance of the marriage of his son's betrothed to the Duke of Bavaria, Richard knew that peace would never come to pass. He had also been compelled to agree to wed his niece Aenor to Leopold's eldest son and to deliver Anna, the Damsel of Cyprus, to the Austrian duke to be wed to his younger son. He could take consolation only from the absence of one earlier demand—that he personally take part in a campaign against the Sicilian king. But that gave him little comfort on this hot Tuesday afternoon, not when he thought about the cost of his freedom, a sum so stupendous that it defied belief, more than three times the annual income of the English government.

THE CONDITIONS OF RICHARD'S IMPRISONMENT improved considerably after he'd come to final terms with Heinrich. He was given greater freedom, no longer kept under such smothering surveillance, allowed to meet in private with his friends and new German allies, and to conduct affairs of state; he'd even sent to England for his favorite falcons, having been promised he'd be able to go hawking and hunting. Heinrich also released the last of his men and Baldwin de Bethune was warmly welcomed at Worms. The Germans were impressed by the constant stream of visitors from England, men of rank and authority making an arduous journey to pledge their loyalty to their captive king, and word soon reached the French court that Richard was being treated more like a guest now than a prisoner.

Philippe was stunned by the news of the Worms settlement, outraged that Heinrich had played him for a fool, making him believe his offer would be accepted. He was horrified, too, once he realized Richard's release seemed imminent. He was shaken enough to agree to a truce with England when he met on July 9 with Richard's chancellor, Guillaume de Longchamp, and his justiciar, William Briwerre, hoping to hold on to the gains he'd made during Richard's captivity.

He also sent an urgent message to his ally and coconspirator. When John read that terse warning—"Look to yourself; the Devil is loosed"—he at once fled to France.

CHAPTER SIXTEEN

❧

JULY 1193

Rome, Italy

The Lady Mariam was seated on a marble bench in the Frangipani family's palace on the Palatine. The sun was at its zenith, but the heat did not bother Mariam, who'd grown up in Sicily. She was waiting for the queens to return from the papal palace. In recent weeks the Pope had been too busy to see them whenever they'd requested an audience. While Berengaria still clung to her faith in the Holy Father, Joanna had given up all hope and his evasiveness infuriated her almost as much as his lack of action, for there was nothing she could do about either. This sudden summons by the Pope had excited them both, convincing them that it meant he'd gotten news about Richard. Mariam did not share their optimistic certainty that the news must be good; no Sicilian harbored any illusions about the Emperor Heinrich.

Mariam would be happy for Joanna and Berengaria's sake if the Pope did indeed have encouraging word about Richard's plight, but she knew it was unlikely that he'd have heard anything about the man who mattered to her, Joanna's Welsh cousin Morgan. As soon as she'd found out that Richard had ventured into enemy territory with only twenty men, she'd been sure Morgan was one of them, and her suspicions had been confirmed by the de Préaux brothers, Guilhem, Jean, and Pierre. After parting from Richard in Corfu, they'd made their way to Sicily, and were heading home to Normandy when they'd learned of the king's capture. They at once changed plans, determined to join Richard in Germany. They'd stopped in Rome long enough, though, to tell Richard's women about his ill-fated journey from the Holy Land.

Joanna and Berengaria had lavished praise upon them for their loyalty, but

Mariam had listened in silence, wondering why male priorities were so hard to fathom. The Préaux brothers were putting their king before their own anxious families back in Normandy, and she did not see that as admirable. She was still resentful that Morgan had chosen to sail with Richard rather than with her, and for a time her relationship with Joanna had suffered. But the two women were as close as any two sisters could be, and Mariam had realized she must let her grievance go. Richard was Joanna's brother, the one who'd rescued her from captivity, so it was only to be expected that she'd love him dearly and his safety would be of paramount importance to her. Mariam reminded herself, too, that Morgan need not have done as Joanna requested, but that brought her back to the baffling subject of male honor.

She was so caught up in her thoughts that she started when a cold nose was thrust into her hand. Smiling at the sight of Ahmer, the cirneco that had been her brother's favorite hound, she fondled his fox-like red ears, remembering William's pleasure and the horror of his Muslim physician when she'd smuggled the dog into his bedchamber during his final illness. Thoughts of William invariably made her sad for what might have been. If only his and Joanna's infant son had lived. If only he'd not married Constance off to Heinrich von Hohenstaufen, giving Heinrich a claim to the Sicilian crown. If only he'd not been so stubborn, ignoring the protests of his subjects, who'd sooner have allied with Lucifer than the German emperor. He'd always been a good brother to her and she thought he'd been a good husband to Joanna, despite keeping a *harim* of Saracen slave girls as his father and grandfather had done. But he'd not been a good king.

Ahmer's head came up sharply and then he wheeled and raced back toward the great hall, barking joyfully. Mariam rose and followed more slowly, sure that the dog had heard his mistress's return. By the time she entered, Joanna and Berengaria were surrounded by the women of their household, all eager to hear the Pope's news. Mariam needed only one glimpse of Berengaria to know Richard's prospects had taken a turn for the better, for his wife's face was glowing, her beautiful brown eyes filled with shimmering light. But Mariam could detect the shadows lurking behind Joanna's smile, and Sir Stephen de Turnham's smile was, at best, a polite grimace.

As Joanna's eyes met Mariam's, she slipped away from the others crowded around Berengaria, leaving it for Richard's queen to break the news that he could soon be free. Emerging into the courtyard, Joanna blinked at the dazzling white brightness of the summer sun and then crossed to a bench in the shade of a silvery-grey olive tree, trailed by Mariam and Ahmer. Once Mariam was seated beside her, Joanna related what they'd been told of the pact Richard and Heinrich had made at Worms on June 25. Mariam listened without interruption, although she could not stifle a gasp at the mention of the staggering ransom demand. Waiting until Joanna had nothing more to reveal, she said quietly, "Those are very harsh terms, meant to break the man and bankrupt his country. Does Berengaria not realize that yet?"

"She is reacting now as Richard's wife, not his queen, and she cannot be faulted for that." Joanna sounded faintly defensive, for she was very protective of the younger woman. "For now, all this means to her is that she may soon be reunited with her husband. Let her have this moment, Mariam. There will be time enough to consider the consequences of this Devil's deal once Richard is freed." She paused and then added bleakly, "*If* he is freed."

"Does the Pope think Heinrich will not honor the pact? He stands to gain a huge amount of money by it."

"Assuming that the French king does not offer even more." Joanna very much wanted to share her sister-in-law's joy, to believe that Richard would soon be freed. But she'd have taken an Outremer scorpion as a pet rather than put her trust in the Holy Roman Emperor. And because she knew her brother far better than his bride did, she nursed a secret dread that she'd shared with no one, not even Mariam—the fear that his imprisonment was ravaging Richard's pride and scarring his soul.

"Joanna . . . are you still sure that you ought to keep Queen Eleanor's letter from Berengaria?"

"Of course I am sure, Mariam! When I think of all the nights that I've dreamed of Richard at Trifels, burning with fever, chained up like a felon . . . Why would I want to inflict such pain upon Berengaria? No, if Richard wants to tell her of his Trifels ordeal, he will. Until then, it comforts her to believe he is being treated with the respect due his rank, and I will not be the one to take that comfort away from her."

Mariam could understand Joanna's reasoning; nor did she blame Joanna for wanting to shelter Berengaria if she could. It was just that if Morgan had been the one kept in irons at Trifels, she'd have wanted to know, the pain notwithstanding. Once she might have argued further, but their falling-out over Morgan had tempered her usual candor, and she chose to change the subject. "Are you going to tell Anna that she is to wed the Duke of Austria's son?"

"Berengaria and I discussed this on the way back from the papal palace, and we decided it is better to wait. I doubt that Richard wants to see that marriage come to pass and he might find a way to circumvent it once he is freed."

Scorning consistency, Mariam agreed with Joanna about keeping the news from Anna. She was fond of the girl, but Anna was flighty and impulsive and it would be hard to predict her reaction. "Does the Holy Father know the identities of the hostages?"

"Not all of them, though he says they will be of high birth." Joanna's lip curled. "Because Heinrich has no honor, he assumes Richard would sacrifice the lives of his hostages as he himself would do, and so he is demanding those whom he sees as the most valuable pawns. Our nephews Otto and Wilhelm are on the list. The sons of some of Richard's barons. Berengaria's younger brother Fernando. Men close to Richard. Even prelates of the Church."

"Has Pope Celestine heard anything about the men taken prisoner with Richard?"

Joanna shook her head reluctantly. Rallying then, she said with all the assurance she could muster, "I am sure they have been freed, though. Morgan is likely with Richard at Worms by now and making plans to return home."

Mariam knew better; Morgan would not leave Germany until Richard did. "Do you think even your mother can raise such a vast sum of money?"

"I have no doubts whatsoever of that." Joanna's voice rang with conviction. "I have more good news, Mariam. The Pope has assumed responsibility for seeing that we get safely back to Richard's domains. We are to be escorted to Pisa and then Genoa, where we'll take ship for Marseille." Despite the scorching heat, Joanna shivered at the thought of setting foot on shipboard again, even though she'd been assured they'd be hugging the coast.

"Thank God," Mariam said fervently, for she'd come to see Rome as a gilded cage. "But . . . Marseille? I thought you told me that Richard had to turn back when he learned he could not land safely at Marseille?"

"I know, and neither Berengaria nor I are at all happy at having to ask the King of Aragon for help. But we have no choice, not unless we want to remain in Rome until Richard can come himself to fetch us."

Mariam was not too proud to admit her ignorance of French geography. "I am Sicilian, Joanna, remember? Marseille is a city on the French coast. How does the King of Aragon come into it?"

"King Alfonso is also Count of Barcelona and Marquis of Provence, which gives him control over Marseille. The Holy Father told us he'd written to Alfonso several months ago, asking for his aid once it was safe for us to venture from Rome, and Alfonso promised that he would make sure we got safely from Marseille to Poitiers. I suspect he feels guilty for betraying Richard and allying with that viper in Toulouse. And indeed, he ought to feel guilty, for he and Richard had been friends since they were fifteen!"

The mention of "that viper in Toulouse" jogged Mariam's memory. She knew Joanna's mother had a claim to Toulouse, for her grandmother had been the only child of one of its counts, her inheritance usurped by her uncle. That had occurred a hundred years ago, and the dukes of Aquitaine and counts of Toulouse had been feuding ever since. Two years ago, the current Count of Toulouse, Raimon de St Gilles, had somehow inveigled Alfonso into an alliance against their mutual enemy, Navarre, and as a result, Richard had been forced to make his way home through Germany. "I know you say Alfonso was once Richard's friend, Joanna. But do you think he can still be trusted? What if he hands you and Berengaria over to the Count of Toulouse?"

"No, Alfonso would never do that. He is not utterly without honor like St Gilles. He guaranteed our safety to the Pope and would not renege upon it. Moreover, we will be escorted to Marseille by Cardinal Melior, of San Giovanni e Paolo in Pisa. He is French," Joanna said, making a wry face, "but he is also a papal legate. I've spoken to him on several occasions and he seemed truly indignant about Richard's plight. He'll not let us come to harm."

"A cardinal and a papal legate? I am impressed, Joanna. Dare we hope that the Holy Father is finally heeding his conscience?"

"I suspect his newfound solicitude is due more to fear of my mother than belated conscience pangs," Joanna said with a sudden grin. When the Pope would no longer meet with them, Joanna had begun to cultivate other sources of information and had easily found a sympathetic ear in one of the papal secretaries, for even men who'd taken holy vows were not immune to a beautiful woman's charm. She'd not revealed the name of her new friend, playfully calling him the "Good Samaritan," and she referred to him as that now, saying that he'd told her Eleanor had been assailing Pope Celestine with letters, by turns beseeching and accusing.

"He said she expressed outrage that the Holy Father had not sent a 'single nuncio, not the humblest subdeacon' to negotiate on Richard's behalf. She wrote movingly of a mother's grief, saying she'd lost 'the staff of my old age, the light of my eyes,' whilst she is 'tortured by the memories of my dead,' the sons who 'sleep in the dust.' She warned him that his failure to act cast a shadow over the Church, demanding to know how he could be unmoved whilst her son is 'tortured in chains.' She reminded him of the great evil Heinrich had done against the Church—the murder of the Bishop of Liege, the imprisonment of five other bishops. She accused him of 'keeping the sword of Peter sheathed,' of yielding to 'human fear.' She wrote, 'Restore my son to me, man of God, if indeed you are a man of God.'"

"She truly dared to say that, Joanna?"

Eleanor's daughter nodded proudly. "She signed one of the letters 'Queen of England by the Wrath of God.'" She added, with another grin, "My Good Samaritan swears the Holy Father shudders at the mere sight of a letter with my mother's seal."

When Joanna laughed, Mariam joined in, both women grateful for a moment of levity in a season of such gloom. Neither one heard the soft footsteps approaching, not turning until Ahmer gave a welcoming whine. Berengaria was smiling at them, her expression curious. "What is so amusing?"

"I was telling Mariam about my mother's letters to the Pope," Joanna explained, sliding over on the bench to make room for her sister-in-law.

Berengaria had been shocked at first by the accusatory tone of her mother-in-law's missives, yet she'd been secretly pleased, too, for she was finding it harder and harder to be patient with the Holy Father's passivity. He was God's vicar on earth, and she wanted to believe that he would never shirk his pastoral duties for venial political reasons. She *needed* to believe that. But he was not making it easy for her.

"It is outrageous that Richard should have to pay so much money to regain his freedom," she said, showing them that she was not oblivious to the burden the ransom would impose upon his kingdom. "It will be a massive undertaking to raise the ransom, especially since Richard's subjects had already been taxed for the Saladin tithe. Do you think your mother will be able to do it, Joanna?" Getting assurances from her sister-in-law, she smiled shyly. "It may be selfish of me to be so happy when I know this ransom will cause misery to so many. But I cannot help it. For the first time, I can see our reunion as a reality, not just a hope glimmering on the horizon. Richard and I have been apart for so long. I was thinking about that this morning and I realized it has been nine months since we left him at Acre. Nine months . . ."

She continued to smile, but there was a catch in her voice, and Joanna understood why, understood all too well. To a woman desperate to bear a child, nine months could have but one meaning. Berengaria was undoubtedly tormenting herself with thoughts of what might have been, thinking that had God been kinder, she might have been pregnant when they sailed from Acre, that she might have had a son to show Richard when they were finally reunited. Joanna had suffered the same stifled yearnings during her marriage to the Sicilian king, anguished that she'd not conceived again after the death of their infant son. She'd felt guilty, as well, fearing she might not be able to give William an heir. She knew Berengaria was haunted by such fears, too, for in the sixteen months between her wedding in Cyprus and her parting from Richard at Acre, her flux had come with heartbreaking regularity.

Joanna had done her best to dispel those fears, pointing out how rarely Berengaria and Richard had been able to share a bed, assuring her that would change once he was no longer fighting a holy war. She did not know if her common sense reminder had helped, though. She'd told herself that her own barren marriage had been as much William's fault as it was hers, for there'd been too many nights when he'd bypassed the marital bed for one that held a seductive Saracen concubine. But that knowledge had not helped to assuage any of her own misery.

Reaching over, she gave Berengaria's hand a gentle squeeze. "We have good reason to be happy," she said, "for the worst is over." And she managed to sound very convincing, given that she did not really believe it.

WHEN THE POPE HAD requested his help, it never occurred to the Aragonese king to refuse. Even had Alfonso considered Richard to be an enemy, he would still have offered his assistance to the Lionheart's wife and sister. Since he saw Richard as a friend with a just grievance against him, he was eager to make amends however he could. That did not mean he was looking forward to receiving Joanna and Berengaria. They were sure to blame him for the part he'd played, however inadvertently, in Richard's capture; moreover, Berengaria's Navarre had always been Aragon's adversary. He considered trying to ease the situation with candor, explaining that he'd felt he had no choice but to ally with the Count of Toulouse, for Berengaria's brother Sancho had been too successful in putting down the rebellion in Richard's lands. He'd gotten as far as the walls of Toulouse itself and, fearing that Sancho would be tempted to move into his own lands in Provence, Alfonso had been alarmed enough to take desperate measures. Could he really expect them to sympathize with his predicament, though, whilst Richard was languishing in German captivity?

In any event, kings had little practice in offering apologies, and so he chose instead to rely upon their good manners, for surely they'd be too well bred to rebuke the man who was acting as their host. He also took the precaution of having his queen, Sancha, present. She'd not been happy at being summoned from Aragon, for the birth of their eighth child had not been an easy one. But he'd insisted, for she was the sister of the King of Castile, who happened to be wed to Joanna's sister Leonora. And he'd heard Richard's queen was quite devout, so he thought she'd find common ground with Sancha, who'd founded a nunnery five years ago.

As it turned out, it was not as awkward as he'd feared. Just as he'd hoped, the women were coolly civil, politely thanking him for his hospitality and keeping their real feelings to themselves. And, as he'd expected, they both thawed with Sancha. The presence of the famed troubadour Peire Vidal helped to ease the tension, too. Cardinal Melior also proved to be an asset, being one of those worldly prelates as much at home in society as he was in the cloister. Alfonso saw to it that his guests had every amenity, and they did not protest when he insisted that they take time to recover from the rigors of their journey from Rome. Things were going so well that he even dared to hope Richard would be mollified when he heard how warmly his wife and sister had been welcomed at Alfonso's court.

❧

ALFONSO CELEBRATED THE END of his guests' first week in Marseille with a lavish feast in their honor. After a five-course meal of southern delicacies, Peire Vidal performed a song he'd written about Richard's captivity, and Joanna and Berengaria applauded enthusiastically when he disdained the French king as "neither true nor faithful," scornfully claiming Philippe "buys and sells like a serf or a burgher," and accusing Heinrich of breaking God's Law in holding Richard prisoner. As he joined in the applause, it occurred to Alfonso that he ought to write a song himself about the English king's plight; that would be a way of expressing his regret to Richard's women without having to offer an actual apology. He was a talented poet, had even learned the *lenga romana* of Aquitaine so he could write in the language of the troubadours, and he was mentally composing verses in his head as the evening's festivities drew to an end.

He was not paying attention, therefore, when Berengaria expressed her gratitude to Sancha for their hospitality, saying it was very kind of Alfonso to accompany them all the way to Poitiers. Sancha frowned, turning to look at her husband in surprise. "You have not told them?" She'd spoken in Catalan, the preferred language of the Aragonese kings, but her tone of voice and her expression alerted both Joanna and Berengaria that something was amiss, and Alfonso suddenly found himself the focal point of all eyes.

Alfonso had deliberately kept his plan secret, knowing it would not be well received. He'd been waiting for Raimond to arrive, hoping he'd be able to dispel their misgivings once they met him. Too late now. "Did I not mention it?" he asked blandly. "Regretfully, I will be unable to accompany you all the way to Poitiers, my ladies. This presented me with a dilemma, since I wanted to make sure you'd be able to continue your journey in safety. Fortunately, a good friend of mine offered to do what I could not. I will escort you through Provence and he will then take over. In fact, he will be meeting us here in Marseille, as he wanted you to get a chance to know him—"

Kings were not interrupted, but Joanna did so now, for an awful suspicion was taking root in the back of her brain; the lands beyond Provence were held by the Toulouse viper. "And the name of this friend you would entrust our safety to, my lord?"

Alfonso resisted the instinct to duck for cover. "Raimond de St Gilles, the Count—"

As he'd feared, he'd just tossed a torch into a hayrick. Both women were staring at him in horror. "You cannot be serious!" Joanna cried, once again cutting him off in midsentence. "The Count of Toulouse is an avowed enemy of our House!"

For once, Berengaria showed herself quite willing to join her sister-in-law in making an unseemly public scene. "He hates and fears my husband," she said tautly. "We know he connived with the French king against Richard. I think he is quite capable of making us his hostages and turning us over to Philippe."

Joanna was even more outspoken. "The man is a monster. He is believed to be responsible for the murder of the Viscount of Béziers some years ago, and many think he was behind the killing of your own brother, my lord king. He has terrorized his neighbors for years, none of whom would trust him with a dog, much less a queen!"

"You have distressed yourselves for naught, my ladies," Alfonso said coolly, irked by Joanna's tactless mention of his brother's slaying; he had indeed suspected the Count of Toulouse of complicity in the plot, although it never had been proven. But he did not appreciate being reminded that he'd allied himself with a man who might have his brother's blood on his hands. "I would never expect you to travel in the company of the Count of Toulouse. I was not speaking of Raimon de St Gilles, but of his son Raimond, the Count of Melgueil."

He benefited momentarily from their earlier indignation. Normally they'd have balked at any member of the House of Toulouse, but because they saw the father as such a threat, his son seemed like the lesser of evils. They exchanged troubled glances, for neither of them knew enough about Raimond de St Gilles to make a persuasive argument against him.

In extinguishing one fire, though, Alfonso ignited another one. Cardinal Melior had been listening in growing concern, for the ultimate responsibility for the queens' safety rested with the Church. He did not like this unexpected involvement of the Count of Toulouse any more than the women did. But when he heard the name Raimond de St Gilles, he reacted as if stung, coming to his feet so hastily that he nearly stepped on the tail of one of Alfonso's dogs, who'd been napping peacefully on the dais.

"The Count of Melgueil poses a far greater danger than his father. At least the Count of Toulouse's faith is not in question. His son is a heretic!"

Berengaria gasped at that. Joanna did not take the cardinal's judgment as absolute the way her sister-in-law did, for she knew the religious life of the south was complex and not always conventional. But she willingly seized the weapon he'd just handed her and said challengingly, "My lord king, is this true? You'd have us escorted by a heretic?"

"Of course not!" Alfonso said through gritted teeth. "You have been misinformed, my lord cardinal. Raimond de St Gilles is no more a heretic than I am. Surely you are not suggesting that the King of Aragon is not a good Christian?"

He'd not usually have been so heavy-handed in pulling rank, but he wanted to end this argument before it spiraled out of control. The cardinal refused to take the hint, though, for more was at stake than a king's displeasure. "Of course your faith is not in question, my liege. But I cannot say as much for Raimond de St Gilles. He often consorts with the Albigensian heretics known as Cathars, and has been seen honoring the *perfecti*, their so-called priests. He allows their vile beliefs to flourish in Toulouse, and vile they are indeed! They deny the Resurrection and the Eucharist, claim the Lord Christ is not the Son of God, and insist the Sacraments are snares set by the Devil!"

"I am not defending those vile beliefs, my lord cardinal! I am saying that Raimond de St Gilles is not a Cathar. He is a faithful son of the true Church." Turning toward the women, Alfonso took up Joanna's challenge. "I would never entrust you to Raimond's care had I any doubts about your safety with him. I admit that his father is not a man of honor. But fathers and sons are not always alike, and Raimond and his sire are very different men. If he is guilty of any sin, it is one of courtesy. Yes, he has shown respect to the Cathar priests, but only because most are aged and he sees them as harmless—"

"'Harmless'?" Cardinal Melior sputtered, so great was his outrage to hear enemies of the Church described in such benign terms.

Realizing he'd misspoken, Alfonso said quickly, "'Harmless' was an ill-chosen word. I meant that Raimond does not see the Cathars as posing a serious threat to the Holy Church. He tells me that their *perfecti* cause no trouble, living austere, simple lives and occupying themselves in prayers and good deeds. Raimond has a kind heart and sometimes it leads him astray. That does not make him a heretic, my lord cardinal."

The expression on Cardinal Melior's face said otherwise, and Alfonso raised his hand imperiously. "I regret that this does not meet with your approval, my lord cardinal, but I cannot escort the queens personally to Poitiers and I am grateful to the Count of Melgueil for offering to act in my stead. So there is no point in discussing this further."

The cardinal was a seasoned diplomat. But he was also a prince of the Church. Struggling with these conflicting claims, he waited until he was sure his voice would not betray his anger. "I defer to your wishes, my lord king. However, I do not share your confidence in the Count of Melgueil's goodwill. So I think it necessary to alter my own plans. Instead of bidding farewell to the queens of England and Sicily here in Marseille, I shall be accompanying them all the way to Poitiers."

Both Berengaria and Joanna at once expressed their gratitude to the cardinal, with such obvious relief that Alfonso realized he'd not been able to ease their qualms. Looking from the unhappy queens to the irate prelate, he suppressed a sigh, thinking, *Poor Raimond. He has no idea what is in store for him.*

BERENGARIA AND JOANNA WANTED to find out all they could about Raimond de St Gilles since they'd be spending so many weeks in his company. Cardinal Melior was only too happy to repeat the stories he'd heard of Count Raimond's transgressions. When the count was not keeping company with heretics, he was chasing after women; he'd had two wives, the cardinal related disapprovingly, and bastard-born children beyond counting. He had a subversive sense of humor that often bordered on sacrilege and the troubadours who flocked to his court were just as impious. Sadly, the man was very popular with his father's subjects, which only confirmed the cardinal's dark suspicions about the people of these sun-blessed southern lands.

Joanna and Berengaria then sought out Sancha, who had a keen ear for gossip and enjoyed sharing it. "I do not know Raimond well," she confided, "but he and Alfonso are good friends. He is one of those men with more charm than the law should allow, and I daresay he could seduce a mother abbess if he truly tried. His first wife was some years older than he was; he was just sixteen at the time of their marriage. When she died four years later, he inherited her county of Mel-gueil. He then married the sister of the Viscount of Béziers—"

"You mean he wed the daughter of the murdered viscount, the one believed to have been slain by Count Raimond's father? Good heavens!"

"They are a practical lot, these southerners. Raimond's sister married into the Trencavel family, too. The idea was to patch up a peace between Toulouse and the Trencavel viscounts. Raimond and Beatrice have had only one child, a daughter, whom he named Constance after his mother." Sancha smiled wryly. "This did not please Raimond's father very much. He treated Constance so badly that she finally left him and fled to the court of her brother, the French king— the one who was once wed to your mother. It was a great scandal, for Constance was with child at the time, later giving birth to another son in Paris. She ada-mantly refused to return to Toulouse, dying a few years ago."

"How old was Raimond when his mother sought refuge in France?" Joanna asked, and Sancha paused to consider the question.

"Raimond is close in age to your brother Richard, so he'd have been about ten at the time."

"So he never saw her again? How sad." Joanna found herself approving of at least one thing Count Raimond had done; naming his daughter after his mother honored her memory while expressing his disapproval of her maltreatment. "Does he have as many base-born children as the cardinal claims?"

"I know of only three, a son and two daughters. Alfonso says he was quick to acknowledge them and provides generously for them, too, which is to his credit, for not all men bother to look after their bastards."

So far, Joanna had heard nothing particularly damning about Raimond de St Gilles from Sancha, for most of the men in her social class kept mistresses and had children born out of wedlock; her father had sired several of his own. "What of the cardinal's other accusation, that he is a heretic? Do you believe it?"

"No . . . Alfonso insists he is not a Cathar."

Joanna caught the dubious note in the other woman's voice and prodded. "But . . . ?"

"It is just that he is strangely indulgent when it comes to the religious faith of others. He actually seems to think that it is none of his concern, that their beliefs are between them and God!"

Berengaria had been listening in silence, but at that, she shook her head, saying that to tolerate heresy was surely to encourage it. Joanna had a more nuanced view, for she'd come of age in Sicily, where Arabic was one of the official languages, her husband had been served by Saracen physicians and astrologers, and Jews were not segregated from society as they were in other Christian countries. She did not argue with Berengaria, though, not wanting to shock her with yet another example of Angevin insouciance; she knew that she and Richard had often disconcerted his sheltered Spanish wife with their candor and irreverent humor. But even if she could acquit Raimond de St Gilles of the most serious charge against him—heresy—he was still not to be trusted, for her House and his had been enemies for as long as she could remember, and she liked being in his debt no more than her sister-in-law did. There was nothing either of them could do about it, though.

THERE WAS SO MUCH TENSION over Raimond de St Gilles's impending arrival that Mariam joked privately to Joanna, "It is as if we are expecting the Antichrist." Joanna smiled sourly, for her sense of humor seemed to have decamped as soon as she'd learned of Alfonso's double cross, as that was how she saw his surprise. Soon afterward, she found herself seated on the dais with Alfonso, Sancha, and Berengaria, awaiting the Antichrist's entrance.

There was a stir as he entered the hall, for he was accompanied by a rising troubadour star, Raimon de Miraval. Joanna never noticed the troubadour, though, for she saw only Raimond de St Gilles. He was taller than average, with a lean build and the easy grace of a man comfortable in his own body. She had never seen hair so dark—as glossy and black as a raven's wing—or eyes so blue, all the more striking because his face was so deeply tanned by the southern sun. He was clean-shaven, with sharply sculptured cheekbones and a well-shaped, sensual mouth that curved slightly at the corners, as if he were suppressing a smile. He was not as conventionally handsome as her brothers or her husband, but as she watched him approach the dais, Joanna's breath caught in her throat, for the first time understanding what the troubadours meant when they sang of "a fire in the blood."

He knelt respectfully before Alfonso, saying smoothly, "As always, it gladdens my eyes to see you and your lovely lady, my liege." Joanna bit her lip; naturally the wretched man would sound like one of God's fallen angels. Low-pitched, with a slight huskiness, it was a voice meant for hot summer nights and honeyed wine and those sweet sins that paved the road to Hell.

Rising, Raimond gallantly kissed Sancha's hand, and as Alfonso introduced him to the others, he acknowledged Cardinal Melior's frigid greeting with elaborate courtesy that held undertones of mockery. He seemed sincere, though, when he kissed Berengaria's hand and offered his sympathies for her husband's misfortunes, saying that it was shameful to hold captive a man who'd taken the cross. Surprised, Berengaria favored him with a warm smile that faltered when she remembered this amiable, attractive man was suspect in the eyes of Holy Church.

"My lady Joanna." Bowing gracefully, Raimond reached for her hand and Joanna felt a physical frisson at the touch of his fingers upon hers. His breath was hot on her skin and his kiss burned like a brand. She recoiled, jerking her hand from his, a gesture that was as involuntary as it was ill-mannered. She blushed deeply then, embarrassed by her own bad behavior. One of Raimond's dark brows arched, ever so slightly, but he did not otherwise acknowledge her rudeness, continuing to regard her with a smile. Joanna sank back in her chair, no longer meeting his gaze. Never had she reacted to a man's presence like this and, as flustered as she was by her body's treacherous betrayal, what was even worse was that she was convinced Raimond de St Gilles was fully aware of the forbidden feelings causing her such distress.

CHAPTER SEVENTEEN

❧

AUGUST 1193

Arles, Provence

Joanna had presided over one of the most sophisticated courts in Christendom, learning at an early age to submerge the woman in the queen. Moreover, she was accustomed to attracting male attention and was an accomplished flirt. But much to her chagrin, she felt like a raw, green girl in the presence of Raimond de St Gilles. Suddenly tongue-tied and ill at ease, she could not banter with him as she'd done with men since she was fifteen. Because she was so disquieted, she barely managed icy civility, and her anger with herself intensified her discomfiture. She took some small measure of comfort that she was not the only one behaving badly in Raimond's company. The worldly, elegant cardinal who'd accompanied them from Rome had become a man smoldering with anger; his courtesy was grudgingly given and he always seemed to be biting his tongue to keep from bursting out with accusations and recriminations. But he and Joanna were the only holdouts against the count's easy charm.

Anna and Alicia had been smitten at once. Joanna kept a hawk's eye on the girls, but she reluctantly admitted that Raimond had so far handled their infatuation very deftly, neither laughing at their clumsy attempts at flirtation nor encouraging them. To Joanna's vexation, he and Mariam had acted as if they were kindred spirits from their first meeting, and by the time they parted from Alfonso and Sancha at Arles, he'd also won over Dame Beatrix. Even Berengaria's straitlaced Spanish ladies were not immune to that smile and seductive voice; they expressed proper horror at his heretical views, but Joanna noticed that they watched him surreptitiously from the corners of their eyes and blushed whenever he glanced their way.

Joanna realized that she was just as guilty as Berengaria's women, for although she kept her distance from Count Raimond, she could not keep her eyes from seeking him out. He was a chameleon, she concluded disapprovingly, changing his colors to match his audience. With the bewitched girls, he was gravely gallant. With the forthright Beatrix, he was respectful. He flirted shamelessly with Mariam, but not with Berengaria. With her, he employed a more subtle approach, asking her to tell him of Richard's exploits in the Holy Land. Joanna was sure he did not give a flying fig for Richard or his triumphs, but Berengaria's pride in her husband prevailed over her initial wariness, and Joanna was sure that she frequently forgot this was a man suspected of the most serious of sins.

Raimond seemed determined to make their journey as pleasurable as possible. In Arles, he'd taken them to see the ancient Roman amphitheater and the Baths of Constantine. From Arles, they'd traveled to St Gilles, the count's birthplace, and he'd entertained them with stories of that celebrated saint, a hermit who'd lived for years in the forest near Nîmes with only a red deer for company. When the king's hunters had pursued the hind, he'd tried to save her and had been wounded himself by a hunter's arrow. The king had been so impressed by the recluse that he'd built a great abbey for him, named in his honor, which was now the first stop for those making the pilgrimage to Santiago de Compostela. Gilles was the patron saint of cripples, Raimond told the women, as well as the saint of lepers, beggars, and Christ's poor. But when he added that St Gilles had never eaten the flesh of animals, consuming only vegetables and fruits, Cardinal Melior stiffened and excused himself. He later told Joanna and Berengaria that the Cathars also refused to eat meat and accused Raimond of deliberately baiting him with the story of this gentle saint. Even to Joanna, who was actively looking for reasons to find fault with Raimond, that seemed to be a stretch, and she and Berengaria agreed that they would try to keep the count and the cardinal apart whenever possible, for they had hundreds of miles still to go.

After leaving St Gilles, they stopped next at Montpelier, before continuing on to the walled town of Béziers. Although its viscount, Roger Trencavel, was not present, they were warmly welcomed by the citizens. Cardinal Melior still insisted that they limit their stay to a single night, for Béziers was said to be a haven for heretics. From Béziers, they rode west to Narbonne. When Eleanor and Berengaria had traveled from Navarre to join Richard in Sicily three years earlier, the Lady Ermengard, the Viscountess of Narbonne, had entertained them lavishly during their stay in her city, and Berengaria had been impressed by

Ermengard, a woman who'd ruled without a man for more than fifty years. She was shocked now to discover that Ermengard had been deposed and forced to flee Narbonne by her own nephew, Pedro de Lara. Neither she nor Joanna was comfortable accepting the hospitality of the usurper viscount, but Pedro was insistent that they pass a few days as his guests. So was Cardinal Melior, for he wanted to meet with the Archbishop of Narbonne, and they soon found themselves settled into the riverside palace that had once been Ermengard's.

⚜

JOANNA AND BERENGARIA HOPED to be able to depart Narbonne by the week's end, but then Mariam suffered a mishap on an excursion with Raimond to visit the suburb across the river known as the Bourg. Joanna had declined to accompany them, then found herself watching from a palace window as they headed toward the old Roman bridge. They were back sooner than she'd expected, the women fluttering about like brightly colored butterflies and Mariam's face white with pain as Raimond carried her into the palace and then up the stairs to the bedchamber she was sharing with Joanna. Mariam insisted they were all making much ado over nothing, but once Joanna shooed the others from the chamber, she saw that the ankle was badly swollen.

She'd fallen, Berengaria explained, whilst they were strolling through the market and a shoat escaped its pen, creating a panic. Mariam had twisted her ankle as she pulled Anna out of harm's way. But Count Raimond had taken charge, Berengaria assured Joanna, stopping the crowd from beating the pig's owner, a country youth overwhelmed by his misfortune, and offering a reward to the one who recaptured the runaway swine. Since they'd not taken their horses in the crowded city streets, he'd carried Mariam back to the palace, much to Anna and Alicia's envy. With a smile, Berengaria predicted that Anna was likely to have a mishap of her own the next time they were out and about in the city, claiming she could not walk so the count must carry her, too.

Joanna had to laugh at that, for she could easily see Anna pulling such a stunt. She thought Mariam's ankle was sprained, a diagnosis confirmed by the viscount's physician. He ordered her to stay off her feet for a few days and Mariam, still protesting she was fine, reluctantly drank the potion of herbs provided by a local apothecary, finally falling into a fitful doze. Joanna had sat with her all afternoon, but once she was sure Mariam was sleeping, she joined the others in the great hall.

Archbishop Berenguer of Narbonne was in a serious discussion with Cardinal Melior and Viscount Pedro, while across the hall, Raimond was joking with the troubadours Raimon de Miraval and Peire Vidal, who'd decided to accompany them as far as Carcassonne. They'd promised to perform that evening, and Joanna was sorry that Mariam would have to miss it. Spotting Berengaria and Beatrix seated in a window-seat, she headed in their direction. Richard's queen was working on a delicate embroidery; she was a fine needlewoman and had tried to improve Joanna's skill during their time in the Holy Land, to no avail. Under Berengaria's patient tutelage, Joanna had been able to recall the *lenga romana* of Aquitaine and Navarre, for she'd lost much of it while living in Sicily. But she still wielded a needle as if it were a weapon, Berengaria gently chided, finally agreeing that needlework would never be one of Joanna's talents.

Looking up with a smile, Berengaria was pleased to hear that Mariam was sleeping. "Count Raimond sent one of his men to the new market for fruit to tempt Mariam's appetite. He truly seems concerned on her behalf." She paused and then said pensively, "I know the cardinal says he is a wicked sinner, but . . . I am no longer so sure of that. He has a good heart, Joanna."

"A veritable saint," Joanna scoffed, for she did not want to listen as Berengaria extolled the count's manifold virtues; it was bad enough that Mariam insisted upon singing that song.

"No, he is not a saint." Joanna was never sure if Berengaria was truly oblivious to sarcasm or simply chose to ignore it. "I am saying I do not believe he is a sinner beyond redemption. I've seen too many examples of his kindness. He never passes a beggar on the street without giving alms. He offered a greeting and a coin to that poor leper we encountered on the road from Béziers, when the rest of us averted our eyes. Whenever he is recognized, people flock to him, and he is always courteous even with the least of them. He says Emperor Heinrich was wrong to hold Richard captive and he sounds sincere. He was willing to take us to the old market yesterday to buy some of the scarlet silks that Narbonne is famous for, and whilst we were there, we saw two louts tossing a kitten up into the air as if it were a camp ball. It was such needless cruelty that I decided to ask the count to put a stop to it. But I did not have to ask, Joanna. He noticed on his own; how many men would have done that? Mayhap if a dog were being beaten, but who pays attention if it is a cat being maltreated? He did, though. When I thanked him, he just laughed and made light of it, but it was a kind act."

"So he is good to beggars and lepers and stray cats," Joanna said, knowing she sounded petty, but unable to help herself. "That hardly gives him a safe conduct into Heaven."

"He is kind to children, too. Did you see what happened when we arrived in Narbonne? Remember how all those boys ran alongside him, shouting, "Count Raimond!" the way they always do for Richard? He laughed and tossed coins to them. But one little lad, younger than the others, had been unable to keep up, and he'd stumbled and fallen. He was sitting there in the street, crying, when the count glanced back and saw his plight. Joanna, he turned his stallion around and, reaching down, he pulled the boy up behind him. You should have seen that child's face. He'll never forget the day he rode with Count Raimond through the city streets to the palace, and the other boys will not, either."

Joanna had seen Raimond go back for the little boy, but hadn't understood why. She was sorry now that she did, for it was so much easier to dislike the man if his good deeds were not being called to her attention daily by Mariam and Berengaria. "Tell me this, then," she said, with such unwonted sharpness that both Berengaria and Beatrix blinked in surprise. "If he truly has such a good heart, how is it that he is so tempted by heresy?"

Berengaria's gaze wavered and color rose in her face. She looked so unhappy at being caught defending a heretic that Joanna felt a stab of remorse. But before she could make amends, her sister-in-law put aside her sewing and rose to her feet. "That is indeed a valid question," she said, "and it is one I shall put to the count. If I have been led astray by his good manners and my wish to believe the best of others, better I know it now."

As they stared at her, she turned and started across the hall toward Raimond. When Beatrix asked if she'd really do that, Joanna jumped to her feet. "I do not know," she admitted, "but I want to hear what he says if she does." And she hastened after Berengaria, with Beatrix just a few steps behind her.

As Berengaria approached, Raimond broke away from the troubadours and moved to meet her, a smile lighting his face. The smile disappeared as soon as she began to speak, though. For a moment, he looked utterly astonished, but he burst out laughing just as Joanna reached them. Those blue-sky eyes caught and held Joanna's green ones, and again she had the uneasy sense that he knew exactly why she was so aloof, occasionally even rude. He turned back then to Berengaria, saying with sudden earnestness, "I've often been asked this and I've always given the same answer. No, I am not a Cathar. Cardinal Melior does not believe me. I hope that you will, my lady."

Berengaria's dark eyes searched his face intently. "I want to believe you. But I do not understand why you are so tolerant of these ungodly, wicked men. Can you explain that to me, my lord count?"

"They are neither ungodly nor wicked, my lady. The Church calls their priests the *perfecti*, but they call themselves the 'good men' or 'good Christians,' for that is how they see themselves. They are greatly respected for the purity of their lives, even by those who are not Believers. They live like the early Church fathers, scorning possessions or material goods, renouncing carnal desires, seeking only to honor God and help their neighbors. They never lie and they forswear all violence, will not even kill animals. I've never met more peaceful souls in all my born days. I do not agree with their beliefs. But I do not see why they should burn for those beliefs. They harm no one but themselves, sacrificing their own chances of salvation, and surely that is punishment enough."

Neither Raimond nor Berengaria had noticed that others had begun to drift over, close enough to hear. They regarded each other somberly, two people yearning to bridge the great gap that loomed between them. "But those beliefs are wrong, my lord count," she said, although not in accusation; she sounded sad. "They are offensive to God. Can you not see that? See the danger they pose?"

"I was told that your lord husband befriended Saracens in the Holy Land, my lady. Yet I am sure you do not doubt the strength of his Christian faith or think he was tempted by their false God. He understood that even infidels can be men of honor. Is that so different from what I do?"

"Yes . . . because the Saracens were infidels. They were not heretics. The threat posed by the Saracens was a military one. They captured the Holy City of Jerusalem, but they could not imperil the souls of the Christians they defeated. Heretics are so much more dangerous, for they are the enemy who attacks from within. Why can you not see that, my lord count?"

"Because he has been infected by their foul heresies, Madame."

Both Raimond and Berengaria whirled at the sound of this cold, hostile voice. Cardinal Melior, the archbishop, and the viscount had joined the growing audience, and the cardinal pushed forward now until he stood beside Berengaria. "Even if he has not openly embraced these heresies, they have seeped into his soul, warping his judgment and eroding his faith."

For the first time, Joanna saw Raimond show anger, his eyes darkening as he stared defiantly at the papal legate. "Have you never wondered, my lord cardinal, why the preaching of the Cathars is so well received in these southern lands? The people see their priests taking hearth mates and concubines, see their bishops engaging in petty squabbles and using excommunication as a political weapon, see a Church as infected by corruption as you claim we are infected by heresy. Mayhap if you worried less about the 'foxes in the vineyard' and more about caring for Christ's poor, the men and women of Toulouse would not find the pure lives of the Cathar priests so surprising or so appealing."

"I do not deny there are village priests who are poorly schooled and ignorant of Latin, or bishops who neglect their spiritual duties by failing to visit their dioceses. But the Holy Church is all that stands between Christians and the triumph of evil. When these Albigensian heretics claim that salvation can be gained only through their teachings, they are committing the worst sort of blasphemy. Even more unforgivable, they are damning forever the souls of the deluded people who have been seduced by their heresy. And for that, I blame men like you, my lord count, for yours could be a voice for righteousness. Instead, you hold your peace whilst these false prophets tempt the unwary and the foolish into apostasy."

Joanna had known that Cardinal Melior was an eloquent speaker; she saw now that he also possessed a lawyer's skills, cleverly defanging Raimond's accusations of Church corruption by admitting there was some truth to them. She could see that Raimond realized he was being outmaneuvered, for he tried to return to his original argument. "My people do not see the Cathar 'good men' as evil, my lord cardinal. They cause no trouble in Toulouse, do not go brawling and drinking in the taverns. They never accost women in the streets or steal or lie, and they turn away wrath with a soft word. They seek only to preach to those who want to listen—"

"And what do they preach, my lord count? They deny the Incarnation and the Resurrection, deny that Jesus is the Son of God, born of the Blessed Virgin. They blaspheme that the Church of Rome is the Devil's church. They teach that men may be saved only by receiving the rite they call the *Consolamentum*, and they even allow women to give this rite."

The cardinal paused dramatically to allow his audience time to consider the awful wickedness of such beliefs. "I do not doubt that the *perfecti* are as soft-spoken and amiable as you claim. That is how the Devil seeks to deceive the faithful. Scriptures warn, *Beware of false prophets, which come to you in sheep's clothing, but inwardly they are ravening wolves.* You mock Holy Church's concern with foxes, whilst you let wolves loose to prey upon the innocent. How do you defend that?"

"I do not share the Cathar beliefs, my lord cardinal. But I do not see their beliefs as truly dangerous to the Church. The Cathar priests are few in number and they do not preach rebellion. By persecuting them, you give them greater importance than they'd otherwise have. Would it not be better for the Church to combat such heresies by putting its own House in order? If there were no lecherous priests or corrupt bishops, the preaching of the Cathars would fall upon deaf ears."

Cardinal Melior was momentarily rendered speechless by Raimond's argument, so alien was it to the teachings of his Church. He regarded the younger man in genuine bafflement, for who but a madman could believe that heresy ought to be tolerated? "Scriptures speak quite clearly, leaving no room for misunderstanding, telling us that *By sword and famine shall those false prophets be consumed.* What you suggest, my lord count, is not only blasphemous, but it would lead to ruination and damnation. A land where Christians must live side by side with heretics and infidels would be truly accursed."

Joanna had not known she meant to speak up until she heard the words coming out of her mouth. "There is such a land, my lord cardinal, and it is blessed by God, not accursed." Suddenly the focal point of all eyes, she took a deep breath before continuing. "In the kingdom of Sicily, the Christians who follow the Holy Father in Rome and those who follow the Patriarch in Constantinople live with Saracens and Jews, and whilst there are tensions and misunderstandings between them at times, there is rarely bloodshed. This is because they do live in such close proximity, enabling them to realize that one can be a good man even if he worships the wrong God."

The cardinal seemed stunned to hear such words coming from a Christian queen. Berengaria grasped Joanna's arm protectively, looking distressed. After a moment, the papal legate collected himself, deciding to ignore the Queen of Sicily's bizarre outburst as an aberration; all knew women were prone to illogical behavior, even highborn ones. Instead, he turned his attention back to the man he saw as a real threat, for even if Raimond de St Gilles was not yet a heretic, he was dangerously susceptible to their blasphemous teachings, and one day he would rule all of Toulouse. Shaking his head as if more in sorrow than anger, he reminded Raimond that even the most devout Christian must remain vigilant, for he that bade a false prophet "Godspeed" was a partaker of the heretic's evil deeds.

Much to his irritation, Raimond did not appear to be listening. He was watching Joanna, and he was smiling.

❧

ONCE MARIAM WAS ABLE to travel, they departed Narbonne for Carcassonne. Cardinal Melior was very unhappy about stopping there, for the Trencavel viscount was even more closely associated with the Cathars than Count Raimond and had been excommunicated twice, once for imprisoning the Bishop of Albi and once for failing to root out heresy in his lands. Viscount Roger's health had been deteriorating in recent years and although he rose from his sickbed to greet his illustrious guests, he soon retreated back to his bedchamber, leaving it to his wife, Adelais, and his eight-year-old son, Raimond-Roger, to entertain them. Adelais was Raimond's elder sister, a stunning, statuesque woman in her late thirties, and, like him, a patron of troubadours. Her son, a handsome, precocious child, obviously enjoyed playing host, and even the papal legate found himself smiling at the sight of the boy in his father's seat at the high table, proudly presiding over the welcoming feast.

Carcassonne was much smaller than Narbonne, but with a formidable castle and equally formidable stone walls encircling the town. Its markets could not compare with those of Narbonne, but the women still enjoyed strolling its narrow streets, taking in the sights and marveling at the surprising number of cats sauntering about—sleek, well-fed creatures that, unlike felines elsewhere, seemed to be doted upon as pets, not just as mousers. They were having a pleasant outing until they noticed an elderly man garbed in black surrounded by an admiring crowd. He seemed to be blessing them, and the women exchanged curious glances. But when Anna and Alicia would have approached, they were stopped by Raimond, who said wryly, "The cardinal would have an apoplectic fit if I let you greet one of the Cathars' 'good men.'"

The girls came to an abrupt halt, staring in fearful fascination at the first heretic they'd ever seen; it was something of a letdown, for the Cathar priest looked more like a benevolent grandfather than a great enemy of the Church. They giggled when Raimond assured them that his cloven hooves were hidden by his long robe, but even Anna kept her distance. Berengaria asked, horrified, if all of those people were heretics, and was relieved when Raimond said that some of them were Believers, but others were simply showing respect to a man well regarded in the community. Her relief soon dissipated, though, as she realized how easily good Christians could be led astray, and she asked Raimond to escort them to a church so she could pray for their imperiled souls.

"Will you be praying for my soul, too, my lady?" he teased, but his smile vanished when she said she was already praying to the Almighty on his behalf, for she believed him to be a good man, albeit a very misguided one. Joanna, close enough to have caught this exchange, noted with amusement that for once, Raimond seemed at a loss for words. But he did as Berengaria requested and took them to the beautiful cathedral of St Nazaire, where they were welcomed by the bishop himself and Berengaria lit candles for her husband in Germany, her family in Navarre, Count Raimond, and those in danger of being seduced by the Cathar heresies.

THAT NIGHT THE TROUBADOURS were to perform, but the castle was not yet astir with preparations for the evening's entertainment. Joanna assumed the Lady Adelais was abovestairs with her ailing husband, and Raimond was not in the hall, either. Cardinal Melior was dictating a letter to the archdeacon, who also served as his scribe. Anna and Alicia were listening raptly as Mariam read aloud the story of the tragic lovers Tristan and Iseult. Sir Stephen de Turnham and the knights of Joanna and Berengaria's household were passing the time with a dice game and Berengaria was playing chess with Raimond-Roger. He'd won the first game, much to his delight; it was obvious to Joanna that her sister-in-law was strongly drawn to Raimond's young nephew, and as she watched them, she found herself thinking that Berengaria would be a good mother. She quickly added God willing, for they were all in His hands, and because the thought of children too often made her sad, she rose and left the hall, her dogs at her heels.

Summer lingered longer in these southern climes and the September sun was still warm on her face, the garden ablaze with fragrant, flame-colored blooms, the harvest sky above her head a brilliant shade of blue, even bluer than the eyes of Toulouse's troublesome count. Once she found a bench, her dogs sprawled happily in the grassy mead, and she wished she could live in the moment as they did. If only she could keep her fears at bay long enough to enjoy the peace of Adelais's garden without thinking of her brother and what horrors awaited him if he fell into the hands of the French king.

Unlike Eleanor and Berengaria, Joanna had met Philippe, three years ago in Sicily. He'd seemed smitten, had paid her so much attention that some thought he might seek to make her his queen. She'd known better; Philippe hated

Richard too much to want to wed his sister. Nor would Richard ever have agreed to the match. She smiled, remembering how relieved Richard had been when she assured him that she had no wish to wed the French king. No crown in Christendom could have compensated for having to share a bed with Philippe.

Her dogs drew her back to the present then, running to welcome a man approaching the garden gate. She sat up straight on the bench, tensing as she watched Raimond de St Gilles enter and walk toward her. "May I?" he asked, waiting until she nodded before seating himself beside her on the bench. Ahmer and Star at once lay at his feet and she wondered how he'd managed to win them over, too. He was holding a single scarlet peony, which he now presented to her with a playful flourish. "I have been hoping for days to find you alone, Lady Joanna. I wanted to thank you."

"You've no need to thank me, my lord count."

"I disagree, my lady," he said, with a smile. "Just between us, Archbishop Berenguer and Viscount Pedro have not shown much enthusiasm for ridding Narbonne of the Cathars. Yet neither one spoke up when I found myself backed against the cliff's edge. You were the only one to throw me a rope."

Joanna wasn't sure how to respond to that, so she remained silent. He reached down to scratch Ahmer's chest and then surprised her by saying, "I hope your lord brother realizes that he has a pearl beyond price in his wife. Did you know she apologized for drawing the cardinal's wrath down upon me? I assured her that he was already convinced I am halfway to Hell."

"And are you? Halfway to Hell?"

"To hear him tell it, I am doomed and damned," he said cheerfully. "I do not share his zeal for burning heretics at the stake. Jews have witnessed a few of my charters, which he sees as proof that I am unduly familiar with them. I much prefer the company of troubadours to clerics. I am more interested in repeating carnal sins than in repenting of them. And I do not believe the Almighty could have created a world of such surpassing beauty without wanting us to glory in it and in all of its earthly pleasures."

"You'd have flourished in Sicily, Count Raimond."

"Like the green bay tree?" he asked with a grin, showing her that, for a man suspected of heretical tendencies, he was familiar with Scriptures.

She shook her head, for she no longer believed that he was one of the wicked. She was not comfortable having him so close—close enough to see that he had lashes a woman might envy and a razor's nick on his chin—but curiosity won out over caution, and she said, "Tell me about the Cathars."

"Well, to begin with, that is not a name they use. They call themselves Christians, for they believe that theirs is the true faith and the Church of Rome has fallen into the Devil's clutches. I said they were gentle souls who rejected violence, but I never said they were diplomatic or tactful, and their names for the Roman Church include the Great Beast, the Whore of Babylon, the Church of Wolves, and my own favorite, the Harlot of the Apocalypse."

Joanna winced at that. She'd heard the smile in his voice, but his humor would have been lost on the papal legate. She was beginning to realize that Raimond enjoyed poking a stick into hives, just as her brothers had always liked to do. "But what do they believe?"

"They believe that the material world is the work of the Devil and must be rejected. They think that Jesus was an angel, not the son of God, and it was but an illusion that he came before men in mortal form. That being so, he could not die, nor could he rise up again. The Virgin Mary is an angel, too, not a real woman. They worship our God, but whilst He is good, they say He is not omnipotent and the struggle with the Devil is unceasing. They think that human souls are those of fallen angels. They believe that we endure our Hell here on earth, and when I see the suffering we inflict upon one another, I am not always sure they are wrong about that."

"Do they believe in Heaven?"

"Indeed, but only the 'good Christians' can get there. They believe in the transmigration of souls. A man who led a just life will be reincarnated into a body better suited for spiritual development. Whereas a man who's done evil will regress, and may even be reborn as an animal. Those who accept this creed call themselves Believers, but few ask for the *Consolamentum* until they think death is near, for it is not easy to live like a 'good Christian.' Once a man or woman becomes one of their priests, they must reject all that they once held dear, even their families, for the Cathars see such earthly attachments as evil, entangling people in the life of the flesh, which will deny them salvation. They are forgiving of sinners, though, yet another way in which they differ from our Church."

Joanna was glad that he spoke of "our Church," for it was becoming very important to her that Raimond de St Gilles did not embrace a false faith that would put his immortal soul at risk. "I've heard the cardinal say the Cathars are wanton and dissolute, scorning marriage and encouraging people to commit the most shameful of carnal sins. Is that true—" She got no further, for Raimond had begun to laugh.

"I've always found it interesting that men who take holy vows of chastity are often the ones to become utterly obsessed with the carnal sins of others. I hate to deny them the pleasure they seem to take in imagining Cathar orgies and depraved revelries, but nothing could be further from the truth. The Cathar priests abhor sins of the flesh even more than our priests do. For them, carnal intercourse is the greatest sin as it can lead to procreation, dragging another heavenly soul down into the horrors of the material world."

Raimond paused to pet one of the dogs when she nudged his leg. "Such a pity that the fear of heresy seems to turn even the most rational of men into raving lunatics. If Cardinal Melior would only consider the evidence dispassionately, he'd realize that I could not possibly be a Cathar, for that would mean abjuring all sins of the flesh."

Joanna thought his smile was more mischievous than salacious and she could not keep from smiling, too, when he said, with a mock sigh, "After all, it is no secret that I do like women."

"So I've heard," she said, very dryly.

"I'm sure you have," he agreed, just as dryly. "But what you may not know is that I differ from most men in that I enjoy the company of women in and out of bed."

"You do not think most men do?"

"Sadly, no. Too many of them show far more interest in the female body than the female brain. They never find out that St Peter was wrong when he called women the weaker vessel. The women I've known have more common sense than most men and they are more resilient, too, for they've had to learn to bend, rather than break. And they can be delightfully unpredictable . . . as a beautiful queen proved to be on a recent evening in Narbonne."

Joanna's breath quickened as their eyes met. But she knew that it was far too dangerous to flirt with this man, for she was acutely aware of his physical presence, wanting to stroke his wind-tousled black hair, to feel his arm slide around her waist, to taste his mouth on hers. She stiffened her spine and her resolve. Before she could say she wished to return to the great hall, though, he drew back, almost imperceptibly, and said casually, "Tell me about Sicily, Lady Joanna."

She was both relieved and unsettled that he seemed able to read her moods so easily. But because she did not really want to go, she found herself doing as he asked. As she spoke, memories came flooding back and she took pleasure in reliving them, in telling him of that beautiful jewel in a turquoise sea, a sun-kissed kingdom prosperous and peaceful during the years of her husband's reign, not yet threatened by the looming shadow of the German emperor. She'd already noticed that Raimond was an unusually attentive listener. As he listened to her now, his eyes never left her face, so intent upon what she was saying that it was as if the world had contracted, shrinking until there was only this lush, flowering garden and a man and woman seated on a narrow stone bench in the shade of a cherry tree.

But if her body and her heart seemed in collusion to tempt her into an unforgivable sin, her brain still functioned clearly and began to raise the drawbridge and lower the portcullis. "It grows late," she heard herself say, pointing toward a sky glowing with the glorious crimson and gold of a southern sunset. "I think we ought to go back."

"Of course," he agreed, rising at once to his feet. But when he offered her his arm, she realized that escape would not be so easy. After the conversation they'd just shared, how could she revert back to her defensive aloofness? Rising, too, she brushed her skirts, and then reluctantly rested her hand lightly on his arm, wondering how she'd be able to keep him at a distance in the weeks and miles that lay between Carcassonne and Poitiers.

CHAPTER EIGHTEEN

❧

At Cardinal Melior's urgings, they soon departed Carcassonne and now headed north, stopping at the abbey of St Papoul, and then on to Avignet, before the famous rose-colored walls of Toulouse appeared on the horizon. Joanna was excited to visit the city that loomed so large in her family's history. She'd seen it as a child, on her bridal journey to Sicily, but she remembered little of that stressful odyssey. She did not even remember Raimond, though he swore he'd met her at St Gilles, where she'd bade a tearful farewell to Richard and had been turned over to the Sicilian envoys. He'd been impressed by her bravery, he confided, an eleven-year-old girl leaving all that was familiar to wed a stranger in a distant land. He laughed when she apologized for having no recollection of their meeting, joking that there was nothing memorable about his twenty-year-old self, but she thought it ironic nonetheless, for now she knew she'd never forget him.

They were to stay in the great citadel known as the Castle Narbonnais, just outside the town walls, and Raimond had promised to take them on a personal tour of the city he obviously loved, for he told them proudly that Toulouse had eleven hospitals and six lazar houses, feigning surprise when they politely declined a visit to the leper hospices. He'd assured Joanna and Berengaria that his father would not be present, and so it was a shock to them all when they saw the red banner flying from the castle battlements, emblazoned with the familiar gold cross of the Count of Toulouse. The count was in the inner bailey to welcome them, smiling complacently. If he'd been expecting to surprise them into civility, he was to be disappointed. Cardinal Melior and his retinue politely did their best to ease the awkwardness, but the queens and his son measured their words like misers hoarding coins. Dinner was a lavish one, with numerous courses, fine wines, and a dramatic subtlety shaped like a dragon. It was also an unmitigated disaster, for Joanna, Berengaria, their ladies, and their household knights were silently seething, and Raimond was making no attempt to hide his own anger. He apologized profusely to the women once the meal was over, swearing his father had promised to stay away, and assuring them that they would leave the city on the morrow.

Joanna had gone to bid Berengaria a good night and was surprised to find only Mariam when she returned to her own bedchamber. "I told the others to wait," Mariam explained, "for I wanted to talk to you in private." Helping Joanna to remove her veil and wimple, she unpinned the other woman's bright hair and began to brush it out, saying one of Sir Stephen's knights had told her he'd heard shouting from the count's bedchamber and thought one of the voices was Raimond's. "He was truly distressed about this, Joanna. He'd not have betrayed you and Berengaria this way."

"I know that, Mariam, and so does Berengaria." Joanna picked up a mirror to study the image reflected in the polished metal. She was in her twenty-eighth year, and she found herself suddenly thinking how fleeting time and beauty were, as ephemeral as memories. "What did you wish to talk about?"

"I wanted to tell you that whilst it is not easy to find privacy, it can be done. With my help, I am sure we can arrange for you and the count to be alone without anyone knowing."

The mirror clattered into the floor rushes as Joanna swung around to face the other woman. "What are you talking about?"

"Joanna, the man is besotted with you and it is obvious to me that you are just as bedazzled by him. That is so rare. Do not let—"

"I am not 'bedazzled' by him," Joanna said sharply, but ruined the impact of her indignant denial by then asking, "Why do you think he is 'besotted'?"

"Because I have eyes to see, dearest. The two of you have been playing this game for weeks, each watching the other when you think no one else will notice. And he never misses an opportunity to ask me questions about you. What color is your hair? Are you close to Richard? Were you happy with William? Not that I answer them, of course, but he keeps on asking. I understand there can be no future for you since his father is such a bitter enemy of your House. But that does not mean you cannot snatch a few precious memories for yourself. As long as you are very discreet, and I can help—"

Joanna was truly shocked. "Have you lost your mind, Mariam? How could you think I'd commit so grave a sin?"

"Do you see Morgan and me as doomed sinners? Granted, you're a queen, but I do not think God will judge you too harshly for seeking a little happiness for yourself. You are free, after all, a widow, a woman grown, and as long as you take care—"

"No queen is ever free, Mariam, and Raimond most certainly is not! I think God would judge me very harshly indeed if I were to take a married man as my lover."

"He is married? He has never said a word to me about a wife!"

"Trust me, he has one."

Mariam looked stricken. "Oh, Joanna, I am so sorry!"

Joanna was no longer angry, remembering that Mariam had not been present when Sancha had related Raimond's marital history. Smiling, she said, "Are you sorry that he is married? Or sorry that you tried to tempt me into a mortal sin?"

"Both!" Touched to see tears in Mariam's eyes, Joanna embraced her, and if she had tears in her eyes, too, Mariam tactfully pretended not to notice.

AFTER A HASTY DEPARTURE from Toulouse, they pushed on to Montauban, where they were the guests at the local Benedictine abbey. From Montauban, they rode to Agen, where they were welcomed by its bishop, Bertrande de Beceyrus, who'd been at the deathbed of Joanna's brother Hal in Martel ten years earlier. After listening to his detailed account of Hal's last hours, Joanna had wept, tears of relief. Her father had written to assure her that Hal had made his peace with God, but it meant more to hear it from one who'd been an eyewitness. From Agen, they made a shorter journey to Marmande la Royale, and both Joanna and Berengaria were delighted to discover that this small town owed its existence to Richard, who'd granted a charter while Duke of Aquitaine and Count of Poitou. Their next stop was the Benedictine priory at La Reole, where they were pleased to find another connection to Richard, who was responsible for its stone walls. La Reole had also been the site of a private meeting between Richard and agents of the Navarrese king to discuss marriage with Sancho's daughter. Berengaria found it comforting to be in the same place where he'd bargained for her hand, and confided that he did not seem so far away whilst they were at La Reole. Raimond indulged her by prolonging their stay for a few days before they continued on toward the crown jewel of Aquitaine, the splendid port city of Bordeaux.

⁂

THEY WERE GIVEN an enthusiastic welcome into Bordeaux, the citizens turning out in large numbers to cheer their duke's wife and sister. The Archbishop Hélie de Malemort, a member of a prominent Limousin family, personally escorted them to the Ombrière, the riverside palace of the Duke of Aquitaine since the eleventh century. And although they were still a hundred and fifty miles from Poitiers, as she rode through the streets of Bordeaux toward the castle where her mother had been born, Joanna felt as if she'd finally come home.

⁂

IT HAD BEEN a whirlwind week of festivities and sightseeing for the two queens and their entourage. The local nobility and clerics arrived to pay their respects, there had been bountiful feasts in their honor, and Joanna had been able to hear Mass in St André, the great cathedral where her mother had wed the French king more than fifty years ago. On this Saturday eve, most of the palace guests had retired to their own chambers, but Joanna felt restless and she and Mariam had gone out into the gardens. They were far more elaborate than Adelais's small garden at Carcassonne, putting the women in mind of the magnificent gardens of Palermo, with raised flower beds, fruit trees, pebble-strewn paths, trellised arbors, and elegant fountains that cascaded water into deep marble basins. It was so peaceful that they lingered even as twilight's lavender haze darkened and stars began to glimmer in the heavens high above their heads. But that peace was not to last, for they soon heard footsteps on the path, and as her dogs ran to investigate, Joanna knew the identity of the intruder even before Raimond de St Gilles came into view.

In the three weeks since they'd left Carcassonne, Joanna had allowed herself to enjoy the count's company, but she had taken great care to make sure they were never alone, and she sensed his growing frustration. That was why she'd asked Mariam to accompany her tonight, for a garden conversation in full sunlight did not offend propriety, whereas one lit by starlight and camouflaged by swirling shadows could compromise her honor and break her heart.

He greeted them both with courtesy not even the cardinal could have faulted, but then he took them by surprise by throwing down a direct challenge. "I have become quite fond of you, Lady Mariam, and I think your Welsh knight is a very lucky man. But what I have to say is not for your ears. I'd be eternally grateful if you were to take a tour of the gardens. Any chance of that happening?"

Mariam looked to Joanna for guidance, saw her hesitation, and leaned over to whisper, "If you want to talk with him, the dogs and I can stand guard to make sure no one else will see the two of you together. If you do not, nothing will pry me from your side."

Joanna would have sworn that she'd have walked barefoot in sackcloth and ashes before she'd have met privately with Raimond in these seductive surroundings. So she was startled to hear herself say softly, "Take the dogs for a walk. But do not go far."

Mariam nodded, squeezed her hand encouragingly, and then gave Raimond a warning look that conveyed her message without need of words. He acknowledged it with a nod of his own and for several moments, there was no sound but the splashing of the fountain and the crunch of Mariam's receding footsteps on the pebbled path.

"Shall we find a place to sit?" He glanced toward a trellised arbor, raising his hands when Joanna frowned, a gesture she took as a promise that he'd not take advantage of the semiseclusion. She was not sure if she could trust him to keep that promise, for how well did she really know him? But then, could she trust herself? Deciding that she preferred this conversation to be conducted by the light of a full moon, she shook her head, pointing toward the edge of the fountain. He did not argue and showed his good manners by making sure the marble was clean and dry before allowing her to sit. Once they were settled, she realized that the moonlight was a double-edged sword; it enabled her to read his face, but he could read hers, too, and her own emotions were in such turmoil that she did not welcome his scrutiny.

"I am not sure if Lady Mariam did me a favor," he said, "for I am probably about to make an utter fool of myself." As he turned toward her, she caught the glimmer of a smile. "I asked myself what I'd come to regret more—saying nothing or playing the fool? I have a lot of practice doing the latter, so I decided that was a regret I could more easily live with."

Joanna had always been charmed by self-deprecating humor and Raimond's smile was so bewitching by moonlight that she realized there were two fools in this garden. She ought never to have agreed to this. Mariam's offer to arrange a tryst had forced her to admit how drawn she was to this man, and she'd realized how fortunate she was that he was married. If not for his wife, she might have yielded to temptation, and she did not believe that a queen had that freedom. What if their liaison had become known? Such a scandal would damage her prospects for remarriage and hurt Richard's chances of making a needed alliance with a foreign prince. And what if she'd gotten with child? She could not have raised the child as her own, yet how could she have borne to give her baby up? No, Beatrice Trencavel was a blessing in disguise. Reminding herself of that now, she tensed, preparing to make an embarrassing retreat from the gardens, seeing that as the lesser of evils.

Raimond did not give her the chance. "I think that we ought at least to acknowledge it," he said, "for it is rather rare—like being struck by lightning and living to tell the tale. I'm not sure when the bolt hit you. For me, it was in the great hall at Narbonne. It was not as if I were blind to your charms until then. But you'd made it clear I was to keep my distance and so I vowed to be on my good behavior. And then you came to my defense like an avenging angel, telling the cardinal that Sicily was blessed, not accursed, and I knew my heart was yours for the taking—along with any other body parts you might want to claim."

His tone was light, but with undertones that sent a shiver up Joanna's spine. Deciding that her best defense was to act as if he were merely flirting, she said coolly, "I believe your heart is already spoken for, my lord count. And I must warn you that I am not susceptible to the 'My wife does not understand me' school of seduction." She could see that her mockery had stung and, perversely, she now found herself regretting her success in rebuffing him. But she dared not let him see how vulnerable she really was to his blandishments.

"Actually, my wife understood me all too well," he said, with a coolness to match her own. "Women usually read men with insulting ease. You seem to be the exception to that rule, Lady Joanna, for you have misread me, for certes."

"Have I?" she said, striving for nonchalance. "I see a man who by his own admission likes women, a man of undeniable charm, but a man with a wife. We may be entitled to our own beliefs, my lord count, but not our own facts, and those facts are yours, whether you like it or not."

"Actually, they are not. You see, I no longer have a wife. I ended our marriage this past January."

Joanna stared at him in shock. Whatever she might have expected him to say, it was not that, never that. Her initial response was pure panic, for her defenses had just taken a mortal hit. "And how did you perform this feat of magic?" she said, with as much sarcasm as she could muster. "How does one make a wife disappear?"

"I did not turn her out to beg her bread by the roadside," he snapped. "She entered a . . . convent."

He'd hesitated almost imperceptibly, and she seized upon that as a shield. "How convenient," she said witheringly. "Whatever did men do with unwanted wives before convents? My mother's grandfather packed two of his off to Fontevrault Abbey and my father would have sent her there, too, if he'd had his way." Remembering then that Raimond and Beatrice had a child, Joanna felt a surge of indignation that was no longer feigned. "What a wonderful example you are setting for your daughter, my lord, teaching her at an early age that women are as easily replaced as horses or hunting dogs!"

By now they were both on their feet, glaring at each other in the silvery moonlight. "Are you always so quick to pass judgment?" he asked challengingly. "But then your family is not known for their sense of fair play, are they?"

Joanna was grateful for the reminder that he was an enemy of her House. "We are done here," she said and started to stalk away.

"Joanna!" She hesitated before turning reluctantly to face him. He was obviously still angry, but he showed now that his anger had not affected his eerie ability to see into her soul. "Do you know what I think? It is not outrage that is chasing you from this garden. It is fear. You saw my wife as a barricade, one that safely kept us apart. Now that the barricade is gone, you do not have the courage to admit you want me as much as I want you. I could respect you for deciding the risk was not worth it. But not for lying to me and to yourself."

"This may come as an unpleasant surprise, Count Raimond, but not every woman finds you as irresistible as you seem to think you are. I assumed that you were worldly enough to take our flirtation for what it was, an amusing way to pass the time on a tedious journey. If you have read more into it, that is your problem, not mine."

Without waiting for his response, she spun around and strode off, head high, heart beating so loudly she feared he might hear it. She was thankful to see Mariam hurrying toward her, drawn by their raised voices. When Raimond called after her, "I do not believe you," she flinched but did not look back.

FROM BORDEAUX, they headed north, accepting the hospitality of Geoffrey Rudel, the Lord of Blaye, who had a small castle on the right bank of the Gironde Estuary. It was claimed that the hero of the Chanson de Roland, a nephew of Charlemagne, was buried in the Basilique St-Roman, but even Roland was overshadowed by Geoffrey's father, the celebrated troubadour Jaufre Rudel. Jaufre had fallen in love with the Countess of Tripoli, a woman he'd never seen. Taking the cross on her behalf, he'd accompanied the French king and Eleanor to the Holy Land on their ill-fated crusade. According to legend, he'd taken ill and had been carried ashore at Tripoli. Being told of his devotion, the countess visited him in his tent and he'd died in her arms.

Joanna was familiar with this romantic legend and under other circumstances she might have enjoyed staying in the love-struck troubadour's castle. As it was, her stay at Blaye was not a pleasant one. Raimon de Miraval and Peire Vidal had left them at Carcassonne, and when the women expressed disappointment that they could not hear Jaufre's famous songs about his beloved countess, Raimond offered to perform one of them himself. His rendition of "During May, When the Days Are Long" was enthusiastically received. Only Joanna, applauding politely, took no pleasure in it. It seemed to her that Raimond was looking directly at her when he sang of Jaufre's "faraway love" and lamented, "I do not know whenever I shall see her, so far away our countries are." When he concluded, "Never shall I enjoy love, unless I enjoy this faraway love," some of the women blinked back tears, but Joanna yearned to pitch her wine cup at Raimond's dark head, knowing full well that he was laughing at her.

She was all the more furious with him because he was right. She *was* afraid to confront her feelings for him. Now that she knew she'd not be committing adultery, she feared that he might tempt her into a less serious sin, but one that she knew she'd regret afterward. For a queen, too much was at stake. So she did her best to keep her indignation burning at full flame, reminding herself repeatedly that he'd treated his wife rather shabbily, most likely putting her aside because she'd failed to give him a male heir, after just one daughter in fifteen years of marriage.

She also did her best to limit their interactions, although that meant spending more time with Cardinal Melior and his clerics. Raimond took note of her new strategy, looking at her with mock sympathy when he saw her choosing to sit beside the cardinal at meals or ride beside him on the road. The papal legate seemed pleased that she was once more treating Raimond coldly and regaled her with stories of the impiety that hung over Toulouse like a storm cloud. There was not even a separate quarter for the Jews, he said; they dwelt wherever they pleased! The people of these benighted southern lands chased after pleasure the way a dog pursued rabbits, and since they allowed their women so much freedom, they were no better than they ought to be. Count Raimond encouraged their frivolous pursuits and wanton behavior and he probably tried to ensnare them in Cathar nets, too.

Joanna listened dutifully to these lectures, knowing she'd brought them upon herself by her defense of Sicilian tolerance. She did not dare to tell the cardinal that, like Raimond, she believed the Almighty would not have created a world of such surpassing beauty without wanting them to glory in it and in all of its earthly pleasures.

IT WAS MID-OCTOBER and the nights were noticeably cooler. From Blaye, they spent a night in a castle at Mirambeau, and then stopped at the Abbaye aux Dames de Saintes. Eleanor had been a generous patron of the convent in the years before and after her captivity, so the nuns welcomed this opportunity to receive her daughter and her son's queen. Saintes had once been a Roman town, and they marveled at the remarkable Arch of Germanicus, towering above an ancient Roman bridge, still in use so many centuries after the empire's fall. But few were curious enough to visit the ruins of a Roman amphitheater, for their enthusiasm for sightseeing had waned and their only interest now was in reaching Poitiers, eighty-five miles to the north.

Their next stop was at Niort, whose castle had been begun by Joanna's father and completed by Richard. They'd just settled in when a stir was created by the arrival of Joanna's cousin, André de Chauvigny. They'd not seen him since their departure from Acre a year ago and they had an emotional reunion. André had a surprise for them. They'd dispatched letters to Germany before they left Rome, letting Richard know of their plans, instructing the courier to meet them at Poitiers, and he'd arrived that past week, André said, bearing letters from Richard; he even had one for Mariam from Morgan. These were the first letters that Richard's wife or sister had received from him, and they snatched them up eagerly. Berengaria took hers up to the privacy of her bedchamber, while Joanna retreated with hers to a window-seat in the great hall.

After she'd read it, she leaned back in the seat, closing her eyes, not opening them until she sensed she was no longer alone. When she realized she was now sharing the window-seat with Raimond, she scowled. Before she could rise, though, he said, "Your news is not good?"

Because he seemed genuinely concerned, she did not flounce away, although she responded with a wary "Why do you say that?"

He reached out, touching her cheek with his finger, as lightly as a feather. "Because of this," he said, and only then did she realize a few tears had seeped through her lashes. "I can only imagine how difficult these past months have been for your brother," he said, sounding quite serious for once. "You probably have a better idea than most do, for you, too, were held against your will."

Joanna nodded somberly. "It is nothing he wrote," she said. "It is rather what he did not write. . . ." She said no more, for she would have felt disloyal to Richard had she discussed her fears with anyone else, and certainly not with Raimond, for she could not ever forget that he was the Count of Toulouse's son. He nodded, too, and seemed content to sit beside her in a companionable silence. Joanna found his presence surprisingly comforting, and she began to wonder if there was a way to apologize for her rudeness without encouraging him to make overtures again. She would never know if she'd have proffered an olive branch, for it was then that she saw André coming toward them.

He and Raimond exchanged cool greetings and the latter soon excused himself. "I hope he gave you no cause for complaint on this journey," André said, watching Raimond depart with obvious suspicion. "I confess that I was not pleased when I heard that he'd be your escort. I considered riding south to meet you, but you know what they say—mice start raiding the pantry as soon as the cat is away—and that rat in Limoges is just biding his time ere he stirs up strife again."

Joanna smiled, knowing he was referring to the Viscount of Limoges, one of Richard's more untrustworthy vassals, and assured him that Raimond de St Gilles had been both courtly and kind. André looked skeptical, but he had more important matters on his mind than the Count of Toulouse's spawn. "Cousin Joanna, your courier brought me a letter from Richard, too. He wrote that he was being well treated now and expected he'd soon be free. But after I reread it, I realized he'd actually said very little. I'd almost think he'd been writing under duress, but your man insisted that this was not so. I was wondering if he was any more forthcoming in your letter?"

Joanna shook her head slowly, and they regarded each other in a troubled silence. It never occurred to either of them to question Berengaria about her letter, for they both knew that if Richard was so guarded with his sister and closest friend, he'd have been even more reticent with the young woman who was his wife but never his confidante.

❧

ANDRÉ RATHER POINTEDLY SUGGESTED that Count Raimond might want to return to Toulouse now that he was there to escort the women on to Poitiers, a suggestion quickly supported by Cardinal Melior. Raimond smiled blandly, saying that he was sure the ladies would be safe with Lord André, but he felt honor-bound to stay with them until the end of their journey. They all departed Niort the next morning, spending the night at the castle of the de Lusignans, who'd long been a burr under the Angevin saddle. Hugh de Lusignan had fought with Richard in the Holy Land, though, and so he was willing to play a role unfamiliar to the de Lusignans, that of a dutiful vassal. The following afternoon, the feast day of St Luke the Evangelist, they crossed the St Cyprien Bridge and rode into a wild welcome in Eleanor's capital, the city she so loved.

❧

JOANNA WAS ACCUSTOMED to taking command, but she was careful to defer to Berengaria now that they were in Richard's realm, and so it was Berengaria who planned an elaborate dinner to thank Cardinal Melior and Count Raimond. She'd have made it a belated birthday celebration for Joanna, too, who'd turned twenty-eight in Blaye, had Joanna not convinced her to keep that a secret for a while longer. The next day, the cardinal departed for the French court; he'd been entrusted with a diplomatic warning for Philippe, although neither the papal legate nor the Pope expected the French king to heed it. Joanna was very grateful to the cardinal for providing them with the Church's protection; she was still glad to see him go.

Later that afternoon, André asked Joanna to accompany him out into the gardens, acting mysterious enough to awaken her curiosity. A boy was pacing nervously around a towering yew tree and as soon as she saw him, Joanna understood. He was a sturdy youngster, tall for his age—which she knew to be twelve—with curly, red-gold hair and blue-grey eyes. Joanna's throat tightened, for this handsome lad was the veritable image of his father. He watched uncertainly as she approached, and then made a credible attempt at a bow, say-ing "My lady" in a gruff, youthful voice that was just starting to change.

"I prefer 'Aunt Joanna,'" she said and drew Richard's son into a warm embrace that seemed to fluster and please him in equal measure. Leading him toward a bench, she gestured for him to sit beside her. "I am delighted to meet you at last, Philip. Your father has often spoken of you."

"He has?" Philip flashed a surprised smile and she nodded emphatically, even though that was not so; Richard was notoriously closemouthed about his private life. But she knew that was what this bewildered boy needed to hear. She was sure he adored his famous father, even if he did not know Richard very well, and these past months must have been very difficult for him. She gave André a fond smile, thankful that he'd thought to take the youngster into his household, and then set about winning her nephew's confidence, which did not prove challeng-ing, so hungry was he for a family connection; André was the only one of his kin whom he'd met until now.

André joined them and they enjoyed a much-needed respite from their cur-rent worries, taking turns telling Philip amusing stories about Richard's own boyhood and his time in the Holy Land. When Philip jumped abruptly to his feet in obvious alarm, they were taken aback, until they followed his gaze and saw Berengaria and her ladies just entering the gardens.

She came to a sudden halt, staring at Philip, for his appearance revealed his identity without a word being said. André started to rise; he'd become very pro-tective of the boy and did not want to see him diminished or made to feel shame for a sin that was not his. Joanna knew her sister-in-law better than he did, and she patted his hand reassuringly, watching serenely as Berengaria approached Richard's son.

"You are Philip." It was not a question, but he nodded, looking both defiant and dismayed. He was already as tall as she was, so Berengaria had to rise up on her toes to kiss him on the cheek. "I am so happy to meet you," she said, and, as Joanna watched her nephew flush with astonishment, delight, and relief, she smiled, thinking that Raimond had been right. Richard had a pearl beyond price in his Spanish bride.

❧

BERENGARIA HAD EXPRESSED her gratitude for all Raimond had done and assured him earnestly that she would continue to pray for him. Next it was

Mariam and Beatrix's turn to bid him a safe return to his own lands, and then Anna gave him a highly inappropriate hug that would earn her a lecture afterward; Alicia contented herself with a shy smile and blush. Only after he'd exchanged terse farewells with André did Raimond turn toward Joanna.

"I hope that your lord brother is soon free, my lady," he said, and as he bent to kiss her hand, she murmured a polite "Go with God, my lord count." But then he leaned closer and said softly, "Farewell, my beautiful coward." Even though she knew no one else could have heard, Joanna still felt her face burn with heat. She stayed in the doorway of the great hall, watching as Raimond mounted his stallion and signaled to his men to ride out. Just before he rode through the gateway, he glanced over his shoulder, waved jauntily, and smiled. And Joanna could not help herself; she smiled back.

CHAPTER NINETEEN

❧

AUGUST 1193

Amiens, France

John and the French king had little in common other than a shared desire to keep Richard in a German dungeon until he drew his last mortal breath. John privately considered Philippe to be as much fun as an Anchorite recluse, so he was not enjoying himself at the French king's wedding. Watching the royal couple seated at the high table, he studied the bride admiringly, for she was not only highborn—the sister of the King of Denmark—she was just eighteen, and lovely, a tall, slender, blue-eyed blonde. She was not John's type, for he did not like his women to be taller than he was and he preferred more voluptuous paramours, but he still thought Philippe was luckier than he deserved. He would not even have to talk to the girl after taking her maidenhead, for she spoke no French and he spoke no Danish. Of course, she'd eventually learn French, but until she did, Philippe would have the ideal bedmate, young and pretty and mute.

John laughed aloud at that, attracting a few curious looks from the other guests. He was already tipsy, and he could think of no reason not to get thoroughly drunk. Mayhap then he could forget for a little while that *The Devil is loosed*. Not yet, but soon. Unless he and Philippe could find a way to outwit that double-dealing spider on the German throne. He felt indignation flicker as he thought how Heinrich had used them to squeeze outrageous concessions from Richard. Of course, they were using him, too, so he supposed he was really vexed because Heinrich had been better at it. He laughed again, for he'd long ago learned to employ mockery as a shield; with a family like his, that had been a survival skill. And as long as he could see some humor in his plight, he'd not have to think about facing Richard's fiery rage or their mother's icy anger. Wine helped, too, a very effective way to blur the hard edges of reality.

He was disappointed by the entertainment offered, although not surprised, for Philippe's lack of interest in music was well known, and by the time the feast ended and the newlyweds were escorted to their bridal chamber, he'd drained so many wine cups that he was unsteady on his feet. So were many of the wedding guests and it was a raucous bedding-down ceremony. Ingeborg, now renamed Isambour, had been put to bed by the women and she watched, wide-eyed, clutching the sheet up to her chin as the men trooped into the chamber, laughing loudly at their own jokes and leering at the bride. John had discovered earlier in the evening that Ingeborg spoke a little Latin, so when he happened to catch her eye, he winked and wished her, *"Bona fortuna,"* adding, because she seemed so nervous, *"Omnia vincit amor."* Of course he did not believe that love conquers all, any more than Virgil had, and he doubted that she'd find love in her marriage to Philippe. But the women he knew would much rather have a crown than a man's heart.

The bedding revelries showed no signs of winding down, and he was already growing bored. He'd left Ursula behind in Paris and regretted it now, for this was a night when he wanted a warm female body in his bed. Fortunately, that was an easy need to satisfy; a king's son never went hungry. Thinking that Ingeborg was a delightful little morsel compared to his own wife, a great heiress whom he tended to forget unless she was standing right in front of him, he pushed his way toward the door. The night was young and he was not yet drunk enough to exorcise his ghosts.

❦

JOHN AWOKE with the greatest reluctance. Squinting up at his squire, he flinched from the bright, blinding light and then groaned, for his head was spinning and his stomach was roiling as if he'd spent the night aboard ship in a monster gale. Beside him, his bedmate was stirring, too, saying, "Good morrow, my lord," so cheerfully that he realized she was one of those odious souls who actually liked to rise with the sun. "The building had better be on fire, Giles," he muttered. But the boy persevered, for all in John's household were accustomed to his early-morning bad temper, reminding him that Lady Ingeborg's coronation was scheduled for noon. John decided he could quite happily go to his grave without seeing Philippe's bride crowned and he burrowed back under the coverlets with another groan. He remembered little about the woman in his bed, but he thought it was safe to assume she was a whore and not a nun, so he mumbled, "Pay her, Giles," before pulling the pillow over his head.

When he awoke again hours later, he called at once for the herbal drink that he'd often used to combat these morning-after woes: a mixture of pennyroyal, betony, and peppermint in white wine. He felt marginally better once he'd forced it down and let Giles help him dress. He was debating whether he ought to go back to bed, when the door banged open with enough force to make him wince. "Hellfire and damnation, Durand, must you make enough noise to awaken the dead?"

The knight grinned. "I'm glad to see you're finally up, for I have news you'll want to hear straightaway."

"Unless you've come to tell me that Heinrich has agreed to turn Richard over to Philippe, I am not interested."

Durand was unfazed by the grumbling, for he knew how much John enjoyed gossip. "Not as good as that, I grant you. But you'll still find it of interest. The coronation went as planned, although Philippe was squirming like a man with a stick up his arse during the entire ceremony, looking dour even for him. Some of us had begun to joke that his little Danish tart must not have been to his taste. Yet no one expected what came next. He announced that the marriage was over and he planned to seek an annulment as soon as possible."

"He did *what*?" John stared at the other man, incredulous. "Is this a joke, Durand? Why would he do that?"

"The entire court is asking that, too, my lord. When one of the Danish envoys explained what had just happened to the bewildered little bride, she looked as if she'd been hit on the head by a hammer. Needless to say, the Danes are outraged and Philippe's clerics are dismayed, seeing a God-awful fight looming with the papacy, since no one thinks he has grounds for annuling the marriage."

John started to shake his head, then decided that was not a good idea. "And I missed all that? Just my luck." He sat down on the bed, fighting back laughter. "Philippe must have gone stark, raving mad. You've seen the girl, Durand. Would you kick her out of *your* bed?"

"Not bloody likely. I'd have been glad to swive her for him if he was not up to it," Durand said, with another grin.

John grinned, too, marveling that Philippe, of all men, should have blundered so badly. For one so cautious and calculating, this defied belief. "That must truly have been the wedding night from Hell!"

⚜

RICHARD ENJOYED GREATER LIBERTY once he'd agreed to Heinrich's exorbitant terms in late June. While he was still kept under surveillance, it was no longer so blatantly intrusive. Heinrich had even agreed to let him go hawking occasionally and Henry Falconarius, one of the royal falconers, hastened to Worms with several goshawks and a favorite peregrine falcon. And he had a steady stream of welcome visitors. He took great pleasure in the company of his friends and was grateful that so many churchmen and highborn vassals would make that long journey from England or Normandy. He knew it impressed the Germans and reinforced his status, showing Heinrich that even as a captive king, he retained the loyalty of his subjects. For he never forgot for a moment how precarious his position still was, at the mercy of a man who could decide on the morrow to accept the French king's offer.

If he'd had any doubts that he was balancing on the thinnest of wires, like the rope dancers so popular at local fairs, they were dispelled in mid-August by Heinrich's unexpected arrival at Worms. While their meeting was outwardly amiable, it swirled with undercurrents deep enough to drown in. Heinrich began by giving Richard unwelcome news: after being stricken with a serious illness, Archbishop Bruno of Cologne had resigned his archbishopric, choosing to spend his remaining days as a simple monk at the monastery in Altenberg. Richard did his best to hide his dismay, for the elderly archbishop had been one of his strongest supporters. Now he could only hope that the monks would elect a prelate who'd also be sympathetic to his plight.

Heinrich was not one for making idle conversation and he soon revealed the purpose of his visit. The Bishop of Bath had been grievously disappointed to learn that the Christchurch monks had disregarded Richard's wishes and elected Hubert Walter as the new Archbishop of Canterbury, he reported, adding that he'd been surprised, too, by their defiance. Richard expressed his own surprise and offered his sympathies for the bishop's thwarted hopes, all the while bracing for whatever was coming next.

"I was sure that you'd share our disappointment," Heinrich said smoothly.

"So I daresay you'll be pleased to hear that there is a way to compensate my cousin for his loss. He tells me he wants to annex the abbey at Glastonbury to his See of Bath."

"Does he, now?" It took all of Richard's self-control to remain impassive, for Glastonbury was one of the most important English abbeys, and since the recent discovery in the monastery cemetery of the graves of King Arthur and his queen, Guinevere, it had become an even more popular pilgrimage site. He could well understand why Savaric wanted to get his greedy hands on such a prize. "I doubt that the monks would take kindly to that, my lord emperor."

Heinrich dismissed the monks' objections with a negligent wave of his hand. "Savaric will deal with their complaints. What he proposes is that he grant you the city of Bath in exchange for the abbey, with the two churches united as one. I told him that I felt confident we could count upon your cooperation, my lord king. So . . . can we?"

Richard wondered if Savaric was truly so stupid that he did not realize there'd be a day of reckoning for this bit of banditry. He did not doubt that Heinrich knew it, but his concern was not with his foolish cousin's future. He cared only about reminding his prisoner that he was one, whatever amenities and civilities he now enjoyed. Richard returned the emperor's smile, although under the table, his hands had clenched into involuntary fists. "Of course," he said, with a nonchalance that cost him dearly. "We are allies, after all."

UNDER THE CIRCUMSTANCES, Richard was not looking forward to his thirty-sixth birthday on September 8; why would a prisoner celebrate one more day of captivity? To his surprise, it turned out to be an enjoyable occasion. The Bishop of Worms insisted upon hosting a festive birthday dinner for his royal guest and afterward, he engaged several of the German minnesingers to perform for them. Music always raised Richard's spirits, and he was in a mellow mood even before the arrival of a messenger from one of his new allies, the Duke of Brabant.

The duke's news could not have been better. The newly elected Archbishop of Cologne was the provost Adolf von Altena, who'd been very friendly with Richard since their first meeting during his trial at Speyer. He could not have asked for a more effective champion than Adolf, and Richard felt as if he'd been given an unexpected birthday gift.

After the meal and the entertainment, they went out into the palace gardens.

Some of the men began to play a boisterous game of quoits, throwing horseshoes at a wooden hob. Richard was sitting on a turf bench, watching the game and bantering with Morgan and Warin Fitz Gerald when he was given a letter from the German emperor. At the sight of the imperial seal, it was as if the sun had suddenly gone behind a cloud, for any communication from Heinrich could not be good. Feeling as if he were about to lift a rock and find a scorpion lurking underneath, he broke the seal. Those closest to him also tensed, and were relieved when Richard looked up from the letter, for he seemed startled, not dismayed.

"Some of you may have heard that the French king agreed to wed the sister of the King of Denmark. My lady mother and my justiciars believe that Philippe hoped to get the use of the Danish fleet for an invasion of England. If that was indeed his motivation for this marriage, he has a most peculiar way of courting the Danes, for he disavowed his bride the day after the wedding."

This astonishing news halted the quoits game and they clustered around him to hear more. Returning to the letter, Richard read rapidly and by the time he was done, he was grinning. "According to the emperor's sources at the French court," he said, careful to accord Heinrich the respect due his rank since there were Germans present, "Philippe privately contended that he'd not consummated the marriage, but he was reminded that nonconsummation alone is not enough for an annulment. His advisers must also have pointed out that if he made such a claim, people would naturally assume that he'd been unable to pay the marital debt." Richard had been circumspect in his choice of words out of deference to the Bishop of Worms and the other clerics, but as he glanced up, he saw that there was no need for discretion. They were obviously as amused as his own men that the French king had gotten himself into such an improbable, embarrassing predicament.

Richard's kindhearted chaplain, Anselm, felt pity for the repudiated bride and asked what would become of her now.

"Philippe had her taken from Amiens and she is being held at the monastery of St-Maur-des-Fossés near Paris. She is showing admirable spirit, balking at being sent back to Denmark like defective goods. She insists the marriage was indeed consummated and they are man and wife in the eyes of God and the Church. But the emperor's spies—I mean his sources," Richard corrected, with another grin, "say that Philippe plans to convene a council of bishops and barons to argue that the marriage is invalid because he and Ingeborg are related within the forbidden degree. Although that is not so, I'd wager the French bishops will pretend to believe it." No longer smiling, he said, "And, of course, that bastard Beauvais is ready and willing to do Philippe's bidding in this, for perjury is the least of his sins."

There was no topic of conversation after that except the French king's marital woes, and the jests got bawdier and cruder once the bishop and archdeacons departed. It was well known that Philippe had an aversion to horses, and men now joked that he must be particularly skittish at mounting mares. It was suggested that Philippe's crown jewels were so meager that Ingeborg had been unable to find them, or that her first sight of a naked man may have stirred mirth instead of desire, especially if his flag was flying at half-mast. Warin speculated whether Philippe could have discovered she was not a maiden, and evoked loud laughter by adding, "Of course, would he have been able to tell?" Several wondered whether a lack of virginity could invalidate a marriage, and looked disappointed when Longchamp said it could not. But Morgan turned all heads in his direction when he said that it was one of the grounds for dissolution of a marriage under Welsh law.

In Wales, he explained, a marriage could be ended by mutual consent. Moreover, a husband could disavow his wife if she claimed to be a virgin and he learned on their wedding night that she was not, or if he found her in compromising circumstances with another man, or if her marriage portion fell short of what was promised. Longchamp and Anselm shook their heads disapprovingly, but the men enthusiastically embraced laws that made it easier to get rid of an unwanted wife, for the Church allowed a marriage to be dissolved only if an impediment had initially existed—consanguinity, a spiritual affinity, a coerced consent, or the inability to consummate the marriage through impotence.

They were shocked, though, when Morgan said that a Welsh wife could shed an unwanted husband, too, able to end the marriage if he contracted leprosy, if he had foul breath, if he was unfaithful three times, or if he was incapable in bed. That went against the natural order of things, confirming their suspicions that Wales was a wild, mysterious land with downright peculiar customs, although they liked Morgan well enough. But when Morgan told them about the Welsh test for impotence, which compelled the husband to spill his seed upon a clean white sheepskin, they shouted with laughter at the thought of Philippe enduring such a humiliating ordeal to prove his manhood.

Richard had not laughed so much in months. This had indeed been a day of surprises, he thought. The news that Adolf von Altena was the new Archbishop of Cologne was more important, of course. But there was such sweet satisfaction in Philippe's plight. "The French king is now the laughingstock of Christendom," he declared, "and best of all, it is his own doing."

❧

THAT EVENING, Richard was in his bedchamber with the men who now composed his inner circle: Longchamp, Fulk, Morgan, Guillain, Baldwin, Warin, and the de Préaux brothers. He was working on a song he called his "prison lament," while they were chatting among themselves and Arne was glaring at Hans; the German youth was one of the servants Heinrich had provided and Arne greatly resented anyone but himself tending to his king's needs.

"How does this sound?" Richard struck a chord on his harp as the others looked toward him. "Feeble the words, and faltering the tongue, wherewith a prisoner moans his doleful plight. Yet for his comfort, he may make a song. Friends have I many, but—"

He got no further, for just then the door burst open and Anselm rushed into the chamber. "My liege, I was just talking to Master Mauger," he blurted out, naming one of Richard's recent guests, the Archdeacon of Évreux. "He is returning to Normandy at week's end, and he says he'd be happy to continue on into Poitou and deliver letters to your queen and sister. By the time he gets there, they ought to have reached Poitiers."

He beamed at Richard, but his smile faltered when Richard shook his head. "I've already written to them, giving letters to the courier they sent from Rome."

"I know that, sire. But surely your lady would be happy to hear from you again—"

"I said no, Anselm!" Richard had not meant to raise his voice, but his chaplain's well-meaning meddling had struck a nerve. He'd labored over those earlier letters for hours, unable to find the right words, and he did not want to go through that again. What was he supposed to write to Berenguela? Tell her about the weather in Worms? The dreams he had about being buried alive in French dungeons blacker than any pits of Hell? How he'd had to make yet another shameful concession to that whoreson Heinrich and betray the monks of Glastonbury?

Anselm was looking at him in dismay, and his bewilderment only added to Richard's frustration. If even Anselm did not understand, how in God's name could Berenguela? He rose, no longer in the mood for music, aware of the silence, the stares. Deliverance came from an unexpected source—the parrot, which suddenly said, with surprising clarity, "Ballocks!" The men burst into startled laughter, and the awkward moment was gone, if not forgotten.

❧

HUGH DE NONANT, Bishop of Coventry, was living proof that outer packaging could be quite deceptive. He was stout and ruddy-cheeked, his balding head resembling a monk's fringed tonsure, his blue eyes wreathed in what looked like laugh lines, and at first glance, he seemed good-natured and benevolent, even grandfatherly. But his benign, innocuous appearance and easy smile were camouflage; the man himself was cynical, shrewd, ambitious, untrustworthy, and utterly ruthless in pursuit of his own ends.

For once, he was off balance, though, his courtly poise ragged around the edges. "The sight of you gladdens these aging eyes, my liege," he murmured, but the unctuous greeting fell on deaf ears and he seemed to sense that, for he no longer met Richard's gaze.

"You took your time in responding to my summons, my lord bishop," Richard said, glazing each word in ice. "I began to suspect that you'd joined my brother when he fled to the French court."

"Indeed not, sire! You have been led astray if you've come to doubt my loyalty." The bishop turned to glare at the chancellor, saying it was all too easy to guess who'd been slandering his good name. Longchamp glared back, his body rigid, black eyes combative.

"My chancellor has earned my trust. You have not."

"My liege, that is most unfair. Your lord brother is the heir to the throne should evil befall you, and I gave him the respect due his rank, no more than that. My loyalty to you has never wavered, not even for a heartbeat."

Richard did not bother to disguise his skepticism, for he wanted Nonant to squirm, to feel in the very marrow of his bones the fear of losing royal favor. "If that is so, then I expect you have brought with you a generous contribution to my ransom."

Nonant's florid complexion reddened still further. "Sire . . . that was indeed my intention. I left London with a sizable sum of money. But we were ambushed on the road and robbed of every last farthing." He turned then, pointing an accusing finger at Longchamp. "And it is all this man's doing!"

Longchamp looked astonished and then outraged. Before he could make an indignant denial, Richard put a restraining hand on his arm. "You'll have to do better than that, my lord bishop. The chancellor has been with me since he arranged a truce with the French king in early July. I can assure you he was not prowling English roads as a highwayman."

"I did not mean he was the one leading the bandits, my liege. But I have no doubt they were sent by his sister's husband, the castellan of Dover Castle!"

One glance toward Longchamp was enough to assure Richard that the chancellor knew nothing of this. "You have proof of this, of course?"

"I had the man excommunicated, my lord, so sure am I of his guilt."

"That may be your idea of proof, my lord bishop, but it is not mine. You are fortunate that I do not have a suspicious nature, or else I might have doubted this very convenient robbery of yours." Richard stared at the bishop until he became visibly uncomfortable, sweat beading his forehead and his breath quickening. "I have been blessed with a good memory, and you may be sure of this— that I will remember who proved themselves to be loyal during these difficult times, and who did not."

"I *am* loyal, sire, I swear it!"

Longchamp would normally have taken great pleasure in his enemy's discomfiture, but he was too uneasy himself to enjoy Nonant's desperate attempts to placate his king. Once the bishop had been dismissed, the chancellor eyed Richard nervously. "Sire, I know nothing of this alleged robbery."

"I know that, Guillaume." Despite that reassurance, Richard's expression was inscrutable. "Do you think your brother-in-law is capable of so rash an act?"

Longchamp hesitated, but he was not going to lie to his king. "It is possible," he said at last.

"Well . . . I think it might be a good idea if your brother-in-law made a generous donation to my ransom fund, then."

This time Longchamp caught the glint of amusement and he smiled broadly. "My thoughts exactly!"

"You need not fear for your position with me, Guillaume—even if you cannot rein in your more impulsive relatives. I will never forget what you did for me at Trifels. I have my vices," Richard said with a quick smile, "but ingratitude is not one of them." The smile vanishing as swiftly as it had come, he said, with the utmost seriousness, "I spoke the truth to that knave, Nonant. I always pay my debts."

Especially blood debts, Longchamp agreed silently. He thought it all too likely that Heinrich would escape earthly punishment for the grievous wrong he'd done the English king. But the French king and Richard's treacherous brother would not be so lucky.

☙

THE DUCHESS OF BRITTANY had ridden for hours in silence, for she was dreading the coming confrontation with her husband. *Husband*. Even after five years of marriage, it seemed strange to call Randolph that. Constance had not wanted to wed him, had been still grieving for Geoffrey. But she'd been given no choice, for her father-in-law had insisted; Henry was determined to marry her off to a man whom he could trust. Ironically, that had not been true for his own son, for Geoffrey had been conspiring with the French king at the time of his death. Henry had expected that Geoffrey would be a puppet prince, governing Brittany according to his will. But Geoffrey had a mind of his own and he'd put Brittany's interests before his father's Angevin empire, winning over the hostile Breton barons and winning over Constance, too.

It had been seven years since Geoffrey had died in that accursed tournament, and there were times, especially at night, when the wound still bled. If only he'd not taken part in that mêlée. How different her life and the lives of their children would have been. But "what if" and "if only" were games for fools. In her heart, she was still Geoffrey's widow. In the real world, she was the wife of Randolph de Blundeville.

It had not been a disparaging marriage, for Randolph was the Earl of Chester, holder of vast estates on both sides of the Channel, cousin to the king, not an unworthy match for the Duchess of Brittany. Nor was he a brute or a lout. But their marriage had probably been doomed from the first, she thought, remembering that nervous eighteen-year-old youth, wed to a woman nine years his senior, a woman of greater rank, a woman who did not want him. He'd been humiliated by spilling his seed too soon, and any chance they may have had of reaching an accommodation had ended with that clumsy wedding-night coupling. They'd shared a bed less and less often as time went on, for she was luckier than most reluctant wives. She ruled a duchy and had vassals eager to make her alien husband feel very unwelcome. Nor did she need him to get her with child, for she had Geoffrey's son and daughter to ensure the Breton succession: six-year-old Arthur and nine-year-old Aenor.

Yet Geoffrey had taught her too well, showing her what pleasures could be found in a man's arms, and her bed was lonely and cold. She'd occasionally considered taking a lover; she'd never done so, though. She told herself it was because even the most discreet liaison still posed serious risks, and while that was true enough, it was also true that the only man she wanted was buried in a marble tomb at the cathedral of Notre-Dame de Paris.

"Madame?" As André de Vitré drew alongside her mare, Constance summoned up a smile, for this Breton lord had become her mainstay after Geoffrey's death. "Are you sure you want to do this?" he asked quietly.

"I know no other way to get the answers we need," she said, and since he did not know, either, he nodded somberly, and they rode on, not speaking until the castle walls of St James de Beuvron came into view.

❦

RANDOLPH DE BLUNDEVILLE WAS astonished when he was told that his wife was seeking admittance; he could not remember her ever paying a visit to one of his castles before. He was not happy about it; he'd given up on his marriage by the end of the first year. His new wife had not denied him his marital rights and even in private, she was always coolly civil. He'd not realized until then what a devastating weapon indifference was. She did not even care enough to quarrel with him, and he could not forgive her for that. Caught between her apathy and the overt hostility of her Breton lords, he was miserable and resentful and his visits to the duchy became more and more infrequent. Shackled in this wretched marriage to a woman who was unlikely ever to give him an heir to his earldom of Chester, he was ashamed now to remember how excited he'd been to make this match. What a fool he'd been! But he would not let the bitch or her arrogant barons scorn him for bad manners, too, and after giving the order to open the gates, he hastily sent to the pantry and the kitchen for wine and wafers.

When his guests were ushered into the great hall, he was waiting for them. He greeted Constance with a courteous bow and then a casual kiss on the cheek. He knew the men with her—André de Vitré and his brothers Robert and Alain, Guethenoc, the Bishop of Vannes—and acknowledged them coolly but correctly. He did allow himself a touch of irony, saying dryly, "This is indeed a surprise."

Conversation was awkward, for Constance was no better at small talk than Randolph. Once she felt etiquette had been satisfied, she wasted no more time. "May I speak with you in private, my lord husband?"

Randolph nodded. "We can walk in the gardens," he said, wanting to make it clear that he was not burning to be alone with her. She was not a great beauty, with unfashionable dark hair and eyes, small boned, and so slender she looked deceptively fragile. But there was an intensity about her that drew male attention, especially men who saw her aloofness as a challenge. Randolph was not one of them, and it vexed him greatly that he still found her desirable.

"The gardens, then," she said, and he offered her his arm. He was shorter than most men, but he was still taller than she was. As they crossed the hall, he wondered if the stories he'd heard were true, that she and Geoffrey had kindled enough heat to set their marital bed afire. How could she have been such a wanton with one husband and so cold with the other?

Once they reached the gardens, he gestured toward a bench, but she shook her head. She'd always had a directness that he considered unfeminine, and now she said bluntly, "I have heard a troubling rumor, Randolph—that one of the terms for Richard's release is the marriage of my daughter to the Duke of Austria's son. I have written to Eleanor, but she is not likely to be in any great rush to respond." Constance detested Geoffrey's family and she was no favorite of theirs, either, so Randolph thought she was probably right. She had begun to pace and he realized how difficult she was finding it to ask him for a favor. "You are Richard's cousin. That ought to make it easier for you to get answers."

Randolph hesitated and then decided to borrow some of her own bluntness. "There is no need for that. It is true."

Constance gasped and looked so stricken that he felt a prick of unwelcome pity; it was the first time that he'd ever seen her truly vulnerable. "Are you sure of this, Randolph?" When he nodded, she sat abruptly on the closest bench. But then she raised her chin, scowling. "Why did you not tell me?"

He scowled, too. "I've not seen you in months, Constance. Do not play the wronged wife. You are not very convincing at it."

"This has nothing to do with us, Randolph. This is my daughter!"

"I assumed you'd been told." He took a step toward her, though, for she was whiter than chalk. "It is not as bad as that. In fact, it is a good match for Aenor. She'll be marrying into one of the most powerful families in the Holy Roman Empire. You ought to be happy—"

"Happy? My daughter is being sent away to a foreign land to wed a stranger and I have been given no say in it!"

"Richard was given no say in it, either," he said impatiently. "You know that full well, too. If you must blame someone, blame the German emperor and the Austrian duke. But I still say it is an advantageous marriage. For God's sake, woman, she'll be the Duchess of Austria one day! Do you truly think you could have done better for her?"

"She is only nine years old!"

"But that is the way of our world, Constance. Highborn girls are often raised at the courts of their future husbands—as you were. All of Richard's sisters were very young when marriages were contracted for them—"

"I do not care about them! I care about my daughter!"

There was so much anguish in that cry that he was at a loss. "You'll come to accept it in time," he said after a strained silence. "You have no choice, Constance."

She bit her lip, looking down so he'd not catch the glimmer of tears. She was so tired of waging this war without Geoffrey, tired of struggling against the inevitable. But slowly the embers began to smolder, igniting a familiar fire that would be her salvation. Anger had always been her shield, her source of strength, often her only refuge. She could not stop them from taking her daughter. But hatred would help her to survive Aenor's loss, would enable her to keep on fighting for her son and for her duchy.

Rising to her feet, she said scornfully, "I ought to have known better than to come to you for help." Before he could respond, she turned on her heel and stalked away, leaving him to fume and to curse Henry for entrapping him in this hellish marriage.

ELEANOR ENJOYED the Countess of Aumale's company, for they had much in common. Like Eleanor, Hawisa was a great heiress, Countess of Aumale in her own right, possessing valuable estates in Normandy, Yorkshire, and Lincolnshire. And like Eleanor, she was strong-willed, not one who deferred easily to male authority. She'd had the backbone to balk when Richard wanted her to marry one of his vassals, William de Forz, and the common sense to yield after Richard distrained her lands. Hawisa had wed Richard's handpicked husband, but that did not tame her independent spirit. She'd accompanied Eleanor on her journey to Sicily, for she shared the queen's keen curiosity about exotic, foreign lands, and she had not let pregnancy curtail her travels any more than Eleanor ever had. Eleanor had only been close to two women in her long life: her sister Petronilla and Henry's cousin Maud, the Countess of Chester. But as she'd gotten to know Hawisa better, she'd lowered the drawbridge, allowing the younger woman into the castle bailey, if not yet into the keep.

On this rain-swept afternoon in November, they were sipping wine in Eleanor's great hall in the White Tower. Eleanor had met for much of the morning with Henry Fitz-Ailwin, the city's mayor, and Richard Fitz Neal, the Bishop of London and Lord Treasurer of the Exchequer, and she was glad now to be able to put her troubles aside for a few hours of easy conversation with Hawisa, who could always make her laugh.

Hawisa had already finished her wine and signaled to a servant for another cup. "I heard that the French king called a council at Compiègne to rid himself of that poor little bride of his. Is that true?"

Eleanor nodded. "He claimed that Ingeborg and his first wife were related in the fourth and fifth degrees, which would be grounds for annulling the marriage—if it had been true."

"And it was not?"

"No. The chart Philippe produced was a forgery and a clumsy one at that. But he knew his audience—eight of the fifteen council members were his kinsmen and several of the others were part of the royal household. To no one's surprise—except possibly Ingeborg's—the Archbishop of Reims, who happens to be Philippe's uncle, dutifully declared that the marriage was null and void. When they told Ingeborg, since she had no French, she resorted to Latin, crying out, *'Mala Francia! Roma!'* Yet if she expects the Pope to champion her cause, she is in for a grievous disappointment. Celestine will express great indignation on her behalf. But words are cheap, especially his."

Hawisa did not have a high opinion of the Pope, either. "If I were Ingeborg, I'd have thanked God fasting to be spared a lifetime sharing Philippe's bed. Why is she fighting so hard to hold on to a man who shamed her like that?"

"Pride, I expect," Eleanor said pensively. "It might be difficult for her brother to find another husband for her after such a scandal. And since she swears he consummated the marriage, I suppose she sees herself as his wife in God's eyes."

"If I thought a scandal would rid me of my husband, I'd gladly walk the streets naked from dawn to dusk."

Eleanor's eyes gleamed with amusement. "Marriage is a man's game for certes. They make the rules and we have to play by them."

"Sometimes the game can be fun," Hawisa conceded. "I liked being married to my first husband—most of the time."

"I could say the same about my second husband—until he became my gaoler, of course." Eleanor took a swallow of wine, regarding Hawisa over the cup's rim. "I had a letter from Constance not long ago. She is outraged that her daughter is to be part of the price paid for Richard's freedom. The foolish woman acts as if we had a choice in the matter. But it is no easy thing to let a daughter go, Hawisa. We can only hope that they find a measure of contentment in the lives we choose for them. I do not know about Alix, but I think Marie, Leonora, Tilda, and Jo-anna did. I suppose mothers always want to believe that, though. . . ."

"I'm glad I birthed a son, not a daughter. At least our sons are not bartered away like prize mares."

"But sons find other ways to steal our peace and break our hearts."

That was true enough to bring a lump to Hawisa's throat. Swallowing it, she joked that it was well babies did not know what awaited them, or they'd never be willing to leave the womb, and then she opened the door wide in case the queen wanted to come through, saying, "Madame . . . have you heard from your son?"

"Which one?" Eleanor drank again, staring down into the depths of her wine cup as if it held answers, not dregs. "Did you hear that John concocted a new scheme, this time to steal the ransom by forging my seal? Say what you will of him, he does not lack for imagination."

Hawisa did not want to talk of John, for whatever she said was bound to be wrong. "I've heard that many have been balking at paying their share of the ransom, especially the clerics, who are loath to give up their churches' gold and silver plate. It is such a vast amount of money. . . ."

"And I hope Heinrich burns in Hell for each and every one of those hundred and fifty thousand marks." Eleanor's voice was low, but it throbbed with barely suppressed fury. "I have never hated anyone as much as I hate that man. But we'll have his blood money—or enough of it—by the time we leave for Germany next month."

"You are going to Germany, Madame?" Hawisa at once regretted the question. After all, this was the woman who'd crossed the Alps in the dead of winter. But she was three years older now—approaching her biblical threescore years and ten—and the North Sea in December would have daunted men half her age.

Eleanor's brows shot upward in surprise. "Of course I am going, Hawisa! We had a letter from Richard last month, saying Heinrich had set a date for his release, the Monday after the expiration of three weeks from the day of Our Lord's Nativity—January 17." She smiled at Hawisa, a mother's smile as memorable in its own way as the seductive smiles of her youth. "God willing," she said, "I will be celebrating the new year with my son. And then . . . then we'll come home."

CHAPTER TWENTY

❦

JANUARY 1194

Speyer, Germany

R ichard found it hard to believe that in less than a fortnight, he'd be
freed. The greater portion of the ransom had been delivered to Heinrich, and his mother and the Archbishop of Rouen would soon be at
Speyer for the day of his deliverance. But Richard knew that any man who
trusted in Heinrich's good faith was one of God's greatest fools, and he would
not feel safe until he was actually on the road, with Speyer disappearing into the
distance.

He was very pleased, therefore, by the arrival of a contingent from Poitou, for
their company kept him from dwelling upon his suspicions or the appallingly
high price he was paying for his freedom. The new arrivals included the bishops
of Saintes and Limoges; Aimery, the Viscount of Thouars; his younger brother
Guy; and two men who'd fought with Richard in the Holy Land, Giraud de
Berlay-Montreuil and Hugh le Brun, one of the contentious de Lusignan clan.
They brought money for his ransom and the Bishop of Saintes and Hugh were
also able to give him news of his wife and sister, for they'd both played host to
Berengaria and Joanna on their way to Poitiers.

Aimery had the reputation of being a political weathercock and Giraud and
Hugh belonged to families that saw rebellion as their birthright, but because
they'd been willing to make such a long and difficult winter journey, Richard
wiped away all memories of past sins. He took a particular liking to Guy de
Thouars, for unlike so many of his visitors, Guy asked no awkward questions
about his imprisonment. Instead, he wanted to hear about the king's exploits in
the Holy Land and so Richard was able to reminisce with Giraud and Hugh

about their campaign against the Saracens, laughing as they recalled how Richard had to come to Hugh's rescue when his house was under siege by the angry citizens of Messina, teasing Baldwin de Bethune about the time he'd tried to ride a camel, and agreeing that the fleetest horse in all of Christendom was Fauvel, the dun stallion Richard had taken from Isaac, the despot of Cyprus.

Their enjoyable afternoon came to an abrupt end when Master Fulk entered and handed Richard a letter from the German emperor. Opening it with a sense of foreboding, Richard caught his breath. "Heinrich has delayed my release for more than a fortnight. Instead of a week from Monday here in Speyer, it is now to be on Candlemas in Mainz."

His guests were disappointed, but his men were dismayed, for they knew Heinrich. Longchamp rose and limped to Richard's side. "Did he offer any reason for this delay?"

Richard shook his head, handing the chancellor the letter. It was not the postponement itself that disquieted him—although every additional day of imprisonment would weigh heavily upon his soul. It was far more ominous than that. Meeting Longchamp's eyes, he said grimly, "What is that spawn of Satan up to now?"

⚜

UPON THEIR ARRIVAL IN GERMANY, Eleanor and the Archbishop of Rouen and their large entourage engaged ships to convey them up the Rhine River and they reached Cologne in time to celebrate Epiphany with its archbishop-elect, Adolf von Altena. The queen, Archbishop Gautier, and the more highborn of the hostages were lodged in his archiepiscopal palace. It was a much-needed respite, for the trip had been hard upon them all. But despite the warm welcome from the archbishop and the citizens of Cologne, Eleanor was impatient to resume their journey and she felt a great relief when they finally boarded ship for the last leg of their odyssey.

⚜

ELEANOR READ MEN WELL and as Archbishop Adolf made his way across the crowded hall of the imperial palace in Speyer, she felt a sudden chill that had nothing to do with the snow on the ground or the icy snap in the air. She had only a limited knowledge of Latin and no German, but he spoke surprisingly good French, albeit with a strong accent. "The emperor has delayed the king's release, Madame. It is now set for February 2 in Mainz."

Eleanor shook her eyes briefly, feeling every one of her sixty-nine years at that moment. But even worse was to come.

"Nor will you be permitted to see your son, Madame. Heinrich has given orders that you are to continue on to Mainz."

Eleanor raised her chin, straightening her shoulders. "I would speak with the emperor and as soon as possible."

"Heinrich is not here in Speyer. He has been at Würzburg all month, holding an Imperial Diet, and will not be at Mainz for at least a fortnight. Moreover, he has summoned me to join him in Würzburg and so I will be unable to accompany you to Mainz."

Eleanor stared at the two archbishops, seeing her fear on their faces. Heinrich already had most of the ransom and now he had the hostages, too. What if he still refused to set Richard free? She'd not realized she'd begun to shiver until her grandson Otto whipped off his mantle and gallantly draped it around her shoulders. The gesture well-nigh broke her heart. Wilhelm had been born in England and Otto had been only five when their parents had taken refuge at the English court. Even if all went as it ought, she'd be leaving her grandsons in a land that was foreign to them, in the hands of a man who knew no more of honor than a bandit or a Barbary pirate. And if all went horribly wrong, what would befall them then?

❧

AFTER SOME OF THE MOST STRESSFUL DAYS and sleepless nights of her life, what Eleanor had been so desperately awaiting finally happened. On Candlemas Eve, her son arrived at the imperial palace at Mainz.

They all were eager to see the king, but the first small group to be escorted to Richard's chamber was restricted to Eleanor, the Archbishop of Rouen, and his nephews, Otto and Wilhelm. Richard was waiting with Longchamp, Fulk, Anselm, Baldwin de Bethune, Morgan, Guillain, and young Arne. As she came through the doorway, Eleanor's eyes were already stinging and she saw her son through a blur of tears. She'd last seen him nigh on three years ago, standing on the quays at Messina with Joanna and Berengaria, waving as her ship slowly edged out into the harbor. She was not reassured by what she saw now, for he looked like a man who'd been shut away from the sun, a man who'd lost a noticeable amount of weight, a man who'd been living on nerves for far too long. But then he smiled and, as he embraced her, she marveled that it had taken her most of her life to understand that the strongest, most enduring love was that of a mother for her children.

"Philippe was a fool to wager against you." Laughing, Richard hugged her again, but then he bent his head to murmur for her ear alone, "Sixteen years— how did you ever survive it, Maman?" telling her with those few simple words all she needed to know about his time as Heinrich's prisoner.

Richard greeted the archbishop next and then turned his attention to nine-year-old Wilhelm and sixteen-year-old Otto, pretending to believe that they could not possibly be his nephews. They were much too tall, he insisted, making them laugh and easing any awkwardness they may have felt. But they truly did look like strangers to him, for four years was an eternity in the realm of childhood, and that cheeky five-year-old and solemn twelve-year-old lived only in his memories now. Would his own son seem so unfamiliar, too?

"Ask him," Wilhelm urged, and Otto did. "Uncle . . . the German lords and bishops have been arriving all week. Whilst we knew our father would stay away, we hoped our brother would be at Mainz. But he ought to have been here by now. Henrik is not coming, is he?"

"No, Otto, he is not," Richard said reluctantly. "Henrik is not in the emperor's good graces at the moment. You see, lads, your brother managed to steal his bride right out from under Heinrich's nose."

Wilhelm looked puzzled, but Otto smiled. "You mean he was able to wed Agnes after all? I thought the emperor had forbidden the match."

"He did, indeed. But he was outwitted by an eighteen-year-old lass with a mind of her own." Seeing that Wilhelm was still confused, Richard explained that Henrik had been betrothed since childhood to Agnes, the only child of Konrad, the Count Palatine of the Rhineland, Heinrich's uncle. That betrothal had been a casualty, though, of the feuding between their father and the Hohenstaufens.

"Heinrich wanted Agnes to marry Ludwig, the Duke of Bavaria. Although she'd been balking, she'd probably have been compelled to yield eventually. But then Heinrich had an offer for her from the French king. Philippe had gotten his puppet princes and bishops to annul his marriage to the unfortunate Ingeborg. You know about her?"

Richard laughed when they both nodded; if even children like Wilhelm had heard of Philippe's marital follies, he'd never live that scandal down. "Well, now that he was in the market for a new wife, he cast eyes in Agnes's direction. I am not sure Heinrich would have agreed, for I cannot see him wanting Philippe to have any claim to the Palatine. But the marriage proposal horrified Agnes's mother. She asked Agnes if she was willing to wed the French king and Agnes said no very emphatically, declaring she would never marry the man who'd treated Ingeborg so cruelly. When she confided that the only one she wanted to marry was Henrik, her mother took action."

Glancing toward Eleanor, he said, with a smile, "If I did not know better, I'd think this admirable lady was kin to you, Maman. She sent word secretly to Henrik and, as soon as her husband was away, she summoned him to their castle at Stahleck, where Henrik and Agnes were quickly wed. Konrad was not happy once he found out, and Heinrich was furious. But when he insisted that Konrad have the marriage annulled, Konrad refused, saying that would bring disgrace upon his daughter."

Otto was very pleased for his brother, knowing how much he'd wanted Agnes as his wife. But it made him uneasy to think of Henrik as the object of the emperor's cold, implacable anger. "Do you think Heinrich will accept the marriage in time, Uncle?"

"His first reaction was to blame me for it all." Although Richard laughed, Eleanor and the archbishop did not, wondering if this clandestine marriage could be the reason why his release had suddenly been postponed. They were somewhat reassured by what Richard said next. "But now that Konrad is supporting the marriage, there is not much Heinrich can do about it. That is why he is holding an Imperial Diet at Würzburg, to discuss the marriage. I think the chances are good that he'll grudgingly come around to an acceptance of it."

There was a discreet knock at the door then, reminding them that there were many others waiting to pay their respects to their king, and he nodded to Morgan, who crossed the chamber to let in the next group. Richard was delighted to see William de St Mère-Eglise, who said that Hubert Walter had wanted to come, too, but since Richard had just named him as the chief justiciar, he'd realized he was more urgently needed in England. Eleanor now brought forward a dark, handsome youth of seventeen, introducing him as Berengaria's brother Fernando. When Richard thanked him for becoming a hostage, he grinned and said he was glad to get away from his father and elder brother's constant scrutiny. Richard was not sure if his insouciance was due to his youth or to his nature; Berengaria had said Fernando was the family jester, cheerful and carefree to a fault.

Richard hated turning over any hostages to Heinrich's mercies, but it was easier to accept for soldiers like his admiral, Robert de Turnham, who'd just entered the chamber, or Robert de Hargrave, who'd been one of the twenty who'd accompanied him to Hell and back. It was much more difficult to watch the innocent nonchalance of youngsters like Fernando, Otto, and Wilhelm. However often he reminded himself that hostages were an integral part of any peace process, frequently offered up as pledges for good behavior and promises given, he knew in his heart that this was different, for Heinrich recognized no moral boundaries.

He'd just greeted the Abbot of Croyland when he noticed the man standing against the wall by the door, watching the commotion with the wry detachment of a spectator at a Christmas play. Weaving his way through the throng encircling him, Richard came to a halt in front of his cousin. "Why are you lurking in the shadows like this? You've always been the first into the breach."

André shrugged. "I knew you'd ask why I'd want to make a journey to Germany, of all places, and in the dead of winter, too. I was trying to think of a convincing answer."

"If you can come up with a good reason for visiting Germany, I'd be most interested in hearing it."

They embraced, then, finding to their mutual embarrassment that they were both blinking back tears. André tried to steer them away from these emotional shoals and into the safer waters of sarcasm, banter, and flippancy by saying huskily, "See what happens when I'm not around to keep you out of trouble?"

"I'll teach you to say 'I told you so' in German," Richard promised and they laughed, relieved that they were on familiar ground again.

Eleanor had followed Richard, marveling, as always, at the male inability to speak the language of the heart. "One day I hope to understand why men see sentiment as the ultimate enemy," she said dryly, "but I'll not be holding my breath until it happens." She was very pleased when Richard put his arm around her shoulders, for she needed the physical proof of his presence after so many months of fearing she would never see him again. "Richard, do you think Henrik's marriage could be the reason why Heinrich has delayed your release?"

"I suppose it is possible, Maman. This could be his way of punishing me for it. Or he might simply like keeping me in suspense for a while longer. Heinrich enjoys other people's pain. Or he could have an ugly surprise awaiting us."

For a moment, Richard could not help thinking of Trifels Castle, and as he looked down into his mother's face, he knew she was remembering Trifels, too. She'd aged visibly in the time they'd been apart, but he suspected it was this past year that had etched those lines in her forehead and smudged such dark shadows under her eyes. He'd always appreciated her strength and her resilience and her unerring ability to separate the wheat from the chaff. Now he regarded her with something approaching awe, having gotten a taste of what she'd endured as his father's prisoner, not knowing if she'd ever regain her freedom. Little wonder that one of her first acts had been to issue an amnesty for those languishing in English prisons, saying she'd learned by experience that confinement was distasteful to mankind and liberty a most delightful refreshment to the spirit. Realizing that she'd been a prisoner, too, during the months he'd been in Heinrich's power, he hugged her again, gently, for she seemed alarmingly fragile.

It never occurred to him to lie to her, though, or to offer false reassurances, and so he said, "Well, whatever Heinrich has in mind, we'll find out on the morrow."

CONSTANCE WAS NOT SURPRISED when Heinrich sat up in bed; he never stayed the night after he'd claimed his marital rights. She was usually very glad to see him go, but now she reached out and touched his arm. "Heinrich . . . may I ask you something? Why did you delay the English king's release? It has stirred much talk at court."

"Has it?" He yawned, idly winding a strand of her long, blond hair around his hand. His natural instinct was for secrecy, but he saw no reason not to indulge her curiosity since all would know on the morrow. "I needed time to consider a new proposal by the French king and the Count of Mortain. They are desperate to keep Richard caged, so much so that they are offering a large sum of money to make that happen. They vow that if I will hold Richard for another eight months—past the campaigning season—Philippe will pay me fifty thousand silver marks and John thirty thousand. Or they will pay me a thousand pounds of silver for every month that he remains my prisoner. Or if I will agree either to turn him over to them or to imprison him for another year, they will match the full amount of Richard's ransom, one hundred fifty thousand marks."

Constance was thankful for the darkness that kept him from seeing her horror or her revulsion. When she was sure she could trust her voice, she said, "I do not understand. Why would you forfeit the English ransom, which is already here, in favor of mere promises of future payment?"

"That is the beauty of it. I would still get Richard's ransom, for he'd be even more eager to pay for his freedom after another year of captivity. And I'd also have John and Philippe's money, which I'd not have to share with Leopold. So you can see why this is a deal well worth considering."

"What . . . what have you decided to do?"

"That will depend upon Richard. If he agrees to sweeten the ransom, all will go as planned. If he balks, I will give serious thought to accepting one of their offers, most likely holding him until Michaelmas. Although that thousand pounds of silver per month is tempting, I admit."

Constance was speechless. As well as she'd thought she knew him, she was staggered by this. Did he truly believe that the English and French kings were mere pawns, to be moved around on the chessboard at his will? Did he not care that his duplicity would make his name a byword for the worst sort of treachery? "But I thought you wanted Richard as an ally."

"Well, 'ally' is too strong a term. Let's just say we have a shared interest in Philippe's downfall. And that will not change even if I do hold him until Michaelmas, for however much he may resent me for it, his hatred for Philippe burns far hotter. He'll have no choice but to make common cause with me against France."

She said nothing, for there was no reasoning with a man who recognized no needs but his own. She did not doubt that God would eventually call him to account for his sins, but that day of divine reckoning could be years in the future. She felt sympathy for the English king. Even if he had recognized the usurper Tancred, he did not deserve what had happened to him in Germany. But her greatest fear was for her beloved homeland. She'd always known Heinrich would rule Sicily harshly. Until tonight, though, she'd not realized what a thin line separated arrogance from delusion. She could not remember their names, but she was sure there had been emperors in Ancient Rome who'd come to believe they were gods, not mortal men. What would happen to the Sicilians if they found themselves under the power of a madman?

She was so caught up in her misery that she did not even notice when Heinrich left. She lay awake as the hours dragged by till dawn, dreading the day to come and damning her nephew for dooming her to this Hell on earth, shackled to a husband she hated.

AS SOON AS RICHARD ENTERED the great hall, he was surrounded by men eager to speak with him. Eleanor was surprised and impressed by the warmth of their welcome. Clearly Richard had done more than make allies amongst the rebel barons: he'd made friends, too. She already knew Adolf von Altena and Conrad von Wittelsbach, the Archbishop of Mainz. Richard had told her they were the two most powerful prelates in Germany, and it was comforting to know they both were so firmly on her son's side. She was introduced to the dukes of Brabant and Limburg and to Simon, the seventeen-year-old Bishop-elect of Liege; she wondered how he felt about stepping into his murdered cousin's shoes or becoming a prince of the Church at such an absurdly young age. But she had no time to talk with him, for the crowd was parting to admit the Marquis of Montferrat into the circle.

She'd met Boniface three years ago during her chance encounter at Lodi with Heinrich and Constance, and he greeted her as if they were old and dear friends. She'd liked him, for she'd always had an eye for a handsome, charming man, but what mattered now was that he greeted Richard so amicably, for his cordiality was in itself a rebuttal for any who might still suspect Richard of complicity in Conrad of Montferrat's murder. Not even the most cynical of souls believed Boniface would embrace the English king if he harbored any doubts about his innocence; Boniface was known to be a more honorable man than his slain brother.

Boniface was one of Heinrich's most important vassals and so she asked if he'd heard why the emperor had delayed Richard's release. He seemed to think it was a minor matter, the delay most likely caused by the Imperial Diet just concluded at Wurzberg. He did have good news about that, he said cheerfully. The emperor had agreed to accept his cousin Agnes's marriage to her grandson Henrik, and he had also promised to restore Henrik to royal favor. Eleanor hoped this was an omen that the day's events would go well for them.

Richard had been talking with the Duke of Brabant, who was also in the dark about the reason for the postponement, but he stopped in midsentence and touched Eleanor's arm warningly. She tensed, thinking that Heinrich had entered the hall. But the man approaching them was the Duke of Austria.

He greeted Richard with courtesy so correct it was almost painful, and when Richard introduced his mother, he bowed stiffly over her hand. Eleanor yearned to slap him with it, but she smiled instead, for she'd had decades of practice in hiding her real feelings. The conversation was awkward, for Leopold was obviously uncomfortable, and while Richard was polite, that was as far as he was willing to go. The Austrian duke made his escape as soon as he could, and as he walked hastily away, Richard said quietly to Eleanor, "Leopold is in a foul mood because he knows that when the hunt for scapegoats begins, it will occur in Austria, not Germany. Not only is Leopold sure to be excommunicated, he'll be waiting years, mayhap decades, to get his full share of the ransom from Heinrich."

They were speaking in the *lenga romana* of Aquitaine and, not having to worry about eavesdroppers, Eleanor felt free to ask whom he blamed more, Heinrich or Leopold. He answered so quickly that she knew he'd given this some thought. "Leopold had a legitimate grievance; I'll admit that now. Not that it justified what he did. I still gave him the chance to end it honorably. I even offered to pay him a ransom. But he did not have the backbone to defy Heinrich, so he deserves all the misery that is coming his way. When it comes to tallying up sins, though, his are venial; Heinrich's are mortal."

She had no chance to respond, for the Archbishop of Salzburg was bearing down upon them, followed by a smiling man and two youths who looked to be about Otto's age. Richard greeted the archbishop affably, but he showed such genuine pleasure at the sight of the others that Eleanor was startled when they were introduced to her as Hadmar von Kuenring, who'd been her son's Austrian gaoler, and Friedrich and Leo von Babenberg. Watching the easy interaction between them, she felt grateful that Richard had not been surrounded at all times by hostility. It amused her, too, that the duke's sons were obviously in thrall to the legend of the Lionheart; she was sure Leopold was not happy about that. She found both boys likable and she thought she'd have to write to Constance about this meeting, reassuring her that Friedrich had made a fine first impression. As little as she liked the Breton duchess, she'd sent too many of her own daughters away to alien lands to be utterly indifferent to Constance's concerns for Aenor.

The atmosphere in the hall was so friendly that Eleanor had been lulled into a false sense of security, for it was almost as if it were a social occasion. That all changed with the blare of trumpets announcing the entrance of the Holy Roman Emperor. As soon as Heinrich strolled into the hall, Eleanor felt as if the temperature had dropped dramatically. But when Richard led her over, she favored Heinrich with a smile that did not even hint at her desire to see him bleeding his life away into the floor rushes at her feet. Heinrich acknowledged her with slightly wary courtesy, for he'd taken her measure at Lodi. His consort had trailed him into the hall, and Eleanor felt a sharp pang of pity for Constance de

Hauteville. At their Lodi meeting, they'd recognized each other as kindred spirits, birds with clipped wings in a world in which only men were allowed to soar. Eleanor had sensed the other woman's unhappiness and understood it as few others could, for she had trudged down the same road that Constance was now traveling. At Lodi, Constance had been armored in the icy aplomb of an imperial empress; today her shield was showing cracks, discernible only to a sharp eye like Eleanor's. And as her gaze met that of Heinrich's wife, Eleanor suddenly knew they were about to be ambushed.

As Heinrich turned toward the dais, clamping his hand down on Constance's arm when she seemed reluctant to follow, Eleanor plucked at Richard's sleeve to attract his attention. But her warning was unnecessary. He was staring at several men just entering the hall and she was close enough to see his body react to his recognition, his mouth thinning, the muscles of his jaw tightening. "You see the coxcomb in the green cap, Maman? That is Robert de Nonant, the Bishop of Coventry's brother."

He did not need to say more, for although Eleanor did not know de Nonant's brother by sight, she did know he was a sworn liegeman of her son John. She'd let herself hope that if Heinrich did have a double cross in mind, it would not involve John. Even though she'd so often had to watch helplessly as her sons fought one another, showing all the fraternal love of Cain and Abel, John's latest betrayal was the most painful, for there was more at stake now than lands or crowns. If John and Philippe won, Richard would die in a French dungeon, suffering the torments of the damned until he drew his last wretched breath.

After he was seated upon the dais, with Constance sitting rigidly at his side, Heinrich beckoned to Richard and then to Robert de Nonant and his companions. They approached slowly, casting hostile glances at the English king as they passed. Once Richard and Eleanor were standing in front of the dais, too, Heinrich held up his hand for silence.

"This was to be the day that my dear friend, the king of the English, gained his freedom. But there has been an unexpected development. The French king and the Count of Mortain have offered a vast sum of money to prolong his confinement, at least until Michaelmas, and they have even promised to match the full amount of his ransom if he is placed in their custody. If I heeded my personal feelings for King Richard, I would, of course, dismiss their offer out of hand. Alas, I must respond as an emperor, not a friend. I have an obligation to consider any proposal that would fill the imperial coffers and finance our expedition to claim the Sicilian crown for my beloved empress."

Richard was stunned, for even in his worst moments, he'd never thought Heinrich would dare to disavow the Worms Pact, one sworn to upon Heinrich's immortal soul, sealed in the name of the Holy Trinity, and vouched for by the honor of the most powerful vassals and churchmen of the empire. He felt his mother's hand tighten on his arm, her fingers digging into his flesh, for although she did not understand the Latin, she read Richard's body language. The silence in the hall was eerie, absolute, Heinrich's audience no less shocked than Richard.

Heinrich seemed to be enjoying himself. "I want all to be out in the open, no secrets. So I would have the English king read this proposal for himself, lest he have any doubts about what is being offered." He snapped his fingers and as soon as rolled parchments were placed in his hand, he held them out to Richard, smiling.

Richard took them automatically. While he glanced down at the letters, the Archbishop of Rouen hastily translated Heinrich's comments for Eleanor. The letters were indeed from Philippe and John, and as Richard read what was being offered and what it could mean for him, his numbed disbelief gave way to despair and then murderous rage.

His fist clenched around the letters and he flung them to the floor at Heinrich's feet. But before he could speak, his mother was beside him. "Wait, Richard, wait!" She was clinging to his arm with such urgency that she actually succeeded in pulling him back from the dais. "Look around you," she said, her voice shaking, but her eyes blazing with green fire. "Look!"

He did and saw at once what she meant. Virtually every German in the hall was staring at Heinrich as if he'd suddenly revealed himself to be the Antichrist. Not a word had yet been said, but their expressions of horror and disgust left no doubt as to how they felt about their emperor's eleventh-hour surprise. "Let them speak first," Eleanor hissed. "Let the Germans handle this."

"My lord emperor!" The Archbishop-elect of Cologne stalked toward the dais. He was Richard's age, a man in his prime, and though he was a prince of the Church, he looked now like a soldier making ready to do battle with the forces of evil. "We must discuss this matter with you ere it goes any further."

Heinrich loathed Adolf von Altena and for just a heartbeat, it showed on his face. "I see no such need, my lord archbishop."

"I do." This declaration came from the Archbishop of Mainz, who'd moved to stand at Adolf's side.

"As do I," Leopold said loudly, striding over to join the archbishops. He was followed by his shocked sons and the Archbishop of Salzburg. By now all of the former rebel lords had added their voices to the growing chorus. When Heinrich's own uncle, Konrad, the Count Palatine of the Rhineland, also insisted upon it, Heinrich grudgingly gave way and agreed to meet with them in the cathedral chapter house in an hour's time.

Richard's moment of pure, primal fury had passed and he was once more in control of his emotions. "This is a shameful offer, craven and contemptible, made by desperate men who lack the courage to face me on the battlefield. I know I need not remind those in this hall that my cowardly brother never took the cross and the French king broke his holy vow, then plotted against me whilst I fought for Christ in the Holy Land. But I have no doubts whatsoever that my *dear friend* the emperor would never act in a way to damage his own honor or that of the empire."

The last word was to be Richard's. Rising to his feet, Heinrich exited the hall, only his quickened pace offering evidence of his anger, his *ministeriales* hurrying to catch up. Forgotten in the confusion, Constance sank back wearily in her seat and closed her eyes, praying that Heinrich had at last overreached himself. Richard was assured again and again that this would never come to pass by men practically choking on their own indignation, and then they, too, followed after the emperor, until the hall had emptied of all but the English and Richard's German guards.

The Bishop of Bath was hovering nearby, sweating and swearing that he'd known nothing of this, but no one paid him any heed. Longchamp declared that he meant to attend that afternoon session of the Diet to speak on the king's behalf; Richard never doubted that he'd gain admittance. Alarmed by his grandmother's pallor, Otto went off in search of wine for her. Savaric had finally stopped protesting, silenced by a lethal look from Richard. André thrust his way through the throng to reach Richard's side, but he was wise enough to understand that nothing he said could be of comfort to his cousin now. The others slowly realized that, too, and for a time, no one spoke at all.

❧

THE DAY PASSED AS SLOWLY as if time itself had been paralyzed by the German emperor's treachery. After darkness fell, some of the men crowding into Richard's chamber departed to find meals or lodgings in the city, but his mother and friends had no more appetite than he did. He'd said very little after leaving the great hall, slouched in a window-seat or restlessly pacing the confines of the chamber. He was close enough for her to touch, yet Eleanor could feel the distance between them widening as the hours crept by, for he shared none of his inner turmoil. He'd said only that he would not endure another year in Heinrich's prison, and what frightened her was that she thought he meant it. André and the men who'd suffered shipwreck and flight and captivity with him seemed to think he meant it, too; at least that was how she read their grim faces and brooding silence. But she doubted she could rely upon any of them to try to talk sense into her son if it came to that. They were much more likely to offer up their lives with his, blind followers of that mad male code of honor. She found it ironic that, even after marrying twice and raising four sons to manhood, the workings of the male brain remained such a mystery to her.

Compline had rung hours ago. Otto had reluctantly departed when it became obvious that his little brother could no longer stay awake. Fernando had amused himself for a while by playing with Richard's parrot, but he'd finally gone off to bed, too. Of the clerics, only the Archbishop of Rouen remained, and most of the men had left with Hugh le Brun when he declared his intention to find a tavern and a wench and get roaring drunk. Morgan, with the resourcefulness of the Welsh, disappeared for a while and returned with a servant toting flagons of wine and German ale. Richard drained two of the flagons, but he still seemed sober to Eleanor, and she thought that in so many ways, he was very like his father. She was trying to remember if she'd ever seen Harry even tipsy in all the years of their marriage, when the door opened and Longchamp stumbled in.

He looked so exhausted that the Archbishop of Rouen, who detested him, nonetheless reached out to guide him toward a chair. Longchamp bristled and pulled away, for he was far too proud to accept aid from an enemy. "Nothing has been resolved, sire," he said wearily. "Heinrich's greed has blinded him to the truth—that Philippe and John could never raise the money they are promising. I pointed out that the annual revenues of France are less than half those of England and what money Philippe has will be needed for his Normandy campaign. I reminded him, too, that John's rich English estates have been forfeited, so he has not a prayer in Hell of paying his share of this disgusting bribe."

"Did he hear what you were saying, Guillaume?" Richard asked, cutting to the heart of the matter.

"I think it gave him something to think about, sire. But he is as stubborn as he is arrogant, and I fear it has now become more a matter of pride than money. You see, he stands alone in this. All of them—the three archbishops, the bishops of Worms and Speyer, the dukes of Brabant and Limburg, the Marquis of Mont-ferrat, even Leopold and Heinrich's own uncle and brothers—are insistent that he honor the terms agreed upon at Worms last June. I think his brothers are enjoying this rare opportunity to see him squirm, but the others are truly out-raged. The only one to speak up for him was Count Dietrich, and since he is believed to have the blood of that murdered bishop on his hands, his words car-ried no weight with any of them. Archbishop Adolf had a very heated confronta-tion with Heinrich, the first time I've seen that bloodless snake show real anger. For the archbishop was fearless, saying that 'the empire had been sufficiently defiled by the unworthy imprisonment of a most noble king,' and warning Heinrich that if he did this, he'd be staining forever the honor of the empire."

Richard smiled for the first time since the morning's betrayal. "I'd have given a lot to see that. Adolf von Altena is a good man, worth a hundred of Heinrich. But do you expect them to prevail?"

"I am not sure," the chancellor admitted, after a long hesitation. "When we adjourned for the night, Heinrich was still holding out against them. Emperors are accustomed to getting their own way and do not take kindly to opposition from those they see as lesser men. But they are no less adamant than he. We will resume in the morning. More than that, I cannot say."

"You'd best get to bed, then," Richard said, "for you'll have another difficult day ahead of you. We all will," he added, glancing over at his mother, who looked just as drained as his chancellor. Eleanor did not argue. Rising to her feet, she crossed the room and kissed her son good night before departing to her own chamber. But she got little sleep that night. All of them did.

❦

THE NEXT DAY WAS one of waiting. Eleanor would have felt better had Richard been fuming and cursing. His silence seemed both unnatural and unnerving, for she was beginning to understand that he was struggling under a burden she'd been spared—a profound sense of shame. She'd had sixteen long years to dwell upon the consequences of her actions, and she'd suffered from regrets, remorse, even guilt for the part she'd played in estranging her husband and sons. But she'd never blamed herself for accepting what could not be changed or challenged.

Watching Richard as he stared moodily into space, she suppressed a sigh. It was almost as if men and women inhabited two different worlds, so differently did they see things. Was it because women learned from the cradle that their freedom was limited, their independence denied? Even a queen must still obey her husband, and punishment was swift and sharp for one who did not. Being powerless was the natural state for most women. But for a highborn man— especially a man like her son—it was intolerable and degrading. Such a wound would be harder to heal than a bodily injury. She would find a way, though, she vowed—if only they could thwart this monster on the German throne.

It was late afternoon before Longchamp returned. He was accompanied by the Archbishop of Rouen, who'd attended the second day's session, and the Archbishop of Cologne. It was the latter who spoke for them, saying with a smile, "It is done. Heinrich has agreed to honor the terms of the Worms pact—"

Whatever else he'd been about to say was drowned out by the cheers and laughter of the men crowding the chamber. Richard did not join in, but he was smiling as he rose and walked toward them. "Thank you," he said simply, for he knew that if any one man had made this happen, it was Adolf von Altena.

Longchamp gave voice to what Richard was thinking. "Most of the credit must go to the archbishop. He refused to be intimidated and argued with the eloquence of the angels."

"More like a lawyer," Adolf said with a chuckle. "I reminded the emperor that if the Worms agreement could be set aside with such ease, so could other pacts— including the one signed at Koblenz that brought the rebellion to an end."

Richard was no longer smiling. "I am more grateful than I can ever say. But you've made a mortal enemy this day."

Adolf's own smile never wavered. "I believe the Almighty judges us by the enemies we make and, come Judgment Day, I will be proud to answer for mine." He paused to apologize to Eleanor for not acknowledging her sooner before continuing. "We were not going to give way on this, for the honor of our empire itself was at stake. I think Heinrich finally realized that. We benefited, too, by his obsession with Sicily. I do not know if you've heard, but there have been rumors since Christmas that the Sicilian king is ailing. So Heinrich is burning to begin his war, and he chose to cut his losses, settling for salvaging what he could of his tattered pride."

Richard had known this was coming. "And what is the price I must pay for saving his pride?" He was not reassured when the three men exchanged glances before responding.

"He is demanding additional hostages," Longchamp said, "who will be held until payment is made of ten thousand marks, and he insists that the Archbishop of Rouen be one of them."

Richard frowned, assuring the archbishop that he would arrange payment as soon as he was back in England. But as he studied their faces, it struck him that his chancellor and archbishop were not as happy about their victory as Adolf seemed to be. "What else does he want? What are you not telling me?"

Longchamp started to speak, then stopped. The Archbishop of Rouen remained mute, no longer meeting Richard's eyes. Seeing that it was up to him, Adolf said gravely, "You will not want to hear this, my lord Richard. Heinrich swears that he will not release you until you do homage to him for your kingdom of England and your lands in France."

There was an immediate uproar as Richard's knights reacted with anger and disbelief. But Richard's voice rose above the clamor. "I will never agree to that," he snarled, "never!"

He was at once supported in his defiance by every man in the chamber, save only the three prelates. The rage Richard had been holding back for the past two days now spewed out in a fiery lava flow of profanities and threats, almost hot enough to blister the air itself. Eleanor had seen too many Angevin eruptions to be daunted by this one, though, and she waited until her son had to pause for breath. "I would speak with the king alone." Richard swung around to look in her direction, already shaking his head, but she knew he would not countermand her in public, and he did not disappoint. As the men began slowly to file out, she asked the chancellor and two archbishops to remain and also signaled for André to stay, even though his own angry outburst made it unlikely he'd be of much help.

As soon as the door closed, Richard said in a sharp tone he'd never used with her before, "I will not consent to this, no matter what argument you make. Become that misbegotten whoreson's vassal? When ice burns and fire freezes!"

"Richard, it is meaningless—"

"Not to me!"

"You would be doing it under duress, and the Church holds such oaths to be invalid. Do they not, my lords?" She appealed to the prelates, and they confirmed her understanding of canon law, assuring Richard that doing homage under these circumstances would have no legal consequences.

Richard was shaking his head again. "How can you not see?" he accused, his gaze cutting from the churchmen to his mother. "My men could never respect me again if I agreed to this. Nor could I respect myself."

"Richard, the one thing you need not fear is losing the respect of your men," Eleanor said impatiently. "They'd follow you to Hell and back if you asked it of them."

"You do not understand. Women never do."

"Mayhap not. But are you truly willing to sacrifice so much to save your pride?"

"It is not a question of pride. It is a matter of honor."

"You will not be staining your honor by doing this. You will be acting as a king." Crossing to his side, she looked up intently into his face. "Think what will happen if you refuse Heinrich's demand. The best you can hope for is that he'll hold you prisoner in an attempt to coerce your consent. But he's not only unscrupulous, Richard, he is unstable. No rational man would have been so shameless, so blatant about his crimes. He is intoxicated by his own arrogance, and if you do not let him save face, it is impossible to say what he may do."

Eleanor gave Richard no chance to respond, glancing back at Adolf. "Can you say for a certainty, my lord archbishop, that Heinrich would not decide to defy the Diet and turn my son over to the French?"

"Of course I could not, my lady. I agree with your assessment of the emperor. The man is dangerously unpredictable. He was motivated by greed when he sought to extort even more money from King Richard. But it is hard to say what he might do if he is not offered a way to save face."

Eleanor put her hand on Richard's arm. "Think what will befall your kingdom and your Norman duchy if you are unable to return to defend them. Philippe will overrun Normandy for certes. He could also threaten Anjou, mayhap even Poitou. Your father's empire would soon be only a memory."

Richard stared at her, saying nothing. He'd told no one about his eerie dream at Trifels, hearing that familiar, hoarse voice echoing in the darkness of his prison cell. *Save my empire. Do not let my life's work become dust on the wind.*

Eleanor was encouraged that at least he seemed to be listening. "We both know John would not be able to stave off the French for long. He is not a coward, but he has rarely bloodied his sword, has never proven himself on the battlefield. He might not even fight for Normandy, willing to content himself with his island kingdom. And what do you think that would mean for the English? A king who cannot command respect is a king who will not be obeyed. Bandits would make a mockery of the King's Peace, and local lords would feel free to pursue their own wars, just as they did during Stephen's reign. Do you know how the chroniclers described those years, Richard? They said it was a time 'when Christ and his saints slept.'"

Richard would have pulled away, but he could not break her grip without hurting her. "You ask too much of me, Maman."

"I am not the one asking it of you, my dearest son. You were anointed with the sacred chrism on the day of your coronation. You are God's vicar on earth, for you swore to defend the Church and deliver justice and mercy to the people of England." The mention of his coronation oath reminded her of another holy vow he'd taken, and she did not scruple to remind him of it, too, even though she fervently hoped he'd never attempt to honor it. "There is something else you must consider. Your chancellor told me that you'd vowed to return to the Holy Land and retake Jerusalem. You can only do that if you regain your freedom and restore peace to the Angevin empire."

Richard could not dispute anything she'd said and he glanced toward his cousin, saying desperately, "For Christ's sake, André, make her understand why I cannot do this."

André looked stricken. "Richard . . . I cannot. I know what you feel, for I feel it, too. But your mother has convinced me. You have no choice."

The Archbishop of Cologne decided this was an opportune time to intervene. "Queen Eleanor has articulated the reasons for consenting with great eloquence, and I urge you to heed her, my lord king. I can assure you that the homage will not fetter you in any way for it will be made under duress. Heinrich will not benefit from it—but you could."

"What do you mean?"

"I mean that Heinrich's need to save face has blinded him to the consequences of his demand. As soon as you do homage to him, you become the most powerful and highborn vassal of the empire. Think what that could mean if Heinrich dies unexpectedly. He has no son, and even if he did, our crown passes by election, not birth. You'd have a vote when it came to electing the next Holy Roman Emperor and your opinion would sway others. The crown might even be offered to you," he said, with a sudden grin. "Now, that's a thought to keep Heinrich awake at night!"

Richard was not yet ready to appreciate the irony of that. For the moment, he could think of nothing but the ordeal he faced on the morrow—having to kneel and swear homage and fealty to a man he loathed, a man he wanted dead.

Turning away, he sat down in the closest chair, and the slump of his shoulders told Eleanor that she'd won. His pain tore at her heart, but his freedom mattered more. She hoped that in time, he'd come to see that, too. But even if he did not, she would have no regrets. There was nothing she would not have done to get her son out of Heinrich's power—nothing.

⁂

THERE WAS A WIDELY HELD BELIEF that certain days had been identified by ancient Egyptian astrologers as days of ill fortune, upon which no enterprise should be started or blood drawn by doctors. The fourth of February was one of these unlucky Egyptian days, yet to Eleanor, it would be a blessed day, for in the third hour of the morning, her son regained his freedom. She was startled and embarrassed to find herself bursting into tears when it finally happened. But the audience was very moved by the sight of this celebrated, aging queen sobbing in the Lionheart's arms, and Heinrich was convinced that it had been a deliberate maneuver to sway public opinion in Richard's favor. He'd awakened in a foul mood, for not even Richard's act of homage could take away the bitter taste of defeat. But he cheered up somewhat after Markward von Annweiler reminded him how outraged the French king would be when he learned that Richard had done homage to Heinrich for Normandy and Anjou, and it was with a chilly smile of satisfaction that he became the English king's liege lord.

Eleanor was sickened by that smile, for although nothing showed on Richard's face, she knew it would haunt his memory in years to come. The ceremony was a formal one, carefully scripted beforehand. Richard knelt and pledged his faith and fidelity to the emperor. He then offered his leather cap to Heinrich as a symbol of vassalage. Heinrich solemnly accepted the cap and then handed it back to Richard, along with a heavy gold cross, in return for a promise of an annual payment of five thousand marks. Eleanor knew Heinrich would never see a farthing of it. As she glanced around the hall, she thought Richard's German allies seemed pleased that so renowned a king was now a vassal of the Holy Roman Empire, but Richard's own vassals looked like men attending a public hanging. She consoled herself that at least the worst was over now, although bidding farewell to the hostages would be difficult.

After his homage to Heinrich, Richard took the homage of eleven German lords and prelates in return for money fiefs, yearly revenues to be paid from the rents of English and Norman manors. He had told Eleanor that he'd formed an alliance meant to encircle and isolate the French king, while also rewarding the men who'd been so instrumental in winning his freedom. But she'd not realized the full significance of this coalition until she saw how many distinguished, influential men had been drawn into Richard's league against Philippe: the archbishops of Cologne and Mainz, the Bishop-elect of Liege, the dukes of Brabant and Limburg, the Count of Holland, the Marquis of Montferrat, and in a fine example of either political cynicism or realism, Baldwin, the eldest son of the Count of Flanders and Hainaut, who was firmly allied with the French king. Even Leopold of Austria and Heinrich's uncle Konrad, the Count Palatine, and his brother, the Duke of Swabia, did homage to Richard for English fiefs.

Eleanor studied the emperor intently. If Heinrich was troubled that so many of his own vassals and kinsmen were pledging their loyalty to the English king, he showed no sign of it. It was true that their oaths were given with the proviso *salva fidelitate imperatoris*—saving the honor of the emperor. To Eleanor, this was conclusive evidence that the French–German axis forged by Heinrich's father was well and truly dead, and as she watched her son accept the homage of his new liegemen, she felt a surge of fierce pride, marveling that Richard could have accomplished a feat like this whilst being held prisoner.

Richard's first act as a free man was to entrust one of his vassals, Saut de Breuil, with an important mission. He was to travel to the Holy Land and assure Richard's nephew Henri, the Count of Champagne, that he would return to fulfill his vow once he had avenged himself on his enemies and restored peace to his domains. In return for this service, Richard made Saut de Breuil a grant of lands worth forty pounds.

His second act was to summon the Bishop of Bath and request that he be one of the additional hostages demanded by the emperor. Savaric declared it would be his honor, for he was eager to convince the king that he'd played no part in Heinrich's double cross. But it did not go as smoothly with the Bishop of Coventry's brother. Robert de Nonant had not made himself inconspicuous as his companions had prudently done. To the contrary, he seemed to be courting attention, swaggering about the hall and infuriating Richard's knights. Eventually, he caught Richard's eye.

De Nonant took his time in responding to the king's summons and gave Richard the briefest of bows in grudging acknowledgment of his rank. Richard regarded him in silence for several moments before saying coldly, "You are a fortunate man, Sir Robert. I am going to give you a chance to redeem yourself. I will forgive your treachery if you agree to be one of my hostages."

That did not go over well with Richard's men, who felt he deserved no clemency. But to the astonishment of all watching, Nonant showed no gratitude for his unexpected reprieve. "I will not be a hostage for you," he said, staring at Richard defiantly. "The Count of Mortain is my liege lord, and my loyalty is pledged to him."

Richard's eyes glittered. "As you will." Glancing around then, he beckoned to his cousin. "Arrest this man for treason."

André smiled. "With great pleasure, my liege," he said, and de Nonant was abruptly hustled from the hall by André's knights, none too gently, as Richard's men clapped and jeered and Longchamp watched with great satisfaction, hoping that the Bishop of Coventry would soon suffer the same fate.

❦

CONSTANCE HAD SOUGHT Eleanor out to confide that Heinrich was not going to honor their request that Otto and Wilhelm be kept together. Otto was to remain at the imperial court, while Wilhelm would be one of Leopold's seven hostages, accompanying the Austrian duke back to Vienna. Eleanor was grateful for the warning, for that enabled her to alert Otto, so her grandsons would not be taken by surprise. Richard had given his parrot to Wilhelm, much to his delight, and she hoped the unusual pet would help to console the little boy once he was separated from his brother. Otto accepted the news with his usual stoicism, and Baldwin de Bethune, who was also to be one of Leopold's hostages, promised to keep an eye on the lad. Eleanor was furious, but there was nothing she could do.

After bidding farewell to the hostages and to Constance, who'd remained in the hall long after Heinrich had departed, Richard paused in the doorway to savor the moment, one in which he was no longer trailed by German guards. Glancing over his shoulder at Heinrich's empress, he switched from French to the safer *lenga romana*. "I feel as if we are leaving one more hostage behind." Looking back at Constance, Eleanor felt the same way.

The outer courtyard was thronged, for they had a huge retinue—Eleanor's ladies, Richard's knights, men-at-arms, the lords and bishops and abbots who'd accompanied the queen from England, and those in attendance upon the Archbishop of Cologne and the Duke of Brabant, who intended to escort Richard across Germany, none of them trusting in Heinrich's safe conduct. Eleanor had tried to anticipate all of her son's needs. She'd ruled out river travel because she was sure he'd want to be on horseback after his long confinement, engaging mounts for the men, horse litters for herself and her women, and for Richard, a spirited grey stallion that brought a delighted smile to his face. Although he'd been able to dress well in recent months, she'd still made sure to bring a wardrobe suitable for a king. And she assured him that English ships would be awaiting their arrival at Antwerp.

She had forgotten one of Richard's needs, though, something he found as essential as air. But André had not, and as Richard stood beside his new stallion, talking soothingly to accustom the animal to his presence before mounting, André approached with a large hemp sack. "I thought you might want this," he said, opening the bag to reveal a scabbard of Spanish leather.

Sweeping his mantle back, Richard fastened the belt and then drew the sword from its scabbard. He saw at once that a superior bladesmith had labored to create this superb weapon, with a thirty-inch blade and an enameled pommel, reminding him of the sword he'd been given by his mother upon his investiture as Duke of Aquitaine at age fifteen. He admired its balance, his eyes caressing that slender steel blade as a lover might, and when he glanced toward his cousin, André thought that he finally looked like himself.

"Do you know how long it has been since I've held a sword in my hand, André?"

The other man shook his head.

"One year, six weeks, and three days." For a moment, their eyes held, and then Richard sheathed his sword, swung up into the saddle, and gave the command to move out.

RICHARD'S HOMEWARD JOURNEY WAS turned into a triumphal procession by his German allies. He and Eleanor spent three days as the archbishop's guests in Cologne, where they were feasted lavishly and entertained by some of Germany's finest minnesingers. On February 14, they heard Mass in the great cathedral, and the English chroniclers reported gleefully that the archbishop had deliberately chosen the Mass for the August feast day of St Peter in Chains, with the Introit that began, "Now I know that the Lord hath sent His angel and delivered me from the hand of Herod." The German emperor's reaction to that was not recorded.

Richard rewarded Cologne by issuing charters exempting its merchants from paying rent for their London guildhall and other local fees and giving them the right to sell their wares at all English fairs and to exercise their own customs. As England was a major wool exporter to the Rhineland city and its largest market for Cologne's textiles, wine, and luxury goods, these privileges were greatly appreciated, rebounding to the credit of their archbishop for allying himself with the English king. And although neither man knew it at the time, their friendship would pay even greater benefits in years to come.

From Cologne, they passed into the territory of the Duke of Brabant, and again they were feted at each town or castle along the way. By late February, they'd reached the duke's port of Antwerp. Here English ships were riding at anchor in the harbor. After parting from Archbishop Adolf and the duke, Richard spent five days at Zwin. The weather was unsettled, and he took advantage of the delay to scout the estuaries and inlets of the islands, for he had a keen interest in naval warfare and felt certain that if a French-Flemish invasion occurred, it would sail from these waters. The winds finally were favorable, and on March 12, they unfurled sails, raised anchors, and headed out into the Channel. By the next day, they were approaching the port of Sandwich. It had been four years since Richard had last set foot on English soil.

CHAPTER TWENTY-ONE

MARCH 1194

Sandwich, England

Richard's unheralded arrival at Sandwich stirred up much excitement, as none had known when he would be returning or even if he would be returning, for many of his subjects had feared he would die on crusade or in a German dungeon. After greeting the townspeople, he continued on to Canterbury, where he gave thanks at the shrine of the martyred saint Thomas Becket, and greatly pleased the Christchurch monks by declaring that he'd not wanted to enter any English church until he'd visited the mother church of Canterbury. Hubert Walter was away besieging John's castle at Marlborough, but the prior was delighted to play host to their renowned crusader king and his venerated queen mother. It was a source of ironic amusement to Eleanor that after a lifetime of controversy and public disapproval, she was now acclaimed for the very qualities that had once earned her such censure. She had never wielded as much power as she had during Richard's crusade and captivity. But none had challenged her exercise of this unique authority, for her boldness, determination, and political shrewdness—so unseemly in a wife—were deemed admirable in a mother fighting for her son.

✧

WORD OF THE KING'S RETURN swept through the shire with the speed of a wind-whipped brush fire. When they rode out of Canterbury the following morning, they found the road lined with people from neighboring villages and hamlets, all eager to see if the rumors were true. Richard was surprised by their enthusiastic welcome, for in the four and a half years since his coronation, he'd spent only four months in England. But Eleanor assured him that the stories of his exploits in the Holy Land had made him known the length and breadth of his kingdom. The crowds slowed them down—priests wanting to offer their blessings, excited children darting underfoot, women holding up little ones so they could one day say they'd seen the king's homecoming, old men shouting out that they'd sent a son or grandson to fight the Saracens, prosperous merchants and their wives mingling with craftsmen, peasants, monks from the Cluniac abbey at Faversham, pilgrims on their way to Canterbury's holy shrine, and beggars asking for alms. Eleanor knew this was a day the good people of Kent would not forget and, as she watched her son acknowledge their cheers, she thought that he would remember it, too. It was her hope that he'd soon have memories bright enough to rout the darker ones of Dürnstein, Trifels, and Mainz.

The western sky was staining with sunset crimson and gold when they saw the castle walls and cathedral spire of Rochester in the distance. A large throng was waiting, spreading across the road, and as they came into view, men on horseback rode out to meet them. When they were close enough for recognition, Richard spurred his stallion forward. He swung from the saddle just as Hubert Walter dismounted, and knelt at the archbishop's feet. The watching crowd cheered wildly, and the Bishop of Rochester and the other churchmen were beaming, delighted by the king's dramatic gesture of piety. Hubert knew it was more than that; it was also a personal acknowledgment of heartfelt gratitude, and his eyes filled with tears. He held out his hand to raise Richard to his feet and the two men embraced, setting off even more cheering. As if on cue, the city's church bells began to peal, until all of Rochester seemed to be reverberating with celestial, melodious music.

THE TOP STORY OF Rochester Castle's keep was bisected into a large private chamber and a great hall, where an informal council was in session. A trestle table had been set up for Richard, Eleanor, Hubert Walter, Gilbert, the Bishop of Rochester, Guillaume de Longchamp, André de Chauvigny, and William de St Mère-Eglise. All eyes were on Richard's chief justiciar as Hubert began with the bad news.

"You may not have heard this yet, sire, but your brother made another treaty with the French king in January, in which he ceded all of Normandy east of the River Seine to Philippe, save only Rouen, as well as a number of important castles in the Loire Valley, including Loches. Of course John did not have actual control of these lands, but Philippe at once invaded Normandy again and the city of Évreux is now in his hands. John then sent his clerk, Adam of St Edmund, to London. This Adam brazenly came to pay his respects to me, and when I invited him to dine, hoping I could learn more, he drank enough wine to boast of John's close friendship with the French king, your mortal enemy. I sent word to the mayor, who had Adam arrested at his lodgings. There, we discovered letters for the castellans of John's castles, ordering them to stock up on provisions and to strengthen their garrisons in preparation for a long siege."

Richard's response was a sour smile. "It sounds as if John is in need of a better class of spy, at the very least one not so fond of wine."

"I held a council meeting with the other justiciars and formally declared all of John's lands in England forfeit. My fellow bishops and I then excommunicated him." Hubert glanced almost apologetically toward Eleanor, but she showed no reaction to the casting out of her youngest son into eternal darkness.

There was a wine cup at Richard's elbow and he took a swallow in a futile attempt to wash away the bad taste of his brother's latest treachery. "What has been done about his castles?"

Hubert smiled. "At last I have good news to share with you, my liege. All but two of John's castles are now in our control. William Marshal took Bristol Castle in February. I captured Marlborough Castle, whilst William Marshal's faithless brother, its castellan, was mortally wounded in the fighting. I am pleased to report that my own brother Theobald, also John's sworn man, has seen the error of his ways and yielded Lancaster Castle to me. And in Cornwall, Henry de la Pommeraye no longer holds St Michael's Mount for John; he died of fright upon learning that you'd regained your freedom." Seeing Richard's skepticism, he smiled again. "It is true, sire. When he heard this, he gasped, clutched his chest, and went down like a felled tree."

That evoked laughter, which ended, though, when Hubert revealed that the two castles still holding out were the formidable strongholds of Tickhill and Nottingham. Tickhill was under siege by the Bishop of Durham, Hubert told them, and the earls of Chester, Huntingdon, and Derby were leading the assault upon Nottingham.

Richard was pleased to hear that the Earl of Huntingdon was taking part in the siege, for he was the brother of the Scots king and his presence at Nottingham was further proof of King William's friendship. Upon taking the crown, Richard had agreed to let William buy back for ten thousand marks those castles William had been forced to surrender to Henry after the Great Rebellion of 1174 and recognized Scotland's independence. Richard had received some criticism for it at the time, but he thought the goodwill he'd gained was worth far more than ten thousand marks; William had even made a substantial contribution to the ransom. Making a mental note to invite William for a state visit once John's rebellion was crushed, Richard glanced around the table at his mother and the men who'd never lost faith in him, no matter how dire his prospects seemed.

"I may have more than my share of enemies," he said, "but I have been blessed in my friends. I have not felt truly freed from Heinrich's yoke until now, finding myself back on English soil."

They all smiled, several of them blinking hard, and Eleanor reached over to squeeze her son's arm. André rescued them from this looming sentimental storm by saying dryly, "My lord archbishop, I hope you will see that my cousin's words are widely circulated. It never hurts a king to declare his love for his homeland, even one with such wretched weather and wine."

Midst the ensuing laughter, Richard discovered, somewhat to his surprise, that he'd actually meant it. Aquitaine would always have the first claim upon his heart, and in truth, he agreed with André about England's weather and wine. But he'd not realized how much he valued his island kingdom until he'd come so close to losing it.

They were rising to go to their beds—Richard was impatient to reach his, since he had a woman waiting in it—when Hubert Walter remembered he'd not told the king about the shocking news from Sicily. "My liege, two days ago we received a letter from Rome. The King of Sicily is dead."

Even though he'd heard Tancred had been ailing, Richard had not expected this. He felt a throb of regret, for he'd developed a genuine respect for the Sicilian king and he'd been hopeful that Tancred, a much better soldier than Heinrich, would be able to fend off the coming German invasion.

"I am sorry to hear that," he said, "very sorry." He'd met Tancred's eldest son during the five days he'd spent at Tancred's court in Catania, and he tried to remember how old Roger was then. Sixteen, mayhap seventeen, which would make him nineteen now. No longer a stripling, yet young to shoulder such a burden.

"Roger is a good lad; I liked him. I am sure the Sicilian lords will rally around him, but it will not be easy to win his war."

Hubert was shaking his head sadly. "Roger is dead, too, sire. He died unexpectedly in December, so suddenly that some spoke of poison. Tancred's heir is now his four-year-old son."

"Christ Jesus," Richard said softly, feeling a stab of pity for Tancred, who'd died knowing that both his dynasty and his kingdom were doomed, for few would dare to defy Heinrich on behalf of a child king. The German emperor would lay claim to Sicily, financing his campaign with the ransom money he'd extorted from England, and untold thousands would suffer under his heavy-handed rule. Richard could only wonder, with both bitterness and bafflement, why the Almighty had let any of this happen.

❦

JOANNA AND BERENGARIA WERE euphoric upon receiving a papal letter informing them that Richard had been freed two days after Candlemas. They did not expect to hear from Richard or Eleanor until their return to England, and they spent much of their time discussing how long that journey would take. Since they were ignorant of German geography and lacked any German maps, they could only speculate. Berengaria confided that she was a little nervous about their reunion. She'd been taken aback to realize that she and Richard had now been apart as long as they'd been together; the sixteen months from their wedding in Cyprus to her departure from the Holy Land matched by the sixteen months since their Acre farewell. She was eager to see England for the first time and Joanna did her best to satisfy her curiosity about Richard's realm, although Joanna's memories were faded by the passage of time. It was nigh on eighteen years since she'd left England on her bridal journey to Sicily.

Their anxious waiting came to an end on March 25. Joanna and Berengaria were playing a game of chess in the latter's bedchamber when a servant informed them that a messenger from King Richard had just ridden in. Berengaria hurriedly covered her hair with a veil—Joanna did not bother—and they flew down the stairs into Eleanor's magnificent great hall. There they came to an abrupt halt, and for the moment, the messenger mattered more than the message.

"Cousin Morgan!" As soon as he'd made a gallant bow, Joanna caught his hand in both of hers, her smile bright enough to light the darkest corners of the hall. "How glad we are to see you!"

"We are, indeed," Berengaria agreed, with a luminous smile of her own, for she was fond of Joanna's Welsh cousin. "How wonderful that my husband thought to send you to us!"

Morgan grinned. "As soon as we reached London, he said he needed a man to carry letters to Poitiers. I'd gladly have groveled and begged for the honor, but he spared me that, merely saying he hoped I'd remember to come back." When they asked if Richard was still in London, he shook his head, saying Richard was likely at the siege of Nottingham by now. He began to tell them of Richard's welcome into the city, but Joanna noted the way his gaze was sweeping the hall and she beckoned to Dame Beatrix, telling her to find Mariam.

"I'd never seen anything like it," Morgan confessed. "Someone told me London has twenty-five thousand citizens, and I vow every last one of them turned out to see the king. The mayor was there, and the Bishop of London, of course, the city sheriffs, aldermen, priests, merchants, journeymen, apprentices—so many people that I could not have thrown a stone without hitting someone. They escorted the king and his lady mother to St Paul's through streets hung with banners and swept so clean the rakers must have been laboring all night long. At the cathedral, a special Mass was said and the bishop offered up prayers of thanksgiving, praising the Almighty for restoring the king to them. I think even the cutpurses and thieves took the day off."

Morgan grinned again, almost adding that the whores in the Southwark stews had likely done a thriving business afterward, but thinking better of it in time, for Berengaria did not share Joanna's bawdy sense of humor. "Now, what did I forget? Ah yes, the letters. They must be in here somewhere," he teased, pretending to root around in his leather pouch. But then he happened to glance up and saw the woman just entering the hall.

Morgan and Mariam's flirtation had begun with their first meeting in Sicily, but they'd not become lovers until their second summer in Outremer, for an army camp was not the ideal place for clandestine trysts. Although they'd sought to be as discreet as possible, Morgan had often suspected their efforts were futile, and his suspicions were confirmed when Richard chose him for this mission. If even the king knew he was besotted with Mariam, clearly their love affair was one of the worst-kept secrets in Christendom. But if there were any innocent souls still in the dark, that ended now when, with an utter disregard for propriety, Mariam flung herself into his arms. He pulled her close, holding her as tightly as he'd hungered to do during those long, dark nights in Germany, kissing her until they both were breathless. Only then did he remember the letters and handed them over with a sheepish smile before turning back to Mariam.

Berengaria eagerly broke the seal of her husband's letter. She had an expressive face and when she looked up, her distress was obvious to all in the hall. "Joanna, he says I should remain in Poitiers instead of joining him in England!"

Joanna had received two letters, one from her brother and one from her mother. She'd already scanned Richard's brief message and was reading Eleanor's when Berengaria cried out in dismay. "He is going to be occupied putting down John's rebellion," she said, hoping she sounded convincing.

Morgan tore his attention away from Mariam long enough to say, "That is indeed true, my lady. Despite the joyous welcome he received in London, the king stayed there but one day, so impatient was he to get to the siege of Nottingham. It would make no sense for you to travel all the way to London when he'd be over a hundred miles to the north."

Berengaria was not yet ready to concede defeat. "But why could I not join him at Nottingham? I often lived in an army camp during our stay in Outremer."

"That was different, my lady," Morgan said earnestly. "Men do not take their wives campaigning, for it is dangerous as well as distracting."

"Richard once told me that if he'd had it to do again, he was not sure he'd have brought us with him to the Holy Land," Joanna chimed in, "for worrying about our safety just added to his concerns."

"Yes . . . he said that to me, too," Berengaria admitted. "I would certainly not want to be a burden, and of course I will await him here in Poitiers if that be his wish. It is just that we've been apart so long. . . ."

"Waiting will be much easier for us now," Joanna said, "for we will no longer have to fear Heinrich's treachery." She was very disappointed herself, for she yearned to see her mother even more than Richard. After being separated for fifteen years, she'd had only four days with Eleanor at Messina before her mother had hastened to Rome on a diplomatic mission for Richard. She was tempted to go on her own to England, but how could she leave Berengaria alone in Poitiers? She was thankful that her sister-in-law seemed resigned now to the delay, and even more thankful that Berengaria had not thought to ask if Eleanor would be accompanying Richard to Nottingham. Glancing down again at her mother's letter, she resolved to lie if Berengaria did ask later. Once she and Richard were finally reunited, none of this would matter.

Crossing to the younger woman, she put an arm affectionately around her sister-in-law's slender shoulders. "At least we'll now have a trustworthy eyewitness account of Richard's tribulations during this past year." Berengaria brightened at that reminder. But when they looked around for Morgan, he and Mariam had disappeared.

"Well, we may have to wait awhile longer for that," Joanna said, with such a mischievous smile that, although Berengaria felt fornication was a serious sin, she could not help returning the smile, thinking that she was so lucky to have Richard's sister as her friend.

Even as she sought to reassure Berengaria, Joanna felt an unwelcome spark of envy. She did not begrudge Mariam her good fortune, her happiness with Morgan. It was just that she was twenty-eight and she'd been sleeping alone for more than four years. She was lonely. And against her will, she found herself thinking of a man with sapphire-blue eyes, an easy smile, and dangerously seductive charm.

❧

ON THE SAME DAY that Morgan arrived at Poitiers, Richard reached Nottingham. From London, he'd stopped at St Edmundsbury to do honor to his favorite saint, and then continued north. At Huntingdon, William Marshal caught up with him. Marshal had chosen to meet his king rather than attend the funeral for his black-sheep brother, who'd not only been one of John's men, but who'd played a suspicious role in the massacre of York's Jews when he'd held the post of Yorkshire's sheriff. Will was sure that Richard did not blame him for his brother's sins, for the king had recently named another brother to the See of Exeter. But these were perilous times for those with more than one liege lord. Just as some of Richard's vassals were also the liegemen of the French king, Will owed homage to John for his Irish estates, and he did not want the Angevin king to doubt where his first loyalty lay. Richard welcomed him with enough warmth to assure him this was not a concern, and they rode on together to the siege.

❧

FROM THE CASTLE BATTLEMENTS, the constables of Nottingham, Ralf Murdoc and William de Wendeval, watched the commotion below in the siege camp.

Trumpets were blaring, horns blasting, drums pounding, and it was obvious even at a distance that something of note was occurring. William, who was shortsighted, struggled to make out what was happening. "Do you think the king could have arrived?" he asked uneasily, but the other man scoffed at that.

"Do not tell me you believe that nonsense about Richard coming back? They know the castle can hold out till Judgment Day, so they are trying to trick us with lies and falsehoods. Richard will never regain his freedom and that means Lord John will be England's king. I know it, you know it, and those stubborn fools down there know it, too. We need only outwait them and pay no heed to their fanciful claims."

What Ralf said made sense. With so much at stake, the French king and Lord John would pay any amount to keep Richard caged. Yet as William gazed down at the turmoil in the enemy camp, he could not stifle his inner voice. *What if the Lionheart really has returned?*

❧

THE WELCOME RICHARD HAD received in English towns and villages paled in comparison with the reception he got at Nottingham. Many of the soldiers had fought with him in past campaigns, and he was mobbed by men who were delighted that he was free, and even happier that he was here, for none doubted that his presence would guarantee victory; by now, Richard's reputation as a battlefield commander had become a weapon in and of itself.

Once relative calm had been restored, Richard wanted to know all they could tell him about the castle. What he heard was not encouraging. Perched on a steep sandstone cliff a hundred feet above the River Leen, it had three separate baileys, separated by deep, dry moats; the outer bailey was enclosed by a timber palisade, but the middle and inner baileys were protected by stone walls and the square tower keep was on a rocky motte fifteen feet higher than its bailey. Continuing the bad news, David, the Earl of Huntingdon, told him that the castle was strongly garrisoned and Randolph, Earl of Chester, reported that it was said to be provisioned for a lengthy siege, making it unlikely the garrison could be starved into surrendering. But Richard had no interest in that approach, for the more time he spent in England dealing with John's rebellion, the more time it gave Philippe to seize Norman towns and castles.

"Show me," he said, and they led him out to see the stronghold's defenses for himself. The siege camp was a large one, occupying the deer park to the west, the open field and hill to the north, and the streets closest to the castle gatehouse that faced the town. The people unlucky enough to live in this exposed area had fled to safer neighborhoods in the two boroughs of the city, their houses appropriated by the earls for lodgings and command headquarters. Richard studied the castle with a frown, for he saw at once what a challenge it posed. He felt anger stirring when the Earl of Chester said the garrison remained defiant, refusing to believe the king had truly returned.

"They will not be doubting for long," he vowed and pointed to the house closest to the castle. "I'll set up my quarters there."

André grinned, remembering Richard's first great military triumph, when at age twenty-one, he'd taken Taillebourg, a castle said to be utterly impregnable, pitching his tents so provocatively close to the town walls that the garrison could not resist the temptation and sallied forth for a surprise attack upon the young Angevin duke. Only it had not been a surprise, for Richard had been expecting it, and when they tried to retreat back into the town, Richard and his men forced their way in with them and soon had the victory. The garrison at Nottingham would not be so foolish, but André felt sure many of them would be unnerved to see the Lionheart's banner flying so close to their walls.

They'd been joined by Richard's uncle, Hamelin, the Earl of Surrey, who'd returned from escorting Eleanor to the Holy Trinity priory in Lenton, a mile to the south. But as he started to assure Richard that she'd been given a warm welcome by the prior, crossbowmen up on the castle walls began to shoot down into the camp and several soldiers were struck, one of them collapsing almost at Richard's feet, a bolt driven through his eye into his brain. Looking from the dead man to the cocky defenders, cheering their success, Richard's eyes darkened to slate, his hand closing around the hilt of his sword.

"We attack now," he said. "Arm yourselves."

THE EARLS HAD ALREADY filled the outer moat in preparation for an assault, although they'd not yet launched one. Since the first ring of defenses was timber, Richard called for a battering ram, his crossbowmen giving such effective cover that the defenders on the wall were unable to offer real resistance. When the wood splintered under the impact, Richard was one of the first to clamber through the shattered gate into the outer bailey, with his knights right behind him, shouting the battle cry of the English royal House, *"Dex Aie!"*

Men up on the middle bailey walls began to shoot at the invaders, but they were carrying large shields that deflected most of the bolts and at first they advanced almost unopposed. When the besieged realized they were in danger of losing the outer bailey, they hastily organized a sortie and came running through the barbican to confront the attackers.

Richard maimed the first man to challenge him, the downward sweep of his blade taking his foe's arm off at the elbow. Since regaining his freedom, he'd occasionally worried that his skills might have become rusty from all that time in captivity, but he found now that his body and brain still functioned in lethal harmony, his instincts and reflexes as sharp as ever. Feeling like an exile who'd finally come home, he wielded his sword with such ferocity that he left a trail of bodies in his wake and his men were hard-pressed to stay at his side.

Hand-to-hand fighting was always bloody and it was particularly vicious as Richard and his men cut and slashed and pounded their way toward the barbican, his soldiers inspired by his example and the rebels showing the desperate courage of the cornered. Their crossbowmen could no longer shoot down into the mêlée, unable to distinguish the enemy from their own, and that freed Richard's arbalesters to launch their own offensive. Whenever a man dared to pop up in an embrasure to aim at the attackers, he was targeted with such deadly accuracy that they soon cleared the walls. Those watching from the windows of the tower keep realized with horror that the castle's fate hung in the balance.

What saved them was the coming of dark. The tide of battle had turned in the favor of the attackers, and the defenders were being inexorably forced back toward the barbican. Some men bravely held their ground to allow the others to retreat into the middle bailey, but that meant the fleeing soldiers could not raise the barbican drawbridge without trapping their comrades, and the fiercest combat of the day happened in the constricted space of the barbican. By the time the king's men had secured it, the sun had set and dusk was chasing away the last of the light.

The bailey was strewn with the wounded and the dead. Once they'd tended to the injured, retrieved the bodies, and put their prisoners under guard, it was full dark. They were exhausted, bloodied, and jubilant, theirs the intoxicating survivor's joy of men who'd triumphed over their enemies and over Death. They knew the worst still lay ahead, for even though they now controlled the outer bailey, the rebels were ensconced on high ground behind sturdy stone walls. But for tonight, they wanted only to savor the day's victory, none more than Richard.

✿

THE NEXT MORNING, Richard held a council of war and told them that he wanted to build mangonels and petraries, saying they'd not launch any more attacks upon the castle until the siege engines were completed and positioned. That was met with unanimous agreement, for none of them were eager to assault those formidable stone walls, and the Earl of Chester volunteered to send men out to a local quarry to search for suitable stones.

"Good. We'll be throwing more than stones, though. How would you all like to see a demonstration of Greek fire?"

That simple sentence created a sensation. All of them knew of Greek fire, of course. The stories told of this eastern incendiary weapon had become the stuff of legend in the west. It was said that it could be extinguished only by sand or urine, that it burned on water, that its use was accompanied by thunder and black smoke. But aside from André and Will Marshal, none of the men had been to the Holy Land, so they'd never seen it for themselves. They bombarded Richard with questions, wanting to know what it was composed of, how long it would burn, how it was delivered, if it had ever been used in Christendom ere this.

Richard abandoned his feigned nonchalance and smiled, pleased by their excited reaction. "The Greeks have always kept its elements secret, but the Saracens use a variation that works just as well. They make it from pine resin, naphtha, and sulphur. Once we have the mangonels built, we'll mix it up and pour it into jars. We can also wrap caltrops in tow and soak them in it. And yes, we'll be the first to use it in England, although I was told my grandfather used it during one of his sieges in Anjou."

The Greek fire dominated the conversation after that. When André described it as looking like a fiery whirlwind, they were even more eager to see it in action. Richard's uncle Hamelin suggested they stop wasting time and find carpenters in the town so they could start building the mangonels straightaway, and they were impressed when Richard said that was not necessary, for he'd brought carpenters with him.

"There is something else I want them to build," Richard said once they fell silent. "A gallows." They exchanged glances and nodded approvingly, for that would be a useful lesson for the castle defenders, reminding them what befell the garrison when a castle refused to surrender and was taken by storm.

⚜

A GALLOWS WAS ERECTED on the hill north of the castle, and several of the sergeants taken prisoner the day before were hanged, as the garrison watched their death throes from the battlements. It had the desired result, and the trapped men began to argue among themselves, many of them losing heart for continued resistance.

⚜

ELEANOR HAD BEEN EXPOSED to more bloodshed and violence than most women of her rank. She had accompanied her first husband on his disastrous crusade, had seen men die of cold and hunger, had heard the anguished moans of soldiers with wounds only God could heal. Her own life had been put at risk in wild storms at sea and she'd almost fallen into the hands of pirates in the pay of the Greek emperor. While wed to Henry, she'd been ambushed by their rebellious de Lusignan vassals, saved from capture only by the heroic sacrifice of the Earl of Salisbury and his young nephew Will Marshal, whose career of royal service had begun on that spring afternoon more than twenty-five years ago. But none of her past experience made it any easier for her as she awaited word from the siege of Nottingham.

The priory at Lenton was so close to the castle that its walls were visible in the distance. As the fighting raged, she'd stalked the confines of the guest chamber, unable to think of anything but that ongoing assault. She considered having Prior Alexander escort her into the town so she could watch the attack from the bell tower at St Mary's Church, but soon realized that would be madness. She made do by sending her household knights back and forth to the siege camp for news, not drawing an easy breath until they told her that her son now held the outer bailey and the assault had ended when darkness fell.

She was very pleased the next evening when Richard and André stopped by for a brief visit. Not surprisingly, they made light of the castle attack, spent more time grumbling about the squabble between the Archbishop of Canterbury and the Archbishop of York, Richard's half brother Geoff. Hubert Walter had arrived that afternoon, having his archiepiscopal cross carried before him, and Geoff had taken offense at that, for Nottingham was in the province of York. When he protested, Hubert had replied that Canterbury had primacy over York and Geoff's always volatile temper had erupted like the Greek fire they hoped to use against the rebel garrison.

"I had to command Geoff to let it be," Richard said, shaking his head in remembered frustration. "How could my father not see how ill-suited Geoff was for a vocation in the Church? God's legs, even I would make a better archbishop than Geoff!"

"He is not one to turn the other cheek," Eleanor agreed wryly. "But then, neither was Thomas Becket."

André grinned. "I doubt that even a martyr's death could secure a sainthood for Geoff."

"If he keeps acting like such an overweening arse, he might well *get* a martyr's death," Richard prophesied gloomily. "We are going to have to allot an entire day of the council to hear complaints against him. His monks loathe him almost as much as the monks of Coventry loathe that bastard Hugh de Nonant."

Richard had told Eleanor that he meant to hold a great council once he'd taken Nottingham Castle, and this gave her the opening she needed. "Richard, we are going to have to decide what to do with John."

"How about a stint as a galley slave?"

"He deserves no mercy," she conceded, earning herself a sardonic half smile.

"But you want me to extend it to him nonetheless."

She nodded and he said noncommittally, "I'll think about it, Maman."

If it had been up to André, John would have suffered the same fate as the sergeants dangling from the Nottingham gallows. But he realized now that John might well escape the punishment he so richly deserved, and that did not sit well with him. On the short ride back to the siege camp, he asked Richard if he would truly consider pardoning John, and when he got a shrug in response, he could not help exclaiming, "Christ Almighty, why?"

Richard was silent for a time, keeping his eyes on the road. "If my mother asks it of me, it would be hard to say no."

"Why would she want John's betrayal to be forgotten?"

"Forgiven," Richard corrected, "not forgotten. He is still her son, André, and the same blood runs in his veins and mine. However little I may like it, it cannot be ignored."

André tactfully let the matter drop. He still did not agree, but then he did not have to think dynastically, and for that, he was grateful. Upon their return to Nottingham, he looked toward the gallows and the bodies twisting slowly in the wind, a sight not even moonlight could soften, and it occurred to him that John had a history of letting other men pay his debts.

THE THIRD DAY OF the siege began well for the besiegers, with the arrival of the Bishop of Durham, bearing the good news that the garrison of Tickhill had surrendered upon hearing that the king had returned. The mangonels were ready by noon and they were soon bombarding the castle, sending up clouds of dust and rubble whenever they made a direct hit. As he'd done at Acre, Richard established eight-hour shifts so the siege engines would be operating day and night, giving the besieged no surcease. Word had already spread through the camp about the Greek fire and Richard's men were keenly disappointed when he said they would not use it just yet. They found some consolation in watching the rocks rain down upon the castle, though, and amused themselves by shouting jeers and insults at the men enduring the onslaught.

Richard was having dinner with the earls and prelates, keeping a hawk's eye upon Geoff and Longchamp, both of whom detested the Bishop of Durham, a wolf in sheep's garb, for his ambitions were very much of this world. He was holding forth at length about the successful conclusion of the Tickhill siege, but Richard was willing to indulge him—at least for a while. Servants had just begun to ladle out their Lenten fish stew when one of Randolph of Chester's knights entered with word that William de Wendeval was asking for a safe conduct for two of the garrison to enter the camp and see for themselves if the king had truly returned.

It was not long afterward when two obviously nervous men were ushered into the command headquarters. "I am Sir Fouchier de Grendon," one said hoarsely, "and this is Henry Russell. We've come to see the king."

Richard rose to his feet, moving into the light. "Well? What do you think?"

There was no need for them to reply, for they were already on their knees, so stupefied that the watching men burst out laughing. Richard waved them to their feet and cut off their incoherent stammering by raising his hand. "Go back to the castle," he said, "and tell them that time is running out. I will show mercy to those who yield now, but those who continue to hold out will suffer the fate that all traitors and rebels deserve."

Several hours later, Richard accepted the surrender of William de Wendeval and thirteen of his knights. The rest of the garrison were not yet ready to yield, but after another night of heavy bombardment by Richard's mangonels, they accepted an offer by the Archbishop of Canterbury to discuss terms, and upon being assured that their lives would be spared, they, too, agreed to place themselves at the king's mercy. The three-day siege of Nottingham was over and, with it, John's rebellion.

❧

ANDRÉ FOUND THE SURRENDER of the last die-hard defenders very entertaining. "What will you do with them?" he asked. "If you hanged a few, that might cheer up all the men so let down at not seeing the castle turned into a Greek-fire inferno."

"Actually, I'm glad that I did not have to use it, for Nottingham is a royal castle and I'd have to pay the cost of rebuilding it. We'll demand ransoms from their leaders and impose fines on the others."

"Well, if you insist upon being practical about it." André unhooked a wine-skin from his belt and raised it in a salute to the red-and-gold banner now flying over the castle. "Not a bad beginning, my lord king, not bad at all."

Richard followed his gesture, his eyes lingering on that royal lion fluttering in the wind. "I agree," he said. "It is just a beginning, though, and we cannot forget that." Then he smiled. "But the worst is over now, and I thank God for that."

CHAPTER TWENTY-TWO

⚜

MARCH 1194

Nottingham Castle, England

Richard's lashes flickered as he slowly became aware of his surroundings. Wherever he was, it was frigid, dark, and windowless, lit only by a small oil lamp. His head was throbbing and he tasted blood in his mouth. He had another merciful moment of hazy confusion, and then he remembered. This was an underground dungeon in the Louvre, the French king's Paris stronghold.

He'd fought them, to no avail, for he was greatly outnumbered. Pinning him down, they had fastened heavy shackles on his ankles and manacled his wrists, tethering the chains to a wall hook. Even then, he'd continued to resist until his head had slammed into the rough concrete floor. As the memories of that chaotic, frantic struggle came flooding back, he attempted to sit up, but his head was spinning again. He was finding it difficult to get enough air into his lungs and he was sickened by the stench. God alone knew how many prisoners had been entombed here, the confined space stinking of urine, feces, sweat, and fear. As the full horror of his new reality sank in, he tried to stave off panic, but he felt as if the walls were closing in on him.

It was then that he heard the sound of a key turning in the lock, and the darkness was pierced by a dazzling blaze of torchlight. Just as it had happened at Trifels, the Bishop of Beauvais was standing there, laughing down at him. But this time there was no hope of reprieve, no ransom to be paid.

"I wanted to reassure you that Philippe will not be putting you to death, Richard. Oh, he thought about it. But I convinced him this way was better. Whenever he has a bad day, he need only remind himself that you're having a far worse one." The bishop grinned. "I think he liked that idea. Whenever I'm in Paris, I certainly intend to stop by to see how you're doing."

He paused deliberately. "Nothing to say, Lionheart? Well, you listen whilst I talk, then. On the way over here, I was thinking of all that you'll never experience again. You'll never see the sky again or feel the sun on your face. You'll never mount a stallion again—or a woman. You'll not hear the sound of the wind or rain or the music you like so much. No more songs to write, no more battles to fight. The only voice you'll hear will be your own. As the years go by, you'll be forgotten—even by your friends. And when you finally do die, you'll die unshriven of your sins, so you'll burn for aye in Hell."

"Then I'll see you there, you craven son of a poxed whore!" Richard lunged to the end of his chain, calling the other man a cankered, maggot-ridden swine, a contemptible coward, a godless renegade, a gutless milksop, and a treacherous viper, impressing the guards with his raging, embittered invective. Beauvais merely laughed.

Gesturing to the oil lamp, he said, "Take that with us, for he'll not be needing it." He halted at the door, just as he'd done at Trifels. "We'll feed you enough to keep you alive. I daresay you could survive for years; other prisoners have. But you might be one of the luckier ones, Lionheart. Mayhap you'll go mad down here in the dark."

With the loss of all light, Richard was blind, utterly alone in this icy, suffocating blackness. Overwhelmed by despair, he cried out, but no one could hear him, not even God. He was buried alive. He yanked desperately at his chains until his wrists were cut and bleeding, until hands gripped his shoulders and a voice entreated him to be still.

He jerked upright, his heart pounding, pulse racing, so shaken that he did not at once recognize his surroundings. He was in an unfamiliar bedchamber, but it *was* a bedchamber. Weak with relief, he sank back against the pillow. A young woman was cowering in the far corner of the bed, her eyes wide, blood trickling down her cheek. His new squire, Robert, was standing, frozen, several feet away, but Arne was leaning over him, saying soothingly that it was a dream, just a bad dream.

Richard knew that by now. The dream had been so real, though, that he could still feel the heavy manacles clamping his wrists; he thought he could even smell the foulness of that accursed oubliette. He closed his eyes for a moment, breathing deeply until his brain communicated to his body that he was at Nottingham Castle, not in a Paris dungeon. When he opened them again, Arne was still there, this time holding out a cup of wine. Richard drained it in several swallows and, without needing to be told, Arne produced a flagon and refilled it to the brim. As their eyes met, the same thought was in both their minds—the nights at Speyer and Worms when the boy had awakened screaming, sure that he was about to be burned with a red-hot poker.

Arne had opened the bed hangings when responding to Richard's nightmare. Now he closed them again, but left a space so that the bed would not be cocooned in darkness, for after his own struggles with night terrors, he'd craved light. He then withdrew to his own bed on the opposite side of the chamber, giving Robert a shove when he still stood there gaping.

Richard drank again, more slowly this time, watching the glowing embers as the fire in the hearth burned low. Glancing over at the girl, he pointed to the bloodied scratch under her eye. "Did I do that?"

She nodded. "You were thrashing about like a trapped eel and when you flung out your arm, your ring caught me here." She'd slid over beside him again, showing that she'd not retreated to the end of the bed from fear, simply to get out of range. When he offered the rest of the wine, she took it eagerly and drank with obvious pleasure. He could see now that her cheek was swollen, too, but she seemed quite unfazed by it. He supposed that since bruises were an occupational hazard, she did not consider unintentional ones worth bothering about, especially when she was likely to be well compensated for them.

She leaned over to set the cup down in the floor rushes, and then propped herself up on an elbow, saying chattily, "That must have been an awful dream, my lord. I have never had one myself, at least not one that I remembered come morning. But my late husband, may God assoil him, suffered dreadfully from bad dreams. He'd often awaken me, yelling and flailing about like one possessed. He even sleepwalked sometimes. Do you ever do that, my lord?"

"What was your name again?"

Her smile set free two deep dimples. She was called Eve, she told him, a popular name for women who made their living by bartering their bodies.

"Stop talking, Eve," Richard said and rolled over on top of her. She wrapped her arms compliantly around his neck, adjusting her body to accommodate him, for she was skilled in all the ways of pleasuring a man and she'd discovered earlier that night that a king was no different from other men when it came to hungers of the flesh.

Richard got the physical release he needed and, for a time, he did not have to think at all. Afterward, his bedmate had fallen asleep almost at once, but he could not, despite being exhausted by the nightmare. Eventually, he gave up and rose from the bed. Crossing to the window, he pulled the shutters back, gazing up at a sky in which stars still glimmered. Dawn was at least an hour away. He grimaced, for it was going to be a long day—the start of the great council—and then began to pull clothing from a coffer. Robert continued to sleep, snoring softly, but Arne soon awakened, for he seemed to have a sixth sense, always on hand when he was needed. He insisted upon assisting Richard in dressing and then quickly did so himself.

Richard retrieved a small casket from another coffer and poured some coins into a leather pouch. Tossing it to Arne, he said, "Give her this when she awakens, lad, and then see that she gets safely back into town."

Arne tucked the pouch into his belt. "I will, my lord." His gaze drawn toward the girl in the bed, he said wistfully, "She is very pretty."

Richard raised an eyebrow. "You want her?" He was turning to take more money from the casket when the boy hastily declined. "Why not?" He glanced over his shoulder, surprised by the refusal. "I daresay she'd fancy a polite lad like you over some of the men she takes into her bed." When Arne continued to shake his head, Richard looked at the youth curiously, remembering that Morgan had said he was younger than they'd first thought. "How old are you, lad? Sixteen?"

"Come Michaelmas, sire." Arne blushed when Richard asked if he'd been with a woman yet, but he was proud to say he had, for some of the king's knights had gone to a German brothel to celebrate his impending release and Guillain had taken a brotherly interest in engaging a suitable girl for Arne's first time. So he was no longer afflicted by the shyness that had kept him from losing his virginity in that Ragusa whorehouse, but the idea of sharing a woman with his king seemed somehow sacrilegious to him. Knowing Richard would have laughed at him had he confided that, he said instead, "May I ask you a question, sire?"

He lost his nerve then, fearing that he'd be unforgivably presumptuous. But when Richard urged him on, he braced himself and blurted out in one breathless sentence, "You could have any woman you wanted, my liege, so why do you choose to pay for one?" And to his vast relief, Richard looked amused.

Gesturing toward the young woman asleep in his bed, Richard said with a grin, "I wanted to swive her, Arne, not court her." Leaning back against the edge of the trestle table, he decided to share a family story with the lad, for they'd developed an odd intimacy since being reunited at Speyer nine months ago, a bond begotten in the torture Arne had undergone for his sake and reinforced by dreams of French dungeons and burning flesh.

"When my brothers and I reached the age of thirteen or fourteen, our father declared that we were now going to be 'thinking with our cocks,' and gave us each a blunt talking-to. 'If you plant a field, you have to harvest the crop,' he said, telling us that we must look after any children we sired. He said he'd not blame us for 'a wench ploughed and cropped,' but we should stay away from virgins and other men's wives, saying, 'If you have an itch, get a whore to scratch it.' He did not always practice what he preached; what man does? But it was good advice nonetheless, which I will eventually pass on to my own sons, and which I am now passing on to you, Arne."

"I will bear it in mind, sire," Arne promised, so solemnly that Richard laughed as he headed for the door. Arne was still shocked that he'd actually dared to ask the king about his whores, but it had been a source of bewilderment to him. He was happy that he had done so, for the king seemed in much better spirits now, and he hoped that the night's bad dream would cast no shadow in the light of day.

But once Richard was alone in the stairwell, he came to a halt, all traces of amusement gone from his face. That nightmare was a familiar one, but he'd not had it since he'd left Germany and he'd not thought it would come back once he was freed. Why would it still haunt him like this, and after his triumph in taking Nottingham Castle? It made no sense to him. He did not mind that Arne knew about the dreams. The lad understood. But he did not want any others to see him like that, to see him so vulnerable.

Robert had been with him for only a few days. His uncle Hamelin had insisted he needed another squire and Richard had humored him. But just before the council began later that morning, he pulled Hamelin aside and said he no longer wanted the boy's services. And from that day on, when he had an itch that needed scratching, he did not let the woman spend the night.

ON THE FIRST DAY of the great council, Richard removed all but seven of the sheriffs from their posts and offered the offices for sale to the highest bidders. The men who'd paid for these shrievalties at the start of his reign, when he was raising funds for the crusade, were understandably not happy at having to buy them back. But Richard's need for money was acute. It was, he thought morosely, like being caught between Scylla and Charybdis, having to repay the rest of the ransom in order to free the hostages at the same time that he faced an expensive campaign against that festering sore on the French throne. During his captivity, he'd been too concerned about regaining his freedom to dwell much upon the outrageous financial burden imposed upon his domains. Now the mere thought of that one hundred fifty thousand marks added fuel to the fire smoldering in the back of his brain, slow-burning but as impossible to quench as Greek fire. He did not understand why the Almighty had allowed Heinrich to prevail, even rewarding him for his treachery with Sicily. Why was Tancred the one to die and not Heinrich? He knew those were questions no good Christian should ask. Mortal men were taught to accept. God's Will be done. But he did *not* understand.

THE KING'S APARTMENTS in the inner bailey had suffered some damage in the mangonel bombardment, forcing Richard to lodge in the top story of the keep. But the queen's quarters had been unscathed in the siege and so after the close of the great council, Richard had chosen his mother's antechamber for an informal meeting with Hubert Walter; two of the justiciars, Will Marshal and William Briwerre; his chancellor, Longchamp; his clerk, Master Fulk; his brother Geoff; his uncle Hamelin; and his cousin André.

Eleanor had detected subtle signs of stress in Richard earlier in the day and she was pleased now to see how much more relaxed he seemed. She thought the council had begun well and, as she'd sat in a place of honor in the splendid great hall built by her husband, she'd savored her preferential status as the queen mother. She'd never been invited to attend one of Henry's great councils, but Richard took it for granted that she would participate, and if any of the men had doubts about her presence, they were careful to conceal them.

Watching now as her son told the other men about his visit yesterday to the royal forest of Sherwood, she found herself feeling a familiar regret. If only Harry had not clung to every last ounce of power the way a miser hoarded even the most paltry of coins. It was not that he'd dismissed her opinions because they were female opinions. No son of the Empress Maude could ever have viewed

women as mere brainless broodmares. No, he simply could not delegate authority, had always to keep his own hand on the reins even if it alienated his wife and
antagonized his sons.

Richard was saying he understood now why this castle had been one of his
father's favorites. "My father would gladly have hunted from dawn till dusk, and
what better hunting could he find than in Sherwood Forest? It seems to go on
forever, with oaks taller than church spires. It must be an ideal haven for outlaws, though." Accepting a cup of wine, he glanced toward his chancellor. "What
is on the schedule for the morrow, Guillaume?"

"Now that we've dealt with the shrievalties, we can move on to consider the
charges against Count John and the Bishop of Coventry." Longchamp tried to
keep his satisfaction from showing, but not very successfully; Hugh de Nonant's
fall from grace gave him fierce pleasure. "On the third day, we're to discuss the
need for new taxes, and the final day is set aside for complaints against the Archbishop of York by his own cathedral chapter."

Geoff scowled. "That is a waste of time," he told Richard vehemently. "Never
have I met a more deceitful lot than those sly, scheming canons. They have opposed me from the day of my consecration, and you'd scarce believe what I've
had to endure at their hands!"

"We have to hear them, Geoff, but you'll get ample opportunity to respond to
their charges," Richard assured him, with more patience than he usually mustered up for his half brother. Geoff subsided reluctantly, staring balefully at
Longchamp as if he suspected the chancellor had encouraged the disgruntled
monks.

Eleanor leaned back in her seat, studying Geoff covertly through half-closed
eyes. He'd been raised at her husband's court and she'd made no objections,
believing that a man should assume responsibility for children sired in or out of
wedlock. But their relationship had soured when she and her sons had rebelled
against Henry, for Geoff had never forgiven any of them for that. Richard had
honored Henry's deathbed promises and approved Geoff's elevation to the archbishopric of York, even though all knew that he did not have the temperament
for a Church career and Geoff himself had never wanted to take holy vows. Few
had expected him to stir up so much turmoil, though, in his new vocation. He'd
feuded bitterly with the Bishop of Durham, even excommunicating him. He'd
clashed with Longchamp and antagonized York's cathedral chapter by trying to
get his maternal half brother elected as Dean of York. He'd horrified his fellow
prelates by having his archiepiscopal cross carried before him in other Sees

than his own, and then offended Hubert Walter by challenging the primacy of Canterbury over York. Eleanor had lost track of all those he'd excommunicated, including a priory of nuns. She'd always known that he'd inherited his fair share of the Angevin temper, but he'd never been so unreasonable or so belligerent in the past, and she could only conclude that York's archbishop was a very unhappy man.

Richard had told her Geoff's cathedral chapter was accusing him of a multitude of sins—simony, extortion, violence, and neglect of his pastoral duties. Richard seemed skeptical of these charges and appeared willing to give Geoff the benefit of the doubt, which had not often been true in their contentious past. But Eleanor knew he was pleased with Geoff's military efforts at the siege of Tickhill; Geoff had also made a good-faith effort to raise money for the ransom, only to be sabotaged by the opposition of his monks, who'd gone so far as to suspend divine services in the Minster in protest. Eleanor did not think this truce between Richard and Geoff would last long; they were both too strong-willed for that. Seeing Geoff glance in her direction, she discreetly lowered her gaze, thinking it was a shame that Harry had been so stubbornly set upon making Geoff into what he was not, could not be, and never wanted to be.

They'd begun a discussion of the new tax to be imposed, two shillings for every one hundred twenty acres of land. Eleanor knew it would not be popular, but she did not see what other choice they had, not if they hoped to free their hostages. Thinking of her grandsons, Otto and Wilhelm, she felt a weary sense of sadness, knowing how homesick they both must be. At least she need no longer worry that Heinrich would renege on the agreement and not release them after the remainder of the ransom was paid, for word had come that the emperor had finally made peace with their father, Der Löwe.

Richard had just told them he meant to send out a letter to the English clerics, thanking them for all they'd done to secure his release. Stifling a yawn, he asked if there was anything else they needed to discuss, saying he'd gotten little sleep last night. André smirked at that, having seen Eve being escorted up to Richard's bedchamber, but the other men started to rise when Richard did, bidding him good night. Geoff and Hubert exchanged glances, and the latter said reluctantly, "There is one matter, sire."

Richard sat back down again. "What is it, Hubert?"

"Yesterday, whilst you were riding in Sherwood Forest, the prelates held a meeting."

Longchamp stiffened, both offended and hurt that even after being restored to the king's favor, his fellow bishops continued to shun him as if he were a leper, for he'd known nothing of this colloquy. Richard was waiting expectantly, but Hubert took his time, sensing that what he was about to say would not be well received.

"They think it would be a good idea, my liege, if you were to hold a ceremony of some sort now that you've returned to England."

Richard's eyes narrowed. Before he could respond, Geoff intervened, for he did not understand why Hubert was vacillating like this. "He is talking about another coronation," he said bluntly, "a renewal of royal authority, a way to—" He stopped in midsentence then, for his brother had shoved his chair back with such force that it toppled over.

"A way to . . . what, Geoff? To exorcise the shame of my captivity and homage to Heinrich?"

"We did not say that, sire," Hubert said hastily.

"You were thinking it, though," Richard raged. "Why else would I need this *ceremony*, this rite of purification? Well, you tell them this, my lord archbishop. Say that if there is any stain upon my honor, I intend to wash it away with French blood!" With that, he swung around, stalked to the door, and slammed it so resoundingly behind him that they all flinched.

There was a long moment of silence. They'd seen the Angevin temper at full blaze before, but none had expected to be scorched by the flames themselves. Longchamp glared at the two archbishops. "Well done! If you'd bothered to include me in that meeting, I could have told you how the king would react to this 'good idea' of yours."

"It was not *my* idea," Hubert said curtly.

"They thought he would enjoy a royal ceremony. He's always liked being the center of attention," Geoff pointed out, his own temper kindling when Longchamp shook his head in conspicuous contempt. But before he could protest, Eleanor rose from her seat.

"My lord archbishop," she said icily and at once all eyes fastened upon her, for it was obvious that she was as furious as Richard. "Is what my son said true? Do men think there is something shameful about his having to do homage to Heinrich?"

"I do not, Madame," Hubert said stoutly. She did not doubt his sincerity, but he'd answered a question she'd not asked, and she turned toward Geoff, who was candid to a fault.

Nor did he disappoint now. "Yes, some do," he confirmed. "It is not that they are doubting the king's courage—only a fool would do that. But there are those who see his act of homage as sullying English honor, even though it was not given of his free will. Captivity itself carries a certain degree of shame, and this only—"

"God in Heaven!" Eleanor stared at him and then turned away, so angry she did not fully trust herself. How dare they judge Richard for doing what he must to save himself? False-hearted hypocrites! Men and their daft notions of honor!

André was on his feet, too, by now. "I'd like to see any man dare to say that to the king's face!" His eyes swept the chamber challengingly. "How many of you agree with them?"

"I am sure I can speak for us all when I say that none of us do," Will Marshal said in measured, deliberate tones. "The king's homage was regrettable, but not blameworthy, for he was given no choice in the matter. Nor do I see captivity as shameful." For a moment, his gaze rested coolly on Geoff. "Any man who says that has never been held prisoner himself."

Remembering that the Marshal had been held captive by the de Lusignans until Eleanor had paid his ransom, Geoff backtracked, saying earnestly, "I was not voicing my own opinion, merely repeating what some have said. I do agree with the other bishops, though, and believe that the king ought to have a crown-wearing ceremony or even a second coronation. It would be a dramatic way of putting this unfortunate incident behind him and signifying a new beginning."

No one answered him. No one spoke at all, for Eleanor, André, and Long-champ were still fuming, and the others were uncomfortable, regretting that the king had been so angered and that they had been caught in the line of fire. They did not even know if they should wait in case Richard meant to return.

RICHARD HAD NOT GONE FAR. He'd come to a halt out in the inner bailey, ignoring the deferential greetings of soldiers and curious eyes of servants. The cooling night air did not dispel his rage. But he realized almost at once that he'd lashed out at the wrong target. Hubert did not deserve that. None of the men in that chamber did. He could not even blame the bishops and the others who thought he needed to submit to a cleansing ceremony. If he felt that what he'd done was shameful, how could he fault them for believing it, too? After a few moments of bleak reflection, he turned reluctantly and retraced his steps.

They all jumped to their feet as he entered the antechamber, and he waved them back into their seats. "Whether the bishops' suggestion is a 'good idea' is open to debate, but it is never a good idea to confuse the messenger with the message. I did this and I regret it." They at once began to insist that his flare-up was of no matter and perfectly understandable, their predictable assurances washing over him unheard and unheeded. Taking a seat himself, he looked from one face to another, his gaze at last coming to rest upon Hubert Walter.

"If you feel this warrants discussion, I am willing to hear you out. But I must say at the outset that I have no intention of having a second coronation."

"I totally agree with you, my liege. I see no need for a second coronation, either, nor did most of the other bishops. They were talking of something less than that, mayhap a crown-wearing ceremony. Kings used to do that several times a year, but your lord father ended the tradition, not liking the bother of it all. So it would not be an innovation, merely the revival of an old custom—a way to celebrate your return to your kingdom and your subjects."

"You have a tongue agile enough to lick honey off thorns," Richard said wryly, quoting a Welsh proverb he'd learned from Morgan. "You sweetened the drink almost enough to disguise the taste of the hemlock—almost." As little as he wanted to do this, mayhap it was a debt he'd owed from the moment he'd knelt before Heinrich in the great hall at Mainz. "What of the rest of you? Do you all think this is necessary, too?"

Eleanor said simply that it was a decision only he should make. He got an emphatic "No!" from both Longchamp and André. But the other men seemed hesitant to commit themselves. Will Marshal at last said slowly, "The people would love such a ceremony, my liege." Geoff, Hamelin, Fulk, and William Briwerre then echoed that, too, and when Hubert suggested that they could pay honor to the Scots king by asking him to take part in the ceremony, Richard knew he'd been outflanked.

"I will think about it," he said, even though he knew—and they did, too—that he was conceding defeat, not delaying the decision.

The meeting ended soon thereafter. Richard walked across the bailey with André, neither one speaking until they reached the keep. André rarely made use of Richard's given name, calling him "my liege" in public, and "cousin" in private; he did so now. "Richard, you did nothing shameful during your time in Germany, and your honor bears no stain." The younger man's face remained impassive, his thoughts guarded. But André coaxed a reluctant smile from him then by adding with a grin, "However, I must say that I rather fancy your idea of bathing in French blood."

JOHN AND HIS ALLY, the Bishop of Coventry, were ordered to appear within forty days to answer the charges of seizing castles, laying waste to lands in England and Normandy and making a treaty with the French king in violation of the fealty he'd sworn to Richard. John was declared to have forfeited any right to the kingdom or his English estates. And it was announced that Richard would celebrate Easter with the Scots King, William the Lion, and then have a formal crown-wearing ceremony at Winchester on the following Sunday.

"SO I HAVE NO SAY in it at all?"

Berengaria sympathized with Anna's plight, but she still marveled that the girl would even ask such a question; at sixteen, she was old enough to know women wed whom they were told to wed. Joanna sympathized, too, while finding it easier than Berengaria to understand Anna's rebellious streak. So rather than chiding her, she patiently explained again that the marriage was part of the terms of the pact of Worms, part of the price Richard had been forced to pay for his freedom. She'd done her best to reconcile Anna to her fate, reminding her that the Austrian duke was her kinsman and he'd shown genuine concern for her welfare, repeating all of the favorable things they'd gleaned from Morgan and from Richard and Eleanor's letters about Leopold's son. Anna was not yet ready to hear them, though, and they finally withdrew, giving her all they had to offer—time and privacy.

Back in the hall, Joanna did not see Mariam and when she asked Dame Beatrix, the older woman said with a sly smile that Mariam and Morgan were out exploring Poitiers again, which they all knew meant visiting one of the city's inns. Joanna laughed, but Berengaria was not as amused, for she'd recently had a worrying conversation with Guillaume Tempiers, the Bishop of Poitiers, about Mariam and Morgan. Berengaria's friendship with Bishop Guillaume had been a source of great comfort in the six months she'd spent in Poitiers, for he was widely respected for his exceptional piety and integrity and at times he seemed almost saintly to her in his determination to combat both secular sins and ecclesiastical abuses. So when he'd drawn Berengaria aside and spoken of his concern for the Lady Mariam's soul, she'd taken that concern seriously.

"Joanna, did Mariam tell you the bishop had admonished her about her relationship with Morgan?"

Joanna shook her head. She hoped the bishop would not ask her to intervene, for she had genuine respect for the prelate, able to recognize a good man when she met one. But she did not think that Mariam's sins were great enough to imperil her salvation. Mariam was a widow, after all, and she had no male kin to answer to; moreover, she and Morgan did make an attempt to be discreet. It was not their fault that even the stable grooms and kitchen scullions knew they were lovers.

"I think," Berengaria said, "that you ought to ask her why she and Morgan have made no plans to wed. It is obvious that they are besotted with each other, and the holy state of matrimony is surely preferable to these sinful trysts."

"I would like to see them wed, too, Berengaria. But it is not as simple as that. Morgan is a knight, not a lord with lands of his own. He will eventually inherit some of his father's properties. Most likely Ranulf will bequeath his Welsh lands to his elder son and his English manors to Morgan, for the Welsh do not leave everything to the firstborn as they do in England. But that could be years from now, and until then, Morgan is not in a position to support a wife. Why do you think so many knights never wed?"

Berengaria had never considered that. Richard had sometimes teased her that she was almost as sheltered as a Cistercian nun, and she supposed that was so, for her life had been a privileged one as the well-loved daughter of a king. She would find a way for Mariam and Morgan to wed, she decided. Richard was celebrated for his generosity, one of the most important attributes of a great lord. If she asked Richard, surely he would be willing to reward Morgan for his steadfast loyalty.

She was about to tell Joanna of her plan when the other woman jumped to her feet, crying out, "Sir Guilhem!" As Guilhem de Préaux was escorted into the hall, he was soon surrounded by women, for he was a great favorite; Joanna and Berengaria were eternally grateful to him for sacrificing his own freedom to save Richard from capture in the Holy Land. When he produced letters from England, Berengaria took hers out into the garden to read and Joanna retreated to a window-seat with hers.

When Joanna rejoined the others after reading her letters, Guilhem was mesmerizing her women and household knights with an account of Richard's crown-wearing ceremony at Winchester Cathedral. It was a sight to behold, he said, with the King of Scotland and the earls of Chester and Surrey carrying the three ceremonial swords of state. The king had looked regal in his royal robes furred with ermine, wearing the jeweled crown that the Archbishop of Canterbury had placed on his head prior to his entering the church, and a special dais had been set up in the north transept for the queen and her ladies, giving them an unobstructed view of the procession. Afterward, there had been a splendid feast in the cathedral refectory, with numerous courses, a fountain that flowed wine, and musicians, harpists, and jugglers for entertainment, whilst a huge crowd gathered out in the street, hoping for a glimpse of their king, the queen, and the highborn guests.

His audience listened raptly, and even Joanna felt a touch of envy, for she'd have dearly loved to have been there with her brother and mother. It was then that she saw Berengaria had returned to the hall and was standing inconspicuously on the edge of the circle. Joanna started to thread her way toward her, but just then Morgan and Mariam returned and greeted Guilhem with delight; Morgan and Guilhem had become friends in the Holy Land. By the time Joanna was able to extricate herself, her sister-in-law was gone.

Joanna had to play the role of hostess then, seeing that a meal, a bed, and bath were made ready for Guilhem. As soon as she could, she slipped away and climbed the stairs to Berengaria's bedchamber. The younger woman had dismissed her own attendants, and although she opened the door to admit Joanna, she seemed distant, retreating into the Spanish reserve that was a sure sign of distress. Joanna decided a frontal attack was the best approach and asked forthrightly if she was troubled by something in Richard's letter.

Berengaria shook her head, but Joanna outwaited her, and after a strained silence, she said, very low, "There is never anything troubling in Richard's letters. He is always perfectly polite, asking after my health and expressing a hope that I am comfortable here in Poitiers. He says nothing personal, nothing intimate, nothing a husband would tell a wife. In this letter, he did not even mention the crown-wearing, telling me only about the siege and that he has appealed to the Pope, demanding that the Holy Father use the authority of the Church to get his hostages and ransom returned."

"That sounds like Richard," Joanna said, as cheerfully as she could. "He is like most men, dearest, without a romantic bone in his entire body. And twelve years of marriage to William taught me that it is well-nigh impossible to change a man. Luckily the Almighty has given women the patience of Job, enabling us to put up with their . . ." Her voice trailed off then, for Berengaria was regarding her with sorrowful brown eyes that held the hint of tears.

"Joanna, what have I done to displease him?"

"Nothing! Why would you ask that, Berengaria? Remember what he said when we parted from him in Acre, that if Philippe took four months to get home from the Holy Land, he could damned well do it in three, promising that he'd return in time to celebrate Christmas with you. Does that sound like a man who was displeased with you?"

"No . . . but the man I left at Acre does not seem like the man who writes these letters. In the Holy Land, he went to great pains to have me with him whenever he could, bringing us from the palace at Acre to his army camp at Jaffa, having us join him at Latrun. Now . . . now he does not seem to care if we are ever reunited."

"Berengaria, that is surely not so!"

Berengaria did not seem to hear Joanna's protest. "I listened to Guilhem tell us about the crown-wearing at Winchester and all I could think was that I should have been there to witness it. I ought to have been seated in the north transept with his mother, not hundreds of miles away, having to hear about it secondhand."

"There was not time to send for you, dearest. It seems to have happened very quickly, barely a fortnight after he took Nottingham Castle."

"There would have been time had I been awaiting him in London, Joanna. Or if I'd accompanied him to Nottingham as his mother did." She saw Joanna's dismay and smiled sadly, realizing her sister-in-law had been trying to protect her again. "Bishop Guillaume was telling me about a letter he'd gotten from the Bishop of London, and he assumed I knew Queen Eleanor had witnessed the siege."

Joanna did not know what to say. She did not understand her brother's behavior any more than his wife did, but she was sure that the sooner they were reunited, the better. She smiled then, for an idea had just come to her. "My mother said that they planned to sail from Portsmouth, so that means they'll be landing at Barfleur. We can be there to meet them, Berengaria!"

"No."

Joanna blinked. "Why not?"

"I will not chase after him, Joanna. When he sends for me, I will come. Until then, I will wait here."

Joanna did her best to convince Berengaria that she ought to come to Barfleur. But her sister-in-law remained adamant. She knew most people thought Berengaria was the ideal wife, soft-spoken and devoted and deferential. They did not realize how stubborn she could be. Or how proud. Joanna decided to try again later, but if Berengaria insisted upon remaining in Poitiers, she would go herself to Barfleur. She needed to see her mother. She needed to see her brother. And she needed, too, to find out why he seemed so indifferent to a reunion with his young queen.

❧

AFTER CAPTURING ÉVREUX, the French king turned it over to his ally, and John was lodged at the castle on this rainy afternoon in early May. As Durand hastened down a narrow street already deep in mud, the knight cursed as the wind blew his hood back and then swore again at an aggressive beggar who blocked his way. It took him a while to find the small, shabby tavern, hidden away in an alley close by the river. It was poorly lit by smoking wall rushlights; he paused in the doorway until his eyes adjusted to the dimness and he saw the man awaiting him at a shadowed corner table.

Sliding onto the bench beside Justin de Quincy, Durand signaled to the serving-maid for wine. "A charming hovel you picked for this tryst. What . . . you could not find a pigsty?"

"I did look for one," Justin said, "for I wanted you to feel at home."

They traded smiles that were colder than the rain drenching Évreux. They were very unlike; Justin was much younger, dark, intense, and guarded, while Durand was in his thirties, with the swagger and high coloring of a Viking. They'd loathed each other from their first meeting, but they'd often had to work together, for they were both the queen's men and the one attribute they shared was loyalty, absolute and unquestioned, to Eleanor.

Justin's message was a coded verbal one, for it was too dangerous to commit anything to writing. "What are your chances of bringing the lost sheep back into the fold?" he said, pitching his voice even lower than usual.

"This particular sheep is one for wandering off on his own. I'll do my best to track him down, though. Once I find him, where should I bring him?"

"To the market in Lisieux."

Durand nodded, then pushed the bench back, having heard all he needed to know. He did not bother to bid Justin farewell, nor did he bother to pay for his wine. Justin dropped a few coins on the warped wood table, watching the other man saunter out the door, shoving aside two customers just entering. They started to object, but after a closer look at Durand, they decided to let it go.

Justin was not surprised by their wariness; he'd once heard Durand described as "a man born to drink with the Devil." Eleanor's tame wolf thrived on danger and courted confrontation, but Justin could deny neither his courage nor his quick wit. He needed both to have survived so long in his dual role, for if John ever discovered he'd been played for such a fool, Justin thought even Durand would be deserving of pity.

DURAND MADE A PURCHASE in the market before returning to the castle. As he entered the great hall, the knights he encountered acknowledged him coolly, for he had no friends among them, nor did he want any. He did not even get a grudging nod from Ursula. She was playing a game of draughts with her maid, and he might have been invisible for all the notice she took of him. Men who showed Durand disrespect did so at their peril. Rudeness from John's sultry paramour merely amused him, and he deliberately annoyed her by stopping to flirt with her flustered maid.

As he expected, he found John alone in his bedchamber, for the queen's son, usually a man who craved company, had been solitary and brooding in the past fortnight, ever since hearing that his castle at Nottingham had surrendered to Richard.

John was lounging on the bed, an open book upon his lap. He'd been given the same excellent education as his brothers and seemed to find a genuine pleasure in reading. He got to his feet, saying sarcastically, "I must be going deaf, for I did not hear you knock, Durand."

"Fortunately, you do not value me for my manners, my lord." Durand moved to the table, picked up the flagon that John's squire kept filled, and poured two cups, then waited for John to join him.

John bridled a bit, but boredom finally drove him to the table, for whatever Durand's other failings, he was usually entertaining. "I assume you have a reason for this intrusion, Durand."

"I brought you this, my lord." Durand put a sack on the table and pulled out a small hourglass.

"Is this a jest?" John said coldly. "If so, I do not find it amusing."

"That is understandable, my lord, for there is nothing remotely amusing about your predicament. But I thought you needed reminding that the time to make a choice is running out."

John scowled. The knight's boldness was one of the reasons he enjoyed the other man's company; few men had the ballocks to be as forthright as Durand, but it could be vexing, too. "Choice?" he echoed. "Your jokes are falling far shy of the mark today."

"You do have a choice, my lord. You can cling to your alliance with the French king or you can seek to make peace with your brother."

"Is that your idea of a choice?" John jeered. "That is like asking me where I'd prefer to live, Sodom or Gomorrah."

"Passing strange," Durand drawled, "for I'd find it very easy to make that choice. In Sodom, you'd be Philippe's puppet, mayhap even his lackey. In Gomorrah, you'd be the heir to the English throne."

John slammed his wine cup down on the table. "I am no man's lackey!"

"But that is what they'll be calling you at the French court, even if it is done behind your back. Your value to Philippe plummeted as soon as Richard set foot again on English soil. He will still call you his ally, throw you the occasional crumbs from his table, like Évreux. But you'll have no leverage with him, and you'd best think what that will mean. You are not a man who finds it easy to curry favor or to curb your tongue. And Philippe will demand that you do both."

Durand had taken a risk in speaking so bluntly. But he was sure that he was not telling John anything he did not already know. John might be many things; a fool was not amongst them. He just needed to be nudged in the right direction and to be assured that it was the only road to take.

John confirmed this now by saying bitterly, "You think Richard would not make me grovel and fawn over him, too?"

If you're lucky, he would, Durand thought. Aloud, he said, "I daresay you're right. But a bit of groveling is a cheap price to pay for a crown, my lord." He leaned across the table, locking eyes with John. "If ever there was a man who'll not make old bones, it is your brother. I consider it a minor miracle that he has managed to dodge Death as long as he has. Sooner or later, his luck will run out, and when it does, you need to be there to take advantage of it."

John's eyes were an uncommon shade of hazel, but they looked golden now, catching the light from the candle at his elbow. "I think you're forgetting Richard's little Spanish bride. Suppose she gives him a son?"

Durand shrugged. "That is the chance you take, my lord. But even if she does so, how likely is it that Richard will live long enough for his son to reach manhood? And no one wants a child king, not when they could have a man grown."

"You're asking me to gamble all upon what may or may not happen, Durand."

"Since when are you averse to gambling, my lord? You wagered that Richard would not come back and lost. This is a gamble with better odds."

John stared down into his wine cup, as if seeking answers. "What if Richard refuses to forgive me? I was declared an outlaw and traitor by his Nottingham council."

Durand hid a smile, sure now that he'd penned his sheep. He allowed himself a moment or two of triumph, and then leaned in again, doing all he could to banish John's misgivings, doing what his queen wanted of him.

ELEANOR STOOD ON THE BATTLEMENTS of Portchester Castle's high stone keep, heedless of the stinging rain and gusting wind. Portsmouth's harbor was slate grey, churned with whitecaps, spume being flung high into the air by the waves pounding the shore. She could no longer find the sail of her son's galley. Her eyes searched the horizon intently, but she saw only storm clouds and the angry sea.

"Madame!" She turned to see the Countess of Aumale hurrying along the rampart walkway, her mantle billowing out behind her as she struggled against the wind. Hawisa had joined them at Portsmouth soon after their arrival on April 24, eager to accompany them to Normandy. Eleanor had welcomed her company, and she was touched that Hawisa would have ventured out onto the battlements, for the other woman had once confessed to an unease of heights. Clearly, Hawisa had heard that Richard's galley had put out to sea in the teeth of the gale.

"Is it true?" Hawisa sounded breathless, and avoided glancing down into the bailey below. "Has the king really sailed on his own?"

Eleanor nodded. "He grew more and more restless as each day passed, and today he lost all patience. This morning he gave the town of Portsmouth its first royal charter, and this afternoon he declared that he would wait no longer. As you can see," she said, gesturing toward the hundred ships riding at anchor in the harbor, "the masters of his fleet balked at sailing in such a storm. But Richard paid them no heed and the *Sea-Cleaver* headed out to sea soon after None rang."

Hawisa shivered, clutching her mantle as tightly as she could. She could not imagine any rational person choosing to sail in such fearful weather and she was deeply grateful that she was not out on that dark, surging sea with Richard.

Richard's insanity was all too familiar to Eleanor, for it was a madness he'd shared with his father. Henry had often pitted his will against nature's fury, sailing in weather even worse than this May squall. When they'd journeyed to England for their coronation, he'd insisted upon braving a wild November gale, and for years afterward, the mere memory of that harrowing Channel crossing could make Eleanor feel queasy. She still remembered her frustration and her fury when he'd taken her back to England as his prisoner, unable to protest when he refused to wait till a savage storm abated, unable to stop him from taking nine-year-old Joanna and eight-year-old John with them. At least Richard had put out to sea alone; Henry always insisted that his fleet sail with him, even when his sailors were pleading that he stay in port. Eleanor had not understood it then, nor did she now. And as she gazed across Portsmouth's storm-whipped harbor, she was torn between anger at her son's reckless lunacy and fear for his safety. Surely he could not have survived so much only to drown because of his own stubbornness? But all she could do was to pray to the Almighty to save him from his own folly.

RICHARD'S GALLEY WAS so battered by the storm that it was blown backward by the wind and they had to take shelter in a cove on the Isle of Wight. Much to his frustration and somewhat to his embarrassment, the winds continued to be so contrary the next day that he had no choice but to return to Portsmouth. There he ran into a force no less powerful than the weather—his furious mother. Eleanor told him in no uncertain terms that he was not to sail again until the winds were favorable, and he reluctantly agreed to wait. So it was not until May 12 that his fleet left Portsmouth behind in the distance, landing that same day at Barfleur. Neither Richard nor Eleanor would ever see England again.

CHAPTER TWENTY-THREE

✥

MAY 1194

Barfleur, Normandy

Richard's galley was able to dock at the quay, but most of the ships in his fleet would have to anchor out in the harbor and send their passengers ashore in small boats. A large crowd had gathered and now began to cheer at the first sight of his red-and-gold lion banner. Richard was pleased by their enthusiastic welcome, for he saw only smiles on their faces, no recriminations for what he'd yielded at the German court. As soon as he strode down the gangplank, he was surrounded by local lords and clerics, who'd preempted the space closest to the quay, forcing all the others out into the street. One youngster was not willing to wait, and he began to push his way through the throng, heedless of the scowls and curses from the men whose toes had been stepped upon. Squeezing past an indignant archdeacon, who swatted at him and missed, he dropped to his knees in the muddy street, suddenly afraid that Richard would not recognize him.

He need not have worried. He'd left childhood behind in the four years that his father had been fighting in the Holy Land and then held prisoner in Germany. But as Richard gazed down at the eager, upturned face and tousled coppery hair, he knew. "I'll be damned," he said. "You grew up, Philip." When he pulled the boy to his feet and they embraced, those watching had no idea why the king was so happy to see this pushy stripling, but they applauded anyway.

It was too noisy to hear, so Philip pointed to draw Richard's attention to the men standing across the street. Recognizing Morgan and Guilhem de Préaux, Richard began to make his way toward them, his son following closely in his wake as the crowd parted to let them pass. It was not until he reached them that he saw the woman they were sheltering from the press of people. When she flung herself into his arms, that set off another wave of cheering.

"Anna insisted upon coming with us," Joanna said once she'd gotten her breath back, "but I made her wait at our lodgings, for I knew how chaotic it would be here at the harbor."

"And Berenguela?"

She shook her head. Another burst of cheering drowned out whatever she meant to say about Berengaria's absence, and she and Richard turned to see that Eleanor had just stepped onto the quay. "Go on, lass," Richard said and, with Morgan and Guilhem clearing a path for her, Joanna hastened toward her mother. She paused, though, to glance over her shoulder at Richard and Philip. They were watching her, smiling, and she was touched to see that Richard still had his arm around his son's shoulders. But she also felt a prick of unease, for it seemed to her that when she'd told him his wife was not at Barfleur, she'd caught a fleeting look of relief on her brother's face.

❧

FROM BARFLEUR, THEY TRAVELED to Bayeux and then Caen. In each village and town they passed through, people turned out in huge numbers to welcome their duke, for Richard's Norman title mattered more to most of them than his English one.

Joanna had been able to have several long talks with her mother for they were sharing a bedchamber; there were so many in Richard's entourage that accommodations were limited even at Caen's royal castle. But so far she'd had no opportunity for a private conversation with her brother; he was never alone.

She was not surprised, therefore, to enter the great hall and find Richard encircled by an animated, eager audience. She'd noticed that Richard seemed comfortable talking about his time in the Holy Land and his misadventures on his way home, making light of his two shipwrecks and the flight into enemy territory; he'd even appeared willing to talk about his three months as Leopold's prisoner, although he'd been very sparing with details. But as soon as anyone mentioned his experiences in Germany, he shut down; that was the only way Joanna could describe it. The stiffness of his posture and the guarded look on his face told her now that he was being asked questions he did not want to answer. Just as it occurred to her that he might welcome an interruption, Richard saw her and stood up.

"We'll have to continue this discussion later," he announced, and held out his arm to Joanna, who happily took it and followed him from the hall. Once they were in his bedchamber, he sent Arne down to the buttery for wine and sprawled on the settle, confiding, "It is passing strange, *irlanda*. There were times in the past year when I craved company the way a drunkard craves wine. But now . . . now I find myself yearning for a bit of solitude, some quiet time for myself—as if a king ever gets that."

Joanna sat beside him, warmed to be called *irlanda* again. She'd been the favorite of her three older brothers, who'd enjoyed teasing her with affectionate pet names. She'd been "imp" to Hal, "kitten" to Geoffrey, and "swallow" or "little bird" to Richard, always in the *lenga romana* of their mother's homeland. Hal and Geoffrey's voices had been silenced for years, but Richard had been restored to his family and his kingdom and for that, she would be eternally grateful to the Almighty.

She'd taken care not to stare at Arne's scars, but once he departed the chamber, she said, "Morgan told me what happened to Arne. That was very brave of him."

Richard nodded. "He was just fourteen. Many men grown would not have shown his courage."

She waited to see if he would say more and when he did not, she honored his choice by asking no questions. She wanted to ask him about the marriages of Aenor and Anna to Leopold's sons, but he'd shown a marked reluctance to discuss the hostages and she knew he'd rebuffed Anna when the girl had rashly entreated him to reject the marriage plans—as if he could. Joanna had always felt free to speak her mind with Richard and she found it disconcerting to have to weigh her words like this.

"Maman says that she hopes Johnny will be at Évreux to seek your pardon for his treachery. I was very fond of Johnny when we were children, but I do not care much for the man he has become. I am not sure he deserves forgiveness."

"Neither am I," he admitted. "It will be easier to pardon him than to forgive him."

She studied him intently. "Why pardon him at all? Because Maman asks it of you?"

"What better reason could I have than pleasing our mother?" he said lightly. "And I do understand why she wants it done. Until I can sire an heir of my own, we are stuck with my brother or my nephew. Neither Johnny nor Arthur inspires much confidence, but Maman sees Johnny as the lesser of evils and I suppose I do, too."

"I cannot argue with that. Not only is Arthur just seven, he would be Philippe's puppet for certes. But whenever you think of Johnny as next in line for the throne, you must be powerfully motivated to get Berengaria with child." She'd deliberately brought Berengaria's name into the conversation, but he merely smiled, not taking the bait.

"There is another reason for making peace with Johnny," he said. "It gets him away from Philippe's baleful influence. Saladin's brother taught me an Arabic proverb that I rather fancied. The Saracens say it is better to have a camel inside the tent, pissing out, than outside the tent, pissing in." When Joanna smiled, he added playfully, "No regrets that you turned him down, *irlanda*?"

She shook her head in feigned disapproval. "You are so lucky the French never learned of your scheme to marry me off to al-Adil. Imagine what they'd have made of that at your trial in Germany!" She felt safe in saying that because he'd spoken freely of his trial, which had been a spectacular triumph for him, after all.

He confirmed the soundness of her instincts by laughing. "Very true, Joanna. If Saladin were my brother by marriage, it might have made my denials of a conspiracy with the Saracens less convincing. Not that any of them really believed that ludicrous accusation, not even Philippe's pet rat, Beauvais." His face momentarily shadowed at the thought of his hated enemy and Joanna said quickly, "I know you respected al-Adil. But when you start husband-hunting for me again, I hope you'll remember that I would prefer he be a Christian."

He grinned and assured her he'd keep that in mind. "So no Saracens, Jews, or heretics. Any other requirements I should know about?"

His joking mention of heretics had stirred up an unwelcome memory; it vexed Joanna the way Raimond de St Gilles hovered in the corners of her consciousness, awaiting his chance to lay claim to her thoughts. "Well, a crown would be good," she said, matching Richard's bantering tone, and he promised to add "king" to the list of qualifications, warning her that she risked never finding another husband if she was going to be so demanding.

Joanna was delighted that they were so at ease with each other, as if the past twenty months had never been. She felt comfortable enough now to acknowledge the ghost in the chamber. "Richard, we need to talk about Berengaria."

If he'd shut down whenever mention was made of Heinrich, now it was as if she were looking at a castle under siege, drawbridge pulled up, portcullis in place, doors barred. "You assured me she was well," he said, making that simple statement somehow sound accusatory. "Were you lying about that?"

"No, of course not!" She was flustered by his hostility, but it was too late to retreat. More convinced than ever that something was wrong, she leaned over and touched his arm. "She is not ailing, Richard. She is bewildered, though, that you seem to be deliberately delaying a reunion. She does not understand why you did not want her to join you in England, and neither do I—"

She could feel the muscles in his arm tense even before he pulled away and got abruptly to his feet. "I've warned you before, Joanna, about meddling in my marriage!"

"I am not meddling. I just want to help—"

"Did I ask for your help? Did Berenguela? You have a bad habit of interfering in matters that are not your concern and I am bone-weary of it!"

Joanna rose, too, staring at him in dismay. This was not the first time she'd taken him to task for neglecting his wife, for she'd become very protective of Berengaria during their time together in the Holy Land. Usually he'd been amused, occasionally annoyed, but only once had he become angry with her, and that was when he'd been in the initial stages of Arnaldia. She'd never seen him as furious as he was now. Instead of snapping back, as she would ordinarily have done, she found herself trying to pacify him. "I am sorry. I did not mean to meddle. . . ."

He was not appeased, continuing to glare at her. "See that it does not happen again," he said, sounding like such a stranger that she could only nod, at a rare loss for words. She was greatly relieved when Arne returned then with the wine, for the silence was becoming suffocating. Accepting a cup from the boy, she managed to make stilted small talk while she drank it, but when she offered an excuse for leaving, Richard did not object. To the contrary, she thought that he seemed glad to see her gone.

"SIT HERE, and I will brush out your hair," Eleanor suggested. They were alone, for Joanna had requested that they go up to their bedchamber before their women joined them for the night. She sat upon the bench as directed, and enjoyed this brief, blessed regression back into childhood, relaxing as her mother tended to her needs. Eleanor drew the brush through her daughter's long, curly hair, establishing a lulling rhythm before saying, "What is wrong, Joanna?"

"I had a dreadful quarrel with Richard this afternoon, Maman. I was trying to learn why he seems set upon keeping Berengaria at arm's length, and he accused me angrily of meddling in his marriage."

Eleanor continued to wield the brush. "Well, you *were* meddling, dearest."

"I know," Joanna conceded. "But I always meddle, Maman! I love Richard dearly, and when we were in the Holy Land, I am sure he did not mean to neglect Berengaria. It is just that he is utterly single-minded, and he tended to forget he had a wife unless I reminded him of it."

"I can see how he might have been distracted," Eleanor said wryly, "what with fighting a holy war at the time."

Joanna looked over her shoulder and grinned. "I'm sure that crossed his mind when I scolded him for not paying more attention to his bride." Her smile faded then. "But this is different, Maman. It has been two months since his return to England. Berengaria is very hurt that he has not sent for her."

Twisting around on the bench, she looked up searchingly into her mother's face. "They seemed to get along well enough in the Holy Land. She was bedazzled, of course, but he appeared to be pleased, too, for she was sweet and loyal and quietly courageous. I know they did not quarrel ere they parted at Acre. So what has happened to make him so loath to have her with him? Have you spoken to him about it?"

"No, I have not." Anticipating the question forming on Joanna's lips, Eleanor said, "Nor do I intend to, dearest, for what would be the point? You ought to know by now that men cannot be talked into doing what they do not want to do."

Joanna sighed, thinking that was certainly true for a man as stubborn as her brother. She had no intention of trying again to pry answers from Richard; as reluctant as she was to admit it, she'd been perturbed by his rage, not having seen it burn so hot before. But she could not be as philosophical as her mother seemed to be, for she knew how much Berengaria was hurting. "Is there nothing we can do, Maman?"

Eleanor paused, for even with Joanna, her instinct was to protect Richard at all costs. "Yes . . . we can give him time."

Joanna wondered, *How much time?* She knew what her mother would say: as much time as he needed. But how could she explain that to Berengaria? How could she expect her sister-in-law to understand when she did not understand herself?

She offered to brush her mother's hair and, after removing Eleanor's veil and wimple, she admired its color; once a rich, dark brown, it was now as silvered as summer moonlight and she hoped that her own hair would become this spectacular shade, too, when she aged. "Where will you go after Lisieux, Maman? We cannot accompany Richard on campaign, so I thought I'd return to Poitiers. Will you come back with me?"

"No, I intend to stay at Fontevrault Abbey."

The brush paused in midstroke. "You do not mean to take holy vows, do you?"

Eleanor laughed softly. "No, child, I am not intending to become a nun. But I find myself yearning for the quiet of the cloister after all the turmoil of these past years. I think it time to reassure the Almighty that I am not as worldly and jaded as my enemies allege. Then, too, Fontevrault is ideally located, close to both Poitou and Normandy."

Joanna was amused by the mixed motives of piety and practicality. She was also relieved that her mother was not going to reject the secular world for the spiritual one; she was not willing to lose Eleanor even to God. She continued to brush out Eleanor's hair as they chatted about less risky topics than Richard's raw nerves. She was caught off balance, though, when her mother suddenly said, "I have never met Raimond de St Gilles. What did you think of him?"

Joanna was glad Eleanor could not see her face, for she could feel herself flushing. How long was the mere mention of that wretched man going to make her react as if she were a novice nun? "Well," she said, "I'd say he is the sort of man mothers warn their daughters about."

Eleanor laughed again. "Yes, I'd heard he is not like his snake of a father. Raimond is said to lust after women, not power."

"He told me it baffles him that his enemies are so sure he is a Cathar," Joanna confided, "since that would mean he'd have to forswear all pleasures of the flesh." An idea came to her then and she marveled that she'd not thought of it before. She wanted to know if Raimond had wed again, although she could not justify that curiosity even to herself, and she realized now that her mother was likely to know that. Eleanor's interest in Toulouse was a very proprietary one, which meant she made certain that she was kept well informed about the county and its people. "I suppose you heard that Raimond put aside his wife last year?" she ventured.

"Of course. I was surprised he'd hung on to that marriage as long as he did."

Joanna discovered that she was as interested in learning about Raimond's former wife as she was in finding out if he had taken a new one. "Was their marriage as unhappy as that?"

"Well, how many men would be happy to have a wife who shunned his bed?"

Eleanor winced, for Joanna had inadvertently banged the brush against her temple. "You did not know that Beatrice Trencavel is a Cathar?"

Joanna shook her head, so shocked it took her a moment to recover. "Was she always one?"

Eleanor shrugged. "The Trencavels have long been known to be very sympathetic to the Cathars. My guess is that Beatrice was a Believer when she wed Raimond and she grew more devout as the years passed. I assume you know that their priests see carnal intercourse as the greatest of all sins because it leads to procreation. They are practical enough to realize that they cannot expect their Believers to be celibate, but once Beatrice needed to live a more holy life, she would be loath to pay the marital debt, convinced she'd be imperiling her chances of salvation."

Fortunately for Joanna, Dame Amaria entered the chamber then, followed soon afterward by Dame Beatrix and Mariam, and the conversation flowed into other channels. But once Joanna was in bed beside her mother, she could not sleep, assailed by mortifying memories that burned hot color into her cheeks. She could hear her own angry words echoing in her ears, scorning Raimond for putting aside an unwanted wife, attacking him when he'd hesitated before saying Beatrice had entered a convent. No wonder he'd hesitated. He would not want to admit that it was a Cathar convent. How gleefully his enemies would have used that against him. And that night in a Bordeaux garden, she'd been his enemy, too, blaming him for the failure of his marriage, even accusing him of being a bad father to his daughter. Now the voice she was hearing was Raimond's. *Are you always so quick to pass judgment?* She had not even bothered to deny it then. She would gladly have denied it tonight. It was too late, of course. Nigh on a year too late.

❧

As a child, Joanna had spent several years in Poitiers with the girls betrothed to her brothers, Constance, Duchess of Brittany, and the Lady Alys of France. Because they were both older than she was, they'd never become friends. She was still surprised by the coolness of Constance's greeting upon the other woman's arrival at Caen—until she remembered that Constance detested all of the Angevins except Geoffrey. Certainly her meeting with Eleanor was an icy one; Joanna joked afterward to her mother that they'd been in danger of getting frostbite. Although she was too far away to hear, she thought that Constance's audience with Richard was no less chilly. She knew that her brother had no liking for Geoffrey's widow, a distrust rooted in Geoffrey's two invasions of Aquitaine. But she did not know why Eleanor was so hostile, and when she asked, she was taken aback by the response.

"Because she did nothing but pour poison into Geoffrey's ear," Eleanor said, staring across the hall at the Breton duchess. "She did her best to estrange him from his family, to ally him with the French king, and if not for that accursed alliance, Geoffrey would not have taken part in that tournament."

While Joanna would agree that Hal had been as malleable as wax, her memories of Geoffrey were not of a man easily influenced, even by a wife. Glancing over at her mother, she decided that Eleanor needed someone to blame for Geoffrey's death, and Constance's hostility made her a natural target. She held her peace, though, continuing to watch as Constance made a stiff curtsy and withdrew from the dais, pausing to give the most grudging of greetings to her husband, the Earl of Chester, before leaving the hall. Chester seemed no happier to see his wife than she was to see him, and Joanna felt pity for them both, fettered in holy wedlock like two oxen yoked to a plough.

When Richard joined them later, she asked why Constance had come to Caen, for she'd never been one to curry royal favor. "She wanted to know when her daughter must depart for Austria," he said, "and she was not happy to hear Leopold is demanding Aenor arrive in Vienna by October. I told her I'd send Anna to join Aenor in Rouen so they could get to know each other, but that was all I could do."

Joanna's first impulse was to object, for she knew Anna would not be pleased. But after a moment to consider, she realized that both Anna and Aenor would benefit from it. At least they'd not be strangers when they had to start out on the marital journey that neither one wanted to make.

Glancing around to make sure no one else was within earshot, Richard confided to Joanna and Eleanor that he had no intention of honoring that provision of the Worms Pact. "I did not say anything to Constance or Anna yet, for I did not want to give them false hope. But I think there is a good chance that these marriages will not come to pass. I've been told the Pope has sent a stern warning to Leopold, demanding that he return my hostages and repay his portion of the ransom, threatening to lay all of Austria under Interdict if he does not obey."

Richard's mouth turned down, for he considered this sudden papal support to be too little, too late. Where was Celestine when he was chained in that Trifels dungeon? "I warned Leopold that he'd be the one to pay Heinrich's debt," he said bitterly, "but he would not heed me." And for a moment, he found himself back at Dürnstein, listening as Leopold told him pompously that they no longer had the luxury of choosing their own fates. Well, if there was any justice under God's sky, that would come to be one of Leopold's greatest regrets.

❦

JOHN KNEW HE'D MADE the only rational decision. As much as he dreaded facing his brother, Durand was right; groveling for the chance at a crown made more sense than begging for scraps from Philippe's table. And it was surely a promising omen that within days of making his decision, he received a confidential message from his mother, urging him to meet Richard at Lisieux. But now that he was actually here, waiting for his brother to arrive, he began to have second, third, and fourth thoughts. What if Richard would not forgive him? If Richard decided to let him experience for himself what a dungeon was like? What if his mother's message had been a ruse? Why had he believed he could trust her? He'd seen her in action and knew her methods were neither merciful nor maternal.

His confidence had begun to erode as soon as he reached Lisieux, for he'd received no warm welcome from his host, Archdeacon John de Alençon, Richard's former vice-chancellor. The archdeacon had greeted him with cold civility, and after escorting him to the manor's solar on an upper floor, he'd angered John by commenting that he need not feel nervous, saying, "The king will be kinder to you than you would have been to him."

Now John could do nothing but wait and try to keep his imagination—always too active for his own good—from running away with him. A sudden uproar outside sent him flying to the window. Cautiously he opened the shutters, gazing down into the courtyard at the turmoil that always heralded a royal arrival. Retreating from the window, he medicated his nerves with some of the archdeacon's wine, all the while staring at the door.

When it finally did open, he tensed in spite of himself. His mother paused in the doorway. Her face was impassive, but her eyes were amber ice in which he could read the reflection of his every sin, could read accusation and indictment, but no hint of absolution.

"Mother," he said, his pride compelling him to meet that daunting gaze without flinching.

Eleanor let the door close behind her, but stayed where she was. This was harder than she'd expected it would be. How well did she truly know him, this stranger, her son? He'd been just seven when she'd been imprisoned, twenty-three when she'd finally regained her freedom. He'd always been Harry's, never hers. She'd not expected to feel this sadness, this sense of loss. But when she reminded herself of what he had done—a betrayal that only God could forgive—she felt rage begin to kindle, and that she did not want, either.

"Well," she said, "at least you had the courage to come."

John bought some time by pouring wine into another cup, relieved that his hand was so steady. Carrying it across the chamber, he held it out, saying, "I hope you'll not throw this in my face, for it would be a waste of good wine. You know why I am here, Mother. I need you to speak for me. You're the one person Richard would be likely to heed."

"I daresay you are right, John. But if I do that for you, there is something I want in return."

John's mouth was dry and he took a sip from the wine when she made no attempt to reach for the cup. "What is that?" he asked warily. "What do you want from me?"

"The truth. When I stopped you from leaving England for the French court two years ago, I thought we'd reached an understanding. I told you then that my first loyalty was to Richard, would always be to him. But if Richard did not sire a son, I wanted you as his heir, not Arthur, and I promised I would do what I could to make it happen. Why was that not enough for you, John?"

He did not hesitate, for he was clever enough to understand that what he'd done was indefensible. There was no way to whitewash his conniving with the French king, to deny that had they succeeded, Richard would have been entombed in some Godforsaken French dungeon, praying for death. It could not be rationalized or explained away as an aberration. All he had to offer was the truth, however brutal it was.

"For what it's worth, I fully meant to hold to our understanding."

"Why did you not, then?"

"Because Richard's capture unbalanced the equation. I truly did not believe he'd ever come back, ever regain his freedom, not with the enemies he's made. The crown was suddenly there for the taking and so I put in my bid."

Eleanor bit her lip. She'd asked for honesty and she'd gotten it—utterly without shame, conscience, or contrition. How had she and Harry failed so badly? Why had they been unable to foster any brotherly feelings between their sons?

Her prolonged silence was beginning to seem ominous to John. "Well?" he said, when he could endure it no longer. "Will you intercede with Richard on my behalf?"

She gave him a look he could not interpret. "I already have."

John's relief was intense, but ephemeral. So this whole scene had been yet another of her damnable games. Why could she not have told him that at the outset? "Thank you," he said, and even to his ears, it did not sound convincing.

It did not sound convincing to Eleanor, either, but she was not seeking gratitude. She knew how little gratitude meant in their world. "It will help," she said, very dryly, "if you try to seem somewhat contrite. But do not waste your breath telling Richard how very sorry you are. He well knows that you are only sorry you failed."

Suddenly impatient to have this over and done with, she turned toward the door, glancing over her shoulder when he did not follow. "Richard is below in the great hall. Now would be as good a time as any."

"The great hall?" John echoed in dismay. He thought it penance enough to have to humble his pride before Richard, shrank from doing it before a hall full of hostile witnesses. He opened his mouth to protest, then caught himself. Like Richard, she judged others by standards that made no allowances for human frailties. Richard measured a man by his willingness to bleed, to risk his life upon the thrust of a sword. With his mother, the test was more subtle and more demanding. She might forgive deceit and betrayal, but not weakness. Above all, he knew she would expect a man to answer for the consequences of his actions.

"Lead the way," he said, with a tight smile. "God forbid that we keep the king waiting."

❧

RICHARD WAS SEATED UPON the dais at the far end of the hall, only half listening to the Archbishop of Canterbury, for his thoughts kept wandering to what was occurring in the solar above their heads. He looked up when his mother slid into the empty seat to his left and nodded. When a sudden silence fell, he knew his brother had entered the hall. The crowd moved aside hastily, clearing a path to the dais. Richard thought he'd been able to extinguish his anger, but the embers were still smoldering and as he watched while John made what must have been the longest walk of his life, he could feel the heat beginning to build again. As if sensing that, Eleanor reached over and rested her hand lightly on his arm. He covered her hand with his own, wordlessly assuring her that he would not be reneging upon his promise. He would pardon Johnny, for they shared the same blood. But Johnny was going to bleed a little of it first. He was entitled to that much.

"My liege." Stopping before the dais, John slowly unbuckled his scabbard and laid it upon the steps. Then he knelt. "I can offer you no excuses. I can only ask for your forgiveness—even though I know I do not deserve it."

Richard studied the younger man, noting the pulse beating in his throat, the sheen of perspiration on his forehead. When he thought John seemed about to jump out of his own skin, he rose to his feet. "Well, you're here. That counts for something. And our lady mother would have me forgive you. That counts for a great deal. I suppose I should just be thankful that since you are so much given to treachery, you're so reassuringly inept at it." He waited for the laughter to subside, for the color to rush to John's face. "You need not fear, John. A child is not punished if he listens to bad counsel. It is those who led you astray who will feel my wrath." And he reached down, raising John to his feet.

The audience dutifully applauded and Richard took advantage of the clamor to pitch his voice for John's ear only. "Your blood may have bought you a pardon, Johnny, but the price is higher for an earldom, higher than you can pay. I've no intention of restoring your titles and lands, not until I'm damned well sure that you're deserving of them . . . if ever."

As their eyes met, John nodded. "I understand," he said tonelessly. "I shall remember your generosity, Brother. You may be sure of that."

❧

WHILE HE COULD LIE convincingly to others, John had rarely been able to lie to himself. He'd inherited too much of the Angevin sense of irony for that. Nor was righteous indignation an emotion indigenous to his temperamental terrain. So he knew he'd gotten off cheaply, given the gravity of his offenses. But that awareness did not soothe his injured pride. Richard's patronizing pardon hurt more than an excoriating recital of his sins would have done, for it reminded him of his brother's devastating response after being warned that he was plotting with Philippe to claim the English crown. *John is not the man to conquer a kingdom if there is anyone to offer the least resistance.* Did Richard truly believe that? Did his bishops and barons? Did they all see him as so worthless?

He'd endured the ordeal with what grace he could muster, ignoring the stares, even smiling when Richard magnanimously dispatched a large salmon swimming in gravy to his end of the table as a mark of royal favor. But as soon as he could, he escaped the hall for the comparative privacy of the manor gardens, grateful to be cloaked in darkness, away from prying eyes. Now that he need no longer fear imprisonment or exile for his betrayal, he was realizing what a rocky road lay ahead of him. How could he hope to regain Richard's trust? Yet unless he did, he'd be the beggar at the feast. Moreover, it was not just Richard's contempt that he must deal with. He'd seen the scorn in the eyes of the other men in the hall. Even if God struck Richard down on the morrow and he claimed the throne, how long could he rule if he was neither respected nor feared?

Far better to be judged evil than inept, he thought, with a gleam of mordant humor, and then whirled at the sound of footsteps to find his sister standing several feet away. He'd not expected to see her at Lisieux and he'd not liked having her witness his public humiliation, for they'd gotten on well as children. With memories of his shame still so raw, his control finally cracked. "If you've come to offer pity, I do not want any!"

"Good, because I do not think you are deserving of any."

They regarded each other in silence. He'd recognized her as soon as he'd seen her on the dais, even though it had been almost two decades. She'd been a beautiful child who'd grown into a beautiful woman, a woman who—like their mother and half of Christendom—thought Brother Richard could walk on water. His relationship with his family had always been a tenuous one, fraught with ambiguity and ambivalence. Even before disgrace and imprisonment had erased her from his life, his mother had been a glamorous stranger to him. His father had dominated his world, inspiring awe, admiration, and fear in the boy he'd once been. His brothers had been so much older than he—eleven, nine, and eight years—that they seemed to live on a distant shore, leaving him to cling to the small island of his father's favor, an island ever in danger of being submerged by the raging Angevin sea. Only with Joanna was it not complicated—until she'd been sent off to wed the King of Sicily, thus depriving him of his only childhood ally.

"Eighteen years . . . We have a lot of catching up to do," he said, striving to sound composed, even nonchalant. "I'll go first. One marriage, no children born in wedlock, some born out of it, two betrayals, and one very public pardon."

Joanna was not fooled by his flippant tone. "For me, it was marriage, motherhood, and widowhood."

John surprised her then, by dropping his sardonic shield and giving her a glimpse of the brother she remembered. "I ought to have written to you when your son died, Joanna."

"You were not yet fifteen, Johnny."

"I still should have written." He moved toward her then, stepping out of the shadows into the moonlight. "Why did you follow me into the garden?"

She thought it was strange to see her mother's green-gold eyes in another face. "Do you remember what I would call you whenever we'd have a falling-out? Johnny-cat, because you were always poking about where you had no right to be."

"I remember," he said, with the barest hint of a smile. "I never liked it much."

"I could not help thinking of that as I watched you and Richard in the great hall. The Saracens had a proverb about cats having seven lives. You offered up your seventh one in there, Johnny-cat. You do know that?"

"Christ, Joanna, of course I do!"

She ignored the flare-up of defensive anger. "Thank God you see that," she said somberly. "I was afraid you would not. I know Richard and he will not forgive you again, Johnny. The next time you fall from grace will be your last. For your sake—for all our sakes—I hope you never forget that."

She stepped closer then, kissing him on the cheek. Feeling as if she were bidding farewell to her childhood, she turned to go back to the great hall, leaving him alone in the garden. He stood there without moving, watching her walk away.

⟨♛⟩

ONE REASON RICHARD HAD been so impatient during his stay at Portsmouth was that he'd heard the French king was laying siege to Verneuil, a strategically placed castle that he could ill afford to lose. Confident that he'd be coming to their aid, the garrison had spurned Philippe's demand for surrender, mocking him from the battlements and drawing an unflattering caricature of the French king on the castle walls. Richard meant to march on Verneuil as soon as he'd made peace with John, and on the day of his departure, he was pleased by the arrival of his infamous mercenary captain, Mercadier. Boasting a sinister scar that carved a jagged path from his cheekbone to his chin, twisting one corner of his mouth awry, with hungry hawk eyes that few could meet for long, this ice-blooded son of the south had earned a reputation for battlefield mayhem that rivaled some of the legends of the king he served. Richard was untroubled by

Mercadier's notoriety, caring only that he was utterly loyal and utterly fearless, and he welcomed the routier with enough warmth to worry the clerics, who were convinced that all routiers were godless men and Mercadier himself the spawn of Satan.

Richard was giving final instructions to the knights who would escort Anna to Rouen, Eleanor to Fontevrault, and Joanna on to Poitiers, when he happened to catch an enigmatic exchange between André and Mercadier, André asking, "He is with you?" Seeing Richard's curious look, André smiled slyly. "We have a surprise for you, sire," he said. "He's awaiting you out in the courtyard."

Glancing around, Richard saw that others were in on André and Mercadier's secret; even his son Philip was grinning. Richard's first thought was that the Earl of Leicester had accompanied Mercadier, but he was not likely to be lurking outside. Vexed when André refused to tell him more, he bade farewell to the women, and then hastened from the great hall to see what his cousin was up to now.

He halted so abruptly that he was jostled by the men coming through the doorway after him. He never heard their embarrassed apologies, for he had eyes only for the dun stallion being held by a beaming groom. Taking the reins from the youth, Richard ran his hand caressingly over the horse's pale gold withers, laughing when he was nudged by a warm muzzle.

"You remember me, do you?" he said and then swung up into the saddle. André was saying something about the horse transport being forced ashore in Sicily and eventually landing at Marseille, but Richard was not listening. He could feel the Cypriot destrier's coiled energy, his eagerness to run, calling to mind memories of racing the wind and Saracens. "You'll be chasing the French now, Fauvel," he told the stallion, and when he gave the signal, Fauvel exploded into action, rocketing across the courtyard as if launched from a crossbow. The men laughed and applauded and then hurried toward their own mounts, for Richard and Fauvel would soon be out of sight.

❧

FROM LISIEUX, Richard rode to Tuboeuf, just twelve miles from the siege of Verneuil. There he met a knight from the garrison who'd managed to slip away under cover of darkness to seek aid, for the French mangonels were pounding away relentlessly at the castle's defenses. Richard at once dispatched a force of knights, men-at-arms, and crossbowmen to reinforce the garrison, then sent others to cut off Philippe's supply lines. He was deeply grateful to God that the French king's day of reckoning was coming so soon, but when he arrived at Verneuil with the bulk of his army on May 30, he discovered that Philippe was gone and the siege was over. He promised to reward the garrison lavishly, although his triumph was tarnished in his eyes by his enemy's escape.

Captured French prisoners told a disjointed, confusing tale, claiming their king had suddenly left the siege two days earlier, leaving men behind to continue the assault upon the castle. But they were demoralized by their king's departure and fled when they heard of Richard's approach. Richard would later discover that Philippe had ridden off in a fury after learning what had befallen Évreux. Eager to demonstrate his newfound loyalty, John had returned to Évreux and easily gained admittance, for it was not yet known that he'd switched sides. He had no trouble taking control of the town; he beheaded many of the garrison and cast the rest into the castle dungeons. Outraged by his former ally's betrayal, Philippe raced to Évreux, so intent upon making John pay for his treachery that he doomed his chances of taking Verneuil. He found that John had already gone, but he recaptured Évreux and since John was out of reach, he took his vengeance upon the town and its people, turning his men loose to pillage and rape, not even sparing churches; he was said to have fired the abbey of St Taurin himself.

This was not the first time that Philippe's temper had gotten the better of him; he'd had the Peace Elm chopped down after a frustrating encounter with Henry and ordered his own siege engines destroyed after being outmaneuvered by the Earl of Leicester at Rouen. But even the French chroniclers were shocked by the charred ruins of Évreux, and as word spread of its fate, the people of Normandy and towns to the south felt a chill of fear. Wars were always brutal and the innocent and the defenseless were usually the ones to suffer. This war, though, promised to be bloodier than most, for the hatred that the French and English kings bore each other burned hotter than the fires that had consumed so much of Évreux.

CHAPTER TWENTY-FOUR

✦

Berengaria's parents had been very happy together. It had been a marriage of state, of course, but they'd come to love each other and after Sancha died giving birth to Berengaria's youngest sister, Blanca, Sancho had not wed again. Berengaria had been only nine when she lost her mother but her father and elder brother had kept Sancha alive for her by sharing their own memories. She'd realized that theirs was not a typical royal marriage, and she felt she'd entered her own marriage with realistic expectations. She'd have been content with mutual respect, while hoping, too, that affection would grow in her marital garden. But nothing had turned out as she'd imagined it would.

She'd been nervous about wedding Richard, knowing how drastically her world would change once she was his queen. And from their first meeting in Sicily, she'd been caught up in an Angevin riptide. Hers had been a sheltered upbringing and at first she'd been troubled that she enjoyed her betrothed's kisses and caresses, fearing that she was being tempted by the serious sin of lust. But Joanna had proved to be a much better marriage counselor than Padre Domingo, her confessor, assuring her that what she felt was desire, not lust, and desire was part of the Almighty's plan, for many believed that a woman could not conceive if she did not experience pleasure. And once they were wed, she'd discovered that she liked paying the marital debt, liked the intimacy and the closeness, liked having Richard's undivided attention, which only seemed to happen in bed.

In these past weeks, she'd deliberately called up every memory of her marriage, trying desperately to discover a clue, something that would explain why things had suddenly gone so wrong. But she found no answers. Despite the dangers of their journey and the hardships of life in an army camp, she'd been happy most of the time. It was exciting being married to Richard. He dominated every gathering, always the center of attention. He was all that their world most admired—a man of prowess—and she was proud to be married to such a renowned battle commander, very honored to be wed to the savior of the Holy City. She'd believed he was content, too, with the bride he'd chosen for himself, and she was sure that they would have a more normal life once they returned to his domains, once she no longer had to fear that she'd become a widow ere she could truly become a wife. After they went home, she would be able to entertain his guests, dispense alms to those in need, hear petitions, manage the royal household, and fulfill a queen's primary duty, which was to bear his children.

That had been the only snake in her Eden: her failure to conceive. With her usual candor, Joanna had reminded her that she'd not had many opportunities to share Richard's bed in the midst of a war, and she knew that was true. Nor had Richard reproached her for it. In fact, the one time her flux had been so late that her hopes had soared, he'd even said that it might be safer if she did not become pregnant until they'd left the Holy Land, pointing out that it was not a kind country for infants, for women and children, for any man not born and bred there.

Even if she'd not become pregnant as quickly as she'd wanted, she'd remained confident that it would happen in God's time. Her contentment with her new life and her new marriage had been shaken, though, toward the end of their stay in Outremer. She'd been shocked by Richard's failure to retake Jerusalem. She did not think to question his military expertise and when he said it could not be done, she accepted that. Yet she grieved for the failure no less than his soldiers had, and she'd been bitterly disappointed that he refused to accept Saladin's offer and visit Jerusalem's sacred sites. When he finally admitted to her that he felt he did not deserve to see them, having failed to keep his vow, she'd been proud that he would not accept from the infidels what he could not win through God's grace. But she'd still wept in secret for the Holy City that neither of them would see.

Was it possible that he'd sensed her disappointment? That he'd felt she was blaming him for his failure to liberate Jerusalem? But if that were so, surely he'd have said something? Or would he? She was beginning to wonder just how well she really knew him. When he'd been so close to dying at Jaffa, he'd not sent for her, and that had raised doubts she'd been unwilling to confront, even to acknowledge. She'd been able to convince herself that he'd kept her away because of the danger. Now, though, his decision took on more sinister significance. How often had he confided in her? Had he ever offered any intimacy that was not carnal? Yes, they were bound by the sacred vows of holy wedlock. But they were often two strangers sharing a bed.

Even so, none of her unhappy conjecturing explained why he would want to keep her at a distance all of a sudden. Joanna had been right; they'd parted on good terms. So what had come between them? If she'd done nothing to offend him, why was he delaying their reunion like this?

Berengaria was lonely, too, for Joanna had not yet returned, sending word that she would be staying at Fontevrault Abbey for a while. Berengaria did not begrudge her sister-in-law some time with her mother, but she missed Joanna very much; for three years, they'd seen each other daily. She did get a surprise visit in early June from her brother Sancho. He'd been ravaging the lands of the rebel lords Geoffrey de Rançon and the Count of Angoulême and was now on his way north to besiege Loches Castle with Richard. Berengaria was delighted to see Sancho. He brought welcome news of home, had stories to relate of her sisters Constanza and Blanca, and he also had word of their young brother Fernando, who'd written that he was being well treated at the imperial court.

But even Sancho's unexpected arrival would prove to be a mixed blessing. He'd assumed she'd joined Richard in England, and although he tried to hide it, he'd been taken aback to find out that she'd not yet seen her husband. It was humiliating enough for Berengaria that her household ladies and knights knew of her plight, but it was far more mortifying that her family now knew, too. Even worse was to come. Sancho had been evasive whenever she'd mentioned their father and at last he'd confessed that the elder Sancho was not well. Their father's health had always been good, but he was sixty-two now, an age where men were vulnerable to any number of dangerous maladies. When Sancho departed for Loches, Berengaria gave him a letter for Richard, as sparing and laconic as any of his own letters had been, and then passed the endless hours praying for her ailing father and trying not to think about her missing husband.

❧

JOANNA FELT A LITTLE GUILTY about staying so long at Fontevrault, knowing how miserable Berengaria must be. But when Eleanor got a letter from her granddaughter the Countess of Perche, Joanna delayed her departure yet again, for she very much wanted to meet Richenza. The young woman did not resemble Joanna's elder sister, for she'd inherited her father's dark coloring, but she had her mother's beauty and much of her charm, and she and Joanna felt an immediate empathy. Like her brothers Otto and Wilhelm, Richenza had grown up at the English royal court, forming a close bond with Eleanor and Richard that was now causing her great pain.

She'd explained apologetically to Eleanor and Joanna that her husband really had no choice. Had he not obeyed the French king's summons, he'd have risked losing all their French lands. If it were up to her, Richenza would have taken the gamble, for she loved her uncle. But she loved her husband and young son, too, and in any event, the decision had been Jaufre's, not hers. Now Richard was back and Jaufre feared what was to come, so he'd willingly agreed when Richenza suggested she visit her grandmother. Jaufre hoped that Richenza could make her Angevin relatives understand why he'd deserted the English king, but he was not optimistic, for he'd heard one of the verses of the song Richard had composed in his German prison, which was being widely circulated by troubadours and trouvères:

> *"My comrades whom I loved and still do love*
> *The lords of Perche and Cauieux*
> *Strange tales have reached me that are hard to prove;*
> *I ne'er was false to them; for evermore*
> *Vile would men count them, if their arms they bore*
> *'Gainst me, a prisoner here."*

Richenza had done her best, stressing Jaufre's reluctance and his kinship to Philippe, which made it even harder to defy the French king. Eleanor's welcome had been affectionate enough to reassure her that she was not blamed for Jaufre's defection. Her grandmother said nothing about Jaufre, though, and she was reluctant to ask Eleanor to intercede on his behalf with Richard. Richenza adored her grandmother but she knew Eleanor was not as quick to forgive as Richenza's mother had been.

On the second day of her visit, while she was walking with Joanna in the gardens of Eleanor's lodgings on the abbey grounds, she decided to risk confiding in her aunt. "It is so hard," she said with a sigh, "for a man to serve two liege lords." When Joanna agreed, she was encouraged to continue. "Aunt Joanna, do you think my uncle will forgive Jaufre and me?"

"He will forgive *you*, Richenza." Seeing the younger woman's dismay, Joanna reached out and steered her niece toward a bench. "You need to understand this, Richenza. Richard is not in a mood to forgive. After he left Verneuil, he took the castle Beaumont-le-Roger from the Count of Meulan, who'd abandoned him for Philippe just as Jaufre did. Then he rode to Tours, where the citizens had been quick to open their city's gates to the French king. He dispossessed the canons of St Martin's, for their priory is as close to the Capetians as Fontevrault is to our family, and he demanded two thousand marks from the townspeople to regain royal favor. So you see, he is more inclined these days to punish than to pardon."

Richenza appreciated her aunt's honesty, for she thought it was always better to know what she was up against. But she was not going to concede defeat so easily, at least not until she heard the bad news from Richard himself. He was just fifty miles away, besieging Loches. She would go to him at Loches and do her best to make him understand why Jaufre had joined the French king. In the event, she did not have to take such dramatic action; as she and Joanna joined Abbess Mathilde for dinner in her guest hall, the abbey was thrown into turmoil by the unexpected arrival of the English king.

Richenza hung back, watching as Richard was greeted joyfully by his mother and sister and the prioress, Aliza de Bretagne, who showed so much excitement that the elderly abbess shot her a disapproving frown. Aliza was so obviously unrepentant that Richenza immediately liked the young nun, who looked to be her own age, twenty-two. Richard's men were sent to eat with the monks at the priory of St Jean de l'Habit, for Fontevrault was unique in that its abbess ruled over men as well as women, and Mathilde hastily ordered servants to set places for Richard, André, Morgan, Guillain, and Master Fulk at her table. It was then that Richard glanced around and noticed his niece.

Richenza held her breath until he smiled, and when he held out his arms, she came gratefully into them. "I'm so sorry, Uncle. . . ."

"You've nothing to be sorry for, lass." He bent down and kissed her cheek before saying, "Your husband does, though."

"I know," she admitted, taking heart from his matter-of-fact tone. "Jaufre felt he had no choice, Uncle. If he'd defied the French king, he'd have lost his lands in Perche."

"Well, he has lost his lands in England now. I ordered his estates in Wiltshire and Bedfordshire forfeit to the Crown." Sliding his fingers under her chin, he tilted her face up to his. "But not your dowry lands. They are still yours."

Richenza's smile was radiant with relief, for even if the very worst happened and Jaufre lost Perche in this accursed war, her son would still have a substantial inheritance; Richard had provided very generously for her at the time that he'd arranged her marriage to Jaufre.

"Why so surprised, Richenza? After all, you're my favorite niece."

"Well, there is not much competition for that honor, Uncle Richard."

They grinned at each other, for this was a running joke between them; he'd not met any of his sister Leonora's daughters in Castile and his sister-in-law Constance had done her best to poison Aenor's mind against all of the Angevins. Richard was tempted to tell her that he intended to restore Jaufre's English lands to him eventually. But she might confide in her husband, wanting to reassure him that he'd be forgiven in time, and Richard was determined that Jaufre lose some sleep over his fall from royal favor. He liked Jaufre and was not about to ruin his niece's husband. There was a price to be paid, though, for failure to keep faith. "Come on, lass," he said. "Let's have dinner."

Once they'd all been seated and freshly caught fish from the abbey's stews had been served, Eleanor leaned over to ask Richard about the siege. She knew better than most what a formidable challenge Loches Castle posed, for she'd been held there briefly after she'd been captured by her husband's men. "I assume that your presence here means the siege is going well?"

"Oh, it is over," Richard said nonchalantly. "How long did it take, André? Two or three?"

"Two and a half, I think," André said, just as nonchalantly, reaching for a slice of bread.

Eleanor's eyes widened incredulously. "You took Loches in just two and a half days?"

"No . . . two and a half hours." Seeing the amazed looks on the faces of all the women, Richard and André burst out laughing, only too happy to answer all the questions that were at once aimed at them. Eleanor listened in silence as the queen warred with the mother. She understood more about war than the other women, and for Richard to have captured Loches in just a few hours, it must have been an extraordinarily ferocious assault—with her son in the very thick of the fighting.

Joanna was pleased to learn that Richard had taken over two hundred prisoners. Legally, he had the right to execute the garrison when a castle was taken by storm; John's slaughter of the Évreux garrison had left a bad taste in her mouth.

She knew Richard could be very ruthless himself when need be—she was still uncomfortable remembering the execution of the garrison at Acre—and she had worried that his war with Philippe would become a bloodbath. "Why did Berengaria's brother not come with you?" she asked, for she wanted to meet Sancho, who was said to be over seven feet tall; she could not imagine a man towering over Richard by fully a foot.

Richard's smile disappeared. "Sancho left the siege ere I even got there. His men told me that he'd had to rush back to Navarre, having gotten word that his father is gravely ill and not expected to recover. When are you planning to return to Poitiers, Joanna? I think it would help Berenguela very much if you were with her."

"I will leave on the morrow," she promised, and when he said that he'd give her a letter for Berenguela, she hesitated. "She will want to know when you'll be there. What shall I tell her?"

Although Joanna had taken care to keep her tone neutral, Richard still found himself on the defensive. "Tell her I'll come as soon as I can," he said tersely. When she nodded, he frowned, faulting her for what he was sure she was thinking. Did she expect Philippe to courteously cease hostilities whilst he was visiting his wife in Poitou? That craven weasel would be quick to raid the hen roost once he learned the guard dog was gone. The only way to end this war was to track down that Judas and force him to fight.

As he studied his sister, he doubted that she truly comprehended what a daunting challenge he faced to regain all that had been lost during his captivity. Setting his wine cup down, he turned toward Joanna and sought to educate her about the harsh reality of warfare. Philippe controlled much of Normandy east of the River Seine, including the ports of Dieppe and Tréport. He now held castles that put him within striking distance of Rouen itself. Moreover, his acquisition of Artois from Flanders gave him more resources than French kings had in the past. But while Joanna listened attentively, Richard sensed that she still did not understand. Nor would his wife. Well, so be it. His duties as king had to come first, and Berenguela would have to accept that.

After dinner, Eleanor asked Richard about Philippe's siege of Fontaines; that had alarmed her, for the castle was just four miles from Rouen. Richard and André were unconcerned, though, mocking the French king for taking four days to capture such a small, poorly defended stronghold and making Prioress Aliza laugh by swearing she and her nuns could have taken it faster than

Philippe. Now Eleanor was not surprised when Richard said he would have to return to his army on the morrow; she knew he'd been practically living in the saddle in recent weeks and that was not likely to change anytime soon. She was about to ask him if he'd heard how Heinrich's invasion of Sicily was going when a courier was ushered into the hall.

He'd been sent by the seneschal of Normandy and his disheveled state alerted Richard that his message was urgent. Snatching up the letter, he broke the seal and read rapidly. "Christ on the Cross!" The color draining from his face, he glanced up, his eyes seeking André. "Leicester has been captured by the French!"

There was an immediate outcry from his audience, for the women were as horrified as his men. "How did it happen?" Eleanor asked her son, who'd gone back to reading the letter.

"Once the French were retreating after razing Fontaines, he ventured out from Rouen to harass them, but with only twenty knights." Richard shook his head angrily. "How could he be so reckless?" That caused some astonished eye rolling among his friends, sister, and mother, but he did not notice. Crumpling the parchment in his fist, he flung it to the floor. "He has been sent under guard to Étampes Castle."

They knew what that meant—rescue was not an option. "Philippe is holding his unwanted wife, Ingeborg, at Étampes," Eleanor said acidly. "Mayhap he can save money by penning them up together."

Abbess Mathilde was surprised that the king seemed so shaken, for she'd assumed he was hardened to the vicissitudes and cruelties of war. Nor did she understand why he and the other men looked so grim, for the Earl of Leicester had earned renown throughout Christendom for his feats in the Holy Land. Surely a prisoner who was so highborn and so celebrated would be well treated. But when she quietly said as much to Eleanor, the queen merely looked at her, saying nothing, and there was something in those hazel eyes that gave the elderly abbess a chill. She would pray for the earl, she decided, for it was becoming clear to her that the king and his mother felt Leicester was in need of prayers.

⚜

IN EARLY JULY, Philippe invaded Touraine. He'd gotten as far as Lisle when his scouts warned him that the English king's army was awaiting him at Vendôme, blocking the road into the Loire Valley. Philippe hastily withdrew a few miles to Fréteval, and conferred with his battle commanders.

❧

VENDÔME WAS A SMALL TOWN north of Tours. It had no defensive walls, and its citizens were understandably alarmed at the possibility of a great battle being fought in their vicinity. The Count of Vendôme was nowhere to be found, but the abbot of Holy Trinity bravely entered the English king's camp to demand royal protection for his abbey and its holy relic, the Sacred Teardrop, which was said to have been shed by the Lord Christ at the tomb of Lazarus. Richard had some of his father's anticlerical bias and he was fast losing his temper. The abbot was forgotten, though, when a herald arrived from the French king.

He was riding under a flag of truce but his tone was bellicose. Reining in before Richard, he delivered his lord's message with a bravado that would have pleased Philippe, declaring that the French king would do battle on the morrow.

Richard was not impressed. "Tell your king that if he does not appear on the morrow, I will be calling on him." André and Will Marshal and Guillain de l'Etang had moved to Richard's side and they all watched as the herald rode out of camp to a chorus of jeers and catcalls.

"You think he will fight on the morrow, sire?" Guillain asked, surprised by Philippe's defiance, for pitched battles were very rare.

"We'll see it snow in Hell ere that coward faces me on the field." Richard beckoned to Warin Fitz Gerald. "Send scouts into the woods to keep watch on the French camp." Turning back to the other men, he said, "I want us to be ready to march at first light. There will be a battle on the morrow, but it will be my doing, not Philippe's."

❧

RICHARD AWOKE SEVERAL HOURS before dawn. While he did not remember it, he knew the dream had been an unpleasant one, for he'd been having them more often since he'd learned of the Earl of Leicester's capture. It infuriated him that he could not exercise better control over his own brain. Why must he keep dwelling upon what was done and over with? He was trying to get the Church involved on Leicester's behalf, but so far Philippe had rebuffed all offers of ransom. Well, if the day went as he hoped, the French king would soon be a prisoner himself.

The English camp was stirring, men yawning as they broke their fast with biscuits and ale; it was a poorly kept secret that soldiers often relied upon liquid courage to ease their prebattle jitters. Most men passed their whole lives without experiencing a pitched battle, for sieges and the raiding known as *chevauchées* were the normal means of conducting war. But Richard's army was more battle-seasoned than most, for many of the men had fought with him in the Holy Land, and Mercadier's routiers were natural killers; Mercadier did not recruit any other kind.

Richard had just given Will Marshal the command of the reserve. Younger knights often balked at that, fearing they'd be cheated of the glory they all sought. Will was just three years from his fifth decade and he knew an army without men held in reserve was at the mercy of fate, exposed to enemy counter-attacks, so he pleased Richard by accepting the charge for the honor it was meant to be. Their battle commanders were gathering around them when shouting turned all heads toward the north. A man on a rangy bay was racing into the camp, one of the scouts Richard had sent to spy upon the French.

"They are in retreat, my lord, fleeing north!"

Richard was not going to be deprived of his prey, though. He'd anticipated just such a move by the French king, and his men were ready. When he gave the command to mount up, they ran eagerly for their horses.

❧

RICHARD WAS RIDING FAUVEL, and he was well ahead of his men by the time they burst from the woods into the deserted French camp. A few fires still smol-dered, not fully quenched by hastily flung buckets of water. Some tents had been left behind, sacks of flour, kegs of wine—all that could be easily replaced. Rich-ard laughed at this proof of the urgency of the evacuation. Giving Fauvel his head, he thought that Philippe was about to get a very unpleasant surprise.

A retreating army was easy to follow and within a few miles, they could see the French rearguard and baggage carts in the distance. Richard unsheathed his sword. He did not have to prick Fauvel with his spurs; the stallion was already lengthening stride. There was considerable confusion in the French ranks as they realized they were being pursued. Drivers were whipping the cart horses mercilessly, cursing and shouting as the wagons swayed perilously from side to side. That the baggage train was so well guarded told Richard that it carried items precious to Philippe. A knight was riding toward him, sword at the ready. Richard took the strike on his shield and counterthrust. The rider reeled back in the saddle, but Richard did not wait to see if he fell, for another foe was just ahead. He swung and missed; Richard didn't. Maddened by the scent of blood, Fauvel veered toward a man on a roan stallion, screaming defiance. His teeth raked the other destrier's neck and as the horse stumbled, Richard decapitated his rider. All around him, his household knights were engaging the enemy, all around him was the familiar chaos of battle, and he set about punishing these French soldiers for each and every time that he'd not been able to hit back in the past year.

The baggage carts were surrounded, their drivers raising their hands in surrender. The French rearguard was scattering under the English assault. Richard spurred Fauvel on, for his quarry was not the baggage carts or these French knights. He was seeking the French king.

As an orderly retreat disintegrated into a panicked rout, the killing became easier for Richard's men; soldiers were at their most vulnerable in flight. Richard soon outdistanced most of his army, his household knights pushing their horses to keep up with Fauvel. He had no thoughts for his own safety now, no thoughts for anything but finding Philippe. Ahead was a crossroad. An overturned cart blocked the smaller road and a soldier standing beside it hastily raised his hands at the sight of Richard's bloodied sword and gore-splattered hauberk. He shrank back against the wagon wheel as Richard brought Fauvel to a shuddering stop and leveled his sword at the man's chest. "The king . . . Where is he?"

"Ahead, my lord." The man's accent was Flemish, but his French was serviceable. "Far ahead," he repeated hoarsely, pointing toward the dust clouds being kicked up in the distance. When Richard swung Fauvel around and set off in pursuit, the man sank to his knees, gulping air as he made a shaky sign of the cross. Other knights were galloping by and he watched in great relief as they rode past him, intent only upon staying with their king. He grabbed a wineskin from the cart and then took off at a trot for the shelter of the woods, for he knew his cart would be a magnet to men eager for plunder. He suspected he'd been threatened by the Lionheart himself. He smiled then, thinking that would make his story much more dramatic when he told it in years to come, and as he disappeared into the trees, it occurred to him that he'd done the French king a great service. A pity Philippe was not known for paying such debts of honor.

⚜

WHEN HIS STALLION FINALLY began to falter, Richard reined him in and slid from the saddle. Fauvel's gold coat was so streaked with lather that he looked white. Richard stroked his heaving side, torn between frustration that Philippe was getting away and remorse that he'd pushed this magnificent destrier beyond his endurance. "Good boy," he said apologetically, "you did your best." Seeing an alder tree some yards from the road, he led Fauvel toward it, knowing that water was often to be found near alders. There was indeed a small stream, and he let the stallion drink. The sun was hot upon his face, for he was wearing only an iron cap, not a full helmet. He was armed as if he were still fighting in Outremer; he'd learned to prefer a lighter hauberk during his months in the scorching heat of the Holy Land. Staring at that beckoning road, he swore with considerable feeling. So close! He'd covered so much ground that Philippe must be just ahead, riding for his life, the gutless swine.

Dust signaled the approach of riders from the south and he watched until André and a handful of his knights came into view. Detouring from the road, they headed in his direction. After dismounting, they tended to their own exhausted horses, some of them kneeling by the stream to wash away grime and blood. André sank down next to Richard with a groan. "I am getting old," he complained, "for every bone in my body aches." Glancing at the younger man's unhappy face, he said sympathetically, "I'd gladly offer Roland, but he is even more knackered than your Fauvel."

"I know," Richard said morosely, for he'd already assessed the sorry shape of his friends' horses. Reaching up to accept a wineskin from Morgan, he leaned back against the tree. Soon afterward, one of the knights called out and they saw other riders, moving fast. Richard scrambled to his feet, thinking that one of them might have a horse capable of continuing the chase.

Reining in, Mercadier removed his helmet. "You're a hard man to catch, my lord," he said. "I thought we were going to have to ride halfway to Paris ere we could overtake you."

Richard was instantly on the alert. "What is wrong?"

"Nothing that I know of. But I figured you'd be needing a fresh mount along about now." Mercadier gave one of his rare smiles then, which most men found even more chilling than his scowls. He gestured and one of his routiers came forward, leading a jet-black horse. Richard gave a whoop of delight, for Mercadier had brought him Scirocco, one of the two Arab stallions that al-Malik al-Adil had given him after he'd won his improbable victory at Jaffa. They'd accompanied Fauvel on the same horse transport and Richard thanked God and Mercadier now in equal measure for Scirocco's appearance when he was most needed.

"How did you find me?" he asked, checking the stallion's cinch and stirrups.

"I followed the trail of bodies," the routier said laconically, earning himself an amused look from his king. "A local farmer told us about a cross-country path that allowed us to save time and miles, so the Arab ought to be ready to run."

Richard's knights had gathered around and André said they'd follow once their horses had rested. Richard was already in the saddle. "Look after Fauvel," he said and then urged the Arab on. As the black stallion streaked toward the road, Mercadier and his routiers rode after him. André and the other men watched until they were out of sight, which did not take long.

❦

IT WAS DUSK BY THE TIME Richard returned to his camp at Vendôme. He'd finally abandoned his pursuit as the day's light began to fade, forced to admit that Philippe had managed to elude him and was probably sheltered in Château-dun Castle by now. He rode into a scene of exuberant celebration and it was only as he listened to Will Marshal that he realized the full extent of his victory. The seizure of his baggage carts would be a devastating blow to the French king; not only had he lost weapons, siege engines, tents, his own chapel accoutrements, jewels, and a vast amount of money, he'd also lost the royal archives, chest after chest filled with charters that would have to be painstakingly re-created—if possible. They'd also taken large numbers of prisoners, as well as capturing some fine horses and provisions that could now be used for Richard's own army.

But to Richard, the long-term significance lay in the capture of the French archives, for Philippe's government would be crippled by such a loss, in disarray for months to come. He laughed, thinking of the dismay of Philippe's counselors and chancery officials, thinking of Philippe's horror when he learned that all his state secrets were now in the hands of the English king. Much to Richard's satisfaction, these included a list of the Norman and Poitevin lords who'd disavowed allegiance to him and done homage to Philippe.

He was going over these charters in his tent when André joined him, bearing news that he expected to ignite his cousin's temper. One of their prisoners had information about the French king, he said, and a frightened youth was soon ushered before Richard. Shoved to his knees, he stared up mutely at the English king until André said impatiently, "Go on, tell the king what you told us."

It took a while to get the story out of him. Philippe had turned aside when he'd reached that crossroad, declaring he wanted to offer prayers in a nearby parish church. And whilst he hid in the church, his enemies had galloped heedlessly past, never suspecting that he was so close at hand.

Richard's knights watched him warily, waiting for the explosion. He surprised them all by laughing—a soured laugh, but a laugh nonetheless. "Come on," he said to André, "let's get some air." The other men took that for what it was, an invitation meant only for his cousin, and none followed as Richard and André left the tent and began to walk through the camp. Richard paused often to banter with soldiers, to offer praise that they valued almost as much as the plunder they knew he'd be sharing with them. He paid a visit to the tent that was serving as a makeshift hospital, jesting with the wounded, pleased to see that there were not very many; most of the casualties that day were French. After that, he wanted to make sure that Fauvel had been cooled down, rubbed, and fed. Getting a dried apple from the groom, he fed the treat to the dun stallion, assuring Fauvel that he was much faster than Scirocco, joking to André that he did not want jealousy to fester amongst his horses.

André was surprised by his good mood, for he'd been certain Richard would be furious to learn he'd come so close to capturing the French king. When he said that, Richard shrugged. "It was not a total loss. When that story of Philippe cowering in a church gets around, he'll be a laughingstock with his own troops. I'll have other chances to run that fox to earth, for I am going to make it my life's mission from now on."

Richard hesitated, giving the other man a sidelong glance. "The truth is that I had something else to do this day, something that mattered almost as much as capturing King Cravenheart. I needed to prove to myself that I am still the same man I was, that my imprisonment left no lasting scars."

André frowned as he thought that over. "But surely you proved that already at the siege of Nottingham and then again at Loches. If you feared death during those assaults, you hid it very well."

Richard was regretting his impulse, for it was not easy to bare his soul, even to André, who was likely to understand if anyone could. "There are worse fates than death," he said at last, and André cursed himself for not having seen it sooner. When Richard had charged into those besieged castles, he'd risked a fatal wound. But by racing into the very midst of the French army, he was risking capture.

"Well," he said, "you need not fret, Cousin. To judge by what I saw today, it is clear that you are the same crazed lunatic on the battlefield that you always were."

Richard grinned. "I was hoping you'd say that." They looked at each other and then began to laugh, sounding so triumphant that soldiers passing by smiled, glad that their king was so pleased with their victory over the French.

❧

WHEN THE WALLS OF POITIERS came into view, Richard could feel himself tense, for he was not looking forward to this reunion with his wife. He'd lashed out at his sister in part because he could not explain to her why he was loath to see Berenguela, why he so often felt distant and detached from his former life. Even with Joanna, there was a constraint between them that had not been there before. Women could not understand the humiliation of being utterly powerless, for few of them ever exercised power. Even his mother did not comprehend why he felt such shame for submitting to Heinrich's demands. That was especially true for the innocent he'd wed. He'd realized early on that Berenguela saw him through a golden glow, not as he really was. He'd liked her adulation, though, liked her bedrock faith that he was so much more capable than other men, that he would always prevail. Now he did not want to see her brown eyes reflect his own deep-rooted disappointment.

Her father's death had cast a new shadow over his marriage, for he'd begun to feel guilty for staying away. No matter how often he told himself that he'd done what he had to do, he knew he'd not been there when she'd most needed him. That awareness made him even more reluctant to face her and angry with himself for feeling this way, so he was in an edgy mood as they approached the Pont de Rochereuil. As the gate swung open, he saw crowds gathered in the streets, already beginning to cheer. Summoning up a smile, he urged his stallion forward into Poitiers.

❧

THEY WERE AWAITING HIM in the palace courtyard. His wife wore the mourning black of the Spanish kingdoms and Sicily, a stark shade that accentuated her pallor, making her seem fragile and even more petite and delicate than he remembered. Dismounting, he handed the reins to Arne and crossed to

Berengaria. Kissing her hand, he said, "I was grieved to learn of your father's death. He was a good man, a good king."

Berengaria inclined her head. "Thank you, my lord," she said softly, and then turned to present him to Bishop Guillaume. Richard already knew the bishop, who'd been elected to the See of Poitiers ten years ago, and their exchange was coolly civil, for they'd clashed over Church prerogatives when Richard was Count of Poitou. He turned then to Joanna, giving her a brotherly kiss on the cheek. She smiled at him, all the while hoping that the decorum of the public greeting between husband and wife was due to the presence of the bishop and the other clerics. But as she looked up searchingly into his face, she could not tell what he was thinking; his court mask was firmly in place.

Upon getting word that Richard would be arriving on the second Saturday in July, Berengaria had insisted upon arranging a formal reception for him, inviting Bishop Guillaume, the abbess of Ste Croix, the Abbot of St Hilaire de Grand, most of the city's clerics, the Viscount of Thouars and his brother Guy, and even their quarrelsome neighbor Hugh de Lusignan. Joanna had noticed that Richard did not seem to enjoy these elaborate public gatherings as much as he once had, and she'd tried to convince Berengaria that Richard might prefer a quiet family dinner. But Berengaria had insisted that Richard be given a ceremonial welcome befitting his rank, leaving Joanna to worry that her sister-in-law was more nervous than joyful about her long-delayed reunion with her husband.

Trestle tables draped in white linen had been set up in Eleanor's splendid great hall, laid with silver plate. The cooks had prepared an extravagant menu: a roasted peacock, its bones strutted, its skin and feathers then refitted to give the impression that it still lived; marrow tarts; venison stew; trout boiled in wine; sorrel soup; rice in almond milk; blancmange; Lombardy custard; salmon in jelly; red wine from Cahors and Bordeaux, and even the very costly Saint Pourçain wine from Auvergne; and then sugared subtleties shaped like dragons and war galleys and Richard's new coat of arms, for upon his return, he'd added two more royal lions to his standard.

Bishop Guillaume did not approve of such excess, although he politely said nothing, reminding himself that the English queen would make sure that her almoner distributed the leftover food to the poor. He could not resist chastising the English king, though, for having turned out the monks of St Martin's at Tours, for he considered that a typical Angevin provocation. He thought Henry had been the worst offender, having the blood of the martyred Thomas of

Canterbury on his hands, but Richard did not always show the proper respect for the Holy Church, either, and his harassment of the Tours monks was shameful in the bishop's eyes—as was the presence amongst good Christians of Richard's cutthroat captain, Mercadier, who was calmly enjoying his dinner at one of the side tables.

Richard felt that he'd been quite justified in punishing the monks for welcoming the French king. He meant to return their property once they'd learned a lesson in loyalty, but he had no intention of sharing that with Bishop Guillaume. He heard the bishop out with icy courtesy, though, for Berengaria was watching him imploringly, dark eyes filled with distress. He supposed he should have expected her to become the bishop's devoted disciple, for her piety inclined her to give the benefit of every doubt to the Church. As likely as not, she'd even defend that inept fool on the papal throne.

He was determined to be on his good behavior and did his best to keep the conversation going, telling them that the Archbishop of Rouen was back from his stint as a hostage in Germany, news that pleased them all, especially the clerics. He revealed that his chancellor, Longchamp, was meeting with French envoys to discuss a truce, a reluctant but realistic acknowledgment that Normandy needed time to recover from the war that had been ravaging it for over a year, and this, too, was well received by his audience. And he entertained them by relating the story of a "fat fish" that had been stranded on the manor of the canons of St Paul's. Whales were considered the property of the Crown, but Hubert Walter had ruled that this one belonged to the dean and chapter of St Paul's, and Richard amused them by grumbling good-naturedly that his justiciar now owed him a whale, a debt that would not be easy to pay. He and André and his knights were the only ones who'd actually seen a whale and after they described the one they'd encountered as they sailed to Sicily, a lively discussion ensued about whether the "great fish" that swallowed Jonah in Scriptures had been a whale.

Berengaria began to relax once she was sure Richard was not going to quarrel with Bishop Guillaume, and she was grateful that he'd introduced a topic their clerical guests found so interesting. She'd feared that he might seem like a stranger after more than twenty-one months apart, but he seemed reassuringly familiar—the way he cocked a brow or tilted his head to the side when he was considering a question, the curve of his mouth when he was suppressing a smile, the sound of his laugh, how he gestured with his hands when he talked. This was the husband she remembered, the man who'd always treated her kindly even though she knew kindness was not an essential aspect of his nature. The other man was the stranger, the one who'd written her such impersonal, unrevealing letters and made excuses to keep them apart.

She was still hurt that he had not come to her as soon as he'd learned of her father's death, but Joanna had almost convinced her that he could not interrupt a war and even Bishop Guillaume had not criticized him for that. She was pleased now when he began to talk about her father, saying how much he'd respected Sancho and reminding their guests that the Navarrese king had been known as Sancho el Sabio, Sancho the Wise. Richard caught the sheen of unshed tears behind Berengaria's lashes and reached over to take her hand, saying again how very sorry he'd been to learn of Sancho's death.

This was their first truly intimate moment since his arrival, and she smiled, speaking so softly that he alone could hear. "It is a comfort that he is with my mother now," she confided. "And my brother finally admitted he'd been in pain for months, so I am thankful he is no longer suffering. I am sure that Sancho will be a fine king, and that helps, too. I just wish my brother Fernando will not have to hear such sorrowful news when he is so far from home, away from family and friends—"

She stopped abruptly when Richard jerked his hand away. "I had no choice in the matter. The German emperor demanded that Fernando be one of the hostages."

She was dismayed by his angry, accusatory tone. "I know that, my lord husband." Painfully aware that they were attracting attention, she said hastily, "I do not blame you, truly I do not." He regarded her in silence before nodding and then reaching for his wine cup. She drank some wine, too, and the moment passed. But after that, she ate without tasting the food, disquieted by what she'd seen in his eyes—that he did not believe her.

❧

BERENGARIA STUDIED HERSELF in a hand mirror, biting her lips to give them more color. Her women had brushed her long, dark hair until it gleamed and daubed perfume on her throat and wrists, and she raised her arms so they could pull her chemise over her head. Slipping naked between the sheets, she ignored their giggling and whispering, thinking they were acting as if this were her wedding night. Dismissing them, she settled down to wait for her husband, admitting that she was more nervous now than on that May evening in Cyprus.

At least then she'd felt confident that Richard wanted to share her bed. Now she was not sure what he wanted.

When he entered, she felt a frisson that was an odd blend of excitement and unease. It seemed like a lifetime since they'd lain together. He was carrying an oil lamp and he set it down on the small trestle table not far from the bed. She'd have preferred darkness, not wanting him to see her blush, but she was not going to object, not after his flare-up during dinner. She closed her eyes in a silent prayer that this would be the night his seed took root in her womb and when she opened them, he was standing by the bed, watching her. She thought he looked very handsome in the lamplight and gave him a shy smile; she was not a natural flirt like Joanna, had never even been alone with a man until Richard, and she had a disconcerting thought now, wondering if he'd rather she be more worldly, be more like the other women at the royal court.

"You look lovely," he said, catching her by surprise, for in the past, his compliments had been as specific as they were sparing, praising her eyes, her smile, her hair, and once, to her acute embarrassment, her breasts. Hoping that he'd not notice the color in her cheeks, she slid over to make room for him as he started to undress. As usual, he did it quickly, letting the clothes lie where they fell, and then, after nigh on two years, she found herself in bed with her husband.

In a corner of her brain, an unspoken resentment lurked, whispering that it was not fair for him to claim his marital rights until he'd offered an explanation, if not an apology, for his inexplicable conduct. But there had been no opportunity to talk privately with him since his arrival and she knew better than to initiate such a dangerous discussion now. She did not want to quarrel with him. She wanted him to make love to her, she wanted her husband back, and so when he pulled her into his arms, she came willingly, telling herself that there would be time for talking later.

She soon discovered that her body had memories of its own, responding to his touch as if they'd never been apart. His mouth was hot on hers and his skin was hot, too. Her breath quickening as he kissed her throat and then her breasts, she slid her hands down his back, smiling as she felt his erection, proof that he did still want her. She cried out softly when he entered her, feeling pain that became pleasure, clinging tightly until he'd gained satisfaction and cried out, too. She was left wanting more, although she was not sure what that was, but she was happy, happier than she'd been in a long time.

When he started to withdraw, she said, "No, not yet," feeling very daring and relieved to catch the glimmer of a smile, for she did not want him to think her a shameless wanton. The priests preached that even marital sex was blameworthy if done solely to gratify lust, warning that people must remain vigilant to avoid so tempting a sin.

Richard had propped himself up on his elbows to support his weight, but after giving her a quick kiss, he rolled over onto his back. After a few moments, he rose and went looking for a towel, which he brought back to the bed to pat them both dry. He'd done that on their wedding night, too, and she smiled at the memory. When he climbed into bed, she shifted so she could cradle her head against his shoulder.

Reaching out, she traced the path of a scar on his hip, trying to remember how he'd said he'd gotten it. The one on his left side, under his ribs, was the entry point for a Saracen crossbow bolt, and that she remembered all too well. "Whenever we'd been apart for a while," she murmured, "I would always check your body for wounds, always afraid I'd find a new one. At least I need not worry about that this time."

"No," he said, sounding drowsy, "no scars from Germany."

Joanna had warned her that he'd said very little about his captivity. Yet it seemed unnatural to ask no questions, to act as if his imprisonment had never been. "Richard . . . if you'd rather not talk about it—what happened in Germany—I will respect that, of course. But I hope that in time, you'll be willing to share some of those memories with me." She was pleased with how she'd phrased that, assuring him she did not want to pry whilst gently reminding him that a wife was a confidante as well as a bedmate. When she tried to assess his reaction, though, she found herself at a loss, for his eyes were impossible to read, utterly opaque.

When he yawned, she knew her window of opportunity for conversation was rapidly closing; he'd soon be rolling onto his side and sliding into sleep. Even if she dared not demand answers yet, there were a few things she could ask, that she had the right to know. "How long can you stay?"

"Just till Monday. I cannot concentrate upon putting out the fires in Normandy unless I can crush the rebellion in Aquitaine. Geoffrey de Rançon and the viscounts of Angoulême and Brosse were constantly stirring up trouble whilst I was in the Holy Land. They became even bolder after I was taken prisoner by that pompous dolt Leopold, but they were running up a debt, and now it is due and payable."

Berengaria was no longer listening, for she'd heard nothing beyond *Just till*

Monday. He was only going to stay two days and nights? After nigh on two years apart, that was all she was to get—two wretched days? She was dumbfounded that they were to have so little time together, but what occurred to her next was even worse. He'd not come into Poitou to see her. He'd come to deal with those southern rebels. His visit to Poitiers was an afterthought—just as she was.

Her first reaction was a rare flash of anger. She fought it back, struggling to see things from his perspective. It was only to be expected that he'd give first priority to ending a rebellion that could threaten his hold on the duchy. In the Holy Land, she'd learned to accept it, the fact that she was always going to take second place to his campaign against the Saracens. But it had been easier to defer to God.

"I am sorry you must leave so soon," she said evenly. "Mayhap I ought to consider settling in Normandy to make it more convenient for you to visit." The words were no sooner out of her mouth than she realized their full implications. Visit. What husband *visited* his wife? Apparently the one she had. Was this what she had to look forward to, a catch-as-catch-can marriage, with Richard stopping by whenever it suited him?

"Normandy . . . yes, that is probably a good idea," he agreed, yawning again.

She decided that she would think no more about this tonight. There would be time enough after he'd gone to consider her future. Now, though, she wanted only to sleep with her husband like wives did all over Christendom, to have at least one or two nights to pretend that everything was normal. She was reaching for her pillow when Richard suddenly sat up, then swung his legs over the side of the bed. Assuming he wanted to use the chamber pot, she began smoothing out the coverlets rumpled by their lovemaking. But then he gathered up the clothing scattered about the floor and drew his braies up over his hips, started to pull his linen shirt over his head.

"Richard? Where are you going?"

He was dressing as quickly as he'd shed his clothes, already had his tunic on. "I had a bedchamber made ready for me." He would rather have left it at that, but his wife was sitting up, looking so shocked that he came back to the bed. "I have not been sleeping well of late," he said reluctantly. "I did not want to keep you from sleeping, too, Berenguela."

She was still trying to make sense of this. "I do not mind."

"Well, I do," he said, summoning a smile. "I have enough on my conscience without robbing you of sleep, too, little dove." Leaning over, he kissed her lightly and was gone before she could respond.

Berengaria sat without moving for a long time after the door had closed behind him. Kings and queens always had their own chambers. Richard had come to her when he wanted to claim his marital rights, as she'd suspected most kings did. But not once had he ever left her bed afterward. She was stunned now by his abrupt departure, feeling bereft, feeling rejected, feeling as if she'd just been slapped in the face. She realized suddenly that this was the first time he'd called her by his favorite endearment, "little dove." And when had he used it? As he was about to leave her. She lay back, hugging the pillow tightly. After a while, she wept.

PHILIPPE WAS ABLE TO redress his humiliating defeat at Fréteval to some extent by inflicting an equally humiliating defeat upon John while Richard was off in Aquitaine. John and the Earl of Arundel had been besieging the stronghold of Vaudreuil, and when Philippe learned of this, he made an impressive march from Châteaudun to Vaudreuil, covering the one hundred miles in just three days. Arriving at dawn, he caught John and Arundel by surprise. John and the earl fled, as did their mounted knights, but Philippe captured their men-at-arms, supplies, and siege weapons.

Richard had a much more successful campaign than his younger brother. On July 22, he wrote to Hubert Walter that "By the Grace of God, who in all things upholds the right, we have captured Taillebourg and Marcillac and the whole land of Geoffrey de Rançon; also the city of Angoulême, Châteauneuf sur Charente, Montignac, Lachaise, and all the other castles and the whole land of the Count of Angoulême in its entirety." With perhaps pardonable pride, he boasted that he'd captured the city and citadel of Angoulême in a single evening, and had taken prisoner three hundred knights and a vast number of soldiers, signing it "Myself as witness at Angoulême, 22 July."

Despite Richard's overwhelming success in the south, he agreed to a truce that ratified the status quo, allowing Philippe and him to keep the lands they held as of July 23. The terms were favorable enough to Philippe to start rumors that Longchamp had acted on his own and that Richard was not pleased with his chancellor. But Longchamp did nothing that his king did not want him to do. As little as Richard liked the terms of the truce, he needed the breathing space, for although he'd easily quenched rebellion in his southern domains, he knew that the real war would be fought in Normandy, and because of the vast ransom he'd been forced to pay, for the first time he had fewer resources to draw upon than the French king. According to the Treaty of Tillieres, the truce was to hold until November of the following year. All knew, though, that neither Richard nor Philippe intended to honor it.

❦

THE DEATHS OF TANCRED and his son Roger had taken the heart out of the Sicilian resistance to Heinrich and when he marched into Italy, he encountered no opposition. By August 13, the city of Naples opened its gates to him. He then exacted a merciless vengeance upon Salerno, whose citizens had seized his empress three years ago and given her to Tancred. Taking the city by storm, he turned it over to his army and the result was a bloodbath of rape and murder and plunder. The citizens not slain were banished into exile and Heinrich ordered the city walls razed. Tancred's desperate widow fled with her daughters and her small son to Caltabellotta and Admiral Margaritis negotiated the surrender of the Sicilian government to the German emperor.

It seemed to many that Heinrich had Lucifer's own luck that year; the vast ransom he'd extorted from the English king had financed his invasion of Sicily and Tancred's death had made his victory inevitable. Then, to the astonishment of most of Christendom, Heinrich's forty-year-old wife, long thought to be barren, became pregnant, and as Heinrich planned his coronation in Palermo, Constance prepared for her lying-in in the small Italian town of Jesi.

But if Heinrich's touch seemed to be golden in that year of God's grace, 1194, the Duke of Austria's fortunes continued to plummet. That June, Pope Celestine had ordered Leopold to return his hostages to the English king, to repay his share of the ransom, and then to go to the Holy Land in expiation of his sins, spending the same amount of time in the service of Christ as King Richard had been held in captivity. When Leopold defiantly refused to accept any of these terms, the Pope ordered the Archbishop of Verona to excommunicate the Austrian duke and to place his duchy under Interdict.

CHAPTER TWENTY-FIVE

⚜

DECEMBER 1194

Chinon Castle, Touraine

Richard had a playful competition going with his mother as to which of them had the most effective spy. Eleanor insisted none could surpass Durand de Curzon, whom she'd implanted in John's household to keep track of her wayward son. But Richard was sure that there was no one better than the man who called himself Luc and had served the English Crown faithfully for more than twenty years, continuing to serve Richard after Henry's death. When he was told now that a man was seeking an audience and heard the code word that identified Luc, he abruptly interrupted the council and then hastened from the great hall for a private word with his spy.

As his absence dragged on, the men in the hall grew restless. Guillaume de Longchamp attempted to discuss Church matters with the Archbishop of Rouen and the Bishop of Lincoln, but Archbishop Gautier continued to snub the chancellor at every opportunity, and he made a conspicuous show of rising and moving away. Longchamp could only fume. He'd clashed with the Bishop of Lincoln, too, but Bishop Hugh at least accorded him the courtesy one prelate owed another. Thanking the Almighty that he need never set foot again on Richard's benighted island kingdom, Longchamp was making polite conversation with the other bishop when a loud burst of laughter caused him to frown.

Gathered by the open hearth, the Viscount of Thouars, Hugh de Lusignan, and William de Forz, the Count of Aumale, had been exchanging bawdy jests about the unlikely pregnancy of Heinrich's empress. Viscount Aimery's brother Guy had been listening in growing discomfort, but he'd so far held his peace. Guy was protective of women, so much so that his brother had dubbed him "the veritable soul of chivalry," which was not meant as a compliment. He did not think it right to mock a woman who'd soon be facing the dangers of the birthing chamber at the advanced age of forty. But as a younger brother, he'd gotten into the habit of deferring to Aimery, and he knew that if he objected now, he'd become the target of their ridicule instead of Constance. After a particularly crass comment by the Count of Aumale, Guy edged away when he saw that they'd attracted the disapproving attention of the Bishop of Ely, not wanting to be judged by the company he kept.

"Such comments are highly unseemly, my lords," Longchamp said coldly. He did not like women, but he made a few exceptions—for his own kin, for the king's remarkable mother, and for the Empress Constance.

The men were not at all discomfited by his rebuke. "What did we say that was not true, my lord bishop?" Aimery grinned. "We were merely marveling that a barren woman could suddenly and miraculously conceive." But when Count William compared Constance's womb to a "withered pear," Longchamp felt a flare of real anger.

"If you'd bothered to learn Scriptures, you'd know that Sarah, the wife of Abraham, gave birth to a son decades after her childbearing years were over. If it is God's Will, a woman can conceive at any age."

That quieted Aimery and Hugh de Lusignan, but William de Forz did not like to be scolded by a cripple. *That bishop's miter does not make you a man, you misshapen dwarf,* he thought indignantly. Aloud, he said skeptically, "Well, if the empress is indeed with child, that will rank as one of God's greatest miracles."

Longchamp reached for a more dangerous weapon than a clerical reprimand. "You'd do well, my lord count, to remember that the Empress Constance is very dear to Queen Joanna, the king's beloved sister."

Even that would not have been enough to daunt the count, but Bishop Hugh then added his voice to Longchamp's, reminding de Forz that it was not for mortal man to question the ways of the Almighty. Although he'd spoken mildly enough, there was an aura of sanctity about the bishop that gave his most casual utterance great weight, and de Forz lapsed into a sullen silence, equally irked with both prelates.

Guy, falling back into his familiar role of peacemaker, sought to steer the conversation into a more innocuous channel and asked where the Lord of Châteauroux was, for he knew that André de Chauvigny had been with the king continuously since the latter's release. Will Marshal had just moved toward the fire to warm himself and he was the one to answer, saying that André had left to spend Christmas at Déols Castle with his pregnant wife and young son.

Guy's well-meaning intercession only vexed de Forz even more, for he disliked both André de Chauvigny and Will Marshal. Upon Richard's accession to the throne, he'd rewarded all three men with marriages to great heiresses. Isabel de Clare, the granddaughter of an Irish king, had brought the Marshal lands in Normandy, England, South Wales, and Ireland. André's marriage to Denise de Déols had given him the barony of Châteauroux, making him one of the most powerful lords of the Poitevin Berry border region. And de Forz was wed to Hawisa, the Countess of Aumale, who held vast estates in Normandy and Yorkshire. While de Forz had envied the Marshal's prize, he'd still been delighted to become Count of Aumale and have such riches at his disposal.

His pleasure had soon curdled, though, for he'd been saddled with an unwilling wife. The prideful bitch had balked at marrying him, had to be coerced into it by the king. He'd been incensed by her reluctance, for his was an old and proud Poitevin family and he'd been Richard's naval commander in the war against the Saracens. He'd discovered that Hawisa was outrageously outspoken for a woman, stubborn and reckless. Even after he'd been provoked into disciplining her as she deserved, she'd remained rebellious. Blood dripping from her nose and mouth, she'd regarded him defiantly, warning that if he ever struck her again, he'd pay for it with his life. He'd laughed, of course, pointing out that no weak woman could match a man's strength. But she'd given him a chilling smile, saying there were many ways for a wife to rid herself of an unwanted husband, that he could be taken ill at dinner or set upon by brigands as he reeled out of a tavern one dark night or thrown from his horse when the saddle cinch suddenly broke. Although he'd forced another scornful laugh, he'd been genuinely shocked, and he'd not hit her again. At least she'd been able to perform a wife's primary duty and give him a son. But so had Isabel de Clare and Denise de Déols, and he was sure they were proper wives, obedient and deferential.

Looking resentfully now at the Marshal, begrudging him the good fortune that could have been his if only he'd been given Isabel de Clare instead of Hawisa, he gave a harsh laugh, saying, "Well, de Chauvigny can have a dull family Christmas by the hearth, but I prefer to attend the king's Christmas Court at Rouen. Wives are not likely to be welcome there, thank God."

De Forz realized at once that he'd gone too far, for he was suddenly the target of all eyes, none of them friendly. Will Marshal; Longchamp; that self-righteous Hugh of Lincoln; the king's crusty clerk, Master Fulk; and those paltry knights who'd been with the king in Germany and were taking shameless advantage of it—that Welsh whelp, Warin Fitz Gerald, and Guillain de l'Etang. Even the Earl of Chester was giving him a disapproving look, and all knew Chester and his Breton shrew of a wife had not exchanged a civil word in years. Still, he could see how the king might take his comment amiss, for he knew Richard was not likely to make common cause with him over their unwanted wives. Would any of these royal lackeys dare to go blabbing to the king? That was a troubling thought, and he jumped nervously when the hall door banged open then, admitting a blast of cold air and the king.

Summoning the others back to the table, Richard dropped down into his chair, glancing from Will Marshal to Longchamp. "I'd hoped to have news about Leicester. I sent one of my best agents to find out how he is being treated at Étampes, but he had no luck. He says the earl is allowed no visitors and those guarding him are as closemouthed as deaf mutes. Even buying them drinks at the local tavern did not loosen their tongues." The other men tried to assure him—and themselves—that the French king would respect Leicester's high birth, rank, and service in the Holy Land, but his own experience left Richard unconvinced. He did not want to dwell upon his fears for the earl now, though, and he turned toward his chancellor, about to resume the council, when Will Marshal suddenly sprang to his feet with a jubilant shout. "Baldwin!"

Several men had just entered the hall. It was December 12, but Richard felt as if Christmas had come early, for the one in the lead was Baldwin de Bethune. He rose as quickly as Will had and they both hastened toward the Fleming, with the other men right on their heels.

"I knew Leopold would release the hostages once he found himself excommunicated! Are the others with you? Wilhelm?" Richard's gaze shifted toward Baldwin's companions, but none of them were familiar. When he glanced back at his friend, his joy congealed at the sorrowful expression on the other man's face.

"Leopold has not yielded, sire. He remains defiant. I am here because he entrusted me with an urgent message for you. He said to tell you that if you do not send your niece and the Damsel of Cyprus to Vienna straightaway, he will execute all of your hostages."

"Jesu!" Richard stared at Baldwin, torn between horror and disbelief, for he'd never even heard of a case in which hostages had been put to death. "Has he gone mad?"

"Not mad, desperate." Baldwin was suddenly aware of how exhausted he was, and was grateful when the Bishop of Lincoln grasped his arm and steered him toward the warmth of the hearth, where he slumped down on a stool, stretching his frozen feet toward the flames. "It has been a bad year for Austria, sire. First there was heavy spring flooding when the snows melted, then destructive forest fires caused by lightning that burned villages and farms, too. When pestilence began to rage, some of the people began to whisper that God was punishing their duke for seizing a king who'd taken the cross. And then the Archbishop of Verona lay Austria under Interdict and put the curse of anathema upon Leopold himself."

Someone handed Baldwin a cup and he drank in gulps. "So far the Austrians have supported Leopold, as have the clergy—however reluctantly. But Leopold is no fool and he understands how quickly that can change. When bodies cannot be buried and marriages cannot be made and people cannot hear Mass, it will not take long for them to start asking why they must suffer for Leopold's sins. He has already spent twenty-five thousand marks fortifying the walls of Vienna, Hainburg, and Wiener Neustadt, has only four thousand still unspent, and so he cannot afford to repay the ransom as the Pope demands. He is cornered and he knows it. But he is a stubborn, angry man, and now a bitter one. I do not know why he is so set upon these marriages. To reward his sons, to prove he is not Heinrich's puppet, to punish you, to show the Austrians that he will not be cowed by kings, emperors, or popes? I can only tell you that I think he means it when he says he'll kill the hostages. Mayhap not the little lad. I would hope to God that his madness would not take him that far. But the others . . . Yes, I think he would."

There was a shocked silence when he was done. Richard turned aside, fighting back a rising tide of fury. How could this be God's Will? He was no longer a prisoner, so how could he still be so powerless?

Will reached over and rested his hand on the Fleming's shoulder, a gesture that brought a weary smile to Baldwin's face. A smile that vanished when William de Forz told him how lucky he was. His head jerking up, he stared at the other man. "And why is that, my lord count?" he asked, his voice dangerously soft.

"Why? Because you're here and safe, not trapped back in Vienna with those other poor sods."

Baldwin got to his feet, and although he was normally imperturbable, not easily angered, Will made ready to intervene in case his friend lunged for de Forz's throat. "I gave my sworn word," Baldwin said, slowly and deliberately, as if speaking to a child or lack-wit, "that I would return with the king's answer. I intend to honor it."

The count was astonished that the Flemish lord could be such a fool. But he sensed the other man's outrage, even if he did not fully understand it. He could see that the Marshal shared it, and however little he liked that man, he was wary of offending him, for Marshal had been quick in the past to challenge men who'd insulted his honor. He was thankful, therefore, when Richard drew all attention back to himself.

Oblivious to the tension between Baldwin and the Count of Aumale, Richard looked around the hall, seeking men he could trust implicitly; his gaze soon settled upon Guillain de l'Etang and his Welsh cousin. "Morgan, I want you and Guillain to fetch the girls from Rouen." When they assured him they'd leave within the hour, he crossed to Baldwin's side, counterfeiting a smile. "It looks as if you'll be making another long journey, my old friend."

Sitting down again, the Fleming smiled, too, just as unconvincingly. "It could be worse, sire. At least I'll not have to set foot on shipboard again."

"The other hostages . . . Do they know of Leopold's threat?"

"Not your nephew. But the others, yes." Baldwin proved himself adept then at reading minds, for he added softly, "They were not afraid, sire. They knew you'd never let harm come to them."

"No," Richard said grimly, "I would not." As that whoreson Leopold well knew, God rot him. Glancing then toward the Earl of Chester, he said, "Tell your wife what has happened, Randolph." He did not doubt that Constance would blame him for this, but that was the least of his worries at the moment. He was finding this a very bitter brew to swallow, but swallow it he must, for what other choice did he have?

Baldwin had never wanted anything as much as he now wanted a hot meal, a hot bath, and a soft bed. But he had not forgotten his Austrian escort, and he started to rise, saying that Leopold had sent a priest along who spoke Latin so he could communicate with his guards. He smiled when the Bishop of Lincoln volunteered to tell them what was going on, for that meant he did not have to move his aching bones just yet. The men were waiting uneasily by the door and the Austrian priest came forward hesitantly when Hugh beckoned, kneeling nervously to kiss the bishop's ring. He looked greatly relieved, though, as soon as Hugh began to speak, and when he turned back toward his men, he was smiling, for they'd feared the English king might take out his anger upon them.

That had never occurred to Richard, but as soon as the priest addressed the other Austrians, he froze. The guttural sound of German called up memories so vivid, so intense, that for an eerie moment, he was not in the great hall at Chinon. He was back in that hovel at Ertpurch, hearing soldiers shouting in a language he did not understand, knowing there was no way out, that he and his men were trapped and the world as he'd known it would never be the same. Just as on that December day two years ago, he could hear the rasping of his own breath, could feel the cold sweat trickling down his ribs. Whirling, he grabbed for the closest chair and slammed it into the wall, with enough force to splinter the wood. He turned then to face the hall, his head raised defiantly. To his relief, they seemed to accept his violence as natural rage over this latest extortion, as nothing more than that.

❦

KINGS PUBLISHED THEIR ITINERARIES weeks in advance so that their vassals and subjects would know where they'd be hearing court cases or accepting petitions. As soon as she knew Richard would be holding his Christmas Court at Rouen, Joanna did her best to convince her sister-in-law to accompany her there. Berengaria flatly refused, saying she'd go nowhere unless Richard sent for her. Joanna did not give up, though, and when she received a letter from Eleanor in mid-December that mentioned that Richard was then at Chinon, she persuaded Berengaria to spend Christmas at the Loire Valley castle, explaining that would give her a chance to visit with her mother since Chinon was only ten miles from Fontevrault Abbey. She felt no guilt about meddling; it was obvious to her that her brother's marriage was in need of mending, and how could that be done if the estranged husband and wife were hundreds of miles apart?

But the best-laid plans could go awry, and upon their arrival at Chinon, Joanna discovered that Richard had already moved on into Normandy. Moreover, she and Berengaria had just missed bidding farewell to Anna, the girls having departed with Baldwin de Bethune for Austria two days earlier. And once Berengaria learned that Richard had been at Chinon, she reproached Joanna with unwonted sharpness. So as Joanna rode toward Fontevrault the next morning, she was fully expecting to be told that her mother had accompanied Richard to Rouen for his Christmas Court, for that was the way her luck seemed to be running.

"I AM SO GLAD that you're still here, Maman. I was afraid that you'd left with Richard."

"My aging bones were not keen to travel so far in the dead of winter. Since I'd already seen Richard several times whilst he was at Chinon, I decided to celebrate Christmas here. It is not as if Richard plans any elaborate or lavish festivities, after all. I suspect his stay at Rouen will more closely resemble a council of war than a Christmas Court."

Joanna thought it passing strange that Richard would not want to make much of his first Christmas back in his own domains. "It would have been a good time, though, to introduce his queen to his vassals and the people of Rouen," she said, but her mother merely shrugged. Watching as Eleanor stroked Iseult, her elegant new greyhound, Joanna realized that as much as she loved her mother, she would not have wanted to have been Eleanor's daughter-in-law. She at once tried to suppress this sacrilegious thought, reminding herself that Eleanor had seemed very fond of Hal's wife, Marguerite. But Marguerite had grown up at the royal court and by the time she was old enough to be a true wife to Hal, Eleanor was Henry's prisoner. John's wife did not count, since he saw her so rarely. That left Constance and Berengaria. Eleanor returned Constance's hostility in full measure. And while Eleanor had shown no antagonism toward Berengaria, Joanna could no longer deny her mother's indifference toward her son's queen.

"I am dining this afternoon with Prioress Aliza, and of course you will join us now, Joanna. I've become quite fond of Aliza. Even though she has been at the abbey since she was thirteen, she retains a lively curiosity about the world beyond these convent walls and she rarely fails to make me laugh—just as you do, dearest."

Eleanor gave Joanna such a fond smile that she felt a pang of guilt for having entertained such uncharitable thoughts about her own mother. She was grateful when Eleanor turned to a safer subject, sharing family news. John was still on his best behavior, doing whatever Richard asked of him, although he spent little time in Richard's company, which doubtless suited both of them. Geoff was continuing to trail turmoil in his wake. Hubert Walter had confiscated his estates that summer, but Richard had restored them when Geoff had appealed to him, pardoning his latest offense on the promise of payment of eleven thousand marks. She'd had another letter from Marie in Champagne, she confided, obviously very pleased that contact had been restored with the daughter she'd not seen since divorcing the French king more than forty years ago. Joanna was just as pleased when Eleanor let her read Marie's letter. Marie had enjoyed a very good relationship with her half brothers, especially with Richard. But she and Joanna had yet to meet, and Joanna was quite curious about this worldly elder sister, having heard many loving stories about her from her son, Henri, during their time in the Holy Land.

Eleanor had news about Henri, too; Richard had gotten a letter from his nephew just before he'd left Chinon for Normandy. Henri reported that Saladin's sons were squabbling with one another, and Richard had cursed the French king in language that might well have shocked a sailor, so angry was he that he could not yet join Henri in retaking Jerusalem, as he'd vowed. Anna's father had been released from his prison by the Knights Hospitaller, as demanded by the Duke of Austria, and Isaac had promptly confirmed all of the rumors of his being in league with the Saracens by going to the Sultanate of Rum in Anatolia. According to Henri, he was said to be plotting against the Emperor of the Greeks, apparently realizing he had no chance of regaining control of Cyprus from Guy and Amaury de Lusignan.

"Henri did have some good news, though, Joanna. He and Isabella have had their first child, a daughter. Since they named Isabella's daughter Maria after her mother, they named this lass Marie after Henri's mother—which pleased her greatly." Eleanor's smile shadowed. "Henri's decision to stay in Outremer and marry Isabella was a heart's wound to Marie, for she knows how unlikely it is that she'll ever see him again."

Joanna was glad for Henri and Isabella; she loved her nephew and liked his bride very much. She still felt a small dart of envy, thinking how lucky Isabella was to conceive again so quickly, thinking of those long, barren years in her own marriage after the death of her infant son.

"Oh, and there is interesting news from Toulouse, Joanna. The Devil has called their count home."

Joanna's heart seemed to skip a beat. "The father, not the son?"

"The father, of course. I do not see Raimond as one of the Devil's acolytes, although the Church most likely would disagree with me about that."

Joanna agreed that they would, indeed, remembering Cardinal Melior's intense hostility toward Raimond. So he was the Count of Toulouse now. Surprised by how pleased she was to hear this, she decided it was because Raimond was bound to be a better ruler than his father had been.

When she relayed this to Berengaria upon her return to Chinon, Berengaria was pleased, too, expressing the hope that Raimond might be less tolerant of heretics now that he had the responsibility of ruling all of Toulouse. She thought they should write to Raimond and offer their sympathies, pointing out that he'd been very kind during their long journey from Marseille to Poitiers. Joanna agreed and that evening, she dictated a brief letter of condolence to her scribe, even though she doubted Raimond was all that grieved by his father's death. But then she snatched it back and penned a postscript herself, writing that Raimond had been right. "At times I am too quick to pass judgment, as on a September eve in a Bordeaux garden." She was sure that Raimond would understand this oblique apology, and she could imagine him smiling as he read it, a thought that made her smile, too.

THE EMPRESS CONSTANCE STILL had nightmares about what she'd endured in Salerno three years ago. Left behind by Heinrich after he and most of his invading army had been stricken with the bloody flux, she'd found herself in grave danger, for the townspeople panicked once they learned that the emperor and the German army were in retreat. Besieged in the royal palace by a drunken mob, she'd come close to death, rescued just in time by a cousin of King Tancred, who'd then turned his prize prisoner over to the Sicilian king. She'd never forgiven Heinrich for abandoning her in Salerno, or for refusing to make any concessions to gain her freedom. She had forgiven the Salernitans, though, for she knew they'd acted from terror, not treachery, and while she thought they deserved some punishment, she'd been horrified by her husband's bloody vengeance upon that unlucky town and its citizens.

But she'd taken away from Salerno more than bad memories. The famed medical school of Salerno admitted women, licensing them to practice medicine, and in the course of her high-risk, improbable pregnancy, Constance had been very grateful to have a female physician. She was convinced that Dame Martina had gotten her safely through those early, perilous months in which miscarriage was most likely, and she had faith that Dame Martina would help her to give birth to a living male child; she never doubted that God would bless her with a son. Yet on this December night, she was not thinking of the dangers of the birthing chamber, for that afternoon she'd learned what her women had tried desperately to keep from her—that people believed her pregnancy was a hoax. She was too old to bear a child, they insisted, after eight barren years, but Heinrich needed an heir and so he had concocted this ruse. A baby would be smuggled into the birthing chamber, mayhap one of Heinrich's by-blows, and it would be announced that the empress had given birth to a fine, healthy boy.

Constance was outraged that she should be the object of such scurrilous speculation and she was appalled that this mean-spirited gossip could cast a shadow upon the legitimacy of her son. If people did not believe he was her child, he would not be considered the rightful heir to the Sicilian throne. His enemies would use these foul rumors against him, a pretext for rebellion. In time, he might even come to wonder himself if they were true. Alone in the dark, she wept quietly. But come morning, she rose dry-eyed from the bed, hers the steely resolve that had enabled past de Hautevilles to carve a kingdom out of the Sicilian heartland. Summoning the head of her household knights, she ordered him to set up a pavilion in the town marketplace.

"And then you are to spread the word that I shall have my lying-in there, in that tent, and all the matrons and maidens of the town are welcome to attend the birth of my child."

They tried to talk her out of it, scandalized by the very idea of a highborn woman making such a public spectacle of herself, sharing so intimate a moment with the wives of cobblers and tanners and innkeepers. But Constance was adamant. Only once did her icy control crack, when Dame Martina asked if she was sure she wanted to do this.

"Of course I do not want to do this! But it is the only way that I can disprove these vile rumors. The women of Jesi will watch as my son is born, they will bear witness that he is indeed flesh of my flesh, and nothing matters more than that."

◈

ON CHRISTMAS DAY IN PALERMO, Heinrich was crowned King of Sicily. He celebrated by having the bodies of Tancred and his son Roger dragged from their royal tombs. Tancred's widow, Sybilla, had yielded to Heinrich after he'd promised that he'd not harm her or her children; showing surprising magnanimity, he even agreed to let her four-year-old son inherit the lands Tancred had held when he was Count of Lecce.

On December 26, Constance gave birth to a son, witnessed by the women of Jesi; the baby was named Friedrich after Heinrich's father. Several days later, Constance offered further proof that Friedrich was a child of her body by nursing him in public.

❧

ANNA WAS ACCUSTOMED TO milder climes than her future home and she wondered if she'd ever be warm again. It had been a wretched journey so far, the women exhausted by the punishing pace, Baldwin bleakly anticipating his continued confinement, and all of them made miserable by the frigid winter weather. Aenor suffered the most, and by the time they were approaching Salzburg, the little girl had developed a hacking cough and she looked so sickly, pale, and hollow-eyed that Anna thought she'd be a disappointment to her husband-to-be. Anna would be very glad to reach Salzburg, for Baldwin had assured them that they'd be staying at Archbishop Adalbert's palace, which would be a vast improvement over some of their past lodgings, usually monastery guest halls and even a few inns. Anna had never been in an inn, so she'd enjoyed the novelty—until she'd awakened one night bitten by mites and fleas.

Sleet had begun to fall and Anna swore when a gust of wind blew back the hood of her mantle. "God's legs!" she cried, borrowing one of Richard's favorite oaths. "It is colder than a witch's teat." Thekla did not say anything, but her mouth pinched in such obvious disapproval that Anna rolled her eyes. The Cypriot widow had served her for several years, but in the past it had been easy enough to ignore her. Now she was subjected to Thekla's earnest platitudes and tedious lectures on a daily basis. Anna had not yet forgiven her friend Alicia for balking at accompanying her to Austria, for the company on this unhappy journey left much to be desired. Thekla would have made a fine nun. Her other Cypriot maid, Eudokia, had been even unhappier than young Aenor at having to start life anew in Austria, for she fancied herself in love with one of Joanna's knights back in Poitiers. Aenor's childhood nurse, Rohesia, was as protective of her charge as a mother bear, and all three of Aenor's attendants were downright elderly, at least in Anna's eyes. Aenor herself was only ten, too young to be much fun even if she had not been crying herself to sleep every night.

Anna had tried to muster up some sympathy for the girl, without much success. Yes, she was going off to wed a stranger in an alien land, but that was only to be expected. Anna had not been happy, either, about her Austrian marriage, for she'd liked the life she led since her father's overthrow and she'd become very attached to Joanna. But Anna was accustomed to upheaval. Her mother had died when she was just six and she and her brother had been held as hostages for two years, finally freed out of pity when the Prince of Antioch had realized their father was not going to pay the remainder of his ransom. After they joined Isaac in Cyprus, her brother soon died, and Anna had to adjust to living with a man she'd not really known, a man so feared and hated by the Cypriots that they'd cooperated with the English king to depose him. So Anna had learned very early to accept the world as it was, not as she wanted it to be, and she thought Aenor's marriage would be much happier if she learned that lesson, too.

When Salzburg came into view, Anna sighed with relief—until she saw the huge fortress rising against the sky, hundreds of feet above the city, looking as if it were halfway to Heaven. "Lord Baldwin, please tell me we do not have to ride all the way up to that mountain citadel!"

"You need not fear, Lady Anna. Whilst Hohensalzburg Castle belongs to the Archbishop of Salzburg, he also has a residence in the town, close by the cathedral, and that is where we'll be staying."

She gave him a smile so charming that Baldwin found himself thinking that young Leo of Austria was a lucky lad. He was not worried about Anna, sure that she'd always land on her feet. But as he glanced over at Aenor, shivering so violently that her teeth were chattering, Baldwin felt as if he were watching a tame fawn being turned out to fend for herself in a forest rife with wolves.

⚜

THE WOMEN WERE PLEASED with their chamber, for it had its own hearth and so many beds that they would not have to bundle up four to a bed as they'd often had to do at other lodgings. Baldwin was on his way up Mönchsberg Mountain to Hohensalzburg Castle, having been told that Archbishop Adalbert was spending the night in that alpine stronghold. He'd promised the women that he would ask the archbishop to send a messenger on to Vienna, letting Leopold know that they'd reached Salzburg but they'd be resting in the city until Lady Aenor's cough improved. Since one hundred fifty miles still lay ahead of them, this was very welcome news to them all.

They'd been served the best meal they'd had since leaving Chinon, and servants had brought up a wooden tub and lugged pails of hot water so they could bathe afterward. Anna found herself thinking that if this was how she and

Aenor would be treated once they wed Leopold's sons, life in Austria might be more pleasant than she'd anticipated. She was enough of a realist to appreciate the value of luxury and comfort, understanding that it was much easier to be unhappy in a palace than in a crofter's hut.

Aenor was already in bed, as were several of their attendants. Anna had prodded Eudoxia into staying up to play chess with her, since she was not sleepy yet. When a knock sounded, Dame Rohesia assumed it was a servant bringing honeyed wine for Aenor's cough. But as soon as she slid the latch back and opened the door, she sought to close it again, saying in shock, "My lord, you cannot come in here! We have retired for the night."

As soon as she heard Baldwin's voice, Anna rose quickly and hastened to the door. "Do not be ridiculous, Dame Rohesia. Lord Baldwin would not come to our chamber at such an hour if he did not have urgent news." She got an indignant glare from the older woman, but she paid Aenor's nurse no mind. She was sensitive to atmosphere, a necessary skill for anyone who'd lived with a hot-tempered lunatic like her father, and she'd begun to sense that something was amiss. The palace servants were strangely subdued, some even red-eyed, as if they'd been weeping, but since she spoke no German, her curiosity had been thwarted. Opening the door wide, she said, "Come in, my lord. What happened at the castle?"

Baldwin had impeccable manners and he apologized politely to the irate nurse, saying that Lady Anna was right and his news was urgent. By now all of the women were awake, several clutching their bedcovers close, looking scandalized to find a man in their chamber. Aenor blinked sleepily, and when she began to cough, Dame Rohesia hurried to the bed, glowering at Baldwin over her shoulder.

He never even noticed. "My news could not wait till the morrow. The Duke of Austria is dead."

Midst the gasps and outcries, Anna was the only one to smile. "Tell me he suffered ere he died!"

Baldwin grinned. "Indeed he did, my lady. The day after Christmas, his ankle was crushed when his horse fell. The injury soon festered and when the flesh turned black, his doctors told him that his only chance of recovery was to amputate the foot. But all feared to do it—the doctors, Leopold's knights, even his own sons. So Leopold held the axe against his ankle himself, and ordered a servant to strike the axe with a mallet. It took three tries to chop off the foot. It did not save him, though, for he died on the last day of December."

Baldwin was belatedly realizing that he'd probably been too gruesomely graphic, for several of the women were looking greensick. Not Anna, though. She'd listened raptly and as soon as he was done, she began to laugh. "He dared to capture a king and now God has punished him as he deserved. Can you imagine Heinrich's horror when he hears of this? He's next!"

Baldwin was amused by her unapologetic vengefulness, and he laughed, too. "I hope so, Lady Anna; indeed, I hope so!"

Anna was fiercely loyal to the man she called Malik Ric, and she made a remorseless enemy, as she proved now, saying with great satisfaction, "Best of all, he died an excommunicate, so he cannot be buried in consecrated ground and will burn in Hell for all eternity."

"Unfortunately not, my lady. Leopold's son Friedrich sent at once for Archbishop Adalbert, realizing the gravity of his injury. But if Leopold thought the archbishop would show mercy because they were cousins, he was mistaken. Ere he would absolve Leopold of his sins and restore him to God's grace, Adalbert made the duke swear that the ransom would be repaid and the hostages released, and he compelled Friedrich to agree, too, since he'd be the one fulfilling these demands. He told me that he made Friedrich swear another holy vow at graveside ere he'd let the funeral proceed. He said Leopold was buried in the habit of a Cistercian monk, but I do not think that will save him from spending a very long time in Purgatory."

"God willing," Anna said flippantly and as their eyes met, they both laughed again.

Aenor had been half asleep when Baldwin entered, but she was wide-awake now. She started to speak, had to wait until another coughing spasm passed. Almost afraid to hope, she said in a quavering voice, "Does this mean that I need not marry Leopold's son?"

Baldwin nodded. "Yes, Lady Aenor," he said gently, "it means exactly that. We will stay in Salzburg whilst you recover, and then we'll go home."

CHAPTER TWENTY-SIX

⚜

Hugh d'Avalon, the Bishop of Lincoln, arrived at Chinon Castle on the last Wednesday in January. As soon as he was ushered into the great hall, he knew that something had happened, something good. Wherever he looked, he saw smiles, and the only sound he heard was laughter. Instead of waiting for him to approach the dais, Richard rose and strode forward, offering a warm welcome that he did not extend to all prelates. Once greetings had been exchanged, Hugh's curiosity prodded him to ask what they were celebrating.

"A death," Richard said, giving the older man a challenging look. "I suppose you will say that is un-Christian, my lord bishop."

"Well, that would depend upon the identity of the deceased."

That earned him a startled smile from Richard. "Would you grieve for the Duke of Austria?"

"No, but I would pray for his soul. I'd say he is much in need of prayers, my liege, wouldn't you?"

Richard agreed that was so and after leading the bishop to the dais, he shared, with considerable relish, the letter he'd just received from his friend and ally the Archbishop of Cologne. "I am not utterly heartless," he concluded. "So I was not sorry to hear that Leopold was reconciled with the Church on his deathbed. I have a legitimate grievance against the man, but not for all eternity." Signaling for a servant to bring wine for the bishop, Richard indulged himself for a moment by imaging Heinrich or Philippe suffering Leopold's wretched fate, for they deserved it more than the Austrian duke. He had a truly blasphemous thought then, that even the Almighty was making Leopold the scapegoat, and he said hastily, "At least none will doubt now that God is on my side."

Hugh blinked in surprise. "Did you ever doubt that, sire?"

Richard looked at him and then away, gazing toward the molten gold flames surging in the hearth. "No," he said, having hesitated long enough to tell Hugh he lied, "I did not. But others did."

"Not anymore," Hugh assured him. "I daresay Leopold's ghastly death will give the German emperor some uneasy moments. The French king, too. No one will ever again dare to defy Holy Church and harm a man who has taken the cross. So," he added, with a mischievous glint, "your ordeal was not for naught, sire."

"It was well worth it, then," Richard said, but the bishop was unfazed by his sarcasm.

"I am looking forward to meeting your queen. I was told she passed Christmas here at Chinon whilst you were at Rouen."

Richard decided to ignore that implied reproach. "My queen is no longer at Chinon, my lord bishop. Soon after Epiphany, she moved her household to the castle of Beaufort-en-Vallée, not far from Angers."

Hugh thought that Richard and his queen were like two ships at sea, never getting within hailing distance of each other. Leaning forward, he pitched his voice for Richard's ear alone. "May we speak in private, my liege?"

Whenever people asked for a private audience, that usually meant they wanted something. The risk was even greater with clerics, for they could also have a lecture in mind. But Richard's respect for the Bishop of Lincoln was genuine; besides, he liked the man. So he ordered all the others away from the dais and out of earshot.

"Did you know that you are my parishioner, my lord king? You were born at Oxford, which is in the diocese of Lincoln, and this means that on the Day of Judgment, I shall have to answer for your soul. I would ask you, therefore, to tell me the state of your conscience, so I can give you effective counsel as the Holy Spirit shall direct me."

Richard was amused by this unexpected approach. "My conscience is at ease, my lord bishop, although I freely admit that I harbor great hatred toward my enemies and cannot forgive them for the wrongs they have done me."

"Scriptures say that *When the ways of a man are pleasing to the Lord, He shall make his enemies wish for peace.* It grieves me to say this, but you have fallen into sin. It is commonly reported that you are not faithful to your marriage bed."

Richard was no longer so amused, but he kept his temper under a tight rein. "Are there not enough unfaithful husbands in England to occupy you, my lord bishop?"

Hugh smiled. "Ah, but a king's sins attract more attention than those of lesser men. So you do not deny it?"

Richard found it difficult to be angry with such a good-humored admonishment. "No, I do not deny it. But my wife and I are often apart, for I am fighting a war, and whilst you may not understand this, my lord bishop, a man's body hungers for more than food."

"Of course I understand the lure of the flesh, all too well!"

Richard was quite interested in this revelation, for he'd assumed that saintly men like Hugh were immune to such temptations. "You?"

"Yes, me. I may wear a bishop's miter, but I am still a man like all others. Especially when I was young, I had to struggle fiercely in the war against lust."

"We differ there, then," Richard said with a laugh. "That is the only war in which I was willing to make an unconditional surrender."

Hugh smiled again, but he was not distracted from his purpose. "Adultery is a more serious sin than fornication, sire. Each time you betray your marriage vows, you put your immortal soul in peril. Nor is infidelity your only transgression. You do not keep inviolate the privileges of the Church, especially in the matter of the appointment or election of bishops. It is said that you have promoted men out of friendship or because they have paid you for it, and simony is a heinous sin. If it is true, God will not grant you peace."

Richard studied the other man, feeling what his father had often felt in his dealings with Hugh of Lincoln, resentment at his remarkable candor mingling with admiration for his courage. "I do not deny that I have sold offices, and I do not apologize for it; my need for money is an urgent one, first to defend the Holy Land and now to defend my own domains. But I will concede that the sale of bishoprics is a more serious sin than the sale of sheriffdoms. I will consider what you have said, my lord bishop, and I would ask for your prayers."

"Gladly, my liege," Hugh said, bestowing his blessings upon the king before Richard summoned his steward to escort the bishop to his lodgings in the castle. Richard was standing on the dais, watching Hugh depart, his expression bemused. When he was joined by Guillain and Morgan, he saw that they were curious about his private colloquy with the prelate. "The good bishop has been chiding me for my manifold sins. I fear that I shall have to stop."

They both looked surprised. "Sinning?" Morgan blurted out, sounding so dubious that Richard grinned.

"No, listening to churchmen." They laughed, and Hugh, by then at the door of the great hall, glanced over his shoulder with another smile, untroubled by their levity. He well knew that it was no easy task to uproot sin in a royal garden, but he was a patient gardener.

※

ELEANOR REGARDED HER SON pensively, trying to decide if she should broach the subject of his marriage, as Joanna had been urging. He'd just told her he was leaving Chinon for another quick trip to his newly fortified strong-hold at Pont de l'Arche, where he was having great success in penning up the French garrison at Vaudreuil Castle, part of the war of attrition he was waging against Philippe, their truce notwithstanding. In mid-March, he was meeting the Duchess of Brittany at Angers in an effort—probably in vain, he conceded—to reconcile her with her husband, the Earl of Chester, for he hoped Randolph might convince Constance to let her son Arthur be raised at his court. After that, he would be holding his Easter Court at Le Mans. Since Le Mans was just fifty miles from Beaufort-en-Vallée, where Berengaria and Joanna were currently residing, that made up Eleanor's mind.

"Do you intend to celebrate Easter with Berengaria?"

She'd taken him by surprise, as his evasive answer made clear. "I have not given my Easter Court much thought yet, Maman. It is only January, after all."

"Richard . . . even if she no longer pleases you, you cannot consider ending the marriage. The alliance with Navarre is too valuable to lose."

"I am well aware of that," he said, scowling. "Nor has Berenguela done anything to displease me."

Eleanor rose and sat down beside him in the window-seat. "Then why are you suddenly so loath to spend any time with her, dearest?"

With anyone else, he'd have flared up, using anger to ward off this intrusion into his heart and mind. He could feel heat rising in his face, for he had no answer to her question. He did not understand himself why he was no longer comfortable with his wife, why her very presence reminded him of all he'd lost since leaving the Holy Land. "I am fighting a war," he said curtly. "Right now I can think only about defending my lands and retaking what the French king seized whilst I was a prisoner. There will be time enough for my wife once our empire is no longer in such danger."

Eleanor had rarely felt so helpless. He was hurting and she'd have given anything to heal that hurt, but there was nothing she could do. "You are right, Richard," she said, for at least she could stop probing this painful wound. "You must give priority to the threat posed by the French." He did not reply, merely nodding, but she sensed his relief, and she made haste to find a safer topic of conversation. "What is this I hear about your confrontation with a priest, Fulk de Neuilly?"

"Oh, that," he said, and when he smiled, she knew she'd made the right choice. "He is one of those vexing preachers who enjoy making foreboding prophesies and claiming divine powers. This Fulk de Neuilly contends that the Almighty has blessed him with the ability to cure the blind, the lame, and the dumb. He also insists he can drive out demons and get harlots and usurers to see the error of their ways, and for all I know, he thinks he can walk on water, too. In other words, the sort of sanctimonious, prideful fool that any sensible person would take good care to avoid. After predicting that Philippe or I would meet an 'unfortunate death' if we do not end our hostilities, he made a dramatic appearance in Rouen, taking me to task for my sins."

"He accused you of having three daughters?" Eleanor asked, even though she knew exactly what had transpired between Richard and the self-professed holy man, for her son's riposte had quickly been repeated with zest, taking no time at all to spill from Normandy into Anjou.

"Three shameless daughters, he declared, warning that I must marry them off as soon as possible lest evil befall me. Of course I said he lied, that I had no daughters. And he replied that my three daughters were pride, avarice, and lust. So I told him that I would give my pride to the Knights Templar, my avarice to the Cistercian monks, and my lust to the prelates of the Church."

It had been a deft rejoinder, showing that Richard could identify a foe's weaknesses on and off the battlefield, and Eleanor laughed. "I could so easily hear Harry saying that," she confided, "for you are more like him than either of you were willing to admit."

"I'll take your word for that, Maman," Richard said, before painting a vivid verbal picture of the discomfited prophet slinking away to much laughter from the audience of earls and barons. They were interrupted by a servant bringing in wine and wafers, and by the time they'd eaten, Richard was in better spirits. "I suppose you heard that your friend the Countess of Aumale is now a widow, and probably a merry one since she loved William de Forz not."

"Yes, I did hear of the count's death. Sudden chest pains, I believe. And you are right about Hawisa. She saw his death as deliverance."

"She will not be pleased, then, when she learns that I intend for her to marry again."

Eleanor was not surprised, for great heiresses were valuable assets, used by kings to reward loyal vassals and to forge alliances. She felt some sympathy, knowing Hawisa would have no say in the matter, but she'd learned years ago to pick her battles and this was the price Hawisa must pay for her good fortune in being highborn and wealthy. "Whom do you have in mind for her, Richard?"

"A good man," he said, although that had not been his reason for choosing Hawisa's next husband. "When he gets back from Austria, I mean to give her to Baldwin de Bethune. I owe him an heiress, for my father had promised him Denise de Déols and I gave her, instead, to André."

"Baldwin is a good man," Eleanor agreed, "and since he was often at your father's court, I am sure Hawisa knows him. That may make it easier for her."

Richard was not particularly interested in Hawisa of Aumale's opinion of her marriage; he saw her as a pawn to be moved around on the marital chessboard however he saw fit. "Tell her that I will give them a lavish wedding and I will pay for it myself. That might reconcile her to her fate."

Richard had sent word to Eleanor as soon as he'd learned of Leopold of Austria's death, knowing she'd find it as gratifying as he did. He'd not disclosed the entire contents of the archbishop's letter, though, and he made ready to do so now, knowing she'd be troubled by what he had to say. "On his deathbed, Leopold gave orders for Wilhelm to be sent to the Hungarian king's court, trusting that he'd restore the boy to his father in Saxony. But Heinrich got wind of it and demanded that Wilhelm be sent to him, instead. So he'll have both Otto and Wilhelm as hostages now—as leverage."

"Richard, do you know how Otto is being treated?"

"I did my best to persuade Heinrich to take Otto with him when he invaded Sicily, for I thought the lad would be better off with the army than sequestered away in some Godforsaken German castle. Heinrich refused, of course, being Heinrich, but I was told by friends in Germany that he has since 'eased' the conditions of Otto's confinement."

That sounded as ominous to Eleanor as it had to Richard. They looked at each other in silence for a few moments, frustrated that they could do so little for Tilda's children. "There is more," Richard said, "both good and bad. The good is that the Empress Constance was delivered of a son in December; I know that will give Joanna great joy. The bad is that four days after his coronation as King of Sicily, Heinrich claimed that a plot had been discovered against him and he arrested Tancred's widow, her children, and the leading Sicilian lords. He sent Sybilla and her daughters to a German convent and her small son to a German monastery. Admiral Margaritis and the Archbishop of Salerno were imprisoned at Trifels Castle, which will be their tomb."

Eleanor suddenly felt very cold, thinking of the horrors hidden away behind the walls of Trifels Castle, thinking that the fate of these Sicilian lords could have been her son's fate, too. "God help them," she said bleakly, "for no one else can."

RICHARD'S MEETING WITH CONSTANCE at Angers Castle was more cordial than he'd expected, for she was so thankful that her daughter was on her way home from Austria that she was less hostile than usual. Her face had always been the mirror to her soul, and her distaste at the thought of reconciling with Randolph was obvious to every witness in the great hall. But she realized that Richard's interest in having her son raised at his court could be the first step toward naming his nephew as his heir if his queen did not give him a son. So she agreed to discuss his proposal with her barons and even to make Randolph welcome in Brittany if they consented. Richard realized this was the best he could hope for, and he could only marvel that his brother Geoffrey had been so happy with this woman, for he found her as prickly as any hedgehog.

By the seventeenth of March, he'd reached the Earl of Chester's castle at St James de Beuvron, where he discovered that the earl was just as stubborn as Constance. When a man wed a woman of higher rank, he expected to share that rank, to be entitled to the possession, use, and income of his wife's lands. But Constance and her barons had never recognized Randolph's authority as Duke of Brittany, which was a long-festering grievance with him. Richard had to spend several days assuring him that if he returned to Brittany, he would be able to exercise his full rights as duke *jure uxoris*.

After securing Randolph's cooperation, Richard intended to meet the Lord of Fougères on the twenty-fourth of the month. Raoul de Fougères had been one of the most notorious of the Breton barons, a man who'd been constantly in rebellion against his Angevin overlords, but he'd died in the past year and Richard hoped his brother would prove to be more tractable. He decided to take a day for himself first, as the hawking season was coming to an end, and before departing for Fougères, he and Randolph and his household knights rode out to try their falcons against cranes along the rushes of the River Beuvron.

They had an unanticipated addition to their hawking party, for his brother John had made an unexpected appearance at the castle, in what he claimed was a visit to Earl Randolph, expressing surprised pleasure to find Richard there, too. Richard was not deceived; he knew full well that John had heard of his meeting with Constance at Angers, and he was desperate to find out if Arthur was now the favorite in the royal heir race. But he said nothing and hid his amusement at the Earl of Chester's bafflement when he found himself acclaimed by John as a dear friend of long standing.

They had an enjoyable afternoon. Richard's white gyrfalcon distinguished itself by bringing down a huge crane, diving upon the larger bird like a lethal streak of lightning, and Randolph's and André's birds also stooped to the kill. Their handlers released the greyhounds and while the men waited for the prey to be collected and the falcons recalled, Richard and André intrigued the others by telling them how the Saracens used leather hoods as a means of controlling their hawks. Once they were returning to his castle, the Earl of Chester took the opportunity to ask Richard if it was true that he'd brought back some Saracen archers from the Holy Land. He was amazed when Richard confirmed it, for he'd been sure this was just another wild rumor started by the French. Richard laughed at his consternation, saying they were brave soldiers with a rare talent. He was explaining how Saracens could shoot arrows from horseback, a skill no Christians had been able to master, when they encountered the old man.

He appeared without warning from the woods, his long, unkempt hair and straggly beard making them think he was a hermit, one of those recluses who shunned contact with other men, living in isolation but dependent upon the charity of their neighbors, who often admired them for their piety and simple, godly way of life. But he was leaning upon a pilgrim's staff, so he might have been on a pilgrimage to the holy shrine at Mont St Michel.

Their horses did not like this stranger's rank smell and shied away as he hobbled forward. "Give him alms, André," Richard directed. When his cousin raised an eyebrow, he grinned. "You know kings do not carry money." He watched as André opened his scrip and tossed some coins at the man's feet. "Surely I'd be more generous than that?" With an exaggerated sigh, André fished out a few more deniers. But instead of reaching for the offering, the hermit moved closer, staring up intently into their faces. His gaze moved slowly from man to man before coming to rest upon Richard.

"Heed me, O Lord!" He had a surprisingly deep and resonant voice, and in that moment he looked more like one of the prophets of the Old Testament than a ragged hermit or beggar. "Be thou mindful of the destruction of Sodom, and abstain from what is unlawful. For if thou dost not, a vengeance worthy of God shall overtake thee."

They looked down at him in astonishment, but several of the men then surreptitiously made the sign of the cross. Richard merely laughed. Turning in the saddle, he glanced toward his brother, saying, "The hermit has to be talking to you, Johnny, since your sins are much more spectacular than mine."

John laughed, too. "I would hope so, for I've always believed that anything worth doing is worth doing to excess."

André and their household knights joined in the laughter, although the Earl of Chester; Richard's vice-chancellor, Eustace; and a few others were still watching the hermit uneasily.

Angered by their laughter, he raised his staff, pointing it skyward as if he were calling down a celestial thunderbolt upon these unrepentant sinners. "'Be not deceived, for God is not mocked!'"

By now Richard was losing patience. "We are not mocking God, old man. We are mocking you." And raising his hand, he signaled for the hawking party to ride on, leaving the hermit behind in the middle of the road, shouting after them that whatsoever a man soweth, so shall he reap. By then, they were out of earshot.

ALTHOUGH JOHN WOULD NEVER have admitted it, he felt diminished in Richard's presence, for his brother was all that he was not. But he knew that if he hoped to be restored to royal favor, it must be done one slow step at a time. And so one of those steps had led him to Richard's Easter Court at Le Mans, where he discovered that he had more to fear from ghosts than jealousy.

It was at Le Mans that he'd seen his father for the last time. As the army led by the French king and Richard closed in on the city, Henry had sent him to safety. Although he'd feigned reluctance, he'd been glad to go, for by then he knew that his father was dying and it was time to strike a deal with Richard and

Philippe. He'd found it easy enough to convince himself that he had no choice, that he was doing what any sensible man would have done: abandoning a sinking ship. And at first he'd been confident that he'd made the right decision. Richard had scorned those who'd deserted his father in his final days, honoring, instead, the men who'd stayed loyal, like Will Marshal and Baldwin de Bethune. But he'd made an exception for his brother, bestowing upon John six English counties and a princely income of four thousand pounds a year. John had soon learned, though, that other men did not respect him. Oh, they were deferential to him as the king's brother and heir, but he could see it in their eyes; they thought it despicable that he had betrayed his dying father. And it was then that Henry began to invade his dreams. Never shouting or ranting or berating him. Far worse. He was a silent spirit, watching his son with sad eyes, fading away whenever John tried to defend himself, to explain why he'd fled Le Mans and made a private peace with Richard and the French king.

So even though he'd been given a seat at the high table in the great hall, John was not enjoying himself on this Monday in Holy Week. Will Marshal and his countess, Isabel de Clare, had arrived that afternoon and while Isabel caught up with André's wife, Denise de Déols, the men were telling Will about the latest offer by the French king—that disputes be settled by a contest of champions, five on each side. But after Richard insisted that he and Philippe be two of the champions, the French lost all interest in the idea. Will and those who'd not heard this before burst into laughter. John smiled, too; although he was bone-weary of hearing Richard extolled as a cross between Roland and the pagan god of war, Mars, he took considerable pleasure in the thought of Philippe's discomfort. Yet he was still relieved when the meal was finally done and he could retreat to his own chamber, away from all prying eyes.

Since he was bored and had not been able to bring Ursula to Le Mans, he sent Durand into the town to find him a whore and then settled down on the bed with a flagon of wine. But he soon received a surprise summons from his brother.

He found Richard in the palace solar with Will Marshal and André. They were trading memories of the siege of Le Mans, laughing as though they'd not been on opposite sides. John already knew Will had unhorsed Richard when he'd set out in pursuit of Henry, who'd been forced to flee after the French fought their way into the city. The story had become famous, and Will had been sure he'd ruined himself by that public humiliation of a man not known for his forgiving nature. But to his amazement, he'd been restored to royal favor and given Isabel de Clare as his bride. John had not known that Will had also nearly captured André that same day. While he'd managed to get away from Will, he'd broken his arm in the escape, and Richard was teasing him about a similar incident in the Holy Land, when he'd somehow been injured by a Saracen he'd fatally wounded. John listened with a fixed smile, for he did not understand the enjoyment that men took in reliving memories of near-death experiences. In that, he was more their father's son than Richard, for Henry had not liked war, and although when he fought, he fought well, he'd never gloried in it as Richard did.

John was shifting restlessly in his seat, wondering if Durand had come back yet with his harlot, when Richard finally turned to him. "I have good news for you, Johnny. I am going to restore your forfeit estates."

John sat up straight, staring at his brother in astonished delight. "Richard, thank you!"

"Your lands, not your castles. They will remain in my hands."

That was a great letdown, for castles were power, but John knew better than to let his disappointment show, and thanked Richard effusively again. André and Will were trying to hide their disapproval, having already argued that John's capture of Évreux had been dishonorable and his flight from the Vaudreuil Castle siege had been craven. They did not understand why Richard was so indulgent with John, although they suspected the queen mother had played a role in this. Exchanging glances, they silently agreed that no outsiders could ever fully comprehend the family dynamics of the Angevins, at once personal and political, vengeful and forgiving, and always dynastic.

❧

ARNE SAT UP ON HIS PALLET, listening intently. When it came again, a muffled, indistinct sound, but one he'd heard before, he flung the covers back, shivering as he struggled to pull his shirt over his head. Padding barefoot across the chamber, he drew aside the linen hangings that cocooned Richard's bed, allowing the low-burning flames in the hearth to chase away some of the dark. As he expected, Richard was trapped in another bad dream, tossing his head from side to side on the pillow, his mouth contorted, his breathing labored. But his sheets were soaked in sweat, and when Arne reached out timidly to shake Richard's shoulder, he jerked back in dismay, for his king's skin was searing to the touch.

RICHARD KNEW HE MUST BE in Jaffa, for it was so ungodly hot. He tried to open his eyes, but the Outremer sun was too blindingly bright. He could hear people moving about, recognizing the voices of André and Master Ralph Besace, his personal physician. He was puzzled, though, to hear his mother's voice, for Maman had not accompanied him to the Holy Land. Steeling himself against the glare, he squinted to see if she was truly there, and set off turmoil in the chamber.

"He's awake!" This voice was familiar, too, that of another of his doctors, Master John of Brideport, which alarmed him, for he'd last seen Master John in Germany. Holy Christ, was he back at Trifels? He struggled to sit up and was at once urged to lie still. He did, realizing that wherever he was, it was not Germany. His mother was there, as was André, Will Marshal, his doctors, even his fourteen-year-old son, Philip, hovering behind the others. Before he could speak, a hand was laid upon his forehead. "God be praised, the fever has broken!"

By now Richard had recognized his surroundings, his bedchamber in the palace at Le Mans. As his wits cleared, it was coming back to him. He'd developed a sudden, intense headache, joking with André that God was punishing him for giving Johnny back his lands. He remembered feeling very hot that night, throwing off the covers to escape the suffocating heat. After that, nothing. "How long . . . ?"

"You fell sick on Monday eve, sire. Today is Maundy Thursday."

He'd lost three days? "It was not the quartan fever?" he said, somewhat uncertainly, for he had no memory of the chills that always followed those bouts of fever. Both of his doctors assured him that he'd not been stricken with a recurrence of the ague that had plagued him for years. "What, then?"

"We do not know, my liege." Master Ralph shook his head slowly. "It is passing strange that you'd become so very ill so suddenly. Were you feeling poorly ere that fever flared?" Richard mentioned the headache and sore throat, but his doctors still seemed baffled. Eleanor was beside him now, kissing his forehead to assure herself that his fever truly had broken. As he looked from face to face, he saw joy so intense that he realized they had not been sure he'd survive. He was both astonished and disquieted. He'd lost track of the times he'd confronted Death, but he'd never been ambushed like this before. In the past, Death had always given him fair warning. He was too tired, though, to give any more thought to his mysterious malady, not when sleep was beckoning so imperiously. He murmured a drowsy apology before surrendering to it, so abruptly that a frisson of fear swept the chamber. But after making sure that his breathing was regular and his pulse steady, both physicians declared that what he most needed now was rest. Master Ralph dared then to tell the queen mother that she ought to get some sleep, too, for God willing, it seemed likely the king would recover. Eleanor was too exhausted to argue with them. André and Will soon headed for their own beds. Philip balked and, wrapping himself in his mantle, he curled up in a nearby chair to keep vigil while his father slept.

WHEN RICHARD AWAKENED AGAIN, he could tell it was daylight for the windows of the royal chambers in the Le Mans palace were luxuriously fitted with glass. After getting up to use the chamber pot, he did not protest when the doctors insisted he go back to bed, for his body was recovering more slowly than his brain, and his legs felt weak. He was sitting up, finishing a bowl of soup, when John was admitted. "Come in, Little Brother. Sorry to shatter your hopes, but it looks as if I am not going to die."

John did not even blink. "And glad I am of it, Big Brother. Had you gone to God in Holy Week, most of your lords would likely have chosen little Arthur as their next king, for I'm still tainted goods in many eyes. So I'd be grateful if you could stop flirting with Death for a while, at least until I can restore my reputation."

The doctors gaped at him, openmouthed. But his gamble paid off, for Richard was amused by his cockiness, not offended. Pulling up a chair, John did his best to be entertaining, knowing what a poor patient his brother was. At first, he appeared to be succeeding. Soon, though, Richard seemed to be withdrawing into himself, dwelling upon thoughts that were not pleasant—or so John judged from the somber look on the older man's face.

By then, Eleanor, André, and Will had joined John at Richard's bedside. He was quiet, but they thought that only natural, and were encouraged that he had been willing to eat. He had to endure brief visits from the Bishop of Le Mans, the Archbishop of Rouen, the Earl of Chester, the Viscount of Thouars, and several other highborn lords and clerics. He slept again after that and, upon awakening, he found that shadows were infiltrating the chamber. Propping himself up on his elbows, he regarded them searchingly, his gaze moving from his doctors to his mother, his brother, his cousins André and Morgan, then on to Will

Marshal; his chaplain, Anselm; his vice-chancellor, Eustace; and the newly arrived Dean of St Martin's le Grand, William de St Mère-Eglise.

"I would ask this of you all. Could this sickness be a sign from God? A warning that I need to atone for my sins and lead a more godly life?"

John saw at once where this was heading and did not like it in the least. If his brother decided to "lead a more godly life," he'd reconcile with his wife, and the last thing John wanted was for Richard to spend enough time in Berengaria's bed to sire a son. "You cannot mean that mad hermit, Richard. He was spouting nonsense!"

But the three churchmen were already assuring Richard that God may indeed have been warning him, and both doctors agreed that the strange nature of his illness could be explained if it had been divine chastisement. Will was the next to speak. It was not Richard's sickbed he was seeing; it was his brother Hal's deathbed. *God is punishing me for my sins, Will.* His eyes dark with fear, Hal had cried out despairingly that it was too late, that Lucifer was in the chamber with them, waiting to claim his soul. Nigh on twelve years later, that memory still brought tears to Will's eyes, for he'd loved his young lord, even though Hal had lost his moral bearings and had been no better than a bandit in his last weeks of life. Will had helped Hal to make a good death, and now he told Hal's brother what he'd once told Hal, saying with such passion that he choked up, "The Almighty has given you a great mercy, sire—time to repent and seek His forgiveness."

Morgan added his voice to Will's, remembering a warning more credible than the hermit's, Bishop Hugh of Lincoln's. André and Eleanor were not sure how to answer; André in particular was dubious, for he thought John was likely right and the hermit mad. But it was always better to err on the side of caution, and Eleanor thought it logical that the Almighty would care more for the soul of a king. Then, too, Richard could not beget a son and heir unless he mended his broken marriage.

When she did not argue against it, John knew that his voice would go unheeded. Richard would make another spectacular repentance as he had in Messina, wanting to be judged worthy to lead the fight against the infidels. And with his accursed luck, Brother Richard would get his little Spanish bride pregnant ere the month was out. Wishing he could hunt that wretched hermit down with lymer hounds and feed him his own entrails, John lapsed into a morose silence that no one noticed.

JOANNA KNEW THAT SOMETHING was wrong. While Richard was meeting with Constance in Angers, Morgan had paid a visit to Mariam at Beaufort-en-Vallée. It had been a very brief one, and in the two and a half weeks since then, Mariam had been quiet and withdrawn, rebuffing all of Joanna's questions. But Joanna was nothing if not persistent, and when Mariam slipped out into the garden after hearing Easter Mass in the castle chapel, she followed.

She found Mariam sitting on a turf bench by the fishpond. "Yes, I know I am meddling," she said before the other woman could speak. "But you are as dear to me as my own sisters, and I can see you are in pain. Let me help."

"As if I could stop you." Mariam's compelling golden eyes were brimming with tears, though, and once Joanna sat beside her, she began to unburden herself. "Morgan came to tell me that Richard had given him and Guillain very generous grants, large estates in his ducal domains in Normandy and Aquitaine. He was so joyful, Joanna, saying that now we could marry. It well-nigh broke my heart to turn him down."

"But why? I know you love him."

"Yes, I do love him, and I would not burden him with a barren wife."

Joanna reached over to take Mariam's hand in her own. "How often have you been able to share a bed with Morgan? A few times in the Holy Land, an occasional tryst in the past year. That you did not conceive yet proves nothing, *Zahrah*."

The use of that Arabic endearment, her brother William's pet name for her, caused Mariam's tears to overflow. "You are forgetting that during four years of marriage to Bertrand, not once did I conceive."

"That does not mean you cannot conceive," Joanna insisted, for the female physicians she'd consulted at Salerno had espoused the revolutionary view that a childless marriage was not always to be blamed upon the woman. "Many wives conceive after years of a supposedly barren marriage. What of Constance? Who expected her to become pregnant in her fortieth year?"

Mariam merely shook her head. But after a few moments of silence, she said, "I was not being entirely truthful, Joanna. Yes, I have worried that I might not be able to conceive. But that is not why I cannot wed Morgan. Our children would never be welcome here. I have seen how people stare at me, whisper behind my back. In Poitiers, they called me 'the Saracen witch.'"

Joanna was outraged; she'd had no idea that Mariam felt like such an outsider in the Angevin domains. "Why did you not tell me? The mean-spirited louts! You're a better Christian than the lot of them!"

Mariam was warmed by Joanna's indignation and reached over to hug her before saying, "I do not care what they say of me, for my life with you shelters me from the worst of their suspicions and ill will. But my children would care. In Sicily, their Saracen blood would not matter. But I could not ask Morgan to abandon his world for mine. Even if he would have considered it, now that Heinrich has been crowned the King of Sicily, a life there is impossible. Morgan would never be willing to live under Heinrich's rule, and in truth, neither would I."

Joanna knew Mariam well enough not to argue further, but she had no intention of giving up. She was ashamed that she'd felt a brief flicker of relief as Mariam had explained why a return to Sicily was out of the question, for losing Mariam would be like losing part of herself. Yet she loved Mariam too much to be selfish, and as they walked back toward the castle, she was privately vowing to find a way for her friend and Morgan to have a life together.

When they entered the great hall, Joanna started toward Berengaria, who was standing by the open hearth. But her step quickened as soon as she got a glimpse of the younger woman's face. "Berengaria? Is something amiss?"

Berengaria's eyes looked very dark against the whiteness of her skin. She was holding a letter that looked as if it had been crumpled in her fist and then smoothed out. "It is from Richard," she said. "He wants me to join him at his Easter Court in Le Mans."

"Dearest, that is wonderful!" Joanna exclaimed, delighted that her stubborn brother was finally reaching out to his neglected wife.

"Yes, wonderful," Berengaria echoed after a long pause, saying, as always, what was expected of her. But she shared none of Joanna's pleasure, feeling only unease, confusion, and even a touch of apprehension.

❧

IT WAS DUSK TWO DAYS LATER when the walls of Le Mans came into view. Berengaria had not seen Richard since that past July, at the beginning and end of his lightning campaign into Poitou, and in the eight months since then, she could do little but mourn her ailing marriage. Her bruised and battered pride had suffered a serious wound when Richard celebrated Christmas in Rouen without her, for her absence proclaimed to all of Christendom that she'd failed as a queen, as a wife. How else explain why Richard would not have wanted her with him on one of the most sacred days on the Church calendar? Her hurt was already well salted with resentment when he met the Duchess of Brittany in March and did not visit her, even though Beaufort-en-Vallée was just fifteen miles from Angers. On the road to Le Mans, she'd tried to banish her grievances to the back of her brain, telling herself that what mattered now was showing Richard and the world that she knew how to behave as a queen ought, serene and benevolent and regal, never giving a hint of her inner agitation, her anger, or her pain. But with each passing mile, she became more and more nervous, not sure that she had her wayward emotions under proper control.

She received a surprise as they approached the Vieux Pont, for the town gate opened and Richard rode out to meet her once they crossed the bridge. He was accompanied by an impressive entourage of barons and bishops, few of whom she knew, since she'd never been formally presented to his vassals. When he reined his stallion in beside her, she thought he looked tired and tense. He smiled, though, reaching over to kiss her hand with a flourish before introducing her to Hamelin, the Bishop of Le Mans, a portly, affable man who seemed very pleased to see her, for he kept talking about what an honor it was to have her visiting his city.

Richard rode beside Berengaria as they entered Le Mans, telling her that the town had both a castle and a royal palace and pointing out the city's ancient Roman walls. He made a brief detour to show her the magnificent cathedral of St Julien, saying that this was where his grandfather Count Geoffrey of Anjou had been buried and where his father had been christened. The narrow streets were thronged with people eager to get their first glimpse of the Lionheart's bride, and they cheered as she and Richard passed, turning their ride into a torch-lit triumphant procession. Berengaria smiled and waved, thinking how much she would have enjoyed this if only it had happened months ago.

❧

BERENGARIA HAD ALWAYS HARBORED ambivalent feelings toward Richard's mother. She could not approve of Eleanor's scandalous past, but she thought Eleanor played the role of queen to perfection: confident, courageous, and elegant. She'd never aspired to compete with her formidable mother-in-law, knowing that was a contest she'd have been sure to lose, and she was regretful that their five-month journey to Sicily had not developed any intimacy between them. She did not doubt that Richard might never have regained his freedom if not for his mother's fierce determination, and she was deeply thankful that in his time of greatest need, he'd had Eleanor to fight for him. But she'd begun to resent Eleanor in the past year, always at Richard's side while she was relegated to the shadows. So upon their arrival at the palace, she offered a coolly formal greeting to her mother-in-law, only to feel ashamed and outmaneuvered when Eleanor was very gracious in return.

Her first meeting with Richard's brother was just as strained. She was startled by how little John resembled Richard; he was handsome enough, but much shorter than Richard, with dark hair, Eleanor's eyes, and an irreverent, sensual smile that made her think he was envisioning her naked in his bed. She knew hatred was an emotion that good Christians should eschew, but she hated John, for he'd done his best to make sure her husband would never see the sun again. She would never forgive him for that and she did not understand how Richard and Eleanor had, how he was swaggering around Richard's court as if his foul betrayal had never been. *They are not like us, little one.* The words were her brother Sancho's, uttered on her last night in Pamplona, a gentle, rueful warning that she would be marrying into a family utterly unlike her own.

It was daunting to meet so many people at once, and she struggled to commit their names and faces to memory, knowing that they'd be offended if she did not remember them at their next encounter. She was grateful that Richard was so often at her side, and when he was called away, he saw to it that she was watched over by Joanna or André. It was Joanna who came to her rescue when they saw John bearing down upon them. Knowing that Berengaria did not want to interact any more than necessary with the man she'd privately dubbed the Prince of Darkness, Joanna adroitly steered her sister-in-law toward a group encircling the Bishop of Le Mans.

Bishop Hamelin at once interrupted his conversation to acknowledge the two queens, visibly proud to have so many highborn guests sojourning in his beloved city. "We are indeed honored that you could join us for Eastertide, my lady queens. It is always a season for rejoicing, but especially so this year, for just a week ago, we feared that our king might be breathing his last. Yet look at him now!" Beaming, he gestured across the hall, where Richard was conversing with the Archbishop of Rouen and the Bishop of Angers. "As Scriptures promise, *Return unto Me, and I will return unto you, saith the Lord of Hosts.* Because the king repented his sins, he was restored to full health, for *God's mercy is everlasting.*"

Berengaria's mouth had gone dry. "My husband was gravely ill?"

"Indeed, Madame. You were not told?"

Berengaria could only shake her head mutely. Joanna was just as stunned, but William de St Mère-Eglise quickly interceded, explaining it had happened so suddenly that there was no time to summon the queens, and once the crisis was past, the king had not wanted to worry them. Isabel de Clare helped, too, by saying lightly that "Men are all the same, bless them. My husband's letters home make his campaigns sound like pleasure jaunts. Why they think wives are such delicate flowers is a mystery to me, for if men had to endure the ordeal of the birthing chamber, no family would have more than one child."

That evoked laughter and Bishop Hamelin continued with his story, telling Berengaria and Joanna that the king had confessed his sins freely before his bishops and asked for absolution. "Since then he has attended Divine Service every morning without fail and he has made provisions for the poor to be fed daily, both at his court and in the towns. He has also ordered that chalices of gold and silver be made to replace those that had been taken from the churches to pay his ransom." The bishop was clearly delighted to be a part of these admirable happenings, and carried on in this vein for some time, praising the king expansively. "Was he not one of the first to take the cross? Did he not found a Cistercian abbey at Bonport and a Benedictine priory at Gourfailles? Think what greatness he shall achieve now that he has vowed to honor God by living as a most just and virtuous prince!"

Berengaria had not known that Richard had founded two monasteries, and that would normally have been of great interest to her. Now that she knew why Richard had summoned her to Le Mans, the news barely registered with her.

⚜

DINNER WAS THE MAIN MEAL of the day, supper usually an afterthought, but because of Berengaria and Joanna's late arrival, Richard had arranged for a lavish repast, the tables in the great hall laden with all the foods that had been denied them during Lent. His miraculous recovery had not been as rapid as it appeared to others. Eating little, he merely pushed his food around on his trencher to disguise his lack of appetite, not noticing that his wife was doing the same. He tired easily these days and all he wanted to do in a bed this night was sleep. But his bishops were watching him expectantly, seeing his reconciliation with his queen as proof that he had turned away from past sins. For all he knew, the Almighty was watching him, too.

After the meal, there was a performance by troubadours and a daring youth who juggled knives. Richard soon rose, reaching for his wife's hand to draw her to her feet. When she realized his intent, she blushed, murmuring that she should summon her ladies. Richard assured her that he could assist her in undressing. She did not doubt that he had considerable experience in ridding women of their clothes, for she was not so naïve as to think he'd been faithful to her during their estrangement. She did not protest and they exited the great hall to a round of cheers and approving smiles.

As they crossed the threshold of the bedchamber that had been prepared for Berengaria, Richard halted in surprise, for it resembled a bridal bower. It was too early for flowers, but fragrant floor rushes had been scattered about with a lavish hand, incense was burning to perfume the air, silver candelabras kept the shadows at bay, and a small trestle table held two jeweled cups, a large flagon of wine, and a dish of dried fruit. He wondered who had ordered this. It was not his mother's style. It *was* Joanna's style, but she'd not had the time. Mayhap André's wife or Will's Isabel. It might even be Johnny's idea of a jest. Well, at least there was wine. After sliding the latch into place, he crossed to the table, asking Berengaria if she would like wine.

"Yes, please." She watched him reach for the flagon, still not sure what she would do. She well knew what was expected of her; she'd been taught from the cradle that wives were to be dutiful and deferential. Did Scriptures not say that they should submit themselves to their husbands, as unto the Lord? "The bishop told me that you were very ill last week, Richard," she said at last.

He paused, then began to pour wine into one of the cups. "I had a fever for a few days," he said dismissively.

She had not known she meant to speak until she heard her own voice, sounding so calm and cold that it could have been a stranger's. "Yet it was serious enough for you to be shriven of your sins. I would not have you jeopardize your health by paying the marriage debt prematurely. I am sure the Almighty will understand if you choose to defer your penance until you are fully recovered."

His hand jerked, wine splattering like blood upon the snowy white linen cloth. "Penance?" he echoed incredulously. "Why would you say something like that, Berenguela? Why would you even think it?"

"Do you truly need to ask that, Richard?"

He could not believe she'd chosen this night, of all nights, to provoke a quarrel. "I can assure you that I do not see bedding you as penance, little dove."

She winced, for that endearment, once so pleasing to her ears, now seemed like a cruel mockery. "I do not believe you," she said, and knew she'd angered him when color rose in his face. But she did not care. "In the year since your return from Germany, you've made it painfully clear that you do not want me, not as queen, wife, or bedmate. You chose not to have me join you in England or to attend your crown-wearing at Winchester—"

"Christ on the Cross, woman, I was putting down a rebellion!"

She discovered, to her surprise, that she was not intimidated by his rage, for what did she have to lose? "I am not as knowledgeable about statecraft as your mother and sister, Richard. But I am far from a fool, so I would ask you not to treat me like one. If your lady mother could accompany you to the siege of Nottingham, why could not your wife?"

She saw he did not have an answer to that, but it gave her no satisfaction. "Then you returned to Normandy and two months passed ere we were reunited—two months. You did not come to me even when my father died."

"I was fighting a war! I seriously doubt that the French king would have agreed to a truce so I could pay a conjugal visit to my wife."

"But you and Philippe did sign a truce in November. Yet you held your Christmas Court without me. You humiliated me before all of Christendom—"

"That was not my intent, Berenguela!" Furious at being backed into a corner like this, he lashed out suddenly, clearing the table with a wild swipe of his arm. She flinched when the flagon and cups crashed into the floor rushes, but she would not capitulate.

"Do you know how long it has been since we've been together? I do—eight months and five days. I thought that would change when you met the Duchess of Brittany at Angers. Yet you did not visit me afterward. It was just fifteen miles to Beaufort-en-Vallée, but you could not take the time." She'd been proud of her self-control, proud that she'd been able to face him dry-eyed and composed. But her voice was no longer so steady when she spoke now of the greatest grievance of all. "And then you summoned me to your Easter Court and I learned that you'd done so only because you had promised God to atone for your sins. It took the fear of eternal damnation for you to reclaim me as your wife!"

"I've had enough of this foolishness. I'll not discuss this further, not as long as you are being so unreasonable and irrational," he snapped, and strode toward the door.

"If you will not tell me how I have offended you, how can I make amends?"

He halted, his hand on the latch, for that was a cry of pure pain, one that not even his anger could deflect. Turning back to face her, he said hoarsely, "You've done nothing, I swear it!"

She'd never heard such emotion in his voice before, and she did not doubt it was raw and real. "If it is not me, what, then?" Crossing the space between them, she looked up imploringly into his face. "Please . . . tell me."

He was silent for so long that she thought he'd refuse to answer. Just when she'd given up hope, he moved to the closest chair and slumped down in it. "It is this accursed war," he said, so softly that she could barely hear him. "It haunts me day and night. People think I'm winning because I've had a few flashy victories, but they mean little in the long run. Philippe still holds fortresses like Gisors and Vaudreuil and Pacy and Nonancourt. He controls the Norman Vexin, most of Normandy east of the Seine. And for the first time, the French have greater resources to draw upon. The ransom . . . Christ Jesus, it bled the Exchequer dry. To fight this war, I'll have to keep raising taxes and men will hate me for it. But if I do nothing, the Angevin empire will crumble; my father's life's work will be dust upon the wind. . . ."

She'd listened without interrupting as he lied to her, for she knew he was lying. She could believe that he was obsessed with defeating the French king. But she did not believe this was the reason for their estrangement. What could have been more important than recapturing Jerusalem from the infidels? She knew full well the burdens he'd shouldered during his campaign in the Holy Land, the impossible demands that had been placed upon him, the constant strain of dealing with French treachery. Yet he'd not turned away from her then. So why now? She had no answer to that question, knowing only that something had gone dreadfully wrong between them and she did not know how to remedy it. And as she studied his haggard face, etched with fatigue and evidence of his recent bout with Death, she did not think he knew how to remedy it, either.

"I am sorry," she said, for she was, sorry for so much.

He ran his hand through his hair, pressed his fingers against his throbbing temples. She'd sat on a nearby coffer as he'd begun to speak, her skirts spreading about her in a silken cascade. He thought she looked very fragile and very young, her pallor pronounced in the subdued candlelight. "They say Easter is a time for new beginnings, Berenguela. Let's agree to begin anew, too." When she nodded, he took her hand in his. "How would you like it if we bought a house together? A place just for us."

The idea had come to him suddenly, and he saw that it had been an inspired one, for her face lit up. "I would love that, Richard!"

Getting to his feet, he reached down and helped her to rise, too. "So you and Joanna go house hunting, then, and when you find something you like, I'll buy it for us."

Her smile lost some of its light. "I thought . . . thought we'd look for a house together."

How could he find the time for that? Reminding himself that he'd not only promised her this would be a new beginning, he'd promised God, too, he said, "Well, you find a house and then I'll come to see it with you. Fair enough?"

She studied his face and then nodded again. "Yes," she said, "fair enough."

BERENGARIA HAD BEEN EXHAUSTED by their confrontation, both physically and emotionally, and she'd fallen asleep soon after their lovemaking. But when she awoke several hours later, she found she could not go back to sleep. Lying very still so as not to disturb Richard, she began to go over all that had occurred that night, trying to make sense of it. *You've done nothing, I swear it!* She wanted desperately to believe him. She did not understand, though, why he'd pushed her away if that was true. In so many ways, he seemed like a stranger, a troubled one. Not that they'd gotten to know each other all that well during their time in the Holy Land. They truly were starting anew, and so she must make a great effort to forgive him for the hurt he'd caused her. At least now they'd be living as man and wife, as God intended. And if He was merciful, she'd be able to fulfill her duty as a queen. She'd be able to give Richard a son.

She was growing sleepy again. The chamber seemed cold, though. *The hearth must have burned out,* she thought drowsily, sliding over to warm herself against her husband's body. But his side of the bed was empty. She was alone.

CHAPTER TWENTY-SEVEN

❧

AUGUST 1195

Fontevrault Abbey, Anjou

Sitting on a shaded bench in the abbey gardens, Eleanor studied the man lounging on the grass at her feet. Richard often paid her brief visits when his travels took him near Fontevrault, but this was the first time that John had done so. She'd been surprised and even disconcerted, but so far, all had gone smoothly. John could be good company when he chose to be, and having spent some of the spring and summer with Richard, he was very well informed about the rapid pace of events, confirming that the fragile truce between Richard and Philippe was but a bad memory now. He began by diplomatically choosing a story sure to appeal to her maternal pride, about a raid that Richard and Mercadier had made into the Berry region in early July. They'd captured the town and castle at Issoudun, and Richard had then returned to Normandy, leaving Mercadier to wreak havoc against rebels in Auvergne.

John had a raconteur's flair for vivid storytelling, and the one he was relating now cast the French king in such a bad light that he soon had Eleanor laughing. Richard had put so much pressure upon the garrison at Vaudreuil Castle that Philippe had concluded he would not be able to hold it and reluctantly decided to destroy it rather than have it fall into Richard's hands again. To gain time, he'd entered into negotiations with Richard about turning it over, with the two armies gathered as the kings sent envoys to bargain.

"But Philippe's engineers did too good a job undermining the castle walls, and one of them collapsed in a cloud of dust in the midst of the negotiations." John grinned at the memory. "Richard realized at once what had happened, and vowing, 'There'll be some saddles emptied this day,' he gave the command to attack. Philippe was already fleeing, though. He's always been one for avoiding the consequences of his actions."

Eleanor said nothing, but John caught the elegant arch of an eyebrow. "Yes, I suppose the same could be said of me," he conceded, before offering her a disarming smile. "Until I repented my sinful past, of course."

"Of course," she agreed dryly. "So what happened next?"

"Philippe was able to cross the River Seine to safety, but at some cost to his dignity. The bridge gave way under the weight of so many men and horses and they were all plunged into the river. Philippe managed to reach the shore, looking like a drowned rat, I'm told," John said, with another grin. "That improved Richard's mood greatly and he returned to Vaudreuil, where he seized the castle and the French soldiers who'd been left behind in their king's flight. Saying that 'a castle half destroyed is one half rebuilt,' he set about doing just that, so Philippe's double-dealing gained him naught but a river bath."

They were interrupted by a servant with wine and angel wafers. John liked dogs and he broke off a piece of wafer to feed to Eleanor's greyhound. While he'd sought to seem blasé and nonchalant, he'd actually been nervous about making this unbidden visit to his mother, for even before his foolhardy involvement with Philippe, he'd never had the easy, comfortable relationship with her that Richard and Joanna did. He understood why; he'd grown to manhood during those sixteen years of her captivity. But he was still jealous and resentful that his brother and sister had what he never would: this formidable woman's love. Tossing another morsel to the greyhound, he did his best to amuse Eleanor now by sharing court gossip. Rumor had it that the reconciliation between Constance and the Earl of Chester was already foundering, he said cheerfully. And he reported with relish that Philippe's attempt to find another German bride had come to naught, for his captive queen, Ingeborg, cast a long shadow.

"Another rumor had me bedding your good friend, the Countess of Aumale. Supposedly this happened whilst her late, unlamented husband, William de Forz, was off in the Holy Land. De Forz deserved to be a cuckold if any man did and I'd not blame the countess if she'd given him horns. But if Hawisa did, it was not with me."

John would not have minded seeing Hawisa's new husband cuckolded, either, for Baldwin de Bethune had blamed him for abandoning his dying father at Chinon. He was not about to admit that to his mother, and so he changed the subject, saying that Richard and Berengaria had bought a house at Thoree, north of Angers. His initial dismay at their reconciliation had soon faded, for he'd realized Richard would never be an uxorious husband; he loved war, not women. He was not going to spend enough time in Berengaria's bed to get her with child, for it seemed obvious to John that she was barren, and he thanked God most fervently for that blessing.

John did not know it, but Eleanor was beginning to share his pessimism about Berengaria's chances of giving Richard an heir. She was not about to discuss her misgivings with anyone, though, much less the son who'd benefit the most from Berengaria's barrenness. So she did not comment upon his news about the house in Thoree. Instead, she gave him a level, searching look. "Why do I get the sense that there is something you are not telling me, John?"

John blinked. Jesu, did she have second sight? Wanting to get their visit off to a good start, he'd deliberately held back the news that was sure to darken her mood. "As usual, you are correct, Mother. Last month Richard heard from the German emperor. Heinrich is back from his conquest of Sicily and already meddling in French and English matters. He sent Richard a gold crown, reminded him of the fealty he owes to Heinrich, and added a warning that if he cares for his hostages, he will do as he is bidden. Heinrich is nothing if not subtle."

Her eyes narrowed. "'As he is bidden,'" she echoed, and John felt as if a chill wind had just swept through the summer garden. "And what, pray tell, is he bidding Richard to do?"

John did not like the way she catapulted to Richard's defense, for he felt certain she'd never do as much for him. "Nothing that Richard was not already inclined to do," he said coolly. "Heinrich wants him to make all-out war on Philippe."

"Does he, indeed?"

"So he says. He even offered to provide aid to Richard in order to 'avenge the injuries done by Philippe to both of them.' Those were his very words. I daresay you can imagine what Richard's were."

Eleanor called Heinrich a name that caused John to regard her in surprised admiration; he had no idea that her command of invective was so extensive. "What does Richard intend to do?"

"He's already done it. I have to admit that he came up with a clever ploy. He sent Longchamp to Germany with instructions to find out exactly what aid Heinrich means to offer. Since he cannot openly defy Heinrich as long as his hostages are in peril, that buys him some time whilst the French king's fears grow by the hour." John's smile was gleefully malicious. "Richard said we'd see the sun rise at midnight ere Heinrich would actually commit troops to a war against the French, that he wants Richard to fight his war for him. But Philippe does not seem to know Heinrich as well as Richard does, for one of our spies at the French court sent word that Philippe had panicked at the thought of an English-German alliance aimed at France. He even tried to capture Longchamp as he passed through France, to no avail. So Heinrich's outrageous interference can be forgiven if it robs the French king of some sleep."

Eleanor knew better. By now she understood that each time Richard was reminded of his past helplessness, it lacerated anew a wound that had yet to heal. "Heinrich is remarkably heavy-handed for one supposed to be so clever. Why push for what was already sure to happen? All know the truce between Richard and Philippe was as fragile as a cobweb, to be blown away by a breath."

"Well, actually, there is a chance that they might make a genuine truce in light of the word from Spain." Seeing that she hadn't yet heard, he smiled, for it was always enjoyable to be the bearer of momentous news. He did not consider it all that alarming himself, but he knew that others did, and he quickly explained that the Caliph of Morocco had invaded the Spanish kingdoms and her son-in-law, the King of Castile, had suffered a great defeat at the battle of Alarcos. English and French prelates at once set up a clamor, arguing that Christian kings ought not to be fighting each other now that Spain was endangered by infidel Saracens.

"Richard was willing to heed them," he said, sounding faintly surprised. That was no surprise at all to Eleanor, for she well knew how guilty Richard felt that his war with the French was keeping him from honoring his sworn oath to return to the Holy Land and wrest Jerusalem from Saladin's sons.

"I doubt that Philippe gives a fig for the fate of Castile," John continued, "but he has come under intense pressure from the French Church and he is already in papal disgrace over the Ingeborg scandal. Nor does he want to seem less concerned about the infidel threat than Richard. So 'peace talks' are being held this week, and I hear that the bishops are pushing for a marriage between Philippe's son, Louis, and Aenor, who is conveniently available again since she did not have to wed Leopold's son. But it remains to be seen how long any such peace will last. Brother Richard will never rest until he reclaims every single castle that he lost to Philippe during his imprisonment, and Philippe . . . Well, that one lusts after Normandy the way other men lust after women."

Eleanor agreed. Any peace between Richard and Philippe would be fleeting at best. Yet a marriage that would one day make Aenor Queen of France was not a bad match. Even Constance might be satisfied with that. Meanwhile, she

vowed to write that day to her daughter in far-off Castile. But what troubled her
even more than the Saracen invasion of Spain was Heinrich's arrogant intrusion
again into her son's life.

That evening she went alone to the abbey church. Kneeling before the altar,
she offered up prayers for the souls of her husband and the children claimed by
Death before their time. And then she prayed that God would punish the German emperor as he deserved, prayed that he would suffer as Leopold had suffered. She did not doubt that her confessor would consider such a prayer to be
blasphemous, for she knew what Scriptures said about forgiveness: *If ye forgive*
men their trespasses, your Heavenly Father will also forgive you. She knew what
Jesus had said when Peter asked how often he must forgive his brother who'd
sinned against him: *I say not unto thee until seven times, but until seventy times*
seven. But Scriptures also said, *As wax melteth before the fire, so let the wicked*
perish at the presence of God. And who was as wicked as a man who'd dared to
lay hands upon a king who'd taken the cross?

⟡

To THE SURPRISE OF MANY, Richard and Philippe's envoys agreed upon a
peace, contingent upon the marriage of Philippe's eight-year-old son and Richard's eleven-year-old niece. As Richard had to consult with his ally the German
emperor, a truce was declared until November 8, at which time the treaty would
be finalized. One immediate result of the truce was the return of the Lady Alys
to the custody of her brother, the French king, twenty-six years after she'd been
sent to Henry's court at the age of nine.

⟡

PHILIPPE HAD OFTEN WISHED he'd been an only child, for his sisters had
brought him nothing but vexation. Marie and Alix had been much older than
he, tainted by Eleanor's blood; Marie had even allied herself with his enemies in
the early years of his reign. His youngest sister, Agnes, had been sent to Constantinople to wed the Greek emperor's son at age eight; her eleven-year-old
husband succeeded to the throne later that year, only to be overthrown and
murdered by an ambitious cousin, who'd then forced Agnes to wed him. While
Philippe had sympathized with her misfortunes, there was nothing he could do
for her. But her maltreatment would later prove to be a source of embarrass-

ment, for he knew men compared his lack of action with Richard's rescue of his sister Joanna in Sicily, and he was convinced that Richard had deliberately made so much of Joanna's plight just to make him look bad.

But Alys had been the most troublesome of his sisters by far. Henry kept finding reasons to delay her marriage to Richard, which was frustrating in and of itself. But then the rumors had begun to circulate that Henry was balking because he'd taken Alys into his bed. Philippe was never sure if the gossip was true or not. From all he'd heard, Henry had gone through life like a stag in rut, but he was far from a fool, and seducing a French princess who was his own son's betrothed would have been quite mad. Philippe had recognized a golden opportunity to make good use of these rumors, though, for he'd been seeking to estrange Richard from his father, just as he'd done with Richard's brothers. So he'd seen to it that Richard heard the stories, sure that would keep Richard from reconciling with Henry as he'd so often done in the past. Instead, Richard had turned that weapon against him after becoming king, declaring that he could not wed a woman who was reputed to be his father's concubine.

Four years after their confrontation in Messina, Philippe still fumed at the memory, one of the most mortifying moments of his life. His alliance with Richard had always been a precarious one, for they were too unlike for a genuine friendship. But it was not until Richard's rejection of Alys that his hatred of the English king had become so intense, so all-consuming. And although he realized it was unfair, some of his anger had spilled over onto Alys, too, a living symbol of the way those accursed Angevins had mocked and shamed the French Crown. He'd continued to press for her return, of course. But now what was he going to do with her?

⚜

PHILIPPE WAS STANDING IN FRONT of his command tent, watching the horizon for the telltale dust cloud that would herald the approach of his sister's escort. His bodyguards hovered nearby, but gave him space, aware of his preoccupied mood. The Bishop of Beauvais showed no such sensitivity, strolling over to say with a grin, "Soon now, eh? I suppose it would be rude to ask her outright if she'd been bedded by the old king."

"It would," Philippe said tersely. He was grateful to his cousin for all he'd done to make life difficult for Richard in the Holy Land and for helping to rid him of Ingeborg. He also valued the bishop as a superb soldier, more at home on the battlefield than behind an altar. But Beauvais's sense of humor could be a trial at times.

"I was jesting, Cousin," Beauvais said mildly, although he could not keep from rolling his eyes, thinking Philippe would not recognize a joke if he fell over one in the road. "The best place to hide an embarrassment is behind convent walls. I can suggest several nunneries if you'd like."

"That will not be necessary. I decided that marriage would be a better solution than having her take holy vows."

"Good luck finding a husband for her. Whether she was Henry's concubine or not, she's still damaged goods and well past her youth."

"As it happens, I've already found one." Philippe permitted himself a faint, satisfied smile. "Guillaume, the Count of Ponthieu."

"Ponthieu? How'd you manage that? She's old enough to be his mother!"

"She is also the sister of the French king. And I promised him that I'd give her the county of Eu and the castle at Arques as her marriage portion, which he found very appealing."

"I daresay he did. But I thought you agreed to renounce any claim to Eu and Arques as part of the peace terms with Richard."

Philippe shrugged. "It must have slipped my mind."

Beauvais laughed. "I'm considered the cynic in the family, but I think you could give me lessons, Cousin!"

Philippe's brows drew together, for he did not see his actions as cynical. He was merely doing what had to be done, what was best for France. And if Alys failed to give Ponthieu an heir and his lands then escheated to the Crown, so much the better. Just then a shout warned of approaching riders. "Stay to welcome her with me," he instructed the other man. "I was four years old when she was sent off to the Angevin court, so she is a stranger to me in all but blood. I just hope I can recognize her."

"I can help with that," Beauvais said as the escort came into view. "There are only three women. One is too old to be Alys and the other one is too plain. Look at that receding chin and small, pinched mouth. Can you see Henry lusting after her? No, the pretty lass in the green mantle must be your sister and my cousin."

He was proven to be right a few moments later as the women were assisted to dismount. As soon as Alys was out of her sidesaddle, she sank down in a graceful curtsy, saying, "My lord king." Philippe was disconcerted by what she did next, though. Casting propriety to the winds, she flung herself into his arms. "Oh, Brother, I am so happy to be home!"

He patted her shoulder. "I am glad you are home, too, Alys." When he introduced her to their cousin, she pleased Beauvais by curtsying again and kissing his ring respectfully. An awkward silence fell then, broken only when Philippe said briskly, "You must be hungry. There is a meal waiting for you in my tent."

They'd been joined by several of his lords and he gave Mathieu de Montmorency the honor of escorting Alys and her attendants into the tent. Beauvais hung back to murmur that Ponthieu was luckier than he deserved, for Alys seemed biddable and looked years younger than thirty-five. Philippe thought she *acted* younger, too, and wondered if that was because she'd been living for so long like a bird in a gilded cage, of the world but not really in it.

The dinner went better than Philippe had expected, in great measure due to Mathieu de Montmorency's gallantry, for he devoted all his attention to Alys and did not let the conversation lag. Philippe was nonetheless relieved when the meal was done, for in truth, he and Alys had very little to say to each other. He certainly had no interest in hearing her talk of the years she'd passed as a betrothed/hostage/political pawn.

Alys seemed disappointed when Philippe announced abruptly that he'd escort her to the tent that had been set up for her use, but she made no protest and he thought that Beauvais was right about her being biddable, which was in her favor. Accompanied by Beauvais, Mathieu, Druon de Mello, and several other lords, they attracted a lot of attention, for all were curious about the king's sister, who was both unfortunate and infamous. After she expressed pleasure at the tent's furnishings, Philippe gave her an obligatory kiss on the cheek, saying she should get a good night's rest, for they were leaving for Mantes in the morning.

"Mantes?" Alys sounded puzzled and he realized she knew nothing of French geography. "Is that on the way to Paris, Brother? I am eager to see it again, for I confess my memories have grown dim over time."

Best to get it over with. "Well, I am sure that your husband will be happy to take you to Paris, Sister."

"Husband?" She looked as bewildered as a child, and he felt a dart of discomfort.

"Yes, I am delighted to tell you that I've made a fine match for you. At Mantes, you are to be wed to the Count of Ponthieu."

"Who?"

"You will be very pleased with him, Alys," Philippe assured her. "He is highborn, handsome, young..." That caused Beauvais to chortle, which Philippe deliberately ignored. Leaning over, he kissed Alys quickly on the cheek again.

"Unfortunately, I cannot remain with you any longer. But I know you must have many questions about your husband-to-be, and our cousin will be happy to stay and answer them for you."

Beauvais did not think that was so amusing. Before he or the stunned Alys could object, Philippe bowed over her hand and lifted the tent flap, a slight smile hovering at the corners of his mouth. Let Beauvais be the one to tell her she'd be wedding a stripling not yet seventeen.

❦

LONGCHAMP RETURNED FROM HIS TRIP to the imperial court in late October. Heinrich had not been pleased by the prospect of peace, he reported, but he brought Richard further proof that, despite his reputation for tactless and arrogant behavior, he could be both diplomatic and persuasive on his king's behalf. He'd managed to convince Heinrich that he and Richard were natural allies against the French, but only if he stopped making threats and offered instead a gesture of good faith. Much to Richard's surprise, Longchamp had talked Heinrich into agreeing to release some of his hostages and to remit the remaining seventeen thousand marks of his ransom as recompense for what he'd lost to the French king during his captivity. With his chancellor basking in the glow of his successful mission, Richard prepared to meet Philippe to ratify a peace treaty that neither king expected to be long-lasting.

❦

RICHARD AROSE EARLY ON the morning of November 8, as the conference was to begin at nine o'clock. Soon after they left camp, they were met by the Archbishop of Reims, the French king's uncle, who explained that Philippe was still consulting with his council and wished to delay the meeting for a few hours. Richard returned to his camp to wait, but as the afternoon dragged on, he lost patience and ordered his men to saddle up.

The French tents were in sight when the men saw horsemen coming out to meet them. Richard's jaw muscles tightened when he recognized the lead rider, possibly the one man he loathed more than the French king. The Bishop of Beauvais reined in his stallion, calling out abruptly, "There is no need to proceed any farther. My master the French king will not be meeting with you, for he charges you with breach of faith and perjury. You gave him your sworn word that you would be here at the third hour of the day and it is now the ninth hour."

Richard and his men had listened, incredulous. Several started to argue, pointing out that they'd been delayed by Philippe's own uncle, but Richard held up a hand for silence. "Tell the French king that he did not have to go to such ludicrous lengths to repudiate the peace talks. If he wants war, I am quite willing to accommodate him."

Instead of turning around, though, he rode straight toward the bishop, whose hand dropped instinctively to the hilt of his sword. For a long moment, Richard stared at the other man. "One of these days, Beauvais, your luck is going to run out. You're going to meet me, not in a German dungeon or at a peace conference, but on the battlefield."

The bishop was not intimidated. "I'll look forward to it," he said with a sneer.

Richard's teeth bared in what was not a smile. "Then you're an even bigger fool than I thought," he said, and so much hatred flashed between the two men that several of those watching made ready to intervene if need be. But Richard was willing to wait, so sure was he that a day of reckoning was coming. He was grateful to God for striking down Leopold of Austria and he hoped that Heinrich would also suffer divine retribution. He intended, though, to deal with the French king and the Bishop of Beauvais himself.

❧

RICHARD WAS NOT LONG in learning why Philippe had subverted the peace talks. Two days later, the French king led six hundred knights in a spectacular raid upon the port of Dieppe, which Richard had recovered earlier in the summer. Philippe and his men destroyed the town and used Greek fire to set the ships in the harbor alight. Richard was besieging Arques Castle when he heard of the Dieppe attack. Leaving the siege, he set off in pursuit and caught up with the French as they passed through thick woods. He and his men bloodied Philippe's rearguard, but once again the French king eluded him.

❧

RICHARD DID NOT UNDERSTAND why his sleep was still so disturbed and fitful nigh on twenty months after he'd regained his freedom. He continued to be haunted by bad dreams that seemed to have their own reality, so vivid and intense were they, and he'd learned to rely upon Arne to rescue him from the horrors of his own imagination. When he was awakened now by a hand gently touching his shoulder, he jerked upright in the bed, his eyes searching Arne's face. "What—was I having another of those accursed dreams?"

The youth quickly shook his head. "No, sire. One of the garrison of Issoudun Castle has ridden in, insisting he must see you straightaway."

"Fetch him," Richard directed, relieved that he'd not been revisiting Trifels Castle this night. After every nightmare, he hoped that it would be the last one, and those hopes would rise as time passed. Eventually, though, the dreams always came back.

It was late November and his bedchamber at Vaudreuil Castle was cold, the brazier of coals giving off little heat; he could see ice skimming the surface of a nearby laver of water. With a sigh, he swung his legs over the side of the bed, knowing an exigent message signaled the end of sleep. He was almost dressed by the time the man was ushered into the bedchamber. Richard had entrusted Issoudun Castle to Guilhem de Préaux and his brother Jean until he could choose a permanent castellan for the stronghold, and he recognized one of Guilhem's knights.

"Sire, Issoudun Castle is under siege by the French king. They swooped down upon us without warning and took control of the town. The castle has not fallen, though, at least not yet. My lord Guilhem bade me tell you that they refused Philippe's demands for surrender and will try to hold out until you can come to their aid."

CHAPTER TWENTY-EIGHT

❧

R ichard's father had been famed for the speed of his campaigns; the French king was once heard to grumble that it was almost as if Henry could fly, so swiftly did he travel the length and breadth of his far-flung empire. Henry would have been proud of Richard's lightning dash to Issoudun, for each day he'd covered a distance that would normally have taken three days to do. He and his small band of handpicked knights arrived on an icy November night, the sky swathed in storm clouds, a gusting wind making it likely that the French sentries were more interested in sheltering from the cold than in keeping vigil. At least that was what Richard and his men hoped.

They'd gathered in a wooded copse overlooking the French siege camp. Dawn was still hours away and blackness shrouded the countryside, but they could make out the blurred outlines of the town walls and the towering castle keep. Philippe did not operate his siege engines in continual shifts as Richard liked to do, and he'd halted the bombardment at dark. Fires burned in the camp, but there was no sign of movement, the tents tightly staked against the wind. The scene looked deceptively peaceful, for the damage done by trebuchets and mangonels was cloaked by the night. Within the town they knew what they'd find: bodies piled like firewood until they could be buried, looted shops, houses commandeered by Philippe's knights. Some of the citizens would have fled to the castle, others to the adjacent Benedictine abbey of Notre-Dame, but many might have stayed, for Issoudun had been under French control until Richard had captured it in July. If they did, they likely regretted it, for soldiers saw plunder as their right, and they rarely drew fine distinctions when the opportunity presented itself. Whatever its loyalties, Issoudun would have suffered the fate of any town taken by storm. But the suffering of its people was hidden behind its stone walls, not particularly redoubtable, yet still a challenge to the men discussing its defenses in this quiet forest grove.

"This will not be easy," Richard admitted. "The castle and the abbey of Notre-Dame and several churches are separated from the town by formidable walls. Its main gate leads into the town, but it has a second gate in its south wall. We are not going to be able to get in that way, for the River Theols flows around the town to the west and the south. Moreover, even Philippe would know enough to have that gate well guarded. So our only chance to reach the castle will be by getting into the town first, and it is walled, too, although they are not as high as the castle fortifications."

There was a silence as they considered that, for they had no siege engines, nor the numbers to confront the French army in the open. "Well," André said, "I assume you do not mean for us to fly over the walls. So how do you intend to accomplish this feat?"

"Remember how we took Messina." It was not a question, for most of the men with him now had also been with him when he'd forced his way into the Sicilian city through a poorly guarded postern gate. "There is a postern gate at Issoudun, too, in the south wall, and it is not protected by the river, which curves away from the town by then. I noticed it when Mercadier and I took Issoudun, although we had no need to make use of it. I'd wager that Philippe did not bother to do an inspection of the walls; what he knows about conducting war could fill an acorn shell. The town is asleep and Philippe's guards probably are, too. If we could open that gate, we'd be in the city ere the French even knew what was happening."

It was too dark to see their faces clearly, but he heard their murmurs of approval. Stealth was their only weapon—that and the French king's carelessness. "We are agreed, then," he said. "One of us will use the hemp ladder to scale the wall, then make his way to the postern gate and open it for the rest."

"Not you, though!" This was said by André, Morgan, and Guillain in such perfect unison that it could have been rehearsed, and the other knights laughed.

"I did not say I'd be the one to do it," Richard protested, but the corner of his mouth was twitching and after a moment, he conceded, "Well, the idea may have crossed my mind."

That came as no surprise to any of them; these men knew Richard as well as anyone on God's earth. "I ought to be the one," André insisted, pointing out that he was familiar with Issoudun, for his castle at Châteauroux was less than twenty miles away. But after some bickering, they settled upon Guillain; he also knew the town well, and for a big man, he could move as quietly as any cat.

The French had taken Issoudun so quickly that they'd had no need to encircle it, and now that they had the castle garrison penned up within the town walls, they relied upon the River Theols and sentries to guard the stronghold's second gate. Their camp was spread out to the north so they could aim their siege engines at the castle's main gate. Richard and his knights gave it a wide detour, also making sure to avoid the suburbs outside the town walls, for an alert watchdog could easily doom their mission. They took shelter in woods that gave them a view of the postern gate, watching tensely as Guillain cautiously made his way across the open fields. Denied moonlight, he had to navigate by the sound of the river to his left and by the spire rising above the town walls, for the hospital, Hôtel-Dieu, was close by the postern gate.

He was soon swallowed up in darkness, but each man could follow him in his mind's eye, knowing he meant to fling a hemp rope ladder fitted with grappling hooks toward the top of the wall embrasure. The wall was not so high that it could not be done, but it might take several attempts for the hooks to catch, with Guillain sweating it out as he waited to see if any curious faces would appear over the battlements, drawn by the scraping of iron on stone, a sound that would be echoing in his ears louder than thunder. No one asked what they'd do if he failed. They had no backup plan, but they were confident that Richard would come up with one if need be; he always did.

After what seemed an eternity to the waiting men, they saw the postern gate crack open, the agreed-upon signal. Richard glanced around at the others and grinned. "Those French whoresons are snug in their beds. Let's wake them up." And with that, they spurred their horses toward the postern gate as it was flung open wide.

As they plunged through the gate, Guillain ran toward Morgan, who was leading his stallion, and hastily swung up into the saddle. Richard and André knew their way through the maze of narrow, twisting streets, so their men let them lead the way as they galloped by the Hôtel-Dieu, using the spire of St Cyr's church as a landmark. By now sleepy guards were appearing on the wall battlements, drawn by the clamor. The door of a nearby house opened and a man stumbled out, holding a lantern aloft. André reached down and snatched the lantern, flinging it onto a roof and setting the thatch alight. As Richard urged his stallion past St Cyr's, a man came at him from his left and he wielded his shield like a weapon, knocking the soldier off his feet. Another man bravely but rashly tried to grab Fauvel's reins, screaming and falling back when the destrier savaged him. Dogs had begun to bark and shutters were being thrown open. There were cries of "Fire," one of the great dangers of town life, and they could hear muffled shouts from the siege camp as the French army was awakened by the commotion. Soldiers rudely torn from sleep were bolting from houses, half armed and confused, not sure what was happening. But most of them hastily retreated, for they were at a distinct disadvantage against men on horseback. Some of the guards on the walls had begun to fire crossbows, but it was still too dark to aim properly and a moving target was hard to hit. All around them was chaos, and Richard and his men gloried in it.

Shouting the battle cry of the English Royal House, they raced through the small cemetery. Not much blood had been spilled so far and none of Richard's men had been hurt, but that could change in a hurry if the castle garrison did not admit them. They could see sudden activity on the castle battlements, and from the cheering, it was clear that the garrison realized these new arrivals were on their side. Ahead lay the gatehouse that connected the castle to the town, and to their relief, they saw the gates were already open, the portcullis being winched up. Richard had scored his first great military triumph at twenty-one by forcing his way into Taillebourg with the retreating castle garrison, but now there were no French close enough to try the same trick, and as soon as they were safely inside, the gates were slammed shut and barred again.

The street was thronged with soldiers, monks from the abbey, and townspeople who'd taken refuge in the castle precincts. A priest from St Étienne's ran alongside them, offering breathless blessings as they rode into the castle's outer bailey. Once they dismounted, they were engulfed by laughing men. Guilhem and Jean de Préaux were pushing their way toward them. "I was in the neighborhood," Richard said, "so we thought we'd stop by to see how you were doing." That evoked more laughter, and for a time, the scene in the castle bailey was as chaotic as it had been in the streets of the town—except that this was an uproarious celebration of deliverance, so sure were the garrison that they'd been saved by the king's arrival.

The jubilation was not universal, though. Jean de Préaux's squire was watching the excitement with a frown, for Alard did not understand why they were rejoicing. All the English king had done was to put himself at peril, too, and he did not see how that benefited the garrison. Most likely they were in even greater danger. He could not see Richard surrendering and if the castle was taken by storm, Philippe would have the right to hang them all. Vexed and baffled that the king was being acclaimed for joining them in the trap, he finally said querulously, "But will our king's presence not encourage the French king to even greater efforts now?"

"Alard!" Jean said sharply, not liking the youth's tone in the least. "Mind your mouth!"

Richard was untroubled by the question. Smiling at the discomfited youngster, he said, "That is exactly what I am counting upon, lad."

PHILIPPE WAS A LIGHT SLEEPER and he'd been awakened by the noise even before one of his knights hastened into his command tent with word that a fire had broken out in the town. Ordering his squire to fetch his clothes, he dressed quickly, for if the fire got out of control, it could imperil his siege of the castle. When a soldier came running to tell him armed riders were in the town, he was angered that the garrison would dare a sortie like that and he vowed they'd pay a high price for their defiance. But his main concern was in putting out the fire, and he sent men-at-arms to fight the blaze, telling them to tear down adjoining houses to create a fire break. By now faint glimmers of light were visible along the horizon, and he broke his fast with wine and cheese. It was then that his day took an even more troubling turn, for several men entered the tent with an unlikely story, claiming that those armed riders had gotten in through a postern gate and fought their way into the castle.

Philippe was skeptical, not wanting to believe his sentries had been so lax. What followed was even more improbable. One of his household knights plunged into the tent, insisting that the invaders had been led by the English king.

"That is nonsense. Richard could not possibly have gotten to Issoudun so quickly; my spies say he is two hundred miles away in Normandy. Nor would he have forced his way into the castle. Even Richard would not be that mad. Go find out if the fire still burns and do not bring me back ridiculous rumors like this, Ivo."

To Philippe's surprise, Ivo held his ground. "My liege, I have seen the English king often enough to know him on sight. I tell you I saw him in the town, astride that dun stallion of his, and he is now in the castle."

Philippe still did not believe him, but the knight had served him loyally in the past, and so he summoned up enough patience to say, "I do not doubt that you think you saw him, Ivo. But it was dark, and I am sure there was great confusion—"

"Sire!" This shout came from outside the tent. Putting aside the rest of his breakfast, Philippe buckled his scabbard and ducked under the tent flap. A crowd had gathered outside, and as soon as he emerged, they began to point toward the town. Philippe was relieved not to see flames shooting up into the sky. But then he saw what they were trying to call to his attention—the banner flying above the castle keep: three gold lions on a field of scarlet.

Philippe rarely cursed; the most he allowed himself was an occasional "By St James's lance!" Now, though, he blurted out a shocked "Jesus wept!" Staring up at that familiar banner in disbelief, he said, "You were right, Ivo. That lunatic has trapped himself!"

His men were laughing and slapping one another on the back, unable to credit their good luck, for they felt sure their king would reward them handsomely for the capture of his greatest enemy. Philippe had yet to take his eyes from the castle. He'd celebrated his thirtieth birthday that August, but most people felt he looked older than his years, for his somber demeanor aged him, as did his premature baldness. Now, though, he was smiling, a smile so triumphant that he briefly seemed like the carefree youth he'd never been.

"I always knew Richard's arrogance would be his undoing," he told his soldiers. "God is indeed good, for He has delivered the English king into my hands."

RICHARD PASSED THE NEXT FEW DAYS inspecting the castle defenses. He showed the Préaux brothers that by shortening the sling of their trebuchet, they'd increase the trajectory of the stone's flight, allowing it to cover more distance and do more damage. He prowled around the storerooms, making sure they still had plentiful rations even though he did not expect to need them. He visited the wounded soldiers, joked with the men on guard duty, joined his knights in taunting the French, and took his turn shooting his crossbow from the castle walls; many of high birth scorned crossbows as weapons fit only for routiers, but Richard was hands-on in all that he did and he was almost as lethal with a crossbow as he was with a sword.

He was up on the battlements on the first Sunday of Advent, amusing himself by exchanging insults with some of the French knights below, wanting to know why the French king had not yet come calling. They responded with a bombardment of stones that rained down into the bailey but did little damage. When the besieged men mocked their aim, one of Philippe's routiers sent a crossbow bolt streaking through the air toward the English king. It missed Richard by half a foot and he jeered, asking if that had been fired by a blind man, but his knights thought it had come too close for comfort and Morgan and Guillain lured him off the wall by saying André needed to talk to him.

Richard reluctantly left the battlements for the less interesting environs of the great hall. André was sharpening his sword on a whetstone, looking up in surprise as Richard joined him in the window-seat. "Help yourself," he said, gesturing toward a bowl of roasted chestnuts. "When do you think the French will realize that you seem in suspiciously high spirits for a doomed man?"

"When it is too late." Richard reached for a chestnut, peeled back the skin, and popped it into his mouth. "I'm going to hold my Christmas Court at Poitiers. You and Denise will be there, of course?"

"Denise will make me come," André said, with a mock sigh. "We'll bring my eldest lad. He's five now, old enough to—"

He stopped abruptly. Richard's head came up, too, for he'd also heard the shouting. A moment later, Morgan appeared and hurried across the hall toward them, saying that the French camp looked like a beehive that had been knocked over, with soldiers swarming in all directions.

"I daresay they've just found out that Mercadier is about to pay them a visit." Richard leaned back in the window-seat and began to laugh. "Poor Philippe . . . so sure he was the cat and now it turns out that he was the mouse all along."

❧

THE FRENCH FOUND THEMSELVES trapped between Richard and Mercadier, outnumbered and outwitted. This time there would be no hasty retreat, for there was nowhere to run. They were faced with only two choices, both of them equally toxic to the French king—fight a battle they were sure to lose or ask for terms. Philippe had always been a realist and he was not about to sacrifice his life to save his pride. He asked for terms.

❧

ON DECEMBER 5, the English and French kings met alone near the bank of the River Theols, within view of the two armies. It was the first time they'd seen each other since Philippe had abandoned the crusade four years ago, and Richard felt anger stirring as he looked upon the younger man, thinking of all Philippe had done to keep him from regaining his freedom. He curbed his temper, though, for this was neither the time nor the place to indulge it.

"As I see it," he said coolly, "there are two roads we can take. This skirmishing can continue and I can keep on inflicting humiliating defeats on you. But as much as I enjoy doing it, I think we'd both be better served by making peace."

Philippe's mouth twisted. "Peace on your terms!"

"Yes. The victor gets to dictate terms to the loser."

The taste in Philippe's mouth was as bitter as bile. "What are the terms?" They were as onerous as he'd expected, reflecting the military reality of their respective positions, and far more favorable to Richard than the treaty they'd signed that past year. Richard would regain all he'd lost in Normandy except the Norman Vexin, which he would agree to cede to Philippe. He demanded that Philippe cede the rights to six strategic castles in Berry, including Issoudun, and formally recognize that the counts of Angoulême and Perigueux and the Viscount of Brosse owed homage to him as Duke of Aquitaine. Philippe was to renounce any claims to the counties of Eu and Aumale, Évreux, the castles of Arques and Driencourt, and all of the other conquests he'd made northeast of the River Seine. Richard in turn would quitclaim to Philippe six important border castles, and he would agree to quitclaim Auvergne to the French king.

Despite some concessions on Richard's part, there was little in this proposed treaty that Philippe found easy to swallow, for he'd be losing much that he'd gained during Richard's captivity in Germany and be totally shut out of Berry. He continued to listen in a stony silence as Richard said he'd accept the switch in loyalties of one of his vassals, Hugh de Gornai, but that if Philippe's ally, the Count of Toulouse, did not want to be included in the peace, the French king could not offer him any aid in a war with England. When Richard demanded, though, that the Earl of Leicester be freed, that was too much for Philippe's self-control, and he said sharply, "I will not agree to that!"

"You have no choice," Richard said, just as sharply, "for that is not open to negotiation." He maneuvered his stallion alongside Philippe's bay mount, a more docile animal than the fiery Fauvel. The bay shifted nervously when Fauvel pinned his ears back and Philippe glared at Richard, thinking the English king was trying to show up his poor horsemanship before their watching men. But Richard had no thoughts to spare for a skittish horse. "You've been punishing Leicester because he made a fool out of you at Rouen, but it ends now. Your grievance is with me, and if you find these terms unpalatable, we can settle our differences here and now, on the battlefield, and let God decide who is in the right."

Their armies were not close enough to hear what was being said and could only wait tensely to see if they would fight that day or not. Even the most bloodthirsty of soldiers shrank from a pitched battle, which was so rare that most had never taken part in one. So when the two kings eventually dismounted and gave each other the formal kiss of peace that signified an agreement had been reached, both sides erupted in cheering, grateful that none would die this day, less than three weeks until the Nativity of the Holy Saviour.

ELEANOR WAS DELIGHTED that Richard had chosen her favorite city for his Christmas Court. She'd missed so many family Christmases during her years of confinement that she would never take one for granted again. She'd been given an enthusiastic welcome into the city, for she'd always been popular with the townspeople, who were proud that she had worn the crowns of two realms. In the splendid great hall of the royal palace, she eclipsed her daughter-in-law without even trying, and some of the women guests pitied Berengaria, knowing that she would not be England's queen as long as Eleanor lived.

After a meal as bountiful as the Advent diet would allow, Eleanor joined Richard on the dais and, as music and spirits soared, he shared with her news both personal and political, telling her his chancellor had brought back word from Germany that her grandson Henrik and his bride were the proud parents of a healthy son. "You are now a great-grandmother twice over," he teased, and smiled when she pointed out that he was now a great-uncle. "I had not considered that," he admitted. "I doubt that we'll ever meet Henrik's little lad, but Richenza and Jaufre will be bringing their son to the Christmas Court."

"Jaufre is coming?" Eleanor asked in surprise, and he explained that Jaufre felt it could be risked since a truce now existed between England and France, with the final treaty to be signed in January. "I was not thinking of him fearing Philippe's wrath, but yours," she responded, and was surprised again when he said that he'd forgiven Jaufre for his defection to the French king.

"I declared his English lands forfeit to teach him there is a price to be paid for disloyalty. But I returned them to him earlier this year, for a king needs to mix the sour with the sweet."

Richard then told her that he'd succeeded in getting his former clerk Master Fulk de Poitiers elected as Bishop of Durham, and Eleanor found herself thinking that he'd been very generous to the men who'd been with him in Germany. "I was astonished to learn that Heinrich had agreed to remit the rest of the ransom and free some of your hostages," she said, and Richard glanced around to make sure they could speak freely.

"Longchamp deserves the credit for that miracle," he said. "But I suspect that Leopold's gruesome fate may have played a small role, too. There were times when I wondered if Heinrich was mad. Yet even a madman must fear God's wrath, and I daresay there were many German churchmen to whisper that in Heinrich's ear."

He paused to take a swallow of wine. "It looks as if there'll be no marriage between Aenor and Philippe's son, for that idea seems to have died when Philippe rejected the earlier peace. Did I tell you, Maman, that Philippe's envoys hinted during those summer negotiations that he might be interested in another marriage, one with Joanna?"

"No, you did not!"

"It was never a formal proposal, just put out there to see how we'd react to it."

"I can well imagine how Joanna reacted," she said, and he laughed.

"She vowed that she'd sooner wed Saladin's brother! After the way Philippe has maltreated Ingeborg, he'll find few men willing to offer their daughters or sisters to him. Even if a father cares little for his daughter, he'd not want to risk being shamed the way Ingeborg's brother was."

"Speaking of marriages . . ." Eleanor glanced meaningfully across the hall toward the Countess of Aumale and her new husband. "Hawisa and Baldwin seem to be getting on. At least she is smiling. Whenever I saw her with William de Forz, she looked as if she'd just eaten something that disagreed with her."

Richard had given Hawisa and Baldwin a lavish wedding, but hadn't thought much about their marriage after that. "Baldwin seems content enough," he said, "though he's not one to complain. For certes, they are happier than Constance and Chester."

Eleanor followed his gaze and found the young Earl of Chester, standing alone as he watched the dancers. "He does not look as if he is enjoying himself," she agreed. "Constance is not with him?"

"No. Her barons chased him out of Brittany again, and he is very bitter about it."

"So he'll be of no help in convincing Constance to send Arthur to your court," Eleanor mused and Richard shrugged. But her words caught the attention of her younger son. John had drifted toward the dais, always on the alert to overhear something useful. He did not like the sound of that, for if Arthur was raised at Richard's court, his brother might well conclude that the boy would make a satisfactory heir.

Richard had signaled for a servant to refill their wine cups. Eleanor clinked hers playfully against his, saying, "Shall we drink to the peace with Philippe? How long do you expect it to last?"

"Just long enough," he said, and she gave him such an easy, intimate smile that John, watching, felt a twinge of envy.

Eleanor sipped her wine as the dancers spun in a carol, remembering how difficult it had been to get Henry to dance, remembering Christmas Courts past, when their marriage had still been a source of pleasure to them both; four of their children had been conceived during the holiday revelries. Those memories were bittersweet, and she turned back to Richard. "I heard a remarkable story recently, that the chieftain of the Assassins sent Philippe a letter absolving you of blame in Conrad of Montferrat's murder. Is that true, Richard?"

"Well, it is true that Philippe got such a letter." Much to John's annoyance, Richard lowered his voice so that only Eleanor could hear. "Even after I was exonerated at Heinrich's court, Philippe continued to accuse me of the murder. I'll admit it angered me, for not only was it a slur on my honor, it was an insult. As if I'd need to resort to hired killers if there was a man I wanted dead!"

Richard moved his chair closer to his mother's seat before continuing. "Longchamp knew it vexed me that Philippe was still muddying the waters, so he suggested that the Old Man of the Mountain write and tell Philippe that I played no part in Conrad's death."

"Ah, I see.... I confess I was puzzled why a Saracen bandit would take the trouble to clear a Christian king."

"You're much more astute than Philippe, Maman. That was a question he'd never thought to ask. Of course, Longchamp composed such a convincing letter that I half believed it myself," he said with a grin. "It seems to have convinced Philippe, for he has stopped accusing me of the murder. That makes me think the damned fool really thought I'd hired Assassins to murder Conrad. And I know who is to blame for that—his cousin. That bastard Beauvais probably told Philippe that I was found standing over Conrad's body with a bloody knife."

Richard's amusement faded as soon as he mentioned the bishop's name. Swallowing the rest of his wine, he got to his feet. "I've not yet danced with my wife, so I'd best remedy that." He paused, though, before starting toward the steps. "At times I think I do not deserve absolution of my sins," he said, so softly that she could barely hear him, "for I cannot do as God demands and forgive my enemies. Even if it imperils my immortal soul, I can never forgive Heinrich, Philippe, and Beauvais."

He did not wait for her response, stepped off the dais, and moved away in search of his queen. Eleanor stayed where she was, her expression so guarded that John could only speculate what had been said in that last, private exchange.

❧

AFTER A CHRISTMAS MASS, the king's family and guests were served a feast of wild boar, roast goose, and stewed capon, and then watched a play, *The Mystery of Adam*, which was performed out in the open in front of the church of Notre-Dame; it was extremely popular because it was done in French instead of Latin, and it attracted a large audience, who cheered the actors, their king, and his mother with equal enthusiasm. Darkness had enveloped Poitiers by the time they returned to the palace.

John was not enjoying himself, feeling like a tolerated trespasser rather than a welcomed guest. He was bored, too. The day's festivities were drawing to an end and people were chatting amiably, waiting for the king to signal that it was time for them all to seek their beds. Until that happened, John could only roam the hall, eavesdropping at random.

Feminine laughter drawing his attention, he glanced toward the women gathered around Will Marshal's young wife. To judge from their exclamations, he guessed Isabel had just confided she was with child again. Would that be her fourth? Or her fifth? Since her marriage, she seemed to be perpetually pregnant. No wonder Marshal watched over her like an old bull with one prize heifer. John's gaze shifted from the radiant Isabel to his sister-in-law. Berengaria was smiling, and he wondered what it cost her to look so happy for a girl who'd given her husband two sons within their first two years of marriage. Whilst he was deeply thankful that she was not as fertile as Isabel, he surprised himself by feeling a glimmer of sympathy for her now. He knew what it was like to be judged and found wanting.

Nearby, his mother and his niece Richenza were engaged in an animated conversation, and he moved within hearing range. He thought he'd been unobtrusive, but Eleanor noticed him; he wondered sometimes if she slept with her eyes open so she'd not miss anything. "We were just talking about Otto, John, and the Scots king's remarkable proposal."

John had heard rumors about that. Apparently despairing that his wife would ever give him a son, King William had suggested to Richard that Otto wed his two-year-old daughter, Margaret, a marriage that would make him the heir to the Scots throne. "So the story is true, then?" John asked. "But I seem to remember my father proposing a marriage between William and Richenza about ten years ago and the Pope would not permit it because they were related within the forbidden degree. If the Church would not let Richenza wed William, why would it allow Otto to wed William's daughter?"

"Different Pope," Richenza said succinctly, sounding very much like her worldly grandmother at that moment.

John expressed his hope that the marriage would come to pass, and he was not just being polite; he truly meant it. He liked Otto well enough and, looking ahead to a time when Richard's crown might rest upon his own head, having his nephew on the Scots throne could be very advantageous.

He soon lost interest in listening to Richenza praise her brother to the heavens, and excused himself. Richard was the center of attention, as usual, and as John wandered over, he found that his brother, André, and Morgan were telling Will Marshal and the other lords about their triumph at Issoudun. Their account was punctuated with much laughter, all at the French king's expense, and Richenza's husband was looking uncomfortable, for Philippe was Jaufre's liege lord, too. John had already heard about the trap Richard had sprung on the French king; Richard was never shy about trumpeting his successes. He found some amusement, though, in Jaufre's frozen smile and in the way his cousin Morgan kept glancing toward Joanna's Saracen handmaiden when he thought no one was looking. John did not understand why Morgan was brooding over her refusal to marry him; that sounded like the ideal situation to him, a woman willing to share his bed without nagging him to the altar.

He was about to move away when Richard suddenly changed the subject, saying that he had one less enemy now. That sparked John's curiosity and he paused to listen as Richard told the other men he'd heard that Isaac Comnenus had died suddenly that summer. "Rumor has it that he was poisoned by an agent of the Greek emperor," Richard revealed, "but however he died, the world is a better place without him."

John glanced back at the women, his gaze finding Isaac's daughter, Anna. If she was grieving for her father, she hid it well. She was laughing at something

Joanna had said, and she put John in mind of a ripe peach. He was tempted to find out if she tasted as sweet as she looked, but Brother Richard might take that amiss, and Joanna would for certes.

Richard was still talking about Isaac, and John had a dangerous impulse to point out that Isaac was not the only enemy Richard had lost that year, for the Bishop of Coventry's brother had died in a Dover dungeon. Robert de Nonant had been John's sworn man, but he thought de Nonant had been a fool to defy Richard so publicly at the German court, on the very day that Richard regained his freedom. He ought to have known better; kings were never defied with impunity. He'd still been sorry to hear of de Nonant's death, sure it had been a hard one, left alone in the dark as he slowly starved, for men did not thrive on bread and water. He did not give in to that reckless urge to mention de Nonant, though. The last thing he wanted to do was to remind Richard of his own dubious past. As he studied his brother now, he thought that de Nonant's sad death might be a blessing in disguise, for he dared not forget that Richard was not as quick to forgive as he once was. De Nonant had found that out too late. God willing, he'd not make the same mistake.

John smothered a yawn, hoping that Richard would soon bring the revelries to an end. His brother was in high spirits, though, enjoying himself, and not ready to call it a night. Seeing that Eleanor was now seated on the dais, he moved in her direction. Motivated by morbid curiosity, John followed. He got within earshot in time to hear Richard say, "There is something I want to discuss with you, Maman. I do not think anything will come of the Scots king's plan to make Otto his heir."

Eleanor looked surprised. "But I thought Hubert Walter was in York to discuss it further with the Scots?"

"He is, but it is likely to be a journey for naught. I've been told the Scots king's barons are adamantly opposed to the idea."

"I am sorry to hear that, Richard."

"I was, too. Otto has the potential to be a good king. But since he'll not be going to Scotland, I've been thinking about naming Otto as Count of Poitou. Would you be comfortable with that?"

John's breath stopped and, for a moment, he thought his heart had stopped, too. He'd not been genuinely alarmed to hear that Richard wanted to bring Arthur to his court, for he felt confident Constance and her barons would never agree; cutting off their noses to spite their faces was a favorite Breton sport. But naming Otto as Count of Poitou could be a first step toward making him Duke of Aquitaine, and if Richard would do that, he might well be willing to make Otto his heir. John waited tensely for his mother's answer, but once again she disappointed him, saying that she thought it was a good idea. John bit his lip to keep from protesting, trying to take comfort in the reminder that Otto was hundreds of miles away at the imperial court and likely to remain there for years to come, too valuable a hostage for Heinrich to relinquish.

By now Joanna and Berengaria had joined them, followed by André and Denise, Jaufre and Richenza, and Will Marshal and Isabel. John's earlier suspicions were confirmed when Eleanor and Richard congratulated Isabel on her pregnancy, and he watched as Berengaria summoned up a heartbreaking smile. They were soon talking again about Richard's victory at Issoudun and the treaty he'd forced upon the French king, and John hid another yawn.

"It was a good day," Richard acknowledged. "But it was only a beginning. I mean to strip away Philippe's remaining allies, one by one, until he is utterly isolated and alone."

He sounded as if he had a plan in mind to do just that, and Joanna found herself feeling a sudden unease. Philippe's most important allies were Baldwin, the new Count of Flanders, and Raimond, the new Count of Toulouse. While she'd always known that Raimond de St Gilles was an avowed enemy of her House, she realized now that she did not want to see her brother leading an army against Raimond. Was Richard seriously thinking of pushing Maman's claim to Toulouse as her two husbands had done? She did not doubt that Richard would prevail if he met Raimond on the battlefield, but she hoped it would not come to that. She was loath to see the dogs of war unleashed upon the easygoing, pleasure-loving people of the sun-drenched South and their charming, controversial count. She turned away so no one could see her distress, hearing again a voice like melted honey, murmuring in her ear, *Farewell, my beautiful coward.*

John almost cheered when Richard finally rose, saying it was growing late. Slipping his arm around Berengaria's slender waist, he made ready to bid their guests farewell. They looked like the veritable image of marital harmony, John thought. But was he the only one to notice how little attention Richard had paid to his wife in the course of the evening? As he studied Berengaria, he thought, *No, I'm not the only one.*

People were beginning to approach the dais when there was a stir at the end of the hall. A moment later, men were being ushered in, wrapped in travel-stained mantles and fur-lined hats that Richard had not seen since leaving Germany. He took a step forward, but his niece was already in motion. Lifting her skirts, Richenza flew across the hall and flung herself into the arms of one of the new arrivals. The other guests looked startled, some shocked. But even before the youth removed his hat to reveal tousled dark hair, a face reddened with cold, and a smile bright enough to illuminate the hall all on its own, Richard knew. "Good God, it is Otto!"

Otto hastened toward the dais, his sister clinging to his arm, her eyes glistening with tears. When he started to kneel, Richard raised him up at once and embraced him warmly. He tried to kneel before his grandmother next, but Eleanor was having none of that, either, and kissed him, instead. There was such a commotion that it took a few moments before Otto could assure them that his little brother had been freed, too, by Heinrich, and had gone to join Henrik in Saxony.

"But I came straight to you, Uncle," he said to Richard. "I came home."

Richard introduced Otto to Joanna and Berengaria then, and looked around for his son, calling to Philip to come meet his cousin. It was the sort of emotional family reunion that the contentious Angevins rarely enjoyed, one that became even more jubilant when Otto told Berengaria that Heinrich had also agreed to release her brother Fernando. When it was his turn, John welcomed his nephew back with a smile and a hug. But all the while, his ears were echoing with Otto's euphoric, revealing words. *I came straight to you, Uncle. I came home.*

CHAPTER TWENTY-NINE

⚜

MARCH 1196

Norman Border

Constance knew that her Breton barons were not happy about her conference with the English king, for they were adamantly opposed to sending Arthur to the English court. She understood their fears, for she had always loathed Geoffrey's family. She mistrusted Richard, and that prideful bitch, his mother, and did not want to see Arthur entangled in their web. And yet . . . and yet. Arthur was nine now, old enough to be educated in a noble household, and a lifelong grudge against the Angevins was being challenged by her maternal instincts. If she agreed to send Arthur to Richard's court, that would greatly improve his chances of being named as Richard's heir if his queen failed to give him a son. She was determined that Arthur would govern Brittany once he came of age. But it would be a great destiny to become England's king, to rule the empire that was denied his father.

Turning in the saddle, she glanced at the men riding at her side: André de Vitré, his brother Alain de Dinan-Vitré, Geoffroi de Chateaubriant, Guillaume de Loheac, the Bishop of Vannes. They understood that they had to obey Richard's summons, for they owed fealty to him as Duke of Normandy. If she chose to give Richard the wardship of her son, they might grudgingly agree, but they'd not like it any. Neither would she. She shrank from the very thought—except for those days when she found herself tempted by that dangerous dream, a crown for her son. Geoffrey would have wanted it for Arthur. She did not doubt that; her husband's ambitions had burned with a white-hot flame. But Richard already had custody of her daughter. Could she bear to give him her son, too? What would be best for Arthur? For Brittany?

They were less than a mile from Pontorson Castle when they saw the dust clouds warning of approaching riders. The marches were often lawless and they straightened in their saddles, making sure their swords were loose in their scabbards. As the horsemen came into view, Constance felt a moment of instinctive unease at the sight of such a large band of armed men. But then she recognized the man on a bay stallion. "It is my husband," she said, sounding as if she thought the Earl of Chester was only slightly more welcome than a Norman or Breton bandit. Her barons watched grimly as the earl and Constance exchanged the frostiest of greetings, bristling when it became apparent that Chester intended to accompany them. Constance was less than thrilled, too, but she thought they'd not be burdened with Randolph's company for too long. His castle at St James de Beuvron was just ten miles away, and she hoped it was his likely destination.

Randolph guided his stallion alongside Constance's mare and his men dropped back, falling in behind her barons and their knights. Neither husband nor wife made any attempt at conversation, riding in silence, keeping their eyes on the road ahead. Constance was never more aware of her first husband's sardonic spirit than when she was in the company of her second. She could almost hear Geoffrey's voice, offering silken sympathy that she'd been yoked to a man who was so decent, so dutiful, so infernally dull—words that would never have been applied to Geoffrey himself. He would be ten years dead come August, and she still missed him, especially at night. He continued to come to her in dreams, some erotic, others unbearably painful, for even now she found it hard to accept that she'd lost him in a meaningless tournament mêlée. There was no justice in that, not even any sense.

Constance was relieved when Chester signaled to his men as they approached the turnoff to his castle at St James de Beuvron. But then she saw that he expected her to go with them. "Whilst I thank you for your offer of hospitality," she demurred, as politely as she could manage, "there are hours of daylight remaining. So we prefer to ride on."

"I must insist," he said, and as he spoke, his men executed what looked like a military maneuver, moving to surround the Bretons. They reacted with outrage, some even starting to draw their swords despite being greatly outnumbered. When Constance commanded them to halt, they did, but with such obvious reluctance that she knew it would take little for violence to break out. She did not want bloodshed, did not want her men to die for naught. Humoring her husband was the lesser of evils, and she grudgingly agreed to talk with him at the castle.

She was still seething at his heavy-handed assertion of his marital authority. Did the wretched man not realize that he'd just given her barons yet another gold-plated grievance? As they approached the earl's stronghold, she assured André that they'd soon be on the road again. Overhearing their exchange, Chester said coldly, "I think not." Constance turned to stare at him, and then she saw the men up on the castle battlements, saw the crossbows protruding from every embrasure, aiming at the Bretons.

For the first time, Constance felt alarm as well as anger. She hid it well, exchanging a brief look with André before raising her head proudly and riding beside the earl through the castle gatehouse. Her ladies were allowed to accompany her, but when her barons attempted to follow, they were turned back. It was only then that she realized her husband meant to be her gaoler, too.

Constance's fury was burning so hotly that she saw her surroundings through a red haze. Glaring at the earl, she said as loudly as she could, "As little as I liked it, I always did my duty as your wife. But never again. If you hope to claim your marital rights, I will have to be bound hand and foot and gagged first!"

Chester flushed darkly, for her defiance had been heard by all his men. "You flatter yourself, Madame. I would sooner take a badger into my bed!"

Constance curled her lip disdainfully, her outrage sustaining her as she and her women dismounted and were escorted to a bedchamber in the castle keep. It was not Randolph's, and she could take a shred of solace in that. It was a comfortable, well-furnished room, one suitable for a guest of her rank. But she was not a guest. She was Randolph's prisoner.

Juvetta and Emma fluttered around her helplessly as she strode to the window and jerked back the shutters. She could see her men milling about beyond the castle walls, stunned and demoralized by this unexpected ambush. Her hand tightening on the latch until her knuckles had gone bone-white, she spat, "Damn them both to Hell Everlasting!"

"Both, my lady?" Juvetta ventured, taking a hasty backward step when Constance turned away from the window, for she thought the duchess's dark eyes were glowing like red-hot coals.

"Yes, both! My cowardly husband and that Angevin hellspawn he serves!"

✦

WHEN RICHARD ARRIVED UNEXPECTEDLY at Fontevrault Abbey, Eleanor was very pleased to see the Earl of Leicester riding at his side. Despite agreeing to release the earl in the January peace treaty at Louvières, the French king had delayed doing so, even after the payment of a large ransom by the captive earl. Richard was finally forced to seek help from the Church in compelling Philippe to honor the treaty terms. Smiling now at Leicester as he kissed her hand, Eleanor expressed her pleasure that he'd finally regained his freedom.

"I am gladdened, too, Madame," he said, with a ready smile of his own. But he said no more than that about his lengthy confinement, and she honored his wish to keep the details of that unpleasant experience to himself; she'd learned from watching her son struggle with his own demons during the past two years.

Leaving Leicester, Guillain, and Morgan to entertain Eleanor's ladies, Richard drew Eleanor aside for a private conversation. As they settled into a window-seat, she studied him with a mother's discerning eye. He looked tired, and little wonder, for he'd all but lived in the saddle since his return from Germany. Even if he'd been besotted with Berengaria, she doubted that he'd have been able to find much time to spare for her. Her husband had been a restless soul, too, always on the move, but at least he'd had periods of peace during his reign. Richard did not have that luxury. Knowing better than to comment upon his appearance or to question him about his sleeping or eating habits, she smiled instead. "This is a pleasant surprise, Richard. I'd not expected to see you for another fortnight, not till your Easter Court."

"There will be no Easter Court, Maman. Last month the Earl of Chester abducted Constance as she was on the way to meet me in Normandy. And, of course, the Bretons are blaming me, sure he did it at my behest."

"Did he?"

"No." He leaned back in the seat, stretching out long, booted legs. "I'd have considered taking her hostage had I thought the Bretons would have been willing to trade her for Arthur. But I knew they'd never do that. Nor had I given up hope of convincing Constance to yield the boy of her own accord. I doubt there was a mother ever born who did not want a crown for her son. And I'd not have gone about it in such a clumsy way had it been my doing. Treaties are made to be broken, but safe conducts need to be honored."

"What do you intend to do, Richard?"

"Well, first I have to quell a rebellion in the making. Some of the more disgruntled Bretons have even dared to raid Normandy. And then I am going to try again to secure Arthur's wardship ere Constance's barons attempt to send him to the French court. Even sheep know better than to seek safety in a wolf's den, but not those fools." He frowned, shaking his head in exasperation. "Philippe would like nothing better than an excuse to meddle in Brittany. If he controlled the duchy, he'd be able to disrupt the sea routes between England and Aquitaine and use it as a base to launch attacks upon Normandy and Anjou. I'll be damned ere I let that happen!"

Catching her concern, he attempted then to reassure her, saying he expected that a show of force would be enough to make the Breton barons see reason and it would not come to serious bloodshed. Eleanor did not believe him and after he departed, she went for a solitary walk in the gardens, accompanied only by her greyhound.

She wondered if a time would ever come when she did not fear for her son's safety whenever he ventured into enemy territory. She'd not worried as much about Harry's safety. But Harry had never been as reckless as Richard. For certes, he would not have challenged the entire line of the Saracen army to combat. Sitting down on a wooden bench, she sighed as she began to ruffle her dog's soft fur. Somewhat to her surprise, she felt a twinge of reluctant sympathy for Constance. As little as she liked the woman, Constance's abduction by her husband cut too close to the bone. Even after more than twenty years, she still remembered her despair on the day of her own capture, still remembered the sinister sound of the key turning in the lock of her bedchamber at Loches Castle. Had it sounded like that to Constance?

❧

RICHARD'S CAMPAIGN IN BRITTANY was brief but bloody; a French chronicler noted in pious disapproval that he continued to fight even on Good Friday. Although the Bretons were no match for him in the field, he failed to secure custody of his nephew; André de Vitré managed to keep Arthur hidden. He did succeed, however, in reminding the Bretons of the high price they'd pay for rebellion, and upon his return to Normandy, they sent envoys to negotiate terms for peace and for Constance's release.

❧

DESPITE THE AUGUST HEAT, the garden of the palace at Le Mans was a scene of exuberant activity. Anna was playing a game of *jeu de paume* with Berengaria's brother Fernando, batting the ball back and forth with great zest. Seated in the shade of a medlar tree, Berengaria watched her brother with a smile as

Joanna watched her. She was glad that her sister-in-law was enjoying Fernando's visit, glad that he'd thought to seek out his sister on his way home to Navarre, for it had not been a happy year so far for Berengaria.

She'd been very disappointed by Richard's cancellation of his Easter Court, for that was a rare opportunity for her to act in public as his queen, and she'd been distressed to learn that he'd shed blood on one of the holiest days of the Church calendar. Joanna knew Berengaria was even more troubled by Richard's intensifying quarrel with the Archbishop of Rouen over Andely, an island in the Seine owned by the archdiocese of Rouen, for this clash of wills had the potential to flare up into a full-blown crisis with the Church.

Andely was highly profitable for the archbishop, allowing him to collect tolls from passing river traffic. But the island's location also gave it great strategic importance and Richard wanted to build a castle there. He'd offered several manors and the prosperous port city of Dieppe in exchange for Andely, and when Archbishop Gautier continued to balk, he simply seized Andely and began construction, much to the archbishop's fury. Berengaria believed that to defy the Church was to defy God, and she'd sought to convince her husband of that on one of his infrequent, brief visits. Joanna had been an uncomfortable witness. Richard had seemed willing to humor Berengaria when she took him to task for his Good Friday fighting, but as soon as she broached the subject of Andely and his dispute with the archbishop, his temper had quickly kindled. They'd continued their argument in private, but the coolness between them when Richard departed told Joanna that they'd not resolved their differences.

The game had ended, for it was too hot even for youthful enthusiasm. Fernando was now pushing Anna in a garden swing, and she shrieked with laughter as she soared higher and higher. Joanna half expected such behavior to offend Berengaria's Spanish sensibilities, but she continued to watch with a smile, happy enough to overlook minor breaches of decorum. "Fernando says he was well treated at the imperial court," she confided to Joanna. "I almost think he enjoyed his time in Germany."

Joanna thought he might have, indeed, for he was young, handsome, and charming, and she suspected he'd not often slept alone. Berengaria was continuing to speak about Fernando, saying he was very surprised to hear of Sancho's marriage. Joanna had been surprised, too, by the Navarrese king's recent wedding to the fifteen-year-old daughter of Raimond de St Gilles, for there had long been bad blood between Toulouse and Navarre. She was about to tease Berengaria about having Raimond as a family member when she caught movement from the corner of her eye and turned to see her Welsh cousin coming up the path. Mariam was not with him, and the expression on Morgan's face told Joanna that their visit had not gone well. When she beckoned, he hesitated, but then joined them, gallantly kissing her hand, bowing to Berengaria, and smiling at Dame Beatrix; Morgan's manners were always beyond reproach.

"You did not get Mariam to change her mind about marriage?" Joanna said sympathetically, and he shook his head in frustration.

"She is so stubborn!" He muttered something in Welsh that they did not understand, but it sounded like an obscenity. "I am at my wit's end," he confessed, "for she refuses to listen to reason. She respects your opinion, my lady. Can you not get her to see that her refusal makes no sense?"

"Ah, Morgan . . . I am on your side in this, but I do not want to meddle—" Joanna got no further, as Dame Beatrix was laughing outright and Berengaria was smiling, while Morgan chivalrously but unsuccessfully attempted to keep a straight face. Joanna couldn't help smiling herself. "Well, I may have been known to meddle occasionally," she admitted. "But in truth, Morgan, I have already urged Mariam to accept your offer of marriage, to no avail."

Morgan's shoulders slumped, for Joanna had been his last hope. "I will be leaving on the morrow," he said, thanking them again for their hospitality. He half expected them to urge him to stay longer, but they were nodding understandingly.

"I expect that you need to get back to the siege at Aumale," Joanna said, to his surprise.

"You heard about the siege?"

She nodded. "Well, only that the French king had arrived at the castle with an army. I just assumed that Richard will race to the rescue and Philippe will flee the way he always does, like a rabbit with hounds on his heels."

Morgan was quiet for a moment, deciding how much to tell them. He finally decided upon the truth, for it was best that they know Aumale would be a very sensitive subject with Richard for the foreseeable future. "Actually, the king already attempted to raise the siege and failed," he said, and almost smiled at their expressions of stunned disbelief. Not that he blamed them; he could not remember himself the last time Richard had suffered a military defeat.

"When we arrived at Aumale, we saw that we were outnumbered and the French siege camp was so well entrenched that the king's first instinct was to back away. But he felt honor-bound to do all he could for the trapped garrison, and so he led an attack on the camp, only to be driven off."

The women were silent, digesting this startling turn of events. "That must have been difficult for him to accept," Berengaria said at last, in what Morgan thought was a classic understatement.

"It was, my lady. He intends to make another attempt as soon as he gathers more troops. Whilst waiting for them, he went off to besiege Gaillon Castle, which is held by Philippe's routier captain, Cadoc." At that moment, he saw Mariam entering the far end of the garden and he scowled, thinking that he ought to ride away for good; why pine over a woman who did not want him?

Mariam had halted at the sight of Morgan, and Joanna sought to dispel the sudden tension by snatching at the first topic to come to mind—the recent marriage of the French king to a German duke's daughter, Agnes of Meran. Since the Pope had adamantly refused to recognize the divorce that Philippe had procured from the Bishop of Beauvais and other compliant French prelates, this remarriage had created almost as much of a scandal as Philippe's repudiation of Ingeborg. Fernando and Anna had approached in time to hear Joanna's remark and an animated discussion now ensued about Philippe, Ingeborg, and Agnes, who was acknowledged as queen only at the French court. None of them could understand why Agnes's male relatives had been willing to make such a match, knowing she'd be viewed as Philippe's concubine throughout the rest of Christendom. Fernando had just made a bawdy jest about Philippe and Agnes's wedding night, earning himself a mildly reproving look from his elder sister, when a servant approached to murmur a few words in Joanna's ear.

"Good heavens," she blurted out, so great was her surprise. "Mercadier has just ridden in!"

Berengaria frowned, for she shared the view of routiers as lowborn killers. It troubled her greatly that her husband had admitted a man like Mercadier into his inner circle, that he showed the routier such favor. He was Lord of Beynac now, for Richard had given him the lands of a Périgord lord who'd died without an heir, and he'd even married into the local aristocracy, wedding the sister of the Seigneur of Lesparre. But to much of their world, he would always remain the scarred, brutal outsider, one of the Devil's own.

Yet there was no way they could have refused to receive him; he was Richard's most trusted general. Berengaria and Joanna rose to their feet, waiting for him to be ushered out into the garden, wondering how he'd even known they were at Le Mans, and wondering, too, what he wanted. Morgan was of no help; all he could tell them was that Richard had sent Mercadier into Berry last month to deal with a troublesome lord. Not all of them were disconcerted by Mercadier's unexpected arrival. Fernando was intrigued, for the routier's notoriety had reached as far as Navarre, and Anna was excited to finally meet a man so often spoken of as the Antichrist.

As Mercadier sauntered toward them, Joanna took the lead in making him welcome, knowing she'd be more convincing than her sister-in-law. She'd met him at Lisieux, so she knew what to expect. The other women did not and stared with morbid fascination at the livid, satanic scar and eerie, colorless eyes as opaque as stone. He bowed correctly, for he'd been in Richard's service long enough to have any rough edges smoothed away, but Joanna thought he was a wolf masquerading as a domestic dog. "I apologize for intruding upon you, Madames," he told the queens, "but the king's messenger who found me in Berry said that Sir Morgan was with you in Le Mans, and I was instructed to bring him back with me."

"Of course," Morgan said promptly, pleased that Richard wanted him to take part in the second attack upon the French. "Are we to meet the king at Aumale?"

"You have not heard then? The king was wounded at the siege of Gaillon Castle."

There were gasps from the women and they were not reassured when Mercadier told them what little he knew—that Richard had been struck in the knee by a crossbow bolt shot from the battlements by Philippe's routier captain, Cadoc. If infection set in, even a minor injury could quickly become life-threatening, and the wound had apparently been serious enough for Richard to summon Mercadier back from his *chevauchée* in Berry.

As Joanna continued to pelt the routier with questions he could not answer, a shaken Berengaria sat down on the closest bench. She'd long feared that she'd be a young widow, yet in the past, she'd not expected to be one of the last to know. She did not hesitate, though, when Joanna said she would accompany Mercadier and Morgan on the morrow, for she knew a wife's duty. Her place was with her husband in his time of need—whether he wanted her there or not.

❧

As THEY RODE INTO the inner bailey of Vaudreuil Castle, Eleanor was standing in the doorway of the great hall, waiting to welcome them. Berengaria felt no surprise, just a weary prickle of resentment. She said nothing, but Joanna read her face easily and leaned over to murmur that Richard would not have sent for his mother. "He loathes being fussed over when he is ailing." Berengaria knew this was true. That did not change the reality, though, that once again Eleanor had been with Richard whilst Berengaria had remained in ignorance of his injury.

"He will be so glad to see you!" Eleanor exclaimed, and for a moment, Berengaria actually thought those words were meant for her. Then she saw that Eleanor was looking at Mercadier, and she thought bitterly that this was as good a commentary on her marriage as any, that her husband would summon his cutthroat routier to his sickbed, not his queen.

HIS DOCTOR HAD TOLD Richard that he'd been lucky, for the crossbow bolt had embedded itself in the muscle, not the bone, which could have been crippling. He did not *feel* lucky, though. He was in considerable pain, as much as he tried to hide it. He was still fuming over his defeat at Aumale, and now that he was bedridden, he had too much time to brood about it. He was very worried about the fate of the castle and the garrison, and he was finding his powerlessness to be intolerable, calling up memories of his German captivity. He'd not been pleased by his mother's arrival, and he was vexed beyond measure at having to submit to his doctor's prodding and poking, even more frustrated by his body's betrayal; his first attempt to leave the bed and put weight on his injured knee had sent him sprawling to the floor. But the worst was still to come. On this humid, hot August afternoon, he'd gotten word that the garrison at Aumale had been forced to surrender to the French king.

He did not blame them; he blamed himself. He dictated a letter to Baldwin de Bethune, for he had the right to know his wife's castle had been lost. He dispatched another messenger in search of Mercadier, who'd yet to answer his summons. And he sent a tersely worded letter to the French king, declaring that he would pay whatever ransom would be demanded for the Aumale garrison. After that, he finally fell into a shallow, troubled sleep.

He awoke to find his doctor bending over him. "Sire, how are you feeling?"

"Wonderful," he said through gritted teeth, thinking that all physicians had sawdust where their brains ought to be.

With a rustle of silken skirts, his mother approached the bed. "You have visitors."

"Who?" he asked warily, for he felt about as sociable as a baited bear.

"Joanna and your wife."

He said nothing, for what was there to say? Why did women not understand that a man in pain wanted only to be left alone? But then Eleanor told him that Mercadier had also arrived, which was the first good news he'd gotten since he'd been wounded. While he realized Berenguela would not like it any, his need to discuss military matters with Mercadier was urgent, and he hesitated only briefly before telling her to send the routier up first.

GUY DE THOUARS WAS one of the garrison taken prisoner at Aumale Castle, and upon his release, he rode straight to Vaudreuil to thank the king for paying the large ransom of three thousand silver marks. He was seated in the great hall, waiting to be escorted up to the king's bedchamber, quite happy to pass the time flirting discreetly with the king's sister. Joanna was encouraging him, for she was bored and he was attractive, with a very beguiling smile. She wondered why he'd not yet married, deciding it was probably because he was a younger brother, overshadowed by Viscount Aimery, who had inherited the family's title and estates. She thought it a pity that he'd not been the firstborn, for he was more likable than Aimery and far more trustworthy; whilst his brother swung like a weathercock in a high wind, Guy's loyalty to Richard had been unwavering.

Berengaria liked Guy, too, and she was coming over to greet him when there was a stir at the doorway. Turning to see what was happening, she was dismayed by the sight of her husband hobbling into the hall, leaning heavily upon a wooden crutch. Joanna was already on her feet and while Eleanor had not risen, her eyes fastened intently upon Richard's halting progress, almost as if she were willing each awkward step. The younger women were not as disciplined and they rushed toward Richard, entreating him to sit down, reminding him that he was not supposed to be up yet.

"I've made a career of doing things I am not supposed to do," he said, with a tight smile that turned into a grimace when he took a misstep and pain shot up his leg.

"Sire!" Guy had been quick to comprehend what was happening, and he hastened over to drop to his knees before Richard, giving him a reason to sit. Richard did, with an alacrity that betrayed his discomfort. "I have come to thank you, my liege, for ransoming me and the other members of the garrison. I am very grateful."

Richard almost asked Guy if he'd thought they'd be left to rot, catching himself in time, for he'd be lashing out at the wrong target. He motioned instead for Guy to rise and then accepted the wine cup that his practical mother was pressing into his hand. His men were hurrying toward him, delighted that he was on his feet again, and the women stepped back, realizing that he'd not heed them any more than he'd heeded his doctor. In less than a month, he'd mark his thirty-ninth birthday, and he was not going to change his ways at this point in his life.

⚜

RICHARD WAS STUDYING PLANS for his new castle at Andely when a message arrived coincidentally from the Archbishop of Rouen. When he swore after reading the letter, Eleanor came to his side; she knew better than to interfere in military matters, but this was a political problem. He did not object as she reached for the letter and read it for herself. It was not good; the infuriated archbishop was threatening to put Normandy under Interdict if Richard did not return Andely to him.

"What do you mean to do?"

"Nothing. If he is rash enough to carry out the threat, so be it. I'll appeal to the Pope. My offer for Andely was more than generous. Dieppe alone is worth far more than those river tolls."

That would not have been the way Eleanor would have handled it, but she was not the one determined to build a castle at Andely. He'd insisted that it would change the balance of power along the Norman border, for it would cut off French access to Rouen and provide a base for attacks upon Philippe's castles in the Vexin. He meant to reclaim the Vexin and saw the stronghold he'd already named Château Gaillard as the means to that end. He envisioned the coming campaign over the Vexin as a naval war as well as a land combat, and he explained to Eleanor that he intended to build a fleet of shallow-hulled ships that would control river traffic on the Seine.

Eleanor knew that he'd proved himself to be a master at sea warfare during his time in the Holy Land, but she saw one major drawback in his ambitious, imaginative strategy. It took years to build a castle. She said nothing, though, for he was well aware of that, and asked him instead about his efforts to end the alliance between the Count of Flanders and the French king. He'd hoped that the new count would be more receptive to English overtures than his late father, but he'd just joined Philippe at the siege of Aumale. Richard remained confident that the trade embargo he'd imposed upon Flanders would work, however. Reminding Eleanor that Flanders was utterly dependent upon English wool for its cloth industry, he insisted that it was only a matter of time until the economic pressure would bring the count to his knees.

Eleanor agreed and expressed approval when he told her he meant to tighten the embargo to include English grain, for Flanders could not feed its own people, dependent upon imported food for the large cities of Ypres, Bruges, Lille, and Ghent. Thinking that he had his father's flair for long-term planning, she said, "And once the Count of Flanders joins you, Philippe will have only one ally left. A pity we do not have such leverage against the Count of Toulouse, for then Philippe would be utterly on his own."

"As it happens, I have a plan in mind for Toulouse, too."

That immediately sparked Eleanor's curiosity, for Toulouse was never far from her thoughts, her family's lost legacy. Both of her husbands had tried to take it for her—tried and failed. Her soldier son might have better luck. She did not see how he could fight a war on two fronts, though. But when she tried to find out more about his plans for Toulouse, Richard merely smiled and shrugged, saying he did not yet know if that hawk would fly.

✦

JOHN USUALLY WENT to see Richard with all the enthusiasm of a doomed felon being dragged to the gallows. But as they rode toward Vaudreuil, he was in high spirits and laughed when Durand gibed that he seemed as eager as a man about to visit a bawdy house.

"Well, Brother Richard has had a truly miserable summer, so that is bound to cheer me up. Forgetting to duck at Gaillon was just the beginning of his troubles. It is hard to say who is giving him more grief these days, the Bretons or the aggrieved Archbishop Gautier."

Durand knew that the archbishop was threatening to lay Normandy under Interdict, but he hadn't heard about new problems with the Bretons; he pricked up his ears in case this was something the queen had not yet heard, either. "The Bretons? I thought they'd come to terms with Richard in the spring."

It took no more than that, for John enjoyed revealing information that was not yet widely known. "So it seemed. They agreed to offer hostages and Richard agreed to secure Constance's release from her husband's clutches, provided that she would agree to be governed by his wishes in the future. The date set for her release was the feast of the Assumption of the Virgin Mary, but it came and passed without her being freed or the hostages returned, so the Bretons met at Saint-Malo de Breignon, swore fealty to Arthur, and repudiated their oaths to Richard. They then sought aid from Philippe, which is like jumping from the frying pan into the fire. But common sense has always been lacking amongst the Bretons."

What Durand found most interesting about John's blithe account of the Bretons' rebellion was that it proved John had a spy, either in Richard's camp or the Bretons'. That would be information his queen would want to know.

John was enumerating the other setbacks Richard had suffered that summer—his defeat at Aumale, its fall to Philippe, the loss of Nonancourt Castle, which had been retaken by the French while Richard was confined to his bed. "And we know my brother is surely the world's worst patient, so how he must have rejoiced when Joanna, our mother, and Berengaria all descended upon him like a flock of hens fluttering about a lone chick!" John laughed again and Durand joined in, thinking that he'd not mind having Joanna nurse him back to health.

"Do you think your good news will salt Richard's wound?" he joked, and John glanced his way with a grin.

"One can only hope."

❧

JOHN'S FIRST IMPRESSION OF his brother was that Richard did not look good. He was pale after over a month away from the sun, shadows lurked under his eyes, and he seemed to have put on some weight. Their father's famous indifference to food or drink had been due in part to the ease with which he gained weight; he'd waged a lifelong battle to avoid becoming heavy. John had inherited Henry's stocky build, and he'd envied Richard, whose height allowed him to eat without concern about putting on pounds. He was pleased to see now that even Richard was not immune to the effects of prolonged inactivity. Or to the impact of a well-aimed crossbow bolt.

"I'm surprised to see you out of bed," he admitted, earning himself a mirthless smile from his older brother.

"If you start preaching to me about that, too, Johnny, I swear I'll hit you with my crutch."

"I'll stay out of range, then. But where are your preachers? I assumed they'd be sticking closer to you than glue." His light tone notwithstanding, John was vexed that neither his mother nor sister had come into the hall to greet him, and so it was welcome news when Richard said the women were no longer at Vaudreuil.

"Maman knew better than to hover, but Joanna and Berenguela . . ." Richard shook his head ruefully. "They carried on so about a mere flesh wound that they even had me half believing I was at Death's door. I endured it as long as I could, and then got Maman to persuade them that it would be best if I was left to heal at my own pace."

Reaching for his crutch, Richard insisted upon limping across the hall toward the dais, beckoning John to follow. "I suppose you heard that the Bretons are in rebellion again?" he said, after he'd settled himself in his chair and propped his injured leg upon a stool.

John nodded. "They are as contrary and querulous as the Welsh. Do not tell Cousin Morgan I said that, though."

"I sent Mercadier and my seneschal of Anjou, Robert de Turnham, to quell it—and to stop the fools from smuggling Arthur to the French court." Richard regarded John with a gleam of mischievous malice. "I suppose that would please you greatly, though."

"Paris is a beautiful city," John said airily. "It would be a shame to deny young Arthur a chance to see it." As usual, John's impudence amused his brother. John's own smile vanished, however, as soon as he saw the youth crossing the hall toward them. He managed to greet Otto affably, but he quickly brought Richard's attention back to himself by saying, "I have good news. I captured Gamaches Castle for you."

"Did you? Very well done, Johnny!"

John had been expecting Richard to make light of his success. He was pleased now by his brother's obvious delight. His seizure of this French Vexin castle was his first military triumph, apart from his tainted capture of Évreux, and he was proud of it, even prouder now that Richard acknowledged it as a deed worth celebrating. It was sweet, too, to receive congratulations from Otto and several of Richard's knights, although he did his best to accept the praise with nonchalance, never wanting Richard to suspect how much his good opinion mattered.

John was on his way to the bedchamber that had been provided for him when he encountered a black-clad monk just entering the hall. He knew the man slightly—Guillebert, the abbot of the Benedictine abbey of St Benoit at Castres—and he paused to exchange greetings. It was only later that he wondered why one of the Count of Toulouse's men was paying a call upon Richard.

⬥

THE SEPTEMBER SKY HAD become overcast, rain clouds sweeping in from the west, and Guy de Thouars decided to pass the night at the closest castle, St James de Beuvron; a viscount's brother could rely upon the hospitality of castellans rather than having to search for inns like those of lesser status. As he expected, he and his men were admitted at once. He was about to head to the great hall when he happened to glance toward the gardens, where several women were picking the last blooms of summer. He recognized the slender woman in a finely woven blue mantle, and he was pleased that the Duchess of Brittany was not being confined to her chamber, for he thought holding a woman hostage violated the tenets of the chivalric code. She was looking his way, doubtless wondering if a message had arrived for her; he knew she was allowed to correspond with her Breton barons. On impulse, he strode over, opened the gate, and entered the gardens.

Constance watched him approach, her expression guarded, although her women were giving Guy an approving once-over. Bowing, he kissed the duchess's hand. "I doubt that you'd remember me, my lady, but we met at Angers last year. I am Guy de Thouars, brother of Viscount Aimery."

"I remember you," she said, in a cool tone that did not encourage further conversation.

"I am honored." He managed to infuse that trite gallantry with sincerity, and his smile was so appealing that Constance found herself thawing a little, enough to agree when he gestured toward the tablecloth they'd spread out on the grass and the basket of fruit and cheese, offering to bring them inside ere the rain began. With Juvetta and Emma casting him flirtatious glances from under fluttering eyelashes, he followed Constance as she led the way toward the castle keep. There she halted, thanked him, and gestured for Emma to reclaim the basket. Guy bowed again and bade them a good evening.

He'd only taken a few steps, though, before he halted. Turning back, he asked if he might have a word in private. Constance hesitated, but curiosity won out. Sending her women on into the keep, she waited expectantly, and a little warily, to see what this Poitevin knight wanted from her.

Guy's action was unpremeditated. He did not regret it, though, for he felt she had a right to know. She was more than a duchess; she was a mother, too. "You may already have heard," he said, "about your son."

Constance stiffened. "What about him?"

"Word has it that the Bishop of Vannes succeeded in eluding Mercadier and the king's seneschal and got Arthur safely to the French court."

Constance had not realized she'd been holding her breath. "Thank God!"

"Well, I doubt that Mercadier or the king would echo those sentiments," he said wryly. He suspected the Bretons would come to regret it, too, but the duchess was not likely to be interested in his views of the French king. He kissed her hand again, and when he looked up, he saw that she was smiling.

"Thank you, Sir Guy," she said. "I will remember your kindness."

"My lady." Raindrops had begun to splatter about them, and as she disappeared into the keep, he quickened his pace, thinking that what he would remember was her smile.

CHAPTER THIRTY

✦

Eleanor was pleased to receive her son's message, asking her to join him at Rouen, for that indicated he was showing common sense in recovering from his wound; she would gladly make that long, tiring journey if it would keep him out of the saddle long enough for his knee to heal. She'd not expected to find Berengaria and Joanna at Rouen, though, for it was painfully obvious by now that Richard rarely sought out his wife for the pleasure of her company. Their surprise presence confirmed her suspicions—that something was in the wind—even if she did not see the role they'd play in whatever grand design Richard had in mind.

She was not kept in suspense for long. After an enjoyable family dinner, Richard said he needed to speak with her in private and, leaving Joanna and Berengaria to preside over the great hall, they withdrew to the solar. Richard still favored his injured leg, but he was no longer using a crutch and, her concerns over his health assuaged, she wasted no time going to the heart of the matter. "What are you up to, Richard?"

He looked amused. "How well you know me, Maman. As it happens, I do have something of consequence to share with you. Do you remember when I said I was contemplating a way to end Philippe's alliance with the Count of Toulouse?"

She nodded. "You said you were not yet sure if that hawk would fly."

"I need not have worried, for it soared high enough to see the gates of Heaven. Raimond de St Gilles and I are about to launch a diplomatic revolution. After nigh on forty years of war with Toulouse, we are making peace."

Eleanor was highly skeptical of that, remembering how her husband had forced Raimond's father to do homage for Toulouse and how quickly he'd repudiated it. "I suspect that any peace with Toulouse will last about as long as ice in the hot sun. What are the terms?"

"Well, you know that Quercy has been a bone of contention since I regained possession of it some years back. So I have agreed to return it to the count. And I have also agreed to renounce the duchy of Aquitaine's hereditary claim to Toulouse."

Her gasp of horror was so audible that he had to fight back a smile. "Richard, have you lost your mind? You would give up so much for so little? What do we get in return?"

"Not much, Maman—merely Toulouse for your grandson . . . or granddaughter, if that be God's Will."

He'd rarely seen his mother at a loss for words and leaned back in his seat to savor the moment, watching with a grin as she processed what she'd just been told.

"A marital alliance, Richard?" She, too, was now smiling, a smile that shed years and cares, giving him a glimpse of the young woman she'd once been, back in the days when she'd been acclaimed as one of Christendom's great beauties and her marriage to his father had been a happy one. "Raimond and Joanna . . . That is brilliant!"

"I thought so, too," he said complacently. "Alliances are easily broken, but not if they are sanctioned by the Church. The old count was a viper, about as trustworthy as Heinrich. Raimond is neither as treacherous nor as ambitious as his father. And by offering him such generous terms—as well as a beautiful bride—I give him some very convincing reasons to stay loyal."

The more Eleanor considered the proposal, the more she liked it. Richard would gain a useful ally, further isolate the French king, and resolve her family's long-standing claim to Toulouse. "This is truly a blessing, Richard, both for us and for Joanna. She ought to have a good life as Raimond's countess. She'll like Toulouse for certes, and it will be wonderful not to have to send another daughter off into foreign exile. I do not expect to see your sister Leonora again in this world, but Joanna will be able to visit us whenever she wishes. And she . . ."

She stopped abruptly then, puzzled by the expression on his face. "What is it? Surely Joanna is pleased about the marriage?"

"Well . . . she does not know about it yet."

"Why not? Do you have any reason to think she'd balk?"

"No. It is just that she can be unpredictable, Maman. And . . . and Berenguela does not think it is a good idea." Catching her look of surprise, he said, "It made sense to discuss it with her, for she'd seen Joanna and Raimond together, and I made her promise she'd say nothing to Joanna until I do. But as I said, she does not approve." His mouth turned down. "In truth, I cannot remember the last time she did approve of something I've done."

"Why does she object? Does she think that Joanna disliked Raimond?"

"Not exactly. She said sometimes they seemed very friendly and, at other times, quite cool with each other. But she feels he would not be a suitable husband for Joanna because he is out of favor with the Church. She says she does not think he is a heretic, just too sympathetic to the Cathars, too 'tolerant of those who have strayed from God's path,' as she put it."

"That would not bother Joanna," Eleanor said shrewdly, "for she grew to womanhood in Sicily. And when I discussed the count with her, I did not get the sense that she found him objectionable. As I remember, she said he was the sort of man mothers warned their daughters about, and I do not think she meant that as an insult."

"I am glad to hear that," he admitted, showing her he was not as confident of Joanna's reaction as he'd have her believe. "Whilst this marriage would be very beneficial to our family, I also believe it would be good for Joanna. So will you help me to make her see that?"

"Yes, I will, Richard. But she is no longer a child being sent off to wed a man chosen for her by her parents. She is a queen, a widow, a woman grown, one with a mind of her own. If she refuses, we cannot compel her, nor would I try."

"Trust me, Maman, no one is going to compel Joanna to do anything she does not want to do!" he said with a laugh, remembering her volcanic rage when he'd confided his scheme to offer her in marriage to Saladin's brother.

She studied him intently for a moment, and then nodded. "We are in agreement, then, that this marriage is worth pursuing. So . . . let's see if Joanna agrees with us."

❧

JOANNA WOULD NORMALLY HAVE been pleased by Richard's summons to Rouen, but it came so unexpectedly that it stirred up misgivings she'd not even realized she'd been harboring. Was Richard planning to end his marriage, wanting her there to comfort Berengaria afterward? Her concern was based in part on the recent upheavals in the south. In April, the region had been thrown into turmoil by the sudden death of King Alfonso of Aragon at age thirty-nine, leaving an untested eighteen-year-old son as his heir. Berengaria's brother Sancho had embroiled himself in a war with the King of Castile, Richard's brother-in-law, and even more troubling, he was showing signs of chafing under the Angevin-Navarrese alliance. Richard had confided to Joanna that Sancho had seized Berengaria's dower castles and he'd appealed to the Pope to pressure Sancho for their return. Joanna did not know if Berengaria realized her increasing vulnerability, but a queen who could provide neither an heir nor a valuable alliance might not be a queen for very long.

Upon their arrival at Rouen, Joanna was relieved when Richard said nothing to her about ending his marriage. The next day she could sense tension in her sister-in-law, but she decided Berengaria had probably had another quarrel with Richard about his appropriation of Andely, for she'd been distressed by the Archbishop of Rouen's threat to lay Normandy under Interdict. Her foreboding came rushing back, though, as soon as Richard revealed that their mother was on the way. Joanna knew he'd not have asked her to make such a long journey unless something urgent was at stake. And so when she was called to the solar, she was already bracing for bad news.

As soon as she was seated, she could not help herself, blurting out nervously, "Richard, do you mean to disavow your marriage and put Berengaria aside?"

Her brother looked surprised. "No, I do not. Why would you think that, Joanna?"

Feeling foolish, she shrugged. "Well, I know that Sancho is becoming troublesome." Leaving unsaid the real problem, Berengaria's failure to conceive.

"He is," Richard agreed, rising and moving to the table to pour wine for them all. "But Berenguela is not to blame for his erratic behavior of late." Passing around cups, he sat down again. "Actually, I do want to talk with you about marriage. Not mine, though—yours. I've made a brilliant match for you, *irlanda*."

Joanna caught her breath, momentarily overwhelmed by emotion—excitement so intertwined with alarm that it was impossible to separate one from the other. She did want to marry again, for she did not like sleeping alone and she desperately wanted children. But marriage was the ultimate gamble for women; even a queen was subject to a husband's will. She was loath to surrender the rare freedom she'd enjoyed in the six years since Richard had pried open the door of her gilded cage at Palermo. Nor was she eager to leave those she loved for life with a stranger in an alien land. Yet she had no choice, not unless she wanted to take holy vows. For women, it was either marriage or a nunnery. For her, marriage was the better road, albeit one fraught with risk. Discovering that her mouth had suddenly gone dry, she said huskily, "Who?"

"He is not a king, and I did promise you one," he said, with a quick smile, "but he is of noble birth and—"

"Richard! Who?"

"The Count of Toulouse." Watching her intently, Richard saw her eyes widen, her lips part. But she said not a word and she looked so stunned that he felt a prickle of unease.

Joanna was still struggling with disbelief. "Raimond de St Gilles?"

"Well, he is the only Count of Toulouse I know, lass." Richard slid his chair closer. "Such an opportunity is rarer than dragon's teeth. You would be bringing Toulouse back into the family, Joanna, whilst depriving Philippe of a valuable ally. But the marriage is a good one for you, too. You already know Raimond, having spent several months in his company, so there'd be no surprises, and not many brides can say that. From what I've heard about the man, he ought to be easy enough to live with, for he likes music and women and wine and seems to find humor in most of life's predicaments. And you'll feel at home in Toulouse, for it is much like Sicily. Even the weather will be to your liking, warmer than Normandy or Anjou; you've often complained of our winters. . . ."

He paused then, feeling that he was talking too much, spurred on by her strange silence. He glanced toward their mother, seeking some help, and she obliged by leaning over to take Joanna's hand; she was startled to find it was as cold as ice. "What pleases me greatly," she said, "is that I will not be losing you again. Few mothers and daughters are so lucky." It troubled her, though, that Joanna seemed so shaken, and she tightened her grip on her daughter's hand, saying, "But it is a decision that will change the course of your life, so that decision ought not to be a hasty one. You need not give us your answer now; you can take some time to think on it."

Richard was not willing to wait for another heartbeat, not with so much at stake. He saw the wisdom, though, in Eleanor's suggestion, for there was a danger Joanna might make an impulsive refusal and then feel bound by pride to hold to it. "Maman is right," he said, albeit without much enthusiasm. "You need time to consider this."

Joanna looked from one to the other, blinking as if she were awakening from a drowsy daydream. "No," she said and was surprised to find them both staring at her in utter dismay, only belatedly comprehending why. "I meant that I do not need time to consider it." She paused to draw a deep, steadying breath, and then smiled. "I am quite willing to marry the Count of Toulouse." After that, she could say no more, for she'd been swept up into her brother's arms and he was hugging her so tightly that she thought he might crack a rib.

FLOATING DOWN THE STAIRS into the great hall, Joanna saw her sister-in-law hurrying toward her. Understanding now why Berengaria had seemed so preoccupied, she paused long enough to confirm that yes, she would be marrying the Count of Toulouse, and no, she did not believe she'd be wedding a heretic. She saw that Berengaria would need convincing, but she did not have time for that now, and she hastily excused herself.

She finally found Mariam in their bedchamber. The other woman glanced up as the door opened, the book on her lap forgotten as soon as she saw Joanna's face. "What is it? You look . . . Well, I am not sure, for I've never seen you look like this!"

"That is because I've never felt like this," Joanna confided. "I am still not sure it really happened, for it seems so . . . so improbable. I've been with Richard and my mother in the solar, listening as they sought to persuade me that I ought to marry Raimond de St Gilles."

"Joanna!" Mariam sprang to her feet, and once again Joanna found herself enveloped in an exuberant embrace, this one easier on her ribs. As giddy as young girls, they laughed and hugged, and settled then onto the bed, where Mariam demanded to know all.

Joanna was eager to share the events of the past hour, hoping that saying it aloud would make it seem real. Richard and her mother were delighted with the match. By agreeing to wed Raimond, she'd be in high favor with her brother for some time to come, she said, with a mischievous smile. Raimond had agreed to marry her as soon as the suggestion had been broached, not even waiting to learn what marriage portion Richard would provide. This time her smile was downright dazzling. Fortunately, Richard was giving her a very generous dowry: the rich county of the Agen. Richard meant to send word to Raimond that very day, and they would be wed here in Rouen as quickly as the arrangements could be made.

"So," she concluded, "by this time next month, I will be the Countess of Toulouse."

Mariam tried to remember when she'd seen Joanna as happy as this. Only when she'd held her infant son for the first time, and then in the harbor at Messina, as she'd gazed at the ships flying the royal lion of England, realizing that her ordeal was over, that her brother had set her free.

"It is not uncommon to use marriages to end rivalries, to forge new alliances. Joanna . . . did you never think that might happen for you and Raimond?"

Joanna shook her head emphatically. "Never, for there was too much hatred between our Houses. The dukes of Aquitaine claimed Toulouse for their own, Mariam. I could not imagine Richard being willing to cede that claim, not when he knew Raimond was no match for him on the battlefield. Why would he have chosen compromise over conquest? No, it would have been mad to torment myself with false hope."

"And yet it happened," Mariam pointed out and Joanna nodded.

"Yes . . . Richard continues to surprise. People are always praising his skills as a soldier, but he has a sure touch when it comes to statecraft, too, and he does not often get enough credit for that. He was willing to offer Raimond terms generous enough to bridge that sea of bad blood. I never expected that and I am sure Raimond did not, either."

Kicking her shoes off, Joanna curled up on the bed. "So much to be thankful for, Mariam. That I am able to do this for my family. That I'll not have to bid them farewell again. That this marriage is going to give the French king so many sleepless nights."

"And . . . ?" Mariam prompted playfully.

Joanna lay back against the pillows, green eyes glowing. "What am I forgetting?" she murmured, with a soft, sultry laugh. "Ah yes . . . that I get to take Raimond de St Gilles as my lover, with the blessings of Holy Church!"

❧

JOANNA WAS SEATED BESIDE her brother on the dais, her eyes never straying from the entrance at the far end of the great hall. Raimond and his men had been sighted approaching the castle, so he'd soon be walking in that door. She was suddenly nervous, for it had been three years. Would it still be the same between them? Could her memory be trusted?

She was surprised when Richard reached over and squeezed her hand. "You need not fret, *irlanda*," he said softly. "There's not a man alive who could resist you when you put your mind to it. Even as a little lass, you had us all singing your song. And husbands are much easier to handle than brothers."

Joanna smiled, touched that he'd noticed her unease, for he was not always so observant, for certes not where his wife was concerned. It amused her, too, that he still thought she'd agreed to wed Raimond as a dutiful daughter and sister. She'd have to enlighten him about that—eventually.

There was a stir outside, enough noise to indicate Raimond had come with a considerable entourage. Joanna was glad, for she wanted him to show them all that he was a prince of power and influence; she knew some of Richard's vassals, especially the Normans, did not think highly of the southerners, considering them to be lazy, dissolute, and infected by heresy. Given how freely wine flowed at weddings, there was a potential for trouble, but she was confident that Richard would keep these regional animosities from getting out of hand.

Raimond was accompanied by the lords and bishops of Toulouse. Some of the men had brought their wives, and Joanna recognized his sister Azalais and his nephew Raimond-Roger. They'd changed in the three years since she'd last seen them, for Azalais had been widowed and her son was now a self-possessed youngster of eleven. Richard leaned over, asking their identities, but she never heard him. Raimond was striding toward the dais, looking just as he had upon their first meeting in Alfonso's palace at Marseille.

"My lord king," he said respectfully and knelt, for Richard—not Philippe— was now his liege lord, owed homage for Toulouse. He greeted Richard's mother and queen next, with the gallantry for which the south was famous. Joanna watched with composure, for all her qualms had vanished as soon as their eyes had met. When he took her hand, she felt again the heat surging between their bodies, a fever of the flesh that burned just as hot as it had in that moonlit Bordeaux garden. He pressed a kiss into her palm, a lover's gesture that he now had the right to make, and as they smiled at each other, she remembered what he'd said that night. *Like being struck by lightning and living to tell the tale.* Words meant to seduce, but true, nonetheless. It was, she thought, the best description she'd ever heard of the sweet madness that could ensnare men and women, decried by the Church but soon to be sanctioned within the bonds of matrimony.

THE OCTOBER DAY OF Joanna's wedding dawned with harvest blue skies and sun so unseasonably warm that it reminded Berengaria of her own wedding day on the isle of Cyprus. It had rained heavily that night, so she was glad the storm had passed. She hoped it would be a good omen for her sister-in-law's future happiness. She'd been dismayed by the Archbishop of Rouen's refusal to attend the ceremony and distressed that she seemed to be the only one troubled by his absence. But the Bishop of Évreux, one of Archbishop Gautier's own suffragans, seemed comfortable stepping into the archbishop's shoes, and as Joanna and Raimond knelt on the porch of the cathedral of Notre-Dame to receive the bishop's blessing, Berengaria did her best to put her misgivings aside.

She thought Joanna was a lovely bride, her gown a rich shade of emerald, her coppery-gold hair set off by a gossamer veil fretted with seed pearls, tumbling down her back in the style worn only by queens and virgin brides. Raimond wore a deep red tunic that enhanced his dark coloring, and as he bowed his head, Berengaria thought the sun made his hair gleam like polished ebony. Hundreds of people had gathered to watch them exchange holy vows before entering the cathedral for the Marriage Mass, but the bride and groom seemed oblivious to their large audience, never taking their eyes off each other as they were joined as man and wife.

Beside her, Berengaria's husband gave a soft chuckle. "I think I've been had, little dove. My sweet sister seems to have played me like a lute."

Berengaria glanced up sharply, but Richard had gone back to watching the bridal couple. His playful comment struck her like a blow, for it reminded her of the easy intimacy they'd shared in the Holy Land, reminded her of all she'd lost. Like Richard, she, too, returned her attention to the ceremony. The scene had blurred, but she did not try to hide her tears, for women were supposed to cry at weddings, were they not?

JOANNA HAD ALWAYS ENJOYED social occasions like weddings, for they provided opportunities for music and rich fare, for flirting, dancing, and basking in the flattering attention that she inevitably attracted during such festivities. But she was eager for her own wedding celebration to be over, wanting only to be alone with her new husband. Raimond did not make it any easier for her to be patient, murmuring in her ear that she looked beautiful in her bridal gown, but he was sure she'd look more beautiful out of it, telling her that her blazing bright hair made her look like a woman on fire, adding that *he* was on fire, too, only his flames were burning in his nether regions, and pretending to be shocked when she laughed. While Joanna was doing her best to be circumspect under constant public scrutiny, she'd begun to wonder if the revelries would ever end.

Eventually, of course, they did, and she and Raimond were escorted up to their bedchamber by the raucous wedding guests, where they knelt for the traditional blessing. Garin de Cierrey, the Bishop of Évreux, was a courtier as well as prelate and he showed a realistic assessment of his audience by keeping his remarks brief, praying that their marriage would be fruitful and that they would find favor in the eyes of the Lord. Nor did he make a serious attempt to convince the bridal couple that they ought to refrain from consummating their marriage at once, spending their first night in meditation and contemplation of the holy state of wedlock; he was worldly enough to know that very few ever heeded that particular Church admonition.

Once the male guests had been chased out, the women helped Joanna to remove her wedding finery. Clad only in her chemise, she sat on a stool as her long hair was brushed until it glowed in the candlelight with a burnished bronze sheen. A jar was handed to her so she could perfume herself again, and another jar was passed so she could reapply her lip rouge. Once she took off her chemise, she was dusted with a fragrant powder before being tucked into bed. The other women tactfully drew back then, so she could have a few private words with her mother.

This was the first time Eleanor had been present for a daughter's bedding-down ceremony. Joanna and her older sisters, Leonora and Tilda, had been sent off at early ages to wed foreign princes, and once her marriage to the French king had ended, Louis had cut her out of the lives of their two daughters. She sat for a moment on the bed, reaching out to arrange Joanna's hair on the pillow; she knew from experience how erotic men found long hair, for a woman let it down only in the privacy of the bedchamber.

"You are such a beautiful bride," she said fondly, "and I am very pleased to see that you are such a willing one. Mayhap your brother does not owe you as great a debt as he first thought."

Joanna grinned. "When did you guess the truth, Maman?"

"From the moment Raimond entered the great hall and I saw the way the two of you looked at each other, as if the rest of the world had ceased to exist. I am very happy for you, dearest," she said, leaning over to kiss Joanna on the cheek. "Were you lovers?"

Joanna actually blushed. "Of course not, Maman!"

"No?" Eleanor sounded surprised. "Well, that will make tonight all the sweeter." And she smiled, remembering her own wedding night to Joanna's father. It was a wonder she and Harry had not set their bed on fire, so much heat had been kindled. If her daughter found even half as much pleasure with the Count of Toulouse, she would be a lucky woman.

⚜

JOANNA HAD LEFT THE BED CURTAINS open a bit, just enough for her to see without being seen. She'd not had a bedding-down ceremony before. She'd been only eleven when she wed William, so there was no question of consummating the marriage on their wedding night. She'd been nigh on fifteen when he'd deemed her old enough, and that was done privately, with him simply showing up in her bedchamber. The memory brought a smile to her face, for it had been a pleasant experience. She'd been bedazzled by her handsome husband, eager to become his wife in every sense of the word. She'd known about his *harim* of Saracen slave girls by then, but she'd convinced herself that he'd get rid of them once he began sharing her bed. Her smile faded as she remembered how hurtful it had been once she'd realized he had no intention of putting them aside. Most wives expected their husbands to be unfaithful occasionally. Few demanded fidelity, only discretion. But even at fifteen, Joanna had seen a *harim* as a greater sin than a concubine and a far greater affront to her pride.

She could hear the clamor in the stairwell that warned of the arrival of the male guests and hastily put her old memories aside. They burst into the bedchamber like an invading army, many of them drunk by now, all of them eager to torment and tease the bridegroom, for this was an accepted rite of passage. She wondered if any bride or groom ever truly enjoyed being at the center of this circus. The risk of violence was always present, too, for wine was combustible and male humor could quickly cross the border from bawdy to obscene to offensive. From stories she'd been told, trouble often began when the wedding guests no longer confined themselves to jests about the groom's manhood and began making lewd jokes about the bride. Most grooms had been drinking, too, and many were just as hot-tempered as the males in her family. So she was very thankful that she had such a formidable peacekeeper in her brother.

She was not happy to see that some of the men had brought flagons of wine with them, for that might make it harder to get rid of them. For reasons that escaped her, men seemed to think it hilarious to drag out the bedding revelries long past the point where the unhappy bridegroom had lost all patience. She occasionally saw a familiar face as they moved within her limited range of vision. Her nephew Otto looked as if he'd rather be elsewhere; she imagined he was not comfortable envisioning his own aunt in the throes of carnal lust. Her brother Johnny did not seem to be taking an active role in the bantering, either, and she wondered if he, too, felt protective of her. That seemed out of character for Johnny, but she could not rule it out, for every now and then he gave her an unexpected glimpse of the boy he'd once been. She could not catch everything that was being said, for it often seemed as if they were all talking at once, their words wine-slurred and interspersed with bursts of loud laughter. But the jests she did hear were rather tame, nowhere near as raw or crude as she'd expected, and she suddenly realized why; even men in their cups were leery of being disrespectful of the Lionheart's favorite sister. *Richard and Berengaria's own bedding-down revelries must have rivaled a nunnery for decorum and propriety,* she thought, stifling a giggle.

When she finally saw Raimond, she frowned, for he was still dressed. The men would be here all night at this pace. Someone made a toast to "storming the castle" and someone else expressed the hope that Raimond would "plant his seed in fertile soil." She'd given up trying to identify the voices by now, so she did not know who cried out that they ought to drink to the "conquest of Sicily." She could hear wine cups being clanked together and sighed with relief when she saw Raimond sit down so he could remove his shoes and chausses, thinking this would soon be over. They began teasing him about taking so long to undress, laughing uproariously when he said good-humoredly that the only person he was interested in getting naked with that night was his wife. But it all changed for Joanna when she heard an unfamiliar voice say with a sneer that there was no need to strip since he'd be praying over his bride, not swiving her.

Most of the men seemed to assume that the speaker meant Raimond would be heeding the bishop's plea for contemplation, not consummation, and there was some halfhearted laughter, for few thought the joke all that funny. Joanna knew better and from the look on Raimond's face, she could tell that he did, too. This was not a jest aimed at a bridegroom, it was a jeer aimed at a Cathar. Clearly the Norman speaker—and she could tell from his accent that he was Norman—believed that Raimond was a heretic at heart and would shrink from sins of the flesh even on his wedding night.

"So you are saying that I've just been wed to one of the most beautiful, desirable women in all of Christendom and I am going to abstain like a monk? Now, why is that?"

Joanna was proud of Raimond for taking up the challenge so boldly, but she was furious, too, that some drunken Norman lout would dare to bring his biases into her bedchamber, casting a shadow over her wedding night. She tucked the sheet carefully around her and before the man could respond, she pulled the bed hangings back.

That at once drew all eyes toward her and men began to jockey closer, hoping for a chance to see some skin. Joanna ignored them. "My lord brother, may I have a word with you?"

It was highly unusual for a bride to participate in the bedding-down revelries, and there were murmurings of astonishment. Even Raimond looked startled. Only Richard took it in stride. Approaching the bed, he leaned over, his expression quizzical. But by the time Joanna was done whispering in his ear, he was grinning. "I'll do my best," he promised. Turning back to the gaping men, he declared, "My sister is greatly troubled, for she fears that strange men have invaded her bedchamber." He paused then, for dramatic effect. "Even worse, she suspects that they might be French!"

That evoked laughter, as he'd known it would. Looking around the chamber, he pretended to be shocked, exclaiming, "By God, she is right! Well, we'll have none of that. This is Rouen, not Paris. Out, the lot of you!"

They didn't like that, for it was looking as if there would be a confrontation between the count and the Norman knight, and they were not happy with either Joanna or Richard for spoiling their fun. But then Richard seized Raimond by the arm and when they realized he was going to be ejected, too, they were immediately enthusiastic. That would be a great joke, holding the groom hostage down in the hall whilst his bride slept alone on her wedding night. Laughing, they started toward the door.

Richard had to laugh, too, at the expression on his sister's face. He wasn't sure if it was dismayed indignation or indignant dismay, but he thought if looks could kill, he'd be writhing in the floor rushes. Raimond was balking, and Richard winked, hoping he'd take the hint. He apparently did, for he no longer resisted as Richard ushered him toward the door. The others were already trooping into the stairwell and André helped to get the stragglers moving by telling them to clear a path, for he thought he was going to puke. Just as Richard reached the door, though, he came to a sudden halt.

"Wait, what if they come back? We know the French are not to be trusted. Best to leave a bodyguard. My lord count, are you up to guarding my sister's body against all intruders?"

"I am sure I can rise to the occasion, my liege," Raimond assured him and

before the men milling about in the stairwell could object, Richard pushed Raimond aside and plunged into the stairwell himself.

Raimond at once slammed the door and slid the bolt into place, cutting off
the protests as the men realized they'd been hoodwinked. "Alone at last," he
said, as Joanna shook her head, torn between amusement and exasperation.

"For a moment or so, I could cheerfully have throttled Richard," she admitted. "I thought he was serious!"

"It would not have mattered, love. I was not going to be removed from this
chamber, not even if I had a knife at my throat." Raimond glanced around the
room, pointing to a gilt flagon on the table. "Do you want some wine?" When
she declined, he crossed to the bed. "I was hoping you'd refuse. Now I shall demonstrate how quickly a man can shed his clothes if he is properly motivated."

Joanna was sitting up, no longer being as careful of the sheet's slippage. "This
is where a modest, demure young woman would blush and dutifully avert her
eyes, having been taught that it is not seemly to look upon male nudity. Alas, I
am not particularly modest, not at all demure, and dutiful only on occasion."

"I'll bear that in mind," he said, with a laugh that was muffled as he pulled his
tunic over his head. His chausses and shoes were already off, and his linen shirt
soon followed. She knew he'd just celebrated his fortieth birthday that summer,
but his body still had the leanness of youth, and she thought he was either very
active or just one of those lucky souls who never had to worry about putting on
weight. His skin was dark and smooth, unmarred by the battle wounds that so
many men proudly flaunted, although she did see one thin white scar along the
outer side of his right thigh. She yearned to touch it, to trace its path with caressing fingers, but then the scar was forgotten as he slid his braies down over his
hips.

Joanna's eyes opened wide. "Oh my!"

He grinned, glancing down at his erection. "And to think I've not yet seen
you naked, love. But Luc needs very little encouragement, always ready for
action."

Joanna gave a surprised lilt of laughter. "You named it?"

"Why not? One of a man's most intimate relationships is with his cock. Not
only are they constantly urging us to sin, but most women are sure we do our
thinking with them, too. Luc is actually named Lucifer, for he has been trying to
lure me to Hell since I was a raw lad of thirteen or so."

By now he was in bed beside her and stopped her laughter with his mouth. It was not their first kiss, for they'd managed to find a few moments of privacy after his arrival at Rouen. But Joanna soon discovered that those quick, stolen kisses were nothing like this, with their bodies entwined, her breasts pressed against his chest, the feeling of his swelling erection on her thigh.

By the time they ended the embrace, they were both breathless. "Luc, meet your new mistress," he murmured. "Clearly he's fallen utterly under your thrall, my lady. Be merciful with him."

Joanna laughed again, amused that he'd be quoting from the troubadours at a moment like this. "I think I am going to enjoy being married to you, Raimond de St Gilles."

"Of course you will." He'd begun kissing her throat, lowering his head to her breasts. "Three years is a long time to wait, love. I'll do my best to avoid racing to the finish line, but you need not fret. If this first time is for me, I promise the second time will be all yours."

Joanna was not sure what he meant; she was too caught up in what he was doing with his mouth and his hands to pay much heed to his words. She returned his kisses and caresses without shyness, for they were man and wife now, not illicit lovers, and she was soon squirming under him, clinging so tightly that she'd leave scratches on his shoulders. She did not even realize she was crying out his name, aware only of her body's fevered heat and the urgency of her need.

Raimond knew she was ready, but he still delayed, prolonging the delicious torment until he dared wait no longer. She gasped with his first thrust, shuddering, and he said, "Stay still, love. Wait . . ." Once he was sure he had Luc under control, he began to move slowly then, watching her all the while, for he loved to see a woman yield to passion, sorry that so many of them denied themselves such pleasure, sure it was a forbidden sin that would send them to Hell. Joanna was moaning, tossing her head from side to side on the pillow as his thrusts became faster, deeper. He kissed her again, his mouth hot on hers, and then she convulsed under him and he no longer held back, listening only to his body now until he also cried out and collapsed on top of her.

For a few moments, neither moved, unwilling to break the bond. When he finally raised up and withdrew, she felt bereft. Propping herself up on her elbow, she reached out and traced the curve of his mouth with her finger. "Oh, Raimond . . ." No more than that, but there was no need to say more.

He took her finger in his mouth and gently sucked. "It was not like that with your husband?"

"No . . . I enjoyed sharing his bed, but it was never like that. Why was it so different with you?"

"Because I'm a better lover?" He laughed. "No, Joanna, there is no great secret to it. I told you once that most men pay little attention to the female brain. Well, even though they think about the female body for most of their waking hours, they do not really know much about it. Some of them never learn that men reach the top of the mountain faster than women do. It is simply a matter of giving a woman the extra time she needs to get there."

When he put his arm around her, Joanna slid over, resting her head in the crook of his shoulder. "Sometimes with William, I'd be left wanting more, but I did not know exactly what that was. Not until tonight." After a moment, she began to laugh again. "I was just thinking of all the qualities I wanted in a husband. That he'd be highborn, of course. That he'd view the world with humor and if he had a temper, that he'd hold no grudges. That I'd find him pleasing to the eye. That he'd be a Christian; I'd taken that for granted until Richard offered me to Saladin's brother. But never once did I think that he ought to be good at climbing mountains!"

He smoothed her hair back from her forehead and brushed his lips against her temple. "I can see that you are going to do wonders for my male pride, love. And if you harbored any misgivings about whether I was a secret Cathar or not, I trust that I've put them to rest."

She studied his face, surprised to realize that he was only half joking. It must be a heavy burden at times, knowing that so many suspected him of heresy. "If I'd had such doubts, you'd have dispelled them quite spectacularly tonight. But I did not, Raimond. As I see it, you are guilty only of exercising tolerance, and in Sicily that was not a sin."

She'd assumed that all men wanted to go to sleep soon after lovemaking, for that had certainly been true with William and other women had confirmed it, too. She was pleased now to see that Raimond showed no such inclination. Instead of rolling over and bidding her good night, he rose and began to prowl about the chamber, saying they must surely have thought to leave out some food. Finding a bowl of dried fruit and nuts, he poured a cup of wine for them to share, snatched up a towel, and brought his booty back to the bed. Handing her the wine cup, he slowly patted her dry, making each touch of the towel feel like a caress. Reclaiming the cup, he said, "Wait . . . did you say Richard offered you to Saladin's brother?"

He listened in obvious delight as she related her brother's creative scheme to drive a wedge between the sultan and al-Adil, shaking his head in wonder once she was done. "How lucky he was that the French never found out about that. Instead of him being exonerated at Heinrich's court, they might have burned him at the stake!"

Joanna agreed, intrigued to see that Richard had just gone up in Raimond's estimation. "At the very least, it would have convinced the Germans that what our enemies say about us is true, that we trace our descent from the Devil's daughter." So then she had to tell him about Melusine, the Demon Countess of Anjou, confessing that her brothers had liked to boast about her, to the horror of any churchmen within earshot. "And what I did tonight will only add to our family's black legends," she said, giving him a look that managed to be both teasing and seductive. "I slept with Lucifer!"

He laughed so hard that he almost overturned their cup. "And the night is not over yet. Lucifer might well tempt you again, my lady." He leaned over then to give her a long, wine-flavored kiss. "How right I was to take you on faith, love!"

Joanna was no longer smiling. "It is true I did not give William a son, a living son. Yet if I conceived once, surely I can do so again."

"Joanna—"

"No, hear me out, for I need to say this. I know I am no longer young, for I turned thirty-one earlier this month. But if I'd feared I could not bear children, I'd have discussed it with you ere we were wed. Whilst my womb never quickened after my son died, I did not have as many chances to get pregnant as you might think. William had a *harim* of Saracen slave girls, and he—"

This time he stopped her by putting his finger over her mouth. "That was not what I meant, Joanna. I have no such fears. It is more likely it was William's fault, not yours, for none of his *harim* concubines ever got with child, did they? When a man spills his seed into so many different women without any of it taking root, the seed is the culprit, not the women."

Joanna had consulted with several of the female doctors at the famed medical school in Salerno after she'd failed to become pregnant again, and they'd told her the same thing, that sometimes the husband could be the one at fault. But she'd never heard a man acknowledge such a possibility until now. "No, William sired no other children," she confirmed. "And I did wonder at times. . . . But what did you mean, then, about taking me on faith?"

"I could not be sure if you were truly willing or if you'd been pressured by Richard into agreeing. I knew you'd been struck by the same lightning bolt, but that did not necessarily mean you would want to wed me. Three years had passed, after all," he said, with a sudden smile, "and the memory of my potent charm might have faded. Having had two unwilling wives, I was not keen to take a third."

Joanna was very curious about his former wives. "Will you tell me about them?"

"My first marriage was not of my wife's choosing, nor mine, either. But Ermessinde was the Countess of Melguel and my father was determined to have Melguel. She was newly widowed and I was much younger, not yet sixteen, so I could understand why she balked. We eventually became friends, though she lived only four years, and when she died, Melguel passed to me. My father usually got what he wanted," Raimond said, the corner of his mouth twisting into a smile that held no humor.

"And Beatrice Trencavel?"

"We got along well enough in the beginning. I knew she was a Believer, but I thought that was between her and her God. I did not allow her to raise our daughter, Constance, as one, though, and she came to resent me for that. She also grew more devout as the years went by, and paid the marital debt with increasing reluctance, fearful that she was putting her immortal soul at risk. So . . . I looked elsewhere when Luc was in need of indulgence, and I never had to look far."

Remembering how sharply she'd chastised him in the Bordeaux gardens, blaming him for the failure of his marriage, Joanna felt a pang of remorse. "You ought to have made it known that she was a Cathar, Raimond. Your enemies have used your unhappy marriage as one more weapon against you, claiming that you were heartless in putting her aside and depraved in siring bastards. If they knew the truth—"

"It would make no difference, Joanna. Dogs are always going to bark. I did not want to draw the Church's ire down upon Beatrice; she is still Constance's mother. And because she is a Trencavel, her family would become even more suspect in the eyes of men like Cardinal Melior, including my sister and nephew."

His tone had been serious, even somber, as he'd related his melancholy marital history, but she would soon learn that he could never be serious for long. The mention of the papal legate's name had awakened his sense of mischief and he gave her a wickedly gleeful smile. "Think how pleased the good cardinal will be to hear that you've wed one of the Devil's disciples, love. I think we ought to name our first daughter Melusine and ask him to serve as godfather."

When he saw that she was amused, not disconcerted, by his audacity, he reached over and drew her into his arms, marveling at how well matched they were, in and out of bed. His kiss was meant to be approving, affectionate, but she responded with such ardor that it soon became a passionate one. "Luc is stirring," he joked. "Do you want to wake him up?"

Joanna had never been a woman to refuse a dare, especially one she could win with such ease. "If I do, will you take me to the mountaintop?"

His breath quickened as her hand slid caressingly down his chest, toward his groin. "I promise," he said, and proved to be a man of his word.

AFTER THEIR WEDDING, Raimond took Joanna home to Toulouse, where she was given a joyful welcome into the city that reminded her of her torch-lit entry into Palermo nigh on twenty years ago. He then took her on a leisurely circuit of his domains to introduce her to his vassals. She'd not realized how extensive his holdings were, and decided it was not surprising that the dukes of Aquitaine had been so set upon reclaiming it for their duchy. By mid-December they were at Carcassonne, expecting to be back at Toulouse in time for their Christmas Court. Raimond was a noted patron of troubadours and jongleurs, and he was eager for them to celebrate the beauty and charm of his bride, assuring Joanna that the best would be in attendance—Peire Vidal, Raimon de Miraval, Gaucelm Faidit, and even Arnaut de Mareuil, whose plaintive songs of love for Raimond's sister Azalais had gotten him banished for a time from his lady's presence.

Joanna was looking forward to presiding over her own court again, a privilege that had been denied her since William's death. She felt a little guilty, though, that her Christmas would be so perfect and Berengaria's so miserable. As he'd threatened, the Archbishop of Rouen had laid all of Normandy under Interdict in November and then departed for Rome to present his grievances before the papal curia. If he'd hoped his drastic action would compel Richard to yield, he was to be disappointed, for Richard at once dispatched Longchamp, the Bishop of Lisieux, and Fulk, the Bishop-elect of Durham, to Rome, while he continued to spend most of his time at Andely, personally supervising the construction of Castle Gaillard. Eleanor had written that he was defiantly holding his Christmas Court in Normandy, at his hunting lodge at Bur-le-Roi near

Bayeux, determined to show the archbishop that in his duchy, his writ overrode the prelate's Interdict.

Eleanor was not attending, preferring not to make so long a journey again in the worst of winter, and she'd said that she did not know if Berengaria would be present or not. Joanna doubted it, for her sister-in-law would be incapable of defying the archbishop as Richard was doing. Her heart ached for her friend, torn between her husband and her God. But even Berengaria's sad plight could not cast a shadow for long. Joanna was so happy that nothing could tarnish the joy she took in her new life as the Countess of Toulouse.

On the morrow they would depart for Toulouse, but that evening a special Votive Mass was being said for the recovery of the ailing Bishop of Carcassonne. Raimond was unenthusiastic about attending, telling Joanna privately that the ineffective, elderly prelate's boring, rambling sermons were the best recruiting tool the Cathars had. But Joanna felt it would only give Raimond's enemies in the Church a new cause for complaint if they stayed away, and because he could refuse his new wife nothing, they emerged from the castle as twilight fell. The cathedral of St Nazaire was easily within walking distance, but their every public appearance had been drawing crowds and so Raimond was astride a favorite black palfrey and Joanna was riding his bride's gift, a fine-boned chestnut mare. Raimond's young nephew had at first balked, influenced—Joanna feared—by his tutor, Bertrand, the Lord of Saissac, who'd proudly proclaimed himself a Cathar upon meeting her. But Raimond-Roger changed his mind at the last moment and Azalais decided she would attend if her son did. So Carcassonne was treated to a royal procession through the narrow, cobbled streets to the cathedral.

The Mass was said by Berenger, the archdeacon, who also happened to be Bishop Othon's nephew, and it was soon obvious to Joanna that he was even less popular with the townspeople than his uncle. She was troubled by such open animosity toward the Church, for while she was prepared to tolerate the Cathars, she still considered herself a good Catholic, and she was relieved when Raimond reassured her that Toulouse was not like Carcassonne, where the appeal of the Cathar theology seemed deeply entrenched in its civic life.

When they departed the cathedral, they found that the street was still thronged with people, who cheered enthusiastically for their young viscount and for the Count of Toulouse and his bride. Joanna enjoyed the brief ride back to the castle, for she relished these demonstrations of her husband's popularity.

She and Raimond were still in the honeymoon phase of their marriage, and she wanted the rest of the world to find him as irresistible as she did.

Once they'd crossed through the barbican into the bailey, Raimond lifted Joanna from her sidesaddle, giving her a quick kiss as he set her upon the ground. As the others continued on into the castle, Joanna caught her husband's arm, asking if they could take a walk in the garden. He agreed readily, welcoming any opportunity to have some time alone with her, not always easy for two who lived so much of their lives on the public stage.

The air was chill but clear, and the sky above their heads looked like a wine-dark sea adrift in sailing stars. They sat on a bench and gazed upward, taking pleasure in the austere beauty of the night. Joanna was warmly dressed in a fur-lined pelisse and soft wool mantle, but Raimond used the cold as an excuse to pull her onto his lap. "Thank you again, love, for not objecting to have my son at our court. Unlike my daughters, he is not yet old enough to be sent off to a great household for educating. But you'll like him, for he is a good lad, if somewhat shy."

"I love children, Raimond. He is more than welcome to live with us."

He slid his hand under her mantle, fondling her thigh, and when she turned toward him, he was struck by how lovely she looked in the winter moonlight. "My God, but you're beautiful," he murmured, leaning in to claim her mouth with his own.

"I wanted you to kiss me like that," she confided, "on the day we sat here in the garden and, for the first time, truly talked. Do you remember?"

"I remember. I was amazed that I was able to exercise so much restraint, wanting to pounce upon you like a dog on a bone," he teased, and laughed when she chided him for being so romantic.

They sat in a comfortable silence for a time, not needing words. But she kept giving him glances from the corner of her eye, and at last, he said, "What is it, love? Is there something you would say to me?"

She nodded. "I was not going to tell you, not yet, not until I was sure. But I cannot wait any longer. Raimond . . . I am with child."

"Already?" He sounded incredulous and then euphoric, kissing her exuberantly, laughing, and kissing her again. "It must have happened on our wedding night, and what better proof can we have of God's favor than that?"

She laughed, too. "I am not sure if that was the night, although it must have been soon afterward," she said, explaining that she'd had her last flux the week ere their wedding day. "I remember, for I was relieved that I need not worry about it coming at an inopportune time. When I missed November's flux, I tried to rein in my hopes, knowing it was too early. Now I've missed December's, too, for it should have come a fortnight ago. I resolved to wait until the third month to tell you. But tonight in the cathedral, I felt this sense of peace, this utter certainty, as if the Blessed Mother herself was smiling upon me, upon us. When we return to Toulouse, I'll seek out a midwife. I have no doubts, though, none at all. I am bearing your child."

"It has been sixteen years since my daughter was born," he said softly, "sixteen years. I did not lie when I told you I did not believe our marriage would be barren. I just never imagined it would be so soon. . . ." Reaching under her mantle again, he laid his hand gently, almost reverently, upon her abdomen. "When?"

"I will have to see what the midwife says, but I think he will come in the summer." Joanna put her own hand over his, as if they were cradling their baby, protecting him from the dangers waiting outside the safety of her womb. She was sure it would be a boy, as sure as if God had whispered it in her ear, and she resolutely refused to think of all that could go wrong, of that small tomb in Monreale Cathedral. Giving Raimond a smile he would remember for the rest of his life, she said, "Soon enough to have people counting on their fingers—July."

CHAPTER THIRTY-ONE

Richard's new stronghold was recorded in the Pipe rolls as the Castle of the Rock, although he and others called it by the playful name he'd given it soon after construction began—Castle Gaillard, French for "saucy" or "bold." But Richard had in mind far more than the strategic placement of a river fortress. He was building a new walled town, Petit Andely, below the castle, and had dammed two streams to form a protective lake between it and the town claimed by the Archbishop of Rouen, now renamed Grand Andely. The Île d'Andely, an island in the Seine, was to be the site of a fortified royal palace, and a fort was to be constructed upon a smaller island, Boutavant. In an even more ambitious undertaking, a double stockade would block the river traffic. And on the steep white cliff three hundred feet above the River Seine would rise the towering walls of Castle Gaillard, the beneficiary of all that Richard had learned in twenty-five years of constant warfare, the citadel he fondly called his "fair daughter," meant to be as impregnable as Heaven's own gates.

André was very familiar with his cousin's audacious vision of what Les Andelys would become. He admired Richard for daring to dream so big, although he did wonder if the king's white-hot enthusiasm would burn so brightly as the years passed; he expected it to take at least a decade for Richard's grand design to be transformed into reality. He was stunned, therefore, on this blustery February afternoon to see how much had been done since his last visit.

A village of wooden buildings and barracks had been erected to house the workers, guards, and supplies, and everywhere André looked, he saw frantic activity. Men were hacking away with pickaxes, chisels, and hammers, carving deep moats out of solid rock. Others climbed up scaffolding to scramble onto walls covered with tarps to protect against the winter frosts. Smiths were busy forging tools, carpenters supervising the cutting of logs, hodmen staggering under heavy loads, barrowmen carrying away soil and stones, youths hastening over in response to thirsty shouts for "Water, lad!" It was, André, thought, like watching an anthill that had been knocked over, with ants scurrying in all directions.

"We cannot mix mortar again until the weather warms up," Richard said, sounding as if he bore a personal grudge against nature for interfering with his plans. "But we can still excavate the ditches. The moat around the outer bailey is going to be thirty feet wide and twenty feet deep. Come on, I'll give you a tour."

Hoping that did not involve climbing up on the scaffolding, André gamely followed as Richard led him across a bridge into the outer bailey. It was triangular and he saw at once that it would function very effectively as a barbican. Even assuming that the attackers got this far—and he doubted they would, for the site was protected on three sides by sheer chalk cliffs—they'd still be cut off from the middle bailey by a second deep moat and a high wall flanked by two round towers.

After they crossed another bridge, Richard pointed out the well in a corner of the middle bailey, saying the chapel and stables would be located here, too. The inner bailey was to be encircled by still another moat, but its most impressive defense would be the thick, corrugated walls, with round towers spaced every nine feet, making it impossible for enemy sappers to dig mines without exposing themselves to fire from above. Richard showed André where a square gatehouse would be situated, and they crossed another bridge into the inner bailey.

There André was astonished to see that work had already begun on the great keep, which was to have a rare cylindrical shape, with a beak like the prow of a ship, similar to the keep that Richard was building at Issoudun. He marveled that it was actually built right into the bailey wall, never having seen that before, and he was impressed, too, when Richard showed him another innovation: the long sloping plinth at the foot of the keep, which would allow rocks and weapons dropped from the battlements to ricochet off it, causing even greater injury to the attackers while deterring would-be sappers.

Nor was that all, Richard added proudly. There would be hoardings on the inner bailey walls, of course, those temporary wooden structures angled out from the top of castle ramparts to allow the defenders to drop rocks and hot liquids through openings in the floor. But the hoardings on Gaillard's keep were to be different. He called them machicolations, saying they'd be permanent, made of stone to defy fire arrows, and when André—who'd never heard of such a thing—asked how their weight could be supported, Richard told him more about corbeled arches than he needed or wanted to know.

"A pity you were born a king's son," he joked, "for you'd have made a right fine master mason!"

Richard grinned. "That is what Master Sewale says, too," he confided, naming the chief clerk in charge of the castle expenditures. "According to him, I am wasting money on a master mason since I am doing most of his work myself."

"Well, you're not only a master mason, Cousin, you're a magician. How in the name of all that's holy have you managed to get so much done so fast?"

"What is the most powerful inducement?"

"A knife at a man's throat?"

"Money, André, money. When men are paid and paid very well for their labors, they are also highly motivated. Master Sewale claims that I'll have spent over eleven thousand pounds on motivation when all is said and done."

André stared at him openmouthed, for Richard had recently complained that since his coronation, he'd had to spend seven thousand pounds on the maintenance of his English castles—all of them. Richard had turned toward the scaffolding that encased a partially completed wall, and André reluctantly followed, thinking he was getting too old to be clambering about like a mountain goat. But the wall seemed to offer solid footing; the rubble packed between the ashlar faces was covered with straw, dung, and a canvas tarp. When he looked down, André discovered a spectacular view. Far below them lay the new walls of Petit Andely, a raised causeway over the lake connecting it with Grand Andely. Beyond it, the River Seine flowed majestically toward the Narrow Sea, moss green in the wan February sun. André tried to imagine that surging current challenged by a wooden stockade—tried and failed, although he did not doubt that Richard would see it done, even if he had to help hammer in the posts himself.

"Did I take your tongue away with that vast sum?" Richard asked, with another grin. "You know why I am willing to spend so much, do you not, André?"

André nodded. "Castles are built for defense. Not Gaillard, though. Oh, it will be of great value in protecting Rouen and the Norman border. But that is not why you are so smitten with this 'fair daughter' of yours. You intend to take the offensive against the French king, to use it as a base to reclaim the Vexin."

Richard was still smiling, but his eyes had focused on the southern horizon, taking on a glitter that André had seen before—on the battlefield. "How much sleep do you think Philippe will get," he said, "knowing that Castle Gaillard is a three-day ride from Paris?"

❦

THE SKY WAS SOON obscured by lowering clouds and, much to Richard's vexation, a chill, steady rain began to fall. He reluctantly ended the day's work and, as the men sought shelter, he and André mounted and rode down into Petit Andely, then across the bridge onto the Île d'Andely. By now, André was expecting miracles to be an everyday occurrence and so he felt no surprise to find that the isle was already walled in, with comfortable living quarters for his cousin the king.

André was pleased to see Otto in attendance upon Richard, not as pleased to see John, but the latter was on his best behavior these days and greeted André with cousinly goodwill. Remembering that he'd not eaten since breaking his fast that morning, Richard ordered a meal, and it was only after they'd dined that it occurred to him to ask André why he'd made such a long winter's journey from Berry into Normandy. Seeing the shadow that crossed André's face at the question, he dismissed the other men, leaving them alone on the hall dais. "Cousin? What is amiss?"

André took a gulp of wine. "I wanted to let you know that I am going to Rome as soon as the alpine passes are open in the spring."

Richard blinked in surprise. "Rome? Why?"

André took another swallow and grimaced, even though they were drinking a fine red wine from Cahors. "Do you remember when I told you I'd been having trouble with the Abbot of Déols? He's quite the strutting peacock, is our abbot, bound and determined to be king of his own little dunghill."

He was mixing metaphors with abandon, but Richard forbore to tease him about it, realizing that the older man was truly worried. "I remember," he said. "He accused you of encroaching on the liberties of his abbey, no?"

"To hear him tell it, my sins are legion. The truth is that the pompous fool does not like it that Denise has a husband willing to defend her rights. He's gone so far as to claim our marriage is invalid, insisting we are within the forbidden degree of kinship."

Richard was astonished. "That is nonsense! We checked for any consanguinity problems ere the marriage took place."

"I know," André said morosely, "but that has not stopped the wretch from asking the Archbishop of Bourges to excommunicate me and declare our marriage null and void. Denise is understandably distraught about it, especially now that she is breeding again, so I promised her that I would appeal to the Pope."

"The Archbishop of Bourges?" Richard sat up straight, staring at his cousin. "Holy Christ! If the archbishop is involved, this is Philippe's doing, André, for they are spokes on the same wheel."

André began to curse, long and loudly. He'd been infuriated that a minor dispute over privileges could have erupted into an ugly quarrel that threatened his very marriage, but he'd been dumbfounded when the archbishop had taken the abbot's side, for it made no sense. Now it did. He was heartened that Richard shared his outrage, gratefully accepted the offer to write to the Pope on his behalf, and they spent the next quarter hour damning the French king and his partners in crime to the hottest regions of the netherworld.

Once their anger had cooled, Richard remembered to congratulate André on Denise's latest pregnancy, adding that he had happy news of his own. "Joanna is with child, too. And I've made a good match for Philip; he's to wed the Lady Amelie, heiress to the barony of Cognac."

André was pleased for Joanna and delighted that Richard had provided so well for Philip's future, for he'd become quite fond of the boy. "How old is he now—nigh on sixteen, no? Of an age to wed for certes," he said, although his smile vanished as his gaze strayed across the hall, where John and several knights were playing a boisterous dice game. He thought it a great pity that Richard's only son was bastard-born and John likely to be his heir since his queen was barren. Denise had taken issue with him about that, arguing that Berengaria might still get with child. But André did not think so, nor did he blame his cousin for neglecting his marital duties. Whilst he liked Berengaria well enough, bedding her must be like bedding a nun.

His smile came back then, as he thought of his own wife, who was as eager for their bed sport as he was, and had been ever since their bridal night. She'd been sixteen, already a widow, and he'd been very grateful to Richard for giving him such a wealthy heiress. But she'd brought him far more than lands. From the first, she'd shown a common sense that belied her youth, realizing how it bene-fited her to have a husband in such high favor with the new king, and their mar-riage had gotten off to a good start, even though he was more than twenty years her senior. She was with child ere he left for the Holy Land, had given him three healthy sons and a happy home life, one he was not going to lose, by God. He'd promised her he'd deal with it, and if that meant traveling all the way to Rome to appeal to that lickspittle on the papal throne, so be it.

Richard had always read André with ease, and he saw now that the other man's thoughts had taken a gloomy turn again. He was about to reassure his cousin that they'd get this lunacy sorted out, but it was then that he happened to notice the new arrivals being ushered into the hall. Recognizing one as the Archdeacon of Évreux, he got to his feet with a frown. "That's passing strange. Master Mauger was part of the delegation I sent to Rome to appeal that accursed Interdict. Why is he back so soon?"

Without waiting for the man to come to him, he strode across the hall. Con-tent to stay where he was, André was finishing the rest of his wine when Otto strolled over to keep him company, bearing some very interesting news. Appar-ently there was new unrest in Sicily, serious enough for Heinrich to hasten there himself to quell it. According to their source, the Archbishop of Cologne, Hein-rich had vowed to show no mercy to the rebels, determined that nothing would delay his departure for the Holy Land.

André had heard that Heinrich had taken the cross, planning to lead a large German army to Outremer, and he very much hoped it would never come to pass. It was bad enough that Richard had been unable to fulfill his own vow to return and take Jerusalem because of the constant threat posed by the French king. How painful it must be to have to watch now whilst Heinrich sought to do what he could not. Sometimes it seemed to André as if the Almighty intended to test Richard as mercilessly as He'd tested Job.

Otto sought to lighten the mood then, with more cheerful news. Heinrich had suffered another setback, he said, with a sudden smile that reminded André how young this solemn lad was, not yet twenty. André had doubtless heard that last spring Heinrich had pressured the German princes and bishops into agree-ing to make the imperial crown hereditary. But at a second Diet in Erfurt that past October, the Archbishop of Cologne had rallied the opposition and they'd held firm, insisting the crown remain elective. "Heinrich was said to have lost some of that vaunted control of his. How he must hate Archbishop Adolf! But the archbishop does not fear him, and because he does not—"

Otto broke off abruptly, for Richard was returning to the dais and they knew before he said a word that something was very wrong. He'd lost color and when he raised his head, they saw tears clinging to his lashes. "Longchamp is dead. He took ill of a sudden when they reached Poitiers and died ere the week was out. . . ."

André and Otto expressed their condolences and, as word spread, other men approached the dais to do the same, somewhat awkwardly, for the chancellor had remained a controversial figure. Acknowledging that now, Richard said, almost accusingly, "There will be few to mourn him."

Since that was true, no one knew what to say. It was Otto who finally found the right words. "But *you* will mourn him, Uncle, and that is what would have mattered to him."

Richard was silent for a time, thinking of Trifels Castle and the small, stooped figure kneeling by his bed, the most unlikely of saviors. "Yes," he said, "I will. . . ."

❧

RICHARD HONORED THE MEMORY of his nepotistic chancellor in the way that Longchamp would have most appreciated, by arranging for his brother Robert, Archdeacon of Ely, to be chosen as abbot of the prestigious abbey of St Mary's in York.

Longchamp's traveling companions, the Bishop of Lisieux and the Bishop-elect of Durham, continued on to Rome, where Pope Celestine heard their arguments and those presented by the Archbishop of Rouen. Ruling in Richard's favor, he lifted the Interdict and advised the archbishop to accept Richard's offer to swap the port of Dieppe and other manors for Andely, which he grudgingly did.

❧

BALDWIN DE BETHUNE'S MEN were pleased when their lord set out to join the English king in his assault upon the Bishop of Beauvais's castle at Milly-sur-Thérain, for they'd missed out on his April raid upon Ponthieu. Richard had burned the port of St Valéry and seized five English ships in the harbor, confiscating their cargo and hanging the ships' captains as a warning to others who defied his embargo upon trade with France and Flanders. As he'd also carried off holy relics and carts loaded down with booty, Baldwin's men regretted not taking part in this raid; Richard was renowned for generously sharing such plunder with his soldiers. They knew his assault upon Milly-sur-Thérain would not be as rewarding, but they still welcomed this opportunity to profit at the bishop's expense. It was a disappointment, therefore, when they reached the siege on May 19 and found that they were too late, that Richard had already captured the castle.

❧

BALDWIN WAS SEATED IN the king's command tent, listening with keen interest to Richard's account of the stronghold's fall, for the hero of the hour was his old friend Will Marshal.

"When we put up the ladders, so many knights started to climb up one of them that it became overloaded and some of the rungs broke, sending men plummeting down into the ditch below." Richard paused until Baldwin had been served wine before continuing. "One of the Flemish knights, Sir Guy de la Bruyère, was trapped on the top of it, unable to go up or down. He would not have been long for this world if Will had not rushed to his rescue."

"I did no more than any man would have done," Will protested, with appealing if unconvincing modesty, for all knew he took great pride in his battlefield prowess.

Richard ignored the interruption. "Will jumped into the ditch and clambered up the other side, then scrambled onto the ladder using the unbroken rungs, sword in hand. Truly a sight to behold," he said, grinning over at the Marshal. "After freeing Sir Guy, he made a one-man stand atop the battlements, defending himself so fiercely that his foes were soon in retreat. It was then that the castellan, Sir William de Monceaux, reached the ramparts. When he charged forward, Will struck him so powerful a blow that his sword cut right through his helmet, separating his coif from the hauberk and piercing his head. Not surprisingly, none were eager to take Will on after that."

"Well done, Will!" Baldwin said, also grinning at the Marshal.

"The story is not over yet, Baldwin. Since Will is not—how should I put it— in the first flush of youth, he was understandably weary after all this activity. The castellan had fallen at his feet, unconscious, but showed signs of stirring. So to make sure he stayed put, Will sat on him as he awaited the rest of our men. He made himself so comfortable that I am surprised he did not take a quick nap."

Richard raised his wine cup in a playful salute and the tent resounded to enthusiastic cries of "To the Marshal!" Glancing fondly at the other man, he said, shaking his head in mock dismay, "But it is not right for a man of such eminence and proven valor to have to exert himself like this. You ought to leave that to the young knights who still have to win their reputations, Will, for your own fame is already secure."

Will did not mind the teasing, for how many men of fifty would have been able to equal the feats he'd performed that day? "Well, sire, the same could be said of you, for I heard that your knights had to keep you from being the first one into the breach."

Richard laughed, conceding the Marshal the honors in that exchange, and when Will then offered him the castellan, who would bring a large ransom, he shook his head. "No, you well deserve this right. I appoint you his lord and warder."

Will smiled in return, savoring his triumph all the more because he knew there would not be that many more of them; age always won out in the end. "We took many prisoners," he told Baldwin, "so there will be enough ransoms for all of us."

Will paused then, for a sudden uproar had broken out in the camp. The men were instantly on alert, but relaxed when they heard the sound of raucous cheering. "Mercadier must be back," Richard said, telling Baldwin that he'd been out on a raiding expedition. They'd begun to discuss the ransoms when the entry flap was pulled aside and John plunged into the tent.

All formality forgotten, John shoved his way toward his brother, his face flushed with excitement, eyes as green as any cat's. "Richard, you're about to get an early birthday present, mayhap your best one ever! I wish I could claim the credit, but it was Mercadier's doing. At least I got to witness it."

By now the tent was abuzz with curiosity and speculation. Before John could make his dramatic revelation, though, Mercadier was there. It was not always easy to tell when he was smiling, for the corner of his mouth was contorted by that disfiguring scar. But there was no mistaking his mood now. His usual demeanor—cynical, wary, faintly mocking—was utterly gone; he looked fiercely triumphant. He was followed by several of his routiers, who shoved a prisoner into the tent, forcing him to his knees.

Even before the man raised his head, Richard knew his identity, for there could be no other explanation for John and Mercadier's unholy glee. The Bishop of Beauvais was chalk white, with a darkening bruise on his forehead, sweat beading his temples, dirt streaking his face, and flecks of dried blood in his beard. He made an attempt at bravado, though, saying defiantly, "Need I remind you that I am a prince of the Church?"

He got no further, for Richard had begun to laugh. "Is this what priests are wearing now to say Mass?" he jeered, gesturing toward the bishop's mail hauberk and empty scabbard.

Beauvais's jaw muscles clenched, his chin jutting out. "I am a consecrated bishop, and the Holy Father in Rome will not tolerate my ill treatment."

Richard was still laughing. "I do not doubt that the Holy Father in Rome will accord you all the protection he gave me when I was held prisoner in Germany."

Beauvais started to rise, only to be stopped by Mercadier's men. "Get your hands off me, you lowborn churls!" he blustered, but they paid him no heed, forcing him back onto his knees. Hectic splotches of color now burned across his ashen cheekbones, giving him the look of a man on fire with fever. "Name your ransom," he said, his voice rasping, his dark eyes desperate, "and I will pay it."

Richard ignored him, glancing around at the other men, all of whom were grinning widely, relishing this moment almost as much as Richard did. Reaching out, he clasped Mercadier's arm. "Thank you, my friend," he said simply, and for just a moment, Mercadier lowered his guard to show a very human reaction— genuine pleasure. Richard exchanged smiles with John, and then turned back to Beauvais.

"Do you remember what you said to me that night at Trifels? I do. You told me how much pleasure you'd derive to think of me 'cold, hungry, dirty, and fettered like a common felon.' You've forgotten that, have you?"

Beauvais ran his tongue over dry lips, swallowing with a visible effort. "You would not dare! Harm me and you'll forfeit your eternal soul!"

Some of the men began to mutter at that, angered by his insolence, for Beauvais found no defenders even among the most devout. But Richard merely smiled, a smile that chilled the bishop to the marrow of his bones.

"I promise you this," he said. "I will show you the same mercy that you'd have shown me had I ended up in a Paris dungeon."

THE ARCHBISHOP OF CANTERBURY had been given the obligatory tour of Castle Gaillard; it gave Richard great pleasure to watch his guests marvel at what he was building at Les Andelys, especially men like Hubert Walter and André, men who could understand and appreciate what a lethal weapon was now aimed at the heart of the French king's domains. He doubted that Philippe fully comprehended it yet. But he would, and soon.

They were back at his new palace on the Île d'Andely now; as much as Richard enjoyed his on-site supervision of the ongoing work, he and Hubert had a lot of catching up to do, for there'd been some dramatic developments on the diplomatic front in June. He'd made peace with the Bretons, agreeing to restore the lands he'd seized during last year's rebellion, pardoning the Breton barons, offering terms generous enough to win over the powerful de Vitré family, and getting the Earl of Chester to end Constance's captivity. In return, Constance and her lords abandoned their alliance with Philippe and did homage again to Richard. Arthur was still at the French court, but Constance pledged homage in his name, and Brittany was once more a domain of the Angevin empire—at least for now. Richard was realistic enough to know how elusive peace was in their world.

In addition to taking homage from Constance and the Breton barons, Richard had also accepted it from knights and lords of Champagne and Flanders, had won back several of the Norman barons who'd defected to Philippe during his time in Germany, and was in secret negotiations with one of Philippe's most powerful vassals, Renaud de Dammartin, the Count of Boulogne. Most promising of all, he told Hubert, his spies at the Flemish court had reported that the unrelenting pressure he'd been putting upon the Flemish economy was finally paying off. They'd assured him that Baldwin, the young Count of Flanders, would be receptive to English overtures, and so he'd dispatched Will Marshal to meet with Baldwin, offering full restoration of trade privileges for the Flemish merchants and a "gift" of five thousand silver marks for Count Baldwin.

"So you see," Richard concluded with a grim smile, "the noose is tightening around Philippe's neck."

Hubert was delighted, pleasing Richard with his heartfelt praise, for he respected few men as much as he did this one. But he had far less pleasant news to share and he put it off for a while, encouraging the archbishop to bring him up to date about English matters. When servants began to set up trestle tables in the hall, though, making ready for the evening meal, he realized he could delay no longer.

"I've heard from my friend, the Archbishop of Cologne," he said abruptly. "You'll not like what I'm about to tell you, Hubert. No man of honor would. Heinrich has been spilling enough Sicilian blood to flood the entire kingdom. He had Tancred's brother-in-law, the Count of Acerra, dragged through the city behind a horse, then hung upside down. It took him two days to die. He had others flung into the sea or flayed alive. And then he exacted vengeance upon the men he'd imprisoned at Trifels Castle after his coronation. He had Admiral Margaritis and the brother of the Archbishop of Salerno blinded and the counts of Marsico and Carinola put to death."

Hubert frowned. "That is very unjust, for they could have played no role in the rebellion; they've been his prisoners for nigh on three years."

"You've not heard the worst of it yet. He ordered Tancred's young son blinded and castrated, and the boy—who was about seven—died as a result of it."

Hubert shook his head slowly and then made the sign of the cross. "The Devil truly walks amongst us."

Richard was gazing broodingly into the depths of his wine cup. "There were times during my German captivity when I wondered if Heinrich was mad. But instead of terrifying the Sicilians into submission, Heinrich's brutal measures incited them against him and a new conspiracy was formed this spring. Heinrich was to be ambushed whilst out hunting and slain. But he was warned in time and fled to Messina. The rebels were defeated in the field and Catania was taken by assault. Heinrich then took a bloody revenge upon the conspirators, having many of them executed in extremely painful ways. The most gruesome fate he saved for Jordan Lapin, the Count of Bouvino, who was killed by having a crown nailed to his head."

Hubert had met some of these men during their stay in Sicily, and even if he did not consider them friends, he did not think they deserved this. "A man who could devise such a barbaric punishment is one who enjoys inflicting pain. You were lucky, Richard, all things considered."

"The story is not done yet, Hubert. Adolf says that Constance was involved with the conspirators."

The archbishop's jaw dropped. "Blessed Mother of God! Can that be true?"

Richard shrugged. "According to Adolf, she and Heinrich quarreled bitterly after he executed the Count of Acerra and so many others, then mutilated Tancred's son. Few women would not have been horrified by that. And at least one of the men killed was kin to her. Adolf even claims that the Pope knew of the conspiracy and approved, or at least gave tacit approval by his silence. As for Constance, whether her involvement is true or not, Heinrich apparently believed it. He forced her to attend the execution of Jordan Lapin, who was also her kinsman, and to watch as the crown was nailed to his head."

"Jesu!" Hubert was a worldly churchman, a politician, a seasoned soldier, and he was not easily shaken by evidence of mankind's capacity for cruelty. But he was appalled by what he'd just learned of life in the once-peaceful kingdom of Sicily. "Does Lady Joanna know of this? I remember how fond she was of the empress."

"I have not told her yet. Her baby is due this month and I thought it best to wait, for she'd be bound to fear for Constance's future. Heinrich has his heir now, so he no longer needs Constance to legitimize his claim to the Sicilian throne. He could rule through Friedrich, who is not yet three."

Richard lapsed into another brooding silence, thinking of his sister's distress when she learned of Constance's peril, thinking of Tancred and his doomed little lad, remembering Heinrich's smug smile when he'd had to kneel in the great hall at Mainz and do homage to the German emperor. "What I do not understand," he said, with some bitterness, "is why the Church does not do more to rein this man in. He was implicated in the murder of the Bishop of Liege. He has held the Archbishop of Salerno prisoner at Trifels for nigh on three years. The Bishop of Catania was one of those he ordered blinded. Why does the Church not defend its own?"

Hubert had no answer for him, not one that did not compromise his rank as the head of the English Church. Celestine was too fearful to challenge the German emperor openly, remembering when Heinrich's father had sent troops into Rome, forcing a Pope into French exile. But Hubert did not think it seemly for a prelate to speak disrespectfully of the Holy Father, however lacking he might be. Reminding himself that his first loyalty must now be to the Church, not the English king, he offered a perfunctory defense of the elderly Pope. "He has protested those outrages in the strongest language possible. But he is an old man, past ninety. . . ."

"A pity popes do not retire," Richard said caustically. "Whilst I was in Germany, the Archbishop of Cologne did just that, believing himself too old and enfeebled to fulfill his duties, thus opening the door for his nephew Adolf to take his place. But popes cling to power the way barnacles cling to a ship's hull, so I suppose we can only hope that the Almighty calls that spineless old man home soon." It had occurred to him that the indecisive Celestine might take the easy way and find against André and Denise rather than overrule one of his own archbishops.

"The Pope did find in your favor, though, in your case against the Archbishop of Rouen," Hubert said mildly. This talk of the papacy had reminded him of an unpleasant duty that lay ahead of him, and he reluctantly asked if he could see the king in private.

❧

"YOU CANNOT BE SERIOUS?" Richard stared at the archbishop in disbelief. "You are defending that treacherous, foul hellhound? If Beauvais is a pious son of the Church, then I'm bidding fair to reach sainthood!"

"I am not defending him," Hubert said hastily. "I am simply saying that we cannot ignore the fact that he is a prelate of the Holy Church, however little we may like it. I had a letter from Pietro of Capua, the papal legate. He is on his way to the French court and he is expressing outrage that you've imprisoned a bishop, is threatening to lay Normandy under Interdict—"

"What are you asking, that I release him? Not even for the surety of my own soul!"

"No, I am not asking that, Richard. But Beauvais's continuing captivity could cause a strain between England and the papacy. You need to bear that in mind."

"And I have so much reason to be grateful to the papacy! I owe my mother and my vassals and subjects for buying my freedom. I owe the Pope nothing!"

Richard was so angry that Hubert no longer argued, seeing it would be to no avail. But his silence did nothing to quench the king's temper. His face flushed, mouth set, he glared at his old friend as if he were the enemy. "Beauvais is the man responsible for the time I spent at Trifels in chains. He urged Heinrich to treat me harshly in order to break my spirit. He came to mock my misery, took joy in dwelling upon all that I'd never experience again, telling me that I'd never see the sun or feel the rain on my face, that I'd never swive a woman or ride a horse or hear music, that I'd be left to rot alone in the dark—"

Richard stopped suddenly, cutting off his words in midsentence. Had Beauvais truly taunted him like that? Or was he borrowing from the harrowing, dreaded dreams that still haunted his nights even now? He found those dreams so troubling because they seemed so utterly and mercilessly real. But never before had they spilled over into the daylight like this, and he was shaken to realize what a blurred line separated the present from the past. Turning his back on Hubert, he moved to the open window, staring up at the dark silhouette starkly outlined against the reddening sky, the castle created solely by his will, each chiseled stone proof of the power he still exercised over other men, the vagaries of war, and his own fate.

Hubert said nothing, silenced by the raw emotion in Richard's voice as he'd railed against the Bishop of Beauvais. When he moved away from the window, his anger still smoldered but was no longer in full flame. "Beauvais slandered me the width and breadth of Christendom. At Speyer, I found myself entrapped in a web of his lies, and when I was able to free myself, he did all he could to make sure I would die in a French oubliette. I will never forgive him. Never."

"Nor would I ask you to," Hubert said quietly. "It is my understanding that you have agreed to ransom Sir Guillaume de Mello and the other knights taken captive that day by Mercadier, but not Beauvais. I heard that you turned down a ransom offer of ten thousand marks. Is that true?"

"It is. I will never set him free."

"I understand," Hubert said, "I do. I ask only that you ease the conditions of his imprisonment. As long as he is being held in such harsh confinement, the controversy about his captivity will continue. Not for his sake, but for the pallium he has the right to wear."

Richard was not moved by the appeal. "Mercadier did not burst into a church and drag him away from the altar, Hubert. He was taken on the battlefield, leading an armed force to raise the siege at Milly-sur-Thérain. He is a false priest, a godless man who knows no more of piety than a wild boar."

"I'll not argue that point," Hubert said with a faint smile. "I ask only that you think upon what I've said."

Another silence ensued. When Richard at last agreed to do so, Hubert suspected that it was a grudging courtesy, no more than that. But he was satisfied, feeling that he'd discharged the duty so unwillingly imposed upon him by the papal legate.

Both men were relieved by the sudden knock at the door, wanting to put this uncomfortable conversation behind them. At Richard's command, his squire entered the solar. Hubert had not seen Arne in several years, and was surprised by how much he'd changed; he was eighteen now, and had left the awkwardness of adolescence behind. He greeted the archbishop with the confidence gained during four years in the king's service, and then smiled at Richard.

"I know you were eager to hear from my lord marshal, sire."

❧

AS SOON AS RICHARD returned to the hall, he knew that Will's Flemish mission had been successful before a word was said, for the man at Will's side was one Richard recognized, Simon de Haverets, the marshal of the Count of Flanders. Glancing toward Hubert, he said jubilantly, "First Toulouse and now Flanders. Philippe has just lost his last ally."

CHAPTER THIRTY-TWO

❦

JULY 1197

Beaucaire Castle, Toulouse

Raimond was standing in the inner bailey, gazing up at the window of the tower in which his wife was laboring to give birth to their child. The sun had set several hours ago, and the whitewashed castle walls glowed in the soft moonlight, but the day's stifling heat still kept the cooler night air at bay and the window was open to any vagrant breezes. Several times he had heard Joanna cry out, stifled sounds of pain that caused him to flinch and pace restlessly. He hated feeling so helpless, hated being banished from her lying-in chamber, hated knowing so little about childbirth. Her pangs had begun that morning, more than twelve hours ago. Should she not have delivered the baby by now? Or was it natural to take so long? Women guarded the secrets of the birthing chamber well, the one realm in which the wishes of men did not matter and female instinct and intuition ruled.

He'd long ago concluded that women had much in common with the Cathars, both forced to live in a world in which law and custom conspired to keep them silent and submissive, although that was not an idea he'd ever shared. He suspected that even Joanna would find his mental musings to be unsettling, for he'd known since boyhood that his brain was as determined as Luc to lead him astray. Inquisitive, whimsical, and irreverent, it balked at following the well-worn path set down by Church and society, constantly veering off into forbidden territory and getting him into trouble with his father, his tutors, his confessors—until he finally learned to control his tongue, if not his thoughts. So he had not blamed women for defending their only sanctum—until tonight, when he was exiled out in the bailey whilst Joanna was struggling to bring a new life into the world without losing her own. For that much he did understand about childbirth—how dangerous it could be.

His pacing had taken him closer and closer to the tower doorway. He'd made several trips up the stairs to the upper story, and although he'd been denied entry, one of his sisters or Mariam would come out and reassure him that all was going as it ought. But would they tell him if it were not so? If the birthing was dragging on too long? If Joanna was weakening? If she'd begun to bleed?

"MAMAN!"

"I am here, dearest, right here." Eleanor took a towel and wiped the perspiration from Joanna's face. She was no stranger to the lying-in chamber, having given birth to ten children and attended numerous female friends over the years. But when she'd assisted in the birth of her grandson Wilhelm during Tilda's English exile, she'd discovered that it was as difficult to watch a daughter's travail as to endure it herself. And on this summer night at Beaucaire Castle, she was suffering Joanna's pain as if it were her own.

Esquiva, younger than most midwives but with a serene self-confidence that women in childbirth found soothing, knelt before the birthing stool and poured thyme oil into her hands so she could check the dilation of the cervix. "It ought not to be much longer, my lady."

Azalais brought over a cup of wine mixed with bark of cassia fistula, urging Joanna to take a few more swallows. "It is sure to be a boy," she assured her sister-in-law, "for males like to tarry in order to make a grand entrance. Girls are more biddable than their brothers, even in the womb."

Joanna was drenched in sweat, her eyes smudged with dark circles, and her lips were cracked and bleeding. She mustered up a wan smile, for she remained convinced that her baby was a son. Why was it taking so long, though? Bohemond's delivery had been quicker . . . or had it? She was so exhausted now that even her memories were becoming muddled.

The opening door drew all eyes toward Mariam, who'd gone on another mission of mercy to Raimond. "You're doing better than your husband," she said, bending over to brush Joanna's hair back from her forehead. "The man is as jumpy as a treed cat. He wanted you to have this." She opened her hand to show Joanna a coral ring. "He remembered hearing that coral eases childbed pains and sent servants rummaging through every coffer in the castle until they found this." It was too big even for Joanna's thumb, but she closed her fist tightly around it, not because she believed it had magical powers, but because it was Raimond's.

"I was waylaid by Master Pons," Mariam said, "and he insisted that I give you his advice, Dame Esquiva." This caused some chuckling among the women, for none of them would have dreamed of trusting a male doctor over a midwife. "He says that it would be safe to bleed Joanna now since night has fallen, explaining at great length that all women are of a melancholic nature, unlike men, who can also be choleric, sanguine, and phlegmatic. I feared he was going to give me the entire history of bloodletting ere I could make my escape!"

"If women are indeed melancholic by nature, then we have men to blame for that," Eleanor said tartly. She had no intention of seeing her daughter bled, thinking women lost enough blood during childbirth as it was. But she need not have worried, for Esquiva was in full agreement, saying dismissively that Master Pons knew as much about delivering a baby as she did about the science of alchemy.

The physician was forgotten then, when Joanna cried out again. Her contractions were coming much more frequently now and under the midwife's direction, the women massaged her belly with warmed thyme oil, fed her spoonfuls of honey to keep her strength up, and closed the window when she began to shiver. Esquiva had probed the mouth of her womb, assuring herself the baby was in the right position, and urged Joanna to bear down until she saw the crowning.

"Stop pushing, my lady! I see the head," she announced triumphantly. Joanna had no breath to scream, writhing in pain when the baby's shoulders came free. She clutched Raimond's ring so tightly that the coral dug deep scratches into her palm as her son entered the world, his skin blotched and puckered, covered in mucus and her own blood. His sex was confirmed almost at once by Esquiva. "A man-child!"

But instead of rejoicing, Joanna was suddenly overwhelmed by fear, remembering how vulnerable Bohemond had been from the moment he'd drawn his first feeble breath, small and frail and unresponsive, almost as if he'd known that he did not belong there, that God would soon call him home. Tears burning her eyes, she reached out weakly toward her baby, wanting to hold him before she saw upon Esquiva's face the dismay that she'd seen upon the faces of the Sicilian midwives. It was then, though, that he let out a loud, piercing cry, sounding as if he was protesting the indignities he'd been subjected to, sounding robust and strong enough to banish the worst maternal fears.

The women were cooing over the baby as Esquiva cleaned out his mouth, cut and tied the umbilical cord, and began to wipe the slimy coating from his squirming little body. Tears were not uncommon after birth, so only Mariam interpreted them correctly, Mariam who'd been in the birthing chamber as Joanna had been delivered of her dying baby. "He is perfect, Joanna," she said, taking the other woman's hand in her own. "Perfect from head to toe, I swear it."

Taking the baby from the midwife, Eleanor leaned over and placed him in his mother's arms. And as Joanna cradled her son, gently stroking his surprisingly thick thatch of dark hair—his father's hair—she would later remember it as the happiest moment of her life.

❧

WHEN JOANNA AWAKENED, morning sun was pouring into the chamber from the open windows, her baby was sleeping in his cradle under the wet nurse's watchful eye, and her husband was dozing in a chair by her bed. He opened his eyes as soon as she stirred, leaning over to give her a quick kiss. He'd stayed with her late into the night, but she saw that he'd changed his clothing since she'd fallen asleep, and a cut on his chin showed he'd taken the trouble to shave before coming back. She had never been shy about admitting vanity as one of her besetting sins and she ran her hand now through her tangled hair, saying, "I must look dreadful, Raimond."

"You look," he said, "like the mother of my son." He turned then toward the wet nurse, but Gileta had anticipated him and was already approaching the bed with the infant. Joanna sat up and Raimond positioned pillows behind her back so she could hold their son. His eyes were puffy and he had a reddish splotch on his forehead, which Esquiva said would soon fade, but Joanna thought he was already the most beautiful baby she'd ever seen.

"His eyes are so blue," she marveled, "just like yours, Raimond."

"Let's hope the poor lad does not take after me in any other way." He reached out and smiled when the baby gripped his finger in a tiny fist. "You do not know it yet, Raimondet, but you are going to like this world even more than your mama's comfortable womb. You will be spoiled and cosseted by your mother, who happens to be astonishingly beautiful, and your well-meaning, foolish father will make the obligatory speeches about discipline and duty, but he'll be able to deny you nothing. And one day you will be the Count of Toulouse, a land of milk and honey that is even more blessed than Eden, since we have no talking serpents."

"Little Raimond," Joanna echoed softly, smiling at her men. "I suppose it is lucky that we did not have a daughter, since we never did choose a name for a girl."

"Yes, we did, love. Do you not remember . . . Melusine."

"It is becoming obvious to me, my darling, that I'd best be the one to name our children. What do you have in mind for our next son—Lucifer?"

"No, that one's taken," he said with a grin, and she pretended to be disapproving, but could not carry it off.

"I shall miss Luc," she murmured, for they'd have to abstain for the next forty days until she could be churched.

Raimond could understand why a woman ought to forgo carnal intercourse for a time after childbirth, given how demanding and dangerous it could be to the female body. He'd been told by a former light-o'-love that one of every five women died in childbed, and while he did not know if that was actually true, the figure was so chilling that he'd never forgotten it. But he found the custom of churching itself to be both idiotic and offensive. According to priests, a new mother could not enter a church until she'd first undergone a rite of purification lest she desecrate its sacred space with the pollution of her female blood. When he'd questioned it, it had been explained to him that women were in a state of sin because of the blood they'd shed in giving birth, because of the male semen that had taken root in their wombs, and because of the carnal pleasure that they'd experienced during conception.

Raimond had seen a number of fallacies in that logic. The Church taught that the Lord Christ's blood led to salvation. So why, then, was women's blood seen as polluting? And if a woman was polluted by a man's seed, why not require her to submit to the ritual of churching every time she shared her husband's bed? Why punish her for bringing another Christian soul into the world? And why did male semen not pollute the man, only the woman who received it? His attempts to debate these questions had done nothing to endear him to the local bishops, who'd accused him of mocking God and had been outraged when he'd injudiciously pointed out that they sounded rather like the Cathars, who saw all sexual intercourse as sinful. He'd also enraged his father, who thought he ought to keep such unorthodox views to himself. But he'd had to do that too often in his youth. Once he reached manhood, he'd gloried in the freedom to speak his mind, and if it vexed the pompous and the petty, so much the better.

His objection to the churching ritual now was personal, as it would mean that Joanna would be denied the privilege of attending their son's christening, for babies were baptized as soon as possible to make sure their little souls would be saved if they suddenly sickened and died. "I was thinking," he said, "that if we held Raimondet's christening in the castle chapel, you could be present, too."

Joanna was caught by surprise. By now she knew that her new husband thrived on such provocations, and there were times when she admitted to herself that his reckless, rakish charm was part of his appeal. But she'd also decided that it would be her role to protect him from his own rash impulses, and so she said composedly, "That is very sweet of you, Raimond, but I'd then have to fast on bread and water as penance for entering a House of God ere I was purified. Whilst I do want to lose the weight I put on during my pregnancy, that is not a diet I'd enjoy, so I'll rely upon you to give me a detailed account of the ceremony."

He showed that he understood her fully as well as she understood him then, by saying wryly, "If you mean to keep me off that too-tempting road to Hell, love, it is likely to be a full-time occupation."

Joanna merely laughed, never doubting that she could do it. For on this July morning, the first day of her son's life, she was serenely sure that nothing was impossible, that their future would be as blessed as their present.

❧

As USUAL, Berengaria got little advance notice of her husband's plans, a brief message that he was on his way back to Rouen from a campaign in Berry, suggesting she meet him at Le Mans. It was a fifty-mile, two-day journey from Beaufort-en-Vallée, and Berengaria reached that lovely riverside city a week after the Feast of the Assumption of the Blessed Virgin Mary. She discovered she need not have hurried so, for Richard was not yet there. Three more days passed before the sudden, loud cheering in the town's streets told her that he had finally arrived. She had no time to change into a fancier gown, to spare more than a hasty moment's glance into her mirror, determined that when he and his men rode into the palace precincts, she'd be waiting in the courtyard to bid him a proper welcome.

He was accompanied by his mesnie of household knights, by William Marshal and his own knights, and by Mercadier and a contingent of his routiers, so arrangements had to be made to billet most of them in the town. The next few hours were hectic ones for Berengaria as she dealt with the demands of hospitality and saw to it that a dinner was made ready for the more highborn of Richard's companions. It troubled her that Mercadier was included, even if he was now Lord of Beynac; she was convinced that he was a man whose soul was already pledged to the Devil, but she knew better than to object.

The meal was a lively one, for her household knights were eager to hear of Richard's warfare in Berry and he was always willing to boast of his military feats. His brief foray south had been a highly successful one, for he'd taken the formidable stronghold of Vierzon and nine other castles from the French king, that story dominating the dinner conversation. It was only as servants began to collect the uneaten food to give to the poor and the guests broke up into smaller groups that Berengaria finally had a private moment with Richard.

After they'd exchanged the courtesies that she thought so incongruous for a husband and wife, he asked politely about the renovations to their house at Thoree. It was coming along very well, she assured him, although she'd lost all enthusiasm for the project, knowing by now that they'd never live there together.

"Good. You'll have to show it to me again one of these days," he said vaguely. "I imagine you know about Joanna's son?" When she smiled and nodded, he gave her a curious glance. "I was surprised that you did not accompany my mother to Beaucaire for Joanna's lying-in."

His comment was not accusatory; he sounded faintly puzzled, his tone one that men often used when they were discussing the mysterious ways of women. But Berengaria's face flamed, and she no longer met his eyes. "I . . . I was ailing," she lied. It was a source of great shame to her that she'd not been there for the birth of Joanna's child. It was not that she'd begrudged Joanna her good fortune and joy. She loved Joanna, wanted her to be happy. Yet she'd shrunk from traveling to Toulouse in the company of the woman who'd usurped her rightful place, then having to watch Joanna give her new husband a son or daughter, doing what she could not. Now, though, she could not forgive herself for that moment of very human weakness. She did penance the only way she could, instigating what she expected to be a very awkward conversation, saying that she needed to speak with Richard alone.

She could tell that he was instantly on guard. When he offered his arm to escort her from the hall, she could feel the tension in the corded muscles. But she was still not prepared for what happened when they reached the gardens. The August sun was hot upon their faces, reminding her of Outremer, which often seemed as if it were part of another woman's life. It was safe from eavesdroppers, though, and she pointed toward a trellis-shaded arbor, suggesting they sit there.

Instead of following her, Richard came to a halt on the pathway. His eyes had narrowed, a storm-sky grey, and his very stance—legs apart, arms folded across his chest—was defiant. "If you mean to reproach me about maltreating a 'man of God,' Berengaria, you will be wasting your breath. I have no intention of setting Beauvais free."

For a moment, she could only stare at him mutely. He'd been angry with her before. But he'd never called her by her given name, had never looked at her as he did now, as if she were a stranger, one he did not like very much.

"I would never do that, Richard," she said, as steadily as she could. "Why would I plead for him?"

"Because he is a bishop," he said curtly, turning the words into weapons.

She shook her head so vehemently that the veil covering her wimple swirled in the breeze. "I would not do that," she repeated. "He is a false priest, a wicked, ungodly man who did his best to bring about your destruction."

Without knowing it, she'd echoed his own argument to Hubert Walter and some of his suspicion eased. "It is good that you understand that," he said at last. "I was not sure you would, for too often you see only one side—the Church's."

She thought that was unfair, but she was not about to challenge him on it now. Tilting her head so she could look into his eyes, she said, "When I heard that Beauvais was your prisoner, I was delighted, Richard." She thought he still seemed skeptical, and she insisted, "In Outremer, I saw how he sought to subvert you at every turn, even if it meant losing the Holy Land to the infidels. Then he slandered your good name, accused you of baseless crimes, and tried to have you cast into a French dungeon. I am sure the Almighty will punish him as he deserves when it is his turn to stand before the celestial throne. But I am glad he will pay a price here on earth, too, for his evil deeds."

He no longer doubted her sincerity; she had no gift for subterfuge, was honest to a fault. He was surprised by how pleased he was to see this glimpse of the loyal, devoted wife he'd left behind in Outremer. Thinking it had been a long time since they were in such accord, he reached for her hand, drawing her toward the arbor bench. "Well, if you did not want to scold me for my impiety, little dove, what *did* you want to talk about?"

She felt a quiver of resentment, feeling that he owed her an apology for such an unjust accusation. But then she realized that his change in tone and his use of "little dove" was his way of making amends, the most she could expect from him. She was sorely tempted to let it be; why risk this rare moment of peace between them? But she knew it had to be said.

"I wanted to tell you how sorry I am, Richard."

"Sorry? For what, Berenguela?"

"For what my brother has done, seizing my dower castles." Looking up then, she caught his flicker of surprise. "I was probably the last one to know. I wish you'd told me."

"I did not see what good it would do, aside from causing you distress."

As she searched his face, she realized she believed him. He truly had been trying to protect her. Did that mean he was not as indifferent as he so often seemed? That he did not intend to use the loss of her dower castles and the Navarrese alliance as an excuse for ending their marriage? Not that he needed an excuse. She'd failed him. She'd not given him an heir in six years of marriage. That they'd been apart for much of that time, that their separations in the past three years were his doing more often than not, mattered little in the eyes of their world.

She lowered her head, but continued to study him from the corner of her eye. How little she knew this man. How little she understood him. Could it be that he truly did not blame her for her barrenness? But that was a question she dared not ask. She was not naturally given to irony, but even she could see the irony inherent in her current predicament. Her brother's bad behavior had undermined her position as Richard's queen, yet Sancho had acted out of love, angry that her husband neglected her so blatantly. Whilst Richard, the cause of much of her misery, had not reproached her as so many husbands would have done. Did that mean he had no intention of putting her aside? As unsatisfactory as her life was as his sometimes wife, she did not want to end the marriage. How shamed she would be if she were sent back to Navarre in disgrace, having failed in a queen's first duty. No, better to endure the hurt here than the humiliation there. And . . . mayhap the Almighty would take pity upon His wretched daughter, answer a prayer as heartfelt as it was humble.

She became aware then that Richard was watching her. "Is that all you wanted to talk to me about, Berenguela?" he asked, and she thought she could detect a hint of relief in his voice. "Do not let yourself be troubled by the dower castles. Sancho and I will sort it out."

She gave him a grateful smile, but then they both turned at the sound of footsteps on the gravel path. One of his knights was hurrying toward them, followed by a man instantly recognizable as a courier. "Sire, an urgent message has arrived for you!"

Berengaria saw Richard stiffen and she felt a touch of sympathy, thinking it must be wearisome and stressful, always having to be braced for bad news. Rising, Richard reached for the letter as the messenger knelt. "It is from the Count of Flanders," he said, looking down at the unbroken seal. She was close enough to hear him mutter, "Now what?" His unease was contagious, and she watched anxiously as he scanned the contents, hoping his new alliance with the Flemish count was not unraveling already. But then he let out a triumphant shout.

"God bless Baldwin!"

It took a while for Berengaria to learn what had given him such delight, for he pulled her to her feet and hugged her so exuberantly that he lifted her off the ground. Laughing as she'd not heard him laugh in a long time, he slapped his knight on the back and told the courier to rise, saying he deserved a dukedom for such news.

Eventually his jubilant celebration eased enough for him to share his news. Philippe had sought to take advantage of his absence in Berry to punish Baldwin for what the French king saw as his disloyalty. When he approached Arras, then under siege by Baldwin, with a large army, the count retreated. Philippe pursued him until he suddenly realized that the hunter had become the hunted. The Flemish count had skillfully outmaneuvered him, burning the bridges behind the French army and cutting off their supply lines. Forced to live off the land, the French foraging parties were ambushed by the Flemings, who knew the terrain far better than the invaders. When Baldwin then burned the bridges ahead of him, too, Philippe finally had to admit he was trapped, unable to advance or retreat.

Richard was laughing so hard that he had to stop from time to time. "Philippe then tried to weasel out of the trap, offering to give Baldwin whatever he demanded if he'd ally himself again with France. Baldwin refused, saying he meant to keep faith with me, agreeing only to arrange another peace counsel in September.

"Philippe had no choice but to agree, and slunk back to Paris to sulk and lick his wounds," Richard said with a grin. "It does not get much better than that, little dove!"

He sounded blissfully happy, looked to have shed years in the time it had taken to read the Flemish count's letter, and Berengaria, who thought she'd uprooted all sprouts of hope from her garden, now found herself wondering if things might be different if only Richard could eliminate the threat posed by the French king.

In September, Richard and Count Baldwin met with Philippe, but nothing was resolved apart from another truce, this one to last for a year from St Hilary's Day in January. Neither king expected it to endure, for they were locked in a bitter struggle for supremacy that could only end in victory for one and defeat for the other. And when Richard held his Christmas Court at Rouen that year, most believed that his prospects seemed far brighter than the French king's.

This was Berengaria's best Christmas since the one they'd celebrated in the Holy Land, and she hoped it would blot out the dismal memories of her lonely, dreary Christmas last year at Beaufort-en-Vallée, unwilling to join Richard whilst Normandy was under Interdict, fearing that the archbishop might even excommunicate him for his defiance, and missing Joanna more than she'd have thought possible.

Joanna was still absent, celebrating in Toulouse with her husband and baby son, but the rest of Richard's family had gathered in Rouen, as well as vassals, lords, and churchmen, and Berengaria enjoyed this rare opportunity to play the public role of his queen. Even Eleanor's presence did not tarnish her pleasure, nor the fact that she knew many of the guests would be measuring her slender waist with judgmental, disappointed eyes.

On this Monday three days before the Nativity, the castle great hall was decked in evergreen, a yule log burned in the hearth, and music echoed out onto the wet evening air. Not even a steady, cold rain could dampen the festivities. Richard was in high spirits and since the king's mood usually set the tone, there was much laughter and merriment. Breathless from the last dance, Berengaria welcomed the chance to talk with Morgan, who'd returned that afternoon from a visit to Toulouse.

"Tell me," she said with a smile, "can my sister-in-law truly be as happy as she sounds in her letters?"

Morgan returned the smile. "Even happier, my lady. And why not? Her husband dotes on her every whim and Raimondet is a robust little lad, as healthy as the most fearful mother could wish."

"God has indeed blessed her, but no more than she deserves." She hesitated then, wanting to express her sympathy, yet not wanting to pry. "Your talk with the Lady Mariam . . ."

He slowly shook his head. "We do not all get a happy ending in this life, my lady."

"No," she agreed softly, "we do not."

She turned then as the Bishop of Lisieux approached and Morgan seized his chance to slip away. Almost at once, he ran into Guillain, who greeted him warmly before raising his eyebrows in a silent query.

Morgan found it easier to confide in his friend than in the queen, and he led the other man toward a nearby window-seat. "We had a candid talk," he said, "one we ought to have had months ago. At least I know now why she refuses to wed me. Children are the barrier. She fears that she might not be able to give me any since she had none with her first husband. I told her that is always in God's hands, but she is also convinced that no child of hers would be welcome in the Angevin domains. She says that only in Sicily could a child of mixed blood find true acceptance."

Guillain considered that, reluctantly concluding that he agreed with Mariam. "You could never do that, Morgan."

"I know," Morgan said bleakly. "I'd sooner take Lucifer as my liege lord than Heinrich. But I am not sure I could do it even if Tancred still ruled over Sicily. My parents are elderly and I'd likely never see them again if I were to settle in Sicily. Moreover, I doubt that Mariam could bring herself to leave Joanna, and I . . ."

Morgan paused before smiling, somewhat ruefully. "You know I was squire to Richard's brother Geoffrey and then a knight in his household. After that, I served the old king till his death. I did not know Richard well at all, and the bad blood between him and his sire and brothers did give me pause. That seems so long ago. Before Outremer. Before . . ."

"Before Germany," Guillain said, and Morgan nodded, both of their eyes shifting across the hall toward the dais, where Richard was holding court. "I had my own misgivings at first about him," Guillain admitted, "for I'd been one of the household knights of his brother the young king, and it is only natural that we'd be loyal to the memories of our lords, may God assoil them both. Now, though, I cannot imagine serving anyone but our king."

"Nor can I," Morgan agreed, and for a moment, they were silent, remembering what they'd shared with Richard on the way home from the Holy Land, having forged a bond beyond breaking.

It was then that the messenger arrived from the Archbishop of Cologne.

RICHARD FOUND HIMSELF HESITATING before opening the letter. Exchanging glances with his mother, he saw that the same thought was in her mind—that they were about to learn how Heinrich had punished Constance for the part she'd played in the conspiracy against him. Richard also dreaded hearing that Heinrich had left for the Holy Land. He'd rather that Jerusalem remain under Saracen control than to have it retaken by the German emperor, and if that was a sin, it was not one he could honestly repent.

Eleanor watched tensely as he broke the seal and began to read. His sudden intake of breath caused her own breathing to quicken. When he glanced up from the letter, he seemed so stunned that she closed her eyes. God pity Constance. Harry had never forgiven her, yet he'd not treated her as harshly as he could have, as their world felt he had the right to do. But what did Heinrich von Hohenstaufen know of mercy?

Richard had raised his hand to quiet the hall, getting to his feet. "The Emperor Heinrich is dead!" There was a shocked silence, and then pandemonium.

THE UPROAR HAD STILL not subsided by the next day. As guests continued to arrive at the royal court, they were met with the astounding news of the German emperor's death, and they then hastened into the great hall to ask the king if it was true. Richard had lost count of the times he'd had to assure these newcomers that it was indeed so, and then had to share with them what little he knew so far of Heinrich's unexpected demise at age thirty-two.

John was in a very good mood that Christmas, for Richard had wanted him to swear to uphold the terms of the treaty signed with the Count of Flanders, and he took that to mean he was once again in serious consideration as his brother's heir. He was also enjoying the excitement stirred up by the news about Heinrich, for he was drawn to intrigue like a shark to blood in the water. Snatching a wine cup from a passing servant, he presented it to Richard with a flourish. "Are you not weary by now of repeating the same story?"

Richard drank and then smiled. "I could never tire of saying, 'Heinrich is dead.' Rarely have my ears heard sweeter music than those three words."

"You'd best make ready to say it again, Uncle," Otto chimed in, and John thought that if anyone could get drunk on good news, their nephew was well on the way.

Richard followed Otto's gesture and sat up in surprise, for he'd not expected André and Denise to attend the Christmas Court this year. André's pilgrimage to Rome had proved inconclusive, with Pope Celestine dithering as usual, accepting the Bishop of Bourges's charge that André had behaved in a "tyrannical manner" but putting off a final decision. Richard knew how bitter the Pope's inaction had been for his cousin and his wife. But for now, at least, they were aglow with elated astonishment, and André barely restrained himself long enough to make a formal greeting suitable for such a public forum.

"Tell me it is true," he entreated, "even if you lie! Give me those few moments of utter joy."

Richard laughed. "No need to lie. Heinrich died at Messina on the twenty-eighth of September as he made ready to depart for the Holy Land." Anticipating the next question, he said, "Of a fever, or so it is said. Adolf wrote that there was talk of a tertian fever and that is certainly common enough in Sicily. But he says there has also been talk of poison, since it happened so quickly—and since half of Christendom would have thanked God fasting to see that whoreson breathe his last. I do not much care how he died, just as long as it was painful."

After a moment, Richard laughed again. "It seems Celestine has discovered it is easier to defy a dead man, for he has forbidden Heinrich to receive a Christian burial until my ransom is repaid. I doubt I'll see so much as a single pfennig, but I'll consider the debt paid in full if Heinrich is truly left to rot or is buried in unhallowed ground."

"What of the empress?" Denise interjected, for André had told her of Constance's peril.

"We can safely say she shed no tears," Richard said with a grin. "Nor did she waste any time. Heinrich had named Markward von Annweiler as regent for his son, but Constance was having none of that. No sooner was Heinrich dead than she seized control of the government, rallied the Sicilians, and had all of the Germans expelled from the kingdom."

He got no further, for it was happening again—new arrivals in a state of obvious excitement. This time they were kin, his niece Richenza and her husband, the Count of Perche. Leaving Jaufre to follow at a more sedate pace, Richenza all but flew across the hall toward the dais.

"Uncle, is it so? That fiend is dead? How good God is!"

Once Richard had assured Richenza that what she'd heard was gospel, not gossip, she embraced her brother jubilantly, she and Otto agreeing it was indeed sad that their father had not lived to see this day. But she was Eleanor's granddaughter and political considerations were never far from her thoughts. "What will happen now? Will the Germans elect Heinrich's son in his stead?"

"I doubt it. Constance does not care a whit for the imperial crown, cares only that Friedrich be crowned as King of Sicily. Since that imperial crown does not pass by blood, there will be no shortage of candidates for the honor."

"The archbishop seems to fancy the idea of your uncle becoming the next emperor," John said and Richenza gave a delighted, undignified squeal before she saw that Richard was shaking his head.

"As much as I'd love to think of Heinrich watching from Hell as his crown was placed upon my head, I have no interest in becoming the next Holy Roman Emperor. As you well know, Johnny."

"I know you keep saying that," John conceded, "although for the life of me, I cannot understand why anyone would refuse a crown."

"I already have one and I am quite content to be England's king, Duke of Normandy and Aquitaine, and Count of Anjou. I ask only for the chance to meet Philippe on the battlefield so I can then fulfill my vow to return to the Holy Land and recover Jerusalem for Christendom. That is a sacred oath, one I made not only to the Almighty but to my nephew Henri, and nothing matters more to me than honoring it." Richard gave his brother another look, this one sardonic. "And when I am able to do that, you will be accompanying me, Johnny. I think a sojourn in the Holy Land would do wonders for your spiritual health."

John smiled sourly, for he was no more enthusiastic about taking the cross than their father had been. He was glad when Richenza deflected attention away from him by asking who was likely to be chosen by the Germans, then.

"Tell her your idea, Uncle," Otto urged, and Richard obliged, saying that he thought their elder brother, Henrik, would be a fine choice. Richenza did, too, and she and Otto embraced again. Only half listening, John was watching his nephew, thinking it a great pity that Otto was not Henrik's elder brother, for he'd no longer be a rival for the English crown if the imperial crown was in the offing. Richard was telling his audience that Henrik had left for the Holy Land ahead of Heinrich and much would depend upon what Heinrich's only surviving brother, Philip, did. According to the archbishop, he'd declared his support for his young nephew Friedrich, but all men were familiar with the warning from Scriptures, *Woe unto thee, O land, when thy king is a child,* and Philip would likely find himself urged to make a claim for himself.

John studied his nephew, wondering how Otto could be so happy for his brother without wanting the crown for himself. But it behooved him to stay in Richard's good graces, whoever ended up on the German throne, and so he said loudly, "We've been drinking since last night to Heinrich's death, but we ought to be drinking to my lord brother's legendary luck. This has been a golden year for him—first the capture of the Bishop of Beauvais, then the French king's humiliation by the Count of Flanders, and now the German emperor's demise."

"It is not luck," Berengaria said suddenly. "It is God's Will. These men dared to imprison a king who'd taken the cross. And look what has befallen them. The Duke of Austria died a truly wretched death. The Bishop of Beauvais has forfeited his freedom. And now the German emperor has been struck down, too. *The day of the Lord is great and very terrible, and who can abide it?*"

Richard could not help thinking that "the day of the Lord" had been a long time coming. But now that it was here, he hoped that the French king would never know another peaceful moment. Leopold of Austria. Beauvais. Heinrich. How could Philippe not fear that he would be next to feel the wrath of God?

FOUR DAYS AFTER CHRISTMAS, Berengaria fulfilled a promise she'd made to the Almighty in gratitude for the divine justice He'd passed upon the German emperor. She had carts loaded with woolen blankets, sacks of grain and flour, firewood, candles, bolts of cloth, and jars of honey, and she and her escort then set off for the priory of Salle-aux-Puelles just southwest of the city. Only one of her ladies was brave enough to volunteer for the mission, as they would be visiting a lazar house, a hospital for highborn women stricken with the most dreaded of all diseases, leprosy.

She was met at the gateway by the prioress and several of the sisters, who thanked her profusely for her generosity. She did not, of course, enter to mingle with the unfortunate inhabitants. Lepers were kept strictly segregated because their malady was thought to be highly contagious; some even feared it could be passed by breathing the same infected air. Berengaria could only marvel at the courage of the nuns and she resolved to add them to the list of those for whom she offered up prayers to the Almighty.

Promising the prioress that she'd return again soon, she rode back to the city, where she had her knights take her to the great cathedral. There she lit candles for her parents, a childhood nurse, and those courageous nuns. She then prayed for the souls of all afflicted with leprosy. After that, she prayed for the Bishop of Poitiers, who'd died that past spring. Already there were reports of miracles performed at his tomb, and she hoped that he would eventually be canonized; it was very humbling to think that she'd been on such friendly terms with one so holy. She ended her prayers with one for her husband's father. Today was the anniversary of the death of the martyred Archbishop of Canterbury, and she made it a habit to pray for Henry on this day, feeling that he was likely in need of as many prayers as he could get.

Upon their return to the castle, she knew that something was wrong as soon as she stepped across the threshold into the great hall. All of the Christmas joy was gone. There was little conversation, just a subdued silence. The few men in the hall were staring vacantly into space and the servants went about their tasks with the caution of people not wanting to draw attention to themselves. Richard was not present, nor was his mother or most of their highborn guests. Struggling with a growing sense of unease, Berengaria was looking around for a familiar face when the Countess of Aumale entered the hall and at once headed in her direction.

"It is so tragic," she said before Berengaria could speak. "I've just been with the queen. She is devastated, not only for his death but for the grief it will give his mother. And the king . . . well, he looked as if he'd been struck in the chest by a crossbow bolt. He—"

"What is it?" Berengaria interrupted, caught up in the worst of fears, that of the unknown. "What has happened?"

"You do not know? The king received a letter from the Archbishop of Tyre. His nephew Henri, the Count of Champagne, is dead."

Berengaria clasped her hand to her mouth. She was very fond of Henri, who'd been a Godsend to the women during their time in the Holy Land. Handsome, clever, courageous, rarely without a smile on his face, and utterly loyal to her husband, Henri had been one of the few French barons who'd refused to pay any heed to the conniving of the Bishop of Beauvais and the Duke of Burgundy. Suddenly shaky, Berengaria let Hawisa lead her toward the closest seat. Henri had been only thirty-one. How could such a vibrant, vital life be quenched like a candle's flame?

"What . . . what happened? Was he slain by the Saracens?"

"No, it was an accident, a bizarre mishap that no one could have foreseen. He was killed in a fall from a balcony of the palace at Acre. Apparently it gave way without warning. . . ."

"Jesu . . ." Now that the initial shock was over, she could think of others. Of Henri's young wife, Isabella, Queen of Jerusalem. Of their little daughters. Of the Christians of Outremer, doubtless panicked by Henri's death. Henri had not wanted to marry Conrad of Montferrat's widow, for it would mean lifelong exile from his beloved Champagne. But he'd agreed to do so because the kingdom's need was so desperate. And God had rewarded him by letting him fall in love with his new wife. Berengaria's throat closed up as she remembered how happy Henri and Isabella had been. Five years . . . That was all the time they'd had together. Why would God let that happen? She knew it was not for her to question the will of the Almighty, but it was hard to understand, so very hard.

"Joanna will be heartbroken. She loved Henri. We all did. . . ." Her husband, above all. Henri had been more like a brother than a nephew, only nine years younger than Richard, his comrade in arms during those difficult, dangerous months in the Holy Land. Wiping her tears away, she tried to put her own grief aside. She could mourn for Henri later. Now, Richard's need was greater.

"Where is my husband? In his bedchamber?" When Hawisa shook her head, her shoulders slumped. Of course. Who else would he have turned to but his mother? "He is with Queen Eleanor?"

Hawisa shook her head again. "We do not know where he is, my lady. He was as distraught as I've ever seen him. He rushed from the hall as if he were being pursued by all the hounds of Hell and no one has seen him for hours. He is not in the castle, that much we know."

"He went off alone?" Berengaria closed her eyes for a moment. *Oh, Richard . . .* "But someone must know where he'd have gone. Did he take a horse? Have men been sent out to search for him? Surely the queen would do that?"

"The queen does not know yet. She took to her bed and we thought it best not to tell her. He'll soon be found, after all. Rouen is a large city, yes, but he could not pass unnoticed. . . ."

At the moment, Berengaria was more concerned with Richard's safety than with her mother-in-law's grieving. She told herself that if any man could look after himself, it was Richard. But she knew there were French spies in Rouen. If he were recognized ... Would he have gone to a tavern? She'd never seen him drunk, but there was much of his life that remained hidden to her. "So you are saying that the king has been gone for hours and no one is out looking for him?"

"No, I am not saying that," Hawisa protested, not liking Berengaria's accusing tone. "His cousin André de Chauvigny went in search of him. He said he thought he knew where the king would have gone. And no, he did not say more than that, rushed off without another word."

Berengaria was relieved to hear that. When Hawisa had shared her horrible news, she'd felt remorseful that she'd not been there. But she was deluding herself again. Her presence would not have mattered, for Richard would not have turned to her for comfort.

"Please let me know if you hear anything," she told Hawisa and then moved like a sleepwalker to her own bedchamber, where she silenced her ladies with unwonted sharpness and told them to withdraw. She curled up on the bed then and wept for Henri, for his grieving widow and fatherless daughters, for the besieged Kingdom of Jerusalem. And she wept, too, for herself, for her missing husband, and for the mysterious ways of the Almighty, which were beyond the ken of mortal man.

IT WAS AFTER DARK when André's boat tied up at the dock on the Île d'Andely. His hunch was verified at once when he was told that the king had indeed arrived several hours earlier. He'd demanded a horse, refused an escort, and ridden across the bridge to Petit Andely. André now did the same. He did not bother searching for Richard in the town, instead turned his mount toward the southeast slope, the only approach to Castle Gaillard.

The workers were already in their quarters, but guards quickly materialized from the shadows and gestured toward a tethered stallion when André questioned them. They were obviously curious, but he gave them no answers, handing his reins to the closest of the guards and taking the man's lantern.

Even with that light, it was dangerous going. There should have been a full moon, but it was shrouded in clouds. The middle bailey was deep in shadow, eerily silent, like a ghost castle, he thought uneasily. Holding the lantern at an angle so he could watch his footing, he continued on into the inner bailey, and there he found his cousin.

Richard was seated on the ground, leaning back against the keep wall. He showed no surprise at the sight of André, as if it were perfectly natural for them both to be prowling about the castle grounds hours after the sun had set. Putting his lantern on a nearby wheelbarrow, André sat down beside Richard. "It was quite mad to come up here without a light," he said after a time, and he thought Richard shrugged.

"It was not dark when I got here."

"I did not think to bring one, either," André admitted. "But I did remember this." Unhooking the wineskin from his belt, he handed it to Richard, who drank and then returned it. They passed it back and forth until it was empty and André then flung it into the blackness beyond the faint glow of his lantern.

Just then the moon broke through the clouds, giving him a glimpse of Richard's profile. His eyes were reddened and bloodshot, but the corner of his mouth was curving in what was almost a smile. "I should have known you'd be the one to find me."

"In my next life, I'll likely come back as a lymer hound." André wished he'd thought to bring a second wineskin. If ever there was a night to get blind, roaring drunk, this was it. "Tell me you are not blaming yourself."

"No." But after another long silence, Richard admitted, "I'll never know, though, if it would have been different had I been able to return as I'd promised him. I hope to Christ he understood why I could not."

"Of course he did. We may have a few fools in our family tree, but Henri was not one of them."

Richard got suddenly to his feet. "You know who I blame for his death, André? That craven, contemptible hellspawn, that spineless viper on the French throne. If not for him, I'd have been able to return to Outremer. With Saladin dead and no French to thwart our every move, Henri and I could have taken Jerusalem."

"Yes," André said, "I think you could have, Cousin." He knew, though, that there was no comfort to be had in that belief. Watching as Richard stalked about the bailey, cursing every time he stumbled on a loose rock, he thought that it was not a good thing to hate as much as Richard now hated the French king. But it was even worse to be so angry with God.

CHAPTER THIRTY-THREE

※

MARCH 1198

Le Mans, Anjou

Joanna paused in the doorway of the solar, savoring the tranquil scene that met her eyes. Her mother was seated in a window-seat with her grand-daughter, Richenza. Berengaria was catching up with Anna, who'd chosen Joanna's household over her own. Will Marshal's Isabel was chatting with De-nise and Hawisa and Loretta de Braose, the Earl of Leicester's new wife, for Richard's lords usually brought their wives to his Easter Court. There were a few exceptions. Joanna wondered if Johnny would even have recognized his wife, he'd seen her so rarely in the eight years since their wedding. The Earl of Chester was alone, of course, for it would have taken a sword to have gotten him and Constance into the same chamber. And Joanna's sister-in-law, Ela, the Countess of Salisbury, was absent due to her youth; she was only eleven.

Joanna's gaze moved toward Ela's husband, her half brother William Longes-pée. Richard had arranged a brilliant marriage for him two years ago, one that had gained him an earldom, but Joanna had not met him until her arrival at Le Mans. Although he was taller than their father, she thought he looked the way Henry must have looked at twenty-one, for like their other half brother Geoff, and like Richard himself, William had inherited the Angevin high coloring. Her eyes shifted to her nephew and other brother. Otto, too, was tall and powerfully built. Did Johnny mind being surrounded by kinsmen who towered above him? Most of the men were clustered around Richard, but John was sitting apart, sip-ping from a gilded wine cup as he watched the others laughing and talking. Like a man observing a play, Joanna thought, not part of the performance. She felt that he deserved to be isolated, for she doubted that she'd ever forgive him for his betrayal of Richard. Yet she was not entirely deaf to the whisper urging pity, reminding her of the little boy who'd shared her life at Fontevrault Abbey so long ago.

A burst of laughter drew her attention back to the men. Raimond had just said something that they all found very amusing, and Joanna smiled, delighted that her husband and brother were getting along so well. This was the first time she'd been apart from their son and she missed Raimondet more than she'd have thought possible. He'd been too young, though, at nine months, to make a three-hundred-fifty-mile journey. Despite a yearning for Raimondet that was almost physical in its intensity, she was still glad to be at Richard's Easter Court, and as she glanced about the solar, she thought how fortunate she was. The daughters and sisters of kings were usually wed to foreign princes, which meant lifelong exile from their homelands and families. That would have been her fate, too, if William had not died so unexpectedly, freeing her to return home and to find what had been denied her in Sicily—passion, love, and motherhood.

Eleanor looked up then, saw her standing in the doorway, and beckoned with a smile. Richenza graciously yielded her seat and Joanna slid onto it, leaning over to kiss her mother on the cheek. She was in her seventy-fourth year, an age few reached, but her spirit still burned as brightly as in her youth, even as the body enclosing that spirit fought a battle she was doomed to lose. To Joanna, she seemed no different than she had at their last meeting nine months ago, and that was a great relief, for she knew her mother's days were trickling away as inexorably as the sand in an hourglass.

She was actually more troubled by her brother's appearance. She'd not seen Richard for seventeen months, and she found herself thinking that he was showing the burdens of kingship more obviously these days. He'd not lost the weight he'd gained during his convalescence from his knee wound, and although he carried it better than most because of his height, it did age him. He seemed very tired to her, too, like a man who was starved for sleep, and once Richenza moved away, she said in a low voice, "Richard does not look well, Maman. Has he been ailing?"

"He is constantly on the move, Joanna," Eleanor said, just as quietly, "rarely spending two nights under the same roof. Like Harry, he pushes himself mercilessly, making demands upon his body that flesh and blood cannot always meet. Harry was not always at war; there were periods of peace during his reign. But Richard has lived under a state of siege since regaining his freedom."

"I would be hard-pressed to say which of those despicable demon spawn I loathe the most, Maman—Heinrich or Philippe. Raimond says that is like choosing between an adder and a viper, and I daresay he's right."

"I would choose Heinrich," Eleanor said, her eyes taking on the cold glitter of emerald ice, "for if not for his treachery, Philippe would never have been able to pose such a threat to Normandy. Richard has won back almost all that was lost during his captivity, but it has not been easy. Four years of constant warfare can wear a man down, even Richard."

They were interrupted then by a servant offering wine. Watching her mother, Joanna realized that motherhood stretched from the cradle to the grave, that fear for a grown son was just as sharp as concern for a toddler. Upon their arrival last night, they'd been greeted with news of death. The elderly Pope had finally gone to face his own Judgment Day, and the new Holy Father, Innocent III, was more than fifty years younger, far bolder and more energetic, making them wonder what might have happened had he been on the papal throne at the time of Richard's capture. But the other death was personal. Eleanor's daughter by the French king, Marie, the Countess of Champagne, had died on March 11, at age fifty-three. Her sister Alix, the Countess of Blois, had died the year before, but it was Marie's death that brought grief to the Angevin court, for she'd been quite close to Richard, who'd dedicated his prison lament to her during his German captivity. Joanna had hoped that she'd one day get to meet Marie and she knew her mother had also hoped for a reunion with the daughter she'd not seen since her marriage to Louis had ended.

"I am so sorry, Maman," she said; no more than that, but Eleanor understood.

"Marie sorrowed greatly for Henri, just as I mourn for her. It is a hard thing to lose a child, as you well know, dearest. I did not expect to outlive six of my children. I can only be thankful that I still have you and Richard and Leonora. . . ." She paused then, her gaze resting for a long moment upon her youngest before saying, ". . . and John."

Even though she'd made John's name sound like an afterthought, Joanna did not doubt she'd fight to gain the crown for him should Richard die without a legitimate heir, as now seemed more and more likely. She understood why her mother would prefer Johnny over Arthur, still residing at the French court, but she wondered if she'd prefer him to her other grandson. Otto was like Richard in many ways—courageous in battle, reckless at times, impulsive, sharing a love of troubadours and music and poetry. But Joanna thought he lacked the political shrewdness Richard had inherited from their father. Johnny was cleverer than Otto. Yet he was also less trustworthy, caring naught for honor or moral boundaries. Which were the greater flaws in a king? She was about to raise that question with Eleanor when a servant entered the solar and murmured a few words in Richard's ear.

"We have a surprise guest soon to arrive," he announced, deflecting their curiosity with an enigmatic smile and a shrug. He'd gotten to his feet and the others did the same, seeing that he intended to return to the great hall.

Joanna had risen, too, but before she could follow after Eleanor, she was intercepted by her sister-in-law. Drawing her back into the window-seat, Berengaria said softly, "I must ask your forgiveness for not being with you during your lying-in."

Joanna knew full well why Berengaria had not attended Raimondet's birth, and she said swiftly, not wanting the younger woman to have to offer an excuse that would salvage her pride but prick her conscience, "There is no need to say more, and for certes, no need to make apologies. You are as dear to me as any sister could be, Berengaria. Do you not know that by now?"

"You are no less dear to me," Berengaria said, grateful beyond measure that Joanna had not been hurt or offended by her absence. "And this I promise you, Joanna . . . that I will be present for the birth of your next child."

Joanna smiled. "In that case, sweet sister, I would suggest you keep August free."

Berengaria's brown eyes widened. "So soon?" she exclaimed, and then, fearing that Joanna might take her words amiss, she hastily embraced the other woman, kissing her on both cheeks and declaring, "I am so very happy for you!"

Her outcry had attracted attention. Seeing that they all were staring at her, Joanna sent an unspoken query winging her husband's way, and when Raimond nodded, she said, "We were not going to announce it yet, but I see no reason to hold back. We have truly been blessed by the Almighty, for I am with child again."

The response was predictable. Joanna was kissed by her mother, had the air squeezed out of her lungs by Richard's exuberant hug, and was warmed by the genuine pleasure with which her news was received, while Raimond found himself fending off jests from the men, for two children in two years of marriage offered an opportunity for bawdy jokes that few of them could resist. Raimond took it good-naturedly, denying that he'd needed a love potion and insisting that, rumors to the contrary, he and his wife did not spend all of their time in bed.

Even though neither Joanna nor Raimond seemed perturbed by the teasing,

Berengaria did not trust male humor and she did her best to keep the conversation from deteriorating still further by asking if they'd chosen a name for their baby.

"I leave that to Joanna," Raimond said blithely. "I have to, since she says I am not to be trusted in such matters. I ask only that she not name any of our sons William, for it is bad form to call a child after a former husband."

"Or a former wife," Joanna shot back. "So we'll be naming no daughters Ermessinde or Beatrice." She added with a sly smile, "I'd also exclude the names of former concubines, but I fear we'd run out of female names if I did that."

Her sally was greeted with laughter and several of the men looked at Raimond with renewed respect, for a long list of bedmates was a testament to a man's virility, all the more so when it came from the man's own wife. Berengaria could not imagine joking in public about Richard's bedmates, or in private, either. But as she caught the look that passed between Joanna and Raimond, one that was both affectionate and smoldering, she felt the last of her misgivings fade away. She still did not understand how Joanna could be so happy with a man who took such pleasure in provoking the Holy Church, yet she no longer doubted that it was so. And it occurred to her that, as unhappy as Richard made her at times, she'd have been far more miserable had it been her fate to wed the Count of Toulouse.

⚜

WORD HAD SPREAD THROUGH the hall that Richard was expecting an important visitor, and speculation was running rife by the time noise out in the bailey heralded his arrival. There were loud gasps as he strode through the doorway. He was in his early thirties, as dark as a Barbary pirate, with a raffish charm and the confident smile of a man accustomed to making high-stakes gambles and winning them.

"The Count of Boulogne!"

There was no need to announce him, though, for Renaud de Dammartin was known on sight to many of them. He was as controversial in his way as Raimond de St Gilles, although for very different reasons. Renaud had been a childhood companion of the French king, a bold and talented battle commander who'd made an advantageous marriage to one of Philippe's Dreux cousins. As a young man, his father had instructed him to serve the Angevin king, and he'd shown surprising loyalty to Henry, staying with him until his death at Chinon. He'd soon regained Philippe's favor, though, and some said that what happened next was done at Philippe's suggestion, or at the least, with his complicity. Renaud had put aside his Dreux wife and then abducted one of France's greatest heiresses, Ida de Lorraine, the twice-widowed Countess of Boulogne, granddaughter of King Stephen and cousin of the Count of Flanders. By this forced marriage, Renaud became one of Philippe's most powerful vassals—and so his appearance at Richard's court created a sensation.

He was given a very enthusiastic reception by the men, who were excited by such a high-level defection. Moreover, Will Marshal, Morgan, Baldwin de Bethune, and several of the other knights greeted him as a comrade in arms, for those who'd shared Henry's last days shared, too, a sense of solidarity similar to that found on the battlefield.

The reaction of the women was different, for many of them were great heiresses in their own right. After the annulment of her marriage to the French king, Eleanor had nearly been ambushed and abducted twice by lords eager to gain Aquitaine by forcing her into marriage. Joanna had feared that this would be her fate during her confinement in Sicily. Denise and Hawisa and Isabel Marshal did not need much imagination to envision themselves in Ida de Lorraine's plight had they been less fortunate. Berengaria was repelled, both by the act and the man himself. But she'd learned by now that a queen could not indulge her emotions, and she joined Eleanor and Joanna in dutifully making Richard's valuable new ally welcome.

Renaud was the guest of honor at dinner and the entertainment that followed. He had an eye for beauty and made his admiration for Joanna rather obvious, to Raimond's equally obvious amusement; he had every confidence that his wife was fully capable of dealing with Renaud de Dammartin. Joanna enjoyed flirting and marriage had not changed that, but she was not going to engage in that pleasant pastime with a man who saw a wife as a possession to be acquired by any means possible. Far from a fool, Renaud soon realized that the Countess of Toulouse's flawless courtesy held the faintest hint of mockery, and that made her all the more desirable, for he loved a challenge. He'd merely been amusing himself, though. He would not only admit he was reckless, he took pride in it. However, he was not mad enough to attempt a serious seduction of the sister of his new liege lord, the English king.

He passed the rest of the evening discussing battlefield tactics with Richard, impressing the younger lords like Otto and William Longespée with his swagger and swapping memories with the men who'd shared Henry's death vigil with him. Inevitably, the talk turned to Richard's miracle, for even his enemies marveled that he could have constructed such a formidable, innovative castle in just two years.

Richard soon discovered that Renaud was quite knowledgeable about Castle Gaillard, for the French were keeping it under close surveillance. Renaud had even heard of the episode of the blood rain, in which the castle had been splattered by a sudden shower of red rain. "Most men would have seen that as a portent of coming calamity," he said. "How did you keep the workers from panicking, sire?"

"I told them that it was not an ill omen, but rather one that foretold victory, that it signified the blood of our enemies. No offense," Richard said dryly, "but I predicted it would be French blood."

"No offense taken," Renaud said, just as dryly. "Of course, the French king chose to see it as a sign of God's anger with the Angevins. He is very irate about your new castle, my lord, wrathful that you'd dare to build it on the border of the French Vexin. He sees that as a deliberate provocation."

"I would hope so," Richard said, so nonchalantly that Renaud grinned.

"I do not doubt that it has given him some sleepless nights, for he often rants about it, cursing you and vowing to destroy the castle. He swears that he would take it if its walls were made of iron."

Richard leaned back in his seat and, as his eyes met André's, he murmured, "He makes it too easy. It is like spearing fish in a weir." He signaled for silence then, for he wanted all in the hall to hear what he was about to say. The more men who heard, the more likely his words would reach the ears of the French king.

"Count Renaud has just told me," he said loudly, "that the French king is boasting he would take Castle Gaillard if its walls were made of iron. Well, I could hold it if its walls were made of butter."

SOON AFTER OTTO HAD returned to Poitou, he received an urgent summons from his uncle. He rode fast, reaching Richard's new manor on the Île de Andely on a cool April afternoon. He was surprised to find the Bishop of Lincoln seated beside Richard in the great hall, for he knew Hugh d'Avalon was out of favor. That past December, Richard had demanded that the barons of England provide him with three hundred knights to serve in Normandy. Hugh alone had balked, insisting that the church of Lincoln did not owe military service to the king beyond the borders of England, and Otto knew that Richard had been infuriated by the prelate's defiance. Yet here they sat in perfect harmony. He wanted to know how these two strong-willed men had resolved their differences, but he had to wait until later that afternoon to have his curiosity satisfied.

They were standing by the open window in the solar, gazing across the river at Richard's "fair daughter." A soft rain was falling and the ramparts of Castle Gaillard were wreathed in ghostly grey mist. To Otto, it looked as if the citadel were floating upon clouds, a place of magic and majesty, one that would never fall to the scorpion on the French throne. As he glanced over at his uncle, he was sure that Richard was thinking the same thing.

When he asked about Hugh's presence, Richard shook his head admiringly. "That man is unlike anyone I've ever met. He fears nothing, not even an Angevin king's just wrath. When he arrived at the castle, I was about to hear Mass in the royal chapel with the Bishops of Durham and Ely. I was in no mood to bid him welcome, and when he approached and asked for the kiss of peace, I ignored him. But he persisted, declaring I owed it to him since he'd come such a great distance to see me. I told him he deserved no kiss from me. Do you know what he did next? He grabbed my mantle and actually dared to shake me, saying he had the right to the kiss and would not take no for an answer. I could not help myself, began to laugh. So he got his kiss of peace and I forgave him, for courage like that must be rewarded."

Otto smiled, for he, too, respected courage. "Why did you send for me, Uncle? Has that French weasel stirred up more trouble?"

"The trouble does not come from the 'French weasel' this time, but from your homeland. Count Emicho of Leiningen sought me out a fortnight ago; you'll want to speak with him later. Some of the princes convinced Philip of Swabia that he ought to make his own claim for the German throne, and they elected him as King of Germany in Erfurt last month."

Otto did not know Philip, for he'd lived in England and Normandy since he was five years old. He did not doubt that Heinrich was burning in Hell with his other two brothers, both of whom had been murdered, one by the husband of a woman he'd raped. From what he'd been told, though, Philip, the youngest, shared neither their cruelty nor their contempt for the rule of law, the only Hohenstaufen prince without blood on his hands or his conscience. But that did not mean Otto wanted to see him as the next emperor; his loyalty was to his elder brother.

"I am sorry to hear that, Uncle. But the Archbishop of Cologne and the Rhineland princes will still support Henrik, surely?" And he was dismayed when Richard shook his head again.

"Henrik is still in the Holy Land, and they believe they dare not delay until his return to Germany. They need a candidate to oppose Philip now, and it looks as if it is going to be you, lad."

"Me?"

Otto sounded so incredulous that Richard smiled. "Why not you? Your father was the Duke of Saxony, your brother is the Count Palatine thanks to his marriage, and you have a generous patron in the English king, one willing to spend whatever it takes to secure your election. You have the blood, you have the backing, and I'll see to it that you have the money."

Richard laughed then, utterly delighted by this unexpected turn of events. "Heinrich's corner of Hell has just gotten hotter. And can you imagine Philippe's horror when he hears that my nephew will sit on the throne of the Romans? Our alliance will guarantee that he never draws another easy breath."

When Otto remained silent, Richard gave him a quizzical look. "You do want to be emperor?"

Otto hesitated. He loved being Count of Poitou. He loved Poitiers, which had fine wine and pretty women and a mild climate. He loved his uncle, who'd treated him as if he were a son. He thought of French as his native tongue and thought of the Angevin domains as home. Germany was an alien land to him now; even its language sounded foreign to his ears. But who could refuse an imperial crown?

"If it is God's Will, then of course I will accept, Uncle."

❧

OTTO WAS ELECTED as king of the Romans in Cologne on June 6 and crowned in Aachen on July 12, while his rival for the German throne quickly made an alliance with the French king against Richard, Otto, the Archbishop of Cologne, and Baldwin, the Count of Flanders.

❧

ON SEPTEMBER 6, the Count of Flanders and the Count of Boulogne invaded Artois and laid siege to St Omer. Philippe promised the citizens that he would come to their rescue by the end of the month, but he soon found himself fighting a war on two fronts and Richard kept him so busy in Normandy that the city would eventually surrender to Baldwin and Renaud on October 13.

❧

IN EARLY SEPTEMBER, Philippe led a raid into the Norman Vexin and burned eighteen towns. Richard had only sixty men with him and hastily sent for reinforcements as he kept the French army under surveillance. As soon as he was joined by two hundred knights and Mercadier with a band of his routiers, he launched an attack. The French were looting and were caught by surprise, suffering many casualties as they fled toward Philippe's castle at Vernon. Richard's men captured thirty knights, forty men-at-arms, and thirty horses, and inflicted another wound to the French king's reputation. But the war continued and took on an even greater savagery, with both kings ordering the blinding of prisoners, each one blaming the other for initiating the mutilation and thus forcing retaliation. Those caught in the middle of this firestorm of hatred knew only that Normandy had become a bloody killing field where Death held dominion, not the kings of England and France.

❧

GUILLAIN DE L'ETANG HAD been very busy on his sovereign's behalf, having been part of the diplomatic mission that Richard sent to Germany and then dispatched to Rouen. After that, Richard gave him some time off to visit his own estates, and he did not rejoin the king until September 28 at the border castle of Dangu, the day after Richard had made lightning attacks upon Philippe's castles at Courcelles and Boury, taking them both by the time the sun had set.

Guillain found his king in a good mood and assumed it was due to such easy victories. But from Morgan, he learned that Richard had also gotten very welcome news from Toulouse; his sister had given birth to a healthy baby girl, named after her mother.

Guillain was pleased; Joanna was a great favorite with her brother's knights. "It is always a happy time when a baby is born," he said, and for a moment, he and Morgan shared the same sad thought—a heartfelt regret that Richard's queen could not have been as blessed as Joanna. "I am sorry I could not take part in the capture of Courcelles. I missed the action at Vernon, too, so it has been too long since I've had a chance to clout someone. Life gets boring when it is too peaceful," Guillain grumbled, only half in jest. But he brightened when Morgan assured him that a patrol was about to be sent out. "I volunteer! Who is leading the patrol?"

Morgan grinned. "Need you even ask?"

RICHARD WAS RIDING his new Lombardy stallion, a silver-grey destrier called Argento who was so fiery-tempered that the other men took care to keep their distance. They'd not gone far when they spotted dust clouds on the horizon. Richard dispatched Mercadier and a local knight, Sir Henri de Corni, to investigate. They were soon back with unexpected news.

"The French king has left Mantes, sire, and is marching north with a large force. I'd say about three hundred knights, as well as men-at-arms and the local levy."

Richard was startled, for the most logical assumption was that Philippe meant to confront his army at Dangu, but the French king avoided battles the way people shrank from lepers. "I suppose he thinks he may be able to catch us by surprise." Telling Mercadier to return to Dangu and align their men along the bank of the River Epte, he said the rest of them would track the French force. They then faded back into the woods to wait.

It was a hot afternoon; even though October was just four days away, there was no hint of autumn in the air. The road that Philippe would be following was cracked and dry, for it had not rained in weeks, and before his army came into view, they were preceded by waves of billowing yellow dust. The French banners hung limply, for there was not a breath of wind. Philippe was mounted on a dark brown gelding known to be of docile temperament, and Richard's men snickered at the sight, for theirs was a world in which a dislike of horses was incomprehensible to most. Their foes plodded on, uncomfortable in the heat, sweating in their armor, unaware that they were being watched.

Richard expected them to ford the Epte, for his army was on the opposite side of the river. When they kept marching north, he began to reassess his assumption. If they did not mean to confront his army at Dangu, what were they up to? He pondered it for a while and then it came to him, so suddenly that he laughed aloud.

"They are heading for Courcelles," he told his knights. "He does not know we took it so quickly and he's coming to relieve the siege." That made sense to them, for the French were heading north, straight as an arrow toward Courcelles. Richard was rapidly reconsidering his options now that he realized what Philippe had in mind. "We have a God-given opportunity," he said, "for if we attack them whilst they are marching, they are likely to panic and flee." He added scornfully, "That is what Philippe always does." His men were in enthusiastic agreement, and after he sent one of the knights back to Dangu with orders for Mercadier to join them, they resumed their shadowy surveillance, keeping to the woods that bordered the road.

They were in high spirits, caught up in the thrill of the hunt, for their quarry was close at hand, but utterly unsuspecting. Richard's excitement communicated itself to his destrier and Argento fought the bit, wanting to run. "Soon, boy, soon," Richard crooned, reaching over to stroke the horse's neck. "There will be plenty of stallions for you to fight. And for me, a king ripe for the plucking." He indulged himself then, imagining how Philippe's capture would forever change their world. The French threat would be trampled into the dust like its fleur-de-lys banners, the country bled white to pay for their king's ransom, one that would make Heinrich's demands seem paltry and trifling. Assuming the French would want Philippe back. Why should they? He'd shamed himself by fleeing the Holy Land, shamed himself again at Fréteval and Vernon, made a fool of himself at Issoudun. God's blood, the French might well pay to keep Philippe off the throne! Richard laughed again, and his men laughed, too, for they were never happier than when they were riding the whirlwind with him.

But as the afternoon wore on, Richard felt some of his confidence ebbing away. The French were not that far from Courcelles now. There they would learn that the castle was in his hands and realize their danger. If he hoped to catch them by surprise, it had to be soon. If he waited for his reinforcements, they were likely to slip out of the trap.

Signaling for a halt, he waited until his men had reined in within sound of his voice. "They are going to get away," he said, "unless we act now. If we want to attack them whilst they are marching and at their most vulnerable, we cannot wait."

He saw that they were taken aback, some of their eagerness blunted by unease, for they would be greatly outnumbered. "I think it best that we wait for Mercadier and his men," Jean de Préaux said, for he had fought beside Richard often enough to have earned the right to speak his mind. His brother Guilhem also counseled caution, as did Morgan and several of the others.

Richard heard them all out. "Of course it would be better if we had more men," he agreed when the last one was done speaking. "But time is not our ally. With each mile, our hopes dim. Can any of you deny that we need to stop them from reaching Courcelles?"

While none could, Richard knew their silence did not mean he'd vanquished their misgivings. "Yes, there are more of them," he said. "But they are French." They were amused by that, and he saw some frowns replaced by reluctant smiles. He tightened Argento's reins when he noticed that the stallion was eyeing another destrier, and then rose in the stirrups so they could all hear him.

"Victory will be ours, I promise you. Why? Because we have the benefit of surprise. Because we are fighting Philippe Capet. And," he added with a sudden grin, "because we have me."

As was so often the case, his cockiness proved contagious. They were all laughing by now, and when he said that for years to come, men would be telling stories around campfires of this day, they believed him.

❁

THE FRENCH ARMY HAD been on the march for hours and they were spread out by now, with many stragglers. When Richard's knights shifted their lances from their fautrés, couched them under their right arms, and charged from the woods, the assault created pandemonium in the French ranks. Some of their knights tried to rally their men, but there was so much confusion that their commands went unheeded. The local levy was the first to break, for they lacked the experience of battle-seasoned soldiers and had never faced a cavalry charge of armed knights. Riding stirrup to stirrup, Richard's knights swept over the road like a wave, engulfing all in their path as the march disintegrated into chaos.

Richard was shouting a new battle cry, one meant to proclaim that he owed his kingship only to God, and the cries of *"Dieu et mon droit!"* rose above the clamor, drowning out the few answering shouts of *"Montjoie Saint Denis!"* Ahead of him a knight on a chestnut destrier was trying to quell the panic, yelling, "Fall back! To me!" as he sought to gather enough men for a countercharge. Richard gave Argento his head, and the stallion's scream was one of primal fury as he spotted the chestnut. Richard's target swung toward the sound and couched his lance as he saw Richard bearing down upon him. But his horse sidestepped at the sight of Argento, just enough to spoil his aim. His lance struck

Richard's shield a glancing blow and then he was flung back against his saddle cantle by the force of Richard's lance. Argento screamed again, lunging toward the other stallion, and when the chestnut reared up, his rider had no hope of retaining his seat, slamming into the ground with enough force to stun him. When he opened his eyes moments later, his horse was gone and he was staring up at the English king, who had his lance leveled at his throat.

"Do you yield?" Richard preferred an iron cap with a nasal guard that did not hinder his vision and permitted his foes to know whom they were facing. The French knight was wearing one of the new great helms that hid his identity and it was only when he wrenched it off that Richard realized he'd just unhorsed one of his crusading companions.

Mathieu de Montmorency had been only sixteen at the time of their arrival in the Holy Land, but he'd grown to manhood fighting the Saracens, and Richard had become fond of him. The eager youth he remembered was a man now of twenty-four, and no longer an ally. But he still had that jaunty spirit, for he mustered up a game smile, saying, "If I must yield, I am glad it is to you, my liege, for there is no disgrace in being unhorsed by the Lionheart." He got to his feet rather unsteadily, for his head was still spinning, unsheathed his sword, and offered it to Richard. "Will my word be enough?"

"I would take the word of a Montmorency in a heartbeat," Richard assured him, waving aside the offer of the sword, and they regarded each other in silence for a moment, remembering a time when Mathieu had fought for God, not the French king. Richard's lance was still intact and he saluted the younger man with it now, knowing he could trust Mathieu to honor his parole. And then he turned back to the battle, which was already showing signs of becoming a rout.

🙟

ANY CHANCE the French might have had of staving off defeat ended when Philippe chose to retreat rather than rally his men. As he fled toward the closest refuge, his castle at Gisors, the best and bravest stayed behind to buy with their blood enough time for him to escape. Most of the French were fleeing after Philippe, but a number of his knights formed a rearguard to protect their king, offering up their lives and their freedom because he was their liege lord, because they knew no other way. Over a hundred of them would be taken prisoner by Richard and his men, and when Mercadier eventually arrived upon the scene, he seized another thirty knights. Men-at-arms were captured, too, and, as Richard would later report to the Bishop of Durham, two hundred warhorses as well, many of them protected by armor. Once again Richard had defied the odds and the fates and emerged triumphant. But the victory was tarnished by his failure to capture the French king.

He and his men pursued the French almost to the gates of Gisors. He had no siege engines with him, so he could not lay siege to the castle, and the fleeing French soldiers knew that they'd be safe once they reached Gisors. The loss of this great stronghold had been a bitter blow to Richard, for its castellan had treacherously turned it over to Philippe during his German captivity. For a time he'd used the man's name as an obscenity, and even now the sight of its soaring stone battlements caught at his heart. His stallion was lathered and both he and Richard were blood-splattered, but none of it was theirs. It had been a glorious day for Richard, one in which he could do no wrong, supremely sure that he would prevail. He'd unhorsed two more knights before his lance shattered and he'd switched to his sword, cutting a path through the French king's desperate defenders with such ferocity that many of them veered off as Argento charged toward them. But his hope of overtaking Philippe died as soon as Gisors came into view.

Richard reined in, for further pursuit was useless. Too late! Once again that paltry milksop had gotten away. He was soon joined by some of his knights and then Mercadier. They were all jubilant, their spirits soaring higher than hawks, for they'd won some rich ransoms this day; even better, they were still alive to savor their victory. Sensing Richard's mood, they sought to cheer him with such savage mockery of the French king that some of his anger began to cool, to be replaced by a genuine sense of bafflement.

"I could not imagine abandoning my army, leaving my men to fend for themselves as I sought to save my own skin. Not only does Philippe have no honor, he has no sense of shame. He must—Jesu!"

The bridge spanning the River Epte was crowded with men and horses, and as more and more of the refugees from the battle swarmed onto the wooden span, it began to creak ominously, swaying under the weight of so many soldiers. As Richard and his knights watched, openmouthed, several of the arches gave way and the bridge collapsed. There was a huge splash, and then screams. Some of the men managed to flounder to shore; others clung to the broken pilings or snatched frantically at the swimming horses. But many drowned within moments, dragged down by their armor. Richard had seen a bridge break apart like this once before, as his and Philippe's armies were crossing the Rhône. He had quickly organized a rescue effort and they'd lost only two men to the river. It was obvious, though, that the French would not be so lucky on this September Sunday afternoon, drowning within sight of the castle that was to have been their salvation.

Men who'd not yet made it onto the bridge willingly surrendered to Richard's knights, for captivity suddenly seemed the lesser evil. On the far side of the river, soaked, shivering men were being pulled to safety, some vomiting up brackish water, others breathing their last. One man clinging to a horse's tail was dragged into the shallows, only to then lose his footing and be swept away by the current. There were no bodies visible, for the dead had been anchored by their armor. The last battle of the day was won by the river.

Richard had turned Argento away when he was called back by a shout from Mercadier. "Look, my lord!" He was pointing toward the far bank, but Richard saw only half-drowned soldiers being assisted toward the castle. He'd often joked that Mercadier's vision could put a gyrfalcon to shame, and the routier proved it now by gesturing again. "That one surrounded by those gabbling priests—it's the French king!"

Richard squinted, shading his eyes against the glare of sun on water. "God's legs, Mercadier, I think you are right!"

Mercadier had no doubts. "I saw several men plunge into the river to swim to his rescue and I wondered why one drowning man would matter so much that other men would risk their lives to save him. Once they had fished him out, I recognized that bald pate of his."

Richard was still embittered that Philippe had escaped him. But as he stared across the river at his bedraggled, waterlogged rival, a smile began to tug at the corners of his mouth. "He does not look as if he enjoyed his bath in the Epte, does he? He always acted as if he was sure he could walk on water. It must be a great disappointment to find he is a mere mortal after all."

But his true feelings were expressed in an aside to Morgan as he signaled for his men to move out. "If there were any justice under God's sky, the bastard would have drowned."

❦

CONSTANCE DE HAUTEVILLE HAD celebrated her forty-fourth birthday on All Soul's Day, but she knew it would be her last. She was dying. She'd been ill for months, and not even the doctors of the famed medical school in Salerno had been able to offer either hope or relief from the pain. She'd been very bitter at first, for she'd had little more than a year of freedom, a year to rule Sicily, to rid her kingdom of the Germans, to have her son with her—a privilege that Heinrich had denied her, for he'd given Friedrich into the care of the Duchess of Spoleto soon after his birth. One year, one month, and twenty-seven days to have been a queen, a mother, and, God be praised, a widow. Not enough time. Not nearly enough.

She'd faced it as she'd faced every crisis in her life, without flinching, without self-pity or panic. What mattered was her son, still a month shy of his fourth birthday. She'd done all she could. She'd exiled Markward von Annweiler, who'd been made Duke of Ravenna and Romagna by Heinrich. In May, she'd had Friedrich crowned as King of Sicily, letting Otto and Heinrich's brother Philip fight over the imperial crown. And she'd turned to the only man powerful enough to protect her son, the new Pope, Innocent III. In her last will and testament, she'd named Innocent as Friedrich's guardian until he came of age. Now, in what she knew to be her last hours, she could only pray that it would be enough: that her son would be kept safe, his rights defended by the Church, and that he would not forget her too quickly.

❧

JOHN HAD NOT ATTENDED his brother's Christmas Court at Domfront, for now that Otto was no longer a rival, he did not feel so much pressure to please Richard. But a summons from his mother was not to be ignored. As soon as he was ushered into her private quarters at Fontevrault Abbey, he sensed that something was wrong. She was alone, and although a fire was burning in the hearth, the chamber seemed very cold to him.

"So you've come. I was not sure you would."

"Of course I came. You sent for me, did you not?" John's smile faded. "What is amiss? Why do you look at me like that?"

"As if you do not know!" Eleanor had stood motionless by the hearth as John crossed the chamber. But as soon as he moved within range, she took two quick steps forward and struck him across the mouth. "You fool! You utter fool!"

John gasped, grabbed her wrist when she raised her hand as if to strike him again. "Christ Jesus, Mother, what is the matter with you? Why should you be wroth with me?"

"Why, indeed? Betrayal is as natural to you as breathing. More fool I, for imagining it could ever be otherwise!" Eleanor jerked her wrist free, began to pace. "More than four years without a misstep, four years of fidelity. You showed Richard that you were not as worthless as he once thought, that you could do more than intrigue and plot and scheme. All for naught. Name of God, why? What demon possessed you to throw it all away?"

"I do not know what you are talking about. Just what am I supposed to have done?"

"Oh, enough! We know. Philippe betrayed you, and how ironic is that? He sent Richard a message that you'd been plotting against him again, that you'd offered an alliance with the French Crown."

"And Richard believed this? You believed it?" John was incredulous. "I am not surprised that Richard is so quick to suspect the worst of me. But you, Madame . . . God's truth, I'd have expected better of you!"

"Philippe claims to have a letter that proves your complicity in this intrigue, a letter in your own hand."

"Oh, for the love of Christ! What better proof of my innocence could you ask for than that? If I were involved in some scheme to betray Richard, do you truly think I'd ever be so stupid as to incriminate myself in writing?"

Eleanor felt the first flickers of doubt. "Your denial has the ring of truth to it. But then your denials always do, John."

"If you and Richard believed this lunatic accusation, it can only be because you wanted to believe it, Madame. You yourself said it—I've devoted years to regaining Richard's goodwill. You think I enjoyed being at his beck and call, enduring the scorn of his friends, knowing he'd have chosen Arthur if the Bretons had not been such fools? Or that I'd gamble those four years on something so worthless as Philippe's word? Christ on the Cross, Mother! What would I gain by intriguing with Philippe? We both know he has no hope of ever defeating Richard on the field!"

He was as angry as Eleanor had ever seen him, too angry for either artifice or discretion. His was not a defense calculated to endear. But there was a cold-blooded, unsparing honesty to it that was, to Eleanor, more persuasive than any indignant avowals of good faith. It was the very amorality of John's argument that carried so much conviction.

"Where is Richard now? Is he still at Domfront?"

Eleanor no longer doubted. There could be no better indication of John's innocence than this, that he would willingly seek Richard out. When he was in the wrong, the last thing he ever wanted was to face his accusers, to confront those he'd betrayed.

Eleanor's relief was inexpressible. Her easy acceptance of John's guilt had been prompted as much by fear as by her son's dismal record of broken faith and betrayals, the fear that she had misjudged him, after all, that he was not the pragmatist she'd thought him to be. Had he indeed been plotting again with Philippe, that would mean his judgment was fatally and unforgivably flawed, flawed enough to taint any claim to the crown. It was a conclusion she shrank from, for it would signify the end of all her hopes for an Angevin dynasty, and that was the dream that had sustained her even in the worst of times, just as it had sustained her husband.

She sat down abruptly in a cushioned chair. "Thank God," she said simply, with enough feeling to soothe John's sense of injury.

"But of course I accept your apology, Mother," he said, very dryly. Righteous indignation was not an emotion indigenous to his temperamental terrain; he had too much irony in his makeup to be able to cultivate moral outrage, and now that he no longer feared being called to account for a sin that truly was not his, he was beginning to see the perverse humor in his predicament. *"Be not righteous over much,"* he quoted, and grinned. "But how can I help it? After all, how often have I been able to expose my conscience to your exacting eye . . . and live to tell the tale?"

Eleanor could not help herself, had to smile, too. "By what strange alchemy do you manage to make your vices sound so much like virtues?" She shook her head, gestured toward the table. "Fetch me pen and parchment. You'll need to face Richard yourself, assure him that you are innocent—this time. But it will help if he knows I believe you."

After he left, she leaned back in the chair, rubbing her fingers against her temples, for her head was throbbing. Richard would never get a son from Berengaria. Nor did he seem willing to put her aside. So John was all they had.

CHAPTER THIRTY-FOUR

✦

MARCH 1199

Chinon Castle, Touraine

There was a chill in the air, the threat of winter lingering beyond its time. Lacking the patience to summon a servant, Richard crossed to the hearth and reached for the fire tongs, prodding the flames back into life. Returning to his seat then, he resumed the story of his January council with the French king, a meeting arranged by the new papal legate, Pietro di Capua.

"I'd taken a boat upriver from Castle Gaillard, but Philippe refused to join me on board. Apparently his bath in the Epte has made him leery of rivers, for he stayed on horseback and we shouted back and forth across the water. An utter waste of time and breath."

"You did agree on a five-year truce, though," Eleanor reminded him, and he shook his head wearily.

"And we know how much such truces mean—counterfeit coin, not worth a copper farthing. But the new Pope is bound and determined to make peace, so his legate came up with another proposal, suggesting that Philippe's son wed one of my nieces."

"Arthur's sister?"

"No, one of Leonora's daughters. I told them I'd consider these new terms once I return from Limousin."

He'd already told Eleanor about his coming campaign. The Count of Angoulême and his half brother, the Viscount of Limoges, were conniving again with the French king, and he meant to teach them that there was a high price to be paid for such treachery. A lifetime of dealing with these rebellious southern barons had taught Eleanor that such lessons lasted as long as hoarfrost, and she was sure Richard knew it, too. But kings did what they must.

"I hear that the papal legate set your temper ablaze?"

"He did, by God. The lack-wit dared to demand that I set Beauvais free, insisting he is under the protection of the Church."

"Is it true that you threatened him with castration, Richard?"

"Is that what he is claiming? Whilst I think society could benefit if some churchmen were gelded—keeping them from breeding, if nothing else—I did not actually threaten to turn him into a capon, merely reminded him that his papal legateship was all that was saving him from my righteous wrath. But he went scurrying back to Paris so fast that he might well have feared for his meager family jewels."

Richard's sarcasm did not disguise the depths of his anger, as he proved now by launching a diatribe against the papacy. "The Church did nothing for me whilst I was held prisoner in Germany and my lands were being overrun by the French king and Johnny. Yet now their hearts bleed for that Devil's whelp Beauvais? Well, he will never see the light of day again, not as long as I draw breath."

Eleanor was conflicted about the Bishop of Beauvais's fate. The queen saw his continuing imprisonment as a source of discord with the new Pope, never a good thing, but the mother had not a drop of pity to spare for the captive prelate. She voiced no opinion, though, for she knew it would not be welcome; the Archangel Gabriel could appear to argue for Beauvais's release and Richard would have paid no heed. Instead, she seized upon his mention of his younger brother.

"Speaking of John . . . Did he seek you out as he promised me he would?"

"He did, on the day after Epiphany, swearing upon all he holds most sacred—which in Johnny's case is to be found below the belt—that he had not been plotting against me. It must have been quite a novelty—for once actually being innocent of the charges made against him. With his usual flair for the dramatic, he dispatched two knights to the French court to formally deny the accusation, and none were willing to accept his challenge."

Richard interrupted himself to pour wine for them both. Regarding his mother with a sardonic smile, he said, "Do you know where he is now? Off to pay a visit to our nephew in Brittany."

Eleanor's eyebrows shot upward. "Whatever for?"

"He reminded me that he'd never met Arthur, and now that the lad has returned from Paris, he decided it was as good a time as any to take Arthur's measure. Knowing Johnny, I daresay he is also amusing himself by putting the cat amongst the pigeons. Think how Constance and her Bretons will react to his unexpected arrival. They'll be sure he is up to no good, but what? I'd wager none of them get a full night's sleep until he departs."

"John is very good at banishing sleep," Eleanor said dryly. "Richard . . . I had a troubling letter recently from the Bishop of Agen. He says the Count of Toulouse has not been very successful in dealing with some of his rebellious vassals, that he tends to be too forgiving and Joanna has been urging him to take a harder stance. Raimond was away when the lord of St Felix rebelled and instead of waiting for her husband's return, Joanna chose to lead an armed force herself and lay siege to his castle at Les Casses."

She sounded so disapproving that Richard hastily brought his wine cup up to conceal a smile. "Say what you will of our lass; she does not lack for spirit."

"Too much spirit. She was not that long out of childbed, and as it turned out, she found herself in real danger. Several of Raimond's knights had been bought off by the rebels and they set fire to her siege camp. She barely escaped with her life."

Richard scowled. "I hope St Gilles saw to it that those shameless curs paid in blood for their treachery."

"The bishop did not say how Raimond reacted. I doubt that he was happy about Joanna taking such a risk, though. How could he be?"

"Well, I never had much luck reining Joanna in, so I doubt that Raimond will, either. She is your daughter, after all. But I agree that we need to talk to her. Once I get back from dealing with that Judas in Limoges, I'll invite Joanna and Raimond to my court. Mayhap between the three of us, we can convince her that besieging castles is not an ideal female pastime."

Eleanor hoped so. A brother might be proud of a strong-willed sister's boldness, but how many husbands would be so indulgent? Marriages were far more fragile than most people realized, even the good ones, and if she could stop her daughter from making some of her own mistakes, she meant to do so.

"Do not tarry too long in Limousin, Richard."

He smiled. "From your lips to God's Ear, Maman."

❧

CHÂLUS-CHABROL WAS PERCHED ON the summit of a low hill above the River Tardoire, although it could more properly be called a stream, just as its village was more properly a hamlet. It was one of the castles that Viscount Aimar

relied upon to guard the Limoges–Périgord road, but it did not look very imposing, a small citadel with a round stone keep and ten houses enclosed by a double
bailey. It was being held for the viscount by the Lord of Montbrun, Peire Brun,
and a captured peddler insisted there were no more than forty people within its
walls. Richard's men did not expect it to present much of a challenge. It was only
the first target of many, for Richard had vowed to raze all of the viscount's
strongholds, leaving Aimar with nothing but charred ruins, ashes, rubble, and
regrets. This was the fifth rebellion launched by the viscount and Richard was
determined that it would be the last.

IT HAD BEEN AN uncommonly warm day for March, even in the Limousin,
and Richard's crossbowmen had shed their mantles as they shot up at Châlus's
ramparts, protecting the sappers who'd been undermining its walls for the past
three days. Morgan did not think the siege would last much longer. They'd already offered to surrender if they were guaranteed their lives, limbs, and weapons, an offer Richard had spurned.

Morgan shook his head as he remembered that, thinking the fools ought to
have known that Richard always insisted upon unconditional surrender from
rebels; only then would he show mercy. So it had been at Darum in the Holy
Land, at Tickhill, Nottingham, Loches, and the dozens of castles he'd taken
from the French king's castellans and vassals. Morgan tried and failed to think
of a castle siege where Richard had not demanded unconditional surrender;
there were so many sieges that he could not recall them all. Five years of inces-
sant warfare, constant and unrelenting. Glancing up at a kestrel gliding on the
wind far above his head, he wondered what he'd do if a true peace was ever
forged between England and France, if Richard no longer had such need of his
sword.

He supposed he could settle upon his estates in Normandy, take a wife, and
sire some children. He'd turned thirty-five in February, after all, and he'd finally given up hope of changing Mariam's mind. He'd found himself thinking
more and more of family in the past few weeks, and why not? He'd lost his Welsh
family, so surely it was natural to want to start a family of his own. How likely
was it, though, that the dove of peace would ever alight on this side of the Narrow Sea? Yet more likely than it had been, for the French king was hard-pressed
on two fronts nowadays, both on the battlefield and in the diplomatic chambers.

Philippe might be many things, but a fool he was not. He must know the time was drawing nigh for him to cut his losses, all the more so now that the Pope was threatening to place France under Interdict for his continuing maltreatment of the unhappy Ingeborg.

Richard's command tent lay just ahead, and Morgan quickened his step. But he found only Arne, diligently rubbing goose grease into a pair of Richard's leather boots. "You just missed the king, my lord," he said with a shy smile. "After supper, he took his crossbow and went out to see what progress the sappers are making."

Seeing Richard's hauberk draped over a coffer, Morgan grimaced. "He did at least take his shield?"

Arne ducked his head, as if his king's recklessness were somehow his fault. "I reminded him about his mail, my lord, but . . ."

"But you might as well bid the sun to stop rising in the east," Morgan said wryly.

"He did wear his helmet." Arne put the boots down, giving the Welshman a searching look. He was not of good birth, an orphan of little education or prospects. He ought to have lived and died in his small Austrian village, never getting farther than twenty miles from his home. But God had decreed otherwise, sending him to the Holy Land, sending him into the service of a great king. Morgan was a lord; royal blood ran in his veins. Yet Arne had shared with Richard and Morgan and Guillain what no other men in Christendom had—they'd been to Heinrich von Hohenstaufen's Hell and battled their way back. He still bore the scars—on his throat, his face, and his memory—and that gave him the confidence now to speak freely to the king's cousin.

"The king told me that you'd gotten a letter at Chinon from your brother, telling you that your parents are dead. My lord, I am so very sorry."

Even after a fortnight, Morgan still struggled with disbelief. He realized that made no sense, for his father had lived to a truly vast age—eighty winters—and his mother had also been blessed with a long life. That ought to have been a comfort, and he hoped in time it would be. God had smiled upon them both, and He'd shown divine mercy, too, sparing them the separation and the grieving that was the inevitable fate of those brave enough to love. Ranulf had died in his sleep, and within the week, his ailing wife had followed him to eternal glory, for Morgan was sure they'd spend little, if any, time in Purgatory.

"Thank you, Arne. At first I grieved that I'd not been there, that I'd not had the chance to say farewell. They died in Epiphany week yet I did not know. So for two months, I thought they still breathed and smiled and prayed and felt the Welsh sun on their faces; despite what men claim, the sun does shine in Wales from time to time. Were they any less alive to me during those two months because I did not know? We live on in memories and deeds and prayers, lad; above all, in those we love."

Arne was not sure he understood, but he murmured a dutiful "May God assoil them," and vowed to add the names of Ranulf Fitz Roy and Rhiannon ferch Rhodri to the list of those for whom he offered up nightly prayers. For he did understand that there was power in prayer, even for ones such as he.

"Come, Arne." Morgan smiled, determined to lighten the mood. "Let's go find that errant king of ours. There is no use in lugging his hauberk along, but at least we can remind him that even lions get wet when it rains."

THE SKY ALONG THE HORIZON was glowing like the embers of a dying fire as this last Friday in March ebbed away. There was still enough daylight remaining for Richard to assess Châlus's weaknesses, though. His sappers, shielded by a wheeled wooden cat, were working industriously to tunnel under the castle walls. Once they'd excavated far enough, they'd shore up the cavity with timber, then fill it with combustible fuel and set it aflame; when the timbers burned, the wall above would collapse with it. But that would take time Richard was not willing to spare. The sooner he could take Châlus, the sooner his army could move on to Aimar's strongholds at Nontron and Montagut. So he and Mercadier were reconnoitering the castle's defenses to see how feasible it would be to take Châlus by storm.

One of Richard's sergeants had set up his large rectangular shield, and he and Mercadier were standing behind it as they debated where the castle seemed most vulnerable to an assault. They were soon joined by William de Braose. He held the barony of Bramber and extensive lands in Wales, where he'd earned himself a reputation among the Welsh as a man of no honor. But he was as capable as he was ruthless and he'd served Richard well as sheriff of Herefordshire and as a royal justice, proving to be an effective bulwark against the ever-restless Welsh. Glancing at Richard's crossbow, he said, "You'll get few chances to make use of that, sire. Our crossbowmen have kept the castle defenders off the walls for much of the day, aside from one lunatic by the gatehouse."

Richard arched a brow. "Why call him a lunatic, Will?"

"See for yourself, my liege." The Marcher lord gestured and Richard squinted until he located the lone man on the castle battlements. When he did, he burst out laughing, for this enemy crossbowman was using a large frying pan as a shield, deflecting the bolts coming his way with surprising dexterity. De Braose and Mercadier were not surprised by his reaction, for they'd known this was just the sort of mad gallantry to appeal to Richard. But because chivalry was as alien a tongue to them as the languages spoken in Cathay, they saw the knave wielding a frying pan as nothing more than a nuisance to be eliminated, sooner rather than later.

When the crossbowman used his makeshift shield to turn aside another bolt, Richard gave him a playful, mocking salute. He was still laughing when the crossbowman aimed at him and he was slow, therefore, in ducking for cover behind his shield. The bolt struck him in the left shoulder, just above his collarbone. The impact was great enough to stagger him, although he managed to keep his balance, grabbing the edge of the shield to steady himself. There was no pain, not yet, but he'd suffered enough wounds to know that would not last. His first coherent thought was relief that dusk was fast falling, for when he glanced around hastily, it was clear that none of his men had seen him hit. Only de Braose and Mercadier had been close enough to see what had happened, and while their dismay was obvious even in the fading light, he knew they were too battlewise to cry out, to let others know that their king had just been shot.

"Come with me," he said in a low voice, remembering in time to call out to his sergeant, "Odo, leave my shield there for now." He was grateful that his voice sounded so natural, as if nothing were amiss, and he was grateful, too, that he'd not ridden out to inspect the castle defenses, for he knew he'd never have been able to get up into the saddle without help. Mercadier and de Braose fell in step beside him, using their own bodies to shield him from any prying eyes. He was able to set a measured pace, but by the time they reached his tent, his legs were feeling weak and his arm had gone numb.

Arne was not within and the tent was dark. De Braose had a lantern, though, and he used its candle to light an oil lamp. Richard sank down on the bed as they closed the tent flaps. Mercadier had already drawn his dagger. Leaning over, he began carefully to cut Richard's tunic away from that protruding bolt. With a few deft slashes, Richard's linen shirt soon followed. Straightening up, Mercadier paused to take a deep breath. He'd removed arrows and bolts from injured men in the past, but only when there was no other alternative, for such wounds were best left to surgeons. It was then, though, that Richard reached for the shaft and yanked.

"No, wait!" Mercadier's cry was too late. There was a sharp crack and the wooden shaft broke off in Richard's hand.

None of them spoke in the moments that followed. Richard had never denied that acting on impulse was one of his worst flaws. But never had he regretted following an impulse as much as he did now, for he'd just made it needlessly difficult for the bolt's head to be extracted.

It was then that the tent flap was lifted and Arne entered, with Morgan and Guy de Thouars right on his heels. "I saw your shield, sire. Shall I fetch— *Ach mein Gott!*"

There were smothered exclamations from Morgan and Guy, too, quickly stilled, as they all stared at the broken shaft in Richard's hand. "You always have a surgeon for your men, Mercadier," he said at last. "You'd best fetch him."

⬧

WHEN RICHARD'S ARMY APPROACHED Châlus-Chabrol, only a few of the villagers sought refuge in the castle, knowing it could not hold out for long; the rest had fled into the woods with whatever meager belongings and livestock they could save. The priest's house was small, with only two rooms, and scantily furnished. But it had stone walls, windows with shutters, and a fireplace, which made it palatial in comparison to the nearby cottages. While Richard usually preferred his command tent at sieges, he did occasionally commandeer a nearby house, so they hoped the move would not cause comment among his soldiers.

The bedchamber soon felt stifling, warmed by as many torches as they could fit into the cramped space. As Arne scurried about, fetching wine, water, blankets, towels, and candles, Morgan felt a twinge of envy, for at least the lad could keep busy. All they could do was wait for the arrival of Mercadier's surgeon. Richard was slumped on the bed, his mantle draped over his shoulders. His face gave away nothing of his thoughts, nor of the pain he must surely be experiencing by now. William de Braose and Guy de Thouars were leaning against the wall, and Guillain was straddling a rickety chair; he alone had been let in upon this dangerous secret so far, but Morgan knew others would have to be told, too.

Unable to endure either the silence or the suspense any longer, Morgan strode over to the table and poured a brimming cup from the wine flagon. *The Welsh were always a practical people,* Richard thought, reaching for the cup. He drained it in several deep swallows; wine was not much of a crutch, but it was better than nothing. Well, he also had anger, although that was not much help, since most of it was directed at himself, at his accursed, idiotic carelessness. There was some fear, too, a purely physical dread of the ordeal that lay ahead of him. And because he hated to acknowledge that fear, even to himself, he sought relief in cursing Mercadier's missing surgeon, demanding to know why it was taking so long to find the man. "He's probably off drinking himself sodden with a few of the camp whores!"

At that moment, the door opened and Mercadier ushered the surgeon into the room. Their first sight of the man was not encouraging. He was well dressed and clean-shaven, looking more like a prosperous merchant than one in the service of the notorious routier captain. But he was so ashen that his complexion had taken on a sickly, greenish-grey cast, a fine sheen of perspiration was coating his upper lip, and he kept his gaze aimed at his feet. Morgan was suddenly fearful that he might indeed be drunk. But after he took a closer look, he thought, *No, not drunk—terrified.*

"This is Master Guyon." When the surgeon still did not speak, Mercadier impaled him with a piercing stare that somehow managed to freeze and burn at the same time. "Would you have the king think you're a mute?" he snarled, and Morgan realized the surgeon was just as afraid of Mercadier as he was of the king. He might have felt pity for the man if the stakes in this high-risk wager were not Richard's life.

Master Guyon shuffled forward to kneel before Richard. "If I may examine the wound, my liege?" he asked humbly.

"You can hardly extract the bolt if you do not examine the wound," Richard snapped, for the man's demeanor was not inspiring much confidence. But he was all they had, for they could not very well ask the Viscount of Limoges to send them one of his surgeons.

Master Guyon set his coffer of instruments on the table. It held the usual tools of his trade, for physicians spoke disparagingly of surgeons as being "in trade." As if any of those smug pompous peacocks could have faced a challenge like this without their ballocks shriveling up like raisins. He stared down at the coffer's contents: chisel, probe, tenaille, bisoury, saw, clamps, razors, hooks, mallet, cautery rods, tweezers, tongs, needles, sutures, *rugynes* for drawing out bits of bone, a trephine for boring holes in the skull. He was not attempting to decide which ones should be used. He already knew that: a tenaille to extract the bolt and, if that failed, a bisoury to dig it out. But he did need a few moments to calm his nerves. He'd never lacked for confidence in his own skills, yet now he felt as if this were his first surgery. "I will need as much light as possible," he said, and a youth darted forward to hold an oil lamp over the bed.

Guyon's first look at the wound confirmed his worst fears. The shaft had broken off close to the entry point, and there was not enough wood left for the tenaille to grip. Nor was it a good sign that bruising was already visible. Moreover, the king was naked from the waist up, so Guyon could see that he'd gained weight in the years since his knee injury, and that excess flesh would complicate his task, making it harder to locate and extract the bolt's head. There were only three ways to treat an injury like this, and he ruled out two at once. Surgeons would often try to push an arrow through a man's body, but even if the shaft had still been intact, that would not have been possible for the king's wound. Many surgeons believed in waiting a few days until the tissue around the wound began to putrefy, making the extraction easier. Guyon did not agree with this method, for it had been his experience that such a delay too often caused the wound to fester, and when that happened, the patient almost always died.

"I fear, sire, that I shall have to cut it out."

"I did not expect you to conjure it out." Richard was rapidly concluding that the man was both timid and incompetent. "Fetch me more wine, Morgan," he said abruptly. "I've made enough mistakes already and am not about to add facing surgery whilst I'm sober to the list." After draining another flagon, he braced himself then for what he knew was going to be a very unpleasant experience. "Arne, did you find something for me to bite down upon?"

From the moment he'd halted in the tent, realizing that Richard had been shot, Arne had found that speech was beyond him; it was as if his throat were being squeezed so tightly that no words could escape. Mutely, he held out his offering, a pair of Richard's leather gloves. As soon as he did, though, time seemed to fracture and for a horrifying moment, he was catapulted back to the Vienna market on that bitter December day, betrayed by those ornate gloves that only a king would have worn. Sweat broke out upon his forehead and he fought the urge to make the sign of the cross. How could he have been so witless? What could be a worse omen than gloves? He reached out to snatch them back, croaking, "Wait, sire! A piece of wood would be better. . . ."

As their eyes met, Arne swallowed a sob. He was sure Richard knew exactly what he was thinking, for his voice softened and he even managed the flicker of a smile. "No wood. The way my day has been going so far, lad, I'd be likely to break a tooth."

Guyon would have given a lot to drain a wine flagon himself. He could feel Mercadier's eyes boring into his back as he approached the bed again. "I'll need more light. Sire, if you'll lie down . . ." He hesitated then, not knowing how to say what had to be said without giving offense. "I've found that it is best if restraints are used during the surgery."

The look he got from the king was sharp enough to draw blood. "You think this is my first battle wound? I will not need to be restrained," Richard said, in so flat and dangerous a tone that Guyon dared not argue further.

Morgan, Guillain, and Guy carried torches over to the bed; they gave off more heat than light and cast eerie shadows that added to Guyon's unease. He would rather have performed this operation in his own surgical tent during daylight hours. He would rather not have performed it at all. Saying a silent prayer that God would bless his efforts with success, he reached for the bisoury.

Richard flinched as he began to widen the wound, biting down upon the glove, but he did not shrink from the scalpel's narrow blade as Guyon's patients usually did. Blood was bubbling up and Guyon reached for a towel to blot it away. Sweat had already begun to sting his eyes. So much that could go wrong. If he cut into an artery, the king would bleed out at once. Bleeding from a vein would not be as quick or fatal, but it would be difficult to staunch.

"Hold the lamp closer," he told Arne, for its fitful flame was still safer than the smoldering torches. After switching to a probe, he wiped away more of the blood obscuring his view. He did not expect them to understand what he'd be telling them, but he'd gotten into the habit of keeping up a running commentary during his surgeries, a holdover from his early days of training. "It looks as if the bolt entered behind the king's collarbone and went down into the muscles in front of his shoulder blade." He knew the Latin terms for these bones—clavicle and scapula—but like most surgeons, his had been a hands-on apprenticeship, his knowledge gained on the battlefield and in surgical tents, not in university classes, and he preferred to use the names that his patients would have used themselves.

Reaching again for the bisoury, he made a larger incision. He was amazed that Richard had so far been able to keep still. His jaw was clenched so tightly that Guyon thought they might have to pry that glove from his teeth afterward, the tendons in his neck were so taut they looked like corded rope, and his body jerked as the blade dug into his flesh. But his self-control was remarkable, for most patients thrashed around wildly even under restraints.

Guyon could see what was left of the shaft now and fumbled for his tenaille. If he could clasp the shaft, mayhap he could maneuver the bolt up and out. That hope was short-lived, for nothing happened when he tugged. It was as he'd feared: the bolt's iron head was lodged deep in the king's muscles, wedged between his scapula and rib cage. "Sire," he said desperately, "the iron will not budge. I shall have to cut it out, and that will cause you great pain."

Richard was drenched in perspiration by now and his chest was heaving with his every breath. His words were garbled, muffled by the glove, but Guyon understood. Closing his eyes, he made the sign of the cross, and then looked over at Mercadier and William de Braose, the only ones without torches. "You must be ready to hold the king down if need be," he told them and then reached again for the scalpel before Richard could protest. *Holy Redeemer, Lamb of God, have mercy upon your servant. Guide my hand.*

What followed would haunt Guyon for the rest of his life. He'd awake in the night, his heart thudding, remembering the heat of the torches, the blood, his shaking hands, his growing panic as he kept trying and failing to wrest the iron free, sure that if Richard died, he'd pay with his life; Mercadier would see to that. At least he and the other lord had done as he'd bidden them, and held the king down when his body finally defied his will and sought to escape that sharp, seeking blade. Thankfully, he'd soon passed out from the pain, the only favor that night that fate had deigned to grant either of them, king or surgeon.

At the last, Guyon had resorted to brute force, having cut away enough flesh to expose the bolt's head, a lethal piece of iron as long as a man's palm. Positioning his clamps, he said another silent prayer, and then yanked with all of his strength. When it finally came free in a spray of blood, he reeled backward and had to grasp the table for support. The youth called Arne had gone greensick and was vomiting into the floor rushes; the fair-haired knight they'd called Guy looked as if he were about to do likewise. Guyon knew one of the men was the king's cousin, and he braced himself for the other's accusations and recriminations. But he said only, "You did your best," and Guyon felt such gratitude he could have hugged the man.

Mercadier had leaned over the bed, his fingers searching for the pulse in the king's throat. "He still lives," he said, and Guyon understood the warning in that terse commentary. Pulling himself together, he took one of the wine flagons and carried it over to pour into the king's wound. When he asked for his jars of unguents and herbal balms, Arne wiped his mouth on his sleeve and hastened over to his side. They all watched intently as he mixed betony and comfrey with water, explaining that these herbs, Saracen's root and woundwort, would assist in the healing. Once he had a thick paste, he applied it to a thin cloth and the king's cousin helped him to lift Richard's inert body up so he could fasten the poultice. He half expected them to demand to know why he was not suturing up the wound, but when none did, he realized why. They'd seen enough battlefield injuries like this to know that surgeons preferred to keep deep puncture wounds open so they could drain of pus.

By the time he was done, the surgeon was trembling with fatigue. "He ought to sleep through the night," he said wearily. "I'll fetch my bedding and sleep in the outer chamber."

"I'll send a man with you to carry what you need."

Guyon mumbled his thanks, even though he knew that Mercadier's helpful routier would really be his guard. But he was so weary that when Morgan asked him if the king would recover from his wound, he could not summon up the energy to lie.

"I do not know, my lord," he said. "God's truth, I do not know."

CHAPTER THIRTY-FIVE

❧

MARCH 1199

Châlus-Chabrol, Limousin

Richard awoke to a world of pain. His entire body hurt and his shoulder felt as if it were afire. When he opened his eyes, there was an immediate outcry and then others were surrounding the bed—Arne, Morgan, Guillain. They looked so distraught that for a moment he almost believed this shabby, unfamiliar chamber was an alewife's cottage in Ertpurch. But then the memories of last night's botched surgery came flooding back.

They did not ask how he felt, for that was obvious to anyone with eyes to see. They concentrated instead upon what little they could do for his comfort, explaining that the surgeon had thought it best to leave him in the priest's bloodied bed. They'd brought his own bed from his tent and they could help him into it if that was his wish. Once Richard glanced down at the damp, befouled sheets, it was. But he soon discovered that his body was not taking orders from his brain and something as simple as changing beds became as challenging as a winter crossing of the Alps. It left him limp and exhausted, feeling as feeble as a newly birthed lamb. For that was what he was now. Not a lion—a lamb at the mercy of his shepherds.

The shepherds were not lacking in solicitude, though; he'd give them that much. They hovered by the bed, fetching a wine cup and then a chamber pot as Arne folded up the priest's straw mattress. Richard started to warn him to take care in disposing of it, for none must see those bloodstains, but then he realized that there was no need. They understood full well how important it was to keep his injury a secret from his men, from the castle defenders, from the French. He felt a little queasy, but thirst won out and he was taking a few swallows when the door opened and the butcher burst into the chamber—for that was Richard's first uncharitable thought at sight of the surgeon.

Master Guyon snatched up the chamber pot, for although surgeons did not view urine the way physicians did—as an indispensable diagnostic tool—he thought there was always something to be learned by examining a patient's piss. He busied himself in taking Richard's pulse and feeling for signs of fever, all the while keeping up a strained flow of chatter as he nerved himself to loosen the poultice so he could inspect the wound. When he did, he felt weak in the knees, so great was his relief that there were no signs of infection. He knew how little that meant, for he'd seen wounds fester within hours and others not for more than a week. But each day that the king's wound remained free of corruption was a day that moved the king—and himself—further away from the precipice. Aware that his presence was not welcome to Richard, he soon retired to a corner of the chamber to study the urine specimen, his nerves so shredded that he jumped and almost spilled the pot's contents when Mercadier slammed into the room.

Richard had never seen the routier so haggard. "God's blood, you look worse than I do," he gibed, but Mercadier seemed to be lacking humor as well as sleep, for he just grunted. His eyes raked the chamber, lingering for an unsettling moment upon Master Guyon before he picked up a chair and brought it over to the bed.

"I promise you," he said, "that I shall take that castle for you, and when I do, I shall hang every mother's son in it."

Richard was surprised, not by the vow, but by the raw emotion that underlay Mercadier's rage, for the other man had never been one to show his emotions openly; many were convinced he had none. Richard started to sit up then—a great mistake. Falling back against the pillow, he gasped as the fire blazed hotter than the flames of Hell. Once he was sure it was not going to consume him then and there, he said, "When you hang the garrison, mayhap you ought to hang Master Guyon, too."

Mercadier's pale eyes glittered. "Just say the word, my lord."

Morgan glanced over at the surgeon, who suddenly looked as if he were the one in need of medical care. Moving toward the man, Morgan said softly, "There's no cause for fear. The king is not serious."

Guyon's Adam's apple bobbed as he swallowed painfully. "Mercadier is," he whispered, and when the routier shafted another glance their way, Morgan thought the surgeon might well be right.

"The fool mangled your shoulder, my lord." Mercadier's voice was so fraught with menace that the surgeon shivered. "I've seen Martinmas hogs butchered with more skill."

The pain was making Richard feel queasy again and he was inclined to agree with Mercadier's harsh assessment of the surgery. "You're right . . . but if we hang that fool for mangling my shoulder, then we'd also have to hang the other fool, the one who tried to pull the bolt out on his own."

Guyon's shoulders sagged with the easing of tension, but Morgan decided they'd best keep a close eye upon him lest he flee when the first opportunity presented itself. Even a second-rate surgeon was better than none at all, for they knew Richard's life still hung in the balance.

Mercadier had risen to his feet. "Châlus will be yours, my liege. May I burn in Hell Everlasting if I fail you in this."

Richard would normally have retorted that Mercadier was likely to burn in Hell Everlasting no matter what he did or did not do at Châlus. But he had no energy for such banter and he merely nodded, keeping silent until the routier reached the door. "Mercadier, wait." The other man turned, his hand on the latch. "When you hang the garrison, do not hang the crossbowman."

Morgan thought he'd rarely heard a command so chilling. Mercadier obviously felt so, too, for he smiled.

✸

THERE WAS DISAGREEMENT as to when a new year began. Some argued for Christmas, the Nativity of the Christ Child. William the Bastard, England's first Norman king, had chosen the Circumcision of Christ, January 1, the occasion of his own coronation. Others recognized Lady Day, March 25, as the date to start anew, while a minority insisted upon Easter. But for the small, select group aware of Richard's peril, they counted time from Friday, March 26, the night of his surgery, knowing that his fate would be determined in the days that followed.

On Sunday evening, Master Guyon was hovering outside the priest's house, scrutinizing the men passing by. Finally seeing the one he sought, he hastened over to intercept the king's cousin. "My lord, may I have a word with you?"

Morgan and Guy de Thouars paused to allow him to catch up with them. Morgan had last seen Richard just an hour ago, but he knew how rapidly a wound could fester, and he frowned, glancing around first to be sure no others were in hearing range. "What is it, Master Guyon? He has not taken a turn for the worse?"

"No . . . He seems to be feeling better, and that is the problem. I can give him herbal remedies mixed in wine. I can change his poultice and I can offer prayers for his recovery. But he must do his part, too. When I visited him earlier today, I found him propped up in bed, consulting with Geoffrey de la Celle, his seneschal for Gascony, ordering assaults upon the viscount's castles at Nontron and Montagut. He ignored my protests and would not let me examine his wound, telling me to come back once he was done speaking with his seneschal!"

He sounded so indignant that Morgan and Guy had to smile, for they were very familiar with Richard's bad behavior whenever he was injured or ill. "If it is any consolation, Master Guyon, there is nothing personal about his disdain. He has been the bane of physicians for as long as I've known him."

"So I've heard," the surgeon said tersely. "But if he does not remain abed, rest, and heed my advice, he is putting his life at even greater risk. I tried to make him see that, to no avail. I only made matters worse, for I angered him by telling him he must listen to me. He cursed me then, saying 'must' was not a word he recognized. He said that if it pleased him, he'd be taken out to the siege on a litter tomorrow, as he'd done at Acre, and he might even have Mercadier bring him a few whores to pass the time tonight!"

Guyon was not sure how much help he'd get from these men, but he'd not expected to be laughed at, and they both were grinning widely. "Do you not understand? If he were to take a woman into his bed, it could well-nigh kill him!"

The fear in his voice sobered their amusement. "We were laughing," Morgan explained, "because we know the king is not going to do anything so foolhardy. When he is angry, he often says things he does not mean, raving and ranting and uttering bloodcurdling threats that he never carries out. His lord father was the same."

Guy saw that the surgeon was not convinced and, because he sympathized with the man's plight, he offered an anecdote from his own past. "When I was about seventeen, I was wounded in a tournament, my leg gashed to the bone in the mêlée. I daresay you remember how it is for lads at that age; they fill their every waking hour with lustful daydreams about naked women. But until my leg healed, I could have been a monk, so circumspect were my thoughts. And the king's injury is far more serious than mine was. It is that painful shoulder he'll be heeding, not any stirrings of his cock."

"Nor will he demand to be carried out to watch the assault on the castle,"

Morgan reassured the surgeon. "He wants his injury kept secret, at least till he is on the mend. Once he regains some of his strength, he might insist upon that, but by then Mercadier will have taken the castle."

"Thank you, my lords, for easing my mind. The king . . . He is a challenging patient," Guyon said, which made them laugh outright, appreciating his fine flair for understatement. "I fear, though, that he is still wroth with me. I would be most grateful if you would accompany me to see him." And he felt a flutter of relief when they showed themselves willing to humor him.

Guyon was relieved, too, to find Richard was with the Abbot of Le Pin, his almoner and a trusted confidant, for he thought Abbot Milo would be an ally if need be. "My liege," he said, hoping his anxiety was not too obvious, for he knew Richard had no respect for men who were timorous, fainthearted. "How are you feeling?"

That question had earned him a scathing "Filled with bliss" earlier in the day. They were all taken aback now by the candor of Richard's response. "My shoulder seemed better this morning, but it has gotten worse in the last few hours. Master Guyon, I have a question to put to you. And do not lie to me. Do you expect me to regain the full use of my arm?"

"I . . . My liege, I would hope so. But it will take time and you will have to be patient, which does not come easily to you."

Richard studied the other man's face, deciding that he was telling the truth. Or was it that his need for hope was strong enough to drown out his doubts? "I never held patience to be a virtue," he conceded. "I suppose I shall have to change my thinking about that."

And grow angel wings whilst you're at it, Guyon thought skeptically, for he considered that equally as likely as the king's embrace of patience and forbearance. "I need to change your poultice, my liege," he ventured, not sure how far to trust Richard's current cooperation. "I am going to add honey to the mixture, for it has proved very effective in healing wounds."

"Do what you need to do." Richard's gaze shifted to the other men. "Whilst Master Guyon tends to my wound, I want you to tell me how the siege is going."

They were happy to do that and began to describe the ferocity of Mercadier's bombardment of the castle as Guyon carefully unwrapped the poultice. While there was more swelling than there'd been earlier, that was to be expected. But when he lifted the poultice to expose the wound, he sucked in his breath, for a red line now showed clearly on the king's skin, surrounding the affected area like a border of blood. A quick glance told him that Morgan, Guy, the abbot, and Arne did not understand the significance of what they were seeing. But Richard did, for he had tensed, one hand clenching into a fist.

"*Gangraena,*" he said softly.

The surgeon felt as if time had stopped. All he could think was that this Latin word was too dulcet a sound for such an ugly ailment. When his eyes met Richard's, he could not look away. By now the other men had realized something was very wrong, but neither Richard nor Guyon heard their agitated questions. They were aware only of that spreading red streak, as ominous as the Mark of Cain.

"It does not necessarily mean . . ." Guyon gave up the attempt, let his words die along with his hope.

"Tell me this." Richard struggled to a sitting position, ignoring the pain that effort cost him. "I know you've treated many men whose wounds festered. Did any of them survive?"

The surgeon had buried all but one of his patients who'd been stricken with *gangraena*. The sole survivor had lived because the infected arm had been amputated in time. He could not offer false hope, though. The king had told him not to lie.

Guyon's stricken silence gave Richard his answer, one that shook him to the core. He was quiet for a long time, but when he finally spoke, it was with a touch of his familiar bravado. "Well, I shall have to be the first, then."

❦

ARNE WAS JOLTED FROM sleep the following morning by a sound that chilled him to the bone, a loud groan from his king. He was on his feet at once, lunging toward the bed, a despairing prayer on his lips. *Merciful God, let it be a bad dream!* For only those harrowing memories of Ertpurch and Trifels had ever been able to wrest such a cry from Richard. But if it was not a dream?

Richard was trembling, his mouth contorted, his breath coming in ragged gulps. When Arne leaned over the bed, he clamped his hand upon the youth's arm, gasping, "Christ's blood, I never felt pain like this, never. . . ." And Arne began to weep.

❦

BY THE TIME Richard admitted his surgeon, he had regained his composure and his control, for he would never let the rest of the world see what he'd shown

Arne. Only Morgan, Mercadier, and Abbot Milo were permitted to enter with Master Guyon, and he could see on their faces the dread roused by his urgent summons.

"I awoke in great pain," he said, as matter-of-factly as if he were speaking of someone else's suffering. "I think what we feared has come to pass."

The surgeon approached the bed with a leaden step. No one spoke as he began to unwind the poultice. Even though he was expecting to see it, he still felt a sinking sensation at the sight of that swollen, discolored flesh. Once *gangraena* laid claim to a man's body, it moved with diabolic speed and Richard's skin was a deep, raw red. It would soon take on a dark bronze color, and then it would blacken as his body rotted away from the inside. Guyon had no words; he knew there were none. But he still heard himself stammering, "I . . . I am sorry, my lord. . . . So sorry . . ."

The abbot knelt and began to pray. Morgan sagged down onto a coffer. Arne was weeping again, silently this time. Mercadier's hand dropped to his sword hilt and Guyon froze. But then the routier whirled, picked up the chair, and smashed it into the wall, again and again, until it was reduced to kindling.

Richard paid none of them any heed. He'd known what the surgeon would find; nothing else could explain sudden pain of such intensity. But knowing it was not the same as seeing it, as looking into his open grave. He supposed he'd always known he would not make old bones. Scriptures spoke plainly enough on that. *For all they that take up the sword shall perish by the sword.* And he'd accepted it, for there were far worse ways to die. He'd just not expected it to happen here, in a siege of a Godforsaken rebel castle so far from the sacred battlefields of the Holy Land.

There was much in his life that he'd taken pride in, exploits of daring, some of them quite mad, but gloriously so, feats that had dazzled his friends and infuriated his enemies. Yet he took as much pride in what he was able to do now, keeping his voice so dispassionate as he said, "No one can know that I am dying. My brother is in Brittany. If the Bretons hear of my mortal wound ere he does, my mother will lose two sons."

He paused, then, for the dragon was stirring again. He closed his eyes until the assault eased—all he could do. A pity that crossbowman's aim had not been better. "How much time do I have?" He was not surprised when Master Guyon could not answer that. Will Marshal would have to be warned. Hubert Walter. His seneschals of Anjou, Poitou, Normandy; his castellans at Chinon and Gaillard.

"Send for my mother." She was at Fontevrault, though. Would she get here in time? "Send word to my cousin, too. And I'll need a scribe, one I can trust."

Abbot Milo had always been able to offer aid both spiritual and secular, a pragmatic, capable churchman like Hubert Walter and Master Fulk, the sort of cleric who found greatest favor with Richard. He did not disappoint now, adjusting to this grim new reality faster than Morgan or even Mercadier. "I will pen your letters myself, my liege. And couriers will go out within the hour to your lady mother, to the Count of Mortain, and to your cousin; I assume Lord André is at Châteauroux?" He sounded admirably calm, but he kept his gaze averted from the bed. "Is it your wish that we summon your queen, too?"

"No . . . We can arouse no suspicions until my brother is safely away from the Breton court. Word is bound to get out that I've not been seen in days and half the countryside is spying for the viscount or the French. My queen's sudden arrival would attract too much attention, too much conjecture, for she's never visited me at a siege camp." There was truth in that and he hoped it would give Berenguela a measure of comfort. He'd not been much of a husband to her. But it was too late to make amends. He'd need all of his waning strength to keep Death at bay long enough to see Johnny recognized as his heir. A wronged wife could not compete with a kingdom at risk. Nor did he want to deal with her tears. Surely dying was penance enough for past marital sins.

So was pain. By the time he drew his last breath, he'd likely have atoned for all of his own sins and those of his father, too, mayhap even Hal and Geoffrey's as well. Knowing he'd need to fight the dragon alone, he said, "Leave me now. All but Arne."

They obeyed, moving like men in a daze. He'd let Master Guyon come back later. They were a fine pair, he and Mercadier's surgeon, between them making sure that March 26 would be the luckiest day of Johnny's life. Was it too much to hope that the man might know of herbs that would dull some of the pain, but not his wits? He already knew the answer to that. If wishes were horses, beggars would ride.

❦

THE SKY WAS THE COLOR of sapphire, Eleanor's favorite gemstone, and the few wisps of cloud seemed as delicate as handmade lace. Sitting in the window-seat, she savored the warmth of the April sunlight; she felt the cold more keenly now, and she was giving serious consideration to accepting Joanna's invitation to spend next winter in Toulouse.

When she said as much to her companion, the prioress flashed an impish smile. "Can you smuggle me into your horse litter, Madame? I'd dearly love to see Toulouse."

Eleanor returned the smile, for she'd become quite fond of Aliza since taking up residence at Fontevrault Abbey. "There is something I would discuss with you. One of my granddaughters is coming to Fontevrault as a novice."

The prioress already knew that; nunneries prided themselves upon attracting highborn young women, and Alix of Blois was a great catch. "I will be happy to keep an eye on her, Madame," she promised, "and we will bend the rules a bit so that she can visit with you from time to time."

Before Eleanor could respond, Dame Amaria appeared in the doorway. "A messenger has just ridden in from the king, Madame. He says he must speak with you straightaway."

"Send him in, then," Eleanor directed. The man ushered into the chamber soon afterward was one she knew and liked—one of Richard's household knights—but her smile splintered at her first glimpse of his stricken face.

"Madame, your son . . ." He sank to one knee before her, holding out the letter with a hand that shook. "He has been grievously wounded, and he . . . he bids you come to him at Châlus."

There were horrified gasps from the other women, but for Eleanor, there was no surprise, only an eerie sense of familiarity about this moment. It was as if she'd always known she would one day be standing here like this, listening to someone tell her that her son was dying. She swayed slightly and the prioress and Amaria moved quickly to offer support, but she shook their hands off. "Is there . . ." She swallowed convulsively. "Is there no hope?"

He did not know which was cruelest—to offer false hope or to strip away every last shred of hope. "He . . . he is in a bad way, my lady."

Eleanor closed her eyes for a moment and then she raised her head, straightening the shoulders that felt too frail to bear this latest burden. "I will be ready to ride within the hour."

❦

ANDRÉ DID NOT BELIEVE Richard was dying. Despite the gravity of the message, he refused to accept it. On the hundred-mile ride between Châteauroux and Châlus, he thought of little else, convincing himself that his cousin would recover, as he always had in the past. But his faith in Richard's powers of recuperation did not keep him from setting as fast a pace as possible. By changing horses, he managed to cover the distance in just two and a half days, a speed that royal couriers might well have envied, reaching Châlus before sunset on the first Friday in April.

Upon his arrival at the siege camp, he took heart from the air of calm; surely there would be panic and confusion if the king were really dying. But soldiers were going about their tasks as if nothing were amiss. The trebuchets were pounding away at the castle walls, sending up swirling dust and rubble with each strike, and some of Mercadier's men were erecting a gallows. When André asked for Richard, he was told that the king had set up quarters in the village and he was soon following a sergeant through the gathering dusk. Richard had always been careless of protocol, priding himself in being accessible to any soldiers who needed to speak with him. Now men-at-arms were stationed at the door of a small stone house and André was told that he must be given permission to enter.

Waiting as one of the guards disappeared inside, André felt sweat begin to trickle down his spine, cold and clammy. When the door opened again, he found himself facing Richard's cousin, and Morgan looked so heartsick that there was no need for words. Grasping André's arm, he pulled the other man inside and, as their eyes met, he slowly shook his head.

Standing before the bedchamber, André was suddenly afraid to go any farther, dreading what he now knew he'd find behind that door. What struck him first was the stench, one he was all too familiar with: the battlefield stink of rotting flesh, putrid wounds, and approaching death. The chamber was dimly lit by oil lamps. Arne was slumped in a corner and gazed up at André, a man he knew well, without a hint of recognition. Guillain de l'Etang rose as André entered. So did the Abbot of Le Pin.

"He's been sleeping, God be praised," he said in a low voice. "That is the only respite he gets from the pain. . . ."

André took the abbot's seat beside the bed. Richard seemed to have aged ten years in the weeks since they'd last met. Pain had etched deep grooves around his mouth and his hollowed cheekbones showed he'd lost an alarming amount of weight in the week since he'd been wounded. His face was so bloodless that André thought it was like gazing down at a carven marble effigy, drained of all life and color. But his body offered tragic testimony to the mortality of men: the skin on his chest was swollen, blistered, and turning black; his shoulder poultice oozing a foul-smelling pus. André was never to know how long he sat there, watching the rapid rise and fall of that rib cage, almost as if he were willing every breath into the other man's lungs. But then Richard's lashes flickered.

"André . . ." His voice was a husky whisper, this man who'd been able to shout down the wind, and André had to lean closer to catch his words. "A favor . . ."

"Anything . . ." André's own words came out as a croak and he had to repeat himself. "Anything . . ."

"No saying 'I told you so,' Cousin. . . ."

André could not speak, his throat having closed off, and he could only nod.

"I sent for my mother, hope she's hurrying. . . ." Richard glanced toward a wine flagon by the bed and André poured with a shaking hand, tilting the cup to Richard's lips. "We've tried to keep it quiet . . . giving Johnny time to get away. . . ." His eyes looked badly bruised and had a glazed, feverish sheen, but he seemed quite lucid to André. His words were halting, though, with long pauses as he fought for breath. "You know where . . . where that damned fool is? Brittany . . ."

"That damned fool," André echoed, not even knowing what he said.

"If the Bretons hear first, Johnny'll have . . . have shortest reign in history. . . ."

"My liege?" The abbot had come to stand beside André. "I am confident your lady mother will soon be here. Are you sure you do not want us to send for your queen?"

"Too late. . . ."

The abbot apparently knew that was true, for he did not argue. "Is there a message you'd have me deliver to her, sire?"

Richard's lashes swept down, veiling his eyes. "That I am . . . sorry . . ." When he asked for wine again, André hastily obliged. The abbot had stepped away from the bed and his next words were pitched just for André's ear. "Women . . . always think men owe them apologies for something. . . ."

André nodded again, and somehow managed to keep his voice steady as he said, "True enough. Apologies, like charity, cover a multitude of sins."

After that, they were silent for a time. André could tell whenever the pain got worse; Richard would shut his eyes, shudder, and bite down on his lower lip until it bled, so determined was he to stifle any groans or cries. Watching his suffering was as difficult as anything André had ever done, but he meant to keep vigil as long as Richard could get air into his laboring lungs.

"Fauvel . . . He's yours, Cousin. Do not . . . not let Johnny steal him. . . ."

"No . . ." André knew by now what was expected of him, what Richard wanted as his life ebbed away, one waning heartbeat at a time. "So you entrust your kingdom to John, but not your horse?"

A ghost of a smile found the corner of Richard's mouth. "Kingdoms come and go. . . . A stallion like Fauvel is special. . . ." He winced then, turning his head aside as if seeking the shadows that held sway beyond the smoldering lamplight. "André . . . give Argento and my sword. . . ."

"Your son?"

"Yes . . . for Philip . . ." It was little enough to leave the lad. Had he only been born in wedlock . . . Richard had never experienced the sort of severe pain he'd endured since the *gangraena* had struck, but there was an odd sort of mercy to it, for it kept him from dwelling upon what lay ahead for his Angevin empire. With Johnny at the helm, how long ere he ran the ship up onto the rocks? Yet Arthur would have turned the tiller over to Philippe straightaway. At least Johnny would not be the French king's puppet. . . . At least he'd not be that.

❦

THE MAN SHOVED ROUGHLY over the threshold was frightened, but defiant, his the courage of utter despair. There was so much hatred in the chamber that he could barely breathe; the very air seemed seared with its heat. Mercadier's men thrust him forward, one of them seizing the chance to kick him in the ribs as they forced him to his knees. He darted a quick glance over his shoulder, saw nothing but hostile faces; even a man clad in the bleached robes of the White Monks was regarding him with accusing eyes. Raising his head, then, he stared challengingly at the man in the bed. It was no small feat to slay a king, especially this one. Did it count for less that he'd not known he was aiming at the Lionheart?

Richard turned to another man standing close by, saying something too low to be heard, then waited as pillows were propped behind him so that he could look upon the prisoner. Death was not only in the chamber with them, it was perched on the edge of the bed. But when he spoke, his fading whisper was belied by the intensity of his gaze. "Your name?"

"Sir Peire Basile of Pouyades."

"A knight?"

"I am," he said proudly, but no more than that, for he'd vowed he'd not beg for his life. That would serve for naught, only bring shame to his name, his family.

Richard regarded him for what felt like several centuries. "Your life is . . . forfeit, you think. . . . You're wrong. . . . I bear . . . bear no grudge. You . . . are free to go, Peire Basile. . . ."

The other men were no less stunned than the crossbowman and there was an immediate outcry. Only André was not shocked by Richard's astonishing act of clemency. The audience for this last act of his cousin's play was reacting as he would have expected them to do. He found approval on the faces of Morgan, Guy, and the abbot, for the former worshipped at the Church of the Chivalric Faith and the churchman had often preached the divine virtues of forgiveness. But William de Braose, Guillain, and Richard's seneschal were not at all happy with this reprieve, and Mercadier looked utterly outraged.

Peire Basile would later wish he'd said something, anything. But shock and disbelief had stolen his powers of speech, and before he could recover, his guards had dragged him to his feet and pushed him toward the door. André quickly gestured for the others to follow, for he knew Richard had no interest in hearing them debate his decision. *Yet one more mystery for the ages,* he thought, gazing down at the dying man. Men would long wonder what he'd have done had he survived this wound. Would Peire Basile have lived or died then? André honestly did not know, for Richard was capable both of great magnanimity and the utmost ruthlessness.

Arne had gone over to close the door after the last of the men departed. André was amused, yet touched, too, by the conflicted expression on the squire's face—pride that his king had spared his slayer's life like one of the knights in a troubadour's tale, but disappointment that the man would also be spared earthly punishment for a crime so great.

Leaning over the bed then, André murmured, "Well done, Cousin. You burnished the Lionheart's legend whilst earning yourself some much-needed credit with the Almighty."

Richard did not seem to have heard, for he did not open his eyes, nor did he speak. But André thought he caught the hint of a smile.

ELEANOR WAS TERRIFIED that she would not arrive in time. A horse litter was too slow, so despite her age, she rode a fast mare. But although she pushed her body to the utmost and beyond, managing as much as twenty-five miles from dawn till dusk, it still took over five and a half days to cover the one hundred forty miles of eternity stretching between Fontevrault Abbey and Châ-lus. The nights were the worst, for she slept only in snatches, and when she did dream, her son was in great danger—sometimes in a German dungeon, some-times at the Châlus siege camp—and she could not help him.

They reached Châlus at midmorning on April 6. As soon as she was assisted from her saddle, the Abbot of Le Pin and her son's Welsh cousin came hurrying toward her. They greeted her warmly, saying the king would be so pleased to see her. Understanding that they were playing to an audience—the soldiers who did not know how seriously Richard had been wounded, even French spies—she smiled, saying she was on her way south to visit her daughter in Toulouse. Only when she was sure none were within earshot did she dare to ask softly, "Does he still live?" And when they nodded but said nothing, she knew it would not be for long.

She was not surprised to find André there; he was the brother Richard ought to have had. It was Mercadier who shocked her, for as he bent over her hand, she thought she saw tears in the routier's icy eyes. As Morgan reached for the door latch, she realized how much she feared crossing that threshold.

The chamber was stifling and shadowed, for it had to be shuttered against prying eyes. André moved a chair to the bed for her and she lowered herself onto it, wondering if she'd ever be able to rise again.

Richard's eyes opened when she took his hand in hers. He'd been sure she'd get there in time, for she had never let him down, never. "So sorry, Maman. . . ." So many regrets. That he'd not made peace with his father. That he'd not been able to free the Holy City from the Saracens. That Philip could not have been Berenguela's. That the French king had not drowned in the Epte. That he'd not taken the time to put on his hauberk. That his mother must now watch him die.

She held his hand against her cheek. "You've been shriven, Richard?"

"Yes . . . So many sins . . . Took half a day . . ."

He was dying as he'd lived, and that made it so much harder for those who loved him. But then she remembered what she'd been told about his father's wretched last hours. After learning that John had betrayed him, he'd turned his face to the wall and had not spoken again. Only as his fever burned higher had he cried out, "Shame upon a conquered king." An anguished epitaph for a life that had once held such bright promise. No, better that Richard laugh at Death than die as Harry had. His body was wracked with pain, but at least he was not suffering Harry's agony of spirit. She could not have borne that.

Richard's breathing was so rapid that his chest was heaving. Talking was not easy, but there were things he must say. "I've made my will.... Three-quarters of my treasury to Johnny. The remainder ... to feed the poor.... I want ... want crown jewels to go to Otto...."

She nodded her head, squeezing his hand to let him know she understood.

"Maman ... I ..." Richard made a great effort to say clearly and distinctly, "I want to be buried at Fontevrault, at my father's feet...."

"I am sure he has forgiven you, Richard."

He did not think his father forgave as easily as that. "My Normans ... always faithful ... Bury my heart with them, at Rouen.... To the disloyal, treacherous curs of Poitou ... I leave my entrails, all they deserve...."

"It will be done, all as you wish—" Her voice broke, for there had been a change in his breathing, a gurgling sound often called the death rattle.

"Do ... what you can for Johnny, Maman...."

She nodded again. Not trusting her voice, she reached out and gently stroked his hair. The odor from his wound was sickening. She did not care. She did not think she could endure this, counting each rasping breath, listening as his heart beat more and more slowly and then stopped. But she would. She would not leave his side. She would be with him until his last moment, and then she would grieve for him until the hour of her own death. This was a wound that would never heal.

Time had no meaning any longer. She assumed hours were passing, but she refused all offers of food or drink. How long would God torment him like this? Leaning over, she kissed his forehead. "You can stop fighting now, my dearest. Your race is done."

He'd not spoken for some time and she was not sure he could hear her, but then he said, "Did ... I ... win?"

"Yes, Richard, you did. You kept the faith." She did not remember the rest of the scriptural verse. She would later wonder how she could have sounded so calm, so composed. But it was the last gift she could give him. "Go to God, my beloved son."

After that, he was still. They could hear church bells chiming in the distance. Somewhere Vespers was being rung, people were at Mass, life was going on. André had not thought there was a need for words of farewell, not between them. But now he found himself approaching the bed, suddenly afraid that he'd waited too long. "Richard." He held his breath then, until the other man opened his eyes. "Listen to me," he said hoarsely. "You will not be forgotten. A hundred years from now, men will be sitting around campfires and telling the legends of the Lionheart."

The corner of Richard's mouth twitched. "Only . . . a hundred years?" he whispered, and André and Eleanor saw his last smile through a haze of hot tears.

❧

RICHARD DIED AT SEVEN O'CLOCK on Tuesday, April 6, in Holy Week, with his mother at his side. He was forty-one and had reigned less than ten years. He was buried at Fontevrault Abbey at his father's feet, as he'd requested.

❧

RICHARD'S PARDON of the crossbowman was not honored. Once he was dead, Mercadier ordered Peire Basile to be flayed alive.

CHAPTER THIRTY-SIX

❖

Bishop Hugh of Lincoln was one of the few who'd known that Richard had been seriously wounded at the siege of Châlus, for he'd had a chance encounter with the abbess of Fontevrault Abbey, and she'd told him that the king was not expected to survive. He was at Angers when he got the grim news of Richard's death and he set out at once for Fontevrault Abbey, where Richard was to be buried. But he took a detour off the high road to ride to the castle of Beaufort-en-Vallée, for he had not forgotten Richard's widow.

✦

BERENGARIA CAME HURRYING OUT into the castle bailey to greet him. "My lord bishop, what a pleasure to see you!" Her smile was radiant and he felt a pang, knowing that he was about to unleash a storm that would render her world unrecognizable. But there was no point in delaying it, and he suggested that they go to the chapel straightaway. That aroused no suspicions in Berengaria, who thought it perfectly natural that he'd give priority to prayer. He sent his clerk and servant on into the hall, and followed Richard's queen toward the chapel, accompanied by one of her women and her chaplain, for even with a godly man like Bishop Hugh, she paid heed to propriety.

✦

"My lady . . . You must be strong, for I bring you grievous news."

She stared at him, eyes widening. "Richard . . . ?"

He nodded somberly. "He was wounded at the siege of Châlus. The wound festered and there was nothing the doctors could do."

She took a backward step and then spun away from them, leaning against the altar as if she did not have the strength to stand alone. Yet when the chaplain and her lady hastened toward her, she flung up her hand, holding them off. Bishop Hugh silently signaled to them, shaking his head. He could see the tremors that shook her slender body. He waited, though, until she turned to face them. Her face was wet, but she'd gotten her voice under control. "Was . . . was there time for him to be shriven?"

"Ah yes, my lady. You need have no fears about that. He made confession to the Abbot of Le Pin, was absolved of his sins, and died in God's grace. He even forgave the crossbowman who shot him."

She closed her eyes for a moment, tears continuing to seep through her lashes. "Does the queen know?"

He thought it sad that even Berengaria spoke of "the queen" as if there were only one. Knowing he was about to inflict yet more pain, he said, "She knows. She was with him when he died."

"I see," she said softly. "So he sent for her."

But not me. Although she did not say it, the words seemed to echo in the air between them. Taking her arm, he drew her gently toward a cushioned bench along the wall, gesturing to keep the others from following. "I know why he did not send for you, my lady. They were trying to keep it quiet for as long as they could. His brother was in Brittany, and they wanted to get word to him ere the Bretons found out that the king was dying."

She stared down at her clasped hands, at the dulled glimmer of her wedding ring. "And it would have attracted attention had I suddenly joined him at the siege." Again leaving the rest unspoken—*Because Richard and I spent so little time together. Whilst a visit from his mother would have seemed quite natural.*

"Yes, my lady, it would," he said, for he believed the truth was always kinder than a lie. Better that she be shamed to realize her marital woes were known to half of Christendom than to believe that her dying husband had nary a thought for her. He hesitated, but remembering that she would have seen men die of such wounds during the siege of Acre, he said, "Then, too, he would not have wanted you to see him in such pain, Madame."

Her mouth trembled and he reached out, took her hand between his as he spoke of the healing power of God's mercy, assuring her that she and Richard would be together again, and reminding her of the solace of prayer. She raised her head at that. "Will my husband have to endure much time in Purgatory, my lord bishop?"

"I cannot answer that, my lady."

"But our earthly prayers can reduce a man's stay in Purgatory?" And when he nodded, she expelled a ragged breath, closing her eyes again. She found a smile for him, though, when he offered to say Mass for her household. "Thank you, my lord bishop. I would like that very much." Remembering her duties to a guest then, she offered him the hospitality of Beaufort.

"I will gladly accept a meal, my lady, but I cannot stay the night. After the Mass, I must be on my way. I am going to Fontevrault to preside over the king's funeral on Sunday. It would be my honor to escort you."

She was quiet for a time, and then she slowly shook her head. "No, my lord bishop. I will do my grieving here. The funeral is for the queen's son, not my husband."

He did not chide her for her bitterness as many priests would have done, and she had the comforting sense that he understood, that he always understood. He left a few hours later, and with his departure, she felt as if she'd lost her only friend. She stood in the bailey, watching as he rode through the gateway and out of sight. Only then did she return to the chapel, rebuffing her chaplain when he would have accompanied her. Tears had begun to flow again, but she let them fall. The small church was filling with shadows as the day's light waned, the air faintly scented with burning candles and incense. Moving down the nave, she knelt by the altar and began to pray for her husband's soul.

WILL MARSHAL AND HUBERT WALTER were at Vaudreuil Castle, arbitrating a dispute between two Norman barons, when an urgent message arrived from Châlus. Will was stunned by Richard's letter, for he made it clear that his chances of recovery were not good. He instructed Will to go to Rouen and take control of the castle, warning him to keep the news of his injury secret. Will confided only in the archbishop, who was just as shaken, and they set out at once for Rouen.

The following three days were difficult ones. The death of a king was always a troubling time, especially if the succession was not settled. But Richard was also a man they both knew well, a man they greatly respected, and their grieving was personal as well as political. Will had not given up all hope, though, for Richard had so often defied the odds that it was easy to believe he could do so again. Will clung to that hope until Palm Sunday Eve when another messenger rode in from the south as he was preparing for bed. Slumping onto the closest coffer, he stared down at the letter as if he expected those bleak, brutal words to change, as if the world as they knew it had not become an unfamiliar, frightening place. It took a while before he could bring himself to order his horse saddled, to tell his startled squire that, despite the late hour, he would be calling upon the Archbishop of Canterbury at the priory of Notre-Dame du Pré.

THEY SAT IN SILENCE, watching the dying embers in the hearth flicker and fade away. Hubert Walter had sent for wine, but they had yet to touch it. Hubert had always prided himself upon his pragmatism. He was finding it impossible to put his emotions aside, though, to respond to this crisis as a prince of the Church rather than a friend of the man who'd died on Tuesday eve.

"This may sound foolish," he said, "but after watching Richard dice with Death more times than I could count, I came to believe that it was a game he could not lose."

Will blinked rapidly, for his eyes were stinging. "I think we all did. . . ."

"And what solace is there for us now? I greatly fear that the Angevin empire will not long survive him."

Will thought it would be all too easy to give in to despair. However, that was a luxury he could not afford, not with a wife and six children and the vast de Clare estates to protect. "We must act quickly, my lord archbishop. Once the French learn of our king's death, they will swoop down upon us like a hawk upon a crippled heron."

Hubert's mouth thinned as he thought of the joy that the news from Châlus would give Philippe Capet. "It would have been easier if Arthur were better known to us, if his mother had only allowed him to be raised at Richard's court. But that is spilt milk. He is said to be a clever lad, and a spirited one, for all his youth. If men rally to him—"

"I think that would be a bad course to take," Will cut in, for there was too much at stake not to speak bluntly. "Arthur has treacherous advisers around him, and he is already said to be prideful and stubborn. If we crown him, who will truly be ruling in his stead? The King of France, I fear."

"And would you rather it be John? We do not know the manner of man Arthur may become, but we know all too well the man that John is."

"I know," Will conceded. "But a brother is closer in blood than a nephew. Moreover, at least John is a man grown. And our king named him as his heir."

"What choice had he? Lacking a son of his own . . ." Hubert let the words trail off, for as deeply as he mourned Richard, he was angry, too, that he had been so irresponsible, that he had not taken greater care to ensure the succession. He ought to have put his queen aside once it became obvious she was barren or have come to terms with the Bretons. "I do not want to see John as king."

"Few do. But John is all we have."

The archbishop started to speak, stopped himself. He knew most men were likely to agree with the Marshal that John was the lesser of evils, and a civil war would be an even worse calamity than choosing John over Arthur. But he remained convinced that this was a great mistake. "So be it," he said grimly. "But this much I can tell you, that you will never come to regret anything you've done as much as you will regret this."

✿

MARIAM DID NOT APPROVE of Joanna's decision to seek Richard out. It was easy enough to understand. Who better to ask for military aid than the Lionheart, after all? So Joanna's logic could not be faulted. But Raimond had not wanted her to do it, and Mariam thought she ought to have deferred to him on this. Whilst Raimond seemed more good-natured than many husbands, she was sure he still had his share of male pride, and male pride was so fragile it could be bruised if breathed upon—or at least it seemed that way to Mariam.

Glancing over at Joanna, she sighed. It would have been better to coax Raimond's consent. Joanna would have been able to win him over had she only been patient. Joanna's patience could not have filled a thimble, though. For certes, she'd proved it by insisting upon leading that attack upon the rebel stronghold at Les Casses instead of waiting for Raimond to return home. He'd been furious when he'd found out, and Mariam could not blame him. They'd made their peace, of course, most likely in bed. But did Joanna realize how lucky she was to be wed to a man who was also her lover? Mariam sighed again, knowing that would have been true, too, for her and Morgan had fate been kinder.

"My lady?" Sir Roger de Laurac, the captain of Joanna's household knights, reined in beside the two women. "There is a stream up ahead. I would suggest we stop to water the horses if that meets with your approval."

"Of course, Sir Roger," Joanna murmured, smiling. Roger was new to her service, selected by Raimond, and she had to admit her husband had chosen well. She was confident Roger would have offered up his life to protect her, but he was also unusually discerning. He'd clearly noticed how easily she was tiring these days and he'd begun to find excuses to halt so she might rest, while taking care to spare her pride. It was frustrating enough that her energy seemed at such a low ebb in the past fortnight, and she was grateful for his tact, not normally a knightly virtue.

After Roger assisted the women from their mounts, Joanna followed him toward a grove of trees off to the side of the road, and once a blanket was spread upon the grass, she seated herself in the shade of an ancient oak, bracing her aching back against the tree's vast trunk. Mariam joined her, offering to unpack a basket of food. Joanna's stomach was roiling as if she'd been at sea instead of perched in the sidesaddle of her favorite mare, and she hastily shook her head. She was very thankful that they were only five miles from Poitiers. Roger had already dispatched one of her knights to alert the palace of her arrival, and she hoped there would not be a lengthy welcome, for she wanted only to go to bed.

"Joanna . . ." Mariam hesitated, for Joanna had rebuffed all of her earlier attempts to discuss this mission to find Richard. But she was tired of being kept in the dark. "After Poitiers, where next?"

"To Fontevrault Abbey, of course. If anyone knows where Richard is off shedding blood, it is likely to be my mother."

Mariam thought she detected the faintest glimmer of a smile and that encouraged her to persevere. "You and Raimond . . . You did not part in anger?"

"No . . . We were not happy with each other, but no longer quarreling. He finally agreed that I could seek help from Richard, saying it was marginally preferable to my leading another expedition against his rebel lords."

This time there was no mistaking her smile, and Mariam was emboldened to say firmly, "You are very fortunate that he has a sense of humor."

"I know," Joanna admitted. A pity her dignity did not allow her to lie down on the blanket and nap, for her eyelids felt as heavy as stones. After a while, she said drowsily, "I cannot blame Raimond. He always warned me he was a lover, not a fighter."

Mariam sat up, staring at her in dismay. "You mean like . . . William?"

Joanna's eyes snapped open. "Good God, no!"

They had never discussed it—that fatal flaw in the man who'd been a good brother to Mariam, a fond husband to Joanna. It was too dangerous, for Joanna had realized that if she'd ever given voice to her qualms, she'd be releasing a demon to prey upon the peace of her marriage. William had pursued a very aggressive foreign policy, dispatching military forces to Egypt, North Africa, Greece, and Spain, yet he'd never taken a personal role in any of those campaigns. Theirs was a world in which a king was expected to lead his army into battle, but William had sent men out to die in his name whilst he'd remained safe and comfortable in his Palermo palaces. Joanna had not loved William; love was not expected in royal unions, however. She'd known, though, that she'd have been miserable with a man she could not respect, and so she'd kept that particular door securely shut and bolted.

Mariam was thankful to hear Joanna's assurances that she did not equate Raimond's lack of martial fervor with William's cowardice. Even now that was too painful a topic to explore in the light of day and she said only, "I am so glad you see that."

"Of course I do, Mariam. Raimond may not be the soldier that Richard is— how many men are? But he leads his men into battle, risking his life with theirs. No, the problem is that Raimond always sees war as the last resort, even when that is not so."

Joanna's backache was getting worse, and she shifted her position before continuing. "I've been giving it some thought, Mariam, and I've realized that Richard and Raimond have more in common than I'd first thought. They both share the same vice, if it can be called that: an overabundance of confidence. They differ only in their choice of weapons. Richard is convinced that he is invincible with a sword in his hand. And Raimond is just as sure that he can talk anyone around to his point of view if he has the chance to do so."

"I had not thought of it that way. I think you might well be right."

"I know I am. I'd be the last woman in Christendom to dismiss the potent power of Raimond's charm. But charm does not work well with princes of the Church or disgruntled, disloyal vassals, and I've been unable to make Raimond see that. In truth, he shares another trait with Richard that I wish he did not. Neither one has any interest in bearbaiting, but they both enjoy baiting their enemies. Raimond jokes that I see it as my wifely duty to keep him off the road to Hell, and he is not far wrong about that. Our lives would be so much more peaceful if only I could get him to understand that churchmen ought not to be publicly mocked, even when they deserve it, and not all rebels are worthy of his mercy."

"Is this why you are so set upon seeing Richard?"

Joanna nodded. "I am hoping that he'll heed Richard as he's not heeded me. It is easy enough for him to dismiss my opinions about rebellions. But if Richard tells him that a ruler needs to be feared as well as respected, he might well listen. I do not expect him to adorn the roads of Toulouse with the rotting heads of treacherous lords and outlaws. He just needs to understand that there are times when forbearance only encourages further defiance."

Mariam was relieved to know that Joanna's mission had her husband's grudging consent. But now that they were finally able to speak freely again, she meant to take advantage of the opportunity. "When we get to Poitiers, Joanna, I think we ought to summon a physician. It is obvious to me that you are ailing."

"I am not ill, Mariam." Joanna paused before saying reluctantly, "I am with child."

Mariam stared at her. "Why did you not tell me?"

"Even Raimond does not know yet. I was not sure myself when we left Toulouse. I'd missed my March flux, but one miss does not mean all that much. But I ought to have had my April flux a fortnight ago and it did not come. I've also begun to feel queasy in the past few days. It may be why I am so tired, too. I never felt so bone-weary with the other pregnancies, though."

Mariam knew she had an expressive face and she could only hope that her misgivings did not show too nakedly. She sensed that Joanna had some ambivalence, too. Not too many women would have welcomed three pregnancies in three years. She did not doubt that this was why Joanna was so exhausted; her body had not had time to recover. Well, now that she knew, she meant to make this pregnancy as easy for Joanna as she could, whether Joanna liked being fussed over or not. "I think that when we get to Poitiers, we ought to take one of the palace horse litters. That is bound to be more comfortable for you than riding Ginger." She was pleased when Joanna did not protest, but surprised, too, which confirmed her suspicions that Joanna was not feeling well at all.

While Roger had allowed his knights to dismount and stretch and go into the bushes to relieve themselves if needed, he'd kept several on watch, and one of them now yelled, "Riders coming!" The warning stirred up a flurry of activity, for the roads were not always safe, not even for those as well armed as Joanna's escort. She let Mariam assist her to her feet, sorry their respite had been so brief. By now the men had relaxed, for the lead rider was one of their own, Sir Alain de Muret, the knight Roger had sent on ahead to Poitiers.

Joanna soon recognized the man riding at Alain's side. "That is Maurice de Blaron," she told Mariam. "As Bishop of Nantes, he accompanied Constance when she came to meet Richard at Caen a few years ago. I'd heard that he'd been elected recently as Bishop of Poitiers, but I did not expect him to ride out like this to bid me welcome." Turning so Mariam could brush off her skirts, she smiled over her shoulder. "I must remember to tell Raimond that not all churchmen are hostile to the Count of Toulouse."

Mariam smiled, too, touched by Joanna's pride in her husband. She was rarely so naïve, for surely the bishop was honoring the Lionheart's sister, not Raimond's wife. Joining Joanna beside Roger, they watched as the riders approached. Joanna's smile soon vanished, for the bishop and his entourage were as somber as men leading a funeral cortege and Alain slumped in his saddle as if he bore the weight of the world upon his shoulders.

Joanna took an instinctive backward step as she realized she was watching a wave of sorrow sweeping toward her, one that would engulf her world. She knew, of course, what grief they were bringing her. Her mother was in her seventy-fifth year. Rarely a day passed that Joanna did not thank the Almighty for letting her mother live to such an impressive age, but she never forgot that Eleanor's remaining time on God's Earth was borrowed and payment would eventually come due. Because she'd so often dwelt upon this inevitable loss, she'd believed that she would find that loss easier to accept when it came. She now knew that she was wrong.

"My mother . . ." Discovering that the words were impossible to say, she let them hang in the air, like distant echoes of thunder. Alain had already dismounted. He knelt before her, and she saw tear tracks streaking through the dust of the road on his upturned face. He said nothing, though, and it was left to the bishop to break her heart.

He was not a young man and had been afflicted with the joint evil, so he needed help in dismounting. "My lady countess, there is no easy way to deliver such news as this. It is the king. He is dead."

There were outcries behind her, but Joanna never heard them. "No," she said. "That cannot be."

"I am sorry, my lady. The ways of the Almighty are not always easy to understand. But with God's grace, even the greatest losses can be endured. It will be my privilege to pray with you and my honor to say a Requiem Mass for the king on the morrow. If you open your heart to God's healing, He will not deny you His mercy."

Joanna was not listening. "No. Not Richard. I do not believe you." She would have continued to deny it, this monstrous lie. But something strange was happening. The ground was shifting under her feet and the horizon had begun to tilt, as if the world were suddenly out of focus. Mariam and Roger got to her before she fell, but by then she was already spiraling down into darkness.

❧

THE ABBESS MATHILDE PAUSED in the doorway of Eleanor's bedchamber, not wanting to disturb the woman in the bed. "How does she?" she asked softly as Mariam hastily rose to bid her welcome.

"She is sleeping now."

"I was told she fainted in the church?"

Mariam nodded, thinking it a miracle that Joanna had not collapsed sooner. She'd agreed to stay just one night at Poitiers before riding on to Fontevrault, only to be told that her mother had departed the abbey not long after Richard's Palm Sunday funeral. Joanna had insisted upon going at once into the church then, where she'd knelt for hours in the nun's choir, praying for her brother until her body could endure no more. Now she slept but she did not seem to be finding any peace in her dreams, for she whimpered from time to time, turning her head from side to side as if seeking escape from a reality too painful to be borne.

The abbess soon departed, saying she'd be back later. The Prioress Aliza was the next visitor, pulling up a chair and joining Mariam's bedside vigil. "She does not look well," she murmured. "Shall we send for a doctor?"

Mariam hesitated before shaking her head. "I think she just needs to sleep."

They'd been keeping their voices low, but Joanna's lashes had begun to flutter. Her eyes were swollen to slits and filled with such anguish that Mariam's own eyes blurred with tears.

The prioress reached over and took Joanna's hand in her own. "I can tell you what has been happening if you wish. Once he was safely away from Brittany, Count John's first action was to ride to Chinon and take control of the royal treasury. The young Breton duke and his mother chose to head for Angers, where he was warmly welcomed and, on Easter, proclaimed as Count of Anjou.

Count John then had a very narrow escape, for he was almost captured at Le Mans. But the citizens had been so unfriendly that he'd departed at dawn, just hours before the Bretons arrived to occupy the city, where they were joined by the French king. By then, Count John was racing for Rouen, with the intention to be invested as Duke of Normandy ere he sails for England. I've been told that Normandy and England are likely to back his claim whilst Anjou, Maine, and Touraine favor Arthur—"

"What of my mother?" Joanna interrupted, for she was not yet ready to contemplate a world without Richard; as raw as her grieving was, she was not sure she'd ever be ready.

Aliza's eyes brightened. "She has been magnificent, my lady. She and Mercadier led an armed force into Anjou and ravaged the countryside around Angers to punish the townspeople for their treachery and to warn others that there is a high price to be paid for disloyalty." Hearing her own words, Aliza flushed, for nuns were expected to condemn all acts of violence. But how could she not admire what the elderly, grieving queen had done? "Your lady mother then summoned the Poitevin lords to make a progress through her duchy," she told Joanna, "issuing charters, confirming privileges and liberties, recognizing communes, doing all she can to win support for Count John."

"Do you know where she is now?"

"We heard she is at Poitiers."

"Then we shall depart on the morrow for Poitiers," Joanna declared, and although she caught the worried look that passed between Mariam and the prioress, she ignored it.

⟡

THEIR HORSE LITTER WAS swaying so wildly that Mariam was beginning to feel queasy. How could Joanna have fallen asleep? And yet she had, proof of how utterly exhausted she must be. Her pallor was troubling, her skin as waxen as church candles, and her breathing was soft and shallow. Mariam at first had assumed she was prostrated by grief alone, and had been slow to realize that she was also ill; it was becoming obvious by now that this pregnancy would be more difficult than her earlier ones. But Joanna had been adamant about finding her mother, and when they arrived at Poitiers and learned Eleanor had left for Niort, she insisted they continue on.

When they were only a few miles from Niort, Joanna sent Sir Roger de Laurac on ahead to announce their coming, both women praying that Eleanor would still be at the castle. It was a massive stronghold, begun by Joanna's father and completed by Richard, and at the sight of its stone turrets, Joanna blinked back tears, remembering how proud her brother had been of his handiwork. As soon as the horse litter came to a halt in the outer bailey, Mariam pulled the curtain aside and jumped out, not waiting for a stool to be brought over. Roger was hurrying toward them and then Eleanor appeared in the doorway of the great hall, with her granddaughter Richenza right behind her. Mariam turned back, crying, "Joanna, your mother is here!"

No one had yet brought out a stool, but Roger quickly stepped forward to assist the queen up into the litter. As soon as she saw her mother, Joanna began to sob. Eleanor pulled the curtain shut, gathered her daughter into her arms, and held her close as they both wept.

CHAPTER THIRTY-SEVEN

⚜

JUNE 1199

Fontevrault Abbey, Anjou

Raimond had been warned that Joanna was ailing. Although she'd given no details, her letter had revealed that she'd not been well enough to accompany her mother on her progress and Eleanor had sent her back to Fontevrault Abbey to convalesce. But Raimond was still shocked by his first sight of his wife. She'd not come rushing out to greet him as he rode into the abbey precincts, as she would normally have done. She was awaiting him in Eleanor's guest hall, holding on to Mariam's arm as if she needed support, and her always fair skin was so white that it looked almost transparent. When he embraced her, she felt as fragile and unsubstantial as cobwebs, smoke, and morning mist.

"I am so sorry for your brother's death, love."

"It still does not seem real," she confided. She sounded as frail as she looked and he instinctively tightened his arms protectively around her. She clung for a moment, but then she shuddered and gasped, "Take me to my bedchamber, Raimond, quickly!"

Her urgency was as compelling as it was bewildering, and he swung her up into his arms, following Mariam across the hall toward the stairwell. Mariam permitted Dame Beatrix to enter, but she refused to admit Anna and the rest of Joanna's women. No sooner had Raimond set Joanna on her feet than she doubled over, vomiting into the floor rushes with such force that her body seemed to be convulsing. Mariam and Beatrix dropped to their knees beside her, offering wordless murmurings of comfort. Raimond had the sense to step back, realizing there was nothing he could do for his stricken wife. When Mariam glanced over her shoulder and asked him to wait down in the hall, he did not protest, for he knew Joanna never liked him to see her when she was sick.

Anna at once assailed him with questions, none of which he could answer. Sitting down in a window-seat, he found himself wondering if Joanna could be with child again. She'd suffered greatly from nausea in her past pregnancies, yet nothing like what he'd just witnessed. Could she have sickened after eating tainted food?

"My lord count." A young woman was standing before him. She was clad as a nun, but he still took notice of her long-lashed blue eyes and heart-shaped face; he often joked he'd be paying heed to a woman's beauty on his deathbed. When she introduced herself as the Prioress Aliza, he quickly rose and greeted her as gallantly as if she were a lady at the royal court.

Once she was sitting across from him in the window-seat, though, he began to question her, no less intently than Anna had tried to interrogate him. How long had his wife been ill? What was being done for her? Why was Queen Berengaria not here with her? And when would her mother return to the abbey?

The abbess would have bridled at his peremptory tone. Aliza was more forgiving. "She has been with us for over a month, my lord, and I regret to say that she has been ill every day since her arrival. We love her dearly and you may be sure that she has wanted for nothing. Queen Berengaria was here with your wife until she had to depart for the wedding, and your lady's mother—"

"What wedding?" Realizing how abrupt he sounded, Raimond made amends with a quick smile.

"Queen Berengaria's youngest sister, Blanca, is to wed Thibault, the Count of Champagne, at Chartres. I think it eased some of the queen's grief to be able to take part in planning the wedding festivities. She then traveled to Poitiers to meet Blanca and escort her to Chartres. But she is devoted to your wife, as you well know, and I am sure she will return ere the summer is over. You asked about Queen Eleanor, too. Once the progress through her duchy was done, she rode straight to Fontevrault to check upon Lady Joanna. She could not stay for long, though, as she has to be at Tours in July to do homage to the French king for her Poitevin domains. From there, she must ride to Rouen to meet with King John, but she promised your lady that she will be back here in plenty of time for the birth."

Raimond was astonished by the prioress's casual comment about Eleanor doing homage to the French king, for women did not do homage in their own right and his mother-in-law loathed Philippe Capet. But that was quickly forgotten when he heard the word "birth," spoken no less casually. She'd taken it for granted that he knew of his wife's pregnancy. Why would she not? He was spared the need to respond by the appearance of Mariam in the hall; she glanced around and then came swiftly toward him.

JOANNA HAD BEEN PUT to bed. They'd cleaned up the soiled floor rushes, but a faint odor still lingered. Raimond noticed that there was an empty basin and chamber pot on the floor by the bed, water buckets, flagons, herbal vials, and a stack of towels and blankets on the table. It looked more like the nun's infirmary than Eleanor of Aquitaine's elegant bedchamber. As soon as Mariam and Beatrix withdrew, leaving him alone with his wife, he pulled a chair over to the bed. "Why did you not tell me that you are with child?" And despite his best efforts, he knew his tone sounded accusatory.

"I did not know when I left Toulouse. I was not sure until I missed a second flux in April and the queasiness began. I thought of writing, but decided that it was best to wait until I could tell you, for I knew you'd worry."

Christ on the Cross, how could he not worry? Three pregnancies in three years? He reached over and took her hand in his; he was startled that her skin felt so cold. "I know you've always suffered more from morning sickness than most women do. But nothing like this. What does the midwife say? You have seen one?"

"Of course. She is said to be the best midwife in Saumur, very experienced. She told us that nausea like mine—so overwhelming and so frequent—is not common, and thank God for that, for no woman would ever have another child after going through this." Joanna mustered up a wan smile. "But she said she had encountered it twice over the years and she assured us that both women stopped vomiting after the fifth month. So . . . I shall be counting the days until August," she said, forcing another smile.

Raimond was at a rare loss for words, for sharing his fears would only add to her own burdens. Why did God make childbirth so difficult and dangerous for women? He'd never understood that. Last year as Joanna labored to give birth to their daughter, he'd confided his concerns to her chaplain, Jocelyn, only to have the man remind him that it was punishment for the sin of Eve, quoting the scriptural verse in which God said, *I will greatly multiply your pain in childbirth. In pain you shall bring forth children.* Raimond had wanted to hit him.

"Why are your hands so cold, love? They are like ice."

Joanna did not know; her constant coldness was only one of her mysterious symptoms. In addition to the extreme nausea—as dreadful and debilitating as her worst bouts of seasickness on their journey to the Holy Land—she was light-headed and dizzy, often short of breath, had trouble sleeping despite her constant fatigue, and there were times when her heart beat so rapidly that it seemed about to burst from her chest. She'd not given much thought to these symptoms, though, for they were a minor matter when compared to the persistent vomiting and her inability to keep food down. She'd been existing on water and a few mouthfuls of bread, and sometimes she could not even manage that much.

Raimond had leaned over and when he kissed her on the forehead, she felt her stomach lurch. Like most men, he smelled of sweat and wine and horses, and she'd loved to breathe in his scent, finding it more of an aphrodisiac than the cinnamon, figs, and pine nuts commonly believed to stir lust. Now, though, she found herself fighting back queasiness. "Raimond . . . Can you fetch me something to drink?"

The queasiness eased as he moved away from the bed, much to her relief; she did not want to vomit in front of him again like a sick dog. When he asked if she wanted wine, she hastily asked for water. Just the odor of wine was enough to make her gag.

Raimond held the cup to her lips, watching as she took a few small sips. His original intent had been to bring her home to Toulouse once she felt strong enough, but it was painfully obvious by now that she was in no condition to make a three-hundred-mile journey. Even after the worst of her nausea abated, he was not sure she'd be up to it, as weak as she was. She was going to have to deliver their baby here at Fontevrault.

She proved, then, that she'd not lost her knack for reading his mind. "Raimond, you cannot stay with me until the baby is born. That will not be until November. Think how rebel lords like that wretch St Felix would take advantage if you were gone from Toulouse that long."

"I am dealing with some disgruntled vassals, Joanna, not an all-out rebellion."

"How long would it take to become an all-out rebellion if you gave them such an opportunity by your absence? And what of our children? Think how confusing it would be for Raimondet and Joanna if we both were gone from their lives for months? Yes, they would still be well cared for, but they would not understand, especially Raimondet."

He knew that was true. She'd been gone two and a half months and their son had not stopped asking for "Mama." "Well, what would you have me do, Joanna?"

She'd had plenty of time to think about that during long, sleepless nights. She definitely did not want him here until the vomiting and nausea finally eased up. It was hard enough to let Mariam see her in such a pitiful, helpless state; it would have been intolerable to have Raimond witness those awful, endless waves of nausea that left her as weak as a newborn kitten. "I want you to go home to Toulouse, to take care of our children and keep the peace. And then you can come back to visit me in August, once I . . ." She'd been about to say "once I can eat again," but the very thought of food made her queasy and she said hastily, ". . . once I am feeling more like myself."

He could not argue with her, for he knew what she said was true. He could not afford to be gone from Toulouse until she gave birth to their child. But even if he'd disagreed with her, he could not have balked, for the last thing she needed was more worries, more cares. Their midwife in Toulouse, Dame Esquiva, had once made him laugh by saying tartly that husbands were as much use during a woman's pregnancy and lying-in as wings on a fish. "We'll do it your way, love— as we always do. I ought to have been warned when I saw how well behaved your dogs were. A woman who could train those stubborn Sicilian hounds would have no trouble at all bringing a husband to heel." And when he coaxed a smile, he felt as if he'd been given a gift.

He remembered his own gift then, and went into the stairwell to call for his squire. Joanna took advantage of his brief absence to close her eyes and engage in some deep breathing, for that sometimes could keep the queasiness at bay. When a knock sounded, Raimond crossed to the door and opened it wide enough to take a small hemp sack. Bringing it back to the bed, he put it in Joanna's hand.

Within the sack was a small ivory box, delicately carved. "Raimond, it is beautiful." She was curious as to the contents, for it was not big enough to hold much; mayhap a ring? He liked to give her jewelry. But when she lifted the lid, tears filled her eyes, for she understood at once what she was looking at—two locks of hair neatly tied with ribbons. The silky ebony curl was Raimondet's and the smaller chestnut wisp had come from their daughter's head. Pressing her son's ringlet to her lips, she said huskily, "Not many men would have thought of this. You have a sentimental streak, Raimond de St Gilles, but your secret will be safe with me."

"I hope so. If word got about, I'd be a laughingstock," he said, with such mock horror that she smiled again. She started to return Raimondet's lock to the box, but noticed a third ribbon, this one tied around a clump of hair that was red and coarse to the touch. When she held it up questioningly, Raimond grinned. "After I explained to Raimondet why I wanted to cut off a strand of his hair, he insisted that I include some of Ahmer's fur for you."

Joanna laughed—for the first time in many weeks. But then she felt the sickness surging back. Raimond was quick to snatch up the basin by the bed, and she endured the humiliation of vomiting into it while her husband held her upright. Once it was done, he brought her water so she could wash out her mouth, and when she asked for Mariam and Beatrix, he was wise enough not to argue. As soon as he left the chamber to fetch them, she sagged back against the pillow. Her mouth still tasted foul and the sheet was wet, for she'd spilled some of the water. Tears welled in her eyes again, but this time they were tears of shame and frustration and utter misery.

MARIAM AND BEATRIX HAD cleaned Joanna up and changed her bed linen. She was so grateful that Beatrix was here, for the older woman had been her anchor since her journey to Sicily as a child-bride more than twenty years ago. She was not as glad that Raimond had brought Anna and Alicia, for they were so distraught that Beatrix had finally given them a sharp talking-to, warning them that they were there to help their lady and if they could not do so, she'd send them back with Count Raimond when he returned to Toulouse. Both Beatrix and Mariam were relieved that Joanna had prevailed, knowing that Raimond could offer no comfort, not yet, not until she was no longer throwing up day and night.

Joanna had slept for a while and felt well enough to spend an hour with Raimond that evening. Talking took too much of her energy, but she listened as he told her stories about their son's mischief-making and growing vocabulary. She was losing months of her children's lives, time that could never be recovered. She was too sick to dwell upon that now, though. Her world had shrunk to the confines of this bedchamber, and for much of her waking hours, she could concentrate only upon what her body was doing to her. It was even worse than her shipboard suffering.

Once Raimond had gently kissed her good night and departed, she closed her eyes, willing sleep to come, for that was the only respite she got. But sleep eluded her. Instead, she found herself in the throes of nausea again—the twentieth time it had happened that day. Fortunately Mariam and Beatrix had returned to the chamber as soon as Raimond had gone, and they kept her from vomiting all over herself and the bed. Afterward, she began to sob, clinging to Beatrix's hand so tightly that her nails dug into the other woman's flesh. "I cannot endure any more," she wept. "I cannot . . . Merciful God, what have I done to deserve this? Please make it stop, please. . . ."

Beatrix was not sure if Joanna was talking to her or to God. She did what she could, cradling the younger woman as she'd done when Joanna was a little girl, stroking her hair as her own eyes burned with tears. When Joanna at last fell into an exhausted sleep, she rose carefully from the bed and drew Mariam toward the far corner of the chamber.

"I need to know," she said, her voice low but fierce. "Did the midwife truly tell you that Joanna's nausea is likely to abate after the fifth month?" She was not reassured when Mariam nodded, for she'd averted her eyes. "What are you keeping from me?"

Mariam hesitated, but she desperately needed to confide in someone. "The midwife did indeed tell us that she'd treated two cases like Joanna's, saying both of the women found relief in the fifth month, later delivering healthy babies. But she also told me in confidence that she'd lied. Only one of the women gave birth to a live baby. The other one continued to grow weaker even after she was able to eat again. She died in the sixth month of the pregnancy."

RAIMOND DREW REIN and glanced back at the abbey walls. His men exchanged puzzled looks, but he was their lord and it was not for them to question why he'd chosen to halt in the middle of the road. Raimond could not have explained himself why he suddenly felt this reluctance to see Fontevrault recede into the distance. Returning to Toulouse would ease Joanna's qualms about their children and his troublesome vassals; staying here would not. And although he was loath to admit it, he felt a certain relief that he would not have to watch helplessly as his wife suffered. Joanna's women had made it clear—without saying a word—that they did not want him underfoot whilst they dealt with female matters that no man could truly understand.

He'd had a private talk with Joanna's midwife and felt better afterward, for she seemed quite confident that Joanna's nausea would not last much longer. He saw no reason to doubt her, for he'd never heard of a woman afflicted with morning sickness for the entire length of her pregnancy. And when he'd bidden Joanna farewell, she'd been in better spirits, revealing that she was sure she was bearing a son. The midwife had performed a test that she claimed was utterly reliable: putting a few drops of Joanna's blood into a bowl of springwater. If they'd floated, that would have meant she would birth a daughter, but they sank, proof that the baby in her womb was a boy. Raimond did not wait for her to ask, suggesting they name their son after her brother, and he would take back to Toulouse the memory of her grateful smile. He did not doubt that she'd bedazzle their son with embellished stories of his renowned namesake, but a nephew would not feel the need to live up to the legend of the Lionheart the way a son would. If it would give Joanna comfort, he'd not care if she turned Richard's crown into a halo and transformed what he saw as a needless death into a holy martyrdom.

Sensing that his men were growing restless, Raimond at last gave the signal to move on. When he returned to Fontevrault, he would bring Dame Esquiva with him, for Joanna would have greater trust in the midwife who'd delivered their children than in a stranger from Saumur. And he meant to have a confidential conversation with Esquiva, one that he doubted he'd share with his wife.

The Church preached that it was a mortal sin to prevent conception, but he had a more flexible concept of sin than Joanna, and he valued her life and her health more than the teachings of self-righteous holy men who knew nothing of the pleasures of the flesh. It was common sense that three pregnancies in three years would take a toll upon a woman's body. Joanna could not keep getting with child every year like this. But abstinence was for monks and nuns, and even they often found it an impossible vow to keep. He remembered, though, a discussion with one of his bedmates, remembered her saying that a woman could avoid pregnancy by drinking wine mixed with willow leaves. She'd also claimed that there were magic charms and amulets that kept a man's seed from taking root in a woman's womb.

He did not doubt that Dame Esquiva would know of these methods. Because she was a good-hearted, practical woman, he was sure she would agree that Joanna needed time to recover her strength between pregnancies. Who understood the dangers of the birthing chamber more than a midwife, after all? And if Joanna never knew what they'd done, she'd be innocent of sin. Whereas his sins were beyond counting, so why would one more matter? If he must choose between risking his wife's life and risking more time in Purgatory, that was not a difficult choice to make.

ELEANOR HAD NEVER SPENT much time at Tours during her marriage to Henry, for he preferred his castles at Chinon and Angers. The fortress at Tours was notable neither for its defenses nor its comforts, consisting of a great hall over ninety feet in length, with living quarters above and an adjoining square tower in the southeast corner of the bailey. But on this stifling summer afternoon in mid-July, it was the scene of a historic and dramatic ceremony. Eleanor was about to do homage to the French king for her Poitevin domains.

The hall was crowded with Philippe's vassals, but only Mathieu de Montmorency had the courtesy or the courage to offer her his condolences for the death of her son. Barthélemy de Vendôme, the Archbishop of Tours, was seated on the dais beside Philippe, but he did not look to Eleanor as if he was enjoying the honor. Touraine was part of the Angevin empire, yet the archbishopric of Tours itself was under the French king's control, and the archbishop was squirming like a man caught between two very hungry wolves.

Her grandson Arthur and his mother were seated on the dais, too, accompanied by Breton lords whom Richard would have called "the usual suspects," men always eager to dip their oars in troubled waters. For a moment, Eleanor's eyes rested on the boy. Only twelve, he would be taller than his father when fully grown. In truth, she could see little of Geoffrey in him; he had Constance's dark eyes and arrogance. Would it have been different—would *he* have been different—had he been raised at her son's court as Richard had wanted? The lad was spirited; Richard would have liked that. Her gaze shifted to her former daughter-in-law. Constance was making no effort to hide her hostility. Even now she did not realize that she'd sacrificed Arthur's bright hopes for a grudge. Eleanor could have told her that revenge had a bittersweet taste, but she'd learn that for herself soon enough.

The presence of Guillaume des Roches amongst the Bretons was troubling, though, for he was an Angevin baron who'd been utterly loyal to Richard. He ought to have pledged himself to her son, not Arthur. She would, she decided, have a word with him ere she departed Tours. But now it was time.

The hall quieted as she stepped forward and began to walk toward the dais. It was customary for an heiress's husband or sons to do homage in her name, yet now she was defying tradition by doing homage herself. She did not doubt that some of Philippe's vassals were shocked and indignant that a woman could exercise authority in her own right, independent of a man. At the French court, they were saying that she must be desperate to safeguard her own lands. None would ever have believed she'd have put her duchy before Richard's interests. She knew it was easier to believe of John.

Reaching the dais, she sank to her knees before the French king, holding her hands up for them to be clasped between his own. "My lady queen, are you willing to become my liege woman?" he asked, his voice as unrevealing as his expression. This was the first time she'd met him face-to-face. His appearance was not regal; he would never command all eyes merely by entering a chamber as Richard had done. But he was the one breathing God's air and plotting to destroy the Angevin empire, whilst Richard slept in a marble tomb at Fontevrault Abbey. She could feel the pain stirring again and fought it back savagely; she'd have the rest of her life to mourn her son, but not now, not here.

"I am willing, my lord king," she said composedly, her voice giving away no more than his had done. When he raised her up to give her the kiss that sealed the ceremony, she was not surprised that the lips brushing hers were cold to the touch.

An oath of homage must be followed by one of fealty, and she knelt again as a priest brought out a small reliquary. She wondered what holy relics she'd be swearing upon. Some were more credible than others; she very much doubted that straw from the Christ Child's manger or nails from his cross had survived so many centuries. Not that it mattered.

"I promise on my faith," she said, "that I will in future be faithful to King Philippe, not cause him harm, and will observe my homage to him completely against all persons in good faith and without deceit."

Only then did Philippe smile.

Eleanor rose to her feet again. All that remained now was the investiture ceremony, in which the French king would formally "return" her domains to her keeping. Male vassals were usually presented with a material symbol such as a scepter or lance. She was curious to see what Philippe would choose for his first female vassal. Most likely a glove. And then it would be done. As his vassal, she would owe Philippe obedience, military aid, and wise counsel, and as her liege lord, he would owe her protection.

The smile she gave him in return was so genuine, so satisfied, that Philippe's own smile fled and his brows drew together. How wary he was, how suspicious— as well he ought to be. Now that he'd recognized her as the rightful heiress to her duchy, Arthur's claim to Poitou as Richard's heir was meaningless. And by do- ing homage to the French king, she deprived him of a legal basis for intervening in the affairs of Aquitaine and Poitou. As her liege lord, he was obligated to de- fend her rights—even against Arthur.

He would have understood that, of course. But she'd known that he could not resist this public submission by Richard's proud mother, seeing it not only as a gratifying acknowledgment of his sovereignty but as a humiliation to John, proof that she had no confidence in his ability to protect her duchy. What Philippe did not know was that she planned to issue a charter in which she rec- ognized John as her "rightful heir" and transferred to him the homage, fealty, and services owed her by her vassals. John would then do homage to her, pro- claiming her "lady of us and all our lands and possessions." And because she'd done personal homage to the French king, Philippe could not demand services directly of John. She—not John—would be answerable at the French court for any grievances Philippe might have.

John had been delighted with her idea, calling it a masterstroke. She knew, though, that it was not a long-term solution to the danger posed by the French king. When she died, her duchy would be vulnerable again. But she'd managed to checkmate Arthur and Constance whilst gaining John time to secure his hold on power, and that would have to be enough.

Philippe was watching her intently. He did not possess what Harry and Rich- ard had—the easy mastery of other men. Nor would he ever win glory with a sword. Yet she saw a ruthless, icy intelligence in those pale blue eyes and, unlike the men in her family, he knew how to be patient; he knew how to wait for what he wanted. He'd never have been a match for Richard on the battlefield and Richard had outmaneuvered him on the diplomatic front, too. But would John be able to defend himself against such a determined, unscrupulous adversary? Well, John was clever, cunning, and unscrupulous, too. He'd be no lamb to the slaughter; it would be a war of wolves.

❧

MARIAM WAS SITTING IN a garden arbor, the only place she could escape the eyes of others. In all of her thirty-three years, she had never been so frightened, never felt so helpless. If only she could talk to Joanna's husband and mother. But Raimond was over three hundred miles away and the queen was in Normandy, devoting herself to the needs of her youngest son.

She swiped at her wet cheek with the back of her hand. Weeping would not help. When had tears ever changed a blessed thing? Hearing footsteps on the garden path, she drew farther back into the arbor, hoping she'd go unnoticed. But then she heard her name called, and the voice was one that still haunted her dreams. Jumping to her feet, she emerged onto the walkway. "Morgan?" she said incredulously. "I thought you'd gone back to Wales after Richard died!"

He'd reached her by now and took her hands in his. "I did return to Wales," he said, for he'd wanted to see his brother and sister and to visit his parents' graves. But he'd stayed only a few weeks, for Wales was no longer where his roots were. His curiosity had been a golden key, admitting him to a world of endless horizons, soaring vistas, and exotic, alien locales. There was a price to be paid for such freedom, though: the loss of his homeland.

"I came back to check upon my Norman manors," he said, omitting the real reason: that he did not know where else to go. Since Richard's death, he'd been a ship without a rudder, sure only that he did not want to seek refuge in John's harbor. He'd even thought of pledging his loyalty to Arthur, for he was Geoffrey's son. But Arthur was the French king's pawn, and serving him would be serving Philippe Capet, which was even more distasteful than the idea of serving John. "When I landed at Barfleur, I heard that Joanna was ailing, so I rode for Fontevrault straightaway. I have not yet seen her, for Dame Beatrix said she is sleeping. How bad is it, Mariam?"

"She has been in Hell, Morgan. I do not know how else to describe it. Joanna has always had more severe morning sickness than most women, but nothing like this. She was unable to eat, sometimes even to drink water. The nausea never went away. She became sensitive to odors that no one else could smell, odors that had never bothered her before. We could not wear perfume or use soap to bathe her and the candles had to be wax, not tallow. There were days when she vomited as often as thirty times. She has lost so much weight that we had to make her gowns smaller instead of enlarging them to accommodate her pregnancy. The nausea began in the sixth week and nothing eased it, not ginger nor herbal remedies, not prayers to St Margaret, who protects women in childbirth, not even a holy relic that the abbess let us borrow. All we could do was to hope that the midwife was right, that the worst of it would abate in the fifth month. Joanna called August the Promised Land, for it would either bring salvation or doom. Whilst we did not talk of it, we all knew she could not keep on like that."

"And now that August has come?"

"The nausea has lessened considerably, although it has not gone away entirely. At least now she can take liquids like soup without throwing them up afterward. But she is still so weak, Morgan. She gets light-headed when she rises, so she must use a chamber pot, and the more time she spends in bed, the more strength she loses. She will not admit it, but I know she is terrified that she will not survive childbirth, for she is insisting that we go to Rouen to find her mother. We've reminded her that Eleanor promised to return to Fontevrault in time for the baby's birth. But Joanna says she cannot wait, that she needs Eleanor now. I truly think she has convinced herself that she will die without her mother."

Morgan was silent for several moments. "That is not so surprising," he said at last. "I have heard men wounded on the battlefield cry out for their mothers. It is a need that seems bred into our bones. And who better to stand sentinel between Joanna and Death than Queen Eleanor?" Reaching over, he took Mariam's hand. "If Joanna is set upon seeking out her mother, nothing we say will deter her. She is every bit as strong-willed as any of her brothers, as you well know. But what matters is not her determination; it is her need. If Eleanor can ease her fears and assure her that she will be able to deliver this child, we ought to be thanking God for it. I know little about childbirth, but I do know about battlefield injuries, and men who think they are going to recover have a better chance of doing so than those who think they are sure to die."

"I know you are right. But the journey will be so hard on her. Rouen is so far away."

"Well, since Joanna has made up her mind to do this, all we can do is ease her discomfort as best we can. We'll put a bed in the horse litter, stop whenever she needs to rest. If we can only cover ten miles a day, what of it? What matters is that we get her to her mother, not how long it takes."

He put his arm around her shoulders then and she leaned against him. "You've been saying 'we.' You will come with us, Morgan?"

"Of course I will. Joanna is my cousin, Richard's sister. There is nothing I would not do for her."

His assurances were very welcome and she felt great relief that he'd be there to help shoulder the burdens. Yet illogically she felt disappointed, too, for there was a time when he'd have said there was nothing he'd not do for *her*.

"You must have faith, Mariam. Joanna will reach Rouen. She will recover. And she will safely give birth when the time comes. Her mother is not going to lose another child."

CHAPTER THIRTY-EIGHT

❧

Eleanor was watching as her son read the drafts of the charters in which she would name him as the heir to her duchy and he in turn would do homage to her for it. He smiled from time to time and once he laughed outright. John, first of that name to rule England since the Conquest, a king of three months. For most of his life, his age had been cited in defense of his follies or betrayals. Again and again her husband had excused his failings as the sins of youth. Even Richard had done that. But the time had finally come for John to stand or fall on his own merits as a king, as a man grown of thirty-two. A memory slithered out to remind her that Richard had been thirty-two at the time of his coronation. She shoved it back into the oubliette where she kept such memories penned up, for memories were her enemies now. Memories sapped her strength, undermined her resolve, reminded her of all she'd lost.

She focused her thoughts instead on John's brief reign. So far it was going better than she'd dared hope. He'd had a narrow escape at Le Mans, but even there his instincts had served him well; he'd sensed the danger that enabled him to evade a Breton trap. And he'd later punished the citizens of Le Mans harshly for their disloyalty as a king must, razing the castle and the town's walls. He'd been generous with those who had been loyal, though, bestowing the earldom of Pembroke upon Will Marshal, making the reluctant Hubert Walter his chancellor, and naming the Viscount of Thouars as castellan of Chinon Castle and seneschal of Anjou. He'd been able to retain Richard's valuable alliances with the Count of Flanders and the Count of Boulogne. And he'd made his half brother

Geoff welcome upon his return from Rome. She doubted that their reconciliation would last, no more than it ever had with Richard, for Geoff had never
forgiven his brothers for rebelling against their father, and he loathed John for
that deathbed betrayal of Henry. But as the Archbishop of York, he had to be
placated, at least initially. A new, unproven king was wise to adopt a policy of
conciliation, to turn as many of his enemies as he could into allies, even temporary ones.

Philippe had not learned that lesson. He'd been unable to keep Richard from
weaving a web of dangerous alliances and then entangling him in it. He'd been
badly hurt by the defections of the counts of Flanders and Boulogne, by the enmity of Richard's German allies in the Rhineland, and now by the hostility of
the new emperor; Otto had pledged his support to John in any war against the
French king. Most damaging of all was the anger of the new Pope; Innocent was
set upon making Philippe put aside his "concubine," Agnes of Meran, and acknowledge Ingeborg as his lawful wife and queen. But Philippe continued to
defy the Church. Nor had he been conciliatory when he and John had met a
week ago near Castle Gaillard. He'd agreed to recognize John as the rightful heir
to Normandy, but only if John surrendered the Norman Vexin to him and
agreed to make Arthur the liege lord of Anjou, Touraine, and Maine. Not only
had John spurned such outrageous demands, he'd laughed in Philippe's face.
Eleanor would have enjoyed witnessing that.

Almost as if reading her mind, John looked up with a grin. "I'd love to be
there to watch when Philippe learns that you've outwitted him and turned your
homage into a shield to use against him." Rising, he moved to the table and
poured wine, serving her with a flourish and a jest about having a king as her
cupbearer. She suspected there were still times when he could hardly believe it
himself—that he was king at long last.

Eleanor took a sip, then saw that he was still watching her. "What is it?"

"I heard from the papal legate again. He claimed it was a warning, but it was
actually a threat. You know that some of Philippe's men captured the Count of
Flanders's ally, the Bishop-elect of Cambrai?"

Eleanor nodded. "That was foolish of the French, a needless provocation of a
Pope who needs no urging to protect the Church's prerogatives and privileges.
But why should Cardinal Pietro threaten you for a crime committed by the
French king?"

"My thoughts exactly. But it seems the Pope wants to appear evenhanded.

He means to lay an Interdict upon France if Pierre de Corbeil, the bishop-elect, is not freed at once. And he warns that he will do the same for Normandy if I do not agree to set that polecat Beauvais loose."

She'd known this day would eventually come, for Innocent III was strong-willed, shrewd, and not about to let a prince of the Church languish in a dungeon, even one he held in such low regard as the Bishop of Beauvais. Richard would never have freed him, but John had no personal stake in his continuing confinement, and so it was not surprising that he'd yield to the Pope in order to avoid an Interdict. It still left a bad taste in her mouth.

"I told the cardinal—a truly tiresome man—that I would take the Church's demand under advisement. I shall have to let the swine go, but I mean to charge him two thousand marks for the cost of feeding him during those two years he was Brother Richard's guest."

When he laughed, Eleanor could not help laughing, too, imagining the bishop's utter outrage at being billed for the time he'd spent in Angevin dungeons in Rouen and Chinon. John poured wine for himself, perching on the edge of the table. "One of my spies tells me that Guillaume des Roches is becoming discontented with Philippe's high-handedness and may be amenable to switching sides again. Tell me, Mother, what did you say to the man at Tours?"

"I asked if it was true that Philippe had proclaimed him seneschal of Anjou. He admitted it but indignantly denied that he'd been influenced by this. I agreed that he was not a man to be bribed, that what mattered to him was honor. And I assured him that we value men of honor, too."

John's eyes shone golden in the sunlight streaming through the open window. *Cat eyes,* she thought, wondering if others said the same of her own eyes. When he confided that he'd be going into Maine next week and hoped he'd have an opportunity for a private talk with des Roches, she knew that he'd make sure the opportunity came to pass. He thrived on intrigue, this youngest son of hers. Mayhap too much so, for he'd shown a decided preference for the oblique approach, enjoying guile and subterfuge as much for their own sake as for what they could accomplish.

"Is it true what I heard, John, that the Earl of Chester has annulled his marriage to Constance?"

He grinned again. "Indeed he did, faster than a rabbit with a fox on its tail. Whilst he got little pleasure from his Breton hellcat of a wife, I think he rather fancied being Duke of Brittany. Even if it was an empty title, it had a nice ring to it, and there was always the chance that his stepson could be named as Richard's heir. But once I became king, he was no longer so keen on being the stepfather of a traitorous whelp, and he shed Constance as fast as he could find a compliant bishop."

Eleanor thought his assessment of the earl's action was cynical but probably accurate. She wondered how long it would take John to rid himself of his own unwanted wife. Kings found it even easier than earls to find compliant bishops, and unlike Philippe and the unfortunate Ingeborg, John had legitimate grounds for invalidating his marriage: they were cousins. She was about to ask him if he'd given any thought to a foreign marital alliance when a servant entered the solar and murmured a few words in her ear. John had turned back to study the charters that were going to infuriate Philippe. He looked up, though, when he heard her cry out.

"A messenger has just ridden in from Joanna! She is on her way here, is only a few miles outside the town." Eleanor was astonished and pleased, but she was aware, too, of a vague sense of foreboding that she could neither explain nor dismiss out of hand.

John did not share it. "That is good news," he said with a smile. "She must surely be feeling much better if she'd undertake such a long journey."

After a moment to reflect, Eleanor smiled, too, realizing he was right. Even though she'd not seen a case of morning sickness as severe as Joanna's, it never lasted through the entire pregnancy. It was the constant vomiting that had made Joanna so weak; she'd soon have recovered once it stopped.

"Come," she said. "Let's find out more from Joanna's knight and order a bed-chamber made ready for her."

AS THEY ENTERED THE GREAT HALL, John stopped in his tracks at the sight of Joanna's messenger. While most of his brother's vassals had accepted the in-evitable and pledged their loyalty to him, there were a few who'd kept their distance. André de Chauvigny was one, and the man coming toward them was another.

"Well, if it is not Cousin Morgan. I'd assumed you must have gotten lost in the wilds of Wales."

"My lord king," Morgan said, dropping to one knee. But the obeisance seemed perfunctory to John. The Welshman's gaze was already moving past him, seeking his mother.

Eleanor had halted, too, as soon as she saw Morgan's face. "My daughter . . . ?"

Morgan courageously kept his eyes upon hers, resisting an overwhelming urge to look away as she realized the truth. "Madame . . . she is very ill," he said softly, and those close enough to hear quieted, sensing that the queen was to be visited by yet more sorrow.

❧

"Maman?"

"I am right here, dearest. Let your ladies settle you in bed and then we'll talk."

Once Morgan gently deposited Joanna upon the bed, he and her chaplain were ushered from the chamber. As soon as Beatrix and the other women began to undress her daughter, Eleanor took Mariam by the arm and propelled her toward a far corner. "Why did you bring her on such a journey when she is so obviously ill?"

Mariam did not resent the sharp tone, understanding that she was speaking to the mother, not the queen, a mother greatly shaken by her daughter's frail appearance. "We tried to dissuade her, Madame. But she was insistent and . . . and we came to realize it was for the best that she seek you out. We'd expected her to regain her strength once the nausea no longer tormented her day and night. She did not. Instead, she grew weaker, until she feared that she'd not survive childbirth. Her need for you was great enough to justify the journey."

Mariam had been speaking without emotion, almost as if relating the story of strangers. Now she faltered, tears welling in her eyes. "But once we were on the road, she got worse, not better. She knows her health is failing and she no longer believes you can vanquish the dangers of the birthing chamber, my lady. She . . . she is convinced that she will not live long enough to deliver her child. And I . . . When I look at her, I fear she is right."

"No," Eleanor said, and although she remembered to keep her voice low, it resonated with resolve, with a determination that recognized no higher authority than the Angevin royal will. "She is not going to die."

But once Eleanor was seated on the bed beside her daughter, that certainty began to crumble, for Joanna did look as if her life could be measured in weeks, even days. She was painfully thin, her collarbones thrust into sudden prominence, her face almost gaunt. Her eyes were sunken back in her head, so darkly shadowed that they seemed surrounded by contusions. Her skin was as white and cold as falling snow; her lips, too, were pallid. Her breathing was shallow and rapid, her pulse so faint that Eleanor could barely find it when she pressed her fingers to Joanna's wrist. Even her hair, always as brightly burnished as molten gold, was limp and lusterless, feeling like sun-dried straw. "I am dying, Maman," she whispered, "and I am so afraid. . . ."

"I know you are, dearest. But your baby is not due for more than two months. There is time enough for you to recover, to get your strength back. I've already sent for Rouen's best midwife, and my own physician will attend you. . . ."

She stopped then, for Joanna was shaking her head, closing her eyes as if even that small movement had exhausted her. Her hand tightened on Eleanor's own; her fingers felt as fragile and delicate as the hollow bones of God's fallen sparrow. "My sweet child, listen to me," Eleanor said, with all the conviction at her command. "You are not going to die."

"You do not understand. It is not death I fear so. . . . Maman, I am damned. When I die, I will be condemned to Hell."

Eleanor was not easily shocked, yet her daughter had managed it. "My darling girl, why would you say that? Why would you think that?" When Joanna did not reply, she held that cold hand against her cheek, inadvertently triggering a troubling memory of doing that during her deathbed vigil for her son. "Joanna, you are making no sense. What sins could you have committed that would deserve eternal damnation?"

"The worst of sins. . . ."

Joanna said nothing more and Eleanor realized that she was ashamed to confess this "worst of sins" even to her mother. What could she possibly have done to believe God had turned His face away from her? "You can tell me anything, my darling. I would never judge you." Feigning a smile, she said, "How could your sins be darker than mine, after all?"

Joanna turned her head aside on the pillow. "I hoped I would lose my baby. My own child. I was so sick, so sick. . . . I just could not take any more. . . ." She'd begun to sob, but softly, as if she did not even have the energy to grieve. "I actually prayed that it would happen. I know now that I was praying to the Devil, for God would never heed such a wicked prayer. . . ."

Eleanor gathered the younger woman into her arms. "Joanna, you must not judge yourself so harshly. You were ill, not in your right senses. The Almighty will understand that."

"No, He will not. This was my child, Raimond's son, but I would have sacrificed him if I could. I even thought about asking Mariam to get me pennyroyal or black hellebore. I could not do that to her, though, could not damn her, too. . . ."

Eleanor tightened her arms around her daughter. "God absolves us of our sins if we are truly contrite. He will forgive you."

"I cannot forgive myself, Maman. So how could God forgive me? A mother's first duty is to protect her child. I would have murdered mine if I could have. . . ."

"You are tormenting yourself needlessly. Since you are unable to believe me, I will send Abbot Luke of Turpenay to you. He accompanied me to Fontevrault, never left my side as I had to watch Richard die. He will hear your confession, lay a penance upon you for whatever sins you have committed, and then absolve you of them."

"No priest can shrive me of such a sin. Contrition is not enough. There is only one way I can hope to escape eternal damnation, Maman. Two nights ago, she came to me in a dream, told me what I must do."

"Who, Joanna? I do not understand."

"The Blessed Lady Mary, Our Saviour's mother. She said that God would forgive me only if I can take holy vows, can die as one of the sisters of Fontevrault."

Eleanor knew the Church would not allow it. But when Joanna raised her head, her eyes filled with panic and pleading, and entreated her to make it happen, she heard herself promising that she would do her best, words that sounded as hollow as she felt. Her promise seemed to give Joanna her first measure of comfort, though, for she could feel some of the tension ebbing from her daughter's shoulders. Lying back upon the bed, Joanna closed her eyes again, murmuring, "Thank you, Maman, thank you . . ."

Within moments, she slept. Eleanor brushed her hair back from her face, tucking the covers warmly around her, for she'd been shivering as if it were winter, not late August. Only then did Eleanor lean forward, dropping her head into her hands. How much more would the Almighty demand of her?

❦

JOHN DID NOT HAVE many warm memories of his siblings. He did not remember his sisters Tilda and Leonora, who'd been sent off to wed foreign princes when he was very young. He'd not often seen his older brothers, and when he had, they'd either ignored him or teased him as mercilessly as older brothers had done since the dawn of time. It had been different with Joanna, his companion during their time at Fontevrault, and he'd missed her after her departure for Sicily. When they'd been reunited eighteen years later, though, he'd discovered that she was one for bearing grudges. She'd never forgiven him for conniving against Richard with the French king, and he'd come to resent her for it.

But he'd been genuinely shocked to be told that she was gravely ill, not expected to live. She was only a year older than he was, too young to die, and he suddenly found himself recalling the lively, mischievous girl who'd once been fond of her little brother. "There is no hope, then?"

Eleanor shook her head, almost imperceptibly. "My physician has examined her, as have the two best midwives in the city. All three reached the same conclusion—that she is in God's hands."

John knew that there was no love lost between doctors and midwives, so their unusual unanimity did not bode well for his stricken sister. He knew, too, that whenever some poor soul was consigned to God's mercy, that one was not long for the world. "I am sorry," he said, vaguely surprised by how much he meant it. Leaning back in his seat, he regarded his mother admiringly. She was the strong one in their family, not his father, nor his brothers. Her spine, like the finest swords, had been forged in fire. She kept her head high even as her heart bled. But then a dark thought intruded; did she blame God for taking Richard whilst sparing the son she did not love? He reached for the wine cup at his elbow, draining most of it in several deep swallows. Was he still yearning after a mother's love, like a mewling babe in need of a teat? She'd done what mattered, traveling more than a thousand miles to win over her Poitevin vassals to his cause. And he was honest enough to admit that if not for her efforts, he might not have prevailed over that Breton brat.

"I shall pray for Joanna," he said, because it was expected of him, not because he believed it would help his sister.

"There is more you can do for her, John. She is in need of money."

Now that he was king, John was learning to dislike any sentence that mentioned money, for like as not, he'd be the one asked to pay it out. "She has a husband who is rich and indulges her every whim, Mother," he reminded Eleanor, with a thin smile.

"When she left Toulouse in April to seek Richard's aid for Raimond, she did not expect to be gone more than a month or so. Her lack of money did not matter much, though, for few merchants would deny credit to the king's sister."

That was a song John could sing in his sleep; he'd lived for years on credit and expectations and the foolishness of men eager to curry favor with one who might be a future king. "Of course," he said. "I will be pleased to give Joanna a hundred marks of rent, to dispose of any way she chooses."

"That is generous of you, John. But I had something else in mind. When Richard landed in Sicily, he did more than gain Joanna's freedom. He insisted that Tancred compensate her in gold for the loss of her dower lands, which he then used to pay for his army's expenses in the Holy Land."

"And he never repaid her." John's smile was sour, for when did Brother Richard ever repay a debt? He'd bled his kingdom white to finance his wars, and had gotten away with it because he was the Lionheart, because men admired and respected and feared him as they did not admire, respect, or fear his brother. John lied to many others, not to himself, and he knew he was going to find it much harder than Richard to raise money. "So what do you have in mind?" he asked warily, already sure he knew the answer.

"Joanna never bothered to ask Richard for repayment since she had no need of it. Now she does. She must make her will, for the Church holds that dying intestate is like dying unconfessed. She wants to settle her own debts and to make bequests to those in her household. Above all, she wants to have enough money to bequeath to churches, to feed the poor, and to have prayers said for her soul."

"And how much is 'enough'?"

"Three thousand marks will do. If you agree, that will release you of all liability for the debt that Richard owed to Joanna."

Three thousand marks! That would buy food to fill all the hungry bellies in Rouen, would keep candles lit for her soul until the Second Coming, would enrich a veritable host of greedy churchmen at his expense. John scowled, feeling as if Richard had gulled him from the grave. His mother remained silent. Why bother with words when she could deliver her message with her eyes? Eyes as piercing as any arrow, aiming for the very depths of his soul. He picked up his wine cup, tasting the dregs before saying with as much grace as he could muster, "Of course I agree, Mother. How could I refuse?"

❧

IT TOOK HOURS FOR Joanna's will to be drawn up to her satisfaction, so determined was she to acknowledge all those who'd served her so loyally. She left a generous bequest to Dame Beatrix and smaller sums to her other maids of honor, to her chaplain and clerks and servants. She took care that the thousand shillings she'd borrowed from the moneylender, Provetal the Jew, would be repaid. She gave her favorite horse to the hospital at Roncevaux, six mares to the abbey of Mont Sainte Catherine, and two mares to every religious house in Rouen. She made a large gift to the abbess of Fontevrault and bequests to several of the nuns who'd befriended her, left a valuable wall hanging to St Stephen's church in Toulouse, and placed the residue of her three thousand marks at the disposal of her mother and the archbishops of Canterbury and York, to be divided among religious houses and the poor.

Abbot Luke then heard her confession and administered the sacrament of Extreme Unction, which normally gave the dying much comfort. It did not assuage Joanna's fears, though, for she remained convinced that her only path to salvation led toward the abbey of Fontevrault.

❧

ELEANOR HAD BEEN UNABLE to save her son and she knew that she could not save her daughter, either. She could not defeat Death. But now her adversaries were flesh-and-blood, stubborn and hidebound, clinging to custom the way snails and turtles retreated into their shells whenever they encountered the unknown. She had been fighting men like this for her entire life and whilst she'd lost most of the time, this was the one battle she had to win.

She at once sent word to Fontevrault, confident that she would have allies in Abbess Mathilde and Prioress Aliza. But Joanna had taken no comfort in that. She was sure that she'd be dead by the time the elderly abbess could travel all the way to Rouen, and Eleanor feared she was right, for it seemed to her that her daughter lost ground by the hour. She went next to the Archbishop of Rouen, only to be rebuffed. He was sympathetic to the countess's deathbed wishes, he assured Eleanor. But canon law spoke clearly on the subject: a married woman could not take holy vows without her husband's consent.

Eleanor had expected such a negative response. She knew she might be maligning Archbishop Gautier, but she suspected that he remained resentful of his clash with her son over Les Andelys; even though he'd been well compensated for his loss, he'd also been humiliated when the Pope had sided with Richard, and she was not sure he was magnanimous enough to overlook that old grievance.

She had better luck with Mathilde d'Avranches, the abbess of St Amand, Rouen's prestigious nunnery. Abbot Luke of Turpenay Abbey was easy to persuade, too, as were the Bishops of Évreux and Lisieux. But since they'd argued Richard's case before the papal curia, Archbishop Gautier was not likely to give their words much weight. She needed more influential allies before a council could be called to debate Joanna's request.

⚜

OF ALL HENRY'S SONS, it was generally conceded that the one who most closely resembled him was his bastard Geoff, York's reluctant archbishop. His russet hair was well sprinkled with grey these days, for he was not that far from his fiftieth birthday, and he'd gained weight as his youth slipped away. But he remained as outspoken and obstinate as he'd ever been, and although he politely heard Eleanor out, he was already shaking his head by the time she was done speaking.

"Do not mistake me, Madame. My heart goes out to your daughter, my half sister. And her wish to take holy vows is a most commendable one. Alas, it cannot be done without her husband's consent."

"If he were here, my lord archbishop, he would give it gladly." Geoff had never mastered the art of dissembling, and his doubt showed so plainly on his face that Eleanor drew an angry breath. But she kept her voice even as she said, "Do you truly believe he would deny his wife salvation?"

"I do not know the Count of Toulouse well enough to say. He has not always been a friend to the Holy Church, after all."

Eleanor opened her mouth to argue that Raimond de St Gilles was not a heretic, whatever slanderous stories Geoff might have heard. But she knew that road led nowhere. She studied her husband's most devoted son with calculating eyes, and then she almost smiled, for she'd realized how to break through his barriers.

"I am not asking you to do this for me or for John. You do not even have to do it for Joanna. Do it for your father. Harry loved Joanna dearly, as you well know. Do not let his daughter go to her death fearing that she is damned."

He looked startled, but not defensive, and she took hope from that. Knowing he was not a man to be prodded, she kept silent as he considered this most personal of appeals. "If you are truly sure that the Count of Toulouse would give his permission," he finally said, "then I see no harm in granting Lady Joanna's wishes. But I doubt that the Archbishop of Rouen will see it in that light. Do you want me to speak with him?"

"That is very kind of you, but not necessary," Eleanor said quickly, for he had never been noted for his powers of persuasion; his impatience and lack of tact inevitably irked those he was trying to convince. She agreed that Archbishop Gautier must be won over, but she had a more eloquent advocate in mind than Geoff.

🙚

"IT IS TRULY PROVIDENTIAL that you should be in Rouen now, when Richard's sister has such need of you, my lord archbishop."

Hubert Walter nodded gravely, while silently saluting her for that adroit "Richard's sister." Not that he needed reminding of all he owed Richard, but he did not blame her for using every weapon at her disposal on her daughter's behalf. "This grieves me more than I can say, Madame. I hold your daughter in high esteem." And while that was the response demanded by courtesy, it was also true; he'd become quite fond of Richard's spirited sister during their time in the Holy Land.

"If I may speak candidly, my lord Hubert, my daughter needs more than your grief. She desperately needs your help."

"And she shall have it," he said, so readily that she closed her eyes for a moment, blessing Richard for making this man Canterbury's archbishop. "I do not see how the Church would be threatened by granting a woman's deathbed wish, one that does honor to the Almighty and the sisters of Fontevrault. But some of my brethren embrace canon law the way soldiers embrace whores—with great enthusiasm. We will need a cogent, compelling argument to overcome Archbishop Gautier's qualms."

Eleanor had one. "Tell them," she said, "that Joanna's desire to take holy vows is the result of a vision. The Blessed Mother Mary came to her in a dream and told her what she must do. She is but seeking to honor that divine command."

Hubert nodded again and then he smiled faintly. "Yes, that ought to do it."

🙚

AS ELEANOR ENTERED THE STAIRWELL leading up to Joanna's bedchamber, she came to an abrupt halt at the sight of the couple cloaked in shadows. For a moment, she felt rage spark through her exhaustion, anger that one of Joanna's ladies would have arranged a tryst as her mistress lay dying. But then she realized that Morgan was holding Mariam as she wept against his shoulder and she was suddenly very frightened, fearing she was too late.

They'd turned at the sound of her footsteps. Although it was too dark to see her face clearly, they sensed her distress and Morgan said quickly, "No, Madame, no. Your daughter still lives."

Mariam moved out of Morgan's embrace. "It was the letters," she said in a choked voice. "You know about them, Madame? She dictated one to her husband and one to Queen Berengaria. Today she wanted to write two more . . . to her son and daughter, for when they are old enough to read them, to understand. . . ." She fought back a sob. "I thought of her children never knowing their mother, not knowing how much she loved them, and I . . . I could not bear it." And there was so much emotion in her voice that Eleanor knew she, too, had lost her mother at a young age.

Eleanor reached out, letting her hand rest for a moment upon Mariam's arm. "Come with me," she said. "I have news for my daughter, and you both will want to hear it, too."

JOANNA DRIFTED IN AND OUT of sleep more and more as her days dwindled. Sometimes her dreams offered respite. She rode through the streets of Toulouse at Raimond's side, chased after Raimondet when he fled, giggling, from his bath, stood again on that ship's deck as Messina came into view and she saw the fleet in the harbor, saw her brother's red-and-gold banners flying from every mast. At other times, her dreams brought only terror, offering her a foretaste of what awaited her after death—lakes of flame, rivers of boiling blood, visions of fire and brimstone made familiar by the priests who preached incessantly of the horrors of Hell, in which suffering was eternal and there was neither hope nor mercy, for there was no God.

Her latest dream had been kinder, wafting her back to her own childhood, to Poitiers and Sicily. She was still glad to awaken, though, when she opened her eyes and saw Eleanor leaning over the bed. She knew she clung to a precipice and only her mother could keep her from falling into the abyss. "Maman . . . ?"

"The council has met, Joanna. They have agreed to disregard canon law and permit you to take vows as a sister of Fontevrault."

"Truly? You would not lie to me, Maman?"

"No, my dearest, I would not lie. The Archbishop of Canterbury convinced them that you'd been blessed with a vision, that you were doing God's bidding and it was not for them to thwart His Will."

Joanna had wept more in the four months since she'd learned of Richard's death than she had in all the years since she'd flowered into womanhood. But now the tears were different; they were tears of joy for the most precious gift she'd ever received—salvation.

"Thank you, Maman, thank you!" She tired very easily and soon afterward, she slept again. But this time she fell asleep smiling.

❧

"WHAT OF MY BABY?"

This was the question Eleanor had been expecting and dreading. Joanna had spoken of her child's plight before, but her fear of eternal damnation had been like a vast, smothering storm cloud, blotting out the sky. Now that she no longer need fear for herself, it was only natural that she would fear for the baby in her womb.

Eleanor was not the only one loath to address that plaintive query. Master Gervase, her physician, took a sudden interest in a psalter lying open on the table. Joanna's chaplain, Jocelyn, began to finger the Paternoster looped at his belt. The two midwives, Dame Clarice and Dame Berthe, remained silent. Nor did Joanna's attendants speak up, for none of them wanted to discuss one of their Church's most troubling teachings—that unbaptized infants were denied entry into Heaven.

Joanna knew that, of course, for it cast a shadow over every woman's birthing chamber, the knowledge that babies who died before they could be christened could not be buried in consecrated ground; few city cemeteries did not have small, pitiful mounds bordering the graves in hallowed soil, looking lonely, untended, and forlorn. But what gave parents the greatest grief was knowing their dead children would be consigned to Limbo for eternity, never to look upon the face of God.

Joanna's question seemed to echo in the air, the cry of mothers since time immemorial. Abbot Luke at last took up the burden, grateful that at least he no longer need tell her that her child would suffer the torments of the damned. For much of their Church's history, priests could give grieving parents no comfort at all, but in the last fifty years, there had been a change for the better, thanks in some measure to the controversial French theologian Abelard, who'd argued persuasively that St Augustine was wrong and babies guilty only of original sin would not burn like the sinners cast down into Hell. Although Abelard had disgraced himself by seducing the beautiful young Heloise, Abbot Luke was glad that his doctrine had gained such quick acceptance, sparing him the need to defend the indefensible.

"Whilst your baby will not be able to pass through Heaven's Gates, my lady," he said gently, "in *Limbus Infantium*, he or she will suffer only the pain of loss, not the pain of fire."

Joanna looked sadly at the abbot. *But he will have lost the vision of God, so even if there is no physical torment, he will endure spiritual torment for all eternity. Not only will he be denied God's Love, he'll be denied the love of his family. He'll never know his father, his brother and sister. He'll never know his mother.*

She said none of that, though, for Abbot Luke was a good man. He did not deserve to be berated for a misery not of his making. Nor had her question been directed at him or her chaplain. Her gaze moved past the abbot, seeking out the two midwives. Dame Berthe had been summoned first, but although she'd come highly recommended, she'd not found favor with Joanna's ladies—a tall, raw-boned, awkward woman with scant social skills and a blunt tongue. Beatrix and Anna had taken it upon themselves to find Dame Clarice, a soft, motherly soul who was sugar to Berthe's salt. It was Clarice who came forward now, blue eyes brimming with tears, for she knew what Joanna would ask and what she must answer.

"I have heard," Joanna said haltingly, "that there are ways of baptizing a child whilst still in the womb."

"That is so, my lady. Sometimes when a mother is unable to deliver her baby and they are both sure to die, a baptismal sponge can be inserted up into her womb so he can be blessed with God's grace."

"Then . . . you can do that for my son?" Seeing the midwife's lips tremble, the tears start to trickle down those rosy cheeks, Joanna felt such pain that she gave an anguished cry. "Why not? I beg you, save my son!"

"My lady, I would if I could! But that can only be done when the woman has begun labor and her womb is dilated."

Joanna had known she'd been clutching at a frail reed. That did not make it any easier to accept. "Surely there must be something you can do," she whispered, although without any real hope. It was then, though, that the other midwife spoke up.

"There is a way," Dame Berthe said, striding forward to stand beside the bed, "although some are squeamish about it. When a woman dies, her child can survive briefly through the air still in her arteries. If it is done quickly enough, the child can be extracted from her womb in time to be baptized."

There was a shocked silence as they realized what she had in mind. Joanna's ladies recoiled at the thought of her body being cut open like this. The physician and her chaplain were clearly skeptical, for midwives were often suspected of baptizing stillborn children in order to comfort their sorrowing parents. But Joanna's eyes shone with sudden light and Eleanor moved closer so she could look intently into the midwife's face.

"You could do this for my son?" Joanna reached out, took the midwife's hand; it was as big as a man's, the knuckles reddened, the nails bitten to the quick, an old scar burned deep into one thumb. Not a hand to elicit admiring glances, no more than she herself was. But Joanna felt the strength in that ungainly hand, felt as if she'd just been thrown a lifeline.

"I can, my lady."

That was too much for the physician. "The child is not due for two months or more. How could he draw air into his lungs?"

The midwife met his accusing gaze calmly. "Women often mistake the time of conception. The countess could be further along than she first thought. And it is my understanding that it takes but one breath, however faint, to make a baptism valid."

"She is right," Abbot Luke said, speaking for the first time. "One breath is sufficient."

The other midwife had remained conspicuously silent, an obvious way of conveying her disapproval. Joanna's ladies still found it abhorrent, for there was an inbred, innate dread of the mutilation of the body after death. But now all eyes shifted instinctively toward Joanna's mother, watching as she leaned over to murmur in her daughter's ear. When Joanna nodded vehemently, Eleanor straightened up and turned back to the midwife.

"Do it," she said.

⚜

JOANNA WAS TOO WEAK to rise from her bed to take her vows. But her voice was surprisingly strong as she pledged herself to God, and afterward, it was obvious to them all that she was at peace. She even sought to console her weeping women, assuring them that she was in God's keeping and, with a flash of the

Joanna of old, she scolded Mariam and Morgan, saying that if they did not wed, she'd come back to haunt them both. She asked again for the small ivory casket that held locks of her children's hair, instructing them to add a long strand of her own hair.

"Give it to Raimond," she murmured. "Tell him he must not grieve too much, that he made me happy." When Eleanor reached for her hand, she entwined their fingers together as she'd so often done as a small child. "I will tell Richard that Johnny owes his crown to you, Maman. Knowing Johnny, he is probably jealous that you gave me something far greater than a crown. You gave me eternal life."

She seemed to have been rejuvenated by the taking of her vows, and her women dared to hope that her death was not as imminent as they'd feared, that they might have more time to say their farewells. Eleanor alone was not deceived by this sudden burst of vitality, seeing it for what it was: the last flaming of the sun ere night came on. She knew that her daughter's life was ebbing away even as they watched, for her green eyes were darkening. She'd seen Richard's eyes change, too, in the moments before death, as his pupils dilated until they'd eclipsed all traces of grey.

"Dame Berthe?" Joanna beckoned for the midwife to approach the bed. "You will do as you promised?" The midwife was as phlegmatic as always, repeating her promise without the slightest hint of emotion or empathy, but to Joanna, this rough-hewn, taciturn woman was one of God's own angels, and she gave Eleanor a meaningful look, wanting to be sure her mother would reward Berthe as she deserved. What value, though, could be placed upon a baby's immortal soul? No matter, Maman would find a way. She always did.

Eleanor was warned when she felt her daughter's grip loosen. "There is so much light," Joanna said, softly but distinctly. She died soon after that, and Eleanor would always believe it was with the name of her son on her lips.

⚜

JOANNA'S WOMEN HAD RETREATED in haste as soon as she'd drawn her last breath, for none of them could bear to watch as the midwife cut Joanna's baby from her womb. Eleanor had drained the last of her reserves, too. Upon returning to her own chamber, she dismissed her attendants. Her eyes were dry, for she did not think she had any tears left. She could not mourn, nor could she pray.

Sitting on the bed, she could only stare blindly into space, too emotionally exhausted to feel anything yet, as if she were lost in Limbo like those legions of unbaptized babies.

The knock on the door came as a surprise even though she'd been expecting it. Getting wearily to her feet, she crossed the chamber to admit Dame Berthe.

"It was a son, my lady. I baptized him Richard as the countess wished."

The eyes of the two women caught and held. And then Eleanor thanked the midwife, telling her to return on the morrow. Once she was alone again, Eleanor crossed to a window-seat and opened the shutters. Joanna's last day seemed more like high summer than early September, the sun burning away clouds in a sky so blue it could have come from a potter's wheel. She gazed up at that blazing sphere of white heat until the bright, dazzling light began to hurt her eyes. She'd always hoped to have a grandson named Richard, a worthy namesake of the man who would be five months dead in just two days' time. Because he was so premature, she very much doubted that Joanna's son had drawn that one crucial, life-affirming breath. But she did not care that the midwife had lied. And she did not think that God would care, either.

⟡

AT FIRST READING, Joanna's letter had seemed to offer good news, for she assured Raimond that her nausea had finally abated. She told him then, though, that he should delay his visit, for she'd decided to join her mother at Rouen. He'd have preferred that she'd stayed at Fontevrault, for he'd need an additional week of travel to reach Rouen. But he understood her desire to be with Eleanor as her time drew nigh. His indomitable mother-in-law put him in mind of those ancient Greek legends of a warrior race of women called Amazons. And Dame Esquiva agreed with him that Joanna must indeed be on the mend if she felt well enough to make that long journey. So he took solace in that and made arrangements to leave for Rouen before Michaelmas, intending to stay with Joanna until the birth of their child.

Yet he was not easy about this ill-starred pregnancy, which had done such damage to his wife's health and kept them apart for so long. Again and again, he'd cursed himself for allowing her to make that stubborn pilgrimage to seek aid from Richard. If only he'd forbidden it, she'd be awaiting her confinement here in Toulouse, under the care of Dame Esquiva, a midwife she knew and trusted. He smiled ruefully then, for trying to turn Joanna into a docile, submissive wife would be like hitching a purebred mare to a plough. Whilst it might be possible, what man in his right senses would want to do it?

A PALL HUNG OVER the count's castle at Toulouse. People spoke in hushed whispers, their gazes drawn toward the stairwell that led to the count's bedchamber. He'd been up there for hours, ever since he'd gotten the English queen's letter. He'd gone ashen at the sight of Eleanor's seal, broke it with shaking fingers, and then turned away without saying a word. It was left to the queen's messenger to tell them that the Lady Joanna was dead and, with her, the count's infant son.

RAIMOND DID NOT KNOW what time it was, not sure if hours or days had passed. He'd refused food, all feeble attempts at comfort, his chaplain's offer of prayers, but he'd finally admitted a servant with wine. Empty flagons lay scattered about in the floor rushes. *Like discarded gravestones,* he thought hazily. He was not truly drunk, though; God had denied him that mercy. Moving aimlessly to the window, he pulled the shutters back, gazing out at a night of heartbreaking beauty; the moon was in its last quarter, a silvered crescent floating in an infinite ebony sea. During those summer months without Joanna, he'd liked to remind himself that they were gazing up each night at the same starlit sky. It was a poetic way of keeping her closer to him. Now all he could think was that she'd never look upon the sky again.

When he opened the door, he tripped over a shadow that yelped when he stepped on it. He gave a startled cry of his own before recognizing Ahmer, one of Joanna's Sicilian hounds. He knew Joanna was being mourned in Toulouse, for she'd been popular with the men and women of his city. But somehow it was the dog's lonely vigil that caught at his heart. With Ahmer at his heels, he slowly climbed the stairs to the small chamber above his own. A wet nurse was sleeping on a pallet beside his daughter's cradle; she was swaddled like a butterfly waiting to hatch from its cocoon. Nearby, Raimondet was sprawled on his back, snoring gently, and fresh tears came as Raimond recalled how proud the little boy was when he'd been allowed to sleep in a bed of his own.

Reaching down, he lifted his son into his arms. Raimondet whimpered, his lashes flickering, but then he sank back into sleep, snuggling against Raimond's shoulder. He'd have to be told, but he was too young, at two, to understand. He would keep asking for "Mama" as he'd been doing all summer. Until her memory faded, until he could no longer remember the woman who'd sung him to sleep at night and made him squeal with laughter when she'd tickled him and pretended not to see him when he'd hidden behind the billowing bed curtains.

For Raimond, this was the pain that tore him apart, even harder to bear than the realization that he'd never hear her laugh again or make love to her or see her sleepy smile upon awakening in the morning. "I will not let him forget you, Joanna," he whispered. "I promise you that, my love, upon the surety of my soul."

CHAPTER THIRTY-NINE

❧

SEPTEMBER 1199

Le Mans, Anjou

John's smile reminded Constance of a cat who'd just gotten into the cream. As little as she'd liked Richard, she'd never had trouble envisioning him as a king. But John? If he were fit to rule, then unicorns roamed the Breton hills and mermaids sunned themselves on Breton beaches. Having to make peace with him was not easy, but they'd concluded they had no choice. Despite Arthur's early successes, it had become obvious that the scales were weighted in John's favor. Moreover, the Bretons were growing uncomfortable with Philippe's heavy hand on the reins; his support of Arthur was coming at a higher price than Constance was willing to pay. She'd already made a dutiful curtsy to the new king, and she watched now as her son knelt before the dais. As always, she felt great pride. Even at twelve, he was poised and self-confident, so handsome that his smile never failed to catch at her heart. She'd explained why they had to accept John's kingship—to buy time until Arthur was old enough to challenge John himself. He said he'd understood, but he had not liked it any, and she was relieved now when the fealty ceremony went off without a hitch.

John was in good spirits. He'd greatly enjoyed watching his young rival humble himself and he had a surprise in store for the lad's prideful mother, too. Leaning back in his seat, he regarded Constance with a smile that put her instantly on guard.

"I have news for you, my lady, that I am sure will please you as much as it pleases me. Now that your marriage to the Earl of Chester has been annulled and you have done your grieving over his loss—for I know how much you valued him—I think it is time to find you another husband. I am not often given to quoting from Scriptures, but I believe St Paul counseled that *it is better to marry than to burn.*"

Constance heard a low murmur from her barons, a growl of pure displeasure. Arthur was frowning, too, even though he was not likely to have understood John's silken malice, the implication that Constance found her bed a cold one. She alone was not surprised, for she'd been expecting an ambush like this; she'd lived amongst the Angevins since she was a small child.

"Are you offering to begin a husband hunt for me, my lord king? How very kind."

"Not at all. Naturally I want the best for my former sister-by-marriage. But there is no need to 'begin a husband hunt.' I've already found him." John let the suspense drag out, his eyes gleaming. "I am sure you will be very happy with . . . Sir Guy de Thouars."

The growl behind Constance became a snarl. From the corner of her eye, she caught a glimpse of Guy and his brother the viscount. Aimery's expression was almost comical it was so conflicted—pride that his House would be able to boast such a highborn sister-in-law warring with astonished jealousy that his younger brother was to become a duke. Guy, quite simply, looked as if he'd been poleaxed.

"Your generosity leaves me speechless, my lord king," Constance said coldly. "I am sure you will understand that I must consult with my son and my barons and bishops about something so important as my marriage."

"Of course," John said, and she thought of cats again, for he was practically purring. "By all means, discuss it. But I have every confidence that you will reach the right conclusion—now that you and your son have been restored to royal favor."

He smiled genially, but Constance heard the unmistakable sound of a sword being slid halfway up its scabbard. And as she looked at her lords, she saw that they'd heard it, too.

❧

THERE WERE EIGHT MEN in the chamber and all but one were in a state of high dudgeon. Constance sat in a window-seat and listened wearily. They were cursing John in the most intemperate language she had ever heard, and she was accustomed to the Angevins' creative use of profanity; even the bishops of Rennes and Vannes were joining in. While they were enraged that John should meddle in Breton matters so blatantly, it was the choice of husband for Constance that had their tempers at full blaze. They considered it a mortal insult that John should have selected Guy de Thouars, a landless younger brother of a Poitevin lord, and none of them were shy about saying so.

At last the others fell silent, yielding to Guillaume des Roches and the de Vitré brothers, André and Robert. Des Roches was an Angevin lord, but Richard had given him the heiress of the barony of Sable, which lay close to Brittany, and he'd supported Arthur over John after Richard's death. He'd been outraged, though, when Philippe had razed Ballon, a castle that ought to have been Arthur's, and then disdainfully dismissed his protest as if it were of no matter. His had been the most vocal and persuasive voice of those urging Arthur to make peace with John. Now he was the only one urging them not to act rashly, saying the marriage was not as demeaning as the others claimed. He was at once shouted down.

"John is mocking us, my lady," André de Vitré spat, "by offering you such an unworthy husband! The Duchess of Brittany to wed a man with no title, no lands of his own, no prospects?"

André's denunciation was not quite accurate, for the viscounts of Thouars did not pass their lands from father to son, but from brother to brother, so although Aimery had three sons of his own, if Guy outlived him, he'd eventually become the next viscount. Constance knew that, but she did not bother to correct him, for the gist of his complaint was true. The possibility that Guy might one day inherit his brother's title was not enough to transform him into a suitable match for the Duchess of Brittany. She did respond, however, when Robert de Vitré charged John with deliberately forcing her into a disparaging marriage to shame her, to shame them all.

"I am not defending John," she said. "I'd sooner walk barefoot to Mont St Michel clad only in my chemise. But I do not think he chose Guy de Thouars because he wanted to degrade me. I suspect his primary concern is to see me wed to someone 'safe,' someone he can trust to do his bidding."

They saw that as an even more damning accusation. Constance let them rant and fume, for she knew how little it meant. She'd known that John would exact a price for his peace and that she'd likely be the one to pay it. Her eyes came to rest upon her son, slouched down in the other window-seat; he was sulking because none of the men were paying him any mind and not happy at the thought of his mother remarrying.

"We have to face the truth," she finally said, "however little we like it. John's father forced me to wed a man of his choosing whilst he knew I was still grieving for Geoffrey, for his own son. Why should John be any more merciful? If I balk at wedding this man, he'll compel me to wed another, one even less acceptable than Guy de Thouars, as punishment for my defiance."

Their silence was a reluctant acknowledgment that they knew she was right. Only Arthur did not understand. "Maman? What will you do then?"

What I've always done—what I must. "I think," she said, "that I shall have to talk to Sir Guy."

THEY WERE WALKING in the palace gardens, trailed at a discreet distance by several of her ladies and barons, for Constance wanted to talk with Guy herself before subjecting him to an interrogation by her Breton lords. She did not know him well, but she'd not forgotten his kindness at St James de Beuvron, and she thought he was a decent man. Of course, so was Randolph of Chester, as loath as she was to admit that. She would never forgive him for holding her prisoner, yet she knew he was not evil. Slanting a sidelong glance toward Guy, she murmured, "So this took you by surprise, too?"

"Good God, yes!" he said and laughed. "I'd sooner have expected to be told the cardinals in Rome had elected our parish priest in Thouars as the next Pope."

She found his candor refreshing, accustomed as she was to a world in which all had ulterior motives and royal courts were breeding grounds for intrigue and double-dealing. "My barons think John chose you because you lack a title, Sir Guy. I think he was more interested in your fidelity to the Angevin House." Coming to a halt on the walkway, she looked up intently into his face. "I've been told that you were very loyal to Richard."

He nodded, no longer smiling. "I would have followed the king into Hell itself if need be."

That was not what she'd wanted to hear, but at least he'd been honest. "Well, you followed him to Germany," she said dryly, "so that was close enough to Hell, I expect. And John?"

"He is my liege lord," he said, and she gave him another searching look, for he sounded dutiful, not enthusiastic. Who would be enthusiastic about serving

John, though, with his history of broken promises and betrayals? They walked in silence for several moments before he said, "There is this you must know, my lady. If we were to wed, my first loyalty would then be to you, as my wife."

He sounded sincere. She knew how easily sincerity was feigned, yet she sensed no guile in him. "So you'd not resolve any of our marital disputes by locking me up in the castle keep?"

"Jesu, no!" he exclaimed before realizing that she was being flippant. He smiled again, ruefully this time. "My brother thinks I am a chivalrous fool," he admitted, "and he may be right. But I am comfortable in my own skin, my lady, and have no desire to be other than as I am."

Constance thought there were worse fates than being married to a chivalrous fool. "I believe you to be an honorable man," she said, "and I think you have a good heart."

"I sense a 'but' coming," he said lightly. "I was planning to plead my case with you. Yet I do not know how persuasive an argument it is to say, 'You could do worse, much worse than me.'"

Constance was realizing that Guy was also quite likable—and that he had a very engaging smile. He was not at all like Geoffrey. But mayhap that was for the best. "Did you mean it when you said that if we were wed, your first loyalty would be to me?"

"Yes—to you and to our children."

For some reason, that caught her by surprise. "You want children?"

"Of course. Do you not want them, too?"

During her marriage to the Earl of Chester, the last thing she'd wanted was to become pregnant. Whilst she was no longer young, women of thirty-eight could still get with child. Would she want that? "Yes . . . I think I do."

Still, she hesitated. Was it such a risk, though? If he were to prove too troublesome, her barons could always run him out of Brittany as they had Chester. Why not take this attractive, good-humored man? For indeed, she could do much worse. "Very well," she said. "I will marry you, Sir Guy."

"You truly will?" He laughed, looking so boyishly elated that she could not help laughing, too. At least he had the mother wit to understand how lucky he was.

She was not expecting what he did next, for so far they'd discussed the marriage as the political arrangement it was. But he stepped forward then, tilted her face up to his, and kissed her.

"I shall do my best to make sure you have no regrets," he vowed, and kissed her again. The first kiss had been tentative. This one was not, and Constance found herself responding to it. It had been so long since a man had shown her tenderness. She felt as if her body were awakening after years of sleep. His mouth was warm, and when he pulled her to him, she did not care that she was embracing a stranger in a public garden, probably under the shocked eyes of her ladies and barons.

When they ended the embrace, she gazed up at him in wonderment, for this was the first time that she'd felt herself free of Geoffrey's ghost. He'd always hovered close at hand during her unsatisfactory couplings with Randolph, reminding her of all she'd had and lost. Was it possible that Guy de Thouars could exorcise his sardonic spirit, banish him back to the realm of memory where ghosts belonged?

It was obvious to her that Guy had been singed by the same flame. He was still holding her close, his body offering her flattering proof that he desired the woman, not just the duchess. "When," he asked throatily, "can we wed? I'd say the sooner, the better!"

One of John's spies later reported on their garden encounter, and upon being told that he'd seen Constance and Guy laughing together as if they were lovers, not political pawns, John frowned, for that was not what he'd expected to hear.

THE PEACE BETWEEN UNCLE and nephew was to be short-lived, not even lasting a day and night. John deeply offended the thin-skinned Viscount of Thouars by suddenly taking Chinon Castle and the seneschalship of Anjou away from him. While the Bretons did not yet know John intended to bestow it upon his new vassal, Guillaume des Roches, their mistrust of John was so strong that they saw sinister significance in this move. When Arthur was then warned that John intended to ensure his good faith by holding him prisoner, they found it easy to believe, and the young duke, his mother, her new husband-to-be, his disgruntled brother, and most of the Breton lords left Le Mans abruptly for the greater safety of Angers. Philippe was quite happy to fish in these troubled waters again and Arthur was soon back in Paris. John had succeeded in luring Guillaume des Roches away from the Bretons, yet he'd missed his last chance to remove Arthur from the French king's influence. Despite her flight to Angers, Constance honored her promise and wed Guy de Thouars, although John considered that small consolation for his failure to deny Philippe such a dangerous weapon.

DENISE ENTERED THEIR BEDCHAMBER at Châteauroux with a lighter step, for she hoped she was bringing a guest to pierce the dark cloud that had been hovering over their lives since Richard's death. In time, she was confident God would heal the wound, but for now André's pain was so raw that she could not look upon it without flinching.

André was sharpening his sword on a whetstone, and did not glance up at the sound of the opening door; it was as if even his natural curiosity had withered, leaving nothing but apathy and indifference.

"You have a visitor," she said. "Sir Morgan ap Ranulf has just ridden in. Shall I send him up?" And she took heart when he nodded. He continued to concentrate upon honing the blade, not putting the weapon aside until Denise ushered Morgan into the chamber. "I'll send a servant up with wine," she said, and got only a distracted nod in return.

Morgan sat down beside André in the window-seat. "I came to bid you farewell," he said, "for I see no place for me in John's realm."

"What . . . you're not looking forward to serving your new king?"

Morgan smiled sadly, for André's sarcasm was as betraying as another man's tears. "John is not my king, will never be my king."

"Where will you go, Morgan? Back to Wales, I suppose."

"No . . . there is no place for me there, either, not anymore. My father left his Welsh lands to my brother and his English manors to me. I am selling them, as well as the Norman estates that Richard gave me. And once that is done, Mariam and I are moving to Sicily."

André's brown eyes showed their first spark of interest. "Good for you, Cousin," he said, although they were not actually kinsmen, for his blood ties to Richard had come through Eleanor and Morgan's through Henry. "I wish you well and Godspeed. I daresay you'll hear about it eventually, but at least you'll not have to watch as John loses the empire that was his father's lifework, the empire that Richard died defending. I can only hope that it does not happen whilst his mother still lives."

Morgan did not dispute André's dark vision, for he shared it. His heart bled for the other man, for André and Denise's lands were in Berry, which meant that he must choose between drinking hemlock or wolfsbane, doing homage either to John or to Philippe. In October he'd accepted the French king as his liege lord, and Morgan knew he'd sooner have pledged his fealty to Lucifer himself. He did not offer sympathy, for André neither expected nor wanted it. Instead, he said, "I am taking Arne with us. He needs a new beginning, too."

André summoned up his first real smile. "It gladdens me to hear that." He made an effort then to shake off his lethargy, for he owed Morgan that much. "Stay the night," he said, "and we'll find some battles to refight over dinner. But on the morrow, take your woman and Arne and do not look back, Morgan. The world as we knew it died at Châlus."

ELEANOR RETURNED TO Fontevrault Abbey on a day of glimmering grey mist and wintry drizzle. While her entourage continued on to her own quarters on the abbey grounds, she was warmly received by the Abbess Mathilde, Prioress Aliza, and her granddaughter Alix, now a novice nun. They offered their sympathies for the death of her daughter, telling her that Lady Joanna's desire to take holy vows on her deathbed had brought great honor to their order.

Eleanor inclined her head. "It gave her comfort in her last hours." She said no more than that and they said no more, either, for her grieving was painful to look upon, but intensely private, shielded from the world by a fierce pride that conceded little, asked for even less. When they told her how happy they were to have her back at their abbey, she inclined her head again.

"I regret that I cannot stay for long. My son and the French king are meeting after Christmas, hoping to make a lasting peace by the marriage of Philippe's son to my granddaughter, and I have agreed to go to Castile to fetch her."

If she had any qualms about making such a long, dangerous, winter journey across the Pyrenees at her advanced age, she gave no indication of it, and the nuns knew better than to admit their own misgivings. Instead, they expressed their pleasure that her granddaughter should one day become Queen of France.

Thank God Almighty that Philippe is so entangled in his own marital web, caught between the queen he does not want and the concubine the Church will not recognize. Eleanor would have found it difficult to consent to a marriage between her daughter's child and a man she'd not have trusted with one of her greyhounds. Whilst she knew little about twelve-year-old Louis, at least he was not his father. She did not share these thoughts with the nuns, of course, and echoed their polite wishes that this marriage might end the war, even though she knew that there would be no lasting peace between the kingdoms of England and France as long as Philippe Capet drew breath.

She soon rose, expressing the desire to visit the church ere returning to her own chambers, pausing at the door to say, "Two of my daughter's ladies have accompanied me. Dame Beatrix and Dame Alicia served Joanna faithfully in life and they wish to take holy vows as she did. They are both of gentle birth, Beatrix the daughter and widow of knights and Alicia the sister of a Templar." The abbess and prioress quickly assured her that they would gladly welcome the countess's ladies. She'd expected such cooperation, for their abbey was now the royal sepulchre for the Angevin dynasty.

THE RAIN WAS HEAVIER now and puddles were forming on the walkway. Silver droplets clung to bare tree branches, glistened like scattered seed pearls in the wilted, wet grass, but the rain felt cold against her skin. She drew her mantle more closely, remembering the superstition that it was lucky when it rained on the day of a funeral, as if Heaven itself were weeping for the deceased. It had not rained when her son and daughter were buried within the span of five months. She'd wept even if Heaven had not, shedding her tears behind closed doors in those endless hours ere the dawn.

The church was empty and her footsteps echoed loudly upon the tiled floor as she moved up the nave. Smoldering torches in wall recesses did not keep the shadows at bay, but she had no fear of the dark.

"I did all I could to gain him the crown, Harry," she said softly, glancing toward the nuns' choir, where her husband and son's tombs lay. "But it will be up to John to hold on to it."

When she paused, the only sound that came to her was the soft patter of rain upon the roof. Fool. Did she think she'd hear voices from the grave? There were no places to sit, only prayer cushions scattered about the floor, and she suddenly felt very tired. She leaned against the altar, thinking that the Almighty would not begrudge her aching bones the support.

"When I return from Castile, Harry, I shall arrange for Joanna's reburial. It was her dying wish that she be buried with you and Richard. I shall have effigies made for you all, and one for myself. I doubt that I can rely upon John to have it done after I die. He loved Richard not and cannot admit his guilt over betraying you, not even to himself."

It did not seem strange to her, talking to the husband who'd been her gaoler.

They'd been married for thirty-seven years, had loved and fought and lusted after empires and each other. And they'd buried too many children.

"Just two left, Harry," she whispered. "Lives cut short ere their time. But living too long is a cruelty, too. I know that losing Hal well-nigh broke your heart. At least you were not there as he drew his last breath; at least you were spared that. There is no greater pain than to watch your child die."

She slowly sank to her knees before the altar. But she did not pray. She wept for her dead.

EPILOGUE

SHE WAS BURNING WITH FEVER, but she welcomed it, eager to shed the body that had become her enemy. It would be soon now, for she was slipping her moorings, one by one, tethered by gossamer threads that trembled with each labored breath she drew. Gradually she became aware that she was no longer alone. She opened her eyes, but she saw only swirling shadows, candles that glimmered like distant stars in the dark.

"God's bones, woman, how much longer are you going to make us wait?"

She'd not heard that voice, once so familiar, for nigh on sixteen years. "Harry?" she whispered, suddenly uncertain.

"Of course it is me," he said, sounding surprised and faintly defensive. "Who else? Do not tell me you expected that milksop Louis to keep vigil at your deathbed?"

"I am not sure I expected you to keep vigil, either, Harry," she confessed.

"Well, if you make me wait much longer, I'll be off," he warned. "You are nigh on eighty, Eleanor. Are you going to outlive Methuselah from sheer contrariness?"

"Will you stop badgering her? You can see, Maman, that eternity has not improved his temper any."

"Richard?" Tears blurred her eyes, tears of joy. She sensed others were there, too, beloved ghosts so long gone from her life, torn from her heart. Her sins had been many, but she'd atoned for them, endured her Purgatory and Hell here on earth. There was nothing to fear. The sudden silence alarmed her, though. Surely they'd wait for her? "Richard? Harry? Do not go! Stay with me. . . ."

"We are here," came the reassuring answer. "We are here."

RICHENZA SLIPPED QUIETLY INTO the chamber, holding a candle aloft. At her wordless query, Dame Amaria shook her head, saying that the queen had not regained consciousness. "But she was talking, my lady."

"She's done that before," Richenza said sadly. She yearned for some last lucid moments with her grandmother, but Eleanor's fevered murmurings were incoherent, not meant for them.

"This was different, my lady. She said 'Harry' and 'Richard' so very clearly. It was . . . it was as if she were speaking to them, that they were right here in the chamber with us. The doctor insists it was the fever, but I do not think so. See for yourself, my lady."

Richenza turned toward the bed and her eyes widened. It had been a long time since her grandmother had looked as she did now—at peace. It was as if all the pain and grief of her last years had been erased, and the candlelight was kind, hinting at the great beauty she'd once been in the sculptured hollows of her cheekbones and the flushed color restored by fever. Leaning over, Richenza took the dying woman's hand.

"Granddame?" Eleanor did not respond, but Richenza was suddenly sure she was listening to other voices, for the corners of her mouth were curving in what could have been a smile.

AFTERWORD

JOHN'S HISTORY IS WELL KNOWN, of course. His kingship was not a successful one. He lost Normandy, Anjou, Maine, and Richard's "fair daughter," Château Gaillard, and when he died in November 1216, he was fighting for his survival, abandoned by two-thirds of his barons, with a French army on English soil. However, he is always great fun to write about.

Berengaria never married again and struggled in vain to obtain her dower payments from John. She was treated more fairly by the French king, and Philippe bestowed the city of Le Mans upon her in return for her surrender of her dower lands in Normandy. During her long widowhood, she was known as the Lady of Le Mans, and she devoted herself to works of piety, proving to be a generous patron of the Church. She founded the Cistercian abbey of l'Epau near Le Mans, and she was buried there after her death on December 23, 1230. Although several safe conducts were issued to her, there is no evidence that she ever utilized them, and she remains the only Queen of England never to set foot on English soil.

Richard's son Philip seems to have died young, for the last mention of him occurs in 1201. The usually reliable chronicler Roger de Hoveden reported that Philip killed the Viscount of Limoges to avenge his father's death. Viscount Aimar did die in 1199, but historians tend to discount the story because it was not reported anywhere else. Since Roger de Hoveden would not have invented it, there must have been a rumor to this effect, which is interesting in and of itself, for rumors shed light on medieval public opinion. It is sometimes reported that Richard had a second illegitimate son, Fulk, but this has not been documented.

Raimond de St Gilles's subsequent history is a tragic one, for he would find himself caught up in the Albigensian Crusade, one of the darker chapters in the history of the Church. I will discuss his fate in greater detail in the Author's

Note. The year after Joanna's death, he wed Anna, the Damsel of Cyprus. I was not surprised by this, as Anna was said to be very attached to Joanna and people grieving for a loved one often turn to each other for comfort. Whatever their reasons for the marriage, it did not last long—less than two years. We do not know the grounds for their annulment, but in 1204, Raimond wed again, this time a political match with Leonora, the sister of the King of Aragon, who would survive him. I should mention here that Raimond had five wives, not the six that many historians have given him. The confusion can be traced to the chronicler of *Historia Albigensis*, who reported that Raimond had wed "la damsel de Chypre." She would later be misidentified as Bourgogne, the daughter of the King of Cyprus at that time, Amaury de Lusignan. There is no evidence that Bourgogne ever left the Holy Land, where she wed Gauthier de Montbeliard, the constable of the Kingdom of Jerusalem. There are historians who are well aware of this mistake, but it is surprising—and depressing—that so many others simply report the Bourgogne marriage like so many sheep, most likely because Raimond's marriages were peripheral to the subject they were writing about and so they did not do the in-depth research that would have revealed the error.

Raimond was a man with his share of flaws, but what caused his downfall was a sin that we would consider a virtue—he was genuinely tolerant and was unwilling to persecute his subjects for their religious beliefs. He would pay a high price for that tolerance, would be publicly whipped, betrayed by men willing to violate canon law to entrap him, and then excommunicated. He died on August 2, 1222, at age sixty-six. He'd spent the morning on the threshold of a church as the sympathetic priests within raised their voices so he could hear the celebration of the Mass. He passed out from the heat and apparently then suffered a stroke. He had sought absolution repeatedly in the years since his excommunication, but it was always denied him, as it was now by the prior of St Severin's. The Hospitallers showed more mercy and accepted the dying man into their Order. The Church's enmity did not soften, though, and he was denied the last Sacraments, denied a Christian burial in consecrated ground. This would be a source of deep grief to his son, who tried desperately to get the Church to relent. The promise of mercy to his father was used as bait to force him into making greater concessions, but the promises were never honored, and Raimond's unburied coffin rested for years in the commandery of the Hospitallers in Toulouse, where it was eventually discovered that his body had been devoured by rats.

His son, the seventh Count of Toulouse, knew nothing but war from his twelfth year. He could not have remembered the mother who'd died when he was only two, but Raimond seems to have kept her memory alive for him, as he showed himself to be devoted to that memory, often mentioning her in his charters, naming his daughter Joanna, and asking to be buried beside her at Fontevrault Abbey when he died in 1249, at age fifty-two. His daughter had been compelled to wed the brother of the French king, and when their marriage was childless, Toulouse was swallowed up by the French Crown.

Very little is known of Raimond and Joanna's daughter, born in 1198. Most historians only mention the son born in 1197 and the son who did not survive. Others know there was a daughter, but claim her name was Mary or even Wilhelmina. That it was Joanna is proven by the necrology of Vaissy Abbey in Auvergne, which records that on May 28, 1255, died *"Johana, filia Raymundi comitis et Reginae Johannae."* She was the second wife of Bernard III, Seigneur de la Tour, and had two daughters and three sons.

André de Chauvigny made another trip to Rome in April 1202, and Pope Innocent was more sympathetic than Celestine, ruling that André and Denise had been married for more than a dozen years, had five children by then, and there was no valid reason for challenging their marriage. Sadly, André was one of the men seized by John in his one great military triumph, when he captured Arthur and the leading Breton lords at the siege of Mirebeau in August 1202. John refused to ransom André and he was dead before the year was out. Some of the prisoners were said to have been starved to death and it has been suggested that he was one of them; he'd have been about fifty-two. Denise was then pregnant with their sixth child. She married again in 1205 to the Count of Sancerre, but died herself in 1207, when she was only thirty-five.

Constance, Duchess of Brittany, seems to have had a happy marriage with her third husband, Guy de Thouars. But her happiness was short-lived, as she died in early September 1201. It has occasionally been claimed that she died of leprosy, but that has been discredited and it is most likely that she died of the complications of childbirth; she was forty at the time of her death and the birthing chamber would have posed greater dangers for her. There is some confusion about her children with Guy. We know she gave birth to two daughters, Alix and Katherine, but I've seen it reported that Alix was born in 1200 and that Constance died after giving birth to twin daughters in 1201. Other histories say that Alix was born in 1201, and if so, she and Katherine would have been the twins. At least Constance was spared knowing the tragic fate of her children by Geoffrey. Arthur is believed to have been murdered at John's command in April of

1203, and his sister, Eleanor (Aenor), was held prisoner in England for thirty-nine years, first by John and then by his son, Henry III, finally dying in August 1241. Once Arthur was believed dead, the Breton barons crowned his half sister Alix and Guy de Thouars served as regent until the French king assumed control of the little heiress, whom he would marry to his cousin when she was twelve. She died in childbirth like her mother, only twenty-two at the time. Guy wed again and his second wife gave him a son.

Baldwin de Bethune died in 1212 and his wife, Hawisa, Countess of Aumale, paid John the vast sum of five thousand marks so she'd not have to marry again; she died two years later. A few historians have suggested she may have been John's mistress, but I've never been convinced of that.

William Marshal was a prominent figure during John's reign, serving as regent to the latter's underaged son, dying full of years and honors in 1219. The Earl of Chester wed another Breton heiress, Clemence de Fougères, but this marriage was childless, too; he died in 1232, having become a valuable ally of our favorite Welsh prince, Llywelyn Fawr. The Earl of Leicester was not blessed with a long life, dying in 1205. He and his wife, Loretta, had no children, and the earldom of Leicester was inherited by his sisters. The elder sister, Amicia, was wed to the French baron, Simon de Montfort, and eventually the earldom of Leicester would pass to Amicia's grandson, another Simon de Montfort, featured in my novel *Falls the Shadow*. Mercadier survived Richard by just a year. He was murdered in the streets of Bordeaux in April 1200 by one of the men of a rival mercenary, who was now seneschal of Gascony.

Geoffrey, Archbishop of York, had an even more turbulent relationship with John than he had with Richard, and he fled to France in 1207. He died in exile in December 1212. I changed the name of Richard's loyal clerk and subsequent Bishop of Durham, Master Fulk of Poitiers, as it was really Philip and I had a surfeit of Philips. He died in April 1208. Hugh, the Bishop of Lincoln, died in November 1200; he would soon be canonized by the Catholic Church and is the patron saint of sick children, the sick, and swans.

Philippe Capet lived long enough to overcome the stain upon his reputation caused by his abandonment of the Third Crusade and his humiliating defeats at Richard's hands. He was much more successful against John and French historians consider him one of their great medieval kings. He seemed to be happy with Agnes of Meran, but he finally yielded to papal pressure and put her aside in 1200, making peace with the Church by effecting a sham reconciliation with Ingeborg. He continued to treat Ingeborg very badly, but Agnes spared him the awkwardness of having two crowned queens by dying in July 1201. Philippe died in 1223, at age fifty-eight, and was succeeded by his son, Louis VIII, who'd wed Eleanor's granddaughter Blanche. Philippe's abused queen Ingeborg outlived him by fourteen years, and was treated much more kindly by Philippe's son and his grandson, Louis IX.

It seems likely that in marrying Alys to the young Count of Ponthieu, Philippe hoped that the marriage would be childless and Ponthieu would then revert to the French Crown. I am happy to report that Alys gave birth to an heir, though, a daughter, Marie. Alys is one of history's sadder figures, but in a nice turn of irony, her great-granddaughter would become Queen of England, Eleanora of Castile, who wed Edward I.

Philip de Dreux, Bishop of Beauvais, took part in the Albigensian Crusade; naturally, he would. When he was freed from captivity in 1199, he was forced to swear that he'd not fight again against his fellow Christians. Not surprisingly, he did not honor this promise, and played a prominent role at the Battle of Bouvines, mentioned below, where he captured John's half brother William de Longespée. He died in 1217, at age fifty-nine.

Berengaria's younger brother Fernando died at the age of thirty in 1207 when he was killed in a tournament. Her youngest sister, Blanca, had a brief but happy marriage to Thibault, the Count of Champagne, brother of Henri of Champagne; she was a great comfort to Berengaria during the latter's widowhood. Berengaria's brother Sancho's story is another sad one. His health deteriorated and he grew so heavy that he could no longer mount a horse and became a recluse. His marriage to Raimond of Toulouse's daughter Constance failed, and although he had four illegitimate sons, he died without an heir in 1234, Navarre's crown passing to his nephew, his sister Blanca's son.

Leopold of Austria's eldest son, Friedrich, assumed the papal penance imposed upon his father and took the cross. Like so many crusaders, he was stricken by a fatal illness, dying in April 1198 at the age of twenty-two. His brother Leopold inherited the duchy. He would have a long and very successful reign, earning himself the epithet "Leopold the Glorious" before his death in 1230. Friedrich, the son of Heinrich von Hohenstaufen and Constance de Hauteville, would become Holy Roman Emperor and even King of Jerusalem; he was one of the most intriguing, colorful, and controversial figures of the Middle Ages, called *Stupor Mundi*, the Wonder of the World.

As I explained in *Lionheart*, I chose to retain Richenza's German name although she'd changed it to Matilda during her family's exile in England. Her husband Jaufre, Count of Perche, died suddenly in April of 1202, leaving her a widow at age thirty. Jaufre entrusted her with the minority of their son, Thomas. She wed again between April of 1203 and April of 1204 to Enguerrand de Coucy, the French king's cousin, and Kathleen Thompson, in her excellent history *Power and Border Lordship in Medieval France*, argues convincingly that what slight evidence there is indicates this second marriage was not of Richenza's choosing. She died in January 1210, only thirty-eight, and her son, Thomas, was slain at the Battle of Lincoln in 1217.

Richenza's brother Otto was crowned King of Germany in 1198, but he continued to be challenged by Heinrich's brother, Philip of Swabia. Richard's death was a great blow to him, and his hold on power became more precarious after John's loss of Normandy, the tide shifting in Philip's favor. But then Philip was tragically murdered in 1208 by a deranged vassal with a personal grudge, and the German barons turned again to Otto, as did Pope Innocent III. He was crowned as the Holy Roman Emperor in October 1209. He soon fell out with the Pope, though, who threw his support to Friedrich von Hohenstaufen, who was then seventeen. Since Philippe Capet was backing Friedrich, John resumed aid to Otto. The result was the Battle of Bouvines in 1214, which ended in a defeat for Otto and John, although the English king had not taken part in the battle. Otto was forced to abdicate the imperial throne in 1215 and died in May 1218, at age forty-one. His elder brother Henrik died in 1227 and his younger brother Wilhelm married the daughter of the King of Denmark, but he died young in 1213.

Anna is my own name for the Damsel of Cyprus. As I explained in *Lionheart*, the best source for the history of Isaac Comnenus and his daughter remains the article by W. H. Rudt de Collenberg, *"L'Empereur Isaac de Chypre et sa fille, 1155–1207."* He speculated that her name may have been Beatrice, for a Beatrice received a generous bequest in Joanna's will. But that Beatrice seems to have been one of Joanna's two ladies-in-waiting who took the veil at Fontevrault after her death. The Damsel of Cyprus had an interesting marital history. Her marriage to the Count of Toulouse did not last long, and was over by the time Raimond went to the Holy Land in October 1202. In 1203, "Anna" wed Thierry, the illegitimate son of Philip d'Alsace, the Count of Flanders. They sailed with the army during the debacle that was the Fourth Crusade, and upon their arrival in Cyprus, Anna's new husband claimed the island in her name. The then–King of Cyprus, Amaury de Lusignan, was having none of that and declared them persona non grata. They then went to Anna's homeland, Armenia. In 1207, Thierry turned up in Constantinople, now ruled by his cousin, but we do not know if Anna accompanied him or remained in Armenia. After that mention in 1207, Thierry and Anna disappear from history; I am sentimental enough to hope that the remainder of her life was a happy one.

AUTHOR'S NOTE

I HAVE ALWAYS LOOKED upon an Author's Note as a necessary evil, for I find them very difficult to do. I do think they are essential, though, serving several purposes. They enable me to clear my conscience if I have had to take any liberties with historical fact and they lift the curtain to offer a behind-the-scenes look at the making of a novel. They are also important to my readers, who have often told me they enjoy them almost as much as the books themselves. I can understand that, for I feel cheated when I read a historical novel and then discover that the author has not included an Author's Note. So I have no intention of abandoning them; I even included one for my contribution to George R.R. Martin and Gardner Dozois's anthology, *Dangerous Women*, surely the first short story to have its own Author's Note! Yet I will always approach them warily, my view of the Author's Note being perfectly expressed by Dorothy Parker, who said that she hated writing but loved having written.

I'll begin with Richard's dangerous and dramatic adventures upon his departure from the Holy Land; it is remarkable how reality so often transcended fiction whenever the Angevins were involved. I've seen it suggested that Richard's crusade was his *Iliad* and his homeward journey his *Odyssey*. I am inclined to see *Lionheart* as the story of Richard the legend and *A King's Ransom* as the story of Richard the man. I realize that *Ransom*'s early chapters may read as if they were written by a Hollywood scriptwriter, but what I describe really happened—the two shipwrecks, the encounter with pirates, Richard's temporary reprieves in Görz and Udine.

The site of his first shipwreck—La Croma—is today known as Lokrum Island (and the shore where Richard and his men landed has become a famous nudist beach). The Republic of Ragusa is now Dubrovnik, Croatia. Sadly, the cathedral that Richard's money helped to rebuild was destroyed in an earthquake in 1667, but his memory lived on in local folklore, and, during World War I, a Serbian diplomat seeking British aid reminded that government of the warm welcome their king had received in Ragusa more than seven hundred years before.

As with virtually every episode of Richard's life, there are conflicting stories about his capture outside Vienna. The most reliable English source is the Cistercian monk Ralph of Coggeshall, for he is believed to have gotten his information from Richard's chaplain, Anselm, and his is the most detailed account. Roger de Hoveden reported that Richard was sleeping when Duke Leopold's men arrived, which makes sense in light of his illness. Years later, the German chroniclers put about a more colorful story—that he'd attempted to escape detection by pretending to be a servant, roasting a chicken on a spit in the hearth, and he was given away because he'd forgotten to remove a valuable ring. But this rather unlikely tale appears in none of the accounts by Austrian chroniclers, as the German historian Dr. Ulrike Kessler points out in her biography of Richard. I was skeptical, too, even before I realized the "chicken on a spit" story was refuted by the Church calendar itself, for Richard was captured on December 21, during Advent, when Christians were forbidden to eat meat of any kind.

The letter that the Holy Roman Emperor, Heinrich, wrote to the French king gives us a glimpse of Heinrich's nasty nature, while providing invaluable details about Richard's capture. The English chroniclers said that Richard was accompanied by only one knight, Sir Guillain de l'Etang, and a young translator. But since Heinrich claimed that Richard had two knights with him, I was able to bring Morgan along for the ride. Arne is a name of my choosing, as the boy's real name was not reported. We know only that he spoke German, that he was courageous, and very loyal to Richard, for he had to be tortured by Duke Leopold's men before he finally revealed that the English king was in Ertpurch, today called Erdburg.

According to William Marshal's *Histoire*, Richard hated Philip de Dreux, the Bishop of Beauvais, more than any other man, blaming Beauvais for his harsh treatment at Trifels, where he was—in his own words—"loaded down with chains so heavy that a horse would have struggled to move." In light of that graphic description, my fictional Richard may have been luckier than the real Richard, for I did let Markward spare him the leg shackles.

I'm on the record as stating that Richard I is the historical figure whom I found the most surprising, and new readers have occasionally asked me to elaborate upon this statement. I had not expected to learn that he'd been seriously ill so often, that his marriage appeared to get off to a promising start, that he was as careful with the lives of his soldiers as he was reckless with his own life. But I was utterly astonished to discover that he'd formed friendships with some of Saladin's emirs and Mamluks, even knighting a few of them, and that his political skills were almost as impressive as his military skills. What he accomplished at Heinrich's Imperial Diet in Speyer is remarkable, a bravura performance that even his enemies were forced to acknowledge.

I was not surprised, though, to find no evidence to support the popular belief that Richard preferred men to women as bed partners, for by the time I began researching *Devil's Brood* I already knew that this claim was founded upon an erroneous understanding of medieval custom and culture. For a supposition that was first raised only in 1948 by J. H. Harvey in *The Plantagenets*, it gained traction due in some measure perhaps to the success of the wonderful film *The Lion in Winter*, one of my favorites. I made my own small contribution to the new legend by not researching what was essentially a walk-on role for Richard in *Here Be Dragons*, and in recent years I've been punished for that by having to explain often to puzzled readers why the Richard in *Here Be Dragons* is not the same man in *Devil's Brood* and *Lionheart*.

I first addressed the question of Richard's sexuality in the *Devil's Brood* Author's Note. J. H. Harvey decided that Richard was gay because he'd misread a passage in Roger de Hoveden's *Annals* (fully quoted in *Devil's Brood*), which described a visit Richard paid to the French king's court in 1187, writing that Philippe held Richard in such high esteem that they ate from the same table and from the same dish and at night shared the same chamber. In our age, we would naturally assume they had a sexual relationship. But in the Middle Ages, it was quite common for people to share beds, even with strangers in inns. More to the point, such ostentatious intimacy was a way to demonstrate royal favor, a means of flaunting political alliances and mending political fences. Edward IV, one of the most heterosexual of English kings, shared a bedchamber with the rebel Earl of Somerset to dramatize their reconciliation. And Roger de Hoveden's matter-of-fact tone clearly shows that he understood Richard and Philippe were deliberately sending Henry a message, which Henry understood all too well, for he at once postponed his plans to return to England, fearing that they were plotting against him.

Richard's famous encounter with the hermit is also cited by those who've accepted J. H. Harvey's premise. Again, if we place a modern interpretation upon the hermit's warning, we conclude that Richard was being accused of sodomy. Yet this reading disregards the fact that the "destruction of Sodom" had a wider meaning in the Middle Ages, often used to refer to the apocalyptic nature of the punishment, not the nature of the offense. Even the term "sins of Sodom" referred to a broad spectrum of sins, not just sodomy, some not even sexual. The French chronicler Guillaume Le Breton declared that Richard had brought about his death at Châlus because he'd offended against the "laws of nature." But he was referring to Richard's war against his own father. Dr. Gillingham has an interesting discussion of all this in his biography of Richard. Not all historians agree with this reading of the "destruction of Sodom," of course. So were there any suggestions made during Richard's lifetime to indicate he was homosexual or bisexual? The answer is no.

Both of the chroniclers who accompanied Richard on crusade believed that he'd desired Berengaria long before he'd married her, Ambroise even describing her as his "beloved." I thought that was sweet, but unlikely, for medieval marriages were matters of state, and I don't think Richard had a romantic bone in his entire body. Their comments do show, though, that they believed his sexual tastes were "conventional," as Dr. Gillingham put it. Legend had it that Richard demanded women to be brought to him on his deathbed, thus hastening his death; Guillaume Le Breton reported that Richard had preferred the "joys of Venus" to "salubrious counsel"—the advice of his doctors. Like so many of Richard's legends, this seems improbable, for gangrene is fast-acting and he'd have known very soon that he was doomed. Eleanor was one hundred forty miles away at Fontevrault, and for her to have reached him in time he must have sent for her within a day or so of his wounding. So I very much doubt that a man in such severe pain would have been carousing with camp whores. Yet the French chronicler's comment does tell us that he, too, assumed Richard's sexuality was "conventional."

Even more tellingly, the Bishop of Lincoln took Richard to task for adultery, not sodomy, and St Hugh was famed for his blunt speaking and strong sense of morality. The bishop's lecture actually occurred in 1198, but I was unable to dramatize it in the chapter for that year and I had to move it back to Chapter 26 in 1195. So Richard's repentance and reconciliation with Berengaria after his sudden illness in 1195 did not last long, and he was soon straying from his marriage bed again.

Sadly, I think some of the criticism directed against Richard hints at an anti-gay bias. Accusing him of being irresponsible and careless echoes the stereotype that many who are homophobic have of gay men.

I tend to agree with the British historian Elizabeth Hallam, who concluded that what little evidence there is paints Richard as a womanizer, if not on the epic scale of his father and brother John. When considering Richard's sexuality, we must always place it in the context of his times, though. I am proud to live in one of the sixteen states in which same-sex marriage is now legal. They were not as enlightened in the Middle Ages, and the Church taught that a man who bedded other men was guilty of a mortal sin. And this makes the utter silence of the French chroniclers highly significant.

Philippe's court historians, Rigord and Guillaume Le Breton, did all in their power to portray Richard as the Antichrist. They accused him of murdering Conrad of Montferrat, of poisoning the Duke of Burgundy, of sending Saracen Assassins to Paris to kill Philippe, of taking bribes from the Saracens, and even of betraying Christendom by a secret alliance with Saladin. Yet they never accused Richard of sodomy, a sin that would have stained his honor and damned his immortal soul. If they'd had such a lethal weapon at hand, I cannot believe they would not have used it. But I suspect that this debate will continue, for it is the Age of the Internet, people enjoy speculating about the sex lives of celebrities, and we can never be utterly sure of another person's sexuality, especially one who has been dead for over eight hundred years.

The term "post-traumatic stress disorder" is a new one, only dating from 1980, but PTSD has always been with us. In my Acknowledgments, I cite a book, *Achilles in Vietnam*, whose author makes a convincing case that Homer understood the psychological damage wrought by war and the impact combat and imprisonment could have upon men, more than twenty-five centuries before PTSD was even diagnosed. He also shows that William Shakespeare recognized it, too, for his Hotspur in *Henry IV* suffers from many of the symptoms of those afflicted with PTSD. But few of us have the insight of a Homer or a Shakespeare. While chroniclers like Ralph de Coggeshall were aware that Richard had come home from his German imprisonment a changed man, they would not have understood why.

Can I prove that Richard suffered from PTSD? Of course not. It is challenging even to attempt to reconstruct the physical outlines of a medieval life; it would be impossible to map a man's interior world. But we know enough about PTSD and the human psyche now to recognize how difficult captivity would have been for a proud, willful, hot-tempered king like Richard.

We all hold certain basic assumptions that allow us to find order in the midst of chaos, and the shattering of those assumptions can be devastating. The risk of PTSD is much higher if the traumatic event is sudden, unpredictable, of long duration, involves a serious risk to life or personal safety, and the person feels powerless. For fifteen months, Richard was balanced on the crumbling edge of a cliff, knowing that Heinrich was quite capable of turning him over to the French king, a fate truly worse than death, and, indeed, Heinrich played masterfully upon this fear. The emperor only overreached himself at the end, with that eleventh-hour double cross at Mainz, and even then Heinrich still managed to extort one final concession, the forced homage that shamed Richard to the depths of his soul. For a crusader king, his ordeal must have seemed utterly inexplicable. How could he not question why God had let this happen? And how could those questions not erode the foundations of his faith?

Did his imprisonment leave psychic scars? Well, his temper became even more combustible after his captivity. He was less inclined to pardon. His relationship with his wife had seemed amicable enough when they were in the Holy Land, but deteriorated dramatically upon his return from Germany, as often happens with PTSD. Despite a love of pomp and pageantry, he had to be coaxed into the crown-wearing ceremony and his Christmas courts were surprisingly low-key. And his hatred for the French king was all-consuming. If seen in isolation, these actions may not seem meaningful. Seen as a pattern of behavior, they reveal a man haunted by memories he could neither understand nor escape.

There has been some confusion among medieval chroniclers as to the identity of the man who shot Richard at the siege of Châlus. The usually reliable Roger de Hoveden was less so when he wrote of affairs in Aquitaine and the Limousin, for he had to depend upon secondhand accounts and rumors. The best sources for the events at Châlus are Ralph de Coggeshall, who seems to have had an eyewitness to Richard's last days, probably the Abbot of Le Pin, and Bernard Itier, the librarian of Saint-Martial, a monastery less than twenty miles from Châlus. It is from Bernard Itier that we learn there were only two knights and thirty-eight people within the castle at the time of the siege. He identified the crossbowman as Peire Basile, a local knight from the Limousin, but he said nothing of the fate of Peire Basile or the castle garrison.

Roger de Hoveden is the only chronicler who reported that Richard ordered the hanging of the castle garrison and that Mercadier disregarded Richard's pardon of Peire Basile and "after the king's death, first flaying him alive, had him hanged." This has been the accepted story, one I'd never thought to question. But then I found *Histoire de Châlus et sa région*, by Paul Patier, and was taken aback to learn that the author is convinced Peire Basile was not flayed alive. He cites a charter dated June 6, 1239, as proof that Peire Basile survived for years after the fall of Châlus. Is he right? I do not know; he himself admits that the Peire Basile mentioned in this charter is *"très probablement"* the same Peire Basile whose crossbow bolt killed Richard. I decided that "very probably" was not enough to rewrite history. The author also contends that the other knight taken at Châlus, Peire Brun, was later permitted to reclaim his castle at Montbrun. If this is true, it would mean that the Châlus garrison were not hanged, either, and Roger de Hoveden's account was merely a rumor that he'd found credible. I would like to believe he was in error, that Peire Basile was spared such an agonizing death at Mercadier's order. But until a French historian decides to do some serious research about Richard's death and the fate of the men captured at Châlus, I can only accept the "traditional" account by Roger de Hoveden, perhaps with an asterisk added.

Another one of Richard's legends—the man was a veritable magnet for myths—is that he was laying siege to Châlus to claim a treasure that had supposedly been found by the castellan. This story has been discredited in recent years, the most thorough exploration of the legend and its sources in "The Unromantic Death of Richard I," by John Gillingham, in his *Richard Coeur de Lion: Kingship, Chivalry and War in the Twelfth Century*. Richard was conducting a punitive military campaign against an often disloyal vassal, the Viscount of Limoges, not a treasure hunt.

I had always assumed that Joanna had died in childbirth, unable to deliver her baby. It was a surprise, therefore, to find that this was not so. In trying to determine why she'd suffered such a dangerous pregnancy, my friend Dr. John Phillips was a great help. As soon as I told him that Joanna had given birth to three children in three years, he told me that she would have been very anemic, which medieval medicine could neither diagnose nor treat. We will never know for a certainty what caused her death, but I think hyperemesis gravidarum is a definite possibility. Women who are prone to motion sickness are more vulnerable to HG, and we do know that Joanna was so seasick on her way to Sicily in 1176 that they'd had to continue her journey on land. Most people are unfamiliar with HG, although it is probably better known today now that the Duchess of Cambridge was afflicted with it in the early months of her pregnancy. It is an awful illness and was often fatal until the advent of IVs and antinausea drugs. It has been suggested that Charlotte Brontë died of HG, possibly complicated by TB, in the fourth month of a problem pregnancy, for her symptoms matched perfectly with those of HG.

For those who would like to learn more about HG, I highly recommend

Beyond Morning Sickness: Battling Hyperemesis Gravidarum, by Ashli Foshee McCall, a collection of powerful, harrowing first-person stories by women who suffered from HG during their pregnancies. Some of them had been so ill that they'd been desperate enough to seek abortions, and then were guilt-stricken and remorseful that they'd done so. As for Joanna's caesarean, it is one of the earliest reported cases of this procedure; in the Middle Ages, it was only done after the woman had died in an attempt to baptize the baby and save a soul.

It may be a cliché but it is also a truism that history is usually rewritten by the victor. One of the more blatant examples of this revisionism is surely the Tudor depiction of Richard III as a moral monster, done in order to validate Henry Tudor's tenuous blood claim to the throne. Richard III was still more fortunate than Raimond de St Gilles, the sixth Count of Toulouse. Unlike Richard, Raimond has no society devoted to clearing his name and his foe cast a far greater shadow than those upstart Tudors—the medieval Church.

Raimond was one of the victims of the Albigensian Crusade, which began in 1209 and ravaged the lands today known as Languedoc. He made mistakes, ill served by an irreverent sense of humor and slow to see the danger until it was too late. In the end, he could save neither himself nor his people from the French invaders who claimed they were doing God's will as they plundered the rich lands of the south. He died an excommunicate, falsely branded as a heretic, unable to keep the Inquisition from taking root and knowing that Toulouse was doomed.

Thousands of men, women, and children would die, the great majority of them Catholics, not Cathars. The most notorious of the massacres occurred at Béziers, whose citizens refused to surrender the two hundred Cathars living in their midst. When the town was captured, it was said that the papal legate, Arnaud Amaury, was asked how the soldiers were to distinguish Catholics from Cathars and he replied, "Kill them all. God will know His own." Some historians have cast doubt upon this statement, for it was not reported until a few years later, but I have no trouble believing it, for I read the letter that Arnaud Amaury wrote to Pope Innocent, proudly declaring that neither age nor sex was spared and twenty thousand had been slain. There was not quite that much blood on his hands; the death toll was probably about nine thousand, including priests. When Raimond's nephew, Raimond-Roger Trencavel, sought to surrender Carcassonne to spare it the fate of Béziers, his safe conduct was not honored and he was put in chains in his own castle dungeon, dying a few months later at age twenty-four. The townspeople of Carcassonne were turned out with just the clothes on their backs, "taking only their sins," as a chronicler gleefully put it.

Men willing to shed blood so cavalierly would have no compunctions about vilifying those they destroyed, and so it happened to Raimond de St Gilles. Catholic chroniclers painted him in the most lurid of colors, maligning him as a godless Cathar, a man steeped in sin, an enemy of Holy Church, seeking to justify what was done in God's name. As I said in the Afterword, his true sin was tolerance, incomprehensible to the medieval mind. By the time he died, his reputation was in tatters, and for centuries it was accepted that the Count of Toulouse had been a dissolute womanizer and a heretic.

Raimond's character assassination at the hands of the Church spilled over into his marriage to Joanna, too. You will find it claimed by Wikipedia, and even some histories, that she was unhappy and was fleeing to Richard for refuge when she learned of her brother's death. This is not true. *The Chronicle of William of Puylaurens* said of Joanna, "She was an able woman of great spirit, and after she had recovered from childbed, she was determined to counter the injuries being inflicted upon her husband at the hands of numerous magnates and knights. She therefore took arms against the lords of Saint-Felix, and laid siege to a castrum belonging to them known as Les Cassés. Her efforts were of little avail; some of those with her treacherously and secretly provided arms and supplies to the besieged enemy. Greatly aggrieved, she abandoned the siege, and was almost prevented from leaving her camp by a fire started by the traitors. Much affected by this injury, she hastened to see her brother King Richard to tell him about it but found that he had died. She herself died, whilst pregnant, overcome by this double grief." This testimony is all the more convincing for being written by a man who was a devout Catholic and a supporter of the Albigensian Crusade, seeing it as necessary to combat heresy.

But Raimond continues to be portrayed as a neglectful or abusive husband, despite all evidence to the contrary, mainly because he remains a peripheral figure, a minor player in the histories of other men. The translators of William of Puylaurens's chronicle, W. A. Sibly and M. D. Sibly, are renowned scholars, but even they get Raimond's marital history wrong, reporting that he had five wives, which is indeed true; however, they, too, have confused the Damsel of Cyprus with the daughter of Amaury de Lusignan, listing the latter and eliminating the Damsel altogether. Raimond de St Gilles is a man desperately in need of his own biographer, and maybe a Raimond de St Gilles Society to repair some of the damage done to his memory.

Peire Basile's crossbow bolt did more than change the history of England and France. It altered German history, too, for without his powerful uncle's support,

Otto's hold on power was much more precarious. And that bolt would have a devastating impact upon Languedoc. Had Richard not died at Châlus, he would never have permitted a French army to invade lands he saw as within the Angevin orbit. I still think the conquest of Languedoc was inevitable; the Church saw it and its pleasure-loving people as a genuine threat, and the French barons saw it as a plum ripe for the picking. But it would not have happened while the Lionheart lived.

The circumstances of Constance of Brittany's capture and imprisonment by her husband, the Earl of Chester, remain somewhat murky and confusing. The Bretons naturally blamed Richard, but that did not seem likely to me as he was still attempting at that time to coax her into allowing Arthur to be raised at his court; moreover, he would have known that the Bretons would never have agreed to trade Constance for Arthur, as indeed they did not. I chose to follow the chronology set forth in Dr. Judith Everard's excellent history, *Brittany and the Angevins*, which remains the best source for Brittany in the twelfth century.

Ralph de Coggeshall reported that Robert de Nonant, the brother of the Bishop of Coventry, was starved to death in prison, and I see no reason to doubt him, for Richard would not have forgiven de Nonant's defiance during their confrontation at Mainz. But he was imprisoned in 1194 and died at Dover Castle in 1195, so clearly he must have been given some sustenance for him to have survived that long; I concluded, therefore, that he was put on a bread-and-water diet. His brother, the bishop, who was hand in glove with John, was more fortunate, for he died in comfortable French exile in 1197.

Some readers may have felt a sense of déjà vu while reading several passages in *A King's Ransom*—the garden scene between John and Joanna after he'd made his submission to Richard at Lisieux and the scene in Chapter 33 in which Eleanor accused John of conniving again with the French king. Your memories were not playing you false; variations of both scenes first appeared in *Here Be Dragons*. And readers of my mysteries will have noted the occasional appearances of Justin de Quincy and his nemesis, Durand de Curzon, both serving Eleanor as they have done since the publication of *The Queen's Man*.

A few readers may also have been struck by the ambiguous way I described an ugly episode in the war between Richard and Philippe in Chapter 33, where I related that both kings had blinded prisoners, each one accusing the other of committing the atrocity first. The French chronicler Guillaume Le Breton claimed that Richard, in a fury, had ordered French prisoners blinded after several thousand of his Welsh mercenary troops had been slain in an ambush. The

English chronicler Roger de Hoveden also reported the blinding of prisoners, only he placed the blame on the French king as the instigator. Historians generally give greater credence to the English chroniclers, for they were more independent of the Angevin kings, not penning court histories as Guillaume Le Breton and Rigord were, and were therefore much more critical of Henry and his sons than the French chroniclers were of Philippe Capet. And Roger de Hoveden, in particular, is considered one of the most respected historians of the twelfth century. Nonetheless, I found it difficult to decide which of the conflicting accounts—Hoveden's or Guillaume Le Breton's—was likely to be the true one, probably because I could see both Richard and Philippe giving such a command in a royal rage; there is no doubt that their war had become very bitter and very personal by then. So I finally decided to include both accounts of the atrocity and then discuss my ambivalence in the Author's Note, allowing readers to make up their own minds.

We do not know the fate of Richard's Cypriot stallion, Fauvel. According to a later legend, Richard was riding Fauvel at the second battle of Jaffa and after Fauvel was slain, Saladin dispatched a stallion to the English king in tribute to his courage. Only that is not true. Richard did not take Fauvel with him as he sailed to Jaffa; he had only eleven horses at the time of Saladin's surprise attack upon his camp, those they'd found in Jaffa or captured from Saracens. And of course, Saladin never sent him a horse during the battle. The gift of two Arab stallions was made by his brother, al-Malik al-Adil, and that was done afterward; not even the most chivalric of souls was going to provide his foe with another horse in the midst of a battle. Fauvel was safely stabled back at Acre while his master was burnishing the Lionheart legend. I am sure Richard would have arranged for the transport of Fauvel and his two Arab stallions; horses were highly valued in their world, especially horses of Fauvel's caliber. So unless Fauvel was unlucky enough to encounter a fatal storm at sea, he and Richard would have been reunited after the latter regained his freedom. A chronicler mentioned Richard's fiery Lombardy stallion; since he did not give us the Lombardy destrier's name, I called him Argento.

Issoudun. That was the name of the castle and town that was unfortunate enough to be caught in the line of fire between the English and French kings. It was also the reason why I lost a lot of sleep. The chroniclers reported that Richard raced for Issoudun after learning that the French had seized the town and forced his way into the castle. The problem for me was that I knew the town was enclosed by walls, but I did not know if those walls had been erected by 1196.

And this made a great difference in how I would write the scene. So I tried to find the answer to that question, with some invaluable help from my friend John Phillips. That turned out to be as challenging as the search for the Holy Grail. I finally struck gold with a French history of Issoudun; local historians are often the answer to a writer's prayers. This book not only confirmed that the walls were indeed there in 1196, it also included a map of medieval Issoudun, which was like winning the lottery. Of course this did make life more difficult for Richard and me, since I now had to figure out a way to get him into a walled town. But it is such a gratifying feeling to be able to approach a scene like this with confidence, knowing it will have a sound factual foundation. And as an added bonus, another book I bought in my search for Issoudun's elusive walls, *Le Berry du Xe siècle au milieu du XIIIe siècle*, contained the story of André and Denise de Chauvigny's troubles with the Archbishop of Bourges, which I'd found in no other history of the period; the author, by the way, shared my suspicions that the French king was behind this harassment of Richard's cousin. The "Issoudun episode" is the perfect example of why I love historical research—and why it takes me so long to write each of my books.

My readers know by now of my m.o. when it comes to writing historical novels. I rarely use fictional characters, Morgan and his family being the exception to this rule. I am admittedly obsessive-compulsive about historical accuracy, and I think the Eleventh Commandment for historical novelists should be the one articulated so eloquently by my fellow writer Laurel Corona: Do not defame the dead. I do have to fill in the blanks more often than I'd like, for medieval chroniclers could be utterly indifferent to the needs of future novelists. We have to rely upon charters and chronicles to find out where someone was on a particular date. Naturally, kings are easiest to track. But women were well-nigh invisible, even queens.

We know Eleanor passed most of her time at Fontevrault, that Joanna visited her there, and Berengaria eventually established her own household at Beaufort-en-Vallée. But for much of the years between 1194 and 1199, the three queens were like elegant ghosts, leaving few footprints. So I felt free to let Eleanor attend Joanna in the birthing chamber, for it seemed logical that she'd want to be with her daughter at such a time; she was with her daughter Matilda when she gave birth in 1184. And while no chronicler thought to mention that Berengaria and Raimond visited the ailing Joanna at Fontevrault Abbey, I do not doubt that they did. We may not always know where someone was on any given day, but we do know what they were likely to do. For better or worse, human nature has not changed in the past eight centuries.

I did a mea culpa in the *Lionheart* Author's Note, and I am continuing the practice here, for this is the way to reach the largest possible audience. I have a "Medieval Mishaps" page on my website in which I alert my readers to past mistakes. But a time-traveling grey squirrel is far more forgivable than the bizarre blunder I made in *The Reckoning*, where I inexplicably had Edward I tell Roger de Mortimer that the crossbow was more difficult to master than the longbow. I can't explain it, can only publicize it as much as possible to lessen the chance of a new reader taking it as gospel.

A King's Ransom is my farewell to the Angevins, although I do hope to let a few of them infiltrate my next novel, *The Land Beyond the Sea*, set in Champagne and the Holy Land. It is not easy to let them go, not after letting them camp out in my brain for nearly twenty years. I have listed my contact information in the Acknowledgments. Readers can time-travel back to see Richard's spectacular castle, Château Gaillard, as he would have seen it in this trailer for the Battle Castle documentary: http://tinyurl.com/kpsye57. And this link will allow you to listen to "*Ja Nus Hons Pris*," the haunting lament written by Richard during his German captivity, performed by the late Owain Phyfe, a wonderful singer and musician who is greatly missed: http://youtu.be/RVRjmTdM4c8.

OCTOBER 2013

ACKNOWLEDGMENTS

IN SOME WAYS, writing a novel is a very solitary endeavor, for it involves isolation, forcing a writer to keep the real world at bay. But in other ways, it is like a team sport, for there are always people who support us in that endeavor—at least, if we are lucky, there are. I have been particularly blessed with my team, starting with my "coach," my editor at G. P. Putnam's, Marian Wood. Other authors are astounded and envious when I confide that Marian has been my editor since the start of my writing career, more than thirty years ago. In my first novel, *The Sunne in Splendour*, I said that she "shapes and polishes words and ideas with the precision and skill of a master diamond-cutter." That has not changed in the three decades since *Sunne*'s publication.

I cannot imagine how my writing career might have fared if not for my wonderful agents, Molly Friedrich of the Friedrich Agency and Mic Cheetham of the Mic Cheetham Agency. They, too, have been guiding my books into safe harbors for three decades. In the United Kingdom, I am delighted to be back with my original British publisher, Macmillan and Company, and I would like to thank my new British editors, Catherine Richards and Jeremy Trevathan. I want to thank Lucy Carson and Molly Schulman of the Friedrich Agency and Sara Minnich of G. P. Putnam's for helping to make my life so much easier. And a special "thank you" to Janet Robbins for her superb copyediting.

Since I write of historical figures who rarely died peacefully in bed, I spend a lot of my time doing medical research, but I have never been fortunate enough to have my own "medical consultant" for past books. For *A King's Ransom*, I did—John Phillips, a retired physician and friend whose expertise proved to be a Godsend when I was writing about Richard's death from gangrene and Joanna's ill-fated pregnancy. John even contacted Dr. Philippe Charlier, the French forensic sleuth who recently analyzed the remains of Richard I's heart. Thanks to Dr. Charlier's study, we now know that Richard died of gangrene, not septicemia, and the myth that he was struck by a poisoned arrow was just that—a myth.

I am extremely grateful to my friend and fellow writer Sharan Newman, who translated relevant passages of Ralph de Coggeshall's Latin chronicle *Chronicon Anglicanum* for me. I am also very grateful to Kathryn Warner for her translation of the German biography by Ulrike Kessler, *Richard I, Lowenherz, Konig, Kreuzritter, Abenteurer.* And as backup, I was fortunate enough to find Quintus, who provides an excellent online translation service at http://thelatintranslator.com/

I have often said that no novel could have a better midwife than Valerie Ptak LaMont, and I feel very fortunate, both for her friendship and her feedback. Lowell LaMont continues to fight my computer demons for me. I'd like to thank my fellow writer Elizabeth Chadwick for calling to my attention the marvelous name that medievals sometimes used for the English Channel—the Narrow Sea. Malcolm Craig has once again generously allowed me to draw upon his extensive knowledge of medieval Brittany. I want to thank Stephanie Churchill Ling for her encouragement and friendship, and my fellow writer Priscilla Royal, who knows a lot about fending off Deadline Dragons herself. I want to mention Anna Ferrell, too, for her Latin translation assistance. Thanks are also due to my friend Paula Mildenhall, and to Jo Nelson, Linda Hein, May Liang, Sarah Adams Brown, Stephen Gilligan, Fiona Scott-Doran, Lesley West, and Celia Jelbart, the brave souls who volunteered to administer my Facebook fan club pages. Thanks, too, to Koby Itzhak, Rania Melhem, and Kasia Ogrodnik Fujcik for taking up the slack when I could not do my daily "Today in Medieval History" posts on Facebook. Stephanie and Rania also do double duty as my Facebook administrators. I wish I could acknowledge all of my Facebook, Goodreads, and blog friends, for you never doubted that I was going to prevail over the Deadline Dragon, even when I despaired myself, and your faith did much to keep my dragon sword sharp.

I included a minibibliography in the *Lionheart* acknowledgments for the first time, and this was so well received by my readers that I am going to continue the practice. Obviously, I cannot list all of the books that I consulted, but at least I can cite those that I found most helpful in my research for *A King's Ransom*. The gold standard for Ricardian biographies remains John Gillingham's *Richard I,* published in 1999 by Yale University Press. Dr Gillingham has written several books about Richard, including *Richard Coeur de Lion: Kingship, Chivalry and War in the Twelfth Century,* which contains interesting articles about Richard and Berengaria, Richard's death at Châlus, and his military skills. Dr. Gillingham's academic article "The Kidnapped King: Richard I in Germany, 1192–1194," published in the *German Historical Institute of London Bulletin* 30 (2008), was invaluable to me in establishing the chronology and details of Richard's captivity, as was Hans Eberhard Mayer's "A Ghost Ship called Frankenef: King Richard I's Germany Itinerary," *English Historical Review*, Vol. 115, No. 460 (2000). The most comprehensive source for the murder of the Bishop of Liege and Heinrich's alleged involvement in it is "The Election and Assassination of Albert of Louvain, Bishop of Liege, 1191–92," by Raymond H. Schmandt, *Speculum*, Vol. 42, No. 4 (1967). *The Social Politics of Medieval Diplomacy: Anglo-German Relations (1066–1307)* by Joseph P. Huffman, published by the University of Michigan Press, is also recommended. For my readers fortunate enough to read German, there is the biography by Ulrike Kessler, which I mentioned earlier in this note. The best source in English for Duke Leopold's role in Richard's abduction is *A History of Medieval Austria*, by A. W. A. Leeper, published by Oxford University Press (1941).

I already discussed biographies of Richard I in the *Lionheart* acknowledgments, but I am going to repeat the titles here for the benefit of new readers. Lionel Landon's *The Itinerary of King Richard I* was a blessing for a writer as obsessive-compulsive about historical detail as I am. *The Reign of Richard Lionheart: Ruler of the Angevin Empire, 1189–1199*, by Ralph Turner and Richard R. Heiser, has a very interesting concluding chapter called "Richard in Retrospect," which analyzes the way his reputation has fluctuated over the centuries. Kate Norgate's *Richard the Lionheart*, published in 1924, has stood the test of time surprisingly well. I also recommend *Richard Coeur de Lion in History and Myth*, edited by Janet Nelson; *The Legends of King Richard Coeur de Lion: A study of Sources and Variations to 1600*, by Bradford Broughton; and *The Plantagenet Empire, 1154–1224*, by Martin Aurell, translated by David Crouch. And to quote a passage from the *Lionheart* acknowledgments: since so many of my readers have seen the wonderful but historically inaccurate *The Lion in Winter*, here are two excellent books about medieval sexuality: *The Bridling of Desire: Views of Sex in the Later Middle Ages*, by Pierre J. Payer, and *Sexuality in Medieval Europe: Doing unto Others*, by Ruth Mazo Karras. I also recommend *Ennobling Love* by C. Stephen Jaeger, University of Pennsylvania Press (1999).

My favorite book about Richard's mother remains *Eleanor of Aquitaine: Lord and Lady*, edited by Bonnie Wheeler. We still do not have the "definitive" biography of Eleanor, but she does not lack for biographers, including Ralph Turner,

Regine Pernoud, Jean Flori, D. D. R. Owen, Marion Meade, and Amy Kelly, although the last two authors' conclusions about the Courts of Love have been contradicted by more recent studies. I also recommend *The World of Eleanor of Aquitaine: Literature and Society in Southern France Between the Eleventh and Thirteenth Centuries*, edited by Marcus Bull and Catherine Leglu, and *Eleanor of Aquitaine, Courtly Love, and the Troubadours*, by Ffiona Swabey.

I have always been surprised that there has been no biography written of Richard's chancellor, William de Longchamp, called by his French name in *A King's Ransom*, for he was an important figure during Richard's reign. So you can imagine my delight when I discovered that he was the subject of a dissertation by David Bruce Balfour: "William Longchamp: Upward Mobility and Character Assassination in Twelfth-Century England." I highly recommend this work for anyone interested in Longchamp and the ways in which propaganda becomes accepted as fact over the course of time. While acknowledging the chancellor's flaws and errors of judgment, the author convincingly debunks the scurrilous stories that have tarnished Longchamp's reputation, including the oft-quoted one in which Eleanor was alleged to have said she'd not trust her grandsons to the chancellor's care.

I am not going to include books about the Albigensian Crusade since that occurred after the events of *A King's Ransom*, but I will recommend one, Joseph R. Strayer's *The Albigensian Crusades*, republished in 1995 by the University of Michigan Press, for this is an excellent account of this sad chapter in medieval history, well researched, well written, and utterly compelling.

The best resource about the Damsel of Cyprus remains the article published in *Byzantion* 38 (1968), pages 123–179, by W. H. Rudt de Collenberg, "*L'Empereur Issac de Chypre et sa Fille.*"

For those interested in learning more about post-traumatic stress disorder, I would suggest *Achilles in Vietnam: Combat Trauma and the Undoing of Character* by Jonathan Shay, MD, in which he compares the soldiers of Homer's *Iliad* with the Vietnam veterans he counseled for PTSD. In addition to reading medical texts, I read a number of autobiographies, and one of the most riveting is *My Private War: Liberated Body, Captive Mind: A World War II POW's Journey* by Norman Bussel. What I found so haunting was that he still had nightmares about his POW experience forty years after regaining his freedom. *Combat Trauma: A Personal Look at Long-term Consequences* by James D. Johnson entwines the stories of sixteen combat veterans with a discussion of what we now know about PTSD and how it manifests itself in those exposed to traumatic events. Thankfully, there are more resources available today for soldiers returning from tours of duty on distant battlefields, although still not enough, not nearly enough. If we are going to send men and women off to fight for us, we owe them more than parades or applause in airports, which are nice gestures, but no substitute for more comprehensive medical care or better VA services or aid to military families.

Lastly, for books about medieval warfare, I highly recommend *By Sword and Fire: Cruelty and Atrocity in Medieval Warfare* by Sean McGlynn; *Noble Ideals and Bloody Realities: Warfare in the Middle Ages* edited by Niall Christie and May Yazigi; *Western Warfare in the Age of the Crusades, 1000–1300* by John France; *War and Chivalry: The Conduct and Perception of War in England and Normandy, 1066–1217* by Matthew Strickland; *Hostages in the Middle Ages* by Adam J. Kosto; and *Encounters Between Enemies: Captivity and Ransom in the Latin Kingdom of Jerusalem* by Yvonne Friedman.

In the *Lionheart* acknowledgments, I expressed the hope that I'd soon be able to post a more extensive bibliography on my website. Unfortunately, that still has not happened. While the spirit is willing, time is as elusive as the unicorn. But, ever the optimist, I keep hoping that it will eventually come to pass. In the meantime, readers can feel free to ask me for recommendations or even for explanations as to why I may have omitted a familiar author, a well-known history. I can be reached via my website, www.sharonkaypenman.com, or at sharonk penman@yahoo.com, or at P.O. Box 1134, Mays Landing, NJ 08330—with the caveat that patience may be required. With the best of intentions, I once offered to provide blog commentary about the Angevins to readers without access to the Internet, and found myself overwhelmed with so many requests that I was unable to respond to them all, much to my dismay. So I have learned to set more realistic goals, always bearing in mind that unlike my medieval kings and queens, I have no scribes on call.

A KING'S RANSOM

SHARON KAY PENMAN

A Reader's Guide

When I realized I wanted to write the story of Richard III, I committed to it in a rather extreme way: I stopped practicing law and moved to England so I could do on-site research of the places I'd be writing about. I visited the castles and battlefields of the Wars of the Roses, becoming even more of an Anglophile and obsessive-compulsive about research in the process. *The Sunne in Splendour* was published in 1982 and it truly was life-changing. For I was no longer a reluctant lawyer; I was now living my dream: I was a full-time writer. I promptly moved to Wales to research my next book. The result was *Here Be Dragons,* which began my love affair with Wales and set the pattern for the next several decades.

I've had some interesting experiences over the years as I followed my muse up Welsh mountains, across Yorkshire dales, and onto French beaches. I climbed Conway Hill with a sprained ankle so I could gaze out across the estuary and see what Llywelyn and Joanna would have seen as they looked over at the deserted camp of his enemy and her father, King John. I stared down a herd of cows in search of the battlefield on the Lleyn Peninsula where Llywelyn ap Gruffydd fought his brothers on a hot day in 1255. On that same hunt, I discovered that my plan to have fleeing soldiers struggling in the river had to be abandoned since the water was so shallow a snake could not have drowned in it. But to my delight, I then came upon a sign warning of quicksand bogs. I resisted the temptation to have anyone swallowed up Hollywood-style. I did, however, let two characters blunder into the bog and lose interest in bashing each other until they could get back onto solid ground.

I once convinced a friend to join me in "breaking into" the Welsh waterfall at Swallow Falls so I could see how it looked by moonlight for a key scene in *Here Be Dragons;* I still remember her muttering "I cannot believe I am doing this" as we found a hole in the fence and clambered through. This same friend and I took three trains to reach the Italian town of Viterbo where one of the most infamous killings of the Middle Ages occurred. Standing there in the piazza, it took little imagination to envision that March morning in 1271 when Simon de Montfort's sons dragged their cousin from a church and murdered him as vengeance for their father's death at Evesham.

I have tramped across battlefields beyond counting. I have visited great cathedrals and haunting castle ruins as I chased my medieval spirits along the Breton coast, through the Loire Valley, and to Siena, York, and Paris. And I enjoyed almost every moment of these research trips—all the more so because they were legitimate tax deductions!

Then came *Lionheart,* my novel about one of the most celebrated and controversial medieval kings, Richard I. That novel dealt primarily with Richard's role in the Third Crusade. On his way to the Holy Land, he logged more miles than Marco Polo, with stops in France, Italy, and Cyprus along the way. But for the first time, I was unable to visit all of the sites I was writing about. I knew it was not necessary—I'd always known that. Yet it was such an enjoyable part of the writing experience that I felt bereft without it. I was laboring under a crushing deadline though, and could no longer take the time for the leisurely sojourns of the past.

The advent of the Internet has made life much easier for writers of historical fiction. We're able to find long out-of-print books with the click of a mouse, unlike the old days when we searched dusty shelves in small, secondhand bookshops, hoping to find a gem nestled amid the dreck. It was like going on a treasure hunt, and it could be fun, although packing up the books myself and then lugging them to a British post office to mail home was definitely not. I was relieved to discover that the Internet also provides enough visual imagery to satisfy the most demanding writer.

I found videos of Palermo churches, Cypriot beaches, and the cliffs of Arsuf, where Richard fought and defeated his legendary foe, Saladin. When I began writing the sequel, *A King's Ransom,* and was once again denied the opportunity to follow in Richard's footsteps as he began his harrowing journey home from the Holy Land, I looked to the Internet. I watched so many videos of Dürnstein Castle, perched on a crag high above the River Danube, that I sometimes felt as breathless as those tourists gamely forging up that narrow path to the citadel ruins. When Richard's galley was shipwrecked on Lacroma during a storm, I turned to YouTube for videos of Lokrum Island, its name today, and was amused to learn that the beach where he came ashore is now a famous nudist beach. His Ragusa is known to us as Dubrovnik, the beautiful walled city on the Croatian coast that was on my bucket list long before I ever imagined I would be writing of the Lionheart. The Internet came to my rescue again until I was able to get Richard back to familiar ground—to England and France, to the siege of Nottingham and to Château Gaillard, and the cloud-kissed castle he built on the chalk cliffs above the Seine, just a day's march from Paris.

In writing *Lionheart* and *A King's Ransom*, I belatedly learned that modern technology is the writer's friend. I felt comfortable writing of places that I'd not actually seen for myself because I'd watched videos that transported me there, at least in my imagination. But the travel urge is a powerful one, and it can be contained by deadline dragons for only so long. I am currently working upon *Outremer*, a novel set in the Kingdom of Jerusalem in the twelfth century, and in a few months, I will be climbing to the top of the Tower of David in Jerusalem, walking the streets of the Old City in Acre, and breathing in the dust of the battlefield at the Horns of Hattin. I cannot wait!

QUESTIONS AND TOPICS FOR DISCUSSION

1. Richard places a good deal of importance on the notion of honor. How would you define Richard's code of honor? Does he consistently live up to it? Do you have your own code of honor? If so, can you describe it?

2. Richard reflects on his mother's sixteen years of imprisonment by his father, noting her fortitude in surviving it for so long. Compare Eleanor and Richard's responses to captivity. What kind of impact did captivity and isolation have on each?

3. Eleanor is approaching seventy years old during the events of this novel. How do you think her age and experience impact her politicking?

4. As a prisoner, Richard observes that "words were his weapons now" (page 239). How does Richard's battle style, when he is armed with words, compare to his tactics when he is armed with a sword?

5. While imprisoned by Hadmar, Richard gains a new perspective on Duke Leopold's reasons for leaving Jerusalem after Richard disrespected the Austrian flag. Before hearing Friedrich's arguments, Richard had never tried to see Leopold's side. How do you think this new information influenced Richard's subsequent actions toward Duke Leopold? In a broader sense, do you think this incident impacted Richard's diplomatic practices? For example, did it make him more open-minded, or more inclined to empathize with his enemies? Can you think of any examples of Richard demonstrating an ability to appreciate multiple sides of an argument?

6. Discuss Pope Celestine's leadership from Rome. How did his allegiances impact Richard's fate? What motivates his actions? What is your view on the Catholic Church's role in the political landscape at this time? Should the Pope have done more to protect the holy crusaders?

7. Eleanor and Hawisa discuss marriage as being "a man's game" (page 310). Discuss the power dynamics in the royal marriages we observe in the novel.

8. Richard considers himself a devoutly religious man, as demonstrated by his efforts in the crusades. Discuss the nature of Richard's faith and his relationship with God. Does he always act in accordance with the teachings of the Church?

9. Discuss the rivalry between Richard and John. What do you think of John's actions during Richard's long absence? Do you think Eleanor was too willing to believe the worst of John, as he says when she confronts him about his treachery? Did you believe his claims of innocence, as Eleanor did?

10. Compare Richard's leadership style with that of the other kings and dukes he encounters. In what ways is Richard more or less effective than his contemporaries?

11. Discuss Richard's relationship with Berengaria. Were you surprised by his infidelities? Is he right to stay with her, despite knowing she will never give him a son, or does he have a responsibility to the crown to produce an heir?

12. How did you react to Richard's final days? How do you think the author feels about Richard?

13. Richard, though he was King of England, spent very little time in that country. Do you think his actions in Normandy and France were in the best interest of his country, or was he motivated by his personal connections to that land and his hatred of Philippe II?

Sharon Key Penman is the author of nine historical novels and four medieval mysteries set during the reign of Eleanor of Aquitaine. She lives in Mays Landing, New Jersey, and is working on her next project.

sharonkaypenman.com

ABOUT THE TYPE

This book was set in Minion, a 1990 Adobe Originals typeface by Robert Slimbach. Minion is inspired by classical, old-style typefaces of the late Renaissance, a period of elegant and beautiful type designs. Created primarily for text setting, Minion combines the aesthetic and functional qualities that make text type highly readable with the versatility of digital technology.

Chat.
Comment.
Connect.

Visit our online book club community at
Facebook.com/RHReadersCircle

Chat
Meet fellow book lovers and discuss what you're reading.

Comment
Post reviews of books, ask—and answer—thought-provoking
questions, or give and receive book club ideas.

Connect
Find an author on tour, visit our author blog, or invite one of
our 150 available authors to chat with your group on the phone.

Explore
Also visit our site for discussion questions, excerpts, author
interviews, videos, free books, news on the latest releases,
and more.

Books are better with buddies.
Facebook.com/RHReadersCircle

RANDOM HOUSE READER'S CIRCLE ®

 RANDOM HOUSE